Praise for *Deep River*

"Marlantes conveys the elements, arcana and dangerous romance of logging superbly. His descriptions of logging itself—the ingenious mechanics of taking down trees and the skill of experienced loggers—are wonderfully detailed, dramatic and exhilarating."
—*Wall Street Journal*

"Marlantes poignantly depicts the intimacies of personal dramas that echo the twentieth century's unprecedented political storms and yet in surprising ways reprise Finland's oldest mythologies . . . An unforgettable novel."
—*Booklist* (starred review)

"*Deep River* seems a work born from Willa Cather by way of Upton Sinclair. But this new book is its own animal, and it's something of a masterpiece . . . In *Deep River*, [Aino] takes her place beside Antonia Shimerda as one of the great heroines of literature."
—*BookPage* (starred review)

"Inspired by family history, Marlantes (*Matterhorn*) offers a sprawling, painstakingly realistic novel about Finnish immigrants in the Pacific Northwest during the first half of the 20th century . . . Marlantes's epic is packed with intriguing detail about Finnish culture, Northwest landscapes, and 20th-century American history, making for a vivid immigrant family chronicle."
—*Publishers Weekly*

"A riveting read in the classic western literature tradition of Wallace Stegner's *The Big Rock Candy Mountain*, delivering the rich pleasures of an epic story well told . . . The realism of *Deep River* comes with a magical tinge."
—*Oregonian*

"An admirable work, this monomyth is dense . . . with Marlantes's gift for lyricism and evocative language."
—*Library Journal*

Also by Karl Marlantes

Matterhorn

What It Is Like to Go to War

DEEP RIVER

A NOVEL

KARL MARLANTES

Grove Press
New York

Published simultaneously in Canada
Printed in the United States of America

This book is set in 11.5-point Janson MT
by Alpha Design & Composition of Pittsfield, NH.

First Grove Atlantic hardcover edition: July 2019
First Grove Atlantic paperback edition: May 2020

Library of Congress Cataloging-in-Publication data is available for this title.

ISBN 978-0-8021-4897-1
eISBN 978-0-8021-4619-9

Grove Press
an imprint of Grove Atlantic
154 West 14th Street
New York, NY 10011

Distributed by Publishers Group West

groveatlantic.com

20 21 22 23   10 9 8 7 6 5 4 3 2 1

For Anniki

Index of Main Characters

THE KOSKI FAMILY

Tapio Koski (Tah-pee-oh Koh-skee): Ilmari, Aino, and Matti's father

Maíjaliisa Koski (MY-uh-LEE-suh): Ilmari, Aino, and Matti's mother

Ilmari Koski (IL-mah-ree): The eldest Koski sibling

Aino Koski (EYE-no): The middle Koski sibling

Matti Koski (MAT-tee): The youngest Koski sibling

OTHER CHARACTERS

Oskari Penttilä/Voitto (OS-kar PEN-ta-lah)/(VOY-toh): A communist activist and Aino's first love as a teenager in Finland

Gunnar Långström (GOO-nar LYNG-strum): Oskari Penttilä's friend, also an activist

Aksel Långström (AK-suhl LYNG-strum): Gunnar's younger brother, and, after he immigrates to America, Matti's friend and fellow logger

Vasutäti/Mowitch (VA-soo tah-tee)/(MOH-witch): A Native American woman and mentor to Ilmari after he immigrates to Washington

John Reder (John REE-dur): Owner of the logging company that Matti Koski and Aksel Långström work for after immigrating to Washington

Margaret Reder (Margaret REE-dur): John Reder's wife

Alma Wiitala (AHL-muh VIH-tah-lah): The manager of the kitchen at John Reder's camp

Kullerikki /Kullervo (KUH-lur-ee-kee/KUH-lur-voh): Young whistle punk befriended by Matti and Aksel

Louhi Jokinen (LAU-hih YOH-kih-nen): A Nordland businesswoman

Rauha Jokinen (RAU-ha YOH-kih-nen): Louhi's daughter

Jouka Kaukonen (YOO-kuh KAU-koh-nen): A fellow logger and friend of Matti and Aksel

Lempi Rompinen (Lem-pee RAHM-pih-nun): A friend of Aino

Joe Hillström/Joe Hill (Joe HILL-strum): Swedish-American labor activist and songwriter who recruits Aino to the Industrial Workers of the World

Kyllikki Saari (KI-luh-kee SAH-ree): A young Finnish-American woman from Astoria, Oregon who is courted by Matti Koski

Jens Lerback (YENS LUHR-bak)   ⎫ Members of the Bachelor
Heppu Reinikka (HEP-puh RAY-ni-kuh) ⎬ Boys along with Aksel and
Yrjö Rautio (YUR-hoh RAU-ti-oh)   ⎭ Kullervo

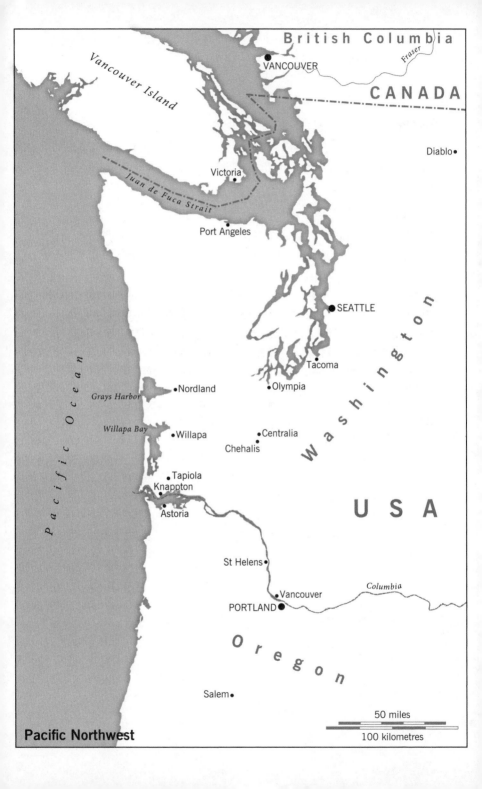

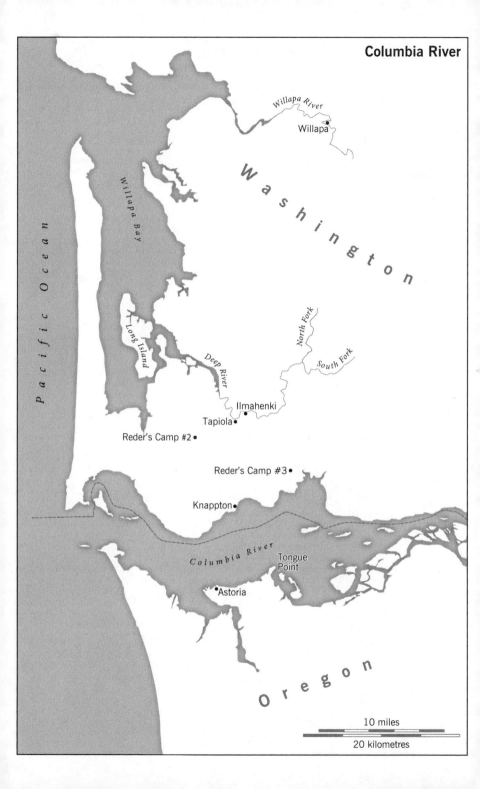

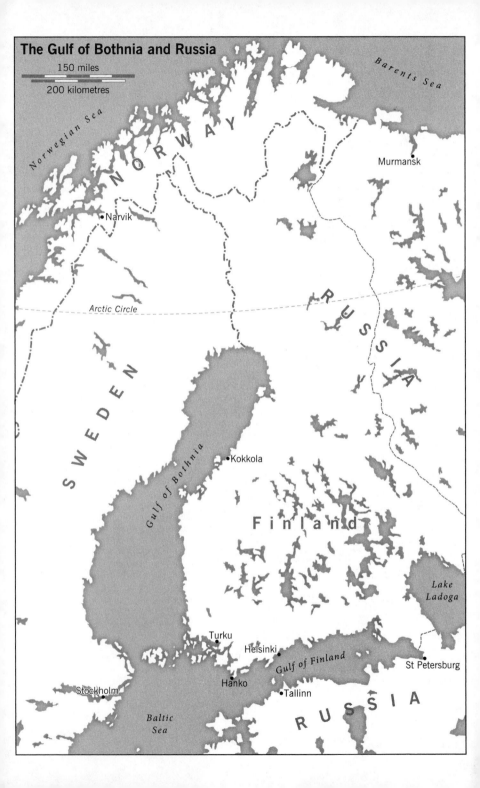

The Gulf of Bothnia and Russia

150 miles

200 kilometres

Norwegian Sea

Barents Sea

N O R W A Y

•Murmansk

•Narvik

R U S S I A

Arctic Circle

S W E D E N

Gulf of Bothnia

•Kokkola

F i n l a n d

Lake Ladoga

•Turku

•Helsinki

•St Petersburg

Gulf of Finland

•Hanko

•Stockholm

•Tallinn

R U S S I A

Baltic Sea

PART ONE

1893–1904

Prologue

A thread of light on the eastern horizon announced the dawning of full daylight and with it the end of a night the Koski family would never talk about and never forget. *A skylark called across the rye field, full throated, pouring out its desire to mate and be fertile. The cold blue sky into which it would rise sat back and let it sing.*

It was on this morning in 1891 that Maijaliisa Koski returned from a three-day absence, helping a Swedish-speaking woman from a poor fisherman's family with a difficult delivery. She found her two oldest daughters and her baby son laid out in their Sunday clothes on the rough planks of the kitchen floor. Although cleaned just hours earlier, the house still smelled of vomit and excrement. Her husband, Tapio; her oldest son, Ilmari Väinö, age twelve; her daughter, Aino, age three; and her now youngest son, Lemminki Matti, two, were sitting on the floor, their backs against the wall, staring dumbly at the bodies. Maijaliisa threw herself to the floor beside her dead children and covered their faces with kisses.

She'd left them with mild fevers just three days earlier, begged by the woman's husband who'd skied and run over thirty kilometers from the coast through the spring thaw to reach her, a midwife renowned throughout the Kokkola region. Knowing that a mother and baby might die, flattered by the heroic effort of the father to reach her, she thought her own children would all pull through.

Few survived cholera.

When she'd finished crying, she stood and looked at her husband. "We'll bury them tomorrow in the churchyard. I want to be with them today."

Her husband said, "Yoh."

* * *

That terrible night marked the children differently. Aino, in whose little arms her baby brother, Väinö Ahti, had died, learned that no one was coming. She was as alone as the meaning of her name—the only one. Ilmari, ill to the point of staggering, had exhausted himself bringing snow from the remaining patches to stem his sisters' fevers. He'd fainted and had visions of angels coming for his siblings. When he regained consciousness, soaked with melted snow, his father was slumped unconscious against the ladder leading to the loft where his sisters Mielikki and Lokka lay dead in the bed all the children shared. From that night, Ilmari knew there was a God and God was to be feared, but He sent angels. Lemminki Matti, not fully aware of what was happening, retained a vague uneasiness about the future. As he grew older, he realized the wealthy feared the future less than the poor. How wealth was attained was less important than gaining it.

The children never knew the name of the woman Maijaliisa went to help that night nor the name of her son who survived and grew to manhood, but their fates were linked.

1

That September of 1901, four years after Ilmari left for America, both for its opportunity and for fear of being drafted into the Russian army, the district was still without a teacher. The Evangelical Lutheran Church of Finland would not confirm an illiterate child, and this made even the poorest of Finnish peasants different from peasants in almost all other European countries: all children learned to read in church-led confirmation classes. For further education, however, the parents had to pay. This was where the bulk of Maíjaliisa's midwifing earnings went. Classes were rotated among farmhouses.

To find a teacher, Maíjaliisa and the other mothers had been writing letters most of the summer. The geese were already on their way south when Tapio came from Kokkola with a letter saying that a young man named Järvinen from the University of Helsinki had accepted the post.

He turned out to be a radical, giving the parents great concern. Aino, now thirteen, along with the other teenage girls, fell in love with him.

Her feelings for the teacher intensified when it was the Koskis' week to board him.

Aino was at the kitchen table working on an essay Järvinen had assigned, when he sat down next to her. He carefully slipped a small pamphlet in front of her, *The Communist Manifesto*, by Karl Marx and Friedrich Engels, in Russian.

"Are you supposed to have that?" she whispered.

He put a finger to his lips. "No. You are."

Aino looked over to see Maíjaliisa knitting and Tapio snoring, the harness he'd been working on still in his hands. "Why me?"

"Your mother told me your father's been teaching you Russian. She says he's fluent because he worked in Saint Petersburg as a young man."

"He stopped teaching me when the czar began making it the language of government."

Järvinen chuckled. He waggled the booklet in front of her. "I can help you with the Russian, but I'm really giving it to you because of your questions in class. Why do people let the czar be so rich and stay poor themselves? Why must families who can barely feed their children do work rent on horse stables and roads that go nowhere for some count who lives in Stockholm? Good questions. This might help answer them." He slid it under her work. "Just between you and me."

When Tapio and Maíjaliisa were safely asleep, Aino lit the kerosene lamp next to her bed and stayed up until just before Maíjaliisa rose for her morning chores. Then she slipped the pamphlet under her mattress. Aware of Matti watching her, she said, "Don't you say a word, or I'll tell Father who took that mink trap from Mr. Kulmala."

"No one here objected to the extra mink pelts."

"Even more reason you'll catch it when they find out the extra pelts are coming from a stolen trap."

Matti glared at the obvious blackmail. "All right. I won't tell; you won't tell."

"Deal."

All through the winter Aino plied Järvinen with questions during lunch breaks, after school, after supper—whenever she could. Is there really going to be a revolution? Why aren't the working classes already throwing off their chains?"

When Aino finished working through *The Communist Manifesto*, Järvinen gave her a Swedish translation of a pamphlet by Rosa Luxemburg titled *Reform or Revolution?* Aino daydreamed about meeting Rosa

Luxemburg and being at her side reforming all of Europe. She also daydreamed about Mr. Järvinen.

That March of 1902, during another one of Järvinen's weeks with the Koskis, he asked if Tapio would like to accompany him to hear a lecture by Erno Harmajärvi in Kokkola—and if Aino could come along. Maíjaliisa shot a quick glare at Tapio. "He's a socialist," she said.

Aino held her breath.

"He's really a Finnish nationalist," Järvinen said.

Järvinen had hit Tapio where his heart beat. He'd named all his children after heroes and heroines of *The Kalevala*, the national epic poem of Finland. The reason he'd worked on churches in Russia was that he'd lost his government job by preaching Finnish independence.

Tapio looked at Maíjaliisa. "He's right. What harm would it be for Aino to hear from someone who is actually *doing* something to get rid of these Russians?"

Aino stood up and whirled around silently clapping her hands. Her mother was shaking her head, tight-lipped.

Maíjaliisa urged Tapio over to the corner of the kitchen.

"They'll have someone there taking names," she said in a fierce whisper. "You know the Okhrana probably has your name from your time in Russia and the police are already keeping an eye on you for that speech about Finnish independence at last Midsummer's Eve dance." She took hold of his loose blouse with both hands and pulled him closer to her face. "I ask you. Don't do this."

Putting his large hands over hers, he gently pulled them away from his blouse. "Living in fear is not living."

"Neither is living without a husband."

"When a woman is humiliated, it doesn't make her less a woman. When a man is humiliated, there are only two choices for him, fight or live in shame. Would you have a husband who is not a man?"

They looked into each other's eyes, neither of them blinking. Then Maíjaliisa sighed. They both knew her answer. She picked up her pipe and walked out the door.

* * *

At the lecture, two men stood just inside the door taking notes, their faces stern and unmoving. They would occasionally ask someone's name, but it was clear that they didn't need to ask either Tapio's or Mr. Järvinen's.

Aino, Tapio, and Mr. Järvinen filed into seats near the lectern. A few minutes later, a boy about Aino's age sat down on a seat by the aisle. She quickly took off her glasses.

She hated them. One day Matti found out she couldn't see a lark that he could. He told her father. Her father asked her that night at family reconciliation—when they all had to recite their sins before they could eat—if she had trouble seeing. She confessed she had been walking by the blackboard during lessons and memorizing it before taking her seat. Her parents drove her into Kokkola to a hardware store where they tried on wire-rimmed glasses until they found a pair that worked for her. It cost them several months of cash, so she felt guilty every time she wouldn't wear them. Like now.

She smiled and looked down at her apron. He was very good-looking.

He politely asked if he could sit next to her. She nodded yes, then wished she'd said something instead of just nodding like an imbecile. He sat silent, intent on the empty podium. The intensity of his eyes drew her attention. She tried not to look at him.

He leaned over and whispered, "This is going to be interesting."

She nodded, then resolving to say *something*, she whispered, "He's really not a socialist. He's a Finnish nationalist." She glanced quickly to see how that went over.

Then the boy leaned back toward her and whispered, "He's really not a Finnish nationalist. He's a revolutionary."

The way he said it excited her, the implication of the righting of all wrongs—of revolution. Then, both tried to sneak a look at the same time and their eyes met again. "I'm Oskari Penttilä," he whispered. He looked around. "I'm called Voitto."

That thrilled her. He had a revolutionary name. Voitto meant victory.

"I'm Aino Koski."

"Are you a socialist?" he whispered.

"Oh, yes. A socialist. But my father, he's a nationalist." She hesitated and looked around. "He goes along with most people saying he just wants to return to autonomy, like what we had under the Swedes. It's safer, but he really wants the Russians gone."

"And the man next to him? Your brother?"

"No, the district teacher. He's from Helsinki. He's staying with us." She looked around, then leaned in and whispered, "He gave me a copy of *The Communist Manifesto*." She watched for a reaction. He nodded his head and craned around her and her father to look at Mr. Järvinen. Then Aino asked, "Have you read it?"

"Of course," he said quietly now, no longer whispering. "I've read everything he wrote, Engels, too." There was a pause. "I can read German."

She was thrilled; he was trying to impress her.

"I read it in a Russian translation," she replied.

"Did you really read *The Communist Manifesto* in Russian?"

"Yes. Plekhanov's eighteen eighty-two translation."

His eyes narrowed. "How do you know Russian?"

"My father is fluent." She hastened to explain. "He's educated. So is my mother," she added. Then she felt bad. She was trying to say that her family weren't just peasant farmers, but a socialist shouldn't care. "Worked for the government, before he got into political trouble. Then he built churches in Russia before he met my mother." She smiled. "It was a game with us, but the Russian lessons stopped when it became mandatory for government workers." She laughed. "The pastor lets me read his Russian novels."

He blinked. "I've never met a girl who's even read the *Manifesto*, much less in Russian."

"Girls aren't socialists?"

"No, no. Lots of girls are socialists: Beatrice Webb who started the Fabians in England and Rosa Luxemburg in Germany. In America, Mary Jones, Mother Jones, who—" He came to a stop, coloring suddenly, which she liked. "I mean, here in Kokkola, I never met a girl socialist."

"Well, you have now," she said proudly, surprising herself to realize that yes, indeed, yes, she was a socialist. She would *do something* instead of just sitting on her hands talking about independence like her father. What good would independence do if Finland was still run by the same oppressor class?

Three weeks later when Aino came down to breakfast, her copy of *The Communist Manifesto* was at her place at the table. She immediately glared at Matti, who vigorously shook his head no. Sternly silent, Maíjaliisa plunked down Aino's bowl of oatmeal mush right on top of the book. How stupid to hide it under the mattress. Of course, her mother would clean there. Aino turned calmly to Matti. "Pass the sugar, please."

Tapio came from their bedroom and sat at the head of the table. When Maíjaliisa put his mush in front of him, she gave Tapio the you're-the-father look and nodded her head toward Aino.

"Where did you get this pamphlet?" Tapio asked.

Maíjaliisa could no longer contain herself. "Do you realize what could happen to you, to us, if the wrong people found out you have this? The czar's secret police, the Okhrana, would arrest—"

Tapio gestured for her to be quiet and she bit back her fear.

Aino was thinking that if she told the truth, Mr. Järvinen would be in deep trouble. But if she lied? But which lie? She blurted out, "Voitto gave it to me."

"Who?" Maíjaliisa asked.

"Oskari Penttilä," Aino mumbled.

Maíjaliisa sat down at the table with her own bowl.

"The boy you introduced me to at the lecture?" Tapio asked.

Aino nodded.

Tapio looked at Maíjaliisa. "See, you may be wrong."

"I don't think so. What would some Kokkola boy be doing with that trash written in Russian?" Maíjaliisa asked.

"Well, Aino read it in Russian," Tapio said. He then focused on his oatmeal.

Maíjaliisa allowed the silence to ripen and then said, "Helmi Rinne swears she found crazy socialist literature in the barn. When she showed it to her son, Pekka, he said Aino gave it to him."

"That's a lie!" Aino burst out.

Maíjaliisa slapped her in an automatic response. She lowered her hand, glaring at Aino as much for her outburst as for the issue at hand. "Just the way it's a lie about this Oskari boy giving it to you? I think Mr. Järvinen has been giving extra lessons." She turned to Tapio. "If the police find this literature, all of us fall under suspicion. We're not paying him to teach dangerous political ideas or put us in danger. We need to talk to the other parents."

"About what?" Aino asked.

"Quiet," Maíjaliisa said to Aino. She turned to Tapio. "We hired him to teach writing and sums, not to preach an ungodly political philosophy to good Christian children."

"Mr. Järvinen says it's not about religion," Aino said. "It's about injustice."

This time Tapio slapped his palm on the table. "That's enough out of you," he said.

Maíjaliisa turned on Aino. "Marx and Engels are atheists!"

"That doesn't make everyone who reads them an atheist," Aino mumbled.

"You go to your room!" Tapio shouted.

When Aino was gone, Maíjaliisa turned to her husband and said, "We hire teachers to teach what we want our children to learn, not what the teachers want them to learn."

Three days later, when Aino came down the ladder dressed for school, Maíjaliisa told her the parents had fired Mr. Järvinen. Aino threw her books on the floor. "It's not fair! You can't!"

"We did," Maíjaliisa said. "Now pick up those books or I'll slap you silly."

Aino stood as tall as she could, looking straight at her mother. Their eyes were on the same level. Maíjaliisa looked right back. She raised her hand slightly, palm open.

Aino picked up the books.

Maíjaliisa let out her breath. "Mrs. Rinne will do the best she can until we get a real teacher," she said. "This time it's going to be a woman and we'll be sure she's a Christian."

2

That April of 1902, the month Järvinen was fired, a very strong wind blew for days, destroying at least half of the tender new rye shoots throughout the district. There was barely enough rye to harvest for their own winter consumption and none to sell for cash. Then, as if a vindictive Pokkanen, the Frost, the son of Puhuri, the North Wind, had it in for the district farmers, he sent a brief snowstorm in August. It soon melted, but the hay was left cool, drooping, and wet. Tapio and Maíjaliisa prayed for dry weather, but the sky remained leaden and overcast. Finally, in late September, Tapio made the decision to cut the hay before winter frosts set in. It went into the barn too damp and by Christmas had started to rot. The family's beloved horse, Ystävä, who they all called Ysti, got thin. The cow developed soft bone and gave less milk. With the tiny rye harvest, Maíjaliisa had resorted to making pettuleipä, mixing the rye flour with bones from fish that Matti caught and the inner bark of the silver birch trees. By January, the women of the district would gather outside after church and whisper about the possibility of famine. The last one had killed nearly two hundred thousand people—over 10 percent of the population—only three decades earlier.

Aino had made up for the lack of a schoolteacher by reading books borrowed from Pastor Nieminen, the minister of the big church in Kokkola and a friend of Pastor Jarvi. Jarvi had written, explaining that Aino had read through his own library and was a good Christian girl.

The good Christian girl, however, had learned that Oskari Penttilä was going to speak in Kokkola. She couldn't go into town on her own, and she certainly could never tell her mother that she was going to a socialist lecture. She bribed Matti with an offer to clean all the fish he caught for two weeks as well as scrape the insides of the pelts he'd collect from his next two trap runs if he would hitch Ysti to the family sledge and take her to town. She told Maíjaliisa that they were going to Kokkola to return books to Pastor Nieminen. She had earlier borrowed five books and hidden two in the barn, taking three into the house to read. On the afternoon of the lecture, she dropped the three in the barn. After the lecture she would take the two back to the house, along with appropriate excitement.

Matti was still acting slightly put-upon. "Acting" was the relevant word, because he was secretly delighted that he'd finally put one over on his big sister. He'd heard that a rich Russian in Kokkola had a three-and-a-half-horsepower Benz Velo motorcar, and he wanted to see one. Unlike his mother, he didn't care one way or the other what his big sister did with her time.

What Aino did with her time was fall in love—for real this time, not as with Mr. Järvinen.

The Kokkolan Työväentalo was a wooden building sheathed with rust-red shiplap that served as a shop during the day and a dance hall or meeting place for social democrats and other left-leaning groups at night. Aino took a place inside, standing by the wall.

When Oskari Penttilä arrived, she shrank back against it, making sure her head scarf obscured her face. Some old man took the floor talking about unions. He sat down to polite applause. Then Oskari took the floor. Oskari talked about overthrowing the chains of capitalism. His voice made the blood rush to her throat so that she was afraid to swallow.

When Oskari finished speaking, clearly pleased with the applause, Aino shoved her glasses into the large front pocket of her heavy skirt and moved to wait by the door, trying not to squint. As Oskari emerged, she pretended to be looking the other way and stumbled into him. Aino was a midwife's daughter and not shy about her body or anyone else's for that matter; she'd been helping her mother with births since she was twelve. With just average looks and those damned glasses, she was at a distinct disadvantage, at least in the winter when her thick clothing covered what she knew was a beautiful figure. If she could just get him talking—well really, just get him listening, since most Finn boys didn't talk idly—there wasn't a boy in the district she couldn't hold, summer or winter.

With a few genuine compliments on his speaking abilities followed by some keenly perceptive questions on socialist theory she had him hooked.

She could have killed Matti when he showed up early with the sledge. She refined that feeling to death by slow torture when Matti began acting like a brat, lightly switching Ysti forward and then pulling him backward in a repeated display of impatience.

She forgot her anger instantly when she turned to look back from the sledge and saw Oskari watching her.

Matti was good with horses. In fact, he was good with anything that involved ropes, cables, animals, machinery, and tools. If Aino saw a huge boulder in the field, she assumed it to be immovable. Matti, on the other hand, would spend time thinking about how to move it. Then, with levers, block and tackle, teamed horses, crowbars, the help of a few friends, and a lot of swear words, the boulder was moved. Even though Matti was two years her junior, Aino felt secure and carefree with him driving. Wrapped in a rug made from the skin of one of the few remaining bears that Tapio had shot as a teenager, with just her dark eyes exposed to the cold, she had her mind on Oskari.

The sleigh took a sudden short shift to the left, breaking Aino's reverie. They were passing dark figures, struggling alongside the roadway, burdened with heavy bundles. Children, the small ones roped together for safety so they wouldn't stray and freeze to death, trudged in a line behind their parents. Ysti's bells jingled as Matti clucked him forward a little faster.

Aino came out of her cocoon and looked back on the dark group until it was swallowed in the early afternoon gloom. She looked over at Matti.

"City people," he said. "No skis." He shook his head slightly. "Probably from the Salminen Brothers' shipyard. No one wants wooden boats anymore."

"But why are they on the road?"

Matti looked at his big sister with the you-are-really-stupid look that only a younger brother could give a big sister. "No work, no wages," Matti said. "No wages, no rent money. No rent money, no place to live. How hard is that to understand?"

Aino flared. "Only an idiot would look at it that way." She set her jaw. "The houses they were thrown out of just sit there empty. None of these people need to be homeless. No private ownership, no evictions."

"Yes. Socialist heaven. They can keep on building wooden boats no one wants to pay them for and then eat our rye without paying us."

The brother and sister rode the rest of the way in silence, passing two more struggling families.

Around seven that evening their old dog, Musti, started barking without getting up from in front of the stove. Aino went to the small window. Yellow light from the kerosene lantern flickered on the snow. A small group of people huddled together, just at the edge of the light. One of them separated from the group and came to the door and knocked.

Maíjaliisa peered over Aino's shoulder. "Don't answer it," she said to Tapio, who was already going to the door. "Beggars."

"What can they want, Maíjaliisa? A little bread?"

"And then the word is out and tomorrow more bread for more beggars? We're already eating birch bark."

"We're eating. They—"

"I was ten during the great hunger years. I watched my grandmother and two cousins die of starvation."

"I lived through it, too," Tapio said. "We're not there yet."

"The shipyards are closing. They'll be swarming into the countryside. They'll swarm here and we'll be beggars like them."

Tapio hesitated. Aino stormed past him and threw open the door. Even in the freezing air a terrible smell assailed her. A man, probably the father, took off his hat. "Please. Please. We have small children. Just a little food? And can we stay in your barn tonight?"

"Go on. Get out." Maíjaliisa was actually shooing at him with her apron as if he were a chicken.

The man pleaded with her silently with stricken eyes. "Please. We are very near ..." He hesitated. "The children, without food, they will freeze."

Maíjaliisa tried to shut the door in his face. Her eyes were wild with fear.

Tapio reached across the threshold, making it impossible for her to shut the door. "They can stay in the barn, Maíjaliisa," he said. Snarling with frustration at him, she shoved Tapio away from the door with both hands on his chest and ran for their bedroom. Tapio turned back to the man. "I'm sorry, but we don't have food to spare."

Aino spun around, heading for the cupboard next to the stove. Tapio said in a clear firm voice, "No, Aino." That stopped her. Tapio told the man where to find the barn and hay for bedding, nodded good evening, and quietly shut the door.

Aino heard something at the window. A girl, perhaps eleven years old, crying, her face twisted with pain, had pressed herself against the glass. Her father gently took her away from the window and the family disappeared into the darkness, walking toward the barn.

When she was sure her mother and father slept, Aino slipped from her bed, quietly pulled on her wool stockings beneath her long wool nightgown, and carrying her wooden clogs crept down the steep ladder. She put her coat on, went to the cupboard, and pulled out the loaf of pettuleipä that Maíjaliisa had made for breakfast. Holding it against her with one arm, she quietly slipped on the clogs, unlatched the door, and ran across the frozen snow.

She was shivering when she entered the dark barn. She located the family by their smell. Approaching awkwardly, unable to see, she brushed up against someone—the mother. She had two of her children tucked against her, her apron around them. She had stuffed every available space with straw to retain their body heat. When Aino put the bread beneath her nose, the woman grabbed her arm. She broke down in sobs. Aino, embarrassed at how the smell revolted her, patted her on the shoulder and then made her way back to her warm bed. Anger at the senseless cruelty of it all kept her awake all night.

A few months later, with the spring thaw, Matti uncovered the frozen body of a small boy next to the barn. One of his thin arms had been revealed by the melting snow. He was probably around three years old.

Tapio wrapped the little frozen corpse in a burlap gunnysack, and the whole family drove the body to the church. They found Pastor Jarvi in the parsonage and Tapio explained what had happened.

"But, I can't bury it here," Jarvi said. "I don't know if it's been baptized."

Tapio put his hand on Aino's arm before she had a chance to say a word. Then he said evenly to Jarvi, "Then what do you suggest we do with *him?*"

Jarvi looked at the floor of the parsonage porch where they were standing. "There's a place," he mumbled, "just over by the river."

"A place," Tapio repeated.

"You know, a place, where we bury the unconsecrated."

"Will you help us bury this little boy?"

Jarvi swallowed and looked over their heads. "I shouldn't," he said.

Aino spun around and walked back to the wagon.

Then Maíjaliisa climbed up a step and stood close to him. "Is it God that doesn't want you to bury this child or the church?"

Jarvi's jaw was rippling just slightly from the rapid movement of his incisors being held against his bottom teeth. "Mrs. Koski," he said. "You put me in a terrible position. I'm sorry." He turned back into the house, leaving the Koskis on the front porch. They turned at the sound of Aino bringing up the wagon.

"We'll bury him by the cherry trees where I can watch over him," Maíjaliisa said.

With that, the family drove back to the farm where Matti dug a small grave. Tapio led them all in the first verse of "Beautiful Savior," playing the accompaniment on his kantele, and then repeated the litany for burial, forever burned into his heart from burying his own children. He read from the family Bible: first from Job, I know my redeemer lives; and then from First Peter, By His great mercy, he has given us new birth; and finally from the Gospel of John, The light shines in darkness. They all said the Apostles' Creed and the Lord's Prayer, Aino joining in for her parents' sake. They silently tossed some dirt on the little brown bundle and Matti filled in the grave.

About a week after that event, Aino was startled by a firm knock on the front door. She opened it and there stood Oskari Penttilä holding his hat and some flowers.

"I came to pay my respects," Oskari said. "It's all over the district. About the baby."

Aino felt a rush of excitement. She knew it wasn't just because of the dead baby that he'd come. "I'll show you where he is," she said. She took off her apron, smoothed her dress, and made sure her stupid braid was at least presentable, then led Oskari to the cherry orchard. Matti had carved a little headstone from a river rock and had placed it on the grave. Oskari put the flowers next to it. The two of them stood side by side, saying nothing.

"It was good of you to come," Aino finally said.

"This baby died because of capitalism."

"He died because of the cold," Matti's voice said from behind them. Aino turned on him. "Matti. We don't need your commentary."

Matti just grinned. "You mean you don't want me standing here saying it. You shouldn't be out here alone with him."

Aino took in a deep breath, flaring, but Oskari only looked at Matti very solemnly. "I know your brother is in America and you're responsible for Aino." He looked at Aino. "Of course, he's right to be here."

Aino watched Matti swell with pride, her annoyance with him for protecting her reputation fading. She looked into Oskari's eyes, loving him.

3

The gardens began producing food by June, and the threat of famine was no more. The summer was warm with just enough rainfall, and the harvest of 1903 was good enough to produce a little cash in addition to plenty of food to make it through the winter. In the cities and towns, however, inflation was rampant. Real wages fell by 20 percent and the workers' unrest was growing, only to be met by Russia's sending more troops to keep things in check.

Every month or so a letter came from Ilmari, usually about four weeks after it was written. Aino loved the strange stamps with their round cancellation mark: "Knappton" curved around the top and "Washington" curved around the bottom. Knappton stood on the north side of the Columbia River, fourteen kilometers south of Ilmari's new farm on the heavily timbered south shore of Deep River, a coastal river that ran parallel to the Columbia, separated from it by a range of hills. Knappton was about two hours from the farm by foot. No road existed. She imagined Knappton as a beautiful port city on a magnificent river. Ilmari wrote that the Columbia was eight kilometers wide at that point. On its south shore was a huge city called Astoria, Oregon.

It was still hard to believe. Ilmari had 160 acres of prime river-bottom farmland that he'd gotten for free! Ilmari had written that there was a law called the Timber and Stone Act entitling every person to 160 acres of prime timberland for just two dollars and fifty cents an acre. Ilmari had staked out his 160 acres about twenty kilometers north of Deep River and sold it to a timber company for five dollars an acre, leaving him four hundred American dollars. Ilmari had used that free money to buy the same amount of land on Deep River from a family that had gotten their land for free twenty years earlier under another law, called the Homestead Act.

Ilmari's 160 acres was sixty hectares, four times the size of their farm in Finland, which Tapio and Maíjaliisa had worked on for years and was owned by a rich aristocrat. There were no aristocrats in America—and the government just gave the people free land. The United States must already be a socialist country!

To be sure, Ilmari made it clear that carving a farm out of wilderness was backbreaking, exhausting work. It seemed the trees were big. He'd sold some of his Deep River timber to both clear the land and get cash to start a little blacksmith shop where he earned more cash making tools, shoeing horses, and repairing equipment for logging companies. That, however, had left stumps over two meters high and four and a half meters across that had to burned out to make way for civilized farming. Well, Aino thought, the free land was probably real, but as for stumps two and a half meters tall and four and a half meters in diameter, Ilmari was having them on. In addition, he'd written that it hardly ever snowed. Aino was way too smart to be taken in by this. She remembered similar wild tales of Yukon gold that had swept the district when she was eight.

Ilmari made no mention of marriage or even women. All he wrote about was clearing those damned trees, some steamboat that *maybe* was going to start service from Willapa Bay to the end of tidewater, where a little Finnish community called Tapiola had formed, another reason Ilmari had moved to Deep River. Many of the Deep River farmers were from families in the Kokkola area. The first structure Ilmari built was a sauna, which he lived in while he worked on his own house. Other Finns in the area helped with what couldn't be done alone. Everyone worked together, for the good of everyone. Aino was convinced, now, that socialism had truly flourished in the new world.

That winter, old Musti died. Aino and Matti buried him next to the dead baby in the cherry orchard, saying nothing to each other.

Two weeks after the burial, Aino was awakened by Matti holding a wiggling mass of warm fur, the slight smell of urine, and a wet tongue over her face. He dropped the puppy, a little female, and it flopped its way clumsily across the quilt, little tail wagging as though it would fall off. Aino hugged the puppy, looking up at Matti, striving to maintain her dignity. The puppy started yelping, as if jealous of Aino looking at Matti. Aino snuggled with it beneath the quilt.

"Oh, Matti," she said.

Matti nodded his head in recognition of her thanks. "What will you name her?"

At that moment, the puppy flopped her way to the edge of the bed where she crowed at Matti like a little rooster, tail vibrating.

"Laulu, because she sings."

In February 1904, the Japanese destroyed the Russian fleet off Port Arthur, Manchuria. Finnish radicals increased agitation for reform and independence. Finnish men in large numbers began refusing to show up for military service. The czar wouldn't compromise, and the Russian governor general of Finland, Nikolai Bobrikov, met agitation with force, making arrests in large numbers.

The increasing unrest in the area brought in a cavalry unit. The Russian army base just south of Kokkola had no room. The troops were to be quartered with the Finnish farmers. For free.

The family stood in a silent, sober line outside the house as the detachment of Russian troopers looked down on them from astride their horses. Laulu started a high-pitched howling, squatting down on her hindquarters and backing away from the horses, only to dart forward and repeat the action. Aino gathered Laulu up in her apron, quieting her.

The officer in charge entered the house without asking. He emerged from the house and shouted two names. A sergeant and a corporal dismounted and looked inside as the platoon rode off.

The two cavalrymen and the Koskis stood in uneasy silence. Aino watched Matti struggling for control, his right hand just short of where his puukko, the traditional man's knife, hung from the back of his belt encased in its wooden scabbard. Tapio put a hand on Matti's shoulder. "Sisu," he whispered. "Show them nothing."

The Russians entered the house. The sergeant came back outside and sauntered over to them, smiling. The corporal remained at the door, looking slightly embarrassed. The sergeant pointed to himself. "Kozlov." Then he pointed to the corporal. "Kusnetsov." Then he pointed to Tapio, raising his eyebrows. Tapio smiled and blinked. "Kozlov," the sergeant said, again pointing to himself. Tapio smiled broadly. The sergeant cursed.

Realizing he didn't speak Finnish, Aino said quietly, "We should show *Koz*lov the cherry trees." Tapio shot her a quick glance. "Koz" was the Russian word for "goat" and cherries poisoned goats.

Kozlov, having heard his name, looked at Aino inquisitively, but Aino went as passive as the rest of her family. Rolling his eyes at the family's stupidity, Kozlov shouted to Kusnetsov and they led their horses to the barn.

Maíjaliisa marched into the house and found one of the Russian's gear thrown on top of her and Tapio's bed. She spat on it. Tapio sighed, took out his handkerchief, and wiped it off, sadly shaking his head at her. She knew he was right, and this made her even more furious. She grabbed her pipe from the mantel and stomped outside. Aino found the other Russian's gear on her bed.

Tapio and Maíjaliisa moved to the loft, Matti and Aino to the barn.

A cold routine settled in. Maíjaliisa had food on the table for the Russians in the morning. When they left, she would put the family's breakfast on the table. Dinner was around noon, normally the largest meal of the day because it had to fuel work until dark. With the Russians eating both breakfast and supper, however, dinner got smaller. The carefully hoarded sugar was gone within two weeks. Sergeant Kozlov loved his sugar. Evening supper was served separately, the same as breakfast.

The corporal, Kusnetsov, tried to be pleasant. It was clear from the way he watched Aino that she was attractive to him. This pleased her, but she treated him with cold civility.

One evening, Aino was picking up the two Russians' plates and Corporal Kusnetsov gently touched the top of her hand. She jerked it away and Matti leaped to his feet from where he was saddle soaping a harness next to the fire. His hand went behind him, touching his puukko. In one swift movement, sending his chair clattering to the floor, Kozlov pulled his revolver, a formidable 7.62 Nagant. He smiled at Matti and pulled back the hammer. Kusnetsov spoke to Kozlov, nodding his head toward Matti, seemingly saying, "He's just a boy." Kusnetsov raised his right palm apologetically to Aino and said, "Anteeksi," pardon me, in Russian-accented Finnish. Aino stalked out of the house. Kozlov holstered his pistol and resumed drinking his heavily sugared tea. Matti picked up the harness and followed Aino outside, his face white with rage and humiliation. He was gone until chores the next morning.

4

Midsummer's Eve arrived. Aino made a new dress for the dance on the hand-cranked sewing machine that Ilmari had shipped from America. Maíjaliisa made her redo the first version because it was too tight. After getting her mother's approval on the second try, she secretly tightened the dress again by hand. She'd also made small adjustments to her light cotton corset. All the mothers were constantly harping at their daughters not to pull their corset laces too tight because it was unhealthy; corsets were for modestly supporting their breasts and making their clothes hang right. All the daughters knew that if you pulled the laces tighter it accentuated your curves and made for a far greater overall effect. All the mothers knew that all the daughters knew this.

Knowing her dress fit perfectly, Aino jumped into the back of the cart covered in her longest shawl and quickly snugged down with her back to the driver's bench, where Matti was driving, her mother squeezed between him and her father.

As soon as they reached the tanssilava—the dance site on a huge expanse of glacier-exposed flat rock several kilometers east of Kokkola—the shawl was crammed between the pillows, along with her glasses, and Aino bolted, holding her skirt up so she could run. Tapio and Maíjaliisa looked at each other quizzically. "Voitto," Matti said. Maíjaliisa looked heavenward and Tapio shook his head, smiling. The three of them walked to join the dancers. Many of these were older men and women in traditional clothing, the young people as well as many of the adults in their Sunday clothes. Children played boys chase

girls and vice versa at the edge of the tanssilava; a slightly older group
played kick the can in the soft light of the midnight sun.

One of the young people in his Sunday best was Aksel Långström, at
his first dance without his parents. Not yet fourteen, he'd come with
his older brother, Gunnar, who was commissioned to watch out for him
but who, to Aksel's delight, had immediately abandoned him. Aksel was
the last child of four. His mother would have died birthing him, had his
father not skied and run over thirty kilometers to bring back the best-
known midwife in the district. The woman had saved his mother's life,
but not her ability to bear more children.

Aksel had been fishing with his brother and father for years
already. It told, not only in the dark, tanned face that framed brilliant
blue eyes but in shoulders that stretched the Sunday tunic his mother
had sewn for him just six months earlier. His Sunday trousers showed
a two-inch gap above his shoes. The Långströms were Swedes, the
descendants of Swedish settlers from several centuries past. Aksel, like
most Swedes, although just coming into manhood was already as tall as
most grown Finns.

His mother had tried to teach him the rudiments of the waltz,
hambo, and schottische in the weeks leading to Midsummer's Eve, humming and singing the music, as there were no instruments in the house.
Farm chores, however, and helping his father with the fishing didn't
leave a lot of time, so Aksel hung back shyly by the refreshments table.
He watched the dark-haired girl with the beautiful figure who could
dance like the wind ruffling the water. Aksel loved his sisters, but they
were literally pale in comparison with this girl. Her black eyes flashed.

The combination of longing and sheer joy in watching her, combined with his shyness, kept Aksel eating by the table until he thought
either his heart or his stomach would burst. She was getting a lot of
attention from the sons of merchants and prosperous farmers, most
of whom were still in school, just as she probably was, putting her out
of his reach. He'd been taught to read and write by the church, but
school was beyond the family's means. She'd been dancing a lot with
that socialist, Oskari Penttilä, who was in the same political club in

Kokkola as Gunnar, a club Gunnar had asked Aksel to keep secret. But now, Penttilä, who must have gone to get the girl a drink, because he had a glass in each hand, was talking animatedly with a group of young men, including Gunnar, ignoring her. Aksel could only shake his head. There she was, a beautiful girl, wasted while those idiots talked politics. He struggled with his shyness. Should he ask her to dance? The sun had dropped below the horizon far to the northwest, making high clouds glow in shades of orange against a soft, light-blue sky. The cold, unblinking luster of Jupiter hung above his head, so bright he felt he could touch it. His star, however, was warm-orange Arcturus at the foot of Boötes, the man who chased the two great bears around the sky. Arcturus was always there for him, summer or winter. He looked for it in the cold nights on the boat and in the cool mornings and evenings of the long summer days. The planets came and went. Gunnar had caught him talking to it one night on the boat and kidded him about it but never told anyone. What was between brothers was kept between them, just like Gunnar's club.

Aksel looked up at his star, stood a little straighter, and said to it, "This is it."

Aino thought a man was coming toward her, but when he came into focus she saw that he was just a boy, good-looking and obviously on his way to being big, but thirteen or fourteen at the oldest. She had seen him arrive with Gunnar Långström, a comrade of Voitto's, so he was probably Gunnar's little brother. They did resemble each other.

The boy just stood there swallowing. Maíjaliisa had told her about this power that women have over men—and had also told her about misusing it. "It's like that Swede's new explosive. It'll move mountains, but you get careless with it and it will get *you* into serious trouble." Serious trouble for Maíjaliisa always meant the same thing: getting pregnant. Aino attributed it to Maíjaliisa's seeing the heartbreak of out-of-wedlock deliveries, which her mother helped with even though Aino was quite sure Maíjaliisa would never help with abortions.

She smiled at the boy. "You're Gunnar Långström's little brother, aren't you?" She said it in Finnish, even though she spoke reasonably good Swedish. Swedes had settled in Finland centuries earlier and Finland was ruled by Sweden until it was ceded to Russia in 1809 after a bloody war, so a sizable minority spoke Swedish.

The boy nodded his head. The Swedish-speaking and Finnish-speaking communities kept pretty much to themselves, but with written material in both languages being common as well as increasing literacy among the younger people, it didn't surprise her that Aksel had picked up some Finnish.

"Aksel," he said. More silence. "Aksel Långström."

She could have made fun of him for the obviousness of that last remark, but she smiled at him instead. "My name is Aino."

"Like in the songs." He answered her in Finnish.

That was good. "Yes."

"She killed herself rather than marry old Väinämöinen," he said.

That was verging on impressive.

"She was beautiful."

Aino could see that his cheeks were flushing. She glanced over at Voitto. Trying not to squint, she could just make out that he was talking to people and appeared to be holding her drink. Obviously, he'd forgotten her. Voitto gestured with one of the drinks, spilling some of it. It must have reminded him why he'd gotten it. He turned toward her. Perfect.

"Are you going to ask me to dance or not? It's a waltz. You can waltz, can't you?"

The boy nodded vigorously, then thrust out his hand. It was the first time she'd ever seen adoration in someone's eyes. It surprised her how much the warm rush of it pleased her, even coming from someone just out of childhood. She took his hand. He escorted her properly to the inside circle of the dancers already circling the dance space. He then took her right hand in his left, placed his right hand in the center of her back, and holding himself erect in the dancer's brace of someone who had been taught something about dancing, moved smoothly into the flow.

Aino smiled, her eyes just able to peer above the boy's shoulders, checking that Voitto was watching them. He was. Her father had taught her how to dance, and many dark winter Saturday nights had been spent with him and Ilmari alternating on the kantele, her mother dancing with the boys and her father with her. To dance on any other day of the week would have been considered frivolous. The band was playing "Lördagsvalsen," or "Saturday Waltz," an old Swedish tune and one of her favorites. She knew Voitto was watching and she gave herself over to the feel of the boy's strong arms holding her against the centrifugal force, the harmony, and the pulse of the three-quarter-time music, the Nordic twilight with its few bright stars above them, the two of them whirling beneath it as one being. She merged with it all.

Aksel escorted Aino back to the group of unmarried girls, where a somewhat irritated Voitto was standing on the group's edge with the two drinks in his hands. Aksel thanked Aino and nodded his head toward Voitto. His whole body felt like a song about to be sung.

He had just returned to his place by the food when stillness quickly spread through the crowd. A group of five young Russian officers had appeared, two of them carrying bottles. They stood there talking among themselves, laughing a little too loudly to be carefree. They must have known they weren't welcome. Still, Aksel didn't begrudge them anything. They were just young men, probably unhappy about being posted so far from home. He, along with all the others, tried not to look at them, but he felt uneasy.

The dance band's leader acted, starting a lively schottische, and the older people, including Tapio and Maíjaliisa, deliberately took the floor to ease the awkward silence. Soon the general hubbub restarted, and the Russians' presence was, if not forgotten, being politely tolerated.

Then, two of the young Russians asked two Finnish girls to dance. The girls politely refused. A couple of the soldiers who hadn't asked the girls to dance made fun of the ones who had, in Russian, probably disparaging their looks or their manhood, and those soldiers came right back with their own insults just like young men everywhere. The bottles were passed again. An empty bottle was thrown into the trees on the edge of the dancing area. That brought looks of disapproval from the adults, but the Russian who did it grabbed for another bottle and took a large defiant swig. Aksel's uneasiness grew.

Still, the Russians now kept to themselves and were politely ignored.

Aksel was aware that Aino had been dancing with other boys than Voitto, and when he'd danced with her earlier, he noticed that her hand was rough and callused, both making her seem a little more within his reach. So Aksel once again looked up to Arcturus in the dawn-like silver of the summer sky for courage and walked over to ask her to dance. She accepted. It was another waltz. She moved like a sailboat responding to the slightest touch of the rudder.

On the second turn around the area, Aksel saw one of the Russians watching Aino intently. The young officer tossed down a drink, handed the bottle he'd been holding to one of his friends, and worked his way slowly through the dancing couples. When he neared Aksel and Aino, he stood there for a moment, swaying just slightly. The waltz came to an end. Aksel bowed, as his mother had told him, and started to escort Aino off the floor. The soldier stopped them, also giving a bow. He was not only an officer but, by the cut and quality of his uniform, upper class. He politely asked Aino, in Russian, if he could have the next dance.

Aino's head went up slightly and her shoulders back and she answered with an abrupt, "Ei onnistu!" "No way" in Finnish. The Russian took it for the clear snub it was. His face clouded. Whatever he said back to Aino in Russian wasn't good. The two stood there, glaring at each other.

Aksel started to look around for Gunnar. He and Voitto were already coming across the tanssilava. The soldier's friends started coming from the other way. Aksel saw a dark-haired boy with the same flashing black eyes, a little older than himself, join Voitto and Gunnar. He guessed this must be Aino's brother.

Voitto was the first to speak. "Maybe you think you own the country," he said in Finnish. "But you don't own our women. Nobody owns Finnish women." The Russian didn't understand him.

Aino, with her fluent Russian, repeated Voitto's words and then added an earthy insult that involved the Russian going home and having sexual congress with sheep.

Two of the Russian officers burst out laughing but not the aristo-crat. He slapped Aino across the face. Aino snarled and hit his face with her fist. The stunned soldier shook his head, trying to clear it. Before he could even think of retaliating, Aino's brother was on him, scream-ing with rage, slugging the Russian, who staggered backward into his friends, trying to shield himself. The brother kicked the Russian in the knee and then, spinning, caught the side of his head with his elbow. Spit and blood flew from the man's mouth. The other Russians waded in, and the fight was on.

Aksel had never been in a fight before. He picked out the nearest Russian, who stunned him with a fist to the temple. He saw stars, not like Arcturus, and found himself sitting on the ground.

Aino stood there with her mouth agape, stunned at the raw male aggression she'd unleashed.

The sound of a vodka bottle breaking stopped the fighting. The Rus-sian with the broken bottle, clearly drunk, was sneering at Gunnar and waving it in his face. Gunnar's hand went behind him, and he drew the long, curved puukko used by all fishermen for gutting and scaling. Matti moved next to Gunnar and pulled out his shorter and broader hunter's puukko, more effective for skinning. Gunnar and Matti stood together facing the Russians, both slightly crouched, left arms up, right arms holding the puukkos away from their bodies. Now there was fear in the faces of both sides.

That was when Tapio stepped in, his own puukko in hand. "I'll use it on the first person who takes a step forward." He looked directly at Matti. "Including you." He repeated himself in Russian and, obvi-ously surprised that the man spoke their language, the young officers backed off.

After a few minutes of awkward silence, the accordion player started up a lively version of "Suomalainen Polkka," and the rest of the band was soon with him. With the almost Russian-sounding minor key, the rapid two-four rhythm, and the repeating four-note figures, the tune was just right to clear the air. Eventually the mood created by the fight dissipated and disappeared altogether when the huge midsummer's night bonfire roared high into the sky, sucking air so furiously that the women's skirts ruffled at their ankles. Then, with a heavy crashing noise, collapsing timber sent up a column of burning cinders into the clear, pale sky. Around the circle, Finns and Russians both were cast in foreboding red.

5

Sergeant Kozlov was a sullen drunk. When he got this way, it felt like a storm cloud moving toward you, the air stirring at your feet and around your shoulders; all you could do was weather it, hoping lightning wouldn't strike.

Kozlov and Corporal Kusnetsov were slumped in the straight-backed wooden chairs at the kitchen table, a bottle of vodka and a plate with their cigarette ashes between them. Aino was knitting a winter sweater for Matti. Maíjaliisa was darning stockings. Both sat next to the woodstove. The fire that had heated supper and coffee was down to just embers, the door and windows were open to let the June air blow through the house. Matti was carving a dinner plate to replace one broken by Kozlov during a previous drunk and Tapio was resoling a winter boot. No Finnish farm family was foolish enough to waste the endless summer twilight. Those who didn't prepare for winter never saw spring.

The Koskis didn't tiptoe when Kozlov was in one of his drunks, but they knew to keep quiet. Laulu, however, lying on the floor in front of Aino with her legs splayed out, suddenly jerked up, came to her feet, and in the way of dogs everywhere began to bark furiously, raising the alarm at something not detectable by humans, something passing over the roof or in the trees across the fields.

Kozlov startled. Springing upright, eyes wild, knocking back his chair, he reached for his revolver, which was always with him like a touchstone of safety and violence. He shouted a string of obscenities at Laulu. Aino dropped her knitting and rushed to Laulu, kneeling next to her, to soothe and quiet her, whispering into her ear, "Shh, shh. It's just Ilmatar flying over us," the spirit of the air. Kozlov sat back down.

She let Laulu go and Laulu padded to the open door, then to the window, checking the perimeter, then padded back to settle in front of Aino, who had again taken her chair next to Maíjaliisa.

Corporal Kusnetsov, his head on the table, was apparently asleep. Kozlov raised his glass to Tapio and asked him in Russian if he wanted a drink. Tapio played dumb, wrinkling his eyebrows in puzzlement. Kozlov then held the glass out to Aino and Maíjaliisa, asking the same question. The combination of hatred for Russians in general, detestation of Kozlov in particular, and the insult to her womanhood made by the proffered drink, as if she and Aino were prostitutes, was too much for Maíjaliisa. She scowled, her jaw set with anger.

Kozlov rose from the table, smiling coldly. He held the glass out to Maíjaliisa, walking toward her, saying he'd by God make her drink and wipe that sanctimonious look off her face. Aino, knowing that her father understood every word, even if Maíjaliisa only intuited the intent, looked at Tapio as he rose to his feet. Matti rose with him, the plate dropping to the floor, his puukko in his hand. Tapio put his hand on Matti's arm.

Matti lowered the puukko.

Laulu gave a low ominous growl.

Kozlov lurched forward, holding out the vodka glass, and stepped on Laulu's outstretched paw. Laulu attacked, latching onto Kozlov's leg just above the ankle. Kozlov threw the glass at her and began kicking her against the stove, screaming with rage and pain. Tapio and Matti both ran to pull Laulu off but didn't reach her before Kozlov had pulled his revolver. The pistol shot froze everyone in place. Laulu sighed, her eyes looking up, and went stiff, blood running from where the rifle-size .30-caliber bullet had exited behind her heart. Kozlov kicked the inert dog away from him. Aino went to the floor, covering Laulu's body.

Tapio was on Kozlov like a wolverine. His rush knocked the drunken Russian sideways and they both went down to the floor, Tapio pounding Kozlov's face with his right fist while trying to push the Russian's gun arm downward toward the man's feet. The pistol went off again. Matti was kicking Kozlov, while Kozlov was trying to bring the pistol up to bear on Tapio, who was trying to keep it turned down and away from him. One of Matti's kicks hit Kozlov's gun arm, and a third shot sent a bullet through Kozlov's cavalry boot into his calf. Tapio wrenched the pistol from Kozlov's hand and threw it between Aino and Maíjaliisa. Matti kicked Kozlov again and Aino started to make a grab for the pistol, but before she reached it, another pistol shot sent a bullet into the planks next to it. Aino jumped back. Everyone froze. Corporal Kusnetsov stood by the kitchen table, smoke curling from his revolver.

Kozlov scrambled over, retrieved his pistol, and tried to stand. He immediately collapsed. He crawled away from the Koskis, his pistol moving to cover them, Tapio rising to his feet to join Matti, Maíjaliisa still by the stove, Aino on the floor hugging Laulu with tears in her eyes—and raw hate.

It was an instant when motion seemed unrelated to time, Kozlov dragging his wounded leg, the Koskis standing by the stove, Aino at their feet on the floor hugging and rocking Laulu's body, Kusnetsov standing behind the kitchen table, smoke from the various pistol shots moving lazily in the twilight air, and stunned silence. There are moments in life when everything is changed and there is no changing back.

Aino heard Corporal Kusnetsov ask Sergeant Kozlov if he could remain conscious and Kozlov answer him that he could and would remain so until this shit-head Finnish revolutionary was in prison for the rest of his life.

With Kozlov keeping his pistol on the family, Kusnetsov took Matti's and Tapio's puukkos. He tied their hands behind them with Aino's and Maíjaliisa's head scarves and forced them to their knees. He turned to Aino and said, "Ysti." Aino glared at him. He fired his pistol into the floor in front of her and she scrambled to get the horse.

Aino held on to Ysti's harness as he stood patiently in front of the wagon. Matti and Tapio were now bound hand and foot on the wagon's floor and Sergeant Kozlov, pale but obviously tough and in total control, was on the driver's seat facing backward toward them, his pistol out.

Kusnetsov climbed up to the driver's seat and took up the reins. He looked with sadness at Aino and Maíjaliisa and nodded his head back toward Tapio and Matti. "Hyvästi," he said quietly, indicating that it was time to say goodbye.

Maíjaliisa hurried to the wagon's side and touched her hand to Tapio's face. "I'll wait as long as it takes. I am your wife for eternity." She then reached for Matti's head, trying to pull it up closer to her over the wagon's sideboard, but Kozlov rapped Matti with his pistol barrel and Maíjaliisa let him go. "Now is when you must remember your sisu," she whispered.

Aino stood next to her mother, fighting tears. Tapio said to Maíjaliisa: "Put your hand on our daughter's head." Maíjaliisa hesitated, knowing what this meant, then she placed her hand on Aino's dark, warm hair. Tapio said, "I cannot give my blessing in the old way, but now my little girl will go into the world a grown woman. I cannot give you silver or gold but take my blessing and keep it. Remember the ways and the prayers of the old people and remember those who love you and all will be well." He nodded to Maíjaliisa, who removed her hand.

Aino and Maíjaliisa watched the wagon until it disappeared behind the birches at the road's turning, keeping everything in: the utter helplessness, the emptiness, the two of them alone in the silence.

Matti came back to them two days later with Ysti and the wagon, his face bruised and eyes blackened, his back raw and still weeping blood and fluid from the whipping. They would never see Tapio again.

6

The burden of planting and harvesting would fall on Maíjaliisa, a forty-six-year-old woman; Aino, a sixteen-year-old girl; and Matti, a boy not yet fifteen. The little cash Maíjaliisa could earn from her midwifery practice wouldn't begin to take care of the monthly rent. And as strong and willing as he was, Matti simply couldn't match a grown man's obligation for the work rent.

Maíjaliisa, of course, tried to hide her fear from her children, as was expected of her, and Aino tried to hide her fear from Matti, as was expected of her. They needn't have worried. Matti was too filled with rage to be worried about the future.

They worked frantically, taking advantage of the long days, sometimes even working through the twilight of the summer night, missing out entirely on sleep. Still, they missed July's rent. In mid-July, just two weeks after the rent was due, a letter arrived from the count's manager, Mr. Melker Gustafsson, in Turku. After reading it, Maíjaliisa took it in to the bedroom and shut the door. Emerging about ten minutes later without it, her face grim and determined, she said nothing. She didn't have to say anything. Aino and Matti just gave each other a look.

Gustafsson arrived at the house on the eighth of August after the Koskis underpaid their August rent. He knocked on the door but entered the house as if he owned it, which his boss did. He presented Maíjaliisa with the letter she'd written several weeks earlier, saying she'd make up the shortfall in July's rent. Maíjaliisa had to admit she didn't have the money. Gustafsson said he wanted it in two weeks and left. Until then, Aino had never seen her mother cry.

Voitto came to help whenever he could, but between school and his work with the socialists, he couldn't come as much as Aino wished. He was also slow and inefficient at farmwork. Neighbors tried to help, but harvest came to every farm at the same time, so in the crucial last days the Koskis couldn't get the hay cut and stacked before rain fell for several days, leaving it sodden and almost sure to rot. The cows might weather the bad hay because they had two stomachs, but their milk would be severely reduced. If Ysti was fed bad hay, it could kill him. They tried selling the cherries from the older trees as well as the potatoes from the garden but really couldn't get much for them. The apples were looking good, but they wouldn't be ripe for another month and, since virtually every other farm had a good apple crop, the market would be bad. So Maíjaliisa and Aino spent days picking deep-red lingonberries that grew in the forest and pale-orange cloudberries that liked to live on little hillocks in the wet pastureland or swampy ground near lakes and rivers, which meant fighting mosquitoes, sometimes so thick that Aino had to put her scarf over her nose and mouth so she wouldn't breathe them in. No one in the district cultivated cloudberries—it was too difficult—so they were able to sell those for cash in Kokkola where the people liked to eat them, either fresh or as jam, with heated leipäjuusto, a local cheese made from cow colostrum.

Maíjaliisa began taking Aino with her on every midwife visit, not just the occasional easy one. With two midwives in the family, there would be two times the income—if only the families who needed midwives could pay in cash.

None of them said it, but winter was coming, and they might not even have a house.

In mid-September Mrs. Puumala went into labor. There was a chance of some actual cash payment as the Puumalas owned their own farm and were good at working it.

"Four centimeters," Aino said. She was looking up at her mother from between Mrs. Puumala's legs. Aino did not have a ruler. She was using her mother's finger scale. Maíjaliisa motioned her aside, gently felt for Mrs. Puumala's cervix, and grunted approval.

"Is there any depth?"

"Just a little."

"So, what do you do now?"

Aino hesitated a moment. "Nothing?"

Maíjaliisa stood up and laughed. "You get coffee."

Aino was learning fast—but it wasn't all about midwifery. While waiting for Mrs. Puumala she picked up Marx's *The Civil War in France* and a German-Swedish dictionary to help her through it, both lent by Voitto. She was deep into it when she heard a horse outside and Mr. Puumala say to his wife, "It's your sister's nephew—the socialist."

Aino's heart lurched. She quickly took her glasses off and stood up. Her hair, which she had piled in thick braids on top of her head, must be a mess from spending the whole morning looking up Mrs. Puumala's kusipää.

Voitto's lean form stood in the doorway, his head nearly touching the lintel. Aino couldn't decide whether to pull her hair together or whether that would be too obvious.

"We heard Fanny-täti was in labor," Voitto said.

"So how long have you had this interest in babies?" Maíjaliisa asked Voitto. There wasn't a hint of it, but Aino knew the question was dripping with irony.

Voitto looked her square in the face and said, "I really came to see Aino."

Aino sat down with her mouth open. For a Finnish boy, this was a declaration of love.

Maíjaliisa turned to Aino. "He isn't shy."

Aino dumbly shook her head no.

Maíjaliisa took out her pocket watch, always with her to time contractions. She turned back to Voitto. "If she isn't back here at noon it'll be the last time you see her because she'll be a prisoner sentenced to hard labor." She turned to Aino and said so no one else could hear, "And you keep your skirt down."

Aino gave Maíjaliisa a look, squeezed past her, and was out the door. Voitto was just out of sight of those inside and she ran to him. He lifted her feet off the ground and twirled one time around before putting her down. He nodded to his horse, mounted, and she was up behind him, long skirt and apron bunched beneath her bottom, her bare legs dangling down, holding him tight with her head resting on his back. She wanted to stay there forever.

They found a spot near the small stream that formed the boundary between Puumala's land and the farm next to it. They were both on their backs, next to a large smooth rock, holding hands, looking up at the August clouds.

"That one," Voitto said. "See. A house with a chimney."

"And to the right, a horse."

"No, that's a cow," he said.

"A horse."

He rolled over and kissed her quickly on the forehead. She laughed. "OK. You win. A cow."

They both waded into the river, ostensibly looking for crawdads. Voitto was carrying the crawdads in his hat, constantly shaking them down as they tried to crawl out. "My uncle can cook them for Fanny after the baby comes," Voitto said.

Aino nodded, happy with the idea. Then she turned serious. "Do you think there will be marriage after the revolution?"

Voitto shrugged. "Probably for a while. But after the state withers away, no reason will exist for marriage. It's all about property rights, isn't it." It wasn't a question.

"Sure." Aino paused. "Of course." She snuggled against him as they waded.

"But there will still be . . ." He colored. "I mean people will still love each other." He turned her to him and, looking into her eyes, put both of his hands gently on the back of her exposed neck. He kissed her, fully and forever.

She felt him through her skirt and apron. Looking up at him, pushing against him, she whispered. "And everyone will have healthy, well-fed babies."

He smiled warmly and shook his head back and forth in wonder, as if he couldn't believe his good fortune to have her for his girl. "And everyone will have healthy, well-fed babies," he repeated.

There was a brief moment; then his whole countenance changed.

"Babies," he gasped.

They both hissed, "Saatana!" and ran for the horse.

Mrs. Puumala delivered a healthy baby girl with no complications. Sitting on the buckboard with Maíjaliisa on the way home, Aino felt she was moving into her mother's sphere as a participant, not just an appendage, and it felt good. Maíjaliisa went over the delivery in detail, questioning Aino about what might have gone, but didn't go, wrong at each step and Aino had the thought that maybe, just maybe, she might follow in her mother's footsteps.

When they arrived at the house, several buggies were in front. Maíjaliisa's hand went to her mouth, she dropped the reins, and she ran into the house. Aino, torn between following her and taking care of Ysti, compromised by tying him next to a water trough and went in after her mother.

Inside the kitchen were two policemen from Kokkola and Gustafsson. Matti was seated on the floor with his hands on his head. One policeman held Matti's puukko; the other one, older, looked uncomfortable. Her mother was literally on her knees in front of Gustafsson, who was seated at the kitchen table having helped himself to some raspberry pudding.

"Mother, get up," Aino said quietly. She asked the two policemen, "Will you let him up if he promises he'll do no harm?"

"He'll do no harm in jail. He assaulted a police officer," the man with Matti's puukko said.

"They came to take the farm," Matti blurted out.

"You'll be quiet," the younger officer thundered, pointing the puukko at Matti.

"Surely, these are extraordinary circumstances," Aino said. "He's fifteen." She looked down at Matti. Matti wouldn't look at her. She looked pleadingly at the older officer who had seemed uncomfortable.

"We're sorry, Mrs. Koski," the older officer said to her mother. "It's the law. Mr. Gustafsson here has given you two weeks."

"And two months before that," Gustafsson said. He took another spoonful of pudding. "I hope you understand my position. I'm responsible for making the estate work efficiently. Clearly, you are no longer able to work the farm. Your husband's agreement with the father of the current owner—which we were prepared to honor fully—to pay him a third of the crops or the cash equivalent is moot. Then there's the undone work rent."

"Surely, my husband will be back soon." Maíjaliisa turned to the older policeman. "It was an accident!" she pleaded. "The Russian was drunk." The police looked down at the table. Maíjaliisa turned to Gustafsson. "He could be back within the month."

Gustafsson sighed. "Mrs. Koski, I have a perfectly healthy man in his thirties with three young children and a wife who will pay half the crops instead of a third. The farm is obviously worth far more now than when your husband made his agreement with the owner's father."

"But we built—" Aino blurted.

"I'm not finished, young lady." Gustafsson cut Aino off. He turned back to Maíjaliisa. "Your husband won't be back in a month or even a year, if ever, and you know it."

Gustafsson gave the older policeman a self-righteous, I-demand-justice look. "We all have our duty." The man looked at Aino, then spoke to Maíjaliisa, still on her knees. "We have no choice. We'll have to take him in."

Maíjaliisa groaned. At best, it meant years in jail.

Maíjaliisa slowly rose to her feet.

Aino watched her struggle for control. She found it. "Aino," Maíjaliisa said. "Please get out the visitor glasses." Then she added, "And the napkins in my dresser." She turned to Gustafsson. "Please. Can't we just have a cordial and talk. He's just a boy."

Gustafsson drew himself up. "It's too late for that."

Aino knew there were no napkins in Maíjaliisa's dresser. What was in her dresser was the family savings, held beneath a false bottom. She swallowed and gave her mother a look to signify that she understood the mission. She went into the bedroom where she nearly tore the false bottom out. She returned to the kitchen, their small savings palmed in the hand that held her apron.

Matti was standing. The younger policeman was taking his handcuffs from his belt.

Maíjaliisa went to her knees again, sobbing hysterically, pleading with them not to take her son. Everyone was looking at her. Aino slipped Matti the bills. There was the briefest of moments when their eyes met, then Matti was running out the door.

The two policemen were trying to get past Aino, who stood firmly in the door until she was thrown against the wall. She watched their backs. There would be no chance for them to catch Matti. She could only hope he'd elude the certain manhunt to come.

Aino looked calmly at Gustafsson. "You'll be the first one we get when the revolution comes."

He slapped her face.

The two police officers returned, winded. Gustafsson pointed at Aino. "Arrest her. She's a revolutionary. She threatened to kill me when the revolution comes."

Maíjaliisa came up to Aino and put her arm around her shoulder, staring defiantly at the three men.

"I heard her. She's a goddamned red," Gustafsson said.

The older police officer sighed. "She's a child—and she's just lost the only home she's ever had."

Maíjaliisa asked Mr. and Mrs. Laakkonen if she and Aino could move into their barn, and they gladly agreed. Laakkonen, taking advantage of the railroad and new creamery in Jakobstad, had switched his rye and barley crops to oats to feed his cows, which increased their milk production, and he was now finding himself with more cash and cows but short of labor.

The law said that the Koskis could take all their personal possessions and Maíjaliisa argued that Ysti was a personal possession. That became irrelevant when Gustafsson said he'd be willing to take Ysti and the wagon in lieu of what was owed for back rent. He also magnanimously agreed to let them use what was now the estate's horse and wagon to haul their goods to the Laakkonens'.

On the last trip, they brought Maíjaliisa and Tapio's bed and Maíjaliisa set it up against the hewn logs of the south wall of the barn, where it could get some heat from the sun. The logs were well fitted with a wide groove on one side overlapping the curved top of the log below in the Finnish style. It required very little chinking. There would also be heat from the cows. Aino and Maíjaliisa were grateful and relieved. They would be safe for winter.

Aino and her mother mounted the wagon behind Ysti for the last time. Down the road, Aino asked Maíjaliisa to stop and she climbed on Ysti's back. Coming up on the farm—with its expanded orchards, tidy rows of new and old trees breathing in the early fall sun, the birches and the alders already starting to turn color; the new outbuildings crisp and solid, the work of months by her father and brothers; the solid old house with its board-and-batten sides, its birch-bark roof, the loft window through which she and Matti would jump with their skis onto fresh snow piled nearly over the sill, the new addition that Maíjaliisa had insisted be built when Aino came of age and that for the past two years had been her very own room; and the neat well-tended graves of old Musti, the baby boy found in the snow, and young Laulu— Maíjaliisa pulled the horse gently to a stop.

"I can't go any closer," she said quietly.

Aino understood. She slid off Ysti's hindquarters to the ground. Maíjaliisa joined her and tied the reins loosely to the seat. Then she gently slapped Ystävä, clucking to him, and said, "Home, Ysti, home."

The horse turned to look at the two of them. Aino couldn't be sure, but she thought Ysti must know that this was a final parting. He slowly and gently bent his large head around toward them and Maíjaliisa scratched his muzzle. Aino let out a cry and grabbed him around the neck, burrowing her head into his wiry hair, feeling his heat for the last time. She pulled back and Maíjaliisa again slapped him on his hindquarters saying, "Home, Ysti, home."

Ysti gave them a long look. Then he turned toward the house and walked away.

Six days later, Aino found work as a housemaid with a merchant family in Kokkola, where she could sleep in the windowless basement near the coal chute, sharing a pallet with another girl. She would have Sundays off to be with her family, given of course that everything had been cleaned up after breakfast and that she was back by four to help prepare supper. Since she had to walk the six kilometers to the Laakkonens' and back, this would give her three or four hours.

Two days after beginning her new job, she joined Voitto's growing cell of the Finnish Active Resistance Party, violent revolutionaries.

7

The pallet Aino shared was only ten feet from the coal bin. She breathed coal dust all night and constantly fought to keep her uniform and underclothes clean. On the other hand, the coal bin was next to the warm furnace. The other advantage of living in the basement was that it was easier to slip away to attend meetings. Which she did, bribing her pallet mate to cover for her with extra food that she managed to sneak out from under the watchful eye of the cook who was also the head housekeeper and had a tiny room to herself just off the kitchen.

Aino's workday started at six in the morning and she had to be dressed and have eaten breakfast before then. She could go to the basement and her pallet only after the kitchen and parlor were spotless, often after ten at night. If the family was entertaining, it was later.

On meeting nights, she could snatch only two or three hours of sleep. She was often late and sometimes missed entire meetings, even though meetings started at ten to accommodate working people like her. It would be her first insight into organizing; working people don't have time to debate theory. That was why most socialist theorists and organizers weren't from the working class.

Aino and Voitto agreed that before meetings he would wait for her by the stone wall of the old Kaarlela church on Kirkkopolku Street. She would usually know from a distance whether he was still waiting for her, because she would see the glow of his cigarette long before she could make out his form in the darkness. From there they would make their way down to the docks, where a sympathetic longshoreman let the small group meet in the attic of one of the many warehouses that lined the harbor. Meeting in the Kokkolan Työväentalo, where the social democrats mostly held sway, was too risky. The police monitored everyone who went there, as Voitto pointed out, to *talk*. The Finnish Active Resistance Party despised social democrats and anyone else who compromised with the corrupt system—and the party wanted to do far more than talk. The time for talking had ended, but a frustrated Voitto had found it difficult to move the group from rhetoric to action. Action meant risk.

On a still, cold night in February 1905, Aino smelled Voitto's cigarette before she saw its glow by the stone wall. She ran into his arms and they held each other, feeling each other's warmth from beneath their many layers of stiff clothing.

He took her by the hand and started off. "Come. We can't be late tonight. What took you so long?"

"My *mistress* had company and wanted me to serve coffee." Voitto was already in front of her, pulling her along. "Hey, hätähousut," Aino laughed, calling him a name that literally meant "emergency pants." "What's going on?"

"Rauta, from Helsinki, is coming tonight."

The chill evoked by the name Rauta came with a tremor of excitement. There might be action. Why else would the party send him this far north? She linked her arm closely inside Voitto's and buried her cheek against his wool coat, feeling the moisture from her breath freezing on his sleeve. Fresh snow squeaked beneath their shoes in the silence of the sleeping town.

Everyone knew that Rauta, which meant "iron," wasn't his real name. None of them knew how high up in the party he went. Everyone was nervous. This was Voitto's only link to the larger party and Rauta's orders were to be obeyed without hesitation.

Rauta wasted no time. "This student debating society must act. I mean illegal action in defiance of laws that protect the rich." He scanned the room, making eye contact. "The party has decided that you will be reorganized for action into independent cells of just three people each. However, you will continue meeting with this larger group, discussing theory, putting out pamphlets, and making speeches. We know that army intelligence, the local police, and even the Okhrana think—with good reason—you're woolly-headed student radicals playing at revolution."

He surveyed the room. "Backsliders and reactionaries will be purged." He paused, the word "purged" hanging in the air. "Am I perfectly clear?"

Aino studied Voitto to see if there was any sign of how *he* felt about all the changes. He showed nothing.

Then Gunnar Långström spoke. "Don't we get a say in what we'll be asked to do?" he asked. Voitto could not contain a visible wince, nor could Rauta contain his anger.

"Who are you?" The voice was ice cold.

Voitto jumped in to protect Gunnar. "We haven't studied democratic centralism as a group, yet," he said to Rauta. He turned to Gunnar. "We must trust party leadership to exercise democratic centralization. Bourgeois democracies are palliatives to keep the people working for capitalists." Aino knew that Voitto was struggling to show Rauta that Gunnar and by association the others weren't reactionaries. "Knowledge of the organization must be limited. You know that, Gunnar. The Okhrana can be very persuasive."

"Yoh," Gunnar said. He and Voitto held each other's eyes.

Rauta stared at Gunnar, then said, "I see we understand each other." Gunnar nodded, shifting his eyes to the tabletop.

"Just last month," Rauta went on, "the czar murdered more than one hundred of our comrades in front of the Winter Palace. The czar's response to the appeasing petition of that collaborating priest, Father Gapon." He paused, making sure no one agreed with Gapon. "The Finnish Active Resistance Party retaliated by killing Grand Duke Alexandrovich and that bastard traitor Soisalon-Soininen. We need to keep up the pressure."

The room was silent.

"Only active resistance," Rauta continued, "not stupid ineffective petitions begging the czar for crumbs, will stop the Russians from squeezing us into slavery and continuing to throw Finnish boys on the corpse piles of imperialism and capitalism in a war with Japan that is not our war. We need to hit the Russian imperialists again." He slapped a palm on the table. "And again. And again. And again." He was now pounding the table, a fleck of spit at one side of his mouth.

Rauta stopped pounding the table and stood up straight. "You have been given the privilege of attacking the army base south of Kokkola. The party will help you with explosives and weapons."

Aino felt a thrill of excitement mingled with fear.

Gunnar stood up from the table, his jaw set. "What about the Finnish workers inside the compound?" he asked.

Rauta's eyes bulged as he turned to Gunnar.

Voitto quickly interposed. "Comrade Långström," he said, carefully choosing his words. "We have repeatedly let it be known, through flyers, newspaper articles, even speaking with these people directly, that collaborating with Russian imperialists and capitalists is morally reprehensible. These people chose easy money."

"You know my mother's sister works there."

"People make choices," Rauta said. "They live with the consequences."

Rauta's face settled once again into its cold mask. He addressed the group, his voice going soft but intense. "At this very moment, the people are rising with the tide of history. Nothing will stop the revolution. Those who fight the party and history will die." He looked directly at Gunnar.

With murmurs of approval, hands thumped on the table in solidarity with Rauta.

Gunnar sat down.

Aino's heart was now pounding in her throat from excitement.

The attack was set for April.

8

By the first week in April, the sea ice was fast disappearing. Aksel's father was driving him and Gunnar hard repairing the net for the spring runs.

Aksel pulled a knot tight with his hand-carved wooden net-mending needle, twisting his wrist to put friction on its inner tongue so the twine wouldn't slip. He wanted to talk with his brother, who was at the other end of the net rack, but he was afraid. Ever since that February morning when Gunnar had come back from spending the night in Kokkola "visiting friends," he'd become grim, as when a seal got in the net and he had to club it to death.

The night before, Gunnar had slipped out of the bed he and Aksel shared, and Aksel had lain awake most of the night. At the noon meal, Gunnar had been uncharacteristically sharp, arguing with their parents about socialism in general and in particular the assassination last summer of Nikolai Bobrikov, the governor general of Finland. Their mother and father weren't pro-Russian, but their father kept saying to Gunnar: "You can't just kill people." When Gunnar gloated openly about Russia's defeat by the Japanese at Port Arthur, their mother pointed out that Finns and Swedes had gone down with the Russians. Gunnar said he didn't care. You couldn't stand in the way of history. Their father told him to leave the table, which he did, slamming the door.

Aksel looked over his shoulder to make sure their father was gone. "You were out again last night," he said to Gunnar.

Gunnar pulled a knot tight and grunted.

Aksel continued to cut and tie, filling in the holes so the net would neither sag nor be pulled too tight after the mending. Aksel usually liked mending net—if the weather was warm. With the thaw just ending, however, his hands ached with the cold.

"What are you doing at night?"

Gunnar stopped working. Looking gravely at Aksel, he said, "For your own good, no more questions. Promise?"

"Promise."

Aksel hadn't promised not to follow Gunnar. Like most Finnish boys, Aksel was a good hunter. Following undetected was a cinch.

He watched from the woods as Gunnar met someone on the road to Kokkola. Something was exchanged. Then he followed to where Gunnar hid the something beneath a pile of brush about four hundred meters into the woods just north of their house.

The next night, Aksel crept out of the house while Gunnar slept. The waxing moon was almost full behind scudding clouds, so it was easy to find Gunnar's hiding place. When he saw the dynamite and two pistols, fear coursed through his body. Aksel knew that with Gunnar it was never about capitalists and workers, despite his socialist rhetoric; it was always about Russia and independence. The target had to be the Russian army base just up the coast road.

Two days later, a Saturday evening, the fifteenth of April, Aksel and Gunnar were washing blood and fish scales from the boat when Gunnar said, a little too casually, "I told mother and father that I'm going into Kokkola to see about a pair of boots that Alvar Johansson's uncle left behind when he migrated to America."

"So, they assume you're drinking."

"Yes." Gunnar put both of his hands on Aksel's shoulders. "You assume it, too."

Gunnar hardly ever touched him. Why now? Aksel's stomach felt a lift of anxiety. The anxiety grew when he saw Gunnar leave for Kokkola with a knapsack too large for boots.

* * *

As Gunnar was walking toward Kokkola, Voitto and Aino were whispering angrily outside the house of Aino's employer, looking up and down the street every so often.

"You can't do this to me," Aino whispered.

"I can, and I will." He grabbed her by her arms, looking intensely into her eyes. "It's no place for a girl and if we fail . . ." He swallowed.

"If we fail, I will fail with you. You can't leave me alone."

"They'll do horrible things to a girl."

"They'll probably treat me better than the boys."

Voitto shook his head at that. "Stubborn," he said.

"Yes," she answered.

"And wrong." Voitto reached his arms around her, pulling her close to him. "We won't fail. Trust me, we won't."

"Then take me with you."

"If you're there, I won't be able to keep my mind on the job and we *will* fail."

"That's not on me."

"Nor me. It's the way it is. It's how we're built."

They stood against each other, feeling their body heat coming through the wool of their clothes and the quilting of their jackets, as a cold April wind blew all around them.

"I promise you," Voitto said. "As soon as it's over, I'll come to the Laakkonens' on your Sunday visit home or get word to you there if I can't come. Kokkola will be crawling with police and soldiers."

"Just come."

He pushed back from her and she leaned after him, seeking him with her mouth. He pulled her in close and kissed her. Then he pushed her back more firmly and held her at arm's length. They looked into each other's eyes, knowing it could be the last time, ever.

Aksel knew that the sun would set just after nine and that it wouldn't be dark enough to see stars until after ten, so whatever Gunnar was up to would probably happen around eleven. Just after Gunnar left, Aksel told his older sister, Anna Britta, who was hanging clothes, that he was going to check out the salt lick for any moose activity. Anna Britta's eyes were troubled. She touched the back of Aksel's hand.

Aksel grabbed the family bicycle and caught up to Gunnar, but he was careful not to reveal himself. He waited in the trees by the road for Gunnar to return from the hiding place. When Gunnar emerged from the forest, Aksel pushed the bicycle out from the trees and confronted him.

Gunnar was savagely angry. "You go back home. Now!"

"You have dynamite in that rucksack."

"Do not get tangled up in this. You go home. I mean it. I'll beat hell out of you if you don't. You're not so big yet that I can't."

"It's the army base."

Gunnar stared at him, lips sealed.

"Finns are working there."

"You think I don't know that?"

"Gunnar, Aunt Jenni works there."

There was a brief silence.

"Go home," Gunnar said. Aksel had never seen Gunnar so intense. "Any slip of the tongue, the slightest hint, could bring the Russians down on the whole family. You must understand this. Army intelligence and the Okhrana have informers everywhere." He held Aksel's shoulders and looked him in the eye. "You must know nothing about this."

"Gunnar, it's murder."

The two brothers stood looking at each other, Aksel standing astride the bicycle, Gunnar, his jaw muscles working, slightly hunched under the heavy pack. Finally, Gunnar spoke. "I know you don't understand, but I have to do this. There's no turning back. Aksel, if you love me, go home and say *nothing*."

Aksel's throat tightened. Don't cry now, damn it. He grasped the handlebar grips so tightly that his fingers were white and his forearms trembled.

Gunnar gently put a hand on one of Aksel's. "I'll be all right. I promise you I'll be back, maybe not for a while, but I'll be back and everything is going to be better."

Aksel watched Gunnar disappear around a bend. He gave a cry of anguish and grabbed a large rock. Remounting the bicycle he pedaled furiously after Gunnar. Gunnar turned around to see him coming and his eyes widened in fear. Aksel hit him square on the forehead and Gunnar went down like a poleaxed cow.

Aksel careened to a stop and ran to his downed brother. He tore open the rucksack and found, along with the dynamite, a rope and grappling hook. They were obviously planning on going over the walls. He took the rope and bound Gunnar, hog-tying him wrists to ankles; slung him over his shoulder; and dumped him into the bushes. He threw the rucksack and its dynamite even farther into the brush and pedaled up the road to the army base.

Aksel lay beside his bicycle just off the road and studied the front gate of the compound. It was all going too fast. He'd pedaled up the road thinking he would tell his aunt Jenni so she could quietly warn the others. He soon realized that if he told her, she might go immediately to the Russians. After all, she had chosen to work for them. Even if she did try to help, someone else could tell the Russians. They would trace the warning back to Jenni and she would quickly be frightened into saying who told her. The army intelligence people for sure, maybe even the Okhrana, would be at the house in a matter of hours.

Aksel realized he didn't even know where in the compound Voitto and his people would be likely to strike. Maybe several buildings were targeted. How many people were involved? He knew next to nothing. He put his face down on the earth and held his head in his hands. What was he doing here?

He looked up at the sound of harness bells. A wagon was coming, spurring an idea. If the wagon contained food or anything bound for the post's kitchen, it would go directly to the cooks. They were all Finns. Maybe he could get a note inside one of the bags somehow. He knocked his forehead against the ground in frustration. He never carried pencils or paper.

With the wagon nearly in sight, he pulled his puukko out and quickly sliced off a slab of bark from a birch. Hurriedly he carved a message on the soft inside of the bark. "Finnish patriots attack tonight." If he had written socialists or communists, whoever found the note would be far more likely to go directly to the Russians. But how was he going to get the note to that someone? He would need to trust the driver to deliver it. The odds were too high that the driver would be afraid and tell the Russians.

The wagon had the name of a local flour mill on it and carried large white bags. Aksel again lay there, face to the dirt. Only one way seemed possible and it was dangerous.

He cut a strip of cloth from his shirttail and bound the bark to a rock. Setting off in a loop through the woods, well out of view of the road, he worked his way carefully up to the low wall of the compound. He waited. No one walked along the perimeter. As far as the Russians were concerned, this was just a sleepy post inside their own country. The only guards were at the gate.

Aksel climbed up a young fir tree, using the branches to conceal him. When he could see over the wall, he paused. The wagon was approaching a building with several chimneys emitting smoke. It had to be the kitchen. Where else would the flour go?

He tried to control his breath. He waited until the flour was unloaded and the wagon left the compound, memorizing the layout he'd seen. He moved up to a point on the wall nearest to the kitchen. He threw the rock over the wall and heard a welcome thud as it hit a wooden wall. He turned quickly and disappeared into the forest, again looping from the road to return to the bicycle. He had done the best he could. Now it would be up to the finder of the note and God.

He met Gunnar on the road. Gunnar had managed to get himself loose and had found the rucksack. Aksel halted in front of him. Gunnar looked at him, his hair matted with drying blood. "You warned the Finns."

Aksel nodded yes.

"Aksel. Aksel." Gunnar looked at him with anguish. "You've killed me."

Dread coursed through Aksel's body. "What? What do you mean?"

Gunnar took a deep breath, looked up at the cool twilit sky for a long moment, as if saying goodbye to it. His eyes moist, he looked down at Aksel with nothing but love.

"You told Jenni."

"No. I realized they'd trace it back. I wrote a note and threw it over the wall to the kitchen."

Gunnar looked back up at the sky. A bird flew from one tree to another. He bent in close to Aksel and smelled his brother's hair, nuzzling his nose in it, taking in all he could. He stepped back, his hands on Aksel's arms. "If it gets to the Russians, they'll be waiting for us. If I tell my comrades before the raid that you warned the Finns, the party will kill me for telling you and they'll hunt you down and kill you for betraying the raid. Discipline will require it. If I don't show up tonight and the Russians are waiting for them, they'll think I sold them out and they'll hunt me down for that."

"Gunnar." Aksel had started crying. "Gunnar. I didn't know. I didn't mean—"

Gunnar tightened his grip. "You listen. Your life depends on this. Are you listening?"

Aksel nodded yes through his tears.

"I'm already under suspicion because I spoke up about the Finnish workers in front of a very scary man from Helsinki. They'll torture me before they kill me. If I'm captured by the Russians . . ." He hesitated. "Only a fool would believe that I won't talk. Either way, I'll be executed and the Russians or the party will come after you. If I know you're safe, I'll feel a lot better when I finally break."

Aksel started to talk but Gunnar put his hand on Aksel's mouth. "You must get out. Tonight. Father has a cousin in Stockholm."

"I won't go."

"If you don't go, I will die knowing you'll be next. Will you leave me to die like that?"

Aksel shook his head no.

"Of course not." Gunnar held him to his chest, soothing the back of Aksel's head. "Of course not." Hugging Aksel close, Gunnar whispered in his ear: "I will never, never hold this against you. Go home. Tell Mother and Father that I"—he took a quick, deep breath—"that I . . ." he momentarily choked. "And tell our sisters, too." Holding him at arm's distance he said, "I'll always love you." Gunnar squeezed Aksel's arms hard and walked away. Aksel held forever the memory of seeing his big brother turn to wave as he disappeared at the bend in the road.

Although Aino knew no details, she knew the raid was tonight. She was barely able to abide the chatter of her fellow servant and the conversation of the merchant and his wife as they placidly ate their Saturday night supper. When the couple rose from the table, Aino curtsied and asked permission to go home so she could attend church in the morning with her mother, which was granted. She was able to leave around ten and half walking, half running in the darkness made it to the Laakkonens' barn after midnight. Maíjaliisa had fallen asleep with some of Mrs. Laakkonen's mending in her lap.

Aino didn't sleep the whole night.

After early church, she tried to pretend that everything was normal as she went about her chores, struggling to ignore a terrible sinking feeling that pulled deep in her body's core.

Late that afternoon the Laakkonens' dogs started barking and Aino ran out of the barn door, her heart soaring. It had to be Voitto, alive, alive.

It was two strange men in a small trap. Maíjaliisa came to the door, her face questioning. The men walked up to the two women.

"Aino Koski?" one of the men asked without the trace of a smile. He spoke with a Russian accent.

Aino nodded, her heart pounding. Something must have gone terribly wrong. She wanted to run, but she was rooted to the ground, her heart sinking, wanting to know what had happened to Voitto, but knowing she couldn't ask for fear of implicating herself.

"You're under arrest for treason and sedition."

Aino and Maíjaliisa gasped, both grabbing at their throats. "No," Maíjaliisa croaked. "This must be a mistake." She was ashen faced. "Aino," she pleaded. "What's going on? What have you done?" Aino looked down at the ground, her lips compressed.

"Aino!" Maíjaliisa cried, grabbing her arm, trying to pull her around to face her.

The men didn't even acknowledge Maíjaliisa. Jerking Aino away from her, they handcuffed her arms behind her back and pulled her stumbling to the small trap. Mr. Laakkonen, who'd been spreading hay for the cows, watched from a distance. Mrs. Laakkonen stuck her head out of the house and quickly pulled back inside.

One of the men lifted Aino and threw her onto the floor of the trap, wrenching her shoulder. She would not cry out.

Maíjaliisa rushed toward the trap and grabbed Aino by her skirt, pulling on her. The man who'd thrown her down was mounting beside the other man who'd already taken up the reins. He shoved Maíjaliisa with his boot and drew a pistol.

"Where are you taking her?" Maíjaliisa cried, running alongside.

The men did not answer her. The driver whipped the horse into a trot, leaving Maíjaliisa alone on the road.

As Aino lay on the boards of the trap, Aksel and his father were ten kilometers out to sea, the sail fluttering slightly at the luff, moving the little fishing boat with maximum efficiency. Aksel's father hadn't spoken in over two hours.

Earlier that day, Aksel had waited, saying nothing, filled with anxiety and guilt, letting his parents believe that Gunnar was missing because he'd drunk too much the night before. By midmorning, however, their anxiety started to rise and Aksel broke, blurting out the story.

When Aksel finished, the entire family was silent. Then, his father rose and took out the puukko he wore on special occasions. Its blade had been incised with beautiful old runes, a magic incantation that asked for safety on the sea. The birch handle had been carved with a slight blade guard to keep it dry in wet conditions.

Aksel shook his head no. The puukko was passed down through the oldest son. It would be Gunnar's when their father died. "If by grace of God's goodness, he is returned to us," his father said quietly, "you can give it back to him." He looked down at the knife. "Gunnar's life was his to give for what he felt was right. You had nothing to do with that. Maybe some Finn lives because of you, and Gunnar will have less blood on his hands when he meets his Savior."

He straightened his back. "Now, you must do as Gunnar told you. You have a man's body. You have the skills of a seaman and you already know that you're a better fisherman than me, or Gunnar." He smiled. "It was you who got the gift of kenning the mind of those we seek beneath the water." He handed the puukko to Aksel. "The police will be on the roads—and the others, too." He looked at Aksel and Aksel nodded that he understood. "My cousin works for a shipping company in Stockholm. I will take you across to Holmsund. Now, say goodbye to your sisters and your mother."

9

Maíjaliisa went to every official who would see her. She was met with condescending sympathy. No one knew. Maybe Okhrana. Maybe Russian army intelligence. Whatever the case, the matter was out of their hands. Sorry about your daughter. From most, she felt a polite, silent disapproval. It was her daughter's choice to be a radical. She went to the army barracks to ask Corporal Kusnetsov for help. Kusnetsov looked out across the fields. When he turned to her, he shook his head no and walked off.

Maíjaliisa went all the way to Helsinki, staying there two nights with her cousin. After a week of fruitless searching, Maíjaliisa returned home to keep up with the chores and her obligation to the Laakkonens. Every night she wrote by candlelight in the barn to Finnish officials in the required Russian, painstakingly using the pastor's Russian/Finnish dictionary.

Then, sixteen days after Aino's arrest, the telegram from Maíjaliisa's cousin in Helsinki arrived: "Alive. On 11:16 train."

When Aino got off the train at Kokkola, Maíjaliisa saw that her cousin had given Aino fresh clothes. They hung on her gaunt body. Aino collapsed into her arms. Maíjaliisa winced when she pulled Aino's head against her chest; her head scarf was covered with wet spots. Maijaliisa pulled it back, exposing bald patches, oozing fluid where skin had been torn away along with hair. The Okhrana's notorious "goose-plucking."

When Aino leaned into her, Maíjaliisa saw the raw sores on her wrists. Watching her climbing painfully into the Laakkonens' wagon, she knew she'd been tortured in other ways. Mrs. Laakkonen immediately offered Aino their bedroom and she and Maíjaliisa shooed the men out of the house. Mrs. Laakkonen helped Maíjaliisa get Aino onto the bed and then left them alone.

Maíjaliisa recoiled when she saw the damage. Then she went to work, gently moving aside Aino's hands every time she tried to cover herself in shame. When she had done all she could, she lay next to Aino and let her sob it out.

She'd been kept alone for nearly a week, not allowed to sleep, slapped during questioning. But she'd not talked. Then they removed her clothes and doused her with water for five days. She proudly never cracked. That was when the goose-plucking started, and it wasn't just on her head. She'd been hung by her wrists with her shackled feet pulled up behind her, leaving her suspended in a sort of upright bow.

"He kept whispering over my shoulder, nuzzling his cheek against my ear, asking me for names," she sobbed. "God, his breath stank." She twisted to look at Maíjaliisa's face. "I never betrayed Voitto. Never." She started crying again. Maíjaliisa stroked her hair, gently murmering, rearranging it to cover as best it could the bald spots on her mangled scalp.

Aino groaned and twisted away to look at the wall. "But then he said just give us names of people you don't know, just who you've heard about. You'll betray none of your friends. I spit on him."

"Shh, shhh. My darling."

Aino was trembling. "There was a stool." She stopped. "There was a stool. They turned it upside down and . . ."

Maíjaliisa hugged here tightly.

"And they lowered me." Aino wailed, choking with the horror of what had happened and with shame at what she'd done. "I gave them every name I'd ever heard . . . Raitanen in Turku, three in Helsinki, and even one in Riga, Latvia." She clutched at her mother. "I never gave them Voitto or anyone in the cell."

When the crying stopped, in a husky voice she asked, "Will I have babies?"

Maíjaliisa caressed her hair, murmuring, "Of course, my baby." She pulled away slightly, her tone becoming clinical. "The cervix and everything behind it is untouched. You'll heal"—she looked Aino straight in the eye—"physically."

That night, Maíjaliisa dug up the ceramic jar she'd secreted in the wall of the barn. It held the money that she had managed to save after Matti fled. She helped Aino pack, carefully folding her good dress and second skirt in newspaper, placing them in a small leather valise, along with all of Aino's underclothes and a jar of viili starter. Every family had its own culture of viili, a Finnish yogurt, that often had been passed down for generations. It would be unthinkable to begin a new life without it.

Just before they climbed into the Laakkonens' wagon, Maíjaliisa handed Aino a letter she'd written to her sons. "You'll get there faster than the mail service. This explains everything. You know your brothers. They'll take care of you."

It was a very quiet ride. Aino was trying to take everything in, everything she could hold of her home in her heart, the gentle landscape with its thousands of lakes hidden in quiet birches, spruce, and pine trees, as if the retreating glacier had left behind tears that mourned its passing, the neat fields where rye, barley, and hay were shooting bright and green up to the white spring sky as they moved toward their full golden destiny in the nearly constant summer light, racing to grow to fullness against the retreating sun before Pokkanen laid the land to sleep under his frost and all the world would dream of spring again.

She ached to be able to say goodbye to Voitto. Instead, she stood before the train that would take her to Hanko on the south coast and said goodbye to what was left of her family, her mother. At Hanko she would take a boat to Hull in England and board another train there for Liverpool where she would embark for America. Crying was beneath both of them. Standing erect, her face controlled, Maíjaliisa said, "You keep your sisu." She gave Aino one last quick kiss and pulled back.

The last Aino ever saw of her mother was at the Kokkola train station, her face stoic and noble.

She sat down on the hard bench of the compartment, refusing to cry, feeling her own face hardened beyond anything she could have imagined just three weeks ago. She vowed that if she ever found out who'd betrayed them, she would kill him.

Three days later, as the steamer picked its way carefully between the rocky islands that surrounded Hanko, she stood on the deck watching the shore pines slide past and the islands recede in the wake. The next time she would see trees and islands would be from the rail of a ship on Willapa Bay in the state of Washington as she made her way south to her brother's farm on Deep River.

PART TWO

1904–1910

Prologue

The majestic westward-flowing river went without a name for millions of years, but for nearly four thousand years she was called Wimah, Big River, by the first immigrants to her shores. Since 113 years before Aino's arrival, she has been called the Columbia.

She begins life in rills along the immense north-south crest of a complex chain of mountains starting with the Selkirks in British Columbia, which merge into the Bitterroots of Idaho and Montana and then turn into the Grand Tetons of Wyoming. The rills become rivulets that become creeks that push and flow through waterfalls and rapids, pulled on by inexorable gravity to form the Duncan, the Kootenay, the Pend Oreille, the Kettle, and the Spokane, all flowing to join her. From the eastern slopes of the Cascade mountains that divide Oregon and Washington and merge into the Sierra Nevada of California, she is met by the Okanogan, the Wenatchee, and the Yakima. The immense Snake River, formed by the Boise, the Owyhee, the Malheur, the Salmon, the Grande Ronde, and the Clearwater, merges with her from the south. From the highlands of eastern Oregon, the Umatilla, the John Day, and the Deschutes add to her strength. She cuts through the scarp lands of the great lava flood of millions of years ago forming deep canyons and passes the sunrise side of the great mountain called Klickitat by the Yakima Indians and Adams by American settlers. She alone of all rivers has the strength to force her way through the Cascade mountains, themselves pushed ever skyward by the vast power of the Pacific and Juan de Fuca Plates diving beneath the North American continent where former ocean floors are turned into hot liquid that makes the land groan and tremble with the strain, until the lava bursts forth, forming peak after snow-covered volcanic peak from Mount Silverthrone by the Straits of Georgia in British Columbia to horizon-filling Ta-koma *of the Lushootseed speakers, the English-speakers' Mount Rainier, which broods, waiting until it can again pour lava into the Salish Sea, all the way to translucent Shasta and dark-skinned Lassen, volcanoes deep into California. The river, cutting faster than these mountains rise, forms the majestic Columbia River gorge that separates the perfectly proportioned maiden Loowit and Klickitat's angry rival for her hand, fierce Wyeast, named by the British navy, Mount Saint Helens, and Mount Hood.*

Now, with the force of all her tributaries, she emerges alone from the western end of the great gorge to meet the broad north-flowing Willamette, giver of rich, black earth. Then, through forests so thick the sun does not reach their floors, flowing a mile wide, flowing two miles wide, flowing west, adding the rain-swollen waters of the Lewis and the Cowlitz Rivers, now flowing five miles wide, she reaches her mother the sea, bearing her salmon fry, depositing her silt and sand, the carved rock of her battles with the land, forming twenty-mile-long beaches on both sides of the ship-killing bar where the great river meets the surging tide, throwing up forty-foot standing waves as she shudders and bludgeons her way back to her origins, the sea, fecund with latent heat, cold to the human touch, but the source of enormous energy, feeding and growing the vast ocean storms that move ever eastward until they collide with the mountains and transform into the steady rain that nurses the rivulets, causing them to grow like sprawling children, until they are born again in the great river that cycles, cycles . . .

Where the great river reaches the Pacific, a vast temperate rain forest grows faster and denser than the Amazon jungle, producing trees inconceivable to Europeans and Asians before they saw for themselves. The first people to see these forests did not penetrate them. Moving ever south in the blink of time when the great glaciers sucked the shoreline thirty miles from their present position and formed a bridge for them to cross from Asia, they settled along the rising shorelines, rivers formed by the melting glaciers, taking only from the very edge of the vast forest the occasional cedar to make a canoe to help gather fish and whales from their mother, the sea, to help them build shelter against the rain and snow falling from their father, the sky. The ice passed from memory. The forest, sea, and rivers provided; time, like the salmon that every year returned without fail, cycled, cycled . . .

Strangers came in canoes large enough to hold small villages and took away the pelts of the sea otter and beaver, leaving iron axes, beads of wondrous color that glowed with light, and an overwhelming knowledge that those who came first had known only a tiny part of a vast world. New villages rose, made of the same cedar and fir, but the dwellings were stiff and angular and had eyes that allowed you to see through their walls. The strangers kept on cutting the cedar and fir, forming the logs into lumber and sending the lumber on the huge ships to that vast unknown world where the trees must not grow. So, too, these people without trees were a people without salmon, and the strangers caught the salmon, cut the salmon to put in metal containers, and shipped the containers, as they did the lumber, to the distant insatiable people who lived where the salmon did not. And the large ships came back for more and cycled, cycled . . .

1

When Matti left home in the summer of 1904, he had fled inland. Avoiding towns, taking on odd jobs at farms for food, he moved steadily north, the land becoming increasingly forested and then increasingly barren as the forest gave way to reindeer country. After several months, he crossed an unmarked border into Norway. At Hammerfest, a lively center where Lapps, Finns, Swedes, Russians, and Norwegians all came together to trade with each other and the wider world, he talked his way on to a boat headed for England, not using and not telling anyone about the money he'd sewn into his clothes. There, he used part of it to buy passage to Boston, near where he found work in a shoe factory in Fitchburg. As soon as he'd earned enough for a train ticket, he set out for his brother's farm on Deep River.

As Matti was leaving Boston, Ilmari was climbing over the trunk of a huge, newly felled Oregon oak. He had spent most of the summer clearing ground for more pasture by felling the smaller trees and drilling fire holes deep into the larger ones. It pained him, but alfalfa didn't grow in shade.

Ilmari had named his farm Ilmahenki, after Ilmatar, the spirit of the air. It stood on the south bank of Deep River, twelve miles by river east of its mouth on Willapa Bay. About a mile downstream was the nascent settlement of Tapiola, which, in the dreams of John Higgins, who'd established a general store next to a natural landing site at the edge of tidewater, would someday become a thriving valley town.

The house was surrounded by newly planted apple trees and hay fields, wrested from the forest through labor that equaled that of any Russian penal colony. The fields were dotted with cattle that grazed around piles of limbs and smoldering seven-foot-high stumps, which were slowly disappearing because of the drilled holes into which Ilmari stuffed hot coals that he relentlessly tended day and night. It was also the way he'd felled the enormous old-growth hemlocks and Douglas firs, many twelve or fourteen feet in diameter. He let fire do his work, while he plowed and planted between the massive trees and stumps. He'd have starved if he'd tried to clear them before planting.

Slow and majestic beating of large wings caused him to look upward, and he watched an eagle descend onto a branch of one of the light-barked alder trees he had left standing by the river to remind him of the birch trees in Finland. The eagle ruffled itself slightly and then remained still, its eyes intent on the river. Ilmari tried to imagine what the river looked like through the eagle's eyes. The sun, usually hidden by clouds in June, warmed his back as he lost track of himself, just being with the eagle and the alders and the river. A flicker of white belly feathers caught his eye as another bird flashed against the edge of the dark forest. Long white feathers with black ends formed what looked like stripes on the bird's tail, which flared wide, slowing the bird's speed so it could perch on the limb of a Douglas fir. It turned its head toward him and a prominent yellow beak identified it as a yellow-billed cuckoo. Ilmari's neck hair rose. He once again got *the feeling*, the one other people didn't get, the feeling he couldn't explain. The yellow-bill normally lived east of the Cascade mountains. Someone was coming. Maybe two. The eagle and the cuckoo.

Ilmari's house had grown from a single lean-to cabin to the bottom floor of a planned two-story farmhouse that he hoped someday would shelter a wife and children. The interior of the house had no furniture other than a raised platform he used as a bed in the single bedroom, a kitchen table and four chairs, and an ornate red-velvet couch a mill owner, short of cash, had offered in lieu of payment. It had taken Ilmari two days to haul it home, first by steamer to the mouth of Deep River and then by his flat-bottomed rowboat. Ilmari took it good-naturedly when his friend Hannu Ullakko kidded him about the yet unknown woman he hoped to entice with the couch.

The couch stood on a hard-packed dirt floor in an otherwise empty living room with a river-stone fireplace and chimney. In the kitchen, however, Ilmari already had laid a floor of clear Douglas fir planks, upon which he proudly set a large wood-burning kitchen stove built from various scrap parts he picked up for next to nothing. He'd placed the stairs to the incomplete second story in the kitchen, because he knew that the kitchen would be the warm center of the family and where the children could dress on cold mornings. He also envisioned a wife sitting before the fireplaces, should fortune smile on him. Single Finnish girls, even single Scandinavian girls, even any girls at all were rarer than cash.

Close to the house was the first thing Ilmari had built: the low, six-by-eight-foot chimneyless sauna made of logs, dug in against a gentle hill and covered with turf. Once it was completed, he'd slept on its two-foot-wide stair-step benches and cooked on its kiuas, not much more that a pile of round river rocks heated during the day by burning the slash from tree clearing. When the day's work was done, he would let the smoke out and stay warm next to the hot stones throughout the night. Every Saturday evening, without fail, he heated the kiuas until some of the rocks glowed. Throwing water from Deep River onto the stones, he filled the sauna with löyly, the sacred cleansing steam, and remembered Suomi.

"Yes, yes, someone is coming," Hannu Ullakko said. "So is Christmas." Ullakko lifted the saucer onto which he'd poured his coffee and sucked the coffee in through a sugar cube that he held between his lips.

Ilmari smiled. He expected no other reaction from his recently widowed friend.

The two often met on Sunday afternoon to have coffee together. Sunday was the day of rest, but neither took more than a couple of hours. Only God could get His work done in six days.

Ilmari had borrowed money from Ullakko, who owned a prosperous dairy farm, to build a blacksmith shop that stood just downstream from Ilmahenki, close to the river. Ilmari didn't like being in debt, but he liked even less cutting his timber, which many did to get much-needed cash. For Ilmari, timber was wealth that grew every day. It could be looked at and smelled. Ilmari didn't trust banks, and holding wealth in the form of paper seemed foolish.

Farmers around Tapiola needed blacksmith work and Ilmari's business had grown with each new logging operation and sawmill. Still, Ilmari was diversifying, ever aware that good fortune would eventually turn to bad. He paid for two Hereford cows and the stud fees to breed them. Loggers loved beef but hated it canned. Beef cattle also meant he wouldn't be tied to twice-daily milking, other than tending one or two cows for his own milk and butter. Ullakko, too, had prospered, not only selling dairy products to the camps but also turning his hay into a cash crop to feed the enormous appetites of the oxen the logging companies used to drag the logs to the edge of water where they could be floated to a mill. Ilmari, however, had repaired two of the new steam donkeys. He knew that the price of hay would plummet.

They were in Ullakko's kitchen, whittling large cooking spoons out of cedar with their puukkos, the male equivalent of knitting. No one was idle, ever. From skilled hands and a sharp puukko came tools and artifacts of all kinds: duck decoys and fishing lures, knobs and handles, kitchen utensils, gate latches. When there wasn't an immediate need for something useful, Ilmari worked on a nativity crèche and a kantele with more strings than the one he used now. The coffeepot empty, the friends broke up. Ilmari didn't bother with a kerosene lamp to find his way to Ilmahenki. The sun set around eight, but the long-lingering July days didn't bring full dark before ten, long after his bedtime. Dawn and the next day of work came around four in the morning.

He said goodbye to Ullakko and set out for Ilmahenki. He passed the grave of Ullakko's wife, buried next to a copse of dogwood. Ullakko had asked him to read the burial service. The nearest pastor was in Astoria, and although he came often, he couldn't always do so.

Just half a mile from Tapiola, Ilmari passed a huge lightning-struck snag, over twenty feet tall, whitened with age and scarred black from fire. Ilmari thought of God's wrath, striking down from heaven. Why would God make a man prosperous enough to lend someone money and then take away his wife and baby? Why would He give and then take away Ilmari's own baby brother and two sisters? Why was there hell? He thought of burning, screaming with pain, forever. How could God be so cruel? But he had sent Jesus to save him, so he wasn't cruel. He was just. He decided to stop thinking, because no one should question God.

When he reached Ilmahenki, he saw a figure standing on the far bank, barely observable against the wall of the forest that covered the high hills across Deep River to the north of Ilmahenki. It was Vasutäti, the name given to the old Indian woman by the Finnish immigrants. It meant "Aunty Basket." Every two or three weeks Vasutäti made the rounds of the farms and logging camps selling her handwoven baskets. She was the last of the Ini'sal Indians, a small tribe of Chinookan-speakers who had lived on Deep River until they were decimated by European diseases.

Ilmari hesitated, then raised his hand in a tentative greeting. She stood there for a moment and then she, too, slowly raised her hand. It seemed to him that the distance between them, the river itself, shrank to nothing and he was captured by dark solemn eyes. Then the woman turned into the forest and disappeared.

He continued toward the house in the twilight, puzzling over the incident. In a surge of longing, he imagined a wife coming to the door to greet him.

He sighed and went in. The house had no curtains at the window, no cupboards to hold Sunday dinner dishes, and no furniture other than the red couch and utilitarian wood chairs. The knitted wool cap that his mother had made him six years earlier hung tattered on the wall. A good wife would have been embarrassed to let him out in public with such a rag on his head. He glanced at the dirt floor, devoid of the ubiquitous rag rugs that Finnish women seemed to turn out in endless profusion, all the while catching up with their neighbors, gossiping, or just quietly weaving them before bed by the embers of the evening cooking fire. If he'd tossed a pebble in the center of that house, its fall would have echoed off the walls and in his heart for hours.

He didn't feel like going to sleep. Maybe sighting the yellow-bill meant someone to love was coming, someone who would love him back.

He took his kantele from the nail where it hung in its soft leather bag and walked to the river, using only the pale light fading in the west. Kerosene was expensive. Idly he started to strum the chords to "Beautiful Savior." *King of creation. Son of God and son of man.* He tried to feel what that meant through the music. *Son of God and son of man.* He softly sang this phrase over and over. Then he went silent, listening only to the chords sung by the vibrating strings of the kantele. He began to pluck a single string, matching his voice to it with a simple, single, open vowel sound. He could hear four overtones from the single humming kantele string and he focused on matching the overtones from his voice to those of the string. Over and over. No thought. Just over and over, he matched his voice to the rich and complex vibrations. Over and over. He felt his way to the sound between the overtones, the sound the ear cannot hear.

Suddenly, light! Light flooded Ilmari's mind, its brilliance obliterating everything around him, yet making everything clear. Every tree, every leaf, stood alone yet was part of an all-pervading fluctuating light that condensed to form it and then expanded to condense again into another object. The light swept through him like a storm hitting the coast after passing over three thousand miles of open sea, bending the tops of the Douglas firs and cedars, wrenching hemlocks, alders, and Oregon oaks from the earth.

Ilmari became aware of the sound of the river and opened his eyes to early dawn. In the east, in a luminous sky, Venus shone next to red Aldebaran, both still outshining the gathering light of the rising sun. He saw them as if for the first time with the clarity of someone newly birthed. He staggered into the house holding the kantele to his chest, weeping. He sat on his bed and stared at the wall. He knew there would be no sleep. The cattle needed tending; the cow needed milking.

* * *

He pondered the vision all that day, not knowing what to make of it. Maybe God wanted something from him. When Jesus appeared to Saul on the road to Damascus, Saul became Paul and brought Christianity to the Roman Empire. He, however, was no Paul. He thought about going to see Pastor Hoikka in Astoria but decided against it. Hoikka would probably think he'd been visited by the Devil. The Devil—people thought of Satan as some sort of bad person, just as they thought about Jesus as some sort of good person. What he experienced last night was beyond anything so small as a person. As if this *something* humans called God could be reduced to something they could grasp, like a father in the sky. Was Jesus *really* God? Was *God* really God? He tried to put the thought away. Maybe it came from the Devil. What had happened last night was ungraspable but experienced. What was he to do with this experience? He prayed for an answer, but no answer came.

Then there was the visit from the eagle and the cuckoo.

Ten days later, on a rainy fall afternoon, Ilmari looked up from his forge to see the figure of a man silhouetted in the door of the smithy.

"Yes?" he asked in English, letting the bellows ease.

The man walked up to him. In the light of the glowing charcoal Ilmari recognized Matti's face. Matti's body was totally unfamiliar. So, Matti was the eagle. They shook hands. "So, you've come," Ilmari said.

"Yoh," Matti replied.

That night, he made up a bed for Matti in the sauna and went to his own bed pondering how a brief unthinking act like Matti's could set someone on a previously unknown path, his life forever changed. As Paul wrote to the Corinthians, "In a moment, in the twinkling of an eye . . . we shall be changed." Maybe Paul was referring not only to life after death.

Before putting the lamp out, Ilmari opened his Bible, as he always did. This entire week he'd been reading Matthew. He liked Luke better for the stories, especially for the Christmas story, but there was something more plain and fundamental about Matthew. It appealed to

Ilmari's practical side, which was always battling the part of him that kept searching for meaning in what is not seen but could be understood at least by him, even if he could never explain it. Like the experience with the kantele. Something similar had happened three times before, ever since he'd seen angels as a kid when his sisters and brother died. As far as he could tell, no one else had experiences like this and they were of no practical use.

Then it was there, in Matthew, chapter 16, as clear as MENE MENE TEKEL UPHARSIN. "And I say also unto thee, that *thou* art Peter, and upon this rock I will build my church; and the gates of hell shall not prevail against it." Here was a clear practical response that could balance out these occasional, often frightening experiences of his. He decided to build God's church in Tapiola and then fell asleep.

2

That fall, Matti helped Ilmari considerably, adding to the house, improving the blacksmith shop, tending the cattle, but it was clear that by December, the food Ilmari had put ahead was running low. What cash Ilmari got from the blacksmithing could be much better used to improve Ilmahenki than to feed Matti. At Christmas, Ilmari had given Matti a puukko that he'd forged himself, to replace the one Matti had left in Suomi. Then he told Matti to find work.

"You'll be sixteen in August. Tell them you're sixteen now. You can do a man's work."

Matti hefted the puukko. He looked up at Ilmari. "Kiitos. For this, for everything."

"Yoh."

The only paying jobs for someone who didn't speak English were logging and fishing. Matti had done neither, but he had a better chance getting on with a logging company.

"You go up to Reder's Camp. Ask for Alma Wiitala. She's a Vanhatalo, Mother's second cousin. You tell her Maíjaliisa's your mother and I'm your brother."

He'd done that, walking to Willapa Bay and then turning south to where John Reder's rail line led back into the hills where Reder's Camp stood. Reder Logging was in full operation now that the higher-elevation January snow was melted and the days were getting longer. Matti stood beside the steam donkey, where John Reder was up on the skid pointing to a huge block hung on a stump about two hundred meters down in a ravine from the steam donkey. He'd seen big trees by now; Ilmari had lots of old growth right at Ilmahenki. He had never seen anyone move one of those trees. Logs lay on their sides, rising well above a man's head. Men, tiny against the hillsides, scrambled to the logs, hauling heavy lengths of steel cable. A small boy tugged on a long wire, making some sort of signal on a steam whistle attached to the steam donkey. The man running the donkey signaled back. Men far down below in the ravine seemed to scramble for their lives as power was applied to one of the huge spools on the donkey, drawing the cable tight, lifting the log, then pulling it bouncing up the hill to where Matti was standing. That log must have weighed tons. These little men, like ants in this vast landscape, were moving what to most people would seem immovable. Matti felt excitement rising in his throat. He looked out over the logging show, as it was called, and saw a huge old-growth Douglas fir slowly fall to the ground, visibly shaking the standing trees around it.

Ilmari had told him all about how dangerous it was. Those logs could roll and crush; those cables could break and fly, taking off arms, legs, and heads. Ilmari, however, hadn't talked about the excitement. Matti wanted to run down into the ravine. He could think of nothing he'd rather do, right now, than be a logger.

The man who ran the steam donkey blasted on a steam whistle and John Reder jumped down to the ground. He stopped when he saw Matti. He didn't look like an owner, at least the kind Matti knew about. He wore the same caulked boots as all the other loggers and the same canvas trousers, cut off at the top of the boots. The only visible difference was that he was older and wider. Not fat. Anyone with an ounce of extra fat was fatter than these loggers.

Reder growled something in English that Matti didn't understand, but Alma Wiitala had prepared him for this.

"Matti Koski," he said, pointing to himself. "Alma Wiitala cousin. Ilmari Koski brother. Good verker, me."

Reder studied him. "How old?"

Matti stood as tall as he could. "Seven ten," he said.

Reder chuckled. "Not likely." He held his hands out, palms up.

Matti showed him his callused hands. "Good verker," Matti said.

Reder grunted. It was approval. To Matti Koski, age fifteen, unable to speak the language in a new world, it was the equivalent of the voice of God. Reder shouted something to the man running the donkey and then walked away. Matti Koski knew then that someday, he didn't know how, he would be like John Reder.

He was put to work splitting firewood to feed the steam donkey. It wasn't logging. It was hard, relentless, exhausting, and boring work.

At the close of the day, a Finn named Toivo Huttula, who called himself a hook tender, explained that Matti was a greenhorn, and none of the men wanted him anywhere near them, because he'd kill them along with himself. If he proved he could work hard splitting wood, then when there was an opening, maybe he would get a job doing something called choker setting. Matti didn't think twice about the meaning of "an opening."

Three weeks after Matti started, Reder came up to him with an envelope. Matti's English was slowly improving because of help from fellow Finns in the bunkhouse. That, however, had a downside. It was too easy to speak Finnish all the time, making learning English slower. He managed to understand that Reder wanted him to take the envelope to his wife, Margaret, who lived in their house in Knappton. Then Reder smiled and handed him a quarter. Matti's pay was seventy-five cents a day. "Fun . . . Knappton . . . wife . . . good worker."

Matti looked at Reder with his mouth open, the quarter in one hand and the letter in another.

"Get," Reder barked. Matti ran for the trailhead.

It took over an hour to run to Knappton, but it felt good. His shoes were nearly gone, but he didn't have enough money for caulk boots yet. Besides, he was afraid he'd be laughed at for being pretentious if he bought them before he was really a logger. When he came out of the forest the Columbia River lay before him. He gasped. The river had to be ten kilometers wide. He couldn't see any possible way to build a bridge across it, unless one could sink pilings where the water was shallow and then span the deeper water with an arched trestle. The little town of

Knappton, built out over the river on pilings, seemed to be clinging to the hillsides, like a limpet on a rock.

Reder had written his wife's name on the envelope and people directed him to a three-story house, built on solid land but land so steep that the lower-floor basement was exposed only on the front end. He knocked on the door. The maid answered, and he pointed at the envelope. The maid smiled and held out her hand. Matti hesitated. He said, "Wife. Mr. Reder."

The maid laughed. She pointed to herself. "Me. Margaret Reder." She held out her hand showing a wedding ring and a diamond engagement ring. "Wife. John Reder." She held out her hand for the letter. Margaret Reder motioned him inside where she opened it in front of him. "He remembered," she said, beaming at the open letter. He tried not to stare. There was a rug made of wool that covered the whole living room. His mother could have clothed the family for years with that much wool.

Margaret sat down neatly on a couch that was twice the size of the old battered red one at Ilmahenki. Her small feet were tucked slightly into the couch, touching each other. Her dress flowed from her trim waist down to her shoes. It reflected light. Her face reflected light. He couldn't help himself and looked up the stairs with their polished walnut banister to where they disappeared into the next story, to the bedrooms. He'd heard that John Reder had come from Holland and started in Michigan, penniless. He'd made enough money to marry Margaret, whose father owned a lumber retailing business. Now, he had her and all this as well.

One envies only what one can achieve. Matti Koski envied John Reder. And he, Matti Koski, was now where Reder had started. Here—in America.

Nearing the end of the letter, Margaret smiled. She folded the letter and said, "My birthday." She beamed up at him, but Matti, not quite sure he'd heard her correctly, said nothing. "Speak English?" Margaret asked.

Matti nodded.

"Birthday," she said, pointing at herself. "Born. New baby. Me."

Matti nodded vigorously. "How old you?" he asked to be polite.

Margaret made an exaggerated mouth drop then laughed. "We don't . . . in America."

Matti looked at the floor.

"Twenty-three," Margaret said. She cocked her head and got him to look at her. "How old you?" She asked.

"Seven ten," he replied.

She gave him an I-don't-believe-you look.

"Five ten, but good verker."

She chuckled. "That's better . . . Mr. Reder OK, but I . . . him home . . . Saturday morning. Wait."

She went into the kitchen. When she came back, she handed Matti a quarter. For a moment he thought about showing her the quarter Reder had already given him. Only for a moment. With the fifty cents, he bought himself a lightweight denim jacket—an American denim jacket.

From that day forward, Matti Koski no longer just split wood. He split wood and soaked up everything possible about logging. At seventy-five cents a day, he had no idea how he would ever get his own company, but he had no doubts that he would.

3

ino's first impression of America was elbows and noise. People were hawking wares in languages she'd never heard before; everyone was pushing and shouting. Surprisingly, there were no soldiers or police to keep things orderly.

She boarded the train for Chicago at Pennsylvania Station. Sitting on her wood seat in the railcar as straight as she could, keeping her tattered hair covered with a kerchief, she watched the increasingly flatter countryside, feeling small and vulnerable. She didn't know enough English to even ask for food. She longed for the gentle landscape and ordered farms of Suomi. She longed for her mother.

She slept badly, unusually for her, often startled awake by unremembered dreams, her clothes soaked with cold sweat. It had been like this crossing the Atlantic as well. She dismissed the problem as a result of the ship's motion and now not paying for Pullman accommodations.

A week after boarding the train in New York, she reached Portland. There, she bought a ticket for Chehalis, Washington, where she bought another ticket on a different railroad to the town of Willapa on Willapa Bay, which opened to the Pacific. It had cost nearly ninety dollars to cross the country. All she had left from her mother's savings was a dollar and seventy-five cents.

She saw only one adult woman on the entire train. At first, she thought that this was because it was a Sunday; of course, the women would have been in church and not traveling. After watching a man vomit, however, she realized that over half of the men were suffering with

severe hangovers after a Saturday night of drinking and who knew what
else. She sat nervously next to two young men who smelled of alcohol,
tobacco, and three months of unwashed sweat soaked into long-sleeved
and long-legged wool underwear. The concept of a weekly sauna had
obviously not penetrated this far.

On their boots were small spikes, five or six millimeters long.
Those spikes on hundreds of similar boots had chewed the heavy
planking of the railcar floor into a mass of tiny spongy splinters that
became the protective coat stopping the boots from grinding right
through to the clicking rails beneath her.

The other woman sat at the far end of the car, a mother with a boy
and two girls under the age of six or seven and barefoot. The woman's
worn but clean black wool skirt went right down to her ankle-high
shoes. Above it she wore a loose long-sleeved cotton blouse. She sat
primly, reading, a pillar of self-contained calm, oblivious to the chaos
of the returning mill workers and loggers, most of whom Aino could
sense were trying not to stare at her, even though she was obviously a
mother and probably married.

Aino straightened herself, holding up her part of a woman's duty
to keep society civilized. She fought an urge to push her way into the
seat next to the woman with the children and start crying.

The train stopped every few miles, letting off boisterous loggers
and mill workers, some still drunk, at isolated sawmills surrounded by
mud and slash, the remains of logs considered too junky to process and
limbs and branches thrown in piles higher than a man's head that lay
whitening in the rain. It looked as if a giant had had a temper tantrum,
smashing the gigantic trees into slowly bleaching jackstraw piles of
splinters, stumps, and snags, and the occasional lengths of abandoned
steel cable, some as thick as a man's wrist, and broken blocks, heavy,
grooved wheels called sheaves encased between two steel cheeks
through which the cable was threaded. The stumps took her breath
away. Her whole family could stand on top of one of them with room
for twenty more people, maybe thirty if some of them sat on the edge
and dangled their legs over it. The image made her think of her mother.
She would be sleeping. Her father? She quickly thought about Ilmari

and Matti. Weren't they going to be surprised. She felt for and found her mother's letter.

Sometimes the train stopped at a larger sawmill, surrounded by wooden houses and shacks laid out on muddy grid sections of streets. Sometimes it stopped at a simple covered waiting platform in the middle of nowhere, a trail leading from it into the dark forest with trees she could not believe could grow so large.

The two young men next to her had been asleep. When they awoke, they spoke to each other in Swedish! It had been unimaginable that, hearing Swedish, she would feel like crying—until now.

She held on, but her face gave her away. The two young men looked at her, worried and concerned. One of them handed her a handkerchief she was sure had snot in it, but she took it, afraid to refuse. She dabbed her eyes with a daintiness that they probably thought was girlish, but she didn't want to get an eye infection.

"Are you all right?" The man spoke heavily accented English.

She didn't understand him, but said in Swedish, "Just homesick, I guess."

The man beamed and, in a loud voice, said, "Svensk flicka." At least six heads turned to look at her.

It felt so good to speak a language from home. She didn't even mind the men roaring with laughter when she asked if the boots with the spikes were an American method of defense. Informed they were used to secure footing, especially on slippery logs, she turned bright red. She wondered but was too shy to ask how a log could be so big a man would need to walk on it in the first place, but then she recalled the stumps.

The Swedes left her before the train got to Willapa but gave instructions for finding a boat to take her to the mouth of Deep River.

Deck space on the boat cost her twenty-five cents. Driven by a huge single-cylinder steam engine, the boat pushed briskly through the choppy water. Far to the west, across the bay, Aino made out a low-lying shore with huge trees silhouetted against a whitewashed sky. She took shelter from the cold slipstream in the stern behind the crude passenger cabin, watching the thin line of smoke from the boat's boiler fade into the receding distance, acutely aware she was the only woman on board.

A fight exploded between two young men shouting curses, one in English and the other in a language she did not know. Some playing cards fluttered away in the slipstream. Other men crowded around the two, none making the slightest move to interfere. The English-speaker lunged, but the other man stepped aside, neatly grabbing him and throwing him overboard. The men crowded to the rail, laughing and pointing, as the man floundered in the wake, receding with every second. Someone threw a life ring. The boat turned around and the man was hauled aboard, shivering uncontrollably. He stripped down to his long wool underwear and descended the ladder to stand next to the boiler, oblivious to being exposed in his underwear.

Her heart still beating, Aino seemed to be the only one who even remembered the fight.

Reaching the mouth of Deep River in the late afternoon, the boat pulled up to a wharf of rough timbers sitting on tall pilings driven into the mud. The skipper hurried because the tide was going out. She scrambled up a wood ladder and someone handed her satchel to her as the boat pulled away. She watched it continue south, self-consciously holding her hat to conceal her hair. A cool northwest wind blowing in from the sea to the west beyond the low-lying peninsula across the bay pushed her wool skirt tight against her legs, ruffling its hem. She had five quarters in the little purse tied to her camisole strap and tucked under her blouse.

A man who'd left the boat with her, and who was loading a small pile of goods into a rowboat, tipped his hat politely and said something she could not understand. Although smiling brightly, she could feel her lip trembling. The man sighed, thinking, then pointed to his chest.

"John Higgins."

She nodded vigorously and patted her own chest. "Aino Koski."

The man smiled, held up one index finger, touched her nose with the other, and brought the two together. "Koski. Ilmari. Matti."

She nodded yes so hard she thought her head would come off.

* * *

When Ilmari saw his sister pulling on one of the oars of John Higgins's rowboat as it rounded the bend below Ilmahenki, he smiled, thinking of Ullakko's rare attempt at a joke: "So is Christmas." He ran into the water and grabbed the boat's gunwale. Standing thigh-deep in the water looking at her, he said, "I thought someone was coming."

She said, "I have a letter from Mother."

They stood, looking at each other, love pouring from their eyes. John Higgins helped her from the boat, shaking his head at their very un-Irish impassivity. Ilmari carried her to the shore and put her down where she stood with the bottom of her skirt dripping while he returned for her valise and asked Higgins to tell anyone from Reder's Camp who happened by the store to tell Matti that his sister had arrived.

Ilmari set Aino's valise down in the house. She was fingering the knot on her head scarf. He gave her a quizzical look. She set her jaw and pulled the scarf from her head.

Ilmari took an involuntary breath, fighting anger and sorrow until he brought both under control. "What happened?" he asked.

"I was goose-plucked in prison."

"Prison," he repeated.

"Yoh. For politics."

When Matti arrived after dark and saw her, he looked at Ilmari, who looked down at the floor. "Who did this to you?" Matti asked.

"The Okhrana."

"For politics," Ilmari added.

"The bastards," Matti said, quietly.

"Mother says it'll grow back," Aino said.

She handed Ilmari Maijaliisa's letter, which he read out loud. The letter said there was still no news of their father and briefly described the raid, its outcome, and why Aino had to leave Finland. No one spoke when Ilmari folded the letter. They never spoke about it again.

It happened to be Saturday, so Matti didn't have to walk to Reder's Camp to start work at dawn as he would have any other night. Aino covered her head, and the three siblings drank coffee and talked and laughed until well after midnight.

Aino slept in Ilmari's bedroom, Matti in the sauna. Ilmari, sleeping on the kitchen floor, was awakened several times by Aino's screams. He went in twice to wake her. She looked at him, fear in her eyes, but wrapped her blankets around her more securely and went back to sleep.

The next morning, Aino made breakfast for her brothers. After they ate silently for a couple of minutes, Ilmari said, "You had night-mares last night."

"Yoh," Aino answered.

There was another long silence. Then Aino took her bowl of mush from the table and went outside with it.

Breaking a domino-size rectangle of sugar into two pieces with a sugar-cube cutter, Ilmari handed one piece to his brother and put the other in his own mouth. Both brothers poured coffee from their cups into their saucers and began sucking the liquid through the sugar cubes.

When he'd finished his coffee, Ilmari said, "It's too late to plant."

"Yoh," Matti replied. They both knew Ilmari had planted only enough to get him through the winter and spring.

"She has no cash-earning skills," Ilmari said.

A long silence ensued as they contemplated this.

"Ullakko's looking for a wife, since he lost Lena with the baby," said Ilmari.

Matti said, "Yoh." Ilmari nodded gravely. More silence.

"Ullakko's the best bet," Ilmari said. "He's got five kids to feed and a dairy farm to run. He won't care if she's red, blue, or green."

"You wouldn't be thinking about the money you owe Ullakko for equipping the smithy?" Matti asked.

Ilmari didn't reply.

It took Ilmari only thirty-five minutes to walk to Ullakko's first thing Monday morning. A dirt road, carved from the forest and paralleling the river, ran a mile into Tapiola and then out to the cluster of farms near Ullakko, where it stopped. County commissioners, who sat a full day by boat to the north in Willapa, the county seat, decided where roads would go and then levied a tax to build them. Because cash was scarce, each family paid the tax by providing a man, a horse, and necessary equipment.

Ullakko had been in America more than fifteen years, building a good-size dairy herd. Famous in the area for bringing in the first Helsinki cream separator, he increased his butter output, getting an exclusive supply contract with Reder Logging. Ilmari found him chopping weeds around the potato plants with his seven-year-old son and nine-year-old daughter, using their three hoes. His five-year-old daughter had a stick she used to loosen the dirt around the weeds, but most of her time was spent taking care of her three-year-old brother and eighteen-month-old sister just getting mobile.

Ilmari shook hands with Ullakko, gravely telling him good day, and Ullakko answered in kind. The two oldest children straightened up. Then Ullakko started chopping weeds again, and the two went back to work.

"My sister Aino has come from Finland."

Ullakko grunted and attacked the next space between potato plants.

"She's seventeen."

Ullakko looked up with soft blue eyes that had seen sorrow.

"She needs work," Ilmari said. "She could cook and take care of the children."

Ullakko thought for a moment. "It would be unseemly for her to live here with no woman in the house." He returned to his weed chopping. Ilmari understood Ullakko hadn't recovered from his wife's and baby's deaths yet, even though it had been nearly two months ago.

"If she stays with me at night, she could be at your place to fix breakfast, watch the children, fix lunch and dinner, and then come back." He watched for a reaction but saw none. "Come over to the house Sunday for coffee."

Ullakko stopped chopping but remained bent over, looking at where his hoe met the ground. After some silence, he said, "I need a wife, not a maid."

"She's going to need a husband in the next couple of years. Why not you? She's a good worker."

Ullakko's oldest daughter turned her head to look at Ilmari and then went back to work. Ilmari and Ullakko looked at each other saying nothing. Then Ilmari said, "You never know."

Just then Ullakko's toddler fell flat on her face and started wailing. They watched her older sister run to pull her up and then try to comfort her, holding her close in her arms. She was not much taller than the toddler.

Ullakko said, "Sunday. I'd have to leave by five to get back to milk the cows."

Ullakko hadn't had pulla bread since his wife died and the two brothers had not had pulla since they left Finland. Aino had gone into Tapiola to Higgins's store to buy yeast and cardamom seeds on Saturday and made it that night, using Maíjaliisa's recipe. It took four hours with the two risings. Since Ullakko was the only Finn other than her brothers Aino had had a chance to talk with, she was having a good time plying him with questions. By the time Ullakko left to milk his cows, he was smitten. He and Ilmari agreed that he would pay Aino two dollars and fifty cents a week plus the same food his family ate.

Just before Ullakko left for home, Ilmari said, "I'm the oldest brother. I take the place of the father here. I'm not without influence."

Ullakko stopped, thrust his hands into his pockets, sighed, somewhat embarrassed, and scuffed a shoe on the dirt road. "Ilmari, I'll be up against younger men. I'm thirty-five."

"Yoh, with an established cream and butter business and a house already built."

"You'd support a proposal, you know, if things went along all right?"

"How would you view the loan?"

Ullakko recognized the deal. "Gone. We'd be family."

The two men shook hands.

Matti had stayed after the meal to help with chores before hiking back to Reder's Camp. Ilmari found him wheelbarrowing cow dung to the compost pile and told him the news, quite pleased with himself. When Ilmari went to tell Aino, Matti followed to watch the fireworks.

With Matti so obviously tagging behind Ilmari, Aino knew something was up. She served her brothers coffee and seated herself. Then Ilmari proudly announced that he'd found her a job working for Ullakko. She responded by putting her coffee cup down and staring at him. "I don't want a job and I especially don't want a job with him. Aren't I pulling my weight?"

"No, no, it's—"

Matti came to Ilmari's rescue. "Aino, you're a good worker. The problem is cash." He waited to make sure she was listening. "Ilmari has to spend cash money for food until he gets the vegetable garden going and the first rye comes in. He also needs to buy tools, glass windows, pay stud fees or buy a bull, and pay road and property taxes. There's not enough cash to feed more than him. The only sources of cash here are logging, fishing, or working in a sawmill."

She knew she couldn't manage the chains and cables, much less swing a ten-pound double-bladed ax for the twelve to fourteen hours a day required by logging. The Chinook salmon in the Columbia often weighed more than a hundred pounds. She'd never get one into the boat. The traditional woman's way of contributing food—tending a large garden and helping with the livestock—was out; it was too late to plant and Ilmari could easily manage the few cattle he had. Where women were invaluable, even treasured, was taking care of the family. There was no family, and if there were, a wife would come with it.

"I could teach."

"There's no school," Ilmari said.

"Then tutor. I'm not going to be someone's servant."

Both brothers sighed. "Aino," Ilmari said. "No one is going to pay good money to have kids . . ." He hesitated.

"Wasting their time," Matti said.

Aino blew up with frustration. "Who do you two think you are? Father? What century do you think you're living in?" She knew Ilmari's intentions were good. She was ashamed that her arrival had saddled him with a problem and that she had nothing practical to offer to help solve it. She felt dependent and useless. They hadn't even included her in the discussion of the problem. "I'm not a servant. I'm better educated than both of you."

"You wouldn't have to go there on Sundays," Ilmari said, looking confused. "And he'll pay you some cash money, too." His voice was almost pleading. "You can buy things."

"You've never been a servant," she said very coldly and evenly.

Ilmari looked at her with a look of love that normally melted her heart. Now, it just added to her fury. She knew he had done the right thing. Then Ilmari said, "Maybe you'll find some nice fella."

That did it. Aino gave him her best withering look. "I already have a *fella*," she said. "Back in Finland."

The two brothers looked at each other, their eyebrows raised. "The one Mother wrote is hiding from the police?" Ilmari asked.

She fought back tears of frustration and anger. She realized that she'd thrown her coffee cup against the stove only when it shattered there. She ran out of the house.

The two brothers looked at each other across the table.

"She didn't mean it," Matti said.

"Yoh," Ilmari replied. Then he said, "She's not the way I remember her. Was she like this when you left?"

"Ei," Matti said, no. "The Okhrana . . ." he tailed off.

Finnish men don't cry, but the sadness the two felt for a sister who existed only in their memories, for a world that could hurt their beautiful fiery sister so badly, sat with them at the table and shared their coffee. They both knew it would be a long time before that unwanted guest departed, if ever.

4

U p by five every morning, Aino reached Ullakko's house by six thirty. At first, she felt dwarfed by the forest and nervous around the children. Having been the youngest girl, she had no experience with little children other than Matti, who was nearly her age. All she could remember about her baby brother, Väinö, was holding his tiny cold body. Within a few weeks, however, she began to relax. Ullakko's children all spoke English fluently, and she began to pick up English from the oldest daughter. She even began to enjoy the walk to and from Ullakko's. The blackberries were rapidly ripening, replacing the yellow, watery salmonberries and the few deep-red thimbleberries still around when she first arrived. She began carrying an old coffee can with a string handle threaded through two holes punched under the open rim to fill up on her way to Ullakko's and again before she returned to Ilmari's.

Her first blackberry pie was a disaster. Ilmari and Matti politely ate the filling, leaving the dense crust. She had no one to turn to, so was stymied about what went wrong. The next day, she remembered Maíjaliisa folding in chunks of lard. They'd had pigs in Finland, but none here, so on her second try she used butter. The brothers ate the crust. Progress.

When the blue huckleberries came in, she spent one evening picking the tiny berries until dark and came in with a full can. She was pleased to see that Ilmari waited outside the door and looked relieved when she appeared. On Sunday, the brothers said they liked the pie— the equivalent for Finnish men of a standing ovation.

*   *   *

In late August, Ilmari returned from Nygaard's General Store in Knappton with a typically fat letter from Maíjaliisa. The store served as the only post office in the area. Aino and Ilmari waited for Matti to come home Saturday night to read it, but it turned out he'd walked to a dance at Knappton and didn't get to Ilmahenki until two in the morning. Ilmari woke her and the three siblings sat around the kitchen table, the kerosene lamp in the table's center lighting their faces.

Aino was the best reader. The letter covered the usual late-summer farm talk: the size of the Laakkonens' oat crop, how a new kid was growing and would be a fine milker, two pages about new babies, changing the draft flow in Laakkonens' barn by adding another cupola so with the coming winter less condensation would be created. Then came the paragraph starting with "Aino, there is bad news . . ."

She stopped reading aloud. Her hand went to her throat as she continued reading to herself. She started to quiver. She looked at her startled brothers and, her hand still at her throat, stood, dropped the letter onto the table, and walked out the door. In the darkness, she fell to her knees and looked up in anguish at the cold August stars. The horror, the guilt, and the loss came out in one long, anguished cry. She put her face on the cool forest duff, and the old fir needles stuck to the tears on her face as she mumbled over and over through her sobbing, "I didn't know."

Inside the house, Matti picked up the letter and read it aloud to Ilmari. The young man from Kokkola, Oskari Penttilä, the one Aino called Voitto, had been in police hands for months. He had been found in Turku, just days after the raid, hiding in the home of a fellow traveler named Raitanen. The police had gone straight to the house and arrested both. Maíjaliisa conjectured that not only had the raid been compromised, but an informer had been planted in the cell. After weeks of inquiry, the Penttiläs, who were connected people, were informed that their son had died of natural causes while in prison. It was unlikely they would ever find out where he was buried.

Matti quietly put the letter on the table and looked at Ilmari. They both could hear Aino sobbing.

The night of the letter marked the moment when Aino retreated from them into a cold and secret world all her own. Her anguished guilt over betraying Voitto was channeled into icy anger toward all who opposed the revolution and hatred for whoever had betrayed them.

5

The same day that Aino read the letter from home, August 29, 1905, Aksel Långström, fourteen, was sick with fear. The *Elna*, a 215-foot iron square-rigger filled with 1,360 tons of manufactured goods and machinery, bound for San Francisco but still several thousand miles away, was smashing through towering waves just south of Cape Horn. Thirty-five feet at the beam, the *Elna* was barely making headway against the prevailing winds that hit the Drake Passage unimpeded after moving across thousands of miles of the empty South Pacific. In the southern hemisphere, August was a month of deadly winter storms.

Years of fishing gave Aksel sure sea legs, but he never in his wildest imagination envisioned the rolling foam-topped swells that virtually stood the beautifully built Swedish ship on her stern and then sent her pitching down the back of the swell as if diving straight to hell. With a huge groan, she shuddered to shake free of the tons of seawater crashing across her forward deck, threatening to tear the sailors from their precarious handholds on sheets or rails and wash them hurtling into the sea, as ephemeral and weak as smoke against a mighty wind. Then, like a seaborne Sisyphus, the ship clawed to the top of the next towering wave, as the sailors fought gravity and slippery decks to maintain their balance and their lives.

Clinging to a shroud, trying to keep from being washed overboard, Aksel watched a small sail set low on the mizzenmast suddenly tear loose from the yardarm and, clinging by a single sheet, stream to the stern like a wailing ghost. Aksel felt the sudden change in the motion of the ship and heard the helmsman cursing as he tried to control the bucking helm. Without the sail, the ship stopped making headway and was in peril of being swept sideways at the mercy of the seas. The captain, who'd made more than thirty voyages around the Horn, shouted orders through a speaking trumpet, and the first mate went past Aksel, clinging to whatever he could reach, shouting the names of two sailors. Two men struggled their way to the base of the mast, one of them holding another sail. After a brief hesitation as they looked at the shredded sail and then at each other, they began climbing.

Aksel clung tenaciously to the fife rail as he looked up with wonder, fear, and admiration for the two men, both of whom he'd gotten to know well on the long but relatively smooth-sailing voyage through the tropics. Then he was hit with a wall of icy water that wrenched him free of the rope he was clinging to. Gasping for air, clawing at the wood on the deck, he was picked up, turned upside down, and bounced toward the stern. He raised his arm and it hooked one of the shrouds, wrenching his shoulder, but he hung on, his other hand grasping his wrist. The wave passed, leaving him gasping. The mate shouted at him to get his ass forward to help a man wrestling with a sheet and he stumbled toward the bow.

He obtained the job because his father's cousin knew someone at the firm that owned the ship and had lied about his age. When he was shown to the forepeak where he would sleep, he was appalled by the narrow bunks above and below him, with only about six inches of headroom. If the sailor above him farted, the one below him felt the wind. He spent the first few days in a ragged haze literally learning the ropes. He'd crawl into his bunk still wet and fall asleep instantly. At first, the food was fresh and good. Then it started to rot. The meals turned to canned vegetables and meat and an obnoxious combination of lye-cured fish and oatmeal. He would shit the liquid remains of the rotten food, hanging his buttocks over the bow, wipe himself clean with cold seawater in the nearby bucket, and go back to work. But now, they faced this green-gray hell of howling wind and numbing water.

The small sail was set and immediately the ship came back to a more controlled heaving. One man started down just as a freakish blast of wind hit the ship from the side. The man above him lost his footing. The ship heeled over, forcing his body out away from the mast and he clung there, his feet flailing in the air. Then, like a piece of paper whisked from the window of a moving train, he was gone.

Two days later they headed north, the coast of Chile to their starboard, the winter seas, if not friendly, at least not totally hostile. Aksel was reeving storm-damaged rigging when the mate sat next to where he was working. He lit a pipe, puffing at it vigorously. The smoke whipped astern and shredded to invisibility before it even reached the wheel.

"I've been watching you," the mate said. "You're quick and you've got good sea legs for someone so young. How come?"

"I fished with my father ever since I can remember. Over by Karleby in Finland." He gave the Swedish name for Kokkola.

"How old are you, anyway?"

Aksel thought quickly. What had his father's cousin said? What could he get away with? He was big for his age, but the still-downy hair on his face might betray him. "Just turned seventeen, sir."

The man grunted and puffed on his pipe, watching Aksel work. "I don't believe you, nor do I care. I'm short a top man."

Aksel took a deep breath and looked at the distant shoreline. "I know, sir. Bergerson."

The mate nodded. "Bergerson. He was a good sailor." He was silent for some time. Aksel continued working.

"You'd get a raise and move aft to the top man's berth area."

Aksel looked up at the mast swinging against the gray sky and gulped.

"Do I get the raise as soon as I start?"

The mate laughed. "Hell no. We pay you for what you can do not what you can learn. I'd guess you'll be earning your keep soon enough, though."

Aksel licked his lips, looking up again at the swinging mast, remembering how easily Bergerson had been swept away. Then he looked at the mate and said, "I'll do it. Thank you."

6

Aino could feel Ullakko watching her as she washed the dinner dishes. She wasn't at all worried that he would harm or even frighten her; he wasn't that sort of man. She just wished he wouldn't moon at her with those sad blue eyes of his. An image of Voitto waiting for her by the old church in the darkness, the glow of his cigarette, a memory of the feel of him through all their winter clothes as they hugged. She looked at the plate in her hand. She looked at her hand, red and raw from harsh soap and hot water. It had been five days since she'd read the letter and she'd thrown herself into her work at Ullakko's to bury the pain. She understood Ullakko's longing, but he was an old man and life was hard. She saw the police storming into Raitanen's house where Voitto was hiding. She had given them Raitanen's name. Fighting anguish and anger, she slammed a plate down on the counter next to the sink a little harder than she'd wanted to. Ullakko moved his head back a little in surprise. She sighed. "It's getting dark," she said, turning to him. The September days were getting shorter. "I'd better get going."

"Yoh," he said.

Aino took off her apron and hung it on the wall in the ensuing but not unexpected silence. The kitchen was gloomy with only the waning light coming through the window. No need to waste kerosene until it was too dark to see. The little five-year-old came running into the kitchen and hugged Aino's knees. She buried her face in Aino's long skirt and then looked up at her. "Take me with you. Take me with you."

Aino touched the little girl's hair, then stood straighter and went for her coat. The little girl trailed after her, no longer grasping her skirt. Aino put on her hat and went to the mirror to make sure it was on properly. She saw her face with her glasses and frowned at it. "It's too far for a little girl to walk and besides, you'll miss bedtime," she said. She knew the girl hadn't expected any other answer.

Her big sister came in the room. "Quitting time," she said in English.

"Qvit-ting time," Aino repeated.

"It means it is time to stop working," the girl said in Finnish. "I quit," she went on, "means 'I won't work anymore.'"

"I qvit. You qvat. They qvut."

The girl laughed, adding to Aino's frustration with this language that was so different from Finnish. This girl had probably never read anything besides that stupid Sears Roebuck catalog, Aino thought darkly.

"I quit. You quit. They quit," she said.

"Qvit, qvit, qvit? It's a stupid language. It's no wonder the Norwegians pick it up so fast."

The girl laughed at the joke and Aino felt better.

Ullakko went to the kitchen window and looked outside. It was raining, and the heavy clouds were bringing darkness on fast. He turned to her. "I'll go with you. I kept you here too long."

She was heading for the door. "No need. I'm fine." She did not want to owe him any favors. It was bad enough being his servant.

"No, no, no. No problem," He said. He put a fresh candle in the square glass-enclosed lantern and lit it. Aino waited impatiently. There was no stopping him from coming.

They walked silently on the dirt road, the quavering light of the lantern just reaching the dark forest at their sides, to be lost in the darkness behind them. They came out of the tunnel of the forest and they saw the dim light of a candle showing through a farmhouse window across a cleared field. Ullakko finally spoke. "It gets dark early," he said.

Aino raised her eyebrows, imploring the heavens, but he couldn't see her doing it. "It's nearly November," she said, not wanting to be impolite.

"Yoh."

The road went into a patch of alders and brush. She heard rustling. Just last week Ilmari killed a cougar that had been prowling around his cattle. Suddenly, in spite of herself, she was glad Ullakko had come along.

When they got to Tapiola, faint light from the warehouse by the boat landing softly lit the dirt street. "You don't need to come any more," she said. "It's only a mile and you need to get back and put the little ones to bed."

Ullakko held the lantern up to see her face. It illuminated his own, along with his yearning blue eyes at the same time. "Really, I'll be fine."

Ullakko nodded and smiled at her. He handed her the lantern. "Here, you take this."

She refused the first time, but on the second offer she took it, secretly glad he'd let her have it. It meant he'd walk back in the dark, but then he was a man.

"Keep it," he said. "I mean it's yours. You'll need it now that the days are getting shorter."

Every time she thought she'd come even with him, he did some other kindness that put her right back in the hole again. She thanked him and took the road to Ilmari's. She could sense him watching her as she moved in her small circle of light into the darkness. She didn't want to turn around and give him any ideas. She passed the old snag on the north side of town without really seeing it, thinking about Voitto, thinking about the coming revolution.

Upon reaching Ilmahenki, she stopped and blew out the candle, feeling the spirit of the air after whom Ilmahenki was named moving all around her. Off in the distance, with only the faintest light from a candle showing through a window, she heard Ilmari playing the kantele and singing. She stood there, the wind rustling the few remaining birch and alder leaves, the slow response of the Douglas fir boughs seeming to move with Ilmari's song. A fine mist had started falling, cooling her face. She became aware of the smell of her damp wool skirt. Suddenly, she was overwhelmed with love for her brothers, here with her in this dark forested land with its distantly separated spots of light. An ache rose in her heart for Finland and her family, and then her whole body ached for Voitto. But that ache turned quickly to revulsion. It seemed as if that stool leg was still there between her legs. In her mind's eye, she pictured herself hanging there, heard herself saying the name Raitanen.

Now weeping, looking into the darkness above, imagining Voitto listening to her, she whispered, "I will never betray you again." She didn't say it aloud, but she felt then that she'd never marry another. She would dedicate herself to the revolution. She saw herself undergoing a novitiate, renouncing the world, expiating her guilt.

She breathed deeply to stop herself from crying. She could not, however, stop the trembling that now seized her as it had been doing at unexpected moments ever since she arrived in America. She remembered her sisu.

By the time the *Elna* crossed the equator, Aksel was a skilled seaman. He'd come to like the solitude of the crosstree so far above the decks and would sit there when he could, watching for whales, seabirds, anything to break the monotony and get away from the cramped quarters belowdecks. He also went there when he was terribly homesick. He would look east, trying to imagine flying across South America and then the Atlantic like a seabird, flying straight home to see his mother, father, and sisters and, hopefully, Gunnar. He could see Gunnar smiling at him and tousling his hair with a big callused hand. Maybe it turned out all right. He could not know because he always moved ahead of any mail. Where would his parents send a letter anyway?

When the *Elna* reached San Francisco in October, Aksel was the best top man of the crew.

The skipper allowed them only enough American dollars to have a hell of a time ashore while the ship was being unloaded. Giving them what they were owed before they got back to Stockholm would only invite desertion. Aksel hit the saloons with the rest of them but soon proved not as able in this particular seaman's skill. He was throwing up bad food and worse beer after just five hours.

He made his way to the docks and was dry heaving over the water when the mate and a couple of Aksel's new friends came up behind him, laughing. Although mildly intoxicated, they seemed unimpaired. Aksel rose stiffly, taking his hands from his knees. He looked at them darkly.

"Hey, Aksel. We got something for you." There were muffled laughs.

"What?"

"Something you've never had before."

"I can't eat a goddamned thing."

Laughing, they frog-marched him back toward the center of the town.

The interior of the brothel was dark. Kerosene lamps set in sconces barely illuminated the unpainted walls of clear redwood boards.

The mate was talking to the woman who supervised everything. They looked at Aksel, both smiling. Money was handed over and the woman walked to where Aksel was sitting at a card table, his back to it so he could see every passing girl.

The supervisor asked a question.

Aksel shook his head. "No English," he said. He saw his friends averting their eyes, suddenly looking at their drinks, smiles on their faces.

The woman reached to take Aksel's chin in her hand. "How old? One, two, three, four."

Aksel caught on and brightened. He spread both hands wide, then showed seven additional fingers. The woman laughed and showed him fourteen with her fingers. He blushed.

She led him up the stairs to a single bed in a small room, then walked out, closing the door.

After he had waited about ten minutes, a woman, maybe in her early twenties, her eyes older than her face, walked in. She was wearing a cream-colored silk robe, tied with a red cord with tassels at both ends. She said hello to him in Swedish. Aksel fell in love.

She wore silk stockings held up the old-fashioned way with a ribbon that went around her thighs and not with the little wire loops and straps that attached to the corsets that he'd seen in advertisements in Stockholm. Between the top of her stockings and the bottom of her corset, just peeping out and then disappearing with the flow of her chemise, he saw her pubic hair. He was embarrassingly erect.

"Lie down," she said in Swedish.

Aksel looked around for help, but no one else was there. She pushed him gently onto his back and, straddling him with her knees, she walked herself up his legs. She held a condom in front of his eyes. "This is called a rubber," she said, stretching it with both hands. "For obvious reasons." She wriggled slightly to get into a better position. "Did you ever hear of syphilis?"

Aksel nodded yes.

"Did you ever hear of gonorrhea?"

Aksel shook his head no.

"It makes you pee pus and it hurts like hell when you do it."

Aksel felt a little sick and his erection started to subside.

She got him hard again and rolled the condom on. Aksel gasped as she settled herself on him. "Easy . . . easy."

Aksel exploded and then fainted.

He knew he was out only a second or two because she was still slowly withdrawing from him when he came to his senses. "If you leave here with nothing else in that square head of yours, remember this. If you don't want to go blind, crazy, or run pus from your pecker for the rest of your life"—she pulled off the condom—"you use one of these." She swung her feet to the floor and threw the condom into a trash can. She then matter-of-factly put the washbasin on the floor, squatted over it, and began washing herself.

"That's it?" Aksel asked.

"That's it, sugar," she said. "It lasts longer the more you do it."

The woman stood up and dried herself with a towel that hung on the wall. Then she put on her silk robe. "Your ship's from Stockholm.

I grew up there. You don't sound like someone from Stockholm," she said.

"Ostrobothnia." Aksel felt as though he couldn't say a coherent sentence. "Near Karleby."

"Ahh. I used to work up in Nordland." Aksel's face went quizzical. "Way north of here. Quite a lot of your folks are there, especially around Astoria. That's in Oregon. Of course, the majority are Finnish-speakers."

"What do you mean, a lot?"

"Hell, sweetheart. It's like all of Finland moved there. No work at home and the Russians drafting the boys . . . More work than people up there."

"What kind of work?"

"Logging, sawmills, mostly." She was moving toward the door. He didn't want her to go.

"Are there fishermen in Astoria?"

"Is that what you did in the old country?"

Aksel nodded. "With my father and my . . ." He hesitated before adding, "big brother."

"Well you'd need them both if you want to get into fishing up there. The river is over eight kilometers wide and when the salmon run, you can cross the river on their backs."

Aksel looked at her askance. "Well, OK, maybe there is a little water between them." She paused, a memory lighting her face. "But I tell you this, and this is no bullshit, they call the biggest salmon up there Chinooks. Those goddamned fish weighed over a hundred and twenty pounds. That's nearly sixty kilos," she said impressively. "I don't even weigh that much."

Aksel's mouth was open.

"Of course you'd need your own boat to get into that game."

Aksel made a quick calculation. "How much do you get for logging or working in a sawmill?"

"Dollar and a half, maybe a couple of bucks a day. But you eat well in the logging camps. They'll board you, too. You pay for it, of course. But you'd never catch me in one of those fleapits they call bunkhouses.

Damp straw and wet long johns." Her voice trailed off and she looked into the distance. "I'd think twice about getting into the logging game." She didn't elaborate, but Aksel knew she was talking about danger. It excited him. How could it be more dangerous than fishing or sailing? "Do you have to speak English?" "You don't have to speak at all, sugar."

All the next day, as the ship was still unloading, Aksel was in a nervous state. He couldn't go home to Finland, at least not until Gunnar said it was all clear. Gunnar must be all right. Sweden wasn't home. He liked the crew, mostly, but months at sea living as close to them as head lice, followed by a few days drunk and then more months at sea, didn't seem appealing. On the one hand, he wouldn't get paid until they returned to Sweden. On the other hand, if many of his home people lived around Astoria, maybe it would be like going home.

Soaking wet and shivering slightly in the Sunday morning darkness, his wet seabag beside him, Aksel watched the *Elna*'s lights as she put out to sea. The seabag being a dead giveaway, he had slipped overboard on the harborside of the ship, not the dockside, so as not to alert anyone. The only thing that made him sad: he was leaving the first mate, who had been kind to him, short of a hand again.

When the ship was well out of the harbor, he hoisted the seabag on his shoulder and set off north. He had two dollars. He decided he could walk to Astoria. It couldn't be too far.

7

The next night, far to the north, Ilmari cried out, sitting bolt upright in his bed. He'd been awakened by the recurring dream that had plagued him since childhood: of going to collect snow in a darkness harboring a terrible lurking presence, biding its time to come into the house. Afraid, he'd gather snow into his hands and turn for safety to the light behind him, where he heard his sisters crying upstairs and his father asking for the snow to cool their fevers. Just past the doorway, the snow he'd gathered would turn to water, dripping from his hands to the floor, and he could not, could never, reach his sisters up the steep stairs.

He knew the dark presence in his dream was death. Death had bided its time, watching him fail. It had come into the house and taken his older sisters and baby brother. He felt a dizzying terror. It was waiting outside to take him.

He put on his outside clothes over the long underwear in which he'd been sleeping and walked to the hand pump on the kitchen counter where he pumped enough water to fill the blue-and-white-flecked coffeepot. He threw into the pot a handful of roasted barley supplemented by the powdered remains of a few carefully boiled and then evaporated hand-ground coffee beans. He loaded kindling into the firebox and blew the coals into life: fire, being blown into life, fire, consuming life, endlessly, forever. But maybe hell wasn't fire. Maybe hell was his dream, endlessly going in and out of the doorway, his sisters crying, the snow melting—in and out, endlessly, forever. How much better to just be extinguished: to be like fire, put out by cold water from melted snow, extinguished forever into oblivion without pain.

He longed to see Pastor Jarvi and the old church. Then *the idea* came thundering back. He'd been asked by God to build God's church here, by Deep River, a church to comfort those like him who mourned, to fortify the weak of spirit like him, so they would enter the kingdom of heaven, so they would no longer fear death. Perhaps when he finished the church, this terrible dream would let him be. It was time to start. He'd start by telling Aino what he'd never told anyone.

Aino woke up to the sounds of Ilmari saying the beatitudes aloud. She smelled the coffee roiling in the water and dressed hurriedly in the dark. She came into the kitchen just as Ilmari was saying, "Rejoice and be glad, because great is your reward in heaven, for in the same way they persecuted the prophets who were before you." She held her tongue—with some effort.

Ilmari was nearly beside himself with something he wanted to tell her. His eyes glowed. There was joy in his usually deliberate movements. When they sat to eat, it came pouring out—six full sentences. She'd expected something religious, but this . . . He'd been called by God. Saint Ilmari, she thought, as blind as Paul on the road to Damascus. He'd find a wife, get married in the church, and become a church elder, a man of faith and stature.

"What foolishness!" She could contain herself no longer. "People starve. The workingman toils endless hours for the comfort of the rich. You and Matti toil endless hours. For what? Some worthless building and a house for the leech pastor and his family who are going to suck off the workingman until people come to their senses and throw all that stupidity out the door." She hadn't expected to say so much.

"God has told me His church needs to be built."

Aino rolled her eyes.

"Like one in the old country."

"Like the one that won't bury a baby dead from starvation?"

Ilmari put his large hands over hers. "Aino," he said gently. "The people need a church."

"The people need a brain."

She picked up her empty cup and walked to the sink.

"How can we be married without a church?" Ilmari asked.

"You have someone in mind?"

Ilmari, a little embarrassed, said, "No one in particular."

"Someone in general then?"

"Well." Ilmari looked at his coffee again, avoiding eye contact. "There are Finnish girls up in Nordland."

"Yes, prostitutes," Aino said.

"Not *Finnish* girls," Ilmari answered, offended that she'd even think a Finnish girl would prostitute herself. He walked over to a small makeshift desk—two two-by-twelves set on trestles—and returned with a letter. "It's from Arne Vanhatalo. He's cousin to Alma Wiitala, you know, up at Reder's Camp. There's a Finnish girl of marriageable age in Nordland, and she's a good worker."

"Oh," Aino broke in. "So you are just going to go up there and get yourself a wife the way you get a horse."

"Easy for you to criticize," Ilmari said. "Good Finnish boys are everywhere. Where do Matti and I find good Finnish girls? And how long can I leave the cow and cattle to even go looking?"

"I'll see what sort of cow you bring back."

"Families are important. Everyone needs to be married," Ilmari said. "Someday," he added a bit lamely, "you, too."

Aino gave him a look.

"I'm serious. For example, Ullakko's a good provider. He's young and—"

"He's older than you are!"

"Yoh." Ilmari paused and then plunged in where angels fear to tread. "You're already seventeen. Who are you going to find except some logger with nothing but his caulk boots?"

"Better that than an old man with cow manure on his shoes," she shot back. "I'm never going to marry anyone." Aino knew Ilmari was only trying to do right by her. She could never explain that she'd promised herself to Voitto and had already betrayed him once. She would not betray him again.

Ilmari gazed at her, taking in her comment about marriage. Then he said gently, "Your boyfriend is dead. The revolution might never come. You're here and there's no going back."

"The revolution will come, and I can wait as long as I please."

"I don't know about the revolution, but I do know that women can't wait like the men."

Aino knew he was right but stayed silent.

"You have three choices," Ilmari continued. "Marry a farmer, marry a logger, or be an old maid. I think being an old maid would be sad." Ilmari looked at his coffee. "Same as an old bachelor."

Aino stood. "Fine. Go up to Nordland and buy yourself a bit and a bridle. After the revolution, marriage will be a thing of the past. We'll love who we want, and the children will be raised by everyone. I'll wait, thank you, and it won't be long."

"Aino," Ilmari said, as if responding to a child.

A week after Ilmari revealed his plan to build a church to Aino, Matti made the first step in his own plan to have a logging company. A man had been crushed by a log. His crew had dragged the body up to the donkey and laid it next to the railroad tracks at the landing, followed by Toivo Huttula. Matti watched Huttula talk to the supervisor the loggers called the side rod. The two men looked at him, and the side rod nodded his head.

When Huttula reached Matti he asked, "How old are you, really?"

"Sixteen."

Huttula looked at the cordwood. Matti was easily two days ahead. "You think you're ready?" he asked Matti.

Matti drove his splitting maul into the block and never looked back.

He started at the bottom, setting chokers.

Setting chokers was the toughest, dirtiest, most exhausting job in the woods. A choker setter's job was to dig, burrow, climb, and crawl under and over the huge logs to wrap a steel cable, called a choker, around the log and back onto itself using a C-hook. The thinner choker cable was attached to a much larger cable called the main line, which was reeled in by the steam donkey, sometimes hundreds of yards away. When the main line was jerked into action by the donkey engineer, the smaller cable choked down on the log, hence its name. The log was ripped from its place on the ground, twisting as it moved, to be hauled at great speed up to the landing next to the steam donkey. When that log moved, the choker setter must have already been moving out of its way, or he would be killed or maimed. Choker setters had to be young, strong, fast on their feet, and fearless. It was where all loggers started—real loggers.

Matti swelled with pride as he headed for the ravine through the jackstraw confusion of slash.

The thrill of the new job lasted about thirty seconds. He would reach the top of a tangle of limbs, feeling them moving beneath him, only to fall through to the ground, the top of the tangle above his head. It took a huge effort to get back on top of the slash. He could hear Huttula cursing at him for his slowness, obviously enjoying himself. Breathing hard, he watched Huttula and other experienced loggers moving across the slash as if they were dancers, timing their moves, using the spring-back of the limbs to move gracefully on to the next tangle. They covered ground easily at ten times his own speed. He arrived at the downed trees in the ravine gasping for air, understanding fully what loggers meant by brush legs.

Fallers were chopping or sawing trees, balancing six to eight feet above the ground on metal-tipped boards hammered into the tree's side. This way they were above the swell of the tree's butt, making it easier to fell. Two fallers to a tree, they swung their double-bitted axes alternately in steady, efficient rhythms, each bite of the ax taking out large chips of wood. Other fallers who'd already made their undercut were balanced on the back sides of their trees, pulling twelve-foot-long crosscut saws between them. Back and forth, each one pulling in turn, cutting toward the undercut, pouring oil or kerosene on the saw to keep it from binding, occasionally driving wedges to keep the cut open. Sawing, without a stop, sometimes for hours before the tree started to tremble then groan as the remaining wood hinge between the undercut and the saw cut gave way with a sustained cracking sound. The fallers would then scramble for their lives, as the huge tree moaned and whistled through the air, nearly silent once the splintering at its base ended, to smash into the earth, sending vibrations through the ground for hundreds of feet. The fallers would gather their equipment, walk to the next tree, and do it again.

Huttula pulled out his puukko and began slashing the hem of Matti's trouser legs about halfway up the boot. "This is called stagging your trousers. You are less likely to get snagged on something and, if you do, you would much rather have your trousers rip than lose a leg." He stood. "Or worse. This is not a game for children." He looked carefully at the buttons holding Matti's suspenders and grunted. "Not too much thread. And no belt. Same reason." Matti knew that "Same reason" meant you could die.

"You pay attention," Huttula said. "All the time. No daydreaming about your girlfriends. I tell you to do something, you do it instantly. Watch everyone, all the time. Work from the uphill side whenever you can. If you lose your balance, always fall toward the rigging. Don't walk, don't run. Fly. The place to rest is the grave."

With that, he pointed to the main line. "Take that choker." He turned and pointed out a huge log. "Attach it to that." He walked away.

Matti was joined by another choker setter and the two of them hauled on the choker, pulling the heavier main line sideways along with them. When they reached the log, Matti's eyes were at the same level as the point where the curve of the log started moving away from him.

Matti could hear the piping of the brass steam whistle from the steam donkey, signaling something, he knew not what. The whistle was triggered by a small boy, the whistle punk, Kullerikki, who stood on a huge stump and pulled on the whistle lever with a wire several hundred feet long. The whole forest was screeching, squealing, crashing, shouting life. Giant logs were jerked from small canyons and pulled uphill across stumps that momentarily resisted the power of the steam donkey, the cable tightening to near breaking until the log suddenly popped over the stump and was reeled in to the landing. Buckers—who often were crushed by rolling logs, and so considered half-crazy by other loggers—cut the logs into mill-specified lengths with large crosscut saws held at nearly forty-five degrees above their heads.

At a shout and a curse from Huttula, Matti began digging under the giant log, burrowing his way, dragging along the twenty-pound C-hook and resisting cable, to get it to his partner on the other side. Matti pulled the heavy cable through and tossed the C-hook up over the log where his partner scrambled to hook it over the cable. With his hand held above, his partner gave the signal to Kullerikki. Kullerikki piped the signal that the log was rigged. Matti ran for cover as the huge log was jerked into motion, spinning about a quarter of the way around to accommodate the angle of the cable. When that happened, Matti learned this first lesson of logging: to stay away from where the cable would end up after it was tight, not from where it was now. He dived for the ground to avoid being hit. The thick flying cable could take off a leg or head like a scythe through barley. He didn't have time to think about how close he'd come to dying, because Huttula was already pointing at the next log as the haul-back cable went screaming by them, pulling the chokers back into position for the next turn.

It went like that until they had twenty minutes for lunch and then it was like that until light failed.

That night, ravenously hungry, Matti ate as he never had eaten in his life. He'd thought he was in great shape, but he felt his body stiffening as he ate. By the time he reached the bunkhouse, he felt as though he weighed three hundred pounds. He threw himself facedown on the hay of his bunk without taking off his clothes. Roused from his bunk before first light, he stumbled to breakfast to begin again. He'd never felt so alive.

The day Matti joined Huttula's crew was the day Aksel ran out of food. He hadn't yet reached the Oregon-California border, and he had one dollar and thirty cents.

The first two days after he left San Francisco weren't so bad. Although his sea legs had proved themselves close to useless for hiking, he had at least run into the occasional farm, where he split wood in exchange for food and permission to sleep in the barn.

Ten days later he found himself hiking through the largest trees he had ever seen or even imagined. He stopped at one giant and spread his arms wide against the trunk. Noting where his right hand stopped, he moved to that spot and measured again. It took twelve measurements to get around to where he had started. The tree appeared to be triple the mast of the *Elna*. If cut down—how this was possible, he didn't know—lying sideways the tree would still be nearly as tall as his two-story house in Finland. The Swedish woman at the brothel told him the Douglas firs near Nordland were even taller but not quite so big around. He imagined cutting down trees like this, feeling a growing excitement that could put the sea behind him forever.

The ninety-mile walk from Eureka to Crescent City took a week. Had he not stopped to chop wood for the occasional farmer or haul sawdust and scrap lumber to the big wigwam burners at two mills, he could have done it in five days. But he had to eat.

When he reached Crescent City, after a meal at a little restaurant run by a Greek family, his belly full and his legs getting stronger every day, he walked into a newspaper office. He managed to convey that he wanted to see a map. When the man pointed to Astoria, part of him wished he'd never seen the map. The man also pointed out that the roads, unlike those between Crescent City and Eureka, did not go north-south. There was only an occasional railroad connecting a seaport town to the big valley on the other side of the Coast Range. Aksel thought briefly of just stopping where he was, maybe going back to Eureka and getting a job, but the woman had said that people from home lived around Astoria.

Winter was coming and he was homesick, powerful incentives to keep walking.

Also aware that winter was coming, Ilmari was weighing the trade-offs of building in bad weather with the fact that winter was when farmers could work on something besides their own farms. He envisioned the new church as a simple Gothic structure, about twenty by forty feet, with a beautiful steeple rising to at least eighteen feet. Everything could be handcrafted by the congregation of ten families except the organ. Pastor Hoikka, the Evangelical Lutheran minister in Astoria, said it wouldn't be a church without an organ.

"Why can't we just use a kantele or an accordion or a fiddle, whatever we've got?" Ilmari asked Hoikka after the service in Ilmahenki's living room. Aino had skipped the service but returned to make a Sunday evening supper for Ilmari and Pastor Hoikka, who was spending the night with them. He'd come from Astoria to Knappton on the small passenger ferry called the *General Washington* after doing two services at the Astoria church that morning and had hiked the last ten miles for an evening service at Ilmahenki.

"Of course, you can," Hoikka said. "But they're dance instruments."

"Not the kantele," Ilmari said, annoyed by Hoikka's constant rejoinders to any objection. Hoikka wasn't a bad fellow. He did double duty to serve the new Tapiola congregation and asked for only boat fare, room and board, and a dollar for the church fund, which everyone knew paid his salary. No one begrudged him that, other than Aino. Even pastors and their families must eat. He was just rigid. Maybe that's what it took to serve a congregation. If he wasn't rigid, he'd do something outside the doctrine and then he really couldn't say he was a Lutheran. Back in Finland, the government enforced the rules. And the Catholics had this centrally organized government of their own. He realized suddenly that people were waiting for him to answer a question. "Mitä?" he asked. What?

"Pastor Hoikka says you can get a really nice Estey reed organ for around a hundred dollars from an organ dealer in Portland," Aino said.

"That would be another ten dollars per family. We're already asking for money for lumber, pews, and Communion cups."

"To be able to gather in God's house," Hoikka said. "To have the fellowship and comfort of a community is money well spent."

Aino broke in. "So, you'll be cutting down trees in God's house to turn them into lumber to make God's house." She began clearing the table, foreclosing any rejoinder.

Ilmari hoped they could have something built by Christmas. He knew that it was a forlorn hope even as he was hoping it, which, he supposed, was why it was called a hope. He read First Peter about hope and being an elder of the church. He'd read Ezra and Nehemiah about building a temple.

Higgins donated a fifty-by-one-hundred-foot piece of land, well up from the river and potential floods, on the south edge of Tapiola, even though he was nominally Catholic.

On the last Sunday in November, the entire congregation trudged from services at Ilmahenki through slashing rain and mud to huddle on the donated lot while Ilmari read the order for the laying of the cornerstone.

How amiable are Thy tabernacles, O Lord of hosts!

I was glad when they said unto me: Let us go into the house of the Lord.

Except the Lord build the house, they labor in vain that build it.

The men of the congregation, enduring the rain and mud, leveled the land and laid the foundation stones in place by dark. Then they all met at Kalle and Lilo Puskala's barn for a dinner cooked by the women.

At this dinner, Ilmari met his first leadership problem: some of the congregation wanted to dance. He argued adamantly that while the Old Testament didn't forbid dancing and the children of Israel did indeed dance, the New Testament said nothing about dancing being good. For Christians, the New Testament was what was relevant. Then he made the mistake of quoting Exodus: "Remember the Sabbath day, to keep it holy. Six days you shall labor, and do all your work, but the seventh day is a Sabbath to the Lord your God." Antti Salmi pointed out that they'd been working all day. After an initial moment of confusion, Ilmari pointed out that building a church wasn't really working; it was a form of worship. This seemed to satisfy Salmi and the rest of the pro-dance congregation, but it caused several nights of intense study by Ilmari to try to find the definitive answer.

In the following weeks, working on Sunday afternoons after the service, they placed sturdy twelve-by-twelve cedar posts on the foundation stones, which then supported the doubled two-by-four plates and knotless two-by-ten Douglas fir floor joists and the two-by-four studs. Some of the women supplied hot food and strong coffee at breaks, while others met at different homes in small groups to sew the altar cloths, vestments for the future pastor, and sturdy cushions to be used at the future altar rail for Communion. Weekend after weekend the walls slowly rose, then the ceiling joists, then the roof. By March, the little twenty-by-forty-foot church was weathertight and fulfilled Ilmari's vision of an eighteen-foot steeple. Arvid Saarenpää, who had a reputation for fine carpentry, had made sure the windows and doors were watertight and had no drafts. Then the remaining chores were assigned. Lars Laakkonen, a cousin of the Koskis' Laakkonen neighbors in Finland, and Johan Pakkanen began carving beautiful designs on the backrests of chairs being made by Matti Haapakangas. Antti Salmi, Jouka Autiovaara, and Abraham Wirkkala met every Sunday afternoon to work on the solid-oak pews. Ilmari assembled a small woodstove and stovepipes for the rear of the little church, and he and Isak Herajarvi both worked on the blue-and-white wine-stem pulpit that would stand at the left of the altar. Adolfiina Laakkonen and Meija Herajarvi took on the task of finding a suitable painting for behind the altar, while Ruusu Pakkanen took on choir robes along with Linna Salmi and Pirkka Autiovaara. After considerable soul-searching, it was decided that selling refreshments at the Saturday dances was really doing God's work. Lilo Puskala and Tuuli Wirkkala organized the women making cake and cookies to raise the cash for the painting, individual glass Communion cups, and a silver host platen. Henni Haapakangas took on the window curtains.

Aino stayed home, feeling left out and wanting female company.

While the church was being built, Aksel spent Christmas alone, huddled on the side of a trail. Just after the New Year, he found shelter against the warmth of a rusting wigwam burner in the little port town of Bandon, Oregon, where he could see a thin line of lighter gray stretched across the horizon of the Pacific Ocean. He hadn't eaten in two days. He hadn't been dry in two weeks. There were now only around eight hours of daylight, less on the many rainy days. Astoria was simply too far away. He hugged his knees to choke off the desire to cry.

A mill worker found him in the morning. A Swede was summoned to translate and the story told. The two men exchanged looks, seeming to say, "What are you going to do? He's a kid." They escorted Aksel to a rough office, MOORE LUMBER neatly painted by hand over the door. The manager asked a few questions in English, nodded, and the Swede took Aksel to a long table about waist-high filled with steel rollers. Boards, timbers, and dimension lumber of all sizes rattled along as fast as men could yank them off the table and stack them. The Swede talked to a foreman and the foreman nodded. That was the day Aksel learned the English words "green chain."

The freshly cut green lumber was soaking wet with sap—and heavy. None of the men had gloves. Soon Aksel's hands were bleeding and blistered, despite his having done hard work to get this far. The lumber moved relentlessly, the huge head-rig saw, band saws, and gang saws all spewing lumber to the green chain. By nightfall, Aksel staggered into a rough dining hall and ate until he thought he would burst. By spring he was a seasoned worker and twenty pounds heavier.

8

Spring in the Deep River valley began with trilliums in mid-March. By late April it brought longing, and Ilmari convinced Aino to move temporarily into Ullakko's house so he could go find a bride. He figured it would take him ten days, maximum.

Aino had raised hell, pointing out that she was perfectly capable of being alone, she'd had enough of being someone's live-in servant in Finland, and it looked very much like the opening move toward an arranged marriage with which she forcefully disagreed. Ilmari in turn argued forcefully that it was in no way the opening move in an arranged marriage and that young women all over America worked for people and boarded with them. What was not argued but was well known to all was that when Ilmari came back with his bride, Aino would be redundant.

When the storm subsided, the rock on the shore had remained unmoved and Ilmari helped Aino move to Ullakko's.

Ullakko had made a platform bed for her in the girls' room and had given up his own mattress for it. She was touched. Being above the kitchen, the girls' room had the double advantage of the heat from the floor and the sheet metal chimney. Aino liked the prospect of sharing the room with the girls. She loved her brothers dearly, but they weren't sisters.

Ilmari walked to Willapa Bay and caught the *Reliable* to Willapa where he spent the night. The next morning in a hard rain he took a second boat out to sea then back across the roiling bar at the mouth of Grays

Harbor and into Nordland, dark against the gray sky in the gloom of late afternoon.

A few streets were paved with sawdust and straw. The rest were mud. The buildings within several blocks of the waterfront were built on pilings. Having arrived at low tide, Ilmari could smell the excrement and garbage lying in the mud beneath the buildings. When the tide came in, most of the excrement and garbage was washed out to the river and then down to the sea—most of it.

He settled in a rooming house on Herron Street, the room just big enough for a single bed. He whittled until there was no light.

He was up at dawn. The meeting was to be at three, so he spent the morning looking at all the merchandise in the stores. At one, he rubbed brilliantine into his hair and combed it in front of the single round mirror hanging next to the two-hole privy that opened over the river below. Then he stood on the boardwalk outside the hotel for over an hour, occasionally going back to recomb his hair. It wasn't like going to a dance.

Louhi Jokinen was in her office at the Tannika House, a brothel in which she held 51 percent. She also was getting ready to leave for the meeting, but she had a problem: Al Drummond lying on her office couch snoozing off a heavy lunch and too much alcohol. Drummond, the owner of the First National Bank of Nordland, was the 49 percent partner. In addition to being a ruthless businessman and an all-around son of a bitch, he was a snoop and Louhi couldn't leave him there alone. He could, however, be childishly belligerent if disturbed. She decided to wake him anyway. She had been handling belligerent men since her parents died when she was fourteen and she took up hooking in Seattle to feed herself.

She shook Al's shoulder and he grunted to low-level consciousness. "It's nearly three," Louhi said. "I'm worried someone might be missing you over at the bank."

Drummond reached up for her, smiling sleepily. "Ah, come on Louhi. Give me a kiss."

She turned her back and went for her coat. A small gat-toothed woman, curvy in all the right places, she could still hold a man's eye although she was no longer young. Her physical appearance combined with a force of personality forged by triumphing over many hard years could attract a strong man and scare the hell out of a weak one. "Come on, Al. If you're horny, go over to the Tannika and pay for it."

"Ahh, Louhi. How unkind."

She shrugged into her long, dark-blue wool coat with a rich chocolate mink collar. "I've got a visitor over at the house at three and you've got a reputation to keep." She paused. "Or at least keep from getting worse." She smiled to let him know she was kidding him. She, however, wasn't kidding. "Come on. If your wife shows up at the bank, there'll be hell to pay."

Drummond sighed and attempted a kiss, deftly avoided. He left the office saying, "Work, work, work. That's all I do." She had to smile. He wasn't without a sense of humor.

When Louhi reached home, she shouted for Rauha to bring her best shoes. She took the clothes brush by the door and began brushing the mud off the hem of her skirt. It left the hem slightly darker with the dampness, but she realized she wouldn't have time to change, and it would have to do. She put her muddy shoes on a low rack in the foyer and went into the parlor just as Rauha came down the stairs.

Louhi sat on the couch, putting on her good shoes while inspecting Rauha, who had seated herself opposite her. Louhi took in the very discreet lip coloring and rouge on Rauha's nearly perfect face and fair skin. She had put her blond hair up but allowed a tendril to dangle down on each side.

"The tendrils are a good idea," Louhi said. Rauha touched one of them and gave a quick nervous smile. "Now get that goddamned color off your lips. He'll think you work at the Tannika."

Pressing and licking her lips to comply with her mother's order, but still leave some color, she asked, "Does he know about the Tannika?"

"If not, he'll know soon enough," Louhi muttered, feeling her corset as she tied her shoes. She sat up straight and took a breath.

"Sigrid married an American," Rauha said.

Louhi focused her dark eyes on her daughter, giving her an I'll-brook-no-nonsense look. "American be damned. You're going to marry someone respectable, not one of my customers. I've asked around and he's an honest hard worker, lives clean, and comes from my home place. He also lives two days away, where what I do for a living won't be thrown in your face. You'll never marry anyone of any standing here."

She watched her daughter bite her lip. No use hiding facts, even hard ones.

"You know she's pregnant," Rauha muttered. Louhi could see Rauha wasn't over her little sister's marrying before her.

"Is that supposed to surprise me?"

Rauha studied her neatly filed, short fingernails.

Louhi stood, straightening her skirt. She put her hand under Rauha's chin to make her look up. "She'll be crawling back home within two years with a baby, no waistline, and a man about as stable as a Siwash canoe."

Rauha started to turn away, but Louhi turned her face back and looked fiercely into her eyes. "I'll be goddamned if you go down the path of your sister. Or me."

Rauha turned her head and walked over to the window. "He's here," she said quietly.

Louhi greeted Ilmari in Finnish at the door, leaving Rauha sitting in the parlor, as was appropriate. She quickly examined how he was dressed. He wore shoes not work boots and a wool suit jacket and tie. The sleeves of the jacket were about an inch too high on the wrists, most likely, she mused, because these were the Sunday clothes he'd brought from Finland when still in his teens. Likely the coat was so little used he hadn't bothered to alter it. She liked the looks of him, strong, thick chest, good posture, darker than most Finns, and with thick black hair.

Ilmari entered the house awkwardly. He started to put his hand out to shake hers but quickly withdrew it, not knowing whether it was polite to shake a lady's hand. Smiling to herself, she thought, I can at least look like a lady. She led him into the parlor.

Rauha stood and smiled. Even though Finns were harder to read than Indians, Louhi had made thousands of introductions between men and women and could tell instantly if she'd correctly connected buyer and product. Ilmari's eyes darted right down to Rauha's shoes. Shy. Louhi watched him struggle between wanting to stare at Rauha and being polite. Clearly, Rauha could have him; the question was would she.

Aware that he shouldn't stare, Ilmari tried to look at the cup as he placed it in the saucer. He failed and once again his gaze strayed to Rauha's ankles. Then he looked up to avoid staring at them only to rest on the outline of her thighs. He quickly moved his eyes upward, trying to avoid looking at her breasts, until he made eye contact. Jerking his eyes to his coffee cup, he began the eye journey anew. Such beauty and a hard worker, too. He wanted to throw the coffee cup at the wall and start dancing. He wanted to propose to Rauha on the spot. He'd seen pictures of women like Rauha in newspapers advertising soap and clothes, and in drawings of Gibson girls on bunkhouse walls, but he had never seen a woman as beautiful as Rauha in the flesh, just feet away from him. He could smell perfume but wasn't sure if it was Rauha's or her mother's. He was acutely aware of the way Rauha's breasts moved when she breathed.

"I play the kantele," he blurted out.

Rauha smiled at him. "That's nice."

He couldn't think of what to say after that.

"I hear you are a blacksmith."

Ilmari nodded his head. "Yoh."

Rauha gave her mother a look. This prompted Ilmari to add, "I can make things from iron . . . that people buy."

As efficiently as bankers making a loan, Rauha and Louhi learned every detail, from the number of rooms in his house to the number, productivity, and age of his cattle to the amount of furniture he owned and whether it was store-bought or homemade.

After Ilmari left, they sat in silence. Then Louhi said, "He's got good timber and land."

"He's also the only blacksmith around Tapiola. The logging and sawmills will make it a growing cash business."

"I agree," Louhi said. It felt good to see herself in Rauha. "I've asked him back. I think he's it, but we'll make it clear there'll be no betrothal until at least fall."

Rauha gave her a questioning look.

"The longer they wait, the longer they stick," Louhi said.

9

In May, the cows gushed milk and the grass was plump with rain and rich soil. They'd seen no snow since February. Even Finns who'd been in the Deep River area ten years still considered Northwest winters comparable to those at home, always in fear of the next subzero freeze that would kill the tender plants pushing aboveground. It never came. Potatoes already showed several inches of vine.

Late one afternoon on an errand to Tapiola, Aino watched two young women holding ribbons next to their faces, getting each other's opinion, speaking Finnish. That was when she learned that every Saturday night in Knappton there was a dance in one of the large net sheds.

Instead of returning to Ullakko's house, she nearly ran to Ilmahenki, where she found Ilmari sweating and red faced at his forge.

"Not by yourself," he said.

"Why do you think I'm here? To smell your armpits? You've got to come," she pleaded. "It'll be fun." As soon as she said it, she realized that fun was probably not a motivator for Ilmari.

Ilmari turned over a glowing steel chain link and hammered it into shape. "I already have a girlfriend," he said with some pride.

"I'm going crazy at Ullakko's," she pleaded.

"He's a good man."

"Yes. He's a good man. And about as entertaining as an oyster."

Ilmari actually cracked a smile.

"Please." She hated to beg, but a dance. A dance!

"All right. Maybe Matti wants to go, too," he said. She danced a half turn and was nearly skipping away when Ilmari said, "And only if

Ullakko gives you time off." Walking backward, she wrinkled her nose at him, then ran for Ullakko's.

Matti and Ilmari picked Aino up at Ullakko's farm Saturday evening and the three of them started on the trail to Knappton. Aino was aware of Ullakko watching them go but refused to turn around. Soon the forest hid the farm from view. The air was fresh. The forest floor gave off a rich, dark smell and orange shafts of setting sunlight pierced through the seventy-meter-high forest ceiling. Far above them she could hear the gentle wind making the trees whisper to each other.

They walked single file, Aino barefoot so as not to soil or wear out her leather shoes. A squirrel chattered at them from a limb, then in an instant disappeared. She heard it chirping from behind her. They weren't in a hurry, so they took nearly two hours to walk the six miles to Knappton.

The trail ran down a steep hill, then through alders growing among stumps logged several years before. They emerged from the forest. It was her first sighting of the Columbia River. She stopped. Ilmari nearly bumped into her. She stopped breathing. Her eyes teared. It was as if her heart had left her to flow out onto the majesty. Far off, maybe six miles away, she could see the Oregon side of the river. To her east, the shimmering water flowed from a gap in the Coast Range, more like an immense magical lake than a river.

She felt Ilmari's hand on her shoulder. He spoke softly into her ear. "Maybe, here is your God." She reached up and touched his hand and felt him give her shoulder a quick grip. She couldn't move. She didn't want to.

Knappton was set on pilings over the river and surrounded by huge rafts of logs, its two sawmills running full tilt. The three walked out on a wharf, passing the Knappton Hotel and smelling the creosote of the pilings and planks. Fifteen feet below them, the tide being low, were rows of open double-ended fishing boats tied fore and aft to ropes on pulleys. The gentle rise and fall of the great river moved the boats, the pulleys softly squealing like a chorus of distant lonely birds. They entered the spacious net shed of Knappton Packing through a huge sliding door. Inside were dozens of net racks, large wooden frames over which were draped the company fishermen's gill nets, which were being repaired during daylight hours for the next salmon run. The spring Chinook run was over, and nets with smaller mesh were being readied for the June blueback run, small five- to fifteen-pound salmon between two and three feet long with a delicate flavor.

A large floor space had been created, surrounded by square platforms on small steel wheels that held more huge nets in piles. The small steel wheels of the net carts splintered the floor made of six-inch-thick planks. It was the biggest building Aino had seen since the train station in Portland.

She quickly put on her stockings and shoes, tucked her glasses away in the canvas bag in which she'd packed their food, and went looking for a mirror where she managed to blend her longer thick hair with the shorter returning hair.

Near the sliding doors where lamplight from kerosene lanterns was just beginning to make headway on the dark planks of the wharf against the gloaming, the women had all gathered, married and unmarried alike. Aino felt their excitement. There were at least five males to every female. No girl needed to fear being a wallflower. The small band—an accordion, two violins, a single snare drum, and a euphonium—tuned to a piano that had miraculously appeared at the huge doors on a net cart pushed by four loggers. The band members weren't paid. They were loggers, mill workers, and fishermen who had a gift and loved to play. Because they were also single men, they would take turns leaving the band to have a dance. The unwritten rule was that only one band member could dance at a time. Because the musicians had no time to practice together, they kept to the traditional tunes with their simple chord progressions.

The band sprang to life at the nod of the lead violinist and began a schottische. A wave of manhood hit the shoals of womanhood and there many foundered. Some, however, sailed clear and out onto the floor. Aino found herself in the care of a large Norwegian mill worker. As soon as the dance was over, another Norwegian, apparently her first partner's friend, took her for the next dance but was himself replaced by a Finnish logger who'd grown up in Tampere. Hambos, polkas, schottisches, waltzes; men getting her punch and popcorn, politely cutting in on each other, taking her on another and then another and another circuit of the floor. She finally pleaded exhaustion and fled to the room set aside for the ladies. It held a three-hole plank that opened to the river beneath. On the rough board walls were pegs for clothing and bags and a single mirror, before which a dozen women were twisting to look at their hair or ducking down to arrange it on top. A few simply leaned against the wall to catch their breath.

Aino, having lived most of her life only with brothers, felt herself being pulled into the flutter and excitement of this other world of girls. She caught a glimpse of herself, her dark hair singular amid all the light brown and blond, her dark eyes among the others' hazel and blue. Straightening her shoulders, pushing her breasts out, and with the confidence of a queen, she reentered the dance.

Something had changed. Five dark-complexioned men stood quietly by the punch. Americans and Scandinavians looked at them silently. The bandleader signaled a waltz for the band and the staring men turned their attention back to the women. Aino ignored a couple of men trying to get her attention and found Matti next to the bandstand. He seemed to know the violin player.

"Dance with me," she said.

Matti took her onto the floor, moving gracefully with a firm frame. It was hard to remember he was her little brother.

"Who are the dark ones?" Aino asked.

"Greeks. They work for next to nothing and take jobs away from white people."

"If they were organized along with all the other workers, that would stop. They would compete together against the capitalists."

"The unions will never take them."

"Why not?"

Matti looked at her incredulously. "They're a dirty people, that's why not. Their church doesn't even teach them to read."

They'd made just two more circuits of the floor when Aino, from the corner of her eye, saw three obviously drunk loggers place themselves directly in front of the Greeks. Drinking inside the building was not allowed, but outside two vendors sold an American whiskey called bourbon and a Canadian whiskey called rye at ten cents a shot. Five shots cost half a day's wages for many of them. Oh, the stupidity of it, she thought.

When the waltz stopped, the place went silent. An American logger told the Greeks in no uncertain terms to get the hell out and keep going. One of the Greeks turned and said something to his friends, who objected, but the Greek raised the palm of his hand to quiet them. He stepped forward and, of all things, made a slight bow. He straightened himself to his full height, easily two or three inches shorter than the Americans, and confronted them with a proud carriage, his hair oiled and his eyes an unexpected blue. "I am called Demetrius Galanis," he said in clear accented English. "I am come here to America for same reason as all, to work, to be free, to live in justice."

"You come here to take our jobs by taking shit for wages."

Galanis looked at the man. "We take what is offered."

"They offer you shit, because you are shit. Get the hell out of here. I mean clear out. Go back to Greece."

Galanis smiled enigmatically. "I am afraid I am welcome even less in my homeland than I am here. Galanis is here to stay."

"You slick son of a bitch," the logger growled. He swung and connected. Galanis went to the floor, obviously surprised by the sudden attack. The logger snarled and kicked him.

Kicking a white man when he was down was always despicable. For some, however, kicking a man like Galanis, who wasn't white, was just sport—for some, not all. A second logger, large, fair-haired, roared from the crowd of onlookers and crashed at a full run into the first, who went down instantly, his legs sprawled out and kicking spasmodically on the ground. His friends came swinging in on the newcomer, but by this time Galanis was on his feet and kicked one of the men in the knees from the side, bringing him to the floor with a scream of pain.

The newcomer scrambled to his feet and he and Galanis stood back-to-back, looking warily around them.

Matti, his hand on Aino's shoulder, called out, "So, this is how you're dancing tonight, Jouka." A couple of guffaws followed. The tall newcomer said, "No offense to Mr. Galanis here, but he's not my type." More laughs. The man who had been knocked down tried to get to his feet. Galanis kicked his hands out from under him with a smile and the man hit the floor face-first. Then he vomited from too much drinking. People moved back in disgust.

Jouka and Matti carried the man outside and dumped him on the wharf where he would sleep it off.

"Who's the girl?" Jouka asked.

"My sister, Aino."

"Is she free?"

"More than you might like," Matti said.

"Hmmm," Jouka murmured, looking at Aino as they walked back to Galanis, who reached out to shake Jouka's hand. Galanis, in his midthirties, was half a foot shorter than Jouka. "Galanis thanks you, Mr. Jouka," he said in English.

"Mr. Kaukonen," he said. "Jouka Kaukonen."

Aino walked up to them. Jouka was hit with the intensity of her dark eyes. "Will you please translate to Mr. Galanis for me?" she asked.

"Yoh."

"If you Finns and Greeks joined together," she said to Galanis, "you could raise everyone's wages. Stop fighting each other for crumbs from the owners like dogs under their table."

Jouka chuckled and then translated. Galanis cocked his head and looked at Aino like the curiosity that, to him, she was. He turned to Jouka. "Greek women only speak like that in private," he said in English.

Jouka chuckled. "She's not Greek."

Galanis looked at Aino. "Of course, you are right about joining together, but Galanis joins nothing," he said in English.

Jouka translated.

"Tell him: 'Galanis is a fool.'"

Hearing the translation, Galanis laughed aloud. "This one has fire." He shook Matti's hand and left them.

"It was good of you to help that man," Aino said to Jouka.

Jouka blushed. "Oh, you know. Underdogs." He paused. "Even under the table."

"Don't make fun. Fools fight each other. Men fight the common enemy."

This girl both fascinated him and made him uncomfortable. "I work for John Reder. He's not the enemy."

"How much does he pay?"

"For a good logger, it can be up to two dollars a day."

"For how long a day?"

Jouka looked at her, wondering if he should even answer such a stupid question. "As long as it's light."

She shook her head at him as if she thought he was a fool. Then his friend, Matti, took her by the elbow and led her back onto the dance floor. In his mind, he heard Galanis's *This one has fire.* Jouka Kaukonen had never fallen in love, until now.

As Matti led Aino through the large space between the open sliding doors, she turned to see Jouka Kaukonen taking a slug from a metal hip flask. He raised the flask to her in a salute and she turned away quickly. She didn't like drinking. But looking at him made her heart light.

More men asked her to dance. They all seemed dull.

At one point, she heard Jouka's voice calling out a tune to the musicians. The fiddle player, grinning, held out his fiddle. Jouka declined. Then a chant started. "Jouka. Jouka." The piano player did a quick riff. "Jouka. Jouka." The whole crowd was chanting his name.

He jumped up to the bandstand made of overturned fish boxes and took the fiddle. He said something to the piano player and the accordion player, they nodded, and he put the fiddle under his chin. Then, with a nod, he was playing a polka.

She'd never heard any music so full of life. She knew a gifted musician when she heard one, and this man, this logger, was gifted. The logger she was with was some Norwegian lunkhead who couldn't lead cows to silage. She wanted to stomp his toes in frustration. When the tune was finished, everyone was clapping, many were shouting for more. Jouka turned to the other players for a brief discussion, and then they broke into a pelimanni schottische, filling the room with memories of birch trees laden with snow, quiet fields, and snug houses. Dancers who'd been intimidated by the polka returned to the floor, and it turned out the Norwegian lunkhead could at least dance the schottische. She could barely keep her eyes forward and her posture formal on the steps and hop, wanting to watch Jouka. Every time she faced the bandstand in a turn, she watched Jouka closely, trying not to make her head swiveling obvious.

When the tune ended, Jouka bowed to warm applause. He handed back the fiddle and she watched him go outside. She felt he was leaving her.

She watched him return from outside, slipping something into a pocket. Then, she watched him move between dancing and returning to the bandstand to play another tune or two, but he never seemed to look her way. Around midnight, however, with the band clearly getting tired and people already leaving, Jouka jumped down from the bandstand and very formally asked her to dance. Aino couldn't help taking a breath that pushed her ribs against her corset.

The dance was a waltz. Jouka placed his large right hand on her left shoulder blade and took her right hand in his left. He seemed to grow a full inch, coming upright and solid. Then he moved. She followed as though she was part of him, as though she had no choice. She wanted no choice. They were moving with the other dancers in a large counterclockwise circle, yet she felt the two of them were truly the center of everything, the refreshment table swinging by, the bandstand swinging by, a glimpse of Matti swinging by, the refreshments table again. The three-quarter time made the dance flow without stopping points, just the beginning of the next three beats on a different foot and the whirling and Jouka's face above her and above him the rafters of the building and the center point of the whirling rafters.

10

Aino, Ilmari, and Matti slept with other tired dancers on the kitchen floor at the hotel. The late-May sun was up by four thirty. They ate the rieska and butter that Aino had packed and were on the trail back to Tapiola by six. Matti broke into an old folk song about a young girl who fell in love with a soldier. Aino threw a fir cone at him.

When they reached Ullakko's, the children ran out. Aino squatted to hug them, avoiding eye contact with Ullakko. His five-year-old daughter took Aino's shoes off her neck and went twirling around, pretending to be dancing.

When Aino went into the house with the children, Ullakko touched Ilmari's sleeve. "Did she, you know, dance with someone?"

"It was a dance," Ilmari said.

"I mean a lot with someone."

"A little with Jouka Kaukonen, toward the end."

"He's good-looking."

"Yoh," Ilmari said. "He's kind of wild though, and he has no farm."

"Sure. I have a farm. Good prospects. But I'm nothing like Jouka Kaukonen. He plays the fiddle. He sings. He recites poems. Even being kind of wild attracts a girl."

"He drinks," Matti put in.

"Yoh. Like most loggers."

When Aino descended the stairs after putting the children down for their nap, she saw Ullakko standing by the kitchen table. It was clear that he'd been waiting for her. He motioned for her to sit at the table and she did. She focused on making her face neutral.

Ullakko sat down and put his hands out to her, but she kept hers in her lap. He quickly withdrew his own. "Aino, you must know how I feel about you."

She had a sinking feeling that this was going to be her first marriage proposal. Voitto had never really proposed to her; they'd just sort of fallen into planning their lives together. She knew she should have felt excited, flattered that someone was so enamored of her he would ask her to marry him. Instead, she was horrified that she was being asked by such an old man.

"Yoh," she said. "And you're a good man." She was desperately trying to come up with how to turn him down without hurting him. At the same time, she was so angry with him that she almost *wanted* to hurt him.

"Washington is a community property state. You know what that means."

"Of course."

"Whatever we build together, half will be yours, no matter what. It's the law."

He walked over to the standing cupboard near the stove, opened a shallow drawer, and pulled out a velvet box, which he put on the table in front of her.

Ullakko's little girl, bursting with excitement, had shown it to her one day. Aino had put it on the child's neck. The little girl went very quiet, stroking the silver chain and single pearl gently, telling Aino that it was her mother's necklace and her grandmother's before that and her grandmother had put it around her mother's neck when she left for America.

Ullakko opened the box, taking what she knew was the most precious thing he owned in his broad callused hands. He walked behind Aino. She felt panic welling up in her. She fought it while he fumbled with his thick fingers to clasp the necklace beneath the coiled bun of her hair. Putting his hand on her neck, he nuzzled his cheek up against her ear from over her shoulder. She could smell his halitosis. Her heart started hammering with fear and adrenaline. She didn't know why. It was like being gripped by a dark shadow.

He dropped down on one knee beside her and said what she'd been dreading, "Will you marry me?"

She shoved the chair away from him and stood looking at the wall trying to sort through a wildly fluctuating and contradictory set of thoughts and feelings. Here was her first real marriage proposal and from a prosperous farmer who could solidly provide for her and her children. Here was a man on his knees, having offered her his most precious possession and the most beautiful thing she'd ever worn. But that was the great temptation: to settle in, to become a rich farmer's wife, a petite bourgeoise. She'd just become part of the oppressive system. It went against everything she and Voitto believed. She remembered kissing Voitto by the river. Why couldn't this have been Voitto? At the same time, her heart ached for Ullakko. She knew he was lonely, that he tried; he was as good a father as any child could expect. Why did her first marriage proposal come from a man she didn't love?

She turned from Ullakko to conceal her disappointment and confusion. Ullakko jumped to his feet, alarmed that he'd done something terribly wrong.

Seeing him so stricken, she panicked. She didn't know what to say to him or what to do with this whole situation. The necklace suddenly felt like a collar, tethering her to the farm, to a life she didn't want. She fumbled for the tiny clasp and couldn't work it. Frustrated with her clumsiness, she yanked too hard on the delicate chain, breaking it. It horrified her. She held the necklace out to Ullakko, her hands shaking, tears of embarrassment in her eyes.

"I . . . I'm . . ." She was stuttering. "I'm so, so sorry." She could feel the wound in his heart and knew she'd put it there. "You're a good man." She looked at the necklace still in her hand and then put it on the table.

Still bewildered, Ullakko said, "Aino, I would love you with all my heart, with everything I have."

"But I won't love you!" she cried.

She fled upstairs.

*   *   *

When she came back with her packed bag, he was sitting at the table, staring at the broken necklace. He looked at her. It was obvious he had been crying. She had never seen a man cry. Her heart went out to him because he was so sad and she'd refused his suit but, at the same time, it infuriated her that he was so unmanly.

"I'm sorry," she said and left.

Upon reaching the road, she realized she had to choose a direction and had nowhere to spend the night. She couldn't go to Ilmahenki, given how Ilmari felt about Ullakko. She could never explain why she quit. She realized she was crying and tried to wipe back the tears.

Then she thought maybe Reder Logging needed a woman in the mess hall or cookshack. She realized that she was now in the same position as Jouka, whom she'd castigated at the dance for just accepting what was offered. She needed to earn money to eat and get shelter.

She knew the logging camp was a few miles southwest of Ullakko's farm. Like all the camps in the area, it was connected to the greater world by its own railroad. There were no roads south of Tapiola of any kind. She figured that there must be a path off the Knappton-Tapiola trail that led to the railroad or directly to the camp. Maybe she'd land a job where Matti worked—where Jouka worked. She'd no longer be a burden. She'd be independent.

Still sniffling, she set off barefoot, wearing her best skirt and blouse from the dance, cloth suitcase in her hand, shoes around her neck, her hopes high.

After the first mile, she began to have doubts. All she saw was dense forest. What if there were some other trail to Knappton or Tapiola from Reder's Camp? The trees seemed to lean into the trail, squeezing it. Of course, that was silly. They didn't lean. She heard something crackle in the underbrush and her heart started racing. Another mile of plodding and still no trail. Her bare feet were covered in mud. The day seemed darker than when she'd left, yet it wasn't even late afternoon. She heard wind rustling the fir boughs high above her. She looked up at dark-gray clouds covering the sky above the moving treetops. She shivered, cold despite the brisk walking, and put on her coat. After about three miles she found a well-worn trail leading west and uphill. Where else would it go except Reder's Camp?

When she lost sight of the Knappton trail, she lost sight of anything familiar.

A raven, startled from its roost, croaked its deep crow-like caw and flew just feet above her head, disappearing into the forest. The raven filled her with foreboding. She fought down childish superstition. The trail now paralleled a creek. The water was dark, filled with silt. It didn't seem natural. She realized she hadn't eaten since the night before and had packed no food. What if she never found Reder's Camp? Should she turn back now to avoid getting trapped in the dark? Turn back to where? Her evaporating sweat chilled her. The slate-gray overcast weighed on her shoulders, pressing her into the forest floor. Then it started to rain.

She was overwhelmed with what she'd done. She'd refused a proposal of marriage, rather badly, hurting the man in the process. She'd quit her job and was now hungry in a forest that seemingly had no end. She'd set off for someplace she didn't know how to find. She had no shelter, she was getting soaked, and the day moved relentlessly toward night. She had no way to see in the dark.

She plopped down next to the creek, not caring about the mud on her good skirt. She thought about going back to Ilmahenki or apologizing to Ullakko. She couldn't. She thought about how she'd gotten to this lonely place where farms were so new the farmers sowed their grain around stumps and their little houses were dwarfed by enormous trees. Her thoughts went back to Finland, where the landscape was on a human scale. Would she ever see her parents again? She fought down the memories of her dead sisters and brother. Then, the horrible prison time once again intruded on her memory. A sickening feeling of guilt swept through her stomach and intestines, knowing what must have been done to Voitto because of her. She started to sob.

Aino looked through tears at the sullen clouds above her. All around her, tree after tree for mile upon mile upon mile made her feel small, helpless, and alone. She thought of wrapping her shawl around her head, covering her face, and throwing herself into the murky creek to drown.

Movement caught her eye and she imagined more than heard a soft flutter of wings. A northern pygmy owl, about half a foot tall, had silently emerged from a hiding place at the edge of the uncut forest. It swooped down, hitting the ground by the creek with a thud. Wings beating at the cool air, the owl climbed to the top of a snag and turned its head, staring straight at her with its fierce immovable eyes. A field mouse hung in its beak. It began to feed on the mouse, occasionally jerking up, swiveling its head to stare at her briefly, making sure she wasn't a threat. It hooted, warning her to stay clear. She laughed. Ilmari would say the owl represented their mother's spirit, come to scold her for forgetting her sisu.

Around midafternoon, beneath high gray clouds from the Pacific climbing over the cooler air of the vast forest, she hit the rail line linking Reder's Camp to Willapa Bay. The rain had stopped, but the sun stayed hidden, its presence signaled only by lighter gray in the southwest sky before her. The forest was cast in continuous shadow. She turned south on the railroad tracks, stepping on the cedar crossties, taking in their soft sweet smell. She guessed that to save money Reder had not bothered to creosote them as major railroads did. The untreated cedar would last long enough for him to cut out the timber. After following the tracks as they climbed into the hills another three or four miles, she heard women's voices. They were speaking Finn! She hurried toward them.

Coming around a gentle curve in the rail line, she faced a large, seemingly haphazard bridge made of log after log piled one upon another from the bottom of a small logged-off canyon with a fast-flowing creek where three girls around her age were washing clothes. The music of their voices blended with the music of the stream. Occasional laughter bubbled up to her, standing there bedraggled on the rail line in her wet and muddy Sunday best.

One of the girls saw her and spoke beneath her breath to the other two. They looked at Aino, skirts tucked above their knees, feet in the cold water. Aino recognized two of them from the dance the night before.

"Päivää," the first girl shouted up to her, short for hyvää päivää, good day.

"Päivää," she shouted back. She looked down, took a deep breath, and began the steep slide down the hill. By the time she'd reached them, she'd snagged her blouse on a blackberry vine and strained an ankle when she caught her foot on her skirt hem and fallen.

The girl who had shouted to her giggled, pointing at her clothes. "You're going the wrong way for a dance, girl. Plenty of men up here, but no music."

"I'm looking for work."

"Yoh," the girl said. "Can you cook?"

Aino hesitated. "Sure. What Finn woman can't cook?"

"Yeah, well, cooking for a husband is different from cooking for a hundred loggers."

"And they can eat," one of the others broke in. "You would never believe it possible how they can eat." All three of them laughed again. Aino smiled. She hadn't realized until just now how much she had missed girls of her own age. She remembered the dance, all the girls primping at the mirror, adjusting skirts, flattening blouses to reveal curves, knowing they were in a situation where none of them could lose. But here, they were working, doing what women did: washing clothes, talking, laughing, being right with the world and full of life.

Aino sat down and put her tired feet and sore ankle in the water. She'd walked about ten miles barefoot, in wet clothes, the last three or four miles on splintered rail ties.

The girls folded the clothes, bundling them with sheets and throwing them, still damp, over their backs to haul back to camp.

"It's about four hundred yards," the first girl said. She used the American measure. "Around that curve," the first girl said, nodding with her chin. She was taller than Aino, but younger, not yet fully developed. She was not beautiful but not ugly, pleasant looking. There was no fat on her, nor was there any on the other girls, but she wasn't thin. She looked strong, in a girlish way. "You ask for Alma Wiitala," the girl continued.

"Alma Wiitala's from my home place," Aino said, excitement growing. "We're shirttail relatives."

"Well, good. You tell her Lempi Rompinen also gave you her name." She paused, just slightly. "That's me," she said softly. "Lempi."

Warmth seemed to flow from deep inside, out through her blue eyes. The two girls regarded each other, just enough for each to know that for some inexplicable reason, here was someone who could be a friend, even though you'd known her no more than a minute. Lempi's voice came back to full volume. "She hires and supervises the flunkies." She used the American word. "That's what the loggers call us girls who work in the mess hall." Her eyes ran up and down Aino. "You can make yourself presentable here." She looked down at Aino's feet. "And put your shoes on so you don't look so desperate."

The three girls climbed a steep well-worn path up the camp side of the creek, bent under their loads. Lempi cracked a joke that Aino couldn't hear, and they laughed in such a way that the joke was probably at Aino's expense.

Aino washed and wrung out her stockings. Then she took her skirt off and brushed it with a cedar branch, getting off most of the leaves and loose dirt. She unbuttoned her blouse and, using one of the wet stockings, sponged the hair in her armpits. She adjusted her corset, put on her wet stockings, and sat by the stream to gather herself together.

11

She smelled Reder's Camp before she saw it, despite the lime thrown on the feces to reduce the odor of the outhouses. Rounding the final curve, she saw a chaotic jumble of slash, snags, rusting steel cables, and mud, the single most recognizable geometric form being the line of railroad track that cut right through the middle of the camp. The ground between the structures couldn't be seen through the mass of limbs, discarded small logs, uprooted trees, and abandoned tops, not worth sawing into logs. Pigs roamed freely, rooting out garbage, the smell of which had been masked until now by the smell of the outhouses supplemented by the smell of the pig shit. How could men live in conditions like this? She saw several rough board-and-batten structures with metal chimneys protruding from their roofs at the far end of the camp, probably the bunkhouses. Closer in, by the tracks, another larger building had been set up high on pilings with a railed porch going around it, probably the cookhouse and dining hall. Shacks, maybe twelve or fourteen feet long by ten feet wide, each set on two large parallel logs, were scattered amid the slash. Most had overlapping split-cedar shakes that formed roofs without gutters or downspouts, some had only canvas roofs. Many shacks had never been leveled but were just dropped from the railcars and left where they settled. A few had curtains on single windows set in the rough board-and-batten siding, suggesting at least some of the men had wives.

In the distance beyond the camp stood a ragged line of uncut trees behind a jumbled wasteland of mud, stumps, branches, discarded treetops that apparently weren't worth limbing, and smaller trees, under

two feet in diameter, left standing for the same reason. Some of the
smaller trees had been hit and broken by larger logs being hauled up to
where they were stacked, waiting to be loaded on railcars. It reminded
Aino of photographs of artillery devastation she'd seen in a book of
Pastor Nieminen's about the American Civil War.

The uncut trees' lower trunks were without limbs and so without
knots, many climbing for more than 150 feet before reaching the first
branches of their dark-green tops. Before that line, constantly pushing
it farther into the ancient forest, was what looked to Aino like a mad-
house of wrist-thick steel cables issuing from smoking steam engines
set on giant logs. The cables were wound on large drums that looked
like thread spools for giants. Spinning rapidly with the power of the
steam, logs were reeled in, bouncing and weaving through the slash
at speeds faster than a man could run—or perhaps run clear of. The
cables, hundreds of feet long, were threaded through blocks, two heavy
steel plates holding a pulley-like sheave between them joined at the top
by a yoke. The blocks were lashed to huge stumps, providing different
angles with which to pull the logs or unwind a cable that had previously been pulled all the way in. Piping whistles, hissing steam, and
dark wood smoke billowed from the boilers. These must be the steam
donkeys, also called yarders, that Ilmari had told her were rapidly
replacing the large teams of oxen or horses that had previously pulled
the logs to water. She could see men crawling under the logs, hooking
them with smaller cables to the main large cable, then scrambling clear
of the logs that smashed their way to piles being collected around rail
spurs.

She saw a small boy standing on a tall stump pull on a wire and
heard a piercing sound. She'd heard about whistle punks, boys as young
as eight or nine who worked twelve- to fourteen-hour days down in the
steep ravines. Their job was to signal the engineer working the steam
donkey that the rigging crew was clear and the log ready to be yanked
into motion. If they made a mistake, it could cost a man his life.

The steam donkey's whistle tooted in response to the whistle
punk's signal and the big cable went stiff with tension, coming off the
ground. She couldn't follow the entire line of it, because the terrain

was so rugged, but could see its end where it wound around an anchoring block that must have weighed a thousand pounds. The block was cinched with a smaller cable to a stump that was at least fourteen feet in diameter. How could men weighing 150 pounds have hauled all this dead weight of steel and cable across that terrain?

Those men were now scrambling for safety, ducking behind stumps, finding shelter in the torn ground, as more steam poured into the donkey's pistons. The massive cable drums whirred, jerking a log weighing several tons from where it lay, bringing it careening through the slash like a runaway railroad car to the landing as fast as the cable drums could turn.

Next to the steam donkey sat a railroad engine and fifteen pairs of trucks, square timber platforms with wheels. Once loaded with one end of a thirty-six- or forty-foot log—the log's other end loaded on a second platform—the two wheeled platforms were joined, converted into a single railcar by the log they were carrying.

Aino stood there transfixed amid the tooting of the whistle punks and the roaring steam donkeys. She became aware of the constant, steady thump and thwack of double-bitted axes and the rasping of twelve-foot-long crosscut saws as men felled trees taller than any building Aino had ever seen. Matti told her that just one of these Douglas firs could produce enough lumber to build three or four houses. She hadn't believed him. But now—with each splintering, anguished crackle, when fibers that had held for centuries first started to part; with each moaning, creaking groan as the tree leaned and tore loose from its stump; with the sound of air rushing through the limbs of a rapidly accelerating top; with each ground-shaking crash signaling a tree's death—she believed. Everything about the place spoke of danger and filled her with respect for these men.

Alma Wiitala had Vanhatalo ears, small, like Aino's mother's. It was somehow comforting, this tracing of family through different branches, yet family all the same. Alma was Aino's height, but she seemed taller. There was a gravitas about her—perhaps because of her position as head of the dining room staff—but there was something more, some sadness deep in her eyes. She'd known sorrow. Aino later learned that Alma had lost two of her children several years earlier to a flu that had moved into pneumonia.

Aino told Alma Wiitala she was Ilmari and Matti's sister and that Lempi Rompinen had recommended her.

Alma observed Aino attentively with warm ultramarine-blue eyes that were beginning to have the wrinkles that form at the outside corners when a person reaches the late twenties. "I met your mother once at a wedding," she said. "When I was a girl, before I left Suomi."

Aino didn't know how to respond. Alma laughed, showing a basic good nature that underlay the hint of sorrow.

"In America, you can talk to your elders, even if you don't know them," she said. "Show me your hands."

It was the first time Aino was grateful for all the work at Ilmahenki and Ullakko's. "I'm a good worker," she said. "I'm healthy, too." She hesitated. "I rarely get tired."

Alma laughed again. "You don't know what tired is."

After a few hard questions, some of which Aino answered by what might graciously be called stretching the truth, Alma took her to meet the head cook, a small man missing one arm, who seemed too busy to talk to her.

"She's from my home place," Alma said. "We're related. Her brothers are hard workers."

The cook grunted. "If it's OK with Reder, it's OK with me."

Alma took Aino back outside. "The cook's the king," she said. "And his two assistants are princes, but I'm the queen. Do you understand?"

Aino nodded.

"We're the most important part of Reder Logging. If the food's bad, the loggers leave. If the food's good, we get the best loggers."

"Why not just pay more?"

Alma gave her a steely look. "Reder pays what everyone pays."

Aino thought now was not the time to talk economics.

Alma made a nod toward the bunkhouses. "Loggers will put up with lice in the bunkhouses, shit two feet from the door, and work that you and I wouldn't do, couldn't do, for ten minutes." She nodded at the cookshack behind her. "But if they get bad pancakes or soggy pies, they'll quit." She napped her fingers. "Just like that."

Aino nodded.

"What we do here can make or break Reder Logging."

Aino nodded again.

"Come on then, let's meet the big boss."

Alma led her past four hanging hog carcasses, explaining that they were tomorrow's bacon and pork stew. She also pointed out with pride that they weren't too fat. If they were fat, that would mean that they were eating too many scraps, which meant that the loggers weren't eating all the food and the cooking was bad. She led Aino along a muddy path, dodging slash and stumps, to a small, rough office set next to the dining hall. She entered without knocking. A large rangy man looked up. He was indistinguishable from the loggers in both clothing and demeanor, with hands so big Aino could barely see the pencil he was using. He did not fit Aino's idea of a capitalist owner, a fat man wearing a suit eating in a fancy club. He looked like a workingman, not the enemy.

She soon learned that John Reder had immigrated to America from Holland when he was sixteen and went to work in the woods of Michigan, saving every penny. At age twenty-four, he had enough money to buy two axes and two saws. Being able to provide his own capital, he bargained to be paid by the trees cut and bucked, not by the day. By age thirty he employed forty loggers and life was good—until Michigan ran out of trees.

He'd always discounted what he heard of the forests of the Pacific Northwest, but a train ride west in the late 1880s changed his mind. He sold everything he owned, came to the lower Columbia River, and by 1906 had more than doubled the size of his Michigan outfit.

Aino noticed a single gold band on his left ring finger.

Alma did the talking in English, most of it too fast for Aino to follow.

"She speak English?" Reder asked after Alma had finished.

Aino immediately chimed in: "Yoh, sure. Good English for verking."

Reder grunted. "Know ... her?"

"I know ... brothers ... Matti ... Ilmari Koski ... black-smith ... Lempi Rompinen."

"Vouch for her?"

"She's family."

Reder grunted a short sign of approval. He turned to Aino and said with a Dutch accent, slowly, so she'd understand him: "Alma vouches for you ... honest ... Matt ... good worker." He had raised his voice, as if that would make him better understood, irritating Aino.

Reder turned to Alma. "She ... fifty cents a day ... other girls. We ... fresh straw? She works ... bed later. All she can eat ... other Sunday off."

Reder went back to his neatly printed columns of numbers without even a grunt of farewell.

Walking back to the dining hall, happy and relieved that she had been hired, Aino listened as Alma translated what Reder had said. She'd get fifty cents a day. She'd live with the other girls in what was called in English the henhouse and sleep on the floor on straw. She was on trial for two weeks. If she worked out, they'd get her a bed with sheets and blankets. One hundred loggers ate every day, so she'd get every other Sunday off. The girls were good about trading shifts if something came up. After the tables were cleared, she would sit down with the rest of the girls and eat as much as she wanted. There was a tub just behind the henhouse with canvas walls for privacy. Before dances, the girls could bring hot water from the kitchen for a single shared bath—in order of seniority.

Matti's jaw dropped when he saw Aino waiting on the tables that night. It pleased her greatly.

"Does Ilmari know?" he asked.

"I only left this morning."

"You need to get word to him. He'll be upset."

"Why? I've landed a good job."

Matti looked at her, then said, "Just get a note to him. It's the right thing to do."

*   *   *

Work at Reder's Camp turned out to be the hardest, most unforgiving work Aino had ever done—and she was used to hard work. She and the other three girls were up in the dark, even in summer. She mixed pancake batter, cut bacon, cracked eggs, made coffee, or frantically tried to keep up her end of an assembly line making dozens and dozens of sandwiches: beef, ham, peanut butter, fried egg, leftover meat loaf, chicken, salmon.

At 5:15 a.m., the steam whistle on the train woke the men. The fireman had been tending the fire in the boiler, getting the steam up, since 4:30. At 5:30, the dining hall filled with men of all types, mostly young, mostly Scandinavian, but Irish, Slovaks, Scots, and Americans as well. Their wiry bodies had the stamina of distance runners combined with the nimbleness of dancers—and an astonishing capacity for food. They focused on eating; save for the occasional "Pass the butter," no one talked. They devoured pancakes stacked eight or nine inches high slathered with butter, syrup, and molasses; put down bowls of oatmeal drowned in cream; consumed plates of eggs, bacon, and ham; ate beans cooked in a sweet tomato sauce for breakfast; and emptied six ten-gallon coffeepots, all in about twenty minutes. She never had time to say more than a few words to Matti.

After breakfast, the dining hall empty, Aino would watch the loggers clamber into the predawn light, still not talking, the spikes on their boots chewing at the heavy plank floor. Within minutes she would hear the first shrills of the whistle punks, the clattering of steam donkeys, the singing of steel cables running through blocks and winding onto and off the huge steam-driven drums, and the rending crash of fallen giants whose deaths she could feel through her feet. Those working more than a mile from the mess hall carried sandwiches of dark heavy bread she and the other flunkies had prepared scant hours earlier. The rest would walk in for lunch.

She would stare at hundreds of dishes and coffee cups, greasy grills on huge woodstoves stretching more than ten feet. Straining to move huge pots of boiling water, pouring the water into sinks, tossing in soap whittled into flakes from one-pound cakes, she would scrub, while other girls, her seniors by hiring date, dried and restacked.

Her hands grew red with the heat and harsh soap, but she had no time to worry about that. Prep work began immediately with wood to haul for the afternoon cooking of the evening meal; vegetables to chop for stew; onions to chop for pounds of meat loaf; massive amounts of dried beans to be boiled soft; salmon to butcher for stew or frying; hogs to gut, skin, hang to bleed, and then butcher; dough to knead for bread, for pies, for cobbler, for dumplings; cream brought up the rail tracks from places like Ullakko's to churn into butter; buttermilk to be mixed with flour and baking soda to make pancakes; and always the constant fight to use the cream, meat, and vegetables before they went bad. Nothing could be kept; there was no ice. Leftovers were never a problem.

Just before dark the locust horde of a hundred men once more descended on the dining hall, some shouting, some quiet, some sullen, some happy—all hungry. Men would shovel six or seven pork chops onto their plates from brimming platters, or three twelve-ounce steaks when beef was served, to be followed by mashed potatoes into which they stirred honey or smashed tablespoonsful of butter. Some nights there would be oysters from Willapa Bay. Other nights there would be thick clam chowder. Cabbage and beets were the main dinner vegetables, because it was fall. They would change to turnips and rutabagas in the winter. The twenty double loaves of bread they'd baked that morning would all be gone by the end of supper, along with the two hundred doughnuts and thirty apple pies.

In about twenty minutes, the huge coffee urns drained, milk pitchers emptied, meat platters left with only traces of grease, the dining hall again would be deserted. Under kerosene lamps the girls washed and put away the hundreds of plates, cups, and bowls, and set the tables for breakfast. Then there would be the mixing of pancake batter, the carving of bacon slices from large sides, the walking in of the huge metal milk cans full of cream, the loading of the empties back on the railcars, and, finally, the staggering to the henhouse. There, the girls stripped to their underwear and collapsed into bed, Aino onto straw on the floor.

Once a week, Aino got her bath after all the others. She distracted herself by doing the math comparing the surface area of her body with the volume of the water, assuring herself that despite the increasingly browner water there was still a chance she'd come out cleaner than she'd gone in. She yearned for a sauna.

Two weeks passed, and Alma told Aino she was on for good. The promised bed showed up on the back of an empty railcar. She felt a little guilty knowing she got the bed because she was a girl, while the loggers had no beds and slept in three-bunk stacks, on planks covered with straw. She got past that the first night.

All this time, she watched for Jouka. She'd get glimpses of him, usually silently shoveling in food as if it were his first meal in a week and his last one for the week to come, but occasionally she'd see him talking and joking with friends outside the bunkhouse in the brief time between dinner and sleep. He was clearly popular. His mother had been pregnant with him when she came from Finland, so he was a citizen and spoke fluent English. She learned he was a faller. That meant skilled with an ax, being able to swing it left- and right-handed, striking every two seconds alternating with another faller, both balancing on springboards wedged into the tree ten feet above the ground. Each stroke had to fall precisely where intended, taking off the maximum chip of wood, the undercut formed perfectly to fell the tree exactly where desired. That went on all day without a stop except twenty minutes for lunch, from dark to dark, six days a week. A typical logger was less than six feet tall. A typical Douglas fir towered over two hundred feet and not infrequently more than three hundred feet above him, ranging in diameter from eight to twenty feet. If the tree didn't go where intended or if it twisted when it started to fall and a faller wasn't quick enough, the faller died.

It amazed Aino that the loggers not only ignored the danger but seemed proud to ignore it, relying on their skill and stamina to win a daily wager against death or maiming—all for about twenty cents an hour. But men did what was expected of them or they weren't men. It was that simple.

* * *

Aino's first Sunday off, June 24, 1906, was the day Pastor Hoikka came from Astoria to consecrate Ilmari's church. Hoikka installed the church council, with Ilmari as president. The congregation had decided to combine the consecration with the traditional Midsummer's Eve celebration, which that year would have fallen on Thursday. They'd prepared a huge bonfire in front of the church. Grumbling that she was doing it only because Ilmari was her brother and she never had time to see him otherwise, Aino attended.

Ilmari was polite, but distant. When Ullakko and his children arrived, he immediately approached them, leaving Aino by herself. When Ilmari reached him, Ullakko looked over at Aino. She smiled. He forced a smile back. His children came running to her. Her smile for them was not forced, but she felt little joy.

When Pastor Hoika performed the ceremony, Aino found herself proud of what Ilmari had accomplished. Lempi and the other girls from the henhouse had also come. Afterward, all the girls walked to the dance in Knappton, occasionally looking back at the towering fire, the sparks rising into the evening sky. It made Aino homesick.

Jouka had been asked to join the band. She watched him come in with the other musicians, all loggers or mill workers, carrying their precious instruments. She'd heard that Jouka made his violin himself, working on it Sundays. Jouka took the last quick drink and tossed the empty bottle over thirty feet into the river in a graceful fluid motion. He jumped onto the stage rather than going up the four stairs at its end. He looked toward Aino and smiled, making her feel as if he were about to play just for her; she was unaware that every girl standing next to her felt the same way.

Turning to his fellow musicians with a quick, "Yksi, kaksi, kolme," he started the night with "Finska Polka." No girl was left alone or given any rest unless she fled to the room reserved for the women. On one of these trips, Aino saw a girl rub something red on her lips with her forefinger. She'd heard about whores and loose women in cities like Astoria, but it shocked her they'd allow someone like that into a dance with decent hardworking people.

She got only one dance with Jouka.

* * *

Two weeks later, Ilmari arrived at the Tapiola landing towing a small raft behind his rowboat. On the raft was a well-wrapped and securely strapped Estey reed organ that had journeyed by rail from Brattleboro, Vermont, to Portland and then on to Willapa, where it was loaded on the *Reliable*. It was unloaded on the Deep River pier, where it sat for a full day before word reached Ilmari to fetch it.

On Sunday evening, the twenty-fifth of August, Ruusu Pakkanen opened services with a rousing and forcefully pedaled "A Mighty Fortress Is Our God," while Pastor Hoikka swept up the aisle resplendent in his new vestments. A large painting of Jesus at the home of Mary and Martha, a fitting testimony to the value of women in the church, hung behind the altar.

12

In June, Aksel had a letter from home confirming his fears. Gunnar had indeed died in the raid. The family had been unable to recover the body for burial.

Aksel quit his job.

By mid-September he stood on a creosoted wharf looking at the Columbia River. Salmon-canning factories lined the riverbank in both directions as far as he could see. On the river itself were hundreds of small two-ended gill net boats with lateen sails. Fourteen miles to the west was the Columbia River bar, two miles of maelstrom where the river hit the Pacific and the site of over six hundred shipwrecks. He'd been told that on clear days, to the east you could see Mount Saint Helens, a snowcapped volcano with the same symmetrical beauty as Mount Fuji. On this typical day, however, all but the immediate hills were hidden from view beneath a flat ceiling of soft gray. He could just make out the smoke rolling from the wigwam burners and boilers of two sawmills at Knappton, six miles across the river from him. His destination, Tapiola, lay hidden behind the steep hills to the north of the town.

Seeing the river, watching the wind fill a sail, and smelling the fish guts thrown into the water from the canneries, Aksel longed to be fishing. The Chinook salmon runs, however, were coming to an end, leaving only winter steelhead and not much chance of work. With San Francisco rebuilding after the huge quake in April, sawmills were operating at full tilt and logging companies were hiring. He couldn't face being tied to a sawmill production line, so logging would have to get him the money for his own boat.

Aksel shouldered his rucksack and paid fifteen cents for passage on the *General Washington*, which plied its daily rounds between Knappton, small landings upstream on the Washington side, and Astoria. He landed at Knappton with four dollars and sixty cents left from his earnings in Bandon. He heard the faint, far-off whistle of a logging train and was told the train belonged to Reder Logging, and John Reder was hiring.

Aksel set off along a trail that headed north into the hills. He was told to turn left at the first trail that looked well used. He did and hit the Reder rail line where he caught a ride on the next train going up to Reder's Camp.

He was hired to chop and split wood for the steam donkeys— seventy-five cents a day, a bunk, all he could eat in twenty minutes, and a chance to move up, starting the next morning. Of course, money would be deducted from his pay for room and board.

Aksel was directed to one of the bunkhouses. The place was gloomy and empty except for one man on his bunk, obviously with a high fever. All the other loggers were working. The clammy air smelled of wet wool blankets, tobacco, and unwashed men. A pig was rooting around scraps thrown next to a potbellied woodstove, and he shooed it out. The bunk was bare planks. He saw a pile of hay in one corner and picked some up. It was limp, damp, and had the slightly sweet scent of decay. He heard rustling. A rat disappeared under the hay. He carried several armloads to his bunk. He leaned his hand against the top bunk, then quickly jerked it away. A flea had hopped on it. He brushed it off but couldn't see it in the gloom to crush it on the floor.

He walked outside into a light drizzle. John Reder had told him all he could eat. After climbing the uneven steps to a wide porch on the west side of the mess hall and cookshack, he looked inside. At first, he thought he must be imagining it. He had often thought about the dark-haired girl he'd danced with on Midsummer's Eve. The girl turned and he saw her face and the glasses. It was her, Aino Koski! Of course, he'd been told there were lots of Kokkola people here, so he shouldn't be surprised. Still, *she* was the first person he saw from home. The long winter, the hard, long walk up the coast, the miserable green chain in Bandon had all been spent to reach one goal—her. He rushed inside, calling her name.

Aino couldn't help smiling. Here was that kid from the Midsummer's Night dance, over two years ago, Gunnar Långström's little brother. He must have grown four inches taller and two inches wider in the shoulders since she last saw him. His onrush slowed. He stopped short of her, his enthusiasm losing out to shyness.

"Hyvää päivää," he said, greeting her formally in just slightly Swedish-accented Finnish. "Do you remember me, Aksel Långström? The Midsummer's dance?"

"Päivää," she answered more informally. "Sure, I do."

He smiled as though she'd just given him Christmas dinner. There was something about him that she just had to like.

An awkward silence followed. Aino looked over her shoulder at the door into the large kitchen to see if Alma was there. Lempi and another girl who were setting the long tables glanced at Aksel, trying to look as if they weren't looking. Lempi was setting the opposite side of the table from where she was standing, making it easier to glance at Aksel unobtrusively without having to turn her head. It made Aino smile. She turned back to Aksel, wondering if he noticed. It didn't seem so. He was looking at his shoes, which were nearly unwearable.

Pressured by the need to return to work, they quickly caught up, Aino telling Aksel about her journey to America, about Matti working at Reder's Camp, about Ilmari's farm. Aksel told Aino about shipping aboard the *Elna* and the long walk north. Aino wondered if Aksel knew about Gunnar's death but was afraid to ask. Aksel didn't mention anything.

Matti and Aksel recognized each other the moment Matti walked into the bunkhouse. They shook hands.

"Food's on," Matti said in Finnish, nodding toward the mess hall.

Aksel followed Matti into the darkness. The crews worked until the light failed. A child, around eight or nine years old, tagged in just behind Matti. Matti tousled the boy's filthy hair and laughed. "Kullerikki, meet Aksel. He's from my home place." He turned to Aksel. "His real name is Heikki Ranta. He's a whistle punk."

Kullerikki meant little Kullervo, a maddened tragic character from *The Kalevala*. Aksel saw that the boy's left ear had been torn and then healed. There was a scar beside his right eye. The boy trudged on determinedly beside them. Clearly, he'd adopted Matti.

They arrived at the mess hall along with dozens of other loggers, some coming from one of the four bunkhouses, many streaming in immediately from work, some jumping off railcars, most walking. There was hardly a word spoken. Matti immediately started taking huge quantities from serving plates and bowls that were rapidly passing by them and soon had his plate covered and heaping. Aksel scrambled to follow suit, noticing that Kullerikki had filled his plate as much as had Matti.

"So, how long have you been here?" Aksel asked, chewing on a chunk of stew meat.

Matti indicated the others with nods of his head. Aksel looked around. No one talked. They all just ate, as fast as they could. He reddened a little and put his mind to the task at hand. He kept glancing around, trying to catch a glimpse of Aino. She ignored him. All the girls were extremely busy. Fifteen minutes later, stomach pressing against his waistband, he followed Kullerikki and Matti into the dark. Faint light from a kerosene lamp in their bunkhouse guided them to its door. Long wool underwear hung from nails and wires, vying for space by the stove, which was cracking and expanding from the sudden heat in its belly. It was burning thick slabs of bark that the loggers carried back from the show. The bark would be replaced by alder before they slept. Matti picked Kullerikki up from beneath his armpits and tossed him up to the third bunk where he soon situated himself, sitting on its edge with legs dangling, kicking gently. Matti reached for a large piece of finely grained cedar on his bunk, took out his puukko, sat on the rough boards of the floor, and started carving a large bowl.

Within half an hour everyone in the bunks slept. Aksel watched the red light from the cracks in the stove door flickering on the ceiling.

* * *

They awoke in the dark. Most of the loggers went to the four- and six-hole outhouses, but some just shit behind stumps next to the bunkhouse. There was no sunrise. Objects just gradually emerged as gray grew lighter around them. Walking with Matti the mile to the logging show after breakfast, Aksel felt the same tension he had felt before going up the mast for the first time, fear and excitement: fear that he'd not make the grade, excitement at realizing that if he made it, he'd be one of those lean taciturn men, a man who could hold his head up in any company anywhere.

But first came making the grade.

They put him to work splitting wood to fuel the steam donkey's boiler, just as Matti had done.

Hauled up to the side of the landing, a single log, about three feet in diameter, lay at an odd angle, its chopped top pointing skyward just over the edge of the flattened ground where much larger and more profitable logs were being stacked and sorted. Aksel used a wide-faced ax to take off the limbs, then, with a six-foot-long crosscut saw, he reduced the tree to rounds. The rounds got hauled, rolled, pulled, and cursed up to the landing where he split them into cordwood, roughly eighteen inches long and eight inches wide.

By midmorning, Aksel wanted to quit. Of course, that was unthinkable. Aksel's hands, work-hardened since he was a boy, still blistered from the nine-pound splitting maul and eight-foot-long bucksaw. His worn-out shoes couldn't grip the wood and he fell awkwardly off logs, barking his shins and scraping his arms and thighs. Still, he kept the monster fed and the donkey puncher, the man running the monster, happy. No breaks.

At noon, he heard four short blasts of the donkey whistle and the cables went slack. Men, many until now unseen, began to emerge from the line of uncut trees and work their way across the slash, moving like acrobats from log to springy limb to stump top, all coming toward the landing. Hearing a short toot behind him, Aksel turned to see the log train puffing slowly up the grade from Reder's Camp. Sitting on one of the empty cars, their legs dangling, were two girls, one of them Aino.

Happiness burst into his body. They were sitting next to steaming pails of stew, beans, and stacks of sandwiches. Lunch. God be praised. Twenty minutes later Aksel was back at work.

And it went like that endlessly. The boiler was a fiery bottomless pit. It seemed a thing alive, its glowing red mouth devouring everything he cut and split, spewing excess steam, driving the cable drums that pulled the huge logs to the loading boom that put them on the railcars. When dark fell, he dragged himself back to the dining hall and then into bed, asleep instantly in his sweat-stained and slightly bloody wool long johns. The loggers awoke before daylight and took down their stiff clothes from the lines strung above them. Since Aksel was the greenhorn, he emptied the piss pots under the bunks into the slash next to the bunkhouse. Every day, he and Matti wolfed down breakfast in near silence, then walked or caught an empty railcar to the show. There they resumed working as if the night hadn't intervened.

Unlike other loggers—who had job titles like choker setter, faller, bucker, and rigger—Aksel had no title. He wasn't a logger and the loggers let him know it, including Matti, which annoyed him. He'd like to see Matti reefing sails a hundred feet above the deck.

In the early afternoon of his fourth day, Aksel heard a sound like a giant steel kantele string snapping. From the corner of his eye he saw the end of a one-inch mainline cable whipping across the top of the slash and slamming into a stump with such force it exploded bark into the air as though the stump had been hit with an artillery round. Then he heard seven long, shrill toots coming from Kullerikki yanking on the whistle wire.

The squealing and clatter died. He looked across the landing and saw the head push, the man in charge, pointing at something, other men gathering and looking. Soon four men were brush dancing across the slash. He climbed to the top of the log he'd been working on and could just make out a small group of men, one of them tending to a man on the ground. He averted his eyes. Looking up at the gray clouds, he forced his gaze back to the downed man. The man had been nearly cut in half by the flying cable.

The four-man crew reached the site and after a brief discussion began the slow journey back to the landing with the mutilated body. Matti and another choker setter had been sent to find the end of the broken main line and Aksel could see them struggling to pull it up so it could be spliced with the end of the cable still attached to the donkey. Every foot of cable weighed two pounds.

From behind Aksel came a shout in English. It was the head push. "Goddamnit . . . don't . . . all day . . . good . . ."

Aksel went back to work. Over the next several hours, he watched three men, who after struggling to pull the broken cable to overlap with the other broken end were finally joining the two ends by rolling a long splice in the cable, a terribly labor-intensive project involving marlinespikes, hammers, and lots of twisting, unraveling, and rewinding. Finally, one of them shouted and waved a hand at Kullerikki, who blasted three short toots. The donkey engineer eased hissing steam into the yarder's pistons, engaged the friction on the main drum to link it through gears to the driving pistons, and the big drum started winding the cable back. The rigging crew, who had been put to work somewhere else, came running back. The main cable went taut. Kullerikki's whistle piped two shorts and the smaller haul-back line went taut. The roaring, squealing, piping, tooting, moving, smashing, and shouting returned as if nothing had happened.

The body lay next to the steam donkey where it remained until the shift ended.

The body was then loaded onto an empty railcar. No one knew the man's family or even exactly where he came from; some friends said Tennessee, others said Alabama. No matter, in cases like this Reder always paid for burial.

13

Barely a word was spoken at supper that night. Men went without something rather than asking for it aloud. They were philosophical about loggers getting killed; it happened—frequently. Still, respect needed to be shown. Aino, however, wasn't at all philosophical about loggers getting killed; it might be her brother. Finished for the night, she found Matti and Aksel outside their bunkhouse, both smoking. The little whistle punk, Kullerikki, was sitting with them, also smoking.

"Do you want a cigarette?" Matti asked.

She knew that he knew she'd refuse. "It cuts your wind."

"It keeps us alert." Matti said, taking a long pull. Aino knew he was showing her that she was no longer the big sister telling him what was good for him. Aksel made room for her to sit but still had said nothing.

"How did the man die?" she asked.

"Cable broke," Matti said.

"Why did the cable break?"

"It broke because the load exceeded the breaking strength."

Two loggers came out of the bunkhouse door and stood there, listening.

"Did anyone check the cable?" Aino asked.

"Aino, back off. Huttula said the lead log on the turn hit something, it put too much strain on the line, and it broke. End of story."

"Somebody is responsible."

"What? Do you want to go fire some dumb swamper because he didn't prepare a perfect skidway?"

"If he didn't do his job, yes. But who's responsible for having to haul the logs out so fast that no one has the time, not just to prepare the skidway, but to check the equipment?"

"You want me to say 'John Reder,' don't you?"

"Only in part. John Reder has to pull the logs out fast so he can make a profit."

"Because if he doesn't, he goes out of business," one of the previously silent loggers said.

"If the working people owned the logging companies," Aino answered, "there'd be time for safety inspections and no need to make a profit. We need lumber to build houses. We don't need to kill people to make profits."

"He didn't kill anyone," Aksel said.

"And Reder always pays for the burial," the other logger said. "He's under no obligation to do that."

Since the conversation was in Finnish and, other than cards, there wasn't much in the way of entertainment, several more of the Finnish loggers had come outside. Aino was suddenly aware that she had people listening to her, and she had something to say. She stood up and faced the small group of loggers.

"Which would you prefer, free burials or no burials?"

There were no answers.

"How many men die in the woods every year?" she went on. Again, there were no answers. Everyone knew that it was quite a few.

"Who looks out for your safety?"

Again, silence.

Toivo Huttula, the hook tender on the side worked by these loggers, had joined the group and was leaning on the bunkhouse door smoking a pipe. He said quietly, "She's right. No one. How long have we been asking for dry straw and to let one man off half an hour early to light the stoves?"

Aino jumped on the statement. "Don't you see, there is no dry straw for the same reason a man died today. The profit motive, capitalism, forces everyone, Reder included, to work for profits. We should work for the common good."

"That's communism," someone muttered.

"That's just common sense," Aino shot back. She felt Matti tugging on her skirt. She got the message. The word "communism" was an emotional lightning rod. Some of the men looked enlivened, others sullen. She realized that converting loggers to the message of Marx and Engels was going to be even more difficult than what the socialists faced in Finland and Russia. These loggers were almost all young, without families, and they'd never eaten better in their lives. The very air was full of the two myths of individual prosperity just around the corner and every American as an equal. Even worse, like Matti they found logging exciting. Unlike workers facing the drudgery of factories or peasants the drudgery of tenant farming, these loggers faced danger every day with skill and aplomb. They came home feeling like men, not proletarians. Then she saw the angle.

"If Reder won't let one of you come back half an hour early, why don't all of you come back half an hour early?"

"That's a strike," someone said.

"Is that legal in America?" another asked.

Aino took a breath and jumped in. She tried to remember all the arguments and tricks of rhetoric she'd learned from Voitto. She found she was good at both. She made her arguments in Finnish and Swedish. She even tried a few sentences of English but found herself handicapped. Frustrated, she reverted to letting some of the bilingual loggers translate, knowing it was less effective than using her own voice.

The loggers listened, some occasionally nodding, some muttering disapproval. She pointed out with biting humor the contrasts between John Reder's house in Knappton and their bunkhouses. She made fun of the human excrement, telling a story on herself about stepping in some before going to work in the dining hall. She made a mock bouquet of damp straw, holding its limp and drooping form for all to see, sarcastically exclaiming over its beauty and other virtues. She pointed out that if they organized as one group, Reder would have to give in or face hiring a hundred loggers with none of their skills. She made it clear, without in any way shaming them for their lack of courage, that it was their lack of courage that kept them in squalor. Then, she connected their living conditions and working conditions—and working conditions and the accident. She ended by saying it wasn't just about straw. It was about the value of their lives. It was about dignity. Those were things worth striking for.

Aino walked back to the henhouse quite pleased with herself.

The next morning, Aksel was promoted.

He'd just started splitting wood in the near darkness when Reder got off a speeder, a tiny hand-pumped railcar used to move maintenance crews or get kids down the track to go to school. He walked up to Aksel, puffing slightly from the exertion of pumping the speeder by himself. Aksel took off his cap. Reder laughed.

"Put that back on. Loggers don't doff their hats to anyone."

Aksel's eyes went wide at the word "logger."

"You're not there yet," Reder chuckled. He pointed to a small canyon, barely discernible in the dawn light. "I've had to move some men around. Get down there with Huttula. Maybe he'll make a logger out of you."

Aksel's first day of setting chokers was every bit as hard as Matti's first day, with the same result: exhaustion and a fierce feeling of pride. He never thought once about the man who'd just died.

14

The same morning that Aksel was promoted, the solution to Aino's poor English was sitting erect on the floor of the engine cab, her ankles crossed neatly beneath her long wool skirt, feet dangling in the air above the steps too large for her to take without a helping hand. Margaret Reder watched the stumps seem to move against the distant trees as the small locomotive chuffed its way up to the camp. She had a valise filled with John's freshly laundered clothes that she'd carried up the trail from Knappton to the east-running spur line that connected to the north-running main line that hauled the logs to tidewater on Willapa Bay. It also contained the Friday editions of the *Weekly Astorian* and the *Oregonian*. John read the *Oregonian* for business news and lumber prices, but he wasn't above being amused by the regularly occurring corruption scandals at Portland city hall. It all balances out, Margaret thought to herself. The politicians make money doing scandal and corruption and the newspapers make money reporting on it. Neatly folded in a towel beneath the newspapers were a dozen oatmeal cookies, John's favorites. She'd heard they'd lost a man the day before and John could probably use a little care.

The steam whistles became louder and she could now hear the whirring of the cables, the squealing of the block and tackle, and an occasional faint shout. Logging terrified her.

The fireman helped her down and offered to take her valise. She politely refused; logs needed to move to market and helping her wasn't helping that. Even though John legally owned the business, as far as she was concerned it was *their* business, and she treated it accordingly, just as her mother had done with her father's sawmill business in Minnesota.

When the smell of the outhouses hit her, she picked up her pace. The pigs rooting around added to the smell, but they were there to get rid of the garbage, so, on balance, maybe they diminished the smell. Then again, loggers liked bacon. The real culprit was, to put it plainly—and she didn't mind plain talk—the shit. Years around loggers and her husband had rid her of prissiness about rough language if it didn't take the Lord's name in vain.

At her suggestion, John had placed the outhouses almost a hundred yards from the bunkhouses. She'd thought the loggers would appreciate the smell being removed from where they slept. She'd failed to take account of traveling a hundred yards in pitch dark in the rain. When nature called under those conditions, feces collected at various points between the bunkhouses and the outhouses. They lived like animals. Immigrants mostly. They had lanterns.

Passing the dining hall, she noticed a young woman reading on the steps, a mug of coffee and a plate of food next to her. The young woman looked at her with intense, nearly black eyes behind thick lenses and then quickly looked back at her book, which Margaret could see from the large lettering on the light-brown paper cover was written in Russian. Her curiosity piqued, Margaret walked to the steps, smiled at the girl, and said hello.

The girl smiled back, saying hello in return. She looked and sounded Finnish, not Russian. Margaret introduced herself and learned that the girl's name was Aino.

"What are you reading?" Margaret asked, pointing at the book.

The girl looked puzzled.

"What—are—you—reading? Book. What name?" she asked.

"Title of book is *What Is to Be Done.*"

Margaret had never heard of it. "Is it good book?"

The girl looked slightly amused. "It is very good book."

"Is it a novel?"

Again the girl looked puzzled. Bad English. Just off the boat. Margaret was disappointed. Here was *someone reading* and she couldn't speak English. Margaret had loved John Reder since she met him in her father's office in Minneapolis the day after she'd come home from convent school in Chicago, but John didn't read anything but newspapers. "Novel," Margaret repeated. "Fiction." The girl still looked puzzled. "Not true, make up story."

That connected. The girl smiled and took off her glasses. "Is not story. But is"—she searched for a word—"is named from storybook, same name, by man name is Nikolai Chernyshevsky. But is not telling story." The enigmatic smile came back.

"I love books," Margaret said. She put her valise and basket down and sat right next to the girl. "Do you?" she asked.

"Yes. I reading lots of books. But not so many books here. I order by mail."

"We really *should* get a library in Knappton," Margaret said. She felt the conversation was about to lag and made another try at keeping it going. "Who is the author?"

The look.

"Man . . . who . . . write . . . book." She pointed at the book. "Man who write." She made writing motions with her hand.

"Man who is writing book is called Lenin, but her name for really true is Vladimir Ulyanov."

"Ohh," Margaret said smiling, ignoring the pronoun. "A pseudonym."

"Soo-doh-nim?"

"Like name for writing only. Like . . ." She paused. What would this girl know? "Like Mark Twain."

The girl smiled broadly. "Yes. Like Mark Twain."

A flunky stuck her head out the door and shouted something in Finnish. The girl—Was it Aino? Why couldn't these Finns be named Mary or something?—jumped to her feet and stuffed the book into her apron.

"I working now," the girl said as she ran nimbly up the stairs and into the dining hall.

Margaret looked at the small, one-room family shacks and observed that a few had only canvas roofs; they were sitting askew and cockeyed on the mud, some not even level, almost overwhelmed by the slash and stumps, some stumps taller than the little shacks' roofs. Looking up at the gray sky with its perpetual, soft, insistent damned mist falling cool and gentle on her face, Margaret felt lonely.

When Aino came inside, Lempi was peering through the window at Margaret Reder as she picked her way carefully toward the office. "Talking to the boss's wife, huh?"

Aino followed Lempi's gaze. "Spoiled little rich girl. Doesn't even know who Lenin is." She laughed and then—wickedly imitating a whining spoiled child—said, "Oh, a pseudonym, like Mark Twain."

For a moment, Lempi looked at her blankly. Then, covering her ignorance, she laughed and said, "She doesn't talk to any of us." That gave Aino an idea. Then Lempi laughed. "Nice dress, though. You think it came from Portland?"

"You think I care?" Aino said. She then almost involuntarily glanced out the window to see Margaret's dress. She instantly averted her eyes back to Lempi, to see Lempi smiling at her knowingly.

"Not much, you don't care," Lempi said.

Furious, Aino stormed into the kitchen.

Margaret knew John didn't like to waste time talking during working hours, so after catching him up on local news, mostly about other lumber families, and getting his dirty laundry, she turned her face up to his. He hated kissing her in public, but it delighted her to tease him. He knew it delighted her, and that delighted him—but he still kept the kiss brief. Margaret impishly swished her head and shoulders back and forth, a motion which also swished her hips and the bottom of her dress. John looked furtively out of the window and Margaret laughed. She kissed the tips of her fingers and pressed them on his lips. "I'll see you at home," she said. "I've got a surprise for you."

"What is it?"

"If I tell you, it's not a surprise."

She walked out the door, aware he was watching her backside. He had no clue at all, but why would he? She never talked about her periods with anyone.

Humming happily as she passed the mess hall, she had an idea. She mounted the rough-sawn steps, holding up the hem of her skirt to avoid catching it on the splinters left from the caulk boots, and walked into the dining hall. The flunkies all stopped working. She hated how being married to John made her seem like royalty to them. She spotted Aino.

"Aino, can I talk with you for a second?"

She saw Aino glance at the other girls, who quickly returned to their tasks. Aino set a huge bowl of beans on a table and came to the door. She said nothing but had drawn herself perfectly erect and was looking at her with that damned Finnish imperturbability, revealing neither pleasure nor displeasure, nothing.

Margaret took a quick breath. "Aino, I know, maybe . . ." She hesitated, then plunged on. "It sometimes feels . . . being a person who reads, and no one else does . . . I mean"—she indicated the world outside the dining hall—"you know . . . books aren't much good here. No one really has the time. Logging isn't really bookish."

Aino didn't say a word, but something in her face changed.

"I thought, maybe we could sometime on a Sunday or even a Saturday . . . before the dance . . . you could even get ready at our house. We could talk about what we're reading." Aino just looked at her. Margaret wanted to shout at her: *I need a friend I can talk with.* Desperate, she said, "You could help me learn Finnish and I could help you with your English." She'd never thought before that she wanted to learn Finnish. She waited, fearful of the very likely rejection.

Finally, Aino said, "I like that."

Relieved, and feeling a sudden wave of excitement, Margaret said, "Next Saturday? Maybe you could come for tea?" She saw Aino's disappointment.

"I working Saturday."

"Maybe I could see if John would let you off work." She saw the girl's face cloud. She remembered she was dealing with a Finn and her pride. "Just a few hours early. I know you would have to give up some pay. I mean John could prorate the daily rate for say just a few hours."

"Prorate?" Aino asked.

"You give up one quarter of the day and John cuts one quarter of your pay. That's prorate." She watched Aino's face cloud. She suddenly felt foolish. She'd just suggested Aino pay to have lessons with her. There simply was no spare time. There was no one "extra" to cover for her, even if she could talk John into giving her the time, which she would probably not accept so as not to be privileged above the other girls. She'd never thought just how trapped these girls were.

Then Aino said, "Maybe you asking husband me working early so qvit early."

Margaret leaped on the idea. "I'm sure he'd be OK with that. And you can eat at our house and not have to pay for your evening meal that night." She saw Aino's head move just slightly toward an affirmative. "Oh, would you please? I know we'll have such a good time. You do like tea, don't you? Oh, of course, your people like coffee. We can do coffee." She laughed. "We can do both."

Aino watched Margaret pick her way through the mud and slash, dress hem in one hand, valise in the other, heading for the railroad tracks. Tea. Aino gave a barely audible snort. Just like an English aristocrat. As soon as she had that thought, it didn't feel quite fair. She wondered if Margaret had china and then pushed that thought out of her mind as well. She needed to keep her focus. Her English was bad. No one in the henhouse spoke English. Margaret did.

On Saturday, after work, Aino walked to Margaret Reder's house, a two-story wood building with cedar shingle siding and a roof of hand-split cedar shakes that sat on the side of a steep hill overlooking the Knappton Lumber Company sawmill. The muddy tidal flat under the splintered planks smelled of rotting fish and decaying river weed. Her eyes stung with smoke from the wigwam burners incinerating the sawdust.

The house was set into a hillside, so from the front it looked three stories tall. A steep stairway led to a covered porch that spanned the front of the house. The climb up the unpaved road had Aino taking deep breaths. Scattered along the road were similar large houses that belonged to owners and higher-level managers.

Margaret greeted her in a different dress from the one she'd worn at the camp. Struggling with envy, Aino wondered how many dresses the woman owned. Margaret led her into the living room, which demonstrated a refined sense of taste. She had made a comfortable and pleasing home of a drafty, all-wood structure. There were stuffed armchairs and a davenport with soft cushions. Under a table that Margaret called a coffee table was a wool rug. A wool rug! Margaret could just waste wool and walk on it instead of using it for clothing. There wasn't a single rug made of rags torn from worn-out clothes. And a table used only for coffee! Aino struggled with anger as well as envy. She thought of Matti and his friends, sleeping on straw, crowded like animals in a pen, risking their lives for a dollar a day while Margaret held herself like royalty, serving tea, her back erect, her manners flawless. Well, she thought angrily, in America capitalists were the royalty, holders of unearned privilege. Their day would come just as it had in France. If she had to drink tea in dainty cups to further the cause, then so be it. The fulfillment of the cause would destroy the unearned privilege of people like Margaret. The revolution would end undeserved and unfair wealth and power. She threw herself into her first lesson with ferocity.

To Aino's surprise, Margaret was a born teacher with a lively and curious mind and, though she didn't want to admit it, a good heart. She was serious about wanting to learn Finnish and asked intelligent questions about Aino's experiences midwifing with Maíjaliisa, making Aino think she might be pregnant. She couldn't help liking her.

15

That next Thursday night, Lempi Rompinen was braiding her long, light-brown hair while looking over Aino's shoulder. Aino was reading a copy of *Työmies*, the Finnish socialist newspaper published in Michigan. "You'd better be careful with that stuff," Lempi said.

"Why?"

Lempi tied off the thick single braid with a strip of cloth. "Everyone knows you've been talking up a strike with the bunkhouse reds."

Aino put the newspaper down. "All they want is clean, dry straw and one man off half an hour early to light fires. We live in a castle compared with the bunkhouses."

"Some castle," Lempi said. She turned back to the mirror, untied the ribbon, shook her hair loose, and started to retie the ribbon. "I'm not saying the boys don't deserve better. They do."

"So, what are you saying?"

"You keep it up and you'll lose your job."

"This country has freedom of speech."

"Sure thing. You can say anything you like. And then get fired."

In the bunkhouse, strike talk was getting heated. The battle lines were drawn between the more radical Finns and the more conservative Swedes and Norwegians. Although sympathetic to the cause of the workingman, the Swedes and Norwegians hadn't been radicalized by living under a foreign dictatorship.

"For one of us, five are waiting at end of rail line to take our jobs," Iverson, a Swedish bucker, was saying in English.

"So don't let them up the rail line," Jouka retorted. "Picket right outside Knappton. We can turn them away at the docks."

"You and what army?" Iverson retorted.

"They can't fight us all."

"Yeah, but if we get into a fight, who do you think will get arrested?" Jouka looked at Matti and Aksel for help.

"You know what he says is true," Aksel said quietly in Finnish. "Reder owns the sheriff."

"But the sheriff doesn't own me," Jouka replied in English, looking around. "Any of us."

"Big talk, Jouka," Aksel said quietly in Finnish. Then in English he said, "I don't want anything to do with it." It created an awkward silence.

Huttula, a devout churchgoer, broke in, in English. "We don't want reputation for troublemaking. You know"—he scanned all of them—"there is a list of names, really, I tell you. Owners send it other owners. It's called blacklist."

"Money talks," Jouka answered. "Reder is selling lumber like hell down to San Francisco. We stop putting logs through his mill, he'll be up here washing our long johns himself."

"He'll put you on a list of troublemakers and you'll never see another job west of the Rockies," Iverson said.

"We only ask straw and bull helper," Matti said in halting English. "Reder not give. We strike."

"Bull cook, you dumb Finn. Yeah, I've heard that red bitch sister of yours talking up that idea. Fat chance that."

Matti came off the edge of his bunk and threw a wide right cross, connecting with the left side of Iverson's face. Iverson's head snapped to the right, and he rolled away, shielding himself with his left arm. Inexperienced, Matti watched him instead of jumping in for the kill. Iverson was up, swinging and cursing. Matti tackled him, knocking the metal stovepipe loose from the stove. Smoke poured into the room.

Three Swedes, Iverson's friends, were on their feet, kicking Matti, trying to get him to release Iverson. That was too much for Aksel. Friends
always trumped politics. He grabbed one man by the shirt, spun him
around, and hit him square in the face. The man's head snapped back,
but only briefly; he came back at Aksel, screaming with rage, smashing
Aksel against one of the bunk beds. The man moved inside, fists pumping into Aksel's stomach. Doubled over, Aksel was about to be driven
into the ground when little Kullerikki attacked the man with an ax
handle, flailing his back. He was too short to get a blow into his head.
The man turned in a rage and grabbed Kullerikki's shirt, holding him
while pumping three short jabs into his face. Jouka grabbed the man's
right shoulder with his left hand, right elbow coming in with all the
torque of his very fit and rapidly twisting body. The man went down
instantly, unconscious.

A sudden, cold bucketful of water hit the fighters, hissing against
the stove, giving them all the out they needed to stop. Hacking, the men
streamed from the bunkhouse, their eyes in tears.

"Take it outside," Huttula said quietly in English.

The fighters stumbled outside.

Huttula got another bucket of water and drowned the fire in the
stove. He came out, face blackened, eyes watering. He pointed to Iverson and Matti. "You two cleaning up the mess."

After helping Iverson restore the chimney and rebuild the fire,
Matti came out and joined Aksel, Jouka, and Kullerikki, who were
seated on the ground smoking.

Aksel talked about fishing the Baltic and his dream of owning his
own boat. Matti talked about one day owning his own logging company.

"A Finnish John Reder," Aksel chuckled.

"No, a Finnish Frederick Weyerhaeuser," Matti said.

Up to this point, Jouka had said little. He was cutting down the
calluses on his hands with a straight razor, so he could play his fiddle
better at the upcoming Saturday dance.

Matti said, "You're kind of quiet."

"Not so big plans like you two," he answered. He moved his fret
hand tentatively.

"You can't log forever."

"Maybe I get a farm." There was a ragged ridge of hard callus at the edge of where he'd been cutting it and he carefully chewed it down to be level with the rest of his skin.

"You? A farmer?" Matti asked.

Jouka seemed embarrassed. "Maybe I want to someday run the steam donkey or maybe"—he hesitated—"be a locomotive engineer. They make good wages and it's as good as indoor work."

Aksel and Matti looked at each other and then back at Jouka.

"No doubt you're good at machines," Matti said. "I watched you help Swanson that time the locomotive died."

Jouka nodded, pleased that Matti had noticed.

"You have to know how to take the locomotive apart and fix it when it breaks down," Aksel said.

"*That's* not a problem," Jouka said.

"So, what is?" Aksel asked.

Jouka swallowed. He started to say something and stopped. Matti, Aksel, and Kullerikki said nothing. Finally, Jouka said very quietly, "I don't read so good."

There was silence in the face of this fact.

Finally, Aksel spoke. "When I was in Stockholm, I once saw a manual for a steam engine for a boat."

"So?" Jouka asked.

"The manual was almost entirely diagrams. You don't need to read."

16

The girls in the henhouse heard about the fight before the loggers came in for dinner. Aino could see that the little whistle punk was sticking to Jouka, Aksel, and her brother. The fight had formed the three of them into a team, with Kullerikki as a sort of ward. She found herself thinking of them as her men.

On the first Saturday evening in October, Aino and her three men went to the Knappton dance. Jouka, his newly made violin carefully wrapped in deerskin, was humming dance tunes. Occasionally Aksel or Matti would remember a tune from the old country and suggest it. Jouka would grin with pleasure and hum it if it had no words or sing the verses through if it did. Trying to stump Jouka with a song he didn't know became a game. Upon finally failing one from Aksel, Jouka claimed unfair advantage because Aksel was a Swede. But within ten minutes, Jouka had that one down as well. Aino caught herself feeling the clever banter and songs were a waste of time. She knew it was irrational. But she wanted to talk with Jouka all by herself. She wanted him to see how intelligent and funny *she* was. She wanted Jouka. Then she remembered wanting Voitto to see her the same way and felt irrationally disloyal.

The sun had set and they made their way in the dark, never looking directly ahead, so they could pick up the trail with their night vision. They also guided themselves by the lighter band of sky above the trail between the trees. The songs ceased. Even Jouka had to concentrate in the dark. Cougars would be hungry this time of year, the easy pickings—fawns and elk calves—long gone. Aino moved closer to Matti, smelling the cigarette smoke that clung to his clothing, feeling the heat from his broad back. Then she felt Aksel move protectively closer to her. She would never tell them, but the vast, dark forest spooked her. The fear of attack and the comfort of her men surrounding her, however, made her heart hum with life.

The net shed was alive with the sound of instruments being tuned, the excited chatter of women, the low murmur of men in small groups, the smell of soap lingering on recently washed clothes, combined with the smell of kerosene lanterns, whose light struggled with the large, open rafter space and the haze of cigarette smoke. Aino watched Matti and Aksel pull tobacco from small pouches and expertly roll it into cigarettes. It meant they were smoking regularly. Her lips tightened just slightly in disapproval. She was the one who swept up the butts and dealt with the ashes in the cups and saucers.

She sat on a bench against one of the walls formed by vertical, rough-sawn boards and changed into her good shoes. She'd already removed her glasses but could see just well enough across the net rack space to make out Jouka playing a bit of a tune to the accordion player, nodding his head to emphasize the rhythm. With a nod of Jouka's head, the band set off in a lively polka.

Men rushed across the dance floor to the girls. A tall stranger with a long, handsome face and strong jawline reached Aino first. He was a good dancer but nothing like Jouka. On the other hand, he was as good-looking. Maybe Jouka wasn't the only fish in the sea.

The music stopped. The stranger pulled out a tobacco pouch. "Do you smoke?" he asked in English.

"I not smoking," she said, knowing she hadn't gotten it right. She felt stupid.

He nodded somewhat deferentially and then put the pouch back in his pocket.

"Finnish girl?" he asked in Finnish.

"Yoh. Kokkola area. You?"

He held up his hand, stopping her assumption that he was Finnish. "Do you speak Swedish?" he asked.

"Lots of Swedes around Kokkola," she said in Swedish.

"I'm from Sweden. From Gävle."

When she was in Finland, she felt different from the Swedes, even antagonistic toward the wealthier ones. But in America, most of the Swedes were small farmers and laborers, just like the Finns. Everyone seemed more alike over here.

She glanced over at the bandstand. Jouka was going outside, probably to get a drink. She glanced up at the man. His eyes had an intensity that reminded her of Voitto's.

"Do you mind if I smoke outside?" he asked.

Soon they were leaning on a rail, looking over the gill net boats about ten feet below them, tied up bow and stern to lines over pulleys that allowed the boats to rise and fall with the swells from the Columbia. All around them in the darkness, the pulleys softly squeaked like young birds. When the Swede pulled on his cigarette, it lit his long face with orange light.

His name had been Joel Hägglund, but because he'd gotten his name on a couple of blacklists he now went by Joseph, or Joe, Hillström. He'd been in America a little more than four years. Soon they were deeply into politics, he gently chiding her for her old-fashioned Marxist views, she staunchly defending them.

"You'll never get what you want through socialism. Marxist, revolutionary, Fabian, whatever," he said. "America dangles the distant prize that anyone can get rich like Rockefeller. All you need to do is work harder and save more. If you don't get rich, it's your fault."

Aino suppressed a laugh. She liked listening to this man.

"If you vote socialist," Hillström went on, "you vote against your chance of getting rich. Even the AF of L," he mockingly enunciated the letters that stood for the American Federation of Labor, "tells its members to stay clear of politics. You'll never even get a socialist workers' party here, much less a revolution." He chuckled.

"The revolution already started in Russia and Finland," she retorted.

"Yah, sure. They've all lived under a rigid class system, doffing their hats as the aristocrat drives by. Here, people all think they're equal.

If you're poor and landless, it's because you didn't have the gumption to move west and homestead."

"That's ending."

He looked at her, smiling with those eyes like Voitto's, so sure of himself. "The false myth of Marxism is never going to beat the false myth of America. Marx and Engels's prediction that America would be the first to go is wrong." She felt a surge of excitement. This man was not only good-looking but also smart. Even better, he was politically conscious. He *talked* about what mattered—with her.

"So, how do we raise starvation-level wages, change unsafe working conditions, filthy living conditions, take care of people who lose their limbs on the job, families who lose their fathers?" She stopped talking. Hillström was leaning against the railing smiling at her.

"Direct union action is the only way," he said, quietly. "The workers have the power, if only they'd organize."

"But the unions have done nothing here."

"The AF of L is as much an enemy of the working class as the capitalists are," Hillström said. "They'll be your union, *if* you have a traditional craft, but they won't let you in if you're just some dumb immigrant who sells muscle and sweat. They also don't let in niggers and women."

"So, what do we do?"

He threw his cigarette butt into the darkness beneath them and she watched its small orange glow as it fell until it hit the water. "Last June," he said, "a group of union organizers who see through the AF of L *and* "—he looked at her—"see through the socialists met in Chicago. Big Bill Haywood, from the Western Federation of Miners, was there. They formed a single union for *all* workers, covering *all* industries, the Industrial Workers of the World. I joined last fall. We include craft workers, unskilled workers, immigrants, niggers"—he paused, smiling—"and women." She felt her own excitement rising with his words. "If there is injustice in any industry, *everyone* goes on strike. Everywhere. We don't wait for Marxist bullshit about a workers' paradise. We don't wait for the Republicans or the Democrats. They're both financed by capitalists." He was looking at her, his eyes burning, burning away any lingering annoyance, any lingering doubt. "We organize! We take direct action. If we don't get justice, we shut America down."

Aino felt her insides were humming.

They stayed at the dock, talking, Aino plying Hillström with questions about the practical side of organizing. Finally, he affectionately said that he had to get at least a couple of hours' sleep before he headed up the river to Portland. "There's an IWW local forming in Astoria. I think you'd add a lot."

Aino could only doze that night, trying to sleep on the hotel kitchen floor next to Matti, thinking about what Hillström had said, thinking about him.

In the morning they ate sandwiches Aino had prepared the day before in the cookshack. She raised the idea of one big union, and Matti rolled his eyes and changed the subject to the size of Reder's house. Aksel seemed more amenable to talking, but he didn't care about unions or groups of any kind. He just wanted his own fishing boat, beholden only to the wind and tide.

She made better progress with Jouka.

"Yeah, we could use fresh straw," he agreed. "Wouldn't hurt the cheap bastard to get that for us. And maybe send someone home early to get the fires going. But word gets out you're talking that way, bang, you're gone. Some damned Greek or dumb Italian is always hanging around looking for work and Reder knows it."

"No *girls* are hanging around looking for jobs. We're in short supply."

He looked at her. "Are you thinking that *you* could organize a strike?"

She smiled at him. "Yoh."

Their eyes met. She thrilled at his admiration. He quickly looked away. She realized she had it all wrong. He wasn't ignoring her; he was shy.

Instead of going back to Reder's Camp, Aino spent her last dollar on a round-trip ticket on the *General Washington*. All the way across the river, she thought about what Hillström had said. She thought about Hillström.

In Astoria she walked to the restaurant Hillström said was an IWW meeting place. It was closed on Sunday, but she knocked on the back door. Seven men, rangy, with callused hands, greeted her. She couldn't help being flattered by her reception and excited by the talk of the One Big Union. They weren't just interested in raising wages, like the AF of L; they wanted to abolish the whole wage system. They wanted to abolish the government, itself another form of capitalist oppression.

She got practical advice on how to organize a strike and promises of help. She left the restaurant with leaflets and pamphlets, her head spinning with the ideas of Proudhon and Blanqui and with stories about founding leaders Big Bill Haywood and Mother Jones.

By the time she returned to Reder's Camp, she felt as though a revolution had taken place in her own mind. That night she lay awake, excited by the thought of leading a strike—and the look in Jouka's eyes when she told him what was on her mind. Then she thought about the look in Hillström's eyes when he told her about the IWW—the fire in Hillström's eyes.

17

There was also fire in Ilmari's eyes. He'd just received the letter from Louhi asking him to come up to Nordland "to talk things over." He'd been setting aside Sunday nights to write to Rauha every week. Rauha had written back almost as regularly, often with small talk about life in Nordland, less frequently, but enough to keep Ilmari starry-eyed, with words of endearment and questions about his life. There were also practical questions, many of which Ilmari suspected came from Rauha's mother.

He arranged for Ullakko, who was rueful, but didn't seem to hold any ill will, to tend the cattle and the cow.

Rauha met Ilmari the next afternoon at the door and invited him in to have coffee with her and her mother. She wore a dress that while seeming demure with long sleeves, high collar, and a skirt that nearly touched the floor managed to somehow promise that the body beneath it was hidden glory. It also brought out the blue in her eyes. Rauha knew what she had to trade and, in a society where men vastly outnumbered women, knew what it was worth. She had Ilmari hooked and could handle him. She was under no illusion that life with him would not be hard work. Hard work was a given and had been all her life. And he might even have a light side to him. He would occasionally smile while staring at the floor.

When coffee was over, Louhi stood up and said, "Let's go for a walk."

Walking beside Louhi, his eyes on the gray green of a distant hill shorn of trees, Ilmari said nothing.

"We both like you," Louhi said.

"Yoh," he replied.

Louhi hesitated. "You must know my business by now."

"A boardinghouse."

Louhi laughed.

Ilmari looked at her quizzically.

"I finance whorehouses and saloons."

He blinked.

Louhi could have been reading his mind. "Rauha has nothing to be ashamed of. *I* own the whorehouse. If you have trouble with it, now is the time to know."

"I'm a strong Evangelical Lutheran."

"So are most of my customers."

Ten minutes later, Ilmari was sitting on the couch with his mouth slightly open as Rauha paced back and forth, explaining the deal. With the earthquake in San Francisco that spring, lumber prices were going sky-high and there were plenty more houses waiting to be built all over the West. The money was in lumber not in blacksmithing. Louhi would invest half of the capital for a sawmill, Ilmari the other half. His blacksmithing skills would give him an advantage, and a mill on Deep River could control all the timber in the watershed.

"We can get married when the mill's built."

"But that could be several years and what do I know about sawmills?"

"Yes, but we think it would only take a year or so. And yes, you don't know much about sawmills, now. But you can make and repair things. Mother's asked around. You're a good worker. You think she let you through the front door just because she knows the grandson of your mother's aunt?"

Ilmari said nothing, looking at her.

"Louhi knows every mill and logging company owner from Port Angeles to Astoria. We'll know things sometimes months before others."

"Through the whorehouse," he said tightly.

Rauha crossed over to Ilmari and knelt on the floor in front of him. Taking his large hands in her small ones, she looked up at his broad, high-cheeked face with her brilliant blue eyes. "Yes. And saloons. It's what my mother does. We've told you about it openly. If you'd asked openly, we'd have never hidden it. But I want out from under that . . . that stigma. She wants me out. We can build a life together." She moved over his knees, arching her back to raise her mouth to his. She kissed him. "I know you can do it," she whispered.

That was the last time Ilmari cared about what Rauha's mother did for a living.

Back at Ilmahenki, Ilmari relit the stump fires from the faint embers he found deep inside them, bringing the fires to life with the leather bellows he'd made. By evening, nearly two dozen smoke plumes rose to merge with the gray clouds. He walked to Higgins's store to send a note to Reder's Camp telling Aino and Matti that he was engaged. He then walked on to Ullakko's in the dark and asked him to watch Ilmahenki for three more days. If he was to build a sawmill, it might be useful to know how much timber lay on the other side of the river—and what it might be worth.

The next morning, he packed his rucksack, strapped an ax on top, and took down his Winchester .30-caliber, in case he ran into a bear or cougar.

Ilmari found the raft he'd made a couple of years earlier, two flat sides of a split-cedar log joined by six-foot planks. He untangled it from the salmonberry vines and sedge and dragged it into the river, the water seeping into his wool socks. Wobbling the raft until he felt it balance, he poled to the far bank about a quarter of a mile downstream and tied it to a small alder.

Walking in the cool gloom of the massive trees on the north side of the river, feeling the spongy carpet of years of falling needles beneath him, he pushed uphill, determined to reach the distant ridgeline. However, even after an hour of climbing over nurse logs and circumventing close-growing trees struggling against each other for light and soil, the image of Rauha, her blue eyes, her thighs outlined under her dress, strode with him along with a feeling of frustration and longing. He felt that he would never meet Louhi's conditions.

Sliding down a steep hillside, he came to rest at a small creek about a yard wide, rippling quietly over rounded rocks. The branches of the Douglas firs interlinked above the creek, so it had the aspect of a tunnel more than a creek bed. He waded slowly upstream. He hadn't eaten since morning, but he didn't care. After half an hour of floundering on slick stones, he found a flat piece of ground. There he cleared enough space to rig his canvas sheet, securing it to nearby branches with a small rope through its grommets. He pulled two wool blankets from his rucksack, untied the ax, and walked about ten yards upstream where he found a young fir with branches to make a good bed.

He pulled a bough back and down, exposing it where it joined the trunk, putting tension on it. With his left leg forward to counter the weight of the ax he brought the ax down swiftly on the branch. The branch snapped, barely impeding the fall of the ax, which drove deep into the side of his calf. He went dizzy with the shock of it and fell to the ground without making a sound. The ax fell out of the wound and blood flowed out. He forced the wound shut. It wasn't an artery, but it was bad. Fear grabbed at his insides. He looked up at the trees, as if for help. There was no help. If he couldn't stop the bleeding, he would be dead within a couple of hours. If he did stop the bleeding, then what? No one would look for him for another two days. He would have to crawl to Deep River.

Holding his calf with both hands, he inched back to his camp on his buttocks. There he fumbled with one hand to unbutton one of his leather suspender straps from his trousers. One hand wasn't sufficient to close the wound and the blood flowed faster as he fumbled. Finally, the suspender was free. He pulled his puukko and slashed a strip of wool blanket, which he put on the wound and then wrapped with the suspender, making a tourniquet. He passed out from shock with his head downhill.

When he regained consciousness, he stuffed the blankets into the rucksack, slung the rifle on his back, and set out on his backside for the river. He lost consciousness twice again before dark. He spent the night huddled in the blankets. With the rising sun for his bearing, the bleeding apparently stopped now, he crawled south.

By late afternoon he could crawl no more. He rolled over on his back and lay there looking up at a tall Douglas fir. He had at times wondered how he would die. Never would he have imagined it would be in a strange country all alone in a forest. He wondered if the angels would come again, as they had when he was a child.

He became aware of his breathing. Looking up, just making out the crown of the big tree, almost idly he began to wonder how tall it would be if he put one just like it right on top of this one. Then, suppose he took those two trees and then put them on top of themselves as before, doubling again. Then do it again. And then again. And again. Doubling, again doubling, doubling, doubling . . . faster, faster, doubling faster. The sky split open into a vast nothingness, a nothingness as the sky is nothingness, real but not seen. He cried out. He tried to crawl away from the tree, crawl with his fingers clawing in the moist needles being turned to soil, crawling from this nothingness he was lost in, crawl and bury his face in the moist forest floor, to feel its coolness on his feverish forehead, to recall the smell and feel of existence, anything to escape this dread, this dreadful nothing that was everything. He passed out.

When he came to, he was on his back, wrapped in an old Hudson's Bay Company wool blanket, its creamy white wool darkened almost to tan, its four stripes of black, yellow, red, and green now faded to pale pastels. His bloody trousers were neatly folded on an exposed root. The old Indian woman, Vasutäti, was sitting cross-legged next to him. She made a satisfied grunt, reached out to feel his forehead, and then took his pulse. "Young. Strong," she said in English. "Lucky."

"Yoh," he said. He couldn't help smiling as he fell asleep.

When he awoke, Vasutäti was gone. He panicked, trying to rise to his feet. He then realized that a mass of spiderwebs had been spread over the wound, bound in place with strips of cedar bark. A small fire glowed just outside the drip line of the tree he lay under, assuring him that Vasutäti would return. He fell asleep.

He awoke to the feel of the old woman's hand on the back of his head, holding it up to a ceramic mug steaming with God only knew what. He wasn't about to argue and swallowed everything in the cup. Again, Vasutäti grunted in satisfaction.

He tried to prop himself upright on his elbows, but she gently pushed him back down. "No sisu now," she said and then laughed.

He had to chuckle, more at the music of her laugh than at her joke about his culture. How had she learned that word? "Do you speak Finnish?" he asked in Finnish.

She laughed again. It was like a creek in summer sunlight. She answered in English, "Some. English better."

She went to tend the fire. A battered saucepan lay on the coals at the fire's edge. She smelled its contents and reached for some sort of shredded plant stock and added it. She walked from sight and returned with the ax. "How this is made?" she asked, weighing the blade in her hand.

He hesitated. "You heat the steel and it gets soft and you—"

She interrupted him. "No, no. Not how make look this way. How make this steel?" She tapped the ax-head. "This bite you. You walk when I know how steel made and sing right song."

He felt he knew what she wanted. He told her how iron is extracted from hematite and how by the addition of charcoal in just the right amounts the iron became steel, watching her eyes to be sure she was following him.

She was. She looked at the ax-head in her hand and hefted it. Then she traced the bloodstain on it. "Steel not friend with blood. Not like life. Kill trees. Kill you."

Ilmari snorted. "I kill myself. Steel not alive."

"Everything alive." She looked at him, her eyes searching somewhere behind his eyes to see if he understood her. She nodded her head. "Now I know where steel is born, I sing to steel. Send pain back to Pain Hill. You not talk."

He took a deep breath, feeling the earth beneath his back, and looked up at the tree. When it started to double, then double again, he cried out in fear. She grasped his left hand with her left hand. "You stay here. Not leave before learn how come back." He squeezed her hand hard, looking at her face as if looking at a life ring. She squeezed back and smiled; then she began to sing.

Vasutäti sang in her own language, a dialect of Chinookan. Her clear high notes trembled with controlled vibrato and the low notes were rich in overtones, amplified by jaw and tongue movements. The words faintly echoed the old songs he'd heard from the master singers of Suomi who, with their arms linked, faced each other in a warm kitchen, while outside the thwarted darkness and bitter cold seemed to moan in frustration. If Ilmari shut his eyes, he could have sworn that the voice was that of a young woman.

On the morning of the fourth day, Vasutäti urged Ilmari to his feet. He leaned on her shoulder, and they slowly made their way through the forest, occasionally stopping when Vasutäti would see some herb or root, grunt to herself, and collect it in a deerskin bag that she carried on her shoulder. They hit a small stream edged by a well-trodden narrow path and came to a tidy, rounded hut made from bent maple saplings covered with overlapping cedar bark. A fire pit, rocks carefully laid to hold several battered cooking pots, sat between the stream and a lean-to shelter holding basket makings and baskets in various stages of completion. Completed baskets were stacked neatly in the shelter's back corner, away from the weather.

Vasutäti motioned with her head to a place by the fire and Ilmari gratefully sat down, light-headed from the exertion. He hadn't realized how much blood he'd lost. Vasutäti went over to a tree and lowered a sack that had been suspended from a branch to protect it from bears. She took out some pemmican, smoked salmon mashed together with dried blackberries; hauled the sack up again; and offered it to Ilmari, who tried not to gobble it down. Vasutäti blew the fire to life and boiled water, which she poured over dried leaves and chopped roots in a ceramic mug.

"Now, you drink," she said, smiling. Ilmari held the cup in both hands, savoring its warmth, and took a careful sip. She laughed. "Not hurt you. Good for making blood." Then, she looked at him coyly, her eyes twinkling. "Also, cure lovesickness."

Ilmari put the cup down in astonishment.

She laughed her merry laugh. "Not so magic me. You talk in sleep. 'Rauha. Rauha,'" she moaned rolling her eyes. Then she got serious. "You tell me story."

She gazed at him until he started talking. He told her the whole story, how he'd longed for a wife, his joy in hearing of a Finnish girl in Nordland, his wonder at Rauha's beauty, his passion for her, his frustration at her mother's bride price. When he finished, she said nothing. She sat with her eyes open but obviously wasn't seeing anything Ilmari could see. Something shifted in her eyes and she was back with him, her face grave. She'd seen something she didn't want to tell him. He nodded his head, indicating he understood but was wise enough not to ask.

From death and angels when he was a child to long nights with the kantele to sad farewells to Suomi to Deep River to a foolish and near-fatal self-wounding, the path led here.

Ullakko raised the alarm when Ilmari failed to return. Aino got the girls to cover for her and rushed down to Ilmahenki. The search party of men from the church was still assembling when Vasutäti emerged from the forest across Deep River. She held both arms high over her head. Although Aino had heard stories about Vasutäti, this was the first time she'd seen the old woman. She knew at once that Vasutäti had found Ilmari and he was safe.

She helped push Higgins's rowboat into the water, Ullakko scrambling to jump in with her. The entire search party followed, nearly overloading the two other rowboats beached in the sedge at the riverbank. They followed Vasutäti to her campsite. Ilmari was waiting for them, sitting with his back to a tree, smiling a little sheepishly at all the fuss he'd caused.

Vasutäti took the opportunity to sell almost all her basket inventory, accepting scribbled IOUs from those who had no cash.

Although unable to walk, Ilmari seemed surprisingly healthy, even oddly content with the world. Two of the men made a stretcher out of cedar limbs and shirts and they packed him back to the river and put him to bed in his own house.

Aino barely slept, working to keep Ilmahenki afloat and at the same time working for Reder. She couldn't have done it without the help of the women from the church who showed up daily with meals and helped with chores when she couldn't be there.

Vasutäti came every day, the hem of her deerskin dress wet from crossing the river. She would tend to Ilmari's wounds. On her third visit, she walked over to where Ilmari had his kantele hanging on the wall. She strummed it quietly. Then she handed it to him.

"Time you played," she said.

"What do you want me to play?" Ilmari asked.

"Not song. Time you played notes between the notes."

Ilmari nodded solemnly. Aino rolled her eyes. Vasutäti, seeing this, smiled gently at her. "You, young woman. Raw soul." She nodded at Ilmari. "Brother raw, too. But not so raw." She looked for a moment at Aino, who could not take her eyes away, feeling at the same time challenged and cared for by this strange old woman. Vasutäti gently nodded her head, as if agreeing with something. She broke the gaze and turned to Ilmari.

"You play, now. Every day." She laughed a clear laugh. It made Aino think of the rapids on Deep River above the farm. "I come back for music lessons." She turned to Aino again. "You not mind I take on music student?"

Aino didn't know what the old woman was talking about, but she knew it wasn't about music.

Ilmari spent most of his time making spoons and ladles, sharpening tools, splicing rope, mending shoes, any work he could do without standing. He also spent a lot of time with his kantele. Aino noticed that he had learned some new songs that he could sing only if he changed the tuning on the kantele. The words were in English, but they made little sense to her, something about iron and pain. At times, she would sigh inwardly and marvel at his foolishness, as he sang just one word, one syllable even, for long periods of time, his leg splayed out on the floor in front of him, his back to a wall, moving his jaw in different positions to change the overtones. But then, that had always been Ilmari.

When Ilmari had healed, every two or three days after the chores he'd make his way to Vasutäti's camp, carrying his kantele. He would stay there until the next morning. Aino gave up asking him what he did there after three tries that elicited only gentle smiles. But then, that had always been Ilmari.

18

The weather grew steadily colder. At Reder's Camp the better of the shorter days were spent logging in light drizzle, the worse in driving rain. The loggers walked to work after breakfast in the dark and did the same coming home. Straw turned damper. Clothes were harder to dry. It was more difficult to get the bunkhouse fires started in the dark. Aino urged the loggers to defy Reder by sending someone back during daylight. They wouldn't do it, afraid Reder would fire the man. "Not if you tell him that if he fires one of you, he fires all of you," Aino said. The loggers wouldn't move.

She went to Huttula directly. "He respects you. You're his best hook tender. Just tell him the men are ready to strike if he doesn't act."

"That would be lying," Huttula answered. "They're not ready to strike and you know it."

"Why?" Aino asked.

"Because they're not crybabies."

She decided on direct action herself and spread the word that there would be a meeting outside the bunkhouses on Sunday afternoon, October 28, to discuss living conditions. She'd pleaded with Matti, Aksel, and Jouka to make sure Huttula came.

He did come, as did the other loggers. Aino, speaking in Finn with Jouka translating into English, tried to make them see that if they didn't protest a simple matter like poor living conditions with one voice, they'd stay forever in wage slavery.

"We're not slaves," someone said.

"You're right," she answered. "You're not slaves. You're well-fed, trapped animals who are kept ignorant that there's a better way."

There were murmurs of disapproval at being called animals.

She backed off, conceding with a hand gesture that she might have gotten a bit hyperbolic.

"Look at it this way," she said, almost pleading with them. "Every dollar Reder got that he didn't work for, some logger worked for a dollar that he didn't get."

Again, she saw heads nodding. Still, the meeting broke up with no action.

A week later, Aino's frustration with the loggers' reluctance to act came to a head one night when she was sitting on the big porch. Her face lit by lanterns from inside, she rounded on her brother and his two friends. "You call yourselves men. *Men* are dying in Finland to get their rights."

"Easy for you to say," Matti replied.

Aksel surprised them all by coming suddenly to his feet. "I'm sick of political parties, unions, business, and government. They all kill people." He walked away, leaving the three others watching him disappear into the night.

"He's not afraid to speak his mind," Matti murmured.

"He's a class traitor," Aino said.

Feeling he had to get away by himself, Aksel walked to the Knappton docks on Sunday. The great river sloshed beneath the splintered planks at full flood. Seagulls, floating momentarily above the water, dived for bits of fish and garbage, flapping skyward to land on pilings or wharves where they immediately fought with other seagulls trying to take the food away. With the food gone, the big western gulls, dark gray on their backs and brilliant white beneath their four-foot wingspans, flapped back into the air struggling to reach cruising altitude. There they went into their graceful glide, moving twenty to thirty miles an hour above the water, eyes searching. The big runs were done for the winter. Nets were draped across net racks, and fishermen stood weaving new mesh with flat wooden net-splicing needles, talking, shouting good-natured

insults to each other or merely lost in the ever present, working the
needle, making new mesh squares.

Aksel quietly watched an older man smoking a pipe as he worked.
Neither said anything. Aksel picked up a splicing needle, full with
twine, walked over to a large tear in the man's net, and started to mend
it. The man watched from the corner of his eye, occasionally taking the
pipe in his hand to puff it back into active burning.

"Feels good," Aksel said in Swedish, laughing a little. "I used to
hate it, my hands freezing, working with my father and my brother,
before the ice broke."

"And now they're in the old country and you're here," the man
said, also in Swedish.

Aksel nodded. He looked at the leaden sky, feeling the cold on his
hands as he worked the damp net. "Yes," he said, looking all the way to
Finland. His father would be mending net alone.

The man took out a tobacco pouch and refilled his pipe, then
turned to Aksel. "Alvar Carlson," he said. "Everyone calls me Cap." He
sat down on a large cable drum and nodded toward another nearby.
Aksel lit a cigarette and started asking Cap questions. Where do the
salmon wait in slack water? Which side of the channel do they favor? If
the wind changes, then what? What do they fetch a pound? And finally,
how much does one of these boats cost? At the answer, Aksel sighed. It
would take years with what he made in the woods.

"You can work for one of the canneries," Cap said, fiddling with
the pipe bowl, not looking at Aksel. "They own the boats and pay you
by the pound."

"Never," Aksel said.

Cap studied him. "Never? You work in the woods; you get a dollar
a day no matter how much timber you send to the mill. If you're good,
become a top boat, the more you catch the more you make."

"I want my own boat."

"Fair enough." Cap tapped out the ashes, still glowing, on a wide
crack between planks and they floated in the gathering darkness to the
darker water.

* * *

When Aksel reached the bunkhouse, several of the loggers were reading IWW pamphlets; others were arguing about what was in them.
Matti handed him one.

"Where did this come from?" Aksel asked.

"You need to ask?" Matti answered. "Aino brought a bunch back
from Astoria and then sent away for more from Portland."

"She shouldn't be fooling around with them. They use dynamite."

"So do loggers."

"Yoh, for logging."

Aksel flopped down on his bunk. He picked up a handful of dank
straw and held it out to Matti. Then he smiled, dropped it on the floor,
and rolled over to face the wall. He had fishing boats on his mind.

Aino was thinking about crybabies—and haircuts.

Monday, after work, she set up a chair and lantern on the dining hall
porch and cut Matti's hair. As loggers walked by, she told them she'd cut
theirs for a nickel. That night, she did three more haircuts, all the while
getting the loggers to talk about how they felt about the bunkhouse
conditions. The problem wasn't the loggers' not caring that they lived
in damp straw, slept two to a bunk on nights too cold for them to sleep
alone, lived with lice, and couldn't get Reder to even let one logger off
work a half hour early. They cared plenty. They just wouldn't show it.

On Tuesday night, she did six haircuts. On Wednesday, she did
eight. With each new haircut, Aino casually mentioned the feelings
of the previous loggers and their names. When one would voice an
opinion about the bad conditions, she asked him if he'd ever talked to
Huttula about it.

The loggers soon figured out what she was doing, but it didn't
matter to them. They'd have walked to Knappton and back just to feel
her hands on their heads. Nor did it matter to Aino. Her model was the
Salvation Army. It, too, knew that unemployed men were there for the
food, not the good of their souls.

Aino would stagger back to the henhouse when she closed shop.
Some nights, she felt she was trying to change the course of an ocean

liner by pushing on its bow. She knew she was trying to overturn centuries of conditioning, knowing one's place in the social order, learning not to complain, learning to endure, learning to keep one's mouth shut.

By midweek, loggers started talking to Huttula, who now had evidence that the men really did want change. He went to Reder on Friday after work asking for fresh straw every week and warm bunkhouses when work was done. Reder refused.

Then, nature waded in on Aino's side. The November rains, the first of the long rainy season, hit on Sunday afternoon, November 11. The rain slashed through the cracks in the crude board-and-batten bunkhouses, forcing some loggers to move from their bunks to the floor. Rain still fell on them through leaks in the shake roof and loggers went to work tired—and grumpy. The rain often hit them horizontally as they worked. High above, limbs creaked and groaned as the trees, many now exposed on one side because of the previous logging, whipped back and forth. Some limbs, the size of small trees, broke and came crashing to the ground. Loggers worked with one eye on the dangerous cables or the unsteady logs and the other looking upward, ears tuned for the telltale crack from above that set eyes searching for the danger and minds racing to decide whether to run or stand still.

The storm passed but not the rain. It settled in under low, oppressive clouds, soaking the ground. It created mud, which in turn created more danger. Logs would slide when they shouldn't and wouldn't move when they should. Hands slipped on wet steel cable. Springboards, eight or ten feet above the ground, became slippery. Hat brims drooped with the weight of water, and wool long johns, shirts, and trousers tripled in weight. At night, men wrung out their clothes, but many could not find room to hang them on the inside clotheslines, so clothes remained in piles, wet. They went on wet in the morning. The caulk boots soaked up water, becoming heavy and squishy to the touch. Putting on wet socks and boots in the dark slowed dressing considerably, so the usual hurried breakfasts became sprints to fuel up and get to work on time. Anger at Reder's intransigence rose.

Huttula went to Reder again on Thursday, November 15. Reder told him he didn't want to hear about it and walked away. Now, Huttula was mad.

Sensing her moment, Aino called for a meeting Sunday afternoon.

Aino stood nervously by one of the railcars, going over her points, fearing no one would come. She pulled her coat closer around her, feeling the rain, light but steady where it touched the parts of her face and head not covered by her head scarf. She'd chosen the time and place carefully. Sunday, Reder was always in Knappton. After Saturday night, most of the loggers were broke, and this made them more amenable to talk about fairness and wages.

Without her glasses, Aino thought she saw Matti and Jouka coming from the bunkhouse, along with maybe ten other loggers. When they joined her, she asked, "No Aksel?"

They both shrugged their shoulders. "He says he hates unions and politics and this One Big Union is both," Matti said.

"He's like all the other Swedes. They just do what master says as long as master throws crumbs under the table for them."

Matti laughed. "Hillström's a Swede."

Aino shot him a dark look. Then she noticed that Jouka wasn't smiling. Could he be jealous?

"Hi, Jouka," she said. "You coming means a lot to me."

Jouka mumbled, didn't know where to look, so he looked at her shoes. She thought if she ever found an outgoing Finnish man maybe he'd look at her knees.

Lighting cigarettes, the loggers squatted on their heels or leaned against the railcar. Iverson and three others climbed onto the loading boom and sat easily on it.

She was acutely aware she was the only woman.

Another figure approached from the bunkhouses. As he came into focus, she could see it was Toivo Huttula—a good sign. Toivo squatted down next to Matti and pulled out his pipe.

As she'd expected, most of the loggers who showed up were Finns, but she was pleased to see a fair turnout of other nationalities. She still wasn't confident about her English. She turned to Jouka. "Will you translate?" He nodded.

Taking a deep breath, she reached behind her on the flatcar and held up some dank hay. "Cows sleep on better hay." She waited a beat. "Are you men or cows?" She had carefully constructed the opening. These loggers were fiercely proud of their skill and their manhood.

Some of the loggers laughed. One shouted back in Finnish, "At least we don't belong to some herd like your communist friends."

"Wolves form a pack, not a herd," she shot back to murmurs of approval. "Cows don't even know they're in a herd. They just eat grass until the master's dog herds them to the milking barn." Saatana, what she would give for Voitto's speaking gift right now. "Every one of you is going to stay a cow in your wet hay, stepping on your own cow pies, unless you organize." As plain Finn as she could make it. Silence reigned, even after Jouka's translation for the non-Finns. Now she had to get them to understand.

"Toivo," she said. "What did Reder say when you asked him for fresh straw and a part-time bull cook to get the bunkhouses warm?"

"He said no." Laughter, followed by more laughter when Jouka translated.

"He would never say no if it meant shutting down his operation," Aino said.

"You're dreaming," Iverson said after hearing the translation from his perch on the boom.

"I'm not dreaming. You are," Aino said, in English. She reverted to Finnish and addressed the others. "Do you ever wonder why someone too cheap to pay for dry straw and a part-time bull cook pays for so much good food?"

Silence. Then, when Jouka had finished, Iverson said, "Because we'd log for someone else."

"And he'd end up with nobody except damned shoe clerks who don't know anything about logging," she added. "Right now, he's got the best crew in the state." The loggers nodded in approval. "And you don't leave, because all the other outfits have the same bad living conditions and pay. And Reder and the other owners get together to keep it that way. Why do you think he goes to Nordland every few months?"

After Jouka translated, someone shouted, "I bet Margaret would like to know the answer to that one," to more general laughter.

"He's there doing what you won't do. He's part of a pack of owners. And because they work together, *one big owner wolf pack*," she enunciated, "they keep the lid on wages and conditions. The only way to counter them is with *One Big Union*." She looked around at them, engaging their eyes. "This isn't just about straw and you know it. It's about organizing. Safety and wages come next."

The loggers were quiet.

She'd been waiting for this moment. "Straw and a part-time bull cook will barely dent John Reder's profits. He'll feel no pain giving us this. What we get, however, is far greater than hay. We'll have proved that we speak with one voice and we're no longer afraid to do so. Organize on straw now, so we can make hay later."

She'd worked that last line up the night before and had expected some laughs. No one said anything. Was it because she'd lost them or because she had them? Her heart raced. Now, she had to ask for action. "We must strike *now*," she said in Finnish. "We striking now," she added in English.

And they did—all of them. After hours of debate in the bunkhouses, the next morning the loggers covered the railroad tracks with the straw from their bunks. The engineers and brakemen left the locomotive on the track, boiler fires dying.

John Reder had walked to Reder's Camp in the dark, as he usually did on Monday morning. When he saw the straw on the track and the locomotive stopped, he simply turned around. Although forewarned by Huttula, he was still surprised. He walked back in grim determination to Knappton, where he took his .44-caliber lever-action Winchester from the coat closet.

Margaret watched him loading the rifle. "Do you really think that'll be necessary?"

He slid down the spring-loading mechanism, locking it in the tubular magazine, and put some extra cartridges into his pocket. "There's IWW pamphlets all over camp. Those sons of bitches use dynamite."

Margaret humphed. "Maybe, but not our loggers." She went into the kitchen, calling over her shoulder: "You're not going back up there without lunch."

He followed her into the kitchen and put his hands over her womb, nuzzling against her neck as she was making a sandwich. The more her belly grew, the more protective he grew. She smiled, then twisted a little, getting him to drop his hands.

"Where's this literature coming from?" she asked, focusing on her work.

"Your friend, Aino Koski."

"Oh, John Reder, she's an idealistic child, a girl. She'll get over it by the time she's married."

"She's no child and she's as red as a fire bucket."

When Reder returned to the strike scene around noon, it looked like a company picnic without food. He could see the small staff of flunkies, including Aino, standing idly on the porch of the mess hall. He climbed onto a log on the train, careful to show that the rifle's chamber was open. He waited until everyone had gathered and was quiet.

"Unless you're all at work in one hour, I'll fire every one of you."

Toivo walked from the crowd, picking up some straw. "We asking you to being treated with some respect." He tossed the straw into the air and it fell to the ground in a clump. "We wanting clean straw and a part-time bull cook. We not asking for more."

"Toivo Huttula, have I treated you badly? Ever? Do I not give you boys the best food in southwest Washington?"

Jouka shouted out: "Sure, but you quarter us like animals."

"You go to hell. You're fired."

Jouka laughed. He turned to the other loggers, speaking Finnish. "I've just been fired. I guess I won't do any work today." The loggers laughed. Several reached for clumps of straw and threw them up in the air. Then one of them threw a clump at Reder. Straw isn't exactly a missile, but when the air became filled with it, all directed at Reder, it delivered the message.

"You're all fired," he shouted. "Be out of the bunkhouses tonight or I'm calling the sheriff. Those bunkhouses are private property."

"So are pigsties," someone shouted.

That elicited more laughter and more straw.

Reder stalked away. He clambered up the steps to the mess hall, brushing past the flunkies and glaring at Aino. He told the cook not to serve any food and returned to Knappton.

Despite Reder's orders, the loggers ate supper in the dining hall. The cook had pointed out that it was Reder's food and Reder didn't want to share it. Huttula had pointed out that since the loggers all paid for their food out of their wages, if their wages were zero, the payment for food should be zero. The cook called in the flunkies and dinner was served on time. He also informed Huttula that there was enough food to last about a week.

Aino took full advantage of the strike to talk to the loggers about the IWW, why it was different from the craft unions, why it was a better way forward than the American Federation of Labor. She signed up fifteen new members by the second day of the strike. On the morning of the third day, however, the atmosphere in the dining hall was more subdued. Aino felt uneasy. They'd seen nothing of Reder or of Sheriff Cobb. Reder had disappeared from Knappton and no one knew where he went. He was clearly playing a waiting game. The loggers knew the stakes: Reder's profits against their empty stomachs.

On the fourth day, Thursday, all the fresh meat was gone and the staples—beans, flour, dried peas—were running low. Aino talked Matti into walking to Ilmahenki where they pleaded with Ilmari to kill a beef.

"The strike committee will sign a note," Aino said. "You'll be paid back. I promise."

"Does lending money make me a capitalist?"

Aino smiled. "You're lending meat."

Ilmari shook his head, slowly, looking at his brother and sister. "Take the oldest one," he said.

Aino and Matti herded the lone beef back to Reder's Camp where it was slaughtered, providing another week of protein, supplementing the hunting parties that were scouring the unlogged areas for deer and elk.

Without work, the loggers had time to talk and the talk turned fearful. They came to Aino with questions she couldn't answer. What would happen if Reder returned with the sheriff? Could you be forced back to work at gunpoint? She reminded them that they weren't slaves or serfs, that this was America. Could they go to jail for eating Reder's food? Wouldn't that be stealing it, when they weren't working for it? Aino tried to still their fears, but her own grew. Could she go to prison? The thought pushed up her pulse and made her stomach lurch.

The girls in the henhouse grew quiet, not saying much to her at night. They'd all been excited and on her side when it started. She was learning about the realities of leadership. Leaders must deliver, otherwise they're abandoned.

On Friday morning, Matti watched little Kullerikki, who'd gone to see his sisters, come running into the camp, his breath heaving. "Scabs. Ten I think. Reder brought them over from Astoria. And Sheriff Cobb," he gasped. "Three armed deputies."

They could all add. Although when logging was going strong in the summer, Reder employed up to a hundred men, he didn't need that many to stay alive. With Reder's side rod donkey punching, four scabs falling and bucking, four rigging, two working the landing, and Reder himself running the locomotive to get the logs to tidewater, he could yard and load enough logs to keep the bill collectors at bay.

The loggers looked at one another. "Well," Huttula said. "I guess we're in it one hundred percent now." He walked into the bunkhouse and came out with his hunting rifle. Jouka followed with the other loggers who had rifles or pistols. They were all used to hunting and firearms, but to Matti they looked nervous.

He and Aksel had only their puukkos. Until now, Aksel had stayed away from the heated discussions, even going down to Knappton again to help Cap with the net mending. Aksel looked at Matti and sighed. "Can't just sit here I guess," he said. Matti felt a tug of love for him, although he would never use that word.

The two of them joined the others.

The loggers quietly gathered behind the rail trucks. Some—more rash or ignorant of what a shootout was like—climbed on top of the locomotive cab and onto the firebox and boiler in front of the cab. Matti and Aksel crouched behind the pilot truck, the small wheels that guided the locomotive on the track, and stared through the running board handrails to where the trail emerged from the stumps and slash.

Matti felt someone slip in behind him. Aino. "You get out of here," Matti said. "This is no place for a girl."

"Make me."

"You damned stubborn . . ." Words failed him. "You realize there could be shooting."

Aino looked at him as if he'd said the most obvious thing possible. "Why do you think I'm here? I started it." Matti said nothing, taking this in. "I never thought it would come to this," Aino said, her jaw set, looking at the trailhead. "But it has." She looked directly into Matti's eyes. "I'm responsible."

Aksel shrugged his shoulders. Matti took Aino by her elbow and dragged her closer to the pilot truck, placing her between him and Aksel. "You stick with us and keep your head down," he hissed.

Aino rearranged herself between them. Matti caught Aksel's eye and touched the puukko in its leather scabbard tucked against the small of his back. Aksel nodded, touching his own puukko, the puukko of his father that should have gone to Gunnar.

They watched the scabs coming closer. Shorter, darker men, Greeks or Italians. Jouka shouted, "That's far enough." He held his rifle high.

There was a brief huddle among the scabs, then one stepped forward. It was the Greek from the dance, Galanis. He opened his palms and shrugged, shouting, "Galanis has to eat."

Jouka lowered the rifle, pointing it in front of him, but not obviously aiming at the group.

The sheriff and three deputies, who'd stopped as well, looked nervously at John Reder.

Reder stepped in front of the group, his rifle cradled in the crook of his left arm. "Get the hell off my property," he shouted. "Get off or I'll have you evicted and arrested." He turned to the sheriff. "Carl, you tell 'em the goddamned law."

Carl Cobb, who'd been the sheriff of Chinook County for nearly six years, having won two elections on the money and backing of the owners in the county, was clearly uncomfortable. Until now, the worst trouble he'd seen was drunken fights on weekends, the occasional petty theft, running the Indians out of town before dark, and the usual wife beatings.

"That's right, boys," he said. "You're on private property."

Before Matti could stop her, Aino stood up in front of the locomotive, exposing herself to the view of the armed group. "Everything you seeing here is paid for by the sveat of verkers," she called out. "Ve verkers owning this machines as much same as Yohn Reder."

Matti tugged at Aino's skirt. She slapped his hand away. He stood up next to her. Then Aksel did the same on her other side. Matti could feel her trembling with fear. Trying to control his own fear, he whispered to her in Finnish, "What you just said is preposterous."

"It's a simple statement of the labor theory of value, which you clearly don't understand," she whispered back, still looking at the sheriff, her head held high, her back straight, her legs quivering.

Sheriff Cobb and Reder had a heated exchange they couldn't hear. Cobb took a couple of steps forward. "You're a bunch of cowards, hiding behind the skirts of a woman," he called out.

Aino immediately knew Cobb had hit the loggers with an insult they couldn't ignore, risking violence even further, foreclosing any chance of winning. She spread her skirt wide with both hands and looking exaggeratedly behind her, called back, "No one hiding behind this skirt." That brought a laugh from some of the loggers.

"That's enough, Aino," Matti whispered tensely. "Get down."

"You get down," she whispered back. "No one's going to open fire on a woman." She drew herself up. "At least I don't think so."

The two groups watched each other in silence. After three minutes that seemed like half a day, Reder ejected a cartridge to clear the chamber and bent down to pick it up. He said something to Cobb and weapons were cleared and pistols holstered. The group disappeared down the trail.

Aino grabbed Matti's arm and buried her face against it. She wouldn't move until Matti gently turned her back toward the dining hall.

That night, after a brief argument with the scabs when he refused to pay their fare back across the river, Reder had to deal with yet another woman.

"The payment for the loan for the new yarder is due next Thursday," Margaret said quietly. "Next Friday, the grocery bills are due and those merchants expect to get paid, whether we think it's fair those loggers are eating our food or not."

"They're stealing it."

"Have you been in the bunkhouses?"

"Goddamnit, Margaret, I told you I grew up in bunkhouses like those, greasing skids when I was eleven."

"John Reder, I'll not have swearing in this house." She sighed. "I know you worked your way up, John, but if you don't settle, it'll be settled for us when we go out of business."

"I've never been beaten."

"Maybe our own loggers aren't the enemy." She held out the *Oregonian* to him. "The IWW is trying to organize a region-wide strike in April. Mills are stockpiling lumber in anticipation. Prices are rising." When Reder finished, Margaret said, "If we can move logs at those prices, we'll recover what we've lost in a week. In several more weeks, the yards will fill and prices come down. Now is the time to settle." She took the paper from him and folded it neatly. "In a way, the IWW is on our side. We have a common enemy, the big corporations. If they're not stopped, they'll eventually own everything from trees to paper plants, controlling the prices, putting the small outfits out of business except for a few of us to log at breakeven when they need more volume. You'll own Reder Logging, but they'll own you."

Reder walked over to the window and stared into the dark. She touched his shoulder. "John, they're the best crew we've had. For heaven's sake, it's straw."

19

Saturday morning, Reder reached the camp before dawn. He fired up the locomotive boiler himself and as soon as he had a little steam up, he laid on the whistle, long steady blasts, then climbed on top of the cab. Loggers stumbled out of their bunkhouses, looking at him in the half light.

"Goddamnit," he shouted, his voice small against the hills and surrounding forest, but clearly heard. "I'll get your straw and give you your bull cook. Now get to work or I'll fire every one of you."

The loggers looked at one another and smiled. They disappeared back into the bunkhouses and came out with their boots on. Aino and the other flunkies were already in the dining hall, preparing a very meager breakfast of pancakes without butter and beans that they'd put on to simmer the night before. In half an hour Reder Logging was back in production.

The girls slammed through the Saturday evening cleanup in record time. The henhouse hummed with discussions about what ribbon, hat, or bracelet to wear. There were never discussions about choice of clothes; the girls had only one good dress or skirt.

The dance that night was in Tapiola, upstairs in Higgins's warehouse. Higgins had rigged a canvas screen for privacy for the women that closed off a space carved out of the goods on the main floor, the front of which served as the general store. Although more than half the people didn't work for Reder, an air of celebration stirred in the building, marking a small victory for working people.

Aino basked in the muted glory.

When the band took a break, Jouka set down his violin and reached into a sack sitting next to the accordion player's chair. He nodded to the band and they played a brief flourish. The hubbub died. "Aino Koski, please come up here," he said. Aino felt her heart thump and she hesitated, looking around her.

Lempi gave her a gentle shove, "Go on," she said. "You're going to like it." Then she added, "I already know what it is."

Aino didn't have time to process exactly what the last remark was intended to convey, but she made her way to where the band had set up.

When she reached Jouka, he pulled out a little doll made from clean straw that arrived on the train that afternoon. He'd put a little apron on the figure and a tiny head scarf. The loggers cheered and then laughed and kidded Aino when she blushed so deeply it could be seen clear across the room. She wanted to kiss Jouka but simply said, "Kiitos." Thank you.

The loggers called out, "Speech, speech!" She looked over the people pushed up behind those forming a small space in the dance floor around Aino and the band. She could see Ilmari and Matti by the stairway, their faces glowing with pride. She saw Ullakko over by the wall, next to his children, two of them asleep on the floor. The older children clapped their hands, proud to know her, but when she saw Ullakko's look, she quickly turned to those immediately in front of her, aware of Jouka, violin in hand, standing just behind her right shoulder.

Although unprepared, she spoke. "First, again, thank you for the doll." She held it above her head and shouted, "Clean straw!" Everyone clapped and some cheered. She continued in Finnish. "But this is just the beginning." She realized it seemed someone else was talking. "Yes, we have won a small victory for the workingman, but we must not let this divert us from our main goal, our final victory. No more will we stand alone, beaten down to slave wages, alone, slave hours, alone, and slave working conditions, alone." Applause, though not general, interrupted her. "When Karl Marx said the workingman has nothing to lose but his chains, he was right, because we have been given nothing and we have nothing. But the chains, the chains, fellow workers, are of our

own making. It is our dumb acceptance of 'the way things are.'" She was
suddenly swept away with her own rhetoric, launching into an impassioned appeal to throw off the combined chains of private ownership,
the fairy tales told by church and government to keep them in their
places and in fear. She finished with a rousing, "Two for ten!" meaning
two dollars for a ten-hour day.

She waited for the applause. About a quarter of the crowd
clapped, some even cheered, but many, including her brothers, looked
embarrassed.

Jouka moved next to her, his hand on her shoulder, and addressed
the crowd. "Now, we celebrate the victory we have won. No more
talk about work. We're here to dance." He turned to the band. "'Skat-
ers' Waltz' in G." He played the two-bar intro and the band took it
away. People began to waltz, forming a flowing circle under the rafters
and split-cedar shakes of the roof. Aino became aware of being alone
between the band and the dancers. Suddenly, Aksel appeared, holding
his hand out in invitation. She glanced at Jouka who, violin under his
chin, nodded just enough, urging her to dance. She took Aksel's hand
and moved into the flowing gyre, aware that everyone she loved wanted
her to keep quiet.

The waltz over, Jouka left the bandstand and joined her and Aksel.
He made a polite nod to Aksel and said, "Mind if I have the next one?"
She saw Aksel's eyes flicker slightly in disappointment, but he graciously nodded back and walked away. She stared up at Jouka. He had
never looked so handsome. The band started and they were dancing.
She knew all the girls would trade months of bad shifts to be dancing
with Jouka, but he had chosen her. He had given her the doll in recognition of what she'd done, the most important thing she'd done in her
life. She focused on his face, aware that she couldn't stop smiling. He
had chosen her.

She walked back to Reder's Camp with Lempi and two other girls from
the henhouse. All of them had Sunday shifts in a few hours. Matti and
Jouka walked ahead of them and two other loggers behind them in case
of a cougar or bear. She felt a letdown. Somehow the speech had turned

people from celebrating their victory to focusing on her being a radical. Two women had asked her how many IWW membership cards she'd handed out, and she didn't get the impression they thought she was doing God's work.

A quiet, insidious voice told her she'd pushed a little too fast. The speech was right, but it was made at the wrong time. Another lesson in politics learned the hard way.

She wrapped her coat around her and moved closer to Lempi and the others. She focused on Jouka's back, realizing she hadn't thought about Voitto the entire night. She smiled, listening to Jouka in his cups, entertaining them all by singing songs in three languages, his lone voice echoing through the dark trees shrouded in the mists of madrugada.

20

On December 2, 1906, as Aino followed Matti down the trail to have Sunday dinner at Ilmahenki, she pondered on change. Reder had let the loggers off early for Thanksgiving. At first, Aino thought that maybe the strike had stimulated his generosity, but Lempi told her that he did the same every year, as well as serve turkey for the loggers who had no homes to go to. Fresh straw came up on the train every Tuesday and Friday. Reder had assigned an older logger with a drinking problem to start the fires before the loggers came awake and just before they quit work. It seemed as if the loggers had never slept on damp hay crawling with vermin or awakened shivering in the cold or fumbled with numb hands to make fires in the dark upon returning to the bunkhouse.

Things were different at Ilmahenki. That morning, at church, Ilmari had heard more than an earful about Aino's rousing thank-you speech.

"Why should I care what a bunch of ignorant toadies to the state religion say about me?" Aino said.

"I've told you before," Ilmari said slowly. "It's not the state religion here. A state religion is forbidden by the Constitution."

"Bunch of toadies," she mumbled, pushing at her mashed potatoes.

Matti looked at Ilmari. "Coffee?"

Aino cleared the table. Matti lit a cigarette. He moved to the door after a scowl from Ilmari. Outside, he took a few deep drags, then threw the butt to the ground, where it sizzled for a moment. He came back inside and said to Aino, "I saw you were dancing close with Jouka last night."

She was pouring coffee into the ceramic mugs from Sears Roebuck and didn't answer.

"Jouka's a good logger," Matti went on. "He'll maybe someday be a donkey puncher. I've watched him around engines. He's good." He paused. "Really good."

She put the mugs in front of her brothers and sat back down at her place. They were silent, drinking their coffee. She glanced at each one's face.

"What?"

"Dancing close," Matti said. "If you're serious, that's fine, but if you're not—"

Aino slapped her hand on the table. "I'm sick and tired of husband, husband, husband. You tried selling me into slavery with old man Ullakko. Can't I just dance with a good-looking boy without everyone thinking I have to marry him?"

Ilmari's eyes flashed. "Trying to find a decent man who could take care of you is not selling you into slavery," he said very evenly. "You'll ruin your reputation and you'll never find a husband."

"What? Dancing with someone makes me the Whore of Babylon?"

"You be careful with language from the Bible," Ilmari said.

She looked right at him and said, "Whore."

"You think it's funny, a girl's reputation?" Ilmari replied. "Who's going to want to marry a girl with a bad reputation?"

"Every logger in this valley—and a blacksmith." Her tone made it clear she was referring to Rauha.

"Her mother has the reputation, not Rauha."

"And she's the madam setting the whore's price."

The table went silent. Ilmari was trembling, reining in his anger. After a time, Matti said, "Well, that puts a cap on it."

Aino put on her coat without speaking, pulled her wool scarf tight against her once again thick hair, tied it under her chin with a single square knot, and walked out.

* * *

Aino heard Matti hurrying to catch up with her. She didn't wait for him. When he joined her, he said, "That was mean to Ilmari and unfair to Rauha."

She knew he was right and felt miserable, but she couldn't bring herself to answer.

They trudged along in silence until Matti gave up and changed the subject. The topic, however, wasn't any less delicate. "Since you don't think Jouka's right for you, how come you don't give Aksel the time of day? You know he really likes you. He's—"

"Good husband material," she finished for him.

"I wasn't going to say that."

"Oh, believe me, it's implied."

After a long pause, Matti tried again. "He's a good man."

"He's a boy."

"He's smart and he's fast. He's—"

"A good logger."

Matti stopped walking. "What is wrong with you? There are six men for every girl here. You could have your pick. But, no, you just want to antagonize everyone."

Aino kept walking.

Matti caught up. "I'm going to partner with Aksel in our own logging company."

"He wants to have his own fishing boat."

"And logging with me, he'll get the money to do it. You could do way worse than marry a good fisherman who owns his boat."

She stopped and whirled on him. "Get off my back. I *do not want to marry anyone.*"

"So, be an old maid."

"In ten years, marriage will not exist. It's just another fairy tale, a prince charming who will make a woman happy forever." She went silent, trudging forward. "My prince charming died," she muttered. She stopped again and barely under control whispered, "You have no idea how painfully. You have no idea."

Matti remained calm. "I do have some idea. Why do you think I ran?"

Suddenly the rage spilled out. "You stupid men have no idea." She stalked off. Matti ran to keep up. "Stay away from me," she hissed. She threw a rock at him—hard. He warded it off with his forearm and stood still. She turned and ran.

"It'll be pitch-black in half an hour," he shouted after her.

She ignored him.

"To hell with you," he shouted at her as she disappeared into the gloom.

Matti stomped into Ilmari's house and slammed the door. "She's crazy," he said, to Ilmari's unspoken inquiry.

Ilmari had clearly mastered his anger. "She was made crazy," he said. "We can guess how."

Matti poured himself a cup of coffee and sat down heavily on one of the kitchen chairs, not bothering to take off his coat or hat. "Yoh," he said.

Ilmari smiled. "She didn't mean it about the bride price."

"Remind me, it's been months."

"Half the capital in a sawmill. I'm saving every penny, but I'm worried she's not going to wait."

"What's the holdup?"

"I've tried everywhere to borrow the money for the equipment." He attempted to smile. "You know the old joke, you only can borrow money if you don't need it."

"Let me think on that," Matti said. He went to the door, opened it, and stared into the darkness.

"She'll be all right," Ilmari said, coming up next to him.

"She was in a state. She won't be watching the woods." He pulled a small matchbox from beneath his coat and struck the match. The sudden glare temporarily blinded him. Shaking the match out, he threw it into the muddy yard in front of the door.

"You shouldn't smoke," Ilmari said.

"To quote our sister, 'Get off my back.'"

He took another drag. "I'm going after her." He tossed the glowing cigarette to the ground and took off running.

He ran past the old snag. Such a waste, he thought. Must be fifty thousand board feet in it, mostly vertical grain. Just past Ullakko's farm, where the Tapiola road became a trail, heading for Knappton and the Reder's Camp cutoff, he caught a slight movement just at the edge of the trail. He stopped and drew his puukko. With it in his right hand, he held both hands above him and started singing, taking slow steps forward. The bigger the animal, the less likely to be seen as prey.

"Matti?" Aino's voice came out of the darkness right where he had seen the movement. He could just make out her dark figure rising from where she must have been sitting or squatting. Matti breathed with relief and put the puukko back in its sheath. "Thought you were a bear or cougar," he said. He was surprised when she came running toward him, and he found himself with his nose in her wool headscarf. She was trembling. He stroked the back of her scarf and looked off into the darkness as she buried her nose in his chest. He knew now was no time for a joke.

Three weeks later, Reder let everyone off early on Christmas Eve. Aino and Matti walked through a steady gentle rain to Ilmahenki, getting there just after dark. They found Ilmari with the top of the stove off, cleaning the ashes from the heat vents surrounding the oven; the ashes were so fine that a gray mist hung in the air, drifting slowly into the open stovetop and up the still-warm flue.

"The stove going to be ready to cook dinner?" Aino asked Ilmari.

"Yoh."

"What are you thinking?"

"Caught a steelhead yesterday," he said. "On the porch. I already cleaned it."

Aino went down to the cellar for potatoes and turnips and started peeling them.

Matti had been thinking about Ilmari's financial problem for a week. He sat down at the kitchen table and inspected the empty coffeepot that had been moved there by Ilmari. "You're out of coffee," he said.

"Yoh."

Silence followed, broken only by the sibilant sounds of the small trowel Ilmari used to clean the oven vent.

"I have an idea about the bride price," Matti said.

Ilmari grunted, went outside, and came back with some alder he'd split two years earlier. He stacked it behind the stove so it would warm and be easier to light on Christmas morning.

"Yoh?" It meant "Go on." He picked up his carving.

"You're sitting on your sawmill only you don't see it," Matti said.

Ilmari gave Matti a look.

"You're good with metal."

"Yoh."

"I know how to log."

"You don't have half the skill of someone like Jouka, much less John Reder."

"Do you know why John Reder is a good logger?" Silence. "Because he can move weight. I already see ways he hasn't seen to move things."

"Thinking's easy; doing's hard."

Aino said nothing, focusing on the meal preparation and listening.

"When Reder bought his new double-drum yarder, he left the old single drum behind at the Fortuna show. It broke down so often it wasn't worth moving."

"So?"

"It's not worth fixing and moving for someone with a better yarder who wants to spend cash on better things. We've got nothing and work for free."

Ilmari resumed carving.

Matti outlined a plan, using Ilmari's blacksmithing skills, for fixing the abandoned yarder and splicing abandoned lengths of cable to move it with its own power to Willapa Bay and then to Ilmahenki.

"That yarder still belongs to Reder," Ilmari said. "It's stealing."

"It's worthless. Reder will get its full value, so it's not stealing."

"What if Reder claims his yarder?"

"He'll never go back to the old site, so he won't know it's missing. If you can make a sawmill, you can make that yarder look like something that came from China."

Now there was a long silence. Then Ilmari said, "How do we get it here?"

That was when Matti's idea really got interesting.

Aino and Matti both sat through Ilmari's "It can't be done" and his "What if?" When he'd finished, Matti proposed the deal. "I want half the money for doing the logging. Your half goes into the lumber mill."

"But I'm helping with the logging."

"You get a dollar a day out of my half."

Ilmari stared at his whittling for some time. "I'll need to see if this yarder can be fixed."

"Yoh," Matti said.

The three siblings were silent. This was no small proposal, and brothers sharing a business was a situation fraught with peril.

When Ilmari said, "The mill needs a name," they knew he'd accepted the deal.

The brothers turned to Aino. She nodded her head. "With this you get a wife," she said to Ilmari.

"Yoh."

"Call it Sampo Lumber. The Sampo was the magic mill forged by Ilmarinen, your namesake."

"Sampo Manufacturing. I can do more than saw wood."

"I like it," Matti said. "The magic Sampo ground out all one could want. Sampo Manufacturing is going to grind out money."

Ilmari smiled at him and said, "Some say it is the mill of the heavens revolving around the polestar."

"I prefer the first version."

Two months later, in February, Matti was walking away from Reder's Camp to Ilmahenki. He and Ilmari had gotten a look at the old yarder in late January after several weeks of delay caused by winter storms, mostly rain but occasionally snow. Ilmari had made two visits to Nordland to see Rauha and assure Louhi that he was making progress on the sawmill. No ultimatum was given, but the message to speed things up was communicated.

Ilmari and Matti decided on making this third Sunday in February the first day of real work to get the yarder moved. When Matti arrived at Ilmahenki, Ilmari hadn't yet returned from church, so Matti spent the time collecting kindling and kerosene. This was the day. They were going to fire the boiler.

When they reached the site, both began to find dry wood and split it to size, When they got sufficient wood, they laid a fire, poured a little kerosene on the wood, threw in a match, and stood back. Black smoke poured from the stack. They added large pieces of split wood, and soon the fire was roaring as the air was sucked through the firebox door. The sides of the boiler began to expand with the heat. Rust flaked off, sometimes in sheets the size of a man's hand. Then there was a terrific bang as one of the interior vertical steam tubes that filled the upper part of the boiler blew apart. Scalding steam exploded into the water that surrounded the tubes, which, combined with the steam, burst into the air as Ilmari and Matti dived for the ground.

When the steam died, they poked their heads up and looked at each other. This meant several weeks of delay because Ilmari needed to patch and refit the tube, which required a hot fire from a small kiln, which meant building a kiln next to the boiler. They sat there, looking away from the yarder, saying nothing. Then Ilmari rose. "It will be dark soon," he said.

"Yoh."

21

On February 28, Aino received a letter from Joseph Hillström. He expected to be in the Astoria area for several weeks. Maybe they could meet at Knappton?

Aino and Lempi arrived at Nygaard's General Store just after dark on Saturday. It was still open, since this was payday. They recognized several loggers from Reder's and said hello, promising them dances. Aino and Lempi were examining a bolt of cloth when the bell attached to the door rang and Margaret Reder entered.

"Aino!" Margaret beamed and came right over. She had on a bright cotton dress for shopping, which both Aino and Lempi compared with their own plain wool skirts and cotton blouses. "How great to see you." She reached for Aino's hands, but Aino pulled her own hands back. How would it look to the loggers, her being so friendly with the boss's wife? After a brief halt in the flow, Margaret quickly went on. Turning to Lempi she said, "I'm Margaret Reder."

"Lempi Rompinen."

Lempi smiled at her, awkward before the boss's wife. Aino simply chose not to answer. She looked around surreptitiously to see if any of the loggers were watching them. Her deal with Margaret was language exchange. The bargain did not extend past that. Margaret didn't understand.

Margaret touched the cloth and started talking in English, which Aino could not yet follow fluently. "Nice pattern . . . with blue eyes," she said looking at Lempi, who, to Aino's mild disdain, blushed. ". . . I tell . . . over to Astoria . . . more choice."

Aino and Lempi said nothing. They worked on Saturdays, stores were closed on Sundays, and they didn't have money for the boat.

"Of course," Margaret said, sensing something gone amiss. "You have . . . the cost of the boat . . . and back."

"We know, Mrs. Reder," Aino said.

"Of course, you do," Margaret said after another awkward pause. Looking around at the store and attempting to remain bright Margaret said, "Well, Aino, can we do a lesson before the dance?"

Aino nodded yes.

"Kuusi?" Margaret said six in Finnish, clearly already past.

"Kahdeksan," Aino answered. "Eight."

"Yksi, kaksi, kolme, neljä, viisi, kuusi, seitsemän, kahdeksan," Margaret counted to eight. "You see, Lempi? I'm . . . progress."

The two Finnish girls didn't know whether that required an answer, so they made none. Margaret walked quickly to the other end of the store.

"For a friend, you weren't very nice to her," Lempi said.

"She's not my friend. I learn English from her and teach Finnish in return."

"When's her baby due?"

"How would I know?"

Lempi gave Aino the look that her snippy answer deserved.

"May, I'd guess," Aino said, now a little embarrassed at her shortness.

"I wouldn't mind if she were my friend." Lempi watched Margaret making her way up the wharf, studiously looking everywhere but back at them. "She seems nice. I mean, it seemed she wanted to be nice. You know."

"Yes. Nice. I know. Nice. Nice is easy. You look at the palace she lives in and the pigsty bunkhouse my brother lives in and the shacks the married couples live in. Her floors are level and she doesn't have to wade through pig shit on her way to the huusika." Aino used a common but crude word for outhouse. "Nice would be housing without wind whistling through the battens. Nice would be sharing the wealth with the people who created it."

"I think she was trying to be a friend," Lempi said tightly. "And you weren't."

Aino trudged up the hill to Margaret's house, dreading what would probably be awkward. Maybe she should apologize. Maybe Margaret would understand that they couldn't be friends. Maybe. The maybes ended when she reached the front door. She knocked and heard the rustle of Margaret skirts as she crossed the floor.

"Hyvää päivää, Aino," Margaret said. "Se on kahdeksan. Tule sisään. Haluatko kahvia?"

Aino couldn't repress a smile. She repeated back in English, "Good day, Margaret. It is eight o'clock. Enter in. Do you want coffee?"

"Not 'enter in,' 'come in,'" Margaret said, and the lesson began.

Aino removed her coat and scarf and sat at the kitchen table as Margaret poured them each a cup of coffee. They both drank it black. Almost everyone did. Cream too often went sour.

Margaret took a sip, set the cup carefully back in its saucer, and said very slowly so Aino would understand, "I thought we were friends, Aino. Why did you snub me like that?"

"What is 'snub'?"

"Snub. Hurt someone by not talking to her."

Aino didn't reply.

Margaret sat very straight. Talking faster, she said, "Aino, I like you and . . . hoped . . . be friends. I know . . . boss's wife . . . thought we were equals."

Aino suddenly felt ashamed of herself, but it was clearly too late—the apology had been owed at the door. "How be equals? You living here. I living up there." Aino nodded in the direction of Reder's Camp.

"John Reder . . . a good hardworking man . . . way up . . . any of his loggers."

"John Reder cutting down trees he never planted on land stealed by the railroads." Before Aino knew it, out came: "And he killing people to do it."

Margaret stood. "It's dangerous work."

Aino stood. "Not so dangerous if loggers not tired and you not having hurry-pants for profits." She used Finglish for hätähousut.

"Aino, our expenses . . . same . . . one log or one hundred. We . . . out of business in weeks, weeks, if we cut any slower." Margaret paused for effect. "And all of you would be out of jobs."

"If the people own the trees and own the machines, never be worry about going out of business."

"That's impossible." Margaret leaned forward. "Aino . . . intelligent young woman but—" She sputtered to a stop. "That's communism!"

Aino, sensing that she had the upper hand because of Margaret's failure to articulate an argument, raised her chin slightly. "Yes. A specter is haunting America, the specter of communism."

"I could have you fired."

"Like a good friend?" Aino went to the coat tree by the door and began putting on her coat and scarf. She wrapped her scarf around her neck, tugging at it. She smiled at Margaret, hard. "Maybe you read Karl Marx not Mark Twain, you know history on our side."

"I think . . . more to say today . . . Aino?" Margaret began picking up the cups and saucers. "Maybe . . . not do any more lessons for a while."

"Not maybe. I qvit."

As she walked down the hill, Aino could feel Margaret watching her. Then she heard the front door shut. Suddenly she felt empty. She wanted to say she was sorry. Tell Margaret how difficult organizing was, explain why it was so important. But she did not turn back—and now she would not. This was war and there were casualties.

She took off her shoes and put them in her bag along with her stockings, then continued down the hill, wondering if Hillström would be at the dance. He would understand.

Accustomed to eating at Margaret's, she was hungry. She looked at the two silver dollars and single four-bit piece in her purse. Soup and a sandwich would cost fifteen cents, nearly a third of her daily pay. Eating her soup, she struggled with the knowledge that she paid for it with money earned by working for John Reder. Without Reder, there would be no Reder's Camp. Who would coordinate the loggers and get the machines if not Reder? We would do it ourselves, she thought. She saw herself leading a meeting of loggers, deciding to buy a new steam donkey or lay a new rail line.

"Soup any good?" someone asked in Swedish.

She looked up in delighted astonishment at Joseph Hillström. Not knowing whether to rise or stay seated, she stayed seated. "Yes. A bit overpriced."

He sat, gave his order to the waitress, and began talking in Swedish. "This time it's going to be different. We will have mills and camps shut down at the same time. Not a stick will move after Monday, April first, until we get two dollars and fifty cents for an eight-hour day."

Aino did the division in her head. "So, about twenty-eight cents an hour."

"Yes, but don't put it that way. Limiting the workday to nine hours is paramount. That gets lost in an hourly wage demand. 'Two Fifty for nine.' Catchy and short, always."

"It should be eight."

"That's the goal. Nine first."

"And if the owners bring in the scabs?"

"It will be harder and harder for the owners. I've been at all the labor exchange places on the river. I've been in the boardinghouses, the saloons. I've handed out more than a thousand red cards." He reached for his coat pocket and placed a red card in front of Aino. "You get all the workers to carry the card; they feel they're part of us. Scabs will no longer exist. All workers will be in the One Big Union. How many do you need?" he asked.

Suddenly fired by his enthusiasm, Aino quickly calculated. "One hundred and twenty." He reached into his valise and threw three bundles of fifty cards each onto her side of the table.

"How much are dues?" she asked.

"A dollar to join, fifty cents if you're unemployed. Twenty-five cents a month, ten if you're out of work. Nothing like the AF of L." Aino nervously held one of the packets, looking at it.

"Will you help me?"

"Aino. I wish I could, but Reder Logging is small potatoes. You'll have to handle it yourself. We're going after Inman, Paulsen, Weyerhaeuser, the big boys. I can't stay."

She stared at the cards.

"Look, I'm giving a speech tonight," Hillström said. "That'll help."

She looked at him. "Speeches are easy, if you speak the language. Organizing is hard."

"I'm just a rabble-rouser next to people like you."

Aino gave a clear signal of what she thought about flattery and false modesty.

Hillström quickly changed his tone. "That's why we need you. Don't you see? We, you and me, and the IWW, together we can eliminate wage slavery. When we're all in One Big Union, there will be no war, no poverty. Imagine a world of peace and plenty for all. Imagine."

Imagine, she did.

22

Ilmari and Matti spent their Sundays in March hauling material up to the yarder to make the kiln and then fix the blown tube. Aino spent her Sundays—and all of her evenings—trying to light fires of a different kind.

Logger by logger, talking sometimes to one logger alone, sometimes to a small group, she began to make headway. More and more loggers took the red cards and signed their names, but she had to have a large majority of them if the Reder loggers were going to join the big industry-wide strike planned for April first.

She'd made no progress with her men. Matti was focused on moving the yarder. Jouka was sympathetic but skeptical about bucking the whole industry and afraid of being blacklisted. Aksel was his usual independent self. Kullerikki would do whatever they did.

Margaret Reder always spent her Sunday evenings going over the books. Increasingly, she didn't like what she saw.

"This is the third week in a row the price of two and better two-by-fours has fallen," she said to her husband, who was reading the paper. "San Francisco's over. Seattle, Vancouver, and Portland are slow. The money's due on that thousand feet of one-and-a-quarter-inch wire in two weeks."

She didn't really expect him to reply. Logging was his turf and he was good at it. Her job was the future. "Prices for lumber go down, stumpage prices follow."

"Damn it, Margaret, don't teach me to suck eggs."

"I'm worried."

"You have more cause than lumber prices." Reder folded the paper. "The IWW is raising hell upriver and that red you didn't want me to fire is handing out IWW membership cards." He slapped the folded paper on his thigh. "I treat them better than anyone else in the country." He looked at her. "Can we take another strike?"

After some quick arithmetic, Margaret said, "You have two weeks of inventory rafted on the river. If they strike, prices will go up, and we'll have no labor or food costs." She tapped her teeth with the pencil eraser, thinking. "The bigger the inventory, the more time we have before we dig into savings."

They both knew what that meant—cutting faster.

Finally, Margaret said, "They're not going to like it."

"I'll put Huttula on another line east of Johnson's crew. Good six-foot timber. We can yank it out faster than this big stuff we're felling right now."

After a silence, Margaret said, "John." The tone was no longer business.

"Hmm?"

"Our baby's due in May."

Motivated by a possible strike and a child, Reder was all over the operation, cursing at people he thought too slow, figuring angles and rigging, selecting stands, doing anything to save time—a fervor of activity to increase production. Normal precautions were overlooked. Impatient at a slow choker setter, Reder would jump onto the sled of the steam donkey and blow the main haul signal himself, shouting at the engineer as the choker setters dived for cover. Responding to Reder's threats of firing them, buckers took on logs sitting precariously on slopes rather than repositioning them to more stable lays with screw jacks. Only superb reflexes and athletic skill avoided catastrophe on more than one occasion. Loggers had a word for it, taken from the railroad signal calling for full speed: highballing. Highballing killed.

The loggers came back even more exhausted than usual. With each near miss, with every torn shoulder muscle, with every cable-burned hand, with every cursing for what Reder considered poor performance, the grumbling grew. Aino was right there, fueling the fire with every ladle of stew and every stack of pancakes, her anger growing with theirs every time another injured man limped in for dinner. After two weeks, Aino sensed that the loggers had had enough of it. Then Matti walked in to dinner with two badly mangled fingers. He was angry. Aino was outraged.

That night, Aino talked individually with all the hook tenders, urging them to go as a group to confront Reder. The last one she talked to was Huttula.

"You see Reder for what he is, Toivo. *Now* we vote to strike. Now."

"Not so easy, Aino."

"*Now*, Toivo. Together with our fellow workers. Only together are we big enough to fight the owners."

"Aino," Huttula said. "What's a fair wage?"

Aino was taken aback at the simplicity of the question. "When you get the full value of what your labor added to the product," she answered carefully.

"I don't understand any of that socialist gobbledygook. It's just German and Russian castles in the sky. What's a fair wage, for us, for Reder. In dollars and cents?"

Aino thought about dignity and fairness but realized if she were to have any success she had to have a simple answer to this simple question.

"The IWW is demanding a raise from a dollar seventy-five a day, with a day being basically dark to dark, to two dollars and fifty cents for a nine-hour day. I would ask Reder for two fifty for an eight-hour day with safe working conditions and tell him that if we don't get it by April first, we'll strike with the IWW."

Once again Toivo Huttula was selected to speak for the hook tenders, but this time they all went with him. The confrontation took place in Reder's office after Saturday's shift. The six men fit themselves into the room and shut the door, surrounding Reder, who sat at his desk.

"Mr. Reder," Toivo said. "No more this highballing. Too dangerous."

"You tell the IWW to stop threatening a strike and I'll slow down."

"We not IWW, but all good loggers. The only reason no one getting killed here."

"If you don't want to do what it takes to keep this operation afloat, you know how to leave."

"John Reder, we log together long time," Huttula said. "You keep this up, for sure, someone getting killed."

"We have been together a long time, Toivo, but you let me run my own goddamned outfit. You want to run one, go build one. It's a free country."

"It's not just highballing," one of the other hook tenders said.

"Oh, there's more?" Reder asked sarcastically.

"Yes, Mr. Reder, there is more."

"Well? I'm listening."

The man looked at the others, getting several nods. "We want two fifty for an eight-hour day."

Reder laughed. "And I want a virgin whore and a drunken Saturday night with no hangover on Sunday."

"You give what we asking," Huttula said, "and we log like hell for you."

"I give you that and there'll be no Reder Logging to log these woods. Not even the IWW is asking that."

Huttula slowly straightened himself to his full height. "After eight hours, men tired and not so fast. Logging is enough danger when not so tired. Two dollars and fifty cents for an eight-hour day. Or by God we strike."

"You can work eight hours for two dollars and fifty cents in hell and I'll help every goddamned one of you get there. I hear one peep more out of you and you'll be looking for hook-tending jobs all over this side of the mountains and you won't find one because I'll make goddamn sure you don't. Now get the hell out of my office."

The group looked at Huttula.

"Get the hell out or goddamnit I'll start firing you sons of bitches right now."

"John," Huttula said. "You making one big mistake."

"I'll run my logging company as I please, Toivo. Now get out of here. I've got work to do."

When the door shut, Reder sat looking at it for a long time.

When Aino heard the outcome of the meeting, she talked with the girls in the henhouse. That night, the girls began moving beans and other storable food from the kitchen to hiding places in the woods.

On Friday, March 29, the accident happened. Harold Iverson, the man Matti had fought in the bunkhouse, was an experienced bucker. He'd just cut a log to length and was tending to his saw downslope as Matti and Aksel struggled to pull the choker to another big log uphill from him. They shouted at Kullerikki to whistle two longs and two shorts for slack. They got it, but the engineer, having just been threatened by Reder with being fired for going too slow, forgot that slack had been requested and, ever mindful of keeping the line moving, tightened up on the main line before Aksel got the choker hook around the choker cable. The hook jerked out of Aksel's hands, stuck momentarily on the underside of the log, and then was underneath and away as the main line tightened, starting the log rolling. Matti shouted at Aksel and dived for a hole while Aksel jumped clear of the rolling log. It pounded right over Matti and down the hill, forty or fifty tons of wood in the shape of a steamroller picking up speed. Iverson heard the shouts and looked up to see the log barreling toward him. Throwing his saw, he ran to the right, but his boot caught and he went down. Had he been half a second faster, had that piece of slash not been there, had the line not been tightened prematurely, had Aksel just managed to hook the line before it tightened—a series of unfulfilled hads. The log crushed Iverson's legs and bounded down the hill where it came to a rest.

Kullerikki was signaling "man-down" as hard as he could, and the donkey engineer pulled the drums out of gear. John Reder heard the man-down piping and his heart sank.

"What happened?" he asked, breathing hard as he reached the yarder.

"Don't know yet. Can't see," the engineer replied nervously. They waited. There was a whistle for go ahead slow from Kullerikki, and the engineer carefully began winding in the main line. Another jerk on the whistle wire signaled him to stop. Small figures below the landing appeared from the defile where they'd been hidden from view, carrying a man between them.

"That's Iverson," the engineer said. "Långström and Koski have him between them."

"Who are those men coming behind them?"

"That's Huttula's crew. They're coming to whip my ass."

By the time Matti and Aksel reached the landing with Iverson, the rest of the crew had beaten the donkey engineer nearly unconscious, ignoring Reder's attempts to stop them. Iverson's eyes were wild with pain, but he said nothing. They laid him next to the moaning engineer on the yarder skids and looked up expectantly at Reder.

"Get back to work," Reder said.

"Maybe we take Iverson to—" Aksel began to say, but he was cut off by Reder.

"We'll handle it. Any damage to the rigging?"

They both shook their heads no. "Then what in hell are you standing here for?"

Reder took over the yarder. The engineer and Iverson were carried to the bunkhouse. Alma Wiitala, who doubled as the camp surgeon, went to work cutting away Iverson's stagged trousers and high boots. Both of Iverson's tibias and his left fibula were broken in several places. One piece of his right tibia had pierced the skin. She had seen worse. She gave Iverson several shots of rye whiskey and a cloth to clench between his teeth, then she pulled the bones back together so they could have a chance of knitting. She finished by pouring kerosene over the open wounds before splinting and bandaging. Then she tended to the donkey engineer, who'd said nothing and asked for nothing. Going against the whistle was a major crime and in a logging crew all justice is local. He just hoped he'd paid in full.

Reder paid Iverson for the full day's pay but said he'd stop his wages after that. He could heal in the bunkhouse if he wanted, but he was probably through logging for Reder for the foreseeable future. If not forever.

That night, Huttula rose from his place at dinner. He pulled his red IWW membership card from his pocket and held it high above him, saying nothing. Soon at least twenty loggers held their red cards high. No one spoke. They were all looking at Huttula.

"Iskemme." he said. Then he repeated it in English. "We strike."

23

Reder's first response was to grab his rifle, several lengths of chain, and some padlocks. Making sure everyone saw him, he locked and chained the mess hall doors.

He handed the rifle to the cook. "Shoot anyone who tries to steal the company's food."

The cook gave the rifle back.

Aino and Lempi, anticipating Reder's move, had carried pots and kettles into the henhouse the night before. With help from the loggers and the tacit approval of Alma and the cook, they'd added more sacks of beans and flour to what they had already hidden in the woods. They built a fire pit in front of the mess hall porch and began cooking. The conflict between labor and capital, spun out so elegantly in political and economic theories, was fundamentally about hunger outlasting avarice.

Everyone chipped in to pay for a doctor from Ilwaco. He changed Iverson's bandages, grunted in satisfaction at Alma's work, and said Iverson would heal but would never log again. Iverson turned his head to the wall and spoke to no one for two days. That was when Lempi came into the dark bunkhouse one morning and handed him a cup of coffee. She soon had him talking to her—then to the others.

A week went by without anyone's even seeing John Reder. Aksel watched his savings for the gill net boat dwindle. Alma Wiitala, Aino, and the other girls prepared food on the outside fires until Aino talked Ilmari into improvising some outdoor stoves. Jouka would sit next to the fire pit, playing his violin if it wasn't raining too hard, watching Aino and the other girls cooking. Matti took advantage of the strike to move cable up to the donkey. He and Ilmari had laboriously spliced two coils of one hundred feet of seven-eighths-inch cable from lengths of scrap. On the first day they each took a coil. The coils could be packed only a short distance before legs and backs gave out. A good part of the time was spent dragging one coil at a time, the two brothers counting aloud and heaving simultaneously on the uphills or when the mud got bad. Matti cursed the cable frequently. Even Ilmari cursed it once. That first day, they got the coils about a third of the way to the site.

At the end of the second week, Alma, Aino, and Lempi added up the strike committee's cash and took inventory of the food on hand. Then they made up two daily menus, one based on restricted rations and the other on very restricted rations.

Two days later, Aino found herself trying to get a sawbuck pack saddle onto the camp mule, Sally, to go down to Higgins's store with some of the precious strike-fund money for beans and other needed food. Ten years earlier, Sally had hauled back the heavy main line to the next log. With the arrival of Reder's first steam donkey, Sally was made redundant, but no one, including Reder, had the heart to turn her into meat as had been done with the oxen. Technically, she belonged to Reder, but even Reder knew she belonged to the camp.

Sally was blowing out her belly to frustrate Aino's attempt to tighten the girth when Jouka came up and punched the mule just below her rib cage. The puffed-up belly disappeared. Aino quickly cinched the pack saddle into place.

"Want company?" Jouka asked.

Aino looked toward the henhouse. "Lempi was coming. Have you seen her?"

"I did. I told her I'd take her place."

"You did?" She looked at him quizzically.

"I did. Can't log."

They set off for the Tapiola General Store, walking on the rail ties to the path that led down to the Knappton-Tapiola trail.

Their purchases made, they headed back. Jouka was as good at conversation as he was at memorizing poems and songs. He even persuaded Aino to sing some of the old *Kalevala* songs her father had taught her. Although she sang them haltingly and was somewhat embarrassed, she needed to sing a song only once and Jouka had it in his memory. He would sing it back to her making changes that were subtle or not so subtle but always for the better. After an hour on the trail, walking one on each side of Sally, smelling Sally's sweet mule smell, singing and joking, they came to the turnoff for Reder's camp and the uphill climb to the rail line. Jouka led Sally to the small creek that paralleled the trail at that point and let her drink her fill. Aino waited for them, sitting on a mossy nurse log sprouting at least twenty tiny new cedar trees. Watching Jouka pulling on Sally to regain the trail, she felt a rush of affection for him. She had rarely had such a good time, not since—she felt a twinge—Voitto.

Jouka astounded her by kneeling to her level and asking her to marry him.

She was shocked by her desire to say yes. She felt herself quivering with the fight between the yes and the no. He was so unlike Voitto, yet there was the same feeling. Jouka's words were coming to her as if through the wrong end of a speaking trumpet.

She just sat there, Jouka before her. Finally, she said, "Jouka, it's . . . it's too sudden."

Jouka looked up at her, fighting, unsuccessfully, to hide his humiliation.

"Jouka, please," she said softly. "Please get up."

Jouka stood and looked away from her. "Is it because I can't read?"

Aino knew she was standing there with her mouth open. So much about him was suddenly clear. She recovered. "No. Heavens no." She smiled brightly at him and offered her hands, which he took. "I knew that," she fibbed. She squeezed his large callused hands.

She did not want to hurt him, but she did not want to marry him or anyone. She would always be true to her vow to Voitto. That was the truth. So, she said just that, imperfectly and haltingly.

When she finished, Jouka said nothing.

"I never have so much fun as when I'm dancing with you," she said, "listening to your music, or just talking, like today. You're wonderful."

"Not wonderful enough," Jouka said.

"I told you. It's not you," she said.

He faced her. "How long will you be married to a ghost?"

"Forever."

Jouka shrugged. "That'll be tough to outwait."

She said nothing for a moment. "Come on. We were having such a good time. Sally wants to get home and we've got loggers to feed."

Aino walked over to Sally and slapped her on her haunch. Jouka went to Sally's other side, slapped her gently, and they walked in awkward silence for about twenty minutes.

"Oh, Jouka, for heaven's sake, sing a song. Sing that one about Sven Dufva holding off the Russians at the bridge."

After a moment's pause, Jouka's baritone sounded through the trees.

Two days later, John Reder appeared. He found Huttula inside the bunkhouse. "Get the other hook tenders."

"For what?"

"Just get them."

Soon, the six hook tenders were standing in a circle around Reder.

"I want you to come with me. I want to show you something before we start talking."

"You're willing to bargain?" one of them asked.

"I'm willing to talk."

They looked at each other, shrugged, and nodded OK. All seven of them boarded the speeder and they pumped their way to Willapa Bay where Reder pointed to several huge rafts of logs, floating quietly on the incoming tide. "Those are all mine," he said. "And I wish they weren't." He turned to them. "And there's more. Indulge me for a small walk." He led them up a small hill to the south of Deep River's mouth where they had a clear view of the south end of Willapa Bay. He pointed out several other large log booms.

"Boys," he said, "those logs aren't moving, because the lumber market is in the shitter. Logging has practically stopped around Arcata and Coos Bay and it's slow clear down to San Francisco. You don't need to take my word for it." He pulled a clipping from the

Oregonian showing bellwether lumber prices and news of mill clo-
sures. "Prices are still going south and you saw the inventory. I just
might be better off not logging. You go back up to camp and tell them
what you've seen."

Huttula called a meeting by the cook fire after a dinner of beans and
only beans. The pigs had all been butchered and eaten. He told everyone what he had seen.

One of the hook tenders said in English, "I don't worry for me
about beans, but my wife, she worries. The baby getting colicky. I
not know about nursing baby, but I know about living with a cranky
woman." There were some laughs.

"So, what?" Aino said in English. "So, life at home not so good? You
qvit on your fellow verkers up the river because your baby gets colic?"

"Give 'em hell, Aino," a man's voice cried.

"She's not feeding the baby," came a woman's voice from the back.
That brought laughs from the women.

"You can't give up," Aino cried out. "We put so much into this. We
not qvitting now, when we almost there."

"Aino," Huttula said. "You've seen the log booms."

"Yes. The logs Reder piling up by highballing, logs paid for by
Iverson's legs. Don't you see? He's just scaring you. He is scared. I know
he having bank loans due."

"Yeah," a voice shouted out. "And Margaret's due as well." More
chuckles.

"Won't you take me serious?" Aino cried. "He is about to breaking."

"If the mill verkers go back to verking," Huttula said, "Reder can
pay bills for months with that pile of logs. What have we got?"

"You got your hearts. You're on the right side of history."

"You can't eat history, Aino," he replied in Finnish. "I'm sorry."
He turned to the men. "I think we're beat," he said, still in Finnish. "It
was a hell of a try, but I think we're beat. The market is against us. It will
be against the IWW, too. I say let's vote on it."

He waited. No one said anything.

"OK, hands up," he said in English. "Who vants to go back to verk?"

Silently, some with shame in their eyes, some with a defiant I-told-you-so look, men raised their arms. There was no need to count.

Aino fought not to burst into tears.

There were a couple of snorts of derision. A woman called out, "Maybe you should have cried earlier to soften Reder up."

Then someone else called out: "You got us into this, you red troublemaker."

Cries of approval and disapproval were all drowned out by Jouka's scream of anger as he barreled into the last heckler. The loggers hooted their approval of the fight, some rooting for Jouka, others for his opponent. Finally, Huttula and two other hook tenders waded in, grabbing both fighters by their shirts and suspenders and hauling them apart. Jouka was bleeding from his nose and mouth. Aino ran to the henhouse.

"Hey, we made a good try," Lempi said, sitting next to Aino on the bed. She patted Aino's knee. "Everyone was for it. Don't listen to those lunkheads. They're just trying to make you a scapegoat."

"I feel so ashamed," Aino said.

"For losing or almost crying?" Lempi asked. "I saw you."

Aino nodded her head. "Both."

"Aino Koski, not a man out there thinks less of a woman who tries and cries. But if you don't go out there and tend to Jouka right now, they'll never forgive you. Nor will I."

Aino willed herself out of the henhouse. Loggers still talked in small groups. She spotted Matti. He was whittling a bowl from a burl with his puukko, talking with Aksel and Jouka, Kullerikki sitting next to them, whittling what looked like a doll's head.

They all looked up as she approached. Jouka started to stand, but Matti put a hand on his shoulder and kept him seated. Jouka's face was raw and his nose had been broken. Aino squatted down next to Jouka, touched the bruises on his face, touched his nose. "It's broken," she said. "Come with me to the henhouse and I'll fix it up." She turned to Matti. "It will need to be straightened."

Matti and Aksel looked at each other for a moment, then at Jouka. Matti nodded toward the ground. Jouka lay on his back and Aksel and

Kullerikki each took a shoulder and pinioned his head. Matti sat on Jouka's chest. He looked down at Jouka. "Ready?" Jouka nodded. Matti grabbed Jouka's nose firmly between his thumb and forefinger, wiggled it slightly, and pushed it back into position. Jouka did not flinch. When Matti leaned back away from his face, Jouka relaxed his body and let out a breath. "Will it ruin my profile?" he asked.

They helped Jouka to his feet and Aino walked him to the hen-house, holding his hand.

Huttula walked to Reder's house and told him about the vote. Reder came back to the camp with him.

On Monday, April 22, the loggers were back at work. Reder told Aino to pack her bags. She was fired.

When Aino arrived at Ilmahenki, she told Ilmari the strike had failed. He nodded and said, "Maybe now we'll get some blacksmith work." Then he said gently, "I can always use help."

The IWW strikes failed everywhere. The market kept contracting. Men who were rehired after the strikes were almost immediately thrown out of work all over the Northwest. Reder Logging managed to keep its head above water through a combination of smart engineering, experienced loggers—and low wages. None of the loggers complained. They saw outsider loggers walk up the tracks, disappear into Reder's office, and then walk back down the tracks.

Two weeks after the strike failed, Aksel walked into Tapiola for the dance above Higgins's store, hoping Aino would be there. She was, but so was Jouka. He came down from the bandstand several times, making it obvious how he felt about her. Aksel got in a couple of dances with her, but a lot of other loggers lined up to do the same.

When the band took a break and Jouka disappeared to take a drink outside, he and Aino were left together by the stair railing.

His mother always said he should ask girls questions about themselves, but he didn't know where to begin. "How's Ilmari?" he plunged in, knowing she was now living with him.

"Fine. Health is good."

Silence, with Aino looking over at the stairs, probably for Jouka.

"Does Ilmari still see Vasutäti?" Aksel asked.

Aino looked back at him and sighed. "Yes. He disappears sometimes for the whole night. Leaves me with all the chores."

"What does he do there?"

"He says he just sits there and does nothing."

"Nothing?"

"Nothing. He says that's the point." Aino laughed. "I love him dearly, but he's always been a hard one to understand."

"Yes, but you have to like him."

Silence, more glancing at the stairs.

"How's Sampo Manufacturing coming along?"

"Still moving the yarder." Aino laughed. "My two capitalists. Living in dreamland where everyone gets rich."

"What's wrong with wanting to improve themselves?"

She looked at him warily.

"I mean," Aksel said, "I want my own fishing boat. Is that bad?"

"No. The problem is you'll be one out of a thousand. It's dreaming like this that makes labor its own worst enemy."

It irritated him. "Why do you make everything look so bad? We've never had it so good. Here in America we have no class structure. There's opportunity."

"For a lucky few. If workers got their fair share of the wealth they create, there would be plenty for everyone. *That's* the dream of the IWW."

"Which is dynamiting its way to power." Aksel knew he should stop there, but he couldn't. "That's what got my brother killed."

"We've never used dynamite. Those are the lies of a capitalist press." She paused for just long enough to make sure Aksel would get the next point. "What got your brother killed was that someone betrayed him."

They stood there, angry with each other and silent, Aksel wishing he'd never gotten into the argument. The tension broke when Jouka came up the stairs, happily inebriated, and asked Aino to dance.

24

Margaret had planned on checking into St. Mary hospital in Astoria the week before her due date, even though she wasn't Catholic. The universe had a different plan. She went into labor two weeks early, eighteen days after the loggers went back to work. A storm was driving straight off the Pacific, whipping the river into six-foot rollers that formed surf on the sandbars. It was impossible to get a message to Astoria for a doctor. No one was crossing the river.

John Reder could only swab Margaret's forehead and pray. He had been doing it for twelve hours.

The house shuddered with the blasts of wind. The rain fell nearly horizontally, driving against the glass windows, spattering in liquid light from the kerosene lanterns in streaks of pale yellow against the blackness of the night.

Margaret was breathing hard. "It's not coming, John. I don't know how long I can keep this up." Her face glistened with sweat. Another contraction hit, and she squeezed hard on her husband's hand, gritting her teeth to try to contain a scream. "Something is wrong. I think the baby is upside down."

He looked at her dumbly. "So, what happens if the legs come first?"

"I don't know, John!" She was suddenly angry, exasperated. "I don't know anything!" she wailed, then was hit with another contraction. "Oh, God, John. The baby could die." She didn't say it, but he knew. She could die, too.

John Reder looked at his hands. Years of hard labor with ax, saw, steel cable, and rigging had made them massive. He couldn't imagine getting one of them in there.

She touched his hand. "I know, John," Margaret said. "I know." She took a breath. "Aino Koski's mother is a midwife and she was teaching Aino before—" She was hit with a contraction.

"It won't come while I'm gone?"

"It can't come," she said through gritted teeth. "That's the problem." Armed with a mission, John Reder never faltered.

Aino wakened when she heard the pounding on Ilmari's door and what sounded like John Reder's voice shouting her name. She heard the scratching of a match as Ilmari lit a lantern. It could only mean Margaret's labor wasn't going well.

She sent a thought heavenward, not believing in any deity but still behaving as if someone was listening. Then she toughened up. No help was coming. She'd known this since childhood. *She* was the help. She began putting on her clothes.

Reder mounted the horse and reached for Aino's hand, hauling her up behind him. A blast of wind sent a crack through the night as a large limb crashed to the ground. The loggers called them widow-makers. There'd be many on a night like this. She locked her arms around his waist and they moved off into the dark.

They reached Knappton at four thirty in the morning. It was clear immediately that it was going to be a breech birth.

She had watched her mother do a breech birth once. She remembered Maíjaliisa looking at her, a hand in the woman's vagina, saying, "You have to get the baby's arm across the body, get the shoulder right. I'm trying to find the arm. If I don't, we'll have to cut her open." She pushed that from her mind. That she could not face.

Aino leaned over Margaret and felt her huge hard abdomen. She shouted to Reder for a wineglass. He came running up the stairs, a puzzled look on his face but with a wineglass in his hand. Aino put the glass on Margaret's belly and put her ear against the base. She looked at Reder. "Baby heart beating good."

"The baby's heart beats well," Margaret said through clenched teeth.

Try as she might, Aino could not get the baby to shift simply by pushing at it through Margaret's skin.

The yellow light from the lamps that had been reflected from the driving rain moving across the windows began to mix with the gray of the Washington dawn.

Margaret was exhausted. Aino was remembering her sisu.

"I go inside," Aino said. "This my first time."

"Go inside!" Margaret, in labor now for over twenty hours, was pushing her feet against the bed, raising her hips and writhing. "Goddamnit, go inside!"

Aino went to the kitchen where Reder had boiled water. She carefully washed her hands with soap. "You keep fire going. Water hot. House not cold."

Reder did not ask if Margaret was going to be all right, because he knew Aino would not know.

Aino put fresh towels underneath Margaret's buttocks. "You ready?" Aino asked.

Margaret nodded, her eyes wide with urgency and pain.

Aino bit her lower lip, looked Margaret right in the eye and began working her hand up the birth canal.

It had never been boring, helping her mother. Not at all, but she paid attention like a teenager. If only, she repeated to herself, if only. She felt a tiny leg and looked at Margaret, whose eyes were closed.

"Mr. Reder," Aino shouted. "More towel."

Reder came up with two towels. "Roll one. Put it in wife mouth. She can bite."

Without a word, Reder rolled the towel and gently as he could put it between Margaret's teeth. Aino went in farther. Margaret's eyes widened with pain and she bit down hard.

Maíjaliisa's voice filled Aino's head. *The problem is the umbilical cord comes with the legs and then gets squeezed. The baby dies from lack of oxygen or is an idiot if it lives.* Aino felt carefully, slowly, between the baby's legs and the cervix opening. There. A lump of umbilical cord had come into the opening. She felt it, like a smooth tough tube of rubber, and slowly pushed it back inside the womb. The legs were partly out, the head back inside. *When the head comes through, it molds to the opening. Sort of like poop squeezing through an asshole.* Aino smiled at the memory. More than once people told her Maíjaliisa had an earthy sense of humor. So, she focused on getting the head squeezed down and then, once through, expanded back to its original shape without hurting the brain.

She guided the head into the cervix, pulling with one hand, using Margaret's muscles to push and turn the baby, pulling the tiny arm to position the shoulder, pulling, gently squeezing, pulling, feeling, Margaret clenching her teeth on the cloth towel, daylight coming into the room, the lanterns growing dim in comparison.

Suddenly Margaret screamed. "Cut it out, Aino, cut the baby out."

John Reder knelt beside his wife and began to pray out loud.

"No. We risking infection, bleeding." Then she heard an inner voice saying, "You don't know what you're doing and you're going to kill this baby and kill Margaret."

Margaret screamed again. Her womb tightened around Aino's hands and wrist, the little body twisted so the shoulder went tight and then it was through. Now the head. The womb had the head flexed against the little chest. Aino gently kept the pressure on, keeping it there. *The head must not leave the chest. The chin could hang it up. The umbilical cord could get in and around the neck. Nature wants the head against the chest.*

She squeezed with her hand, her long fingers grasping around the fontanelle, squeezing the head to a point, squeezing the baby's skull to an egg shape, a hard-boiled egg without the shell. Squeezing. Then . . .

The miracle of birth.

After Aino had cut the umbilical cord and Reder had buried the after-birth outside, the two sat at the kitchen table across from each other.

They were sharing the pot of coffee Reder had made several hours earlier. "You all right walking back to your brother's?" he asked. "I'd go with you, but . . ." He looked upstairs where Margaret was asleep with her daughter on her breast.

"Best staying with Mrs. Reder. I going OK myself."

She went and took one more peek at Margaret asleep and breathing easy. John Reder followed and looked over her shoulder. She turned to him and whispered, "Clean. Everything very clean or bad little plant can kill mother. Mama's milk usually make baby OK, but maybe bad little animals are making red bumps and white . . . " She couldn't come up with the English for bacteria and pus. "Ugly bumps. You will see. You get doctor if little bumps."

Reder nodded.

Rain rattled the windows, but the wind had died down. Reder helped Aino on with her coat. This gesture of politeness gave Aino a feeling of great satisfaction. Up at Reder's Camp, John Reder was the king in his kingdom—and she was nothing. Here, for the past few hours, she had been the queen. She wondered if this was how Margaret felt all the time.

"Just a moment," Reder said. He disappeared into the small office off the living room. When he returned, he held out a twenty-dollar gold piece to her.

"I cannot thank you enough. Please take it. You earned it."

Aino looked at the gold piece—nearly two month's wages. She was out of a job. He was the man who fired her. After a moment of hesitation, she said slowly, "Someday people will see save a life is different from earning wages."

Reder tried to put the gold piece in her hand and she gently turned it away. "What is market price to save someone you love?" she asked softly. "It is all you have. How can price be fair when one side willing to pay everything?"

Reder said nothing.

"How you can make this business?" Aino said. "People not things like logs and lumber. Earnings, prices, supply, demand, they make no sense with people, only with things."

Reder looked at her a long time, cool and steady. He put the coin in his pocket. "Margaret likes you. Now I see why. You're a special girl, Aino Koski. You'll always be welcome in my house." Then his eyes revealed just the smallest twinkle "But if I ever see you up at the camp, I'll call the sheriff and have you arrested for trespassing."

Aino didn't know how to respond.

Reder opened the door. A gust of wind sent rain splattering into the hallway. "Aino," Reder said. "I will recommend you to anyone as a midwife." He smiled at her. "Until the revolution comes, I suggest you charge ten dollars a delivery."

When Aino reached the muddy street she suddenly felt compelled to turn around. He still stood by the door. He waved to her. She hesitated, then waved back. Tired, elated, and confused she set off in the rain for Ilmahenki.

25

Two weeks after the Reders' daughter was born, Matti and Ilmari were ready to move the donkey. In the bunkhouse on Saturday night, June 1, Matti told Jouka and Aksel that he and Ilmari could use some help packing the haul-back line, grease, additional blocks, and wire to the site.

"I'm not doing much tomorrow," Jouka said.

"I'll help," Aksel said.

Matti was a little surprised at their eagerness.

The next day the three of them walked from Reder's Camp to Ilmahenki. When they got to Ilmari's shop, Jouka asked, "How's Aino?"

"Ask her yourself," Matti replied. "She's at the house."

Jouka smiled and walked off. Cocking his head sideways and raising his eyebrows, Matti looked at Aksel. Aksel looked at the ground. Then, without a word, he followed Jouka. Ilmari also followed, smiling, proud that these two young men were vying for his little sister.

When Aino saw Jouka coming, she scooted quickly into the house, going to the mirror on the kitchen wall to get her hair in order. She put her glasses in her apron pocket. Then, she put them on again and took her apron off. Then she thought better of that and put the apron back on. When she started again to take off her glasses, she saw another figure following behind the figure she guessed was Jouka. It was Aksel. She smiled.

Aksel and Jouka came in, taking their hats off, followed by Ilmari. The three standing together, two tall and fair, one not so tall but dark and broad of chest, made the kitchen feel cramped. She took their hats and motioned them to the table. The three men sat, saying nothing, while Aino poured the coffee and cut each a slice of pulla.

"Come to help Matti with the wire rope?" Ilmari asked after everyone had taken a sip and a bite.

"Yoh," Jouka replied. Aksel just nodded.

There was more silence while the men chewed. Aino knew they were friends, but she could almost feel the air quivering. It made her anxious and simultaneously terribly pleased with herself. Finally, Aino asked, "How's it going at camp? Reder keeping to the bargain?"

"Yoh," Jouka replied.

Aino waited to see if anything would follow. It didn't. She looked at Aksel. "The savings for the boat coming along?"

"Yoh," Aksel replied.

And so it went, until Matti poked his head in the door and Aksel and Jouka left. A nice Sunday chat.

Jouka came along to help again the next Sunday as well. Aksel had taken off for Astoria the night before and no one expected him back. This time, Aino was hoeing the garden weeds when she heard Jouka clear his throat. She startled, then turned to face him, fighting the urge to take her glasses off. She was self-aware enough to know that she was vain, but there was no need for Jouka to know. She left them on.

Jouka took the hoe from her. "Kiitos," she said. She followed behind him, pulling the uprooted weeds.

He stopped after a while and faced her. "You weren't at the dance last night."

"Busy."

"Too busy to dance? Aino . . ." He gestured around him, questioning why she would stay home.

"I was gone."

"Gone?"

"Yes."

"Where?"

Aino could feel Jouka struggling between genuine interest and some sort of jealousy.

"I was at the Astorian Suomalainen Sosialisti Klubi."

"And you walked home at night? Alone?"

"Wouldn't be the first time, but no. I stayed in the new ASSK hall."

"Alone?"

"Jouka. It is all perfectly legitimate."

"People will talk."

"People talk no matter what I do."

"So, why not do things people won't talk about?"

"Like?"

"Like come to the dance at Knappton next Saturday. I won't be playing. There's a band from Astoria."

"People will talk about that, for sure."

"Yes, but *that* kind of talk is expected. Matti can come. It'll all be legitimate."

Aino paused. She looked at Jouka solemnly. "Jouka, I'd love to go, but I've committed to making a speech in Willapa."

"A *speech?*"

"What? I can't talk?"

Jouka got flustered. "No . . ." He started hoeing, fiercely. She followed, weeding.

Jouka turned to her. "Is it because of Aksel Långström?"

"Nooo," Aino said. "He's my little brother's friend. He's a kid."

"He doesn't look like one."

Aino didn't respond.

"Matti says you'll be twenty next March," Jouka said.

"How am I supposed to take that little piece of information that I already knew?"

Jouka looked at her, as if she were doing something to hurt herself. "I turned twenty-two in April," he said.

"I like you, Jouka, but this stops now."

Looking into her eyes, pressing his lips together, Jouka dropped the hoe at her feet and walked off, leaving Aino trembling.

* * *

Jouka joined Matti and Ilmari as they walked to the donkey site. Ilmari
had patched the hole in the steam tube and now the three began the
backbreaking work of replacing the lost water with creek water. They
reeved the cable through two blocks and Matti ran one of the blocks,
paying out the wire rope as he went, to a stump, attaching it with a
hook choker looped back on the standing line. They greased every
moving part.

Then the moment came. The three stood looking at the iron monster, saying nothing. Matti lit the fire. This time only a little rust flaked
off as the boiler expanded. They watched it tensely, Matti throwing
wood into the firebox, building steam pressure. Two large steam pistons
began to hammer back and forth, moving drivers, smaller versions of
those found on a steam locomotive, one on each side of the donkey.
Ilmari climbed onto the machine, grabbed the five-foot-long steel gear
lever, and gave Matti a grim look. He threw his weight against the friction clutch that linked the axle of the single drum to the main shaft
being spun by twin drivers. Screaming in protest at being wakened from
its long sleep, the yarder drum bucked briefly and then began turning.

The three of them looked at each other and said nothing.

Matti gave two pulls of his fist for an imaginary whistle and Ilmari
gave two toots back from the tarnished brass whistle, then put tension
on the line.

The line lifted off the ground, quivering with the strain. With
a belch of steam the old donkey lurched from the mud accumulated
around the two large skids bolted beneath it. The donkey bucked and
squealed in protest, but it moved. Matti ran to clear obstacles as it
jerked toward the fixed block. When the donkey closed on the block,
Matti removed the block from the stump and reset it another two hundred feet closer to the bay. Grunting with the strain, pulling the cable
to unwind it from the donkey's drum and attaching it to the reset block,
they started the next leg.

Throughout the summer and into the fall of 1907, the occasional midwife job kept up Aino's contribution to Ilmari—along with cooking,

cleaning, milking, mending, knitting, and tending the vegetable garden. In late September, Aino was bundling the hay in the field, moving behind Ilmari, smooth and steady with the scythe. He'd been in the forest with Vasutäti the whole day before and Aino had lit into him because he'd left her with all the work.

As always, Ilmari took criticism as he took praise, which is to say without affect. He said he was sorry, got out his whetstone, and started sharpening his scythe. His eyes, however, were seeing something hers didn't see.

It was a typical late-September day, the sun out, the air cool, but she could almost feel the rain gathering itself out to sea. Ilmari said there were two seasons here, not four. The wet season would start in October and go through June, succeeded by the dry season, which went through September. She remembered following behind her father and Ilmari, Matti following her, gathering sheaves with her mother, just before Ilmari left for America, helping her mother weave the hay into stacks that would shed the rain and snow. She remembered Suomi, its birches and lakes, rolling hills, icy still rivers in deep winter, the sun low in the south casting blue shadows from cozy houses onto the snow and the smell of pines and wood smoke. She paused to look at Ilmari's tiny purchase of civilization in the vast forest where rain-swollen streams, hidden from view by trees too large and close together to see through or by salal taller than a man and too thick to penetrate, ran unseen to wide tidal rivers. The farms here, unlike the tidy farms at home, seemed more like survivors in a battlefield of stumps and slash, just waiting to be reclaimed by the forest that rolled unconquered and impenetrable, all the way to the other side of the Cascade mountains. She wanted desperately to return to Suomi.

Her brothers were focused on the here and now. Sunday by Sunday, two hundred feet at a time, the length of the main cable, Ilmari and Matti yanked, bucked, and hauled the donkey to Willapa Bay, just south of Long Island. They built a raft around the yarder and, through several more weeks of nearly superhuman effort, managed to get an A-frame set in the mud exposed at low tide. They hoisted the donkey into the air, so it hung beneath the A-frame like a fat spider, and at high tide lowered it to the raft and towed it to the mouth of Deep River behind a hired tug. Again, using the yarder to pull itself, they moved the raft to Ilmahenki.

The entire journey took five months of Sundays, but by November 1907, Matti and Ilmari were ready to start logging. Their first piece of business was to negotiate with Higgins to buy more cable on credit. The Koski brothers' collateral was their promise of sawmill-ready logs, because they had timber and a working yarder on-site.

Logging was less about cutting down trees than about moving them. Ideal logs were four to eight feet in diameter and up to forty feet long. These logs weighed over twenty tons. The bigger logs, if left at forty feet, could weigh more than fifty tons, requiring that they be cut to thirty-two-foot or even sixteen-foot lengths. To move a log from where the tree was felled to water deep enough to float it required bravery, brute strength, and endurance. More important, it required extremely creative engineering. It quickly became apparent that Matti was a natural engineer. He'd solve the most difficult problems of angles, slopes, and gravity with secondhand jerry-rigged equipment made by Ilmari, and with hand tools. If he had had the opportunity to go to school, he would have been building bridges and skyscrapers, but work like that would have bored him.

Jouka and Aksel agreed to help on Sundays for a dollar a day in cash plus the sandwiches that Aino provided along with coffee. They logged the easy trees close to the river first, a mixture of spruce, western red cedar, Douglas fir, and hemlock, the last of which they worked around because hemlock wasn't worth much. As they moved farther from Deep River, the logging got tougher. They made corduroy skid roads from smaller logs to move the bigger ones. Ideal-size trees, four to six feet in diameter and easier to move, were plentiful. There were plenty of eight- to ten-footers, but they took a gamble on those, as there was a higher risk of rotten cores and other defects. The giants, twelve feet across or more, were predominately the Sitka spruce, but included cedar and Douglas fir. It could take two weekends just to get one of these giants down.

26

That fall and winter of 1907 to 1908, Aino gained some renown speaking at socialist club meetings, at dances, after church potlucks. Fellow IWWs helped promote her lectures with flyers. The few who owned homes put her up for the night.

She stood in the rain outside the mess halls and bunkhouses of the logging camps. She stood on boxes outside boardinghouses. She spoke in the living rooms of fellow socialists. She joined in the growing repertoire of songs, singing the strange English words in a forceful soprano. She would follow a Salvation Army band in the larger towns like Willapa and Nordland and retain some of the crowd to preach—yes, it was preaching, she thought—the good news of the coming revolution, the wake-up call of class consciousness, how the system exploited labor, and how to forever banish exploitation of the poor by the rich. She had no interest in changing society gradually; she even thought it would be better to have the capitalist class clamp down harder on labor, because like a boiler building steam the system would one day simply burst.

But it was slow going. Meetings had to be scheduled by mail weeks in advance, and the letters had to be mailed and picked up in Knappton. She would miss important meetings because of a woman going into labor early or late, annoying her comrades.

In late February 1908, already exhausted from a difficult three-day delivery with little sleep, Aino had been up the river, talking to sawmill workers. She had to take the boat back to Knappton, because another mother was due and she could not chance another day away. The midwife business was growing, perhaps too much. Desperate for sleep, she forced herself off the boat at Altoona, where there was a large fish-processing plant. Just half a day more. She'd catch the next boat. When the shift changed, she handed out flyers to both shifts. She passed one to a large man who looked her in the eye as he slowly tore it to shreds.

"You're on private property. Leave."

Aino stood as tall as she could, but she came only to the man's chest level. "I am outside the fence."

"Yeah, but you're not off the property." The man pulled back his coat to reveal a pistol in a shoulder holster.

Aino looked around at the devastation of logged-off land. The man had probably cut down the trees and financed the fish-processing plant with the proceeds.

She left, trembling with fear and anger. She walked seven miles to Rosburg, where she collapsed aboard the *General Washington*, arriving in Knappton just after dark. Feeling guilty about leaving her brother with all the chores, she headed up the Tapiola trail, muddy with a mixture of forest humus, fallen fir and hemlock needles from winter storms, and relentless rain. A waxing half-moon gave her just enough light to stay on the trail, but not enough to distinguish shallow standing water from deeper puddles.

After a couple of miles, she got tired of dodging around the deeper puddles, took off her shoes, and just waded through them, holding her skirt above her knees, the mud beneath the puddles up to her ankles and the cold water sometimes up to her midcalves. She lost all feeling in her bare feet. Every small sound became a hungry cougar or bear in her mind. After two hours of slow going, a crackling in the brush to her left startled her and she lost her balance. She fell forward full-length in the mud, scattering pamphlets from her large purse. She turned onto her back screaming with frustration, kicking like a two-year-old throwing a tantrum, and covering herself with mud. She ended in tears, staring up at the faintly luminous moonlight visible between the dark trees. It occurred to her that if she were married she wouldn't have to midwife. She could organize without the frustrations of trying to work around baby deliveries.

She reached Ilmahenki after several hours. Ilmari took one look at her and began throwing wood into the kitchen stove. He pumped a large potful of water, placed it on top, and went outside to start a fire in the sauna. She undressed in the kitchen, her clothes so stiff with mud they could nearly stand up on their own. She put on one of Ilmari's coats, shivering against the cold. Ilmari returned. "Half an hour for sauna," he said. The water boiled and he made coffee. Then he went back to the sauna to let out the smoke.

She sat in the sauna a long time, still, naked, and warm, staring at the glowing embers in the kiuas, listening to Ilmari's kantele, lonely and spare in the night.

While Aino had been organizing, Ilmari, Aksel, Jouka, and Matti had cut their way to the back side of Ilmahenki. Fearful that he was making progress too slowly for Rauha and her mother, Ilmari had made another trip to Nordland, leaving his blacksmithing work in the middle of the week, so he wouldn't lose a Sunday with Matti. He had the sinking feeling that no matter what he did, he did it too slowly.

By March 1908, the last of the timber stood on the other side of a steep ravine that blocked access to the river, now nearly three-quarters of a mile away. About two-thirds up a hill on the other side stood the granddaddy of them all, over fifteen feet in diameter and more than 120 feet to the first limb—a lot of clear fir waiting to be turned into cash.

It took Matti, Ilmari, and Aksel four full Sundays using axes, saws, and wedges to get the behemoth down. When it went, they watched, hiding behind another tree, their mouths open with awe. In the quiet after it fell, needles still drifting in the air, they walked over to inspect it. The tree towered above their heads lying on its side.

Everyone looked at Matti. Now what? Matti, who'd clearly been thinking about it, turned to Aksel and pointed to a still-standing three-foot-diameter fir. "Can you hang a block about two-thirds of the way up that fir?"

"Are you crazy?" Aksel answered. "That's three times the height of any mast I've ever seen, much less climbed."

Matti stood there, but his eyes were moving from point to point around him.

"If you can get a small block and cable up there, I can haul up a bull block. Then, I can move the yarder over there." He pointed. "We run line totally clear of the ground across the ravine. We can move every tree on this side, including the logs from this monster. In the air."

Jouka laughed. "And people accuse me of drinking too much," he said.

"I heard a logger on the Oregon side named Johnny Yeon has already done something like it," Matti said.

No one said anything; all were thinking. Then Ilmari said, "Horses can't climb trees." Everyone knew he meant there was no way to haul the line back to hook up the next log. They all turned to Matti.

Matti grinned and walked over to the yarder. He jumped up on one of the skids. Pointing down into the gears he said, "I can get a second drum in here, just like the two-drum skidders Reder's got." He paused. "If Ilmari can make it." They all turned to Ilmari.

Ilmari looked at the gears for a long time. "You draw it; I'll make it," he said. Everyone turned to Aksel.

Aksel looked at the tree a long time. The others knew what was going through his mind. This tree looked healthy, but with old-growth trees, you never knew if they were solid all the way up. A perfectly good-looking tree could just be waiting for the next strong blow to break apart, weakened by insect damage or rot.

Aksel took a deep breath. "You expect me to go up there? Risk my neck for a dollar a day?"

At the mention of money, Matti knew he had him. "I'll give you three dollars extra after we sell the logs."

Aksel stared at a point over a hundred feet above him, considering and discarding several ideas for getting not just himself but a massive steel block that weighed several hundred pounds as well as about a hundred feet of heavy cable up that high. He looked around. They'd probably need to find a similar tree near the east end of the show. That would be an extra six dollars. At his savings rate, the fishing boat would be reality months sooner.

"I think I can do it on springboards," he said to Matti. "It'll cost you four dollars."

"Three fifty."

"OK. But you pay for the coffin and burial on Peaceful Hill over east of Tapiola. And you pay to ship everything I own and my money back to my parents." Everyone could see that Aksel was serious.

"You'll have to write me into a will," Matti replied, equally serious. "Where's your money?"

"I don't believe this," Jouka said. He looked at Ilmari, who remained passive. This was between Matti, Aksel, and God.

"There's a twenty-dollar gold piece and thirteen silver dollars in a can on the back side of a stump down by Bean Creek," Aksel said. "I'll show you tonight."

"It would be thirteen pieces of silver," Ilmari said. "Only you're selling your soul to Matti."

They all looked at Ilmari with astonishment: he had cracked a joke.

Aksel showed both Matti and Jouka the location of the money, because accidents didn't always happen to just one person. He wrote out a will to benefit his parents, naming Matti as the administrator with Ilmari as the second and Jouka as the third.

The next Sunday afternoon, Aksel quietly tied a small swamping ax and a short crosscut saw that Ilmari had fashioned from a larger broken one onto his waist. He'd found two solid springboards, both about eight inches wide and five feet long, with one end jacketed with steel plate. He tied one to his belt. He then attached about three hundred feet of carefully coiled line to the back side of his belt, where it would be relatively out of the way. He chopped out a niche for the first springboard at head level and hammered the board into it so that with weight on it the end inside the niche pushed up against the top of the niche, making it solid but possible to pull out when upward force was applied. Pulling down on the board just above his head to test it, he looked at his friends, licked his lips, and jumped, grabbing the board, scrambling to get on top of it. There, balanced on the narrow board, with nothing between him and the ground but his caulk boots and balance, he started chopping out the next niche.

He knew from his days on the ship to focus on the work in front of him. Below him, he could hear the other three working. No use wasting their time watching Aksel do his job. After an hour of work, he was higher than on any mast he'd climbed on the *Elna*.

Chop, pull the lower board loose with the attached rope, hammer it in above, test it, jump, scramble to the next level, teeter uncertainly for a moment, get balanced and centered, repeat.

He reached the first limb at about eighty feet above the ground. It had to be removed so it wouldn't interfere with the lines. He looked down at his three friends, their legs foreshortened beneath them. This was a perspective he knew, but he never had to cut his way to the top of a mast. He undercut the limb just above him and then began hacking at it. It cracked with its weight and started to bend down, swiveling on the wood still attached to the trunk. Aksel gave a hard swing and cut through. The limb sailed slowly down, its long smaller limbs and needles making it almost float as it grew smaller and smaller beneath him. The tree trembled and shook slightly with the shift in weight. The limb crashed to the ground. He saw Matti and Jouka start to move it away from the base of the tree. He looked above him to the next limb.

After several hours, Matti signaled he'd gone high enough. Aksel lowered one end of the thin line and Matti attached a small block and length of chain to it. Aksel chained the block to the tree and looped the line over the sheave, paying it out until both ends were on the ground. Then Matti attached a large block weighing several hundred pounds along with more chain to the line and attached the other end to one of the yarder drums. He wound the line in, pulling the large block up to Aksel, over one hundred feet above the ground.

His arms and legs trembling with the effort, Aksel tied in the large heavy block. Matti attached the heavy main cable to the lighter line, hauled it up the same way, and Aksel ran it through the large block. When all the steel cable was set, Matti gave Aksel the signal on the whistle and Aksel began his equally perilous journey back down, relying on the friction from a length of rope he'd looped around the tree to hold him. He finally reached the ground and staggered off to sit against a stump. His racing heart slowed, the trembling stopped, and he was back to work in ten minutes.

It was two more weeks before they had bucked the monster into sixteen-foot and twenty-four-foot lengths and split the two largest logs down the middle by drilling a line of holes deep into their cores, filling the holes with blasting powder, and blowing the logs apart.

They had laid small alder and fir trees in a corduroy road in front of the huge logs' path, sniped their ends so the logs would not catch on the road logs, then foot by foot, Ilmari babied, cajoled, sweet-talked, and on occasion even swore to wrestle the logs to Deep River.

By the end of each Sunday, more logs floated in Deep River, held together in a boom by scraps of chain and wire rope. In April, with Deep River still swollen and turbulent from winter rains, the four friends ran the boom of several hundred logs to Willapa Bay. They hired a tug to haul the boom to a mill in Willapa. The mill paid with a check.

After showing Rauha and Louhi the check and sealing the betrothal with a shy kiss in front of his future mother-in-law, Ilmari walked into the Bank of Nordland and asked to open an account in the name of Sampo Manufacturing. Al Drummond invited Ilmari into his office. The check was examined. It proved to be from a reputable buyer and Drummond said that when it cleared, Ilmari could write checks on his new account.

"I need cash start now. Pay my brother."

"Not until the check clears."

"But . . . but I wanting get married. I needing cash money now."

"Three weeks."

"I taking my money else place."

"Your decision. You do know that Louhi Jokinen is a silent partner of mine. I don't think she'd feel too happy about you taking your money 'else place,'" he said with a smirk.

It was the first bad feeling about the money. The second came when Rauha said the wedding would be after the mill was operating. He'd objected, though it was soon clear that it wasn't entirely Rauha's doing but her mother's. He acquiesced. Then Rauha hit him with the third bad feeling. He must sign a document stating that if he died or there was a divorce, his share of Sampo Manufacturing would go to her.

Ilmari was taken aback by this hardness.

"There will be no divorce. A marriage is before God."

"And if you die?"

"What about my brothers and sister?"

"Their mother isn't putting up the other half of the initial capital. And my mother isn't either unless she's sure her daughter will be taken care of."

Ilmari took a small step back. She took his hands in hers. "Ilmari, we can build Sampo together." She kissed him suddenly. He went stiff. She kissed him again. "It's not about me; it's about our children." The blue eyes, the soft dress flowing over the soft body, the swell of her breasts, the long blond hair done neatly in braids atop her head, a ribbon the color of forget-me-not matching her blue eyes, making them seem as wide and deep as the lakes of Finland. The deal was done. The wedding was set for Sunday, October 25, 1908—provided the mill was running.

27

Ilmari's check cleared three weeks after the sale of the Ilmahenki logs and Matti opened an account in Astoria in the name of 200-Foot Logging. The following Sunday, Aino watched Matti and Aksel, who were studying the old steam donkey. The two friends hadn't spoken for several minutes.

Finally, Matti said, "We'd get more power if Ilmari could rig an extra gear right there." He pointed to a spot in the machinery.

"Yoh," Aksel said.

They looked at the problem for a while.

"You'd lose power to the friction," Aksel said.

Matti said nothing for a full minute. Then he pointed out another spot, "Maybe put it right there."

"Yoh."

More silence.

Aino thought she would go crazy. They were not even looking at each other, just looking at the equipment.

Finally, Aksel said, "It'll take more inch-and-a-quarter cable. It's expensive."

"Yoh."

"What would it leave us?"

"Two hundred," Matti said.

More silence.

"You said 'us,'" Matti said.

"Until I get my boat."

Matti kicked the skids of the donkey gently, thinking. After a while he said, "Saaranpa has fifty acres of good fir and cedar left over from selling his homestead before moving to Astoria. No one will touch it, because it's on a really steep ravine and over a mile from the river. He'll sell it for two hundred dollars."

"That's the whole farm," Aksel said. "What do you think we'd get for the logs?"

"Eight hundred. That quadruples the capital."

"If everything goes right."

Matti climbed up on the steam donkey and tugged on the large gear lever, moving the cogs into and out of the gears absentmindedly. "Sixty-forty, because I'm putting up the money. You want to look at the site?"

Aksel, his hands in his pockets, looked at his shoes and said nothing. Then he said, "Yoh."

They shook hands and the partnership was formed.

Aino just shook her head and went back into the house.

The two friends took Ilmari's boat upriver, towing it over the occasional rapids to just below where Deep River split into the north and middle forks. The river had narrowed to a steep canyon full of prime old-growth trees, thickly packed, most of them six to eight feet in diameter, but some monsters as well.

"I can see why it's going for just two hundred dollars," Aksel said. "You'll have to yard downhill and you'll get hung up on stumps all day long."

Matti said nothing, his eyes moving from point to point. He gestured at a large tree. "Can you get a block to the top of that one the way you did back at Ilmahenki?"

Aksel looked at the tree, about a third of the way up the steep slope. "Yoh."

Matti nodded. "Saaranpa will think we're suckers. He doesn't know what we know, and he doesn't know we know it."

* * *

Two weeks later, Aksel and Matti collected their final pay from John Reder. On Sunday, they were on the *General Washington* crossing the Columbia to Astoria. The canning factories were not working Sundays, but the June blueback run would be starting about now, followed by the big August Chinook run. Soon, dozens of canneries would be operating on two or even three shifts, seven days a week, from Hammond near the mouth of the river all the way upstream past Tongue Point on the Oregon side and Skamokawa on the Washington side. Next year, Aksel thought. Always next year.

Saaranpa was home and he sat down with the two of them while his wife served coffee. After half an hour of discussion, Saaranpa and his wife disappeared into their living room, leaving Matti and Aksel looking expectantly, even a little anxiously, at each other. Saaranpa came into the kitchen with a sales agreement. They shook hands on $180. Matti paid him in cash and 200-Foot Logging had its first timber purchase.

"Most loggers would just do it for the logging," Aksel said in the boat going back.

"Most loggers," Matti said.

"You've only got twenty dollars left."

"No, twenty dollars of cash and eight hundred dollars of timber. We've already made a profit."

"Golly sakes," Aksel said in English, mimicking someone who didn't curse. "Do I get to buy my boat tomorrow then?"

Matti looked at him. "You think you're joking. Look. You go to the bank and put up your share of the timber as collateral, get the money, then sign a note with someone who sells you the boat, and you're in business."

Aksel laughed. "With no money?"

Matti looked up the river at the timber stretching away on both sides of the factories, nearly covering the waterfront of Astoria. "Aksel, this is America."

Aksel and Matti moved into the sauna at Ilmahenki until they'd built themselves a crude shack next to Saaranpa's timber. Then they moved the old steam donkey to the Saaranpa site and started logging.

Aino had told Lempi that Aksel was going to hang the high block, and she was at Ilmahenki only an hour after sunrise, helping Aino make sandwiches, getting coffee ready for when the boys showed up. When she poured Aksel his cup, she made sure she brushed his sleeve. He smiled up at her, a little shyly. Maybe she'd been too forward.

When the boys left, she and Aino cleaned up.

"He's so hard to read," Lempi finally burst out.

"Yoh. They practice it since they're babies."

"Rrrhhh," Lempi growled in frustration. "Men."

Lempi and Aino walked to the show, bringing the lunches. Aksel was already up at least eight stories on a Douglas fir, balancing on a springboard and chopping another niche, when they got there. He looked tiny, so far above her, and Lempi felt vertigo just watching him. Yet he was moving around and rigging the block as if he were on the ground instead of on eight inches of wood eighty feet up.

When Aksel came down, Lempi realized she hadn't been breathing normally. All loggers had to be brave, skilled, and strong, but she doubted any would do what Aksel just did. At the same time, she knew he was no daredevil—even more impressive. She felt proud that she knew this quiet Swede, the best friend of the brother of her best friend. It just seemed so perfect how it could all work out, if only she could make it so.

Aksel was sorting out his gear when Lempi walked up to him. He looked up at her a little shyly. "That's some good work," Lempi said.

Aksel gave her a big grin, terribly pleased, but he quickly started fiddling with his gear. He couldn't think of anything to say, so he just nodded at her, still grinning, feeling like a bumpkin.

She smiled and picked up his ax. "How come this is called a swamping ax?" she asked, using the English term.

It puzzled Aksel that she cared. "It's because they call cutting limbs and cleaning logs up swamping. It's the ax we use to do it."

"You mean it's different from the ones you use to chop down the trees?"

It pleased Aksel that this girl seemed genuinely interested in what he did. He picked the ax up and showed it to her. "See the bit, here," he said, moving his finger along its curve. "It's wider and rounder than the ones we use for felling. Better for cutting through limbs, but not so good for making headway into a big tree."

"Oh, I see," Lempi said. Still holding the ax out to her, Aksel watched Lempi touch the ax's cheek with her fingertips and move them back and forth on it. Then she quickly pulled back her hand. He didn't know whether to keep holding the ax out to her or put it down.

"Are you scared up there?" she asked.

How to answer truthfully but without looking bad? "Not so much," he said.

She smiled at him, nodding. He thought maybe it was time to pick up his gear and started to do it.

"We brought coffee and sandwiches," Lempi said.

"Oh. Good."

"We're setting up over there," she said, nodding toward where he could see Aino. "See you there." She smiled, then walked away toward Aino.

Aksel assembled his gear to move to the next place. He stood just a moment, watching Aino ready the lunch. He knew that to her he was just her little brother's friend. Then he had a brilliant idea of how he could change that.

28

For six months, Ilmari was a man possessed, refusing to even think discouraging thoughts. He turned his blacksmith shop into a miniature mill-parts production factory, where he hammered out anything he couldn't buy or didn't think was worth spending the money on. He reshaped the chimney and forge. Through the long days of summer, through the shortening days of fall, just as alchemists of old hoped to turn lead into gold, Ilmari turned iron and steel into machinery.

Often alone, sometimes with family and friends or hired help, he turned machinery into a sawmill. First, connected to Deep River, was a holding pond deep enough to float the largest logs. Next to the pond he built a pole-barn structure with platforms to hold the saws and conveyor belts. The most expensive purchases were the saws themselves: a large circular head rig to take the logs down to dimension lumber sizes and smaller gang saws for cutting them to length. He purchased two used steam tractors and modified them to power the saws and conveyor belts.

After several days of breaking in, breaking down, fixing, and starting over again, he put the first log, floated down from Matti's Saaranpa show, completely through the mill without a hitch. On a clear, crisp October day at high tide, a small tug brought the first small raft of logs that was purchased from another logger, and Sampo Manufacturing was truly in business.

Day after day, the magic mill began grinding out money. Louhi and Rauha came down to look at it and Louhi nodded her approval. Ilmari and Rauha's wedding was on.

* * *

Aino was scheduled to speak in Astoria on the Thursday night before the Sunday wedding. It gave her two full days to get to Nordland, but it still worried Ilmari that she might miss his marriage. He sent Matti.

"Why risk it?" Matti asked. He and Aino sat together on the riverbank in front of Ilmahenki.

"I can't back out," she said. "It's been scheduled for weeks. I'll make it." Then she added, almost muttering, "Besides, it's just another church ceremony." She wished she'd kept that to herself. She turned her head to look across Deep River.

Matti watched her. Then he said, "Ilmari believes it's a sacrament. Not an empty ceremony."

"Ilmari is delusional."

"If he believes it is a sign of God's grace then it is a sacrament. It's not at all delusional."

"Humph." She hated the way Matti always made such sense of things—especially at her expense.

"You're giving a speech. One of many." He left it to her to work out the implication that there would be only one wedding for Ilmari. She did. She said, "I'm going to Astoria. Don't worry. I'll be there."

On Thursday night, a storm blew in from the Pacific, shutting down river traffic. The storm was still blowing strong on Friday morning, the twenty-second. Aino had gone down to the docks in the dark. There she waited in the rain for the instant the *General Washington* would sail. She tried to tell herself it was just a ceremony. It didn't work. She felt terrible.

Her brothers waited in the rain on the banks of Deep River. Aino still hadn't shown up by noon. Saying nothing, Ilmari untied his boat and he and Matti climbed in. Ilmari propelled the boat with a single oar from the stern into the strong ebb. Sunday would be the new moon and the tides were both higher and lower than usual.

The Koskis, less one, arrived on Saturday afternoon. Louhi had made barrels of her own beer. Matti was delighted and Ilmari uncomfortable.

She'd also bought a beautiful fat steer for the wedding meal, and it stood tethered in her backyard, contentedly chewing on the grass. Louhi had bought it to save money, but neither Rauha nor Louhi wanted to kill it. Rauha pointed out that it was Louhi's idea and handed her the ax. Louhi swung the ax down as hard as she could, but she was not strong enough or fast enough for a killing blow. Blood ran from the wound as the steer backed away bellowing, jerking at the rope that tethered it to a stake in the ground. Louhi swung again and the ax glanced off the bony forehead. The bellowing steer was trying to shake loose of the stake, while Louhi circled it, trying to dodge its flailing hooves.

Rauha coolly reached her hand out for the ax and Louhi relinquished it, her chest heaving. Rauha brought the ax down hard on the steer's neck just above the shoulders, severing the spinal cord. She swung the ax again, just to make sure. She looked down at the skirt of her dress. It was splattered with blood. "Goddamnit," she said.

They gave a derelict who frequented Tannika House two dollars to skin and butcher the animal and take the relevant parts to the butcher. The man's eyes lit up as she put the money in his hand. He loaded a wheelbarrow with as much meat as it would carry and set off down the street with the bloody hide draped over the top.

"How do you know he won't steal the meat?" Rauha asked.

"He's a regular at the Tannika House bar," Louhi answered. "Stealing the meat would only slow him down." She started back into the house. "And I'll get my two dollars back."

The day of the wedding was rainy and dreary. The Koski brothers had packed Sunday shoes in their valises, made of canvas stitched onto wood slats. They'd found a room at the same boardinghouse Ilmari used earlier, only this time they luxuriated in a room with two cots.

They carefully donned their best wool trousers, white shirts, and suit coats. Matti, having recently arrived, still fit into his suit coat best—the sleeves at least covered his wrists—but his chest and back muscles had developed and the coat strained to close. For the occasion, Ilmari splurged on a tin of Macassar oil and the two left the boardinghouse smelling like gardenias, their thick, dark hair gleaming.

* * *

Seeing Rauha, radiant beneath her myrtle crown, her blue eyes framed with her blond hair nearly doubled in size by the leaves and rose hips woven in it, Matti certainly understood why this woman made his beloved big brother happy, but he saw no warmth and certainly no sweetness. He couldn't define warmth and sweetness, but he knew that's what he wanted in a woman—and this woman had neither. He looked at Ilmari with hope, just as did the bride.

After the ceremony, the chairs and other furniture were hauled away to clear the space for dancing. Louhi had hired a fiddler and an accordionist and they struck up a traditional wedding song, the men and women alternating verses. Ilmari went to one knee before Rauha, who was sitting in the only chair like the queen for the day that she was, and asked her to dance. With everyone singing and clapping, Rauha and Ilmari danced with solemn dignity.

Aino finally made it back to Deep River the same Sunday. She stopped by Ullakko's to tell him he needn't come to milk the cow anymore. When she reached Ilmahenki, the house was cold. Empty. She gathered Ilmari's dirty work shirt, canvas pants, socks, and wool underwear, realizing it would probably be the last time she did Ilmari's laundry. From now on, he would have a wife. She fought down a feeling of being replaced. She pulled the sheets from Ilmari's bed. She wanted him and his bride to sleep in clean sheets. Ilmari hadn't thought of it before he left.

The night air was still as she made her way to the riverbank by the light of the kerosene lantern. She could hear Deep River talking as it made its way to Willapa Bay. The darkness seemed to press down on her with a palpable weight. An owl hooted. There was a sudden fierce flapping of fast wings as two ducks, startled by what might have been a muskrat, rose into the sky. She listened to the rapid whirring of their wings in the near silence as they disappeared around the first bend. She regretted being so stubborn about making the speech now that it was over. It *was* one of many.

Hitching her skirt up above her knees and securing it with a knot, she hung the lantern on a branch and laid the clothes on the washing rock, then began to beat each piece with the worn-smooth club she kept hanging on another branch nearby. She wondered if there would be dancing at Ilmari's wedding. Soon she was lost in the rhythm of the washing, the lapping of Deep River around her ankles, and the lonely gray sky above the river between dark guardian trees.

The sound of a throat being cleared startled her so severely that she threw the shirt she was washing into the river, her heart pounding. She whirled and saw a man standing there, barely illuminated by the lantern.

The man sprinted into the river and grabbed the shirt that was now floating downstream. He brought it back and handed it to her. "I didn't mean to scare you." It was Aksel.

Aino couldn't talk, because her heart was beating so fast, the blood coursing through her throat. She tried desperately to control her trembling, but she could not.

Aksel's bright-blue eyes stared at her with a combination of fear and wonder.

"My God, Aino. How you're shaking."

She swallowed, sighed, and reached out for the shirt. He let her take it. "You scared me," she said.

"I guess *so.*" Aksel looked at her closely.

Aino turned from his gaze and looked down at the pile of laundry. "What brings you here?" she asked, trying to recover from the extraordinary unexpected fright.

"I saw Ullakko at Higgins's. He said you missed the ferry."

"That's a nice way of saying I missed my brother's wedding."

Aksel chuckled. "I just thought I'd stop by to see how you were doing. Have you done the milking?"

Aino was suddenly aware of her exposed legs, then she thought, What's wrong with seeing a girl wash clothes with her skirt above her knees? She left her skirt tucked.

Aksel sat on a log and pulled out a cigarette, striking a match with his thumbnail. He had his good shoes wrapped around his neck. She knew he was trying to avoid staring at her legs. He tossed the match into the river and it made a brief glowing arc before being extinguished in the water.

"Were you at the Knappton dance last night?" she asked.

Aksel seemed to hesitate. "I was in Astoria."

She thought she saw Aksel color just a bit. He was doing *that*. He just didn't seem old enough.

"What's wrong with Lempi? She's your age and you know she likes you."

"It's awkward." He seemed about to say something more but only said, "I don't want to hurt her."

Aino began twisting the shirt, wringing the water from it. Aksel stood, cigarette dangling in his mouth, and reached out his hand for the shirt. She handed it to him. She thought she smelled cheap perfume. Even though she had already wrung the shirt, he easily got more water out of it when he wrung it again.

Aksel took a drag on the cigarette and nervously flicked ashes into the river. He took another deep drag, licked his thumb and forefinger, and snubbed the butt out. He took out his tobacco pouch and carefully stripped the paper, dropping the remaining tobacco into the pouch, letting the scrap of cigarette paper fall into the river. They watched it drift downstream out of the small circle of lamplight.

Aino picked up a pair of stiff canvas trousers and this time she handed them soaking wet to Aksel. Why bother to do it herself, when he did it so easily?

After a few halting starts, the conversation soon normalized. She told Aksel what she knew about Rauha. He talked about people she knew at Reder's camp. As usual, she was frustrated because he didn't seem to know what was going on with the girls in the henhouse, who they were sweet on, who was sweet on them. Even though she always felt she had nothing in common with the other flunkies, she realized that compared with the other 80 percent of the local population, she and the flunkies had a lot in common.

Aksel helped her pack the damp clothes back to the house, staying on the porch as she hung the sheets on the clothesline above the stove. She was surprised to find herself anxious that Aksel would interpret her hanging the laundry inside without him as a signal to leave. She hurried back outside with the lantern and the remaining clothes. He followed her to the clothesline and she happily talked of whatever came to mind while he rolled another cigarette.

"How's the fishing boat project?" she asked.

Aksel gave a short laugh. "I'm about where I was before the strike."

Aino wasn't sure whether it was a statement of fact or criticism.

Aksel took a short drag, blinking his eyes as the smoke was pushed back into them by a gentle breeze that also stirred the laundry. She again smelled the perfume along with the faint odor of whiskey that had clung to his wool coat. She suddenly realized Aksel was no longer a boy. Other than the whistle punks, a logging show had no room for boys.

She could tell he was about to leave. A woman had no easy way to say goodbye to a man. She couldn't shake hands or touch cheeks with him as she could with women. Just this awkwardness, this space between them.

"You're leaving?" she asked.

Aksel put his tobacco pouch in his coat pocket, not answering her. Then he said, "Do you care?"

"Care if you leave?" She was puzzled.

Aksel shrugged.

Men could be so inarticulate. "What?" she asked.

"Aino, ever since we danced at Midsummer's Eve, I've been in love with you."

"Aksel," she gasped. "Oh. I—"

"Didn't know."

She didn't know what to say.

"I know you've always seen me as your little brother's friend."

Aino could only nod.

"I am." Aksel nodded back. "But your little brother and his friend are all grown up now. I'll be eighteen in January." He plunged ahead, his words coming faster. "I know I'm younger than you. And I know you like Jouka . . . and he's a good man." He put his hands in his pockets and looked at the ground. Then he met her eyes. "I'm a high rigger. I can make more money than any other logger in the valley, including Jouka." He paused.

She stammered, "I thought you wanted to fish."

"I do. But, if you'd marry me, I'd high climb until the day I die."

For a high rigger, she thought, that could be a short time.

"Are you asking me to marry you?" she asked, saying it to buy time. Of course, he was.

Aksel nodded.

Time was up. "Oh, Aksel." She turned to look in the direction of the river, which she could hear but not see. She felt him waiting behind her. "Aksel, I can't do it," she said, still looking at the river. He touched her shoulder.

"Tell me to my face."

"I can't do it," she said loudly and clearly. "Aksel, you're a wonderful man. You'd make any girl happy. It's just not me."

"Why not? Is it Jouka?"

"Aksel." She felt that she was pleading. "It's no one."

"You won't marry?"

"I won't marry."

"You'll marry me." With that, he walked away.

Just before he could no longer be seen in the lamplight, he turned and waved to her. She waved back. Aksel turned and disappeared into the dark.

Ilmahenki seemed vast and empty. She walked into the house and lit and trimmed the kerosene lamp. She heard the wind whistle through the cracks in the door and rattle the thin glass window. She decided to make bread, so the others could have it fresh when they returned. She'd borrowed *The Jungle* by Upton Sinclair from the Suomi Hall library and now read it, consulting the dictionary frequently, occasionally punching down the rising dough, fragrant with yeast and rye and graham flour. She thought about Sinclair's book. Logging was way more dangerous than packing meat, but as bad as loggers' working conditions were, they were nothing like the horrors of the slums described by Sinclair. People out here had farms and game—salmon, elk, deer. And they had plants—blackberries, licorice root, salmonberries, thimbleberries, camas root, even skunk cabbage if you boiled it twice. No cash, but food. And food kept the loggers happy. And then, most of the loggers were young and single, needing only enough money to get through the next weekend. Maybe she should go to IWW headquarters in Chicago. Things were heating up there. People were crowded into slums and worked in factories. She could make a difference.

She crawled into the bed, the sheets she'd fashioned from old flour sacks feeling damp and cold. She turned down the wick and the kerosene flame snuffed out.

29

After Aino turned him down, Aksel had avoided Ilmahenki, other than for an occasional visit to the sauna or for a meal. He didn't want to look as though he was sulking. Aksel decided to put into action the idea he'd had while on the spar tree on the Saaranpa show, and he boarded the *General Washington* for Astoria.

He walked into the smoky warm interior of the Lucky Logger to set his plan going. The pianist was playing what the Americans called a rag—a syncopated mesmerizing beat underlying a catchy melody line that seemed to never end, just constantly move. It moved just like the country: forward.

Karen, his favorite, was also the best dancer in the house. That night, she taught him the latest dance that had come north with some sailors from San Francisco, the Grizzly Bear.

Aksel returned from Astoria on Sunday with more than a hangover. In the bunkhouse, he handed Jouka a piece of sheet music. "It's called 'Frog Legs Rag.'"

Jouka looked at it. "I don't read music, but this looks hard."

"What about your piano player?"

"He can read music, but this will look hard to him, too."

"Give it to him and see what he says."

The next Saturday, March 27, the dance was at Tapiola. As Aksel hoped, Aino came along with Ilmari and Rauha, who even at five months pregnant had all the men's attention. The unwritten code allowed married women to dance with others. Aksel now understood one primary assumption that underlay the code. Other than waltzing, where the partners held each other apart in a stiff frame, the old-country dances involved only hand-holding. The Grizzly Bear was intimate.

When the band struck up "Frog Legs Rag," people stood momentarily puzzled on the dance floor, then slowly moved toward the walls. Aksel took a deep breath and walked up to Aino. She was standing next to Lempi.

"May I have this dance?" he asked Aino.

Aino looked at Lempi, then back at Aksel. "What do you dance to this . . . this . . . music?"

"It's called the Grizzly Bear. I'll teach you."

She gave him her hand. Lempi's face was as cold as a Finnish winter.

Aksel began the side-to-side lumbering motion of the dance, moving his feet in a sideways hop, combining a rise on his toe and a thumping heel drop to mark the beat. Aino awkwardly tried to copy him. He showed her again. She copied him again, this time smoothly. He took her out on the floor. Doing the crazy lurching imitation of a bear, he held her tight to his chest. Aino bent her head back and laughed.

Jouka kept playing the fiddle, staring at them, a hard, cold stare.

"Jouka doesn't like you dancing with me," Aksel said.

"Jouka doesn't like me dancing *like this* with anyone." She wrinkled her nose and laughed.

A couple of women started hissing and shouting: "For shame. For shame."

Aksel could see them turning to their husbands, making out "Stop them" and "Do something" with their lips. The husbands hesitated. Then a woman stamped her foot and said something quite heated to her husband. Pointing at Aino, she shouted, "Whore."

Jouka stopped playing. The other musicians stopped. The room went silent. Aksel saw Aino's eyes tear up and felt her trembling. "You take that back," he said to the woman. She looked to her husband.

"She will not," he said.

Aksel guided Aino gently toward the wall, his eyes on the man, sizing him up, trying to think how he was going to take him. Before he took a step, Jouka barreled into the man whose wife had slandered Aino. The man's friends joined to defend him. Aksel charged in, Matti and Ilmari right behind him.

The women backed up against the walls, some aghast, some enjoying themselves. They'd all seen fights before. The rules were clear but unspoken: no kicking a man when he was down, no choke holds, and certainly no knives or other weapons.

Lempi was holding her fists to her mouth. Aino was standing straight with her shoulders back.

The fighters were getting tired. Two or three minutes were exhausting, even for these aerobic machines, and some of the older, married men took the opportunity to start moving between fighters. Another unwritten rule: when the fight was over, it was over and no hard feelings.

Jouka was standing over the man whose wife had called Aino a whore. The man's face was as bloody as Jouka's, but his nose was broken and Jouka's wasn't. Someone gently moved Jouka back and offered the man on the floor a hand, watching Jouka carefully. Still breathing hard, Jouka looked over to where Aino and Lempi stood. One eye would soon be black and swollen and his knuckles were raw. Aksel was bent over, breathing hard as well, clearly trying to recover from a punch or kick to his abdomen. He, too, looked over at Aino and Lempi, then painfully straightened.

Jouka strode over to Aksel and just as Aksel drew himself upright, slugged him with a right cross to his head, sending him back to the floor. Aksel managed to get to his knees, trying to shake his head clear. Jouka headed outside.

Lempi started toward Aksel, but Aino caught her arm. "Let him get up on his own."

Lempi shook her arm free, clearly furious with Aino, but she stopped. She watched Aksel struggle to his feet, then she rushed to him.

The band started up again without Jouka. Aksel had disappeared.

Aino and Lempi went to the ladies' room, a canvas screen that shielded the only mirror in the building. Aino started to put her hair back in order.

Lempi let Aino have it. "For Christ's sake, what the hell's wrong with you?" Serving food to loggers didn't do much for language refinement. "Jouka's good-looking, a great dancer, a good earner, and clearly head over heels for you."

"I know. He proposed." Aino said, primping in the mirror, pleased with the effect this would have on Lempi. Of course, she knew Lempi pushed her toward Jouka because Lempi liked Aksel. Aino patted something invisible into place and turned to her. "I said no. I don't believe in marriage."

"Right, free love," Lempi said sarcastically.

"Why not?"

"That makes you a hussy."

"And giving it away for a house, food, and security in marriage makes you a whore."

"Don't bait me. I won't rise to that nonsense."

When Aino returned to the dance floor, Jouka was waiting for her. Aksel was still nowhere to be seen. The band moved into the accordion player's two standard waltzes: "Skål Skål Skål" followed by "Livet i Finnskogarna" with its lively triplets and wavelike melody.

She knew she had a gift for dancing, as did Jouka. When they danced together, they were like one beautiful body, man and woman in perfect harmony. Waltzing highlighted this. She became the sun in the center of the solar system, supported and contained by the gravity of Jouka's strength and rhythm, the other dancers turning into circling planets. If he ever asked her to marry him when they were dancing, she was afraid she wouldn't be able to say no. She could dance with Jouka every night. Maybe that wouldn't be so bad. Voitto was dead. She tried to make that sound final in her mind. Dead. Jouka was a good earner. If all she had to do was keep house for Jouka, there would be no farmwork, no need to midwife. She would have time for organizing. But what if she had a child? She pushed the unromantic thoughts from her mind.

The dancing wound down about one in the morning and Aino found herself on the muddy street in front of the store and warehouse in the dim light of a kerosene lantern. With just a mile on the wagon road to Ilmahenki, she had no chance of getting lost. She'd long ago mastered walking at night, trusting some instinct that guided her by dim light above the trees. Tonight, however, with the drizzle and thick clouds, there would be no guidance. The mile to Ilmahenki felt like twenty in the cold darkness.

Jouka came down the steps. "Want me to walk home with you?" he asked.

At first, she refused. He insisted. She was glad he did.

He tucked his violin under his coat, the strap from its deerskin cover around his neck, and offered her his arm. They soon saw the light from the lantern Ilmari or Rauha had left on the porch.

Aino turned, intending to break the link between them. He reached out, taking her upper arms in his hands, and asked her to marry him—again.

Her romantic musings about marrying Jouka had become a real choice. She wasn't ready for this. It was so much easier to keep playing with possibilities. She felt as if Lempi was in her head telling her to say yes. Did she love Jouka? It would be wrong to marry for just practical reasons. It didn't feel like what she had felt with Voitto. Was that love or something else? She fell back on ideals to guide her, not on her heart. "Why can't we just be friends? All this . . . this societal pressure about marriage. It's just the police saying that it's OK to do what's OK anyway."

Jouka recoiled and stepped back. A cloud of anger crossed his face. Then he smiled. He raised his palms to the air. "So, it's nothing. Let's you and I go into the bushes."

She took a step back. Fear. Surely, he was joking.

"Come on. Let's do it. Right now." He bowed with a sweeping gesture toward the bushes.

Helsinki. Voitto. She brought up her sisu. "Jouka! You stop talking like that. I won't put up with it."

He covered her mouth and nose with one large hand while grabbing the back of her head with the other. He pulled her close to him, his lips right up against her ear, his breath on the back of her neck. She panicked, struggling, futilely trying to slap his hands away, feeling no stronger than a child. "Big talk," Jouka whispered. "I know you don't believe it." He let her go. "Don't worry. I would never hurt you."

She scratched his face and stepped back, breathing hard, her heart pounding.

He touched his face and looked at the blood on his hand. "You keep up this political nonsense about marriage," he said, "the only way you'll ever make love is being treated like a whore."

She ran to the light. Whirling around, nearly spitting, she shouted, "A free whore, goddamn you!" She ran into her big brother's house, where she never had to make any hard decisions, like marriage. She threw herself onto the bed, burying sobs in her pillow.

30

Having no hard decisions to make had a considerable downside. Rauha treated her like a little sister, and the bigger Rauha grew with the baby, the worse it got. Aino wanted to find fault with her, but Rauha was a good wife. She worked hard. Given the pregnancy, she filled that part of the bargain as well. What was worse, she was stunning. Aino couldn't wait for her to go into labor to bring her back down.

The baby came in August. The birth went without a hitch and took about six hours. Rauha, hard as a walnut shell, as cool as the wind off a glacier, and not particularly interested in babies, popped her child like a healthy bitch on her second litter. Aino, standing by for any emergency, felt she was there only to clean up.

But she had a niece named Mielikki after her and Ilmari's departed sister.

She puttered around the house, cleaning while Rauha slept. After a couple of hours, she peeked into the bedroom. Rauha was nursing the girl steadily, stolidly, a job neither distasteful nor enjoyable. Mielikki was drooling colostrum. It was all so unfair. Margaret Reder, wanting more than anything else to be a good mother, nearly died and then had a difficult time breastfeeding.

"Everything OK?" Aino asked.

Rauha smiled at her. At least helping her with the birth removed a bit of the tension from missing her wedding.

"Aino, come and hold Mielikki." Rauha matter-of-factly removed her nipple from Mielikki's mouth and held the baby out to Aino. The little hand waved awkwardly, touching nothing but air, the little eyes squinted nearly shut, the head searching around for the vanished nipple. Taking Mielikki in her arms, Aino held her against her breasts, rocking her slightly, cooing unconsciously to her. She was suddenly hit with a strange yearning, a warmth, a lovely feeling of holding this tiny creature, half her brother Ilmari.

She pictured what it would take to have this: a man, a marriage, a baby. The thought of sexual intercourse gave her an involuntary start. Why was she thinking about marriage, anyway? Her midwifery business was doing well. Although difficult because of the uncertainty of timing, it gave her money and time to organize and cash to chip in at Ilmahenki, something even more important now that Rauha was handling the household finances.

Recently, she spent four dollars taking the boat to Portland and back to attend two meetings at the new IWW hall where she picked up several boxes of flyers and pamphlets. It cost her another dollar to go to Astoria for the Saturday night meeting of Astorian Suomalainen Sosialisti Klubi. The more she went there, however, the more she felt the members were just debating theory, getting nowhere. Maybe it wasn't worth the boat fare. But the ASSK meetings offered more than politics: the coffee, the coffee cake, the sound of Finn, the socialists' passion for their part in the final days of capitalism. These nice people, the ASSK socialists, were committed to a cause, too, no less than the IWW, but she felt a tinge of guilt, knowing she was spending time there only because of sentiment, missing Suomi. Mielikki was squirming. She shifted the baby more to her shoulder. She was surer than ever the IWWs had it right. They weren't nice, but they got things done. Direct action. They scared the hell out of ownership. She needed to stop being nice with the nice people and commit entirely to the IWW.

But the revolution had failed in 1905, so say ten years for the next one. That made it 1915. Could she do six years of organizing with a baby? If she said yes to Jouka, it would be the kind of hard choice it took to get things done. She gently bobbed with Mielikki. Revolutionaries made hard choices, sometimes for other people. Jouka could sacrifice for the revolution as well as anyone else, as well as her. She'd marry him, free herself from midwifing, free herself from the chores at Ilmahenki. But that meant no baby—and dealing with Jouka about *that.* She pulled Mielikki back and looked into her face, the face of the future. "We're going to make it right," she whispered to her, bouncing her gently.

She handed Mielikki back to Rauha. It felt wrong, like handing over her fate, that Mielikki was being taken from her. She knew she wanted a baby. Well, there was nothing but convention stopping her from having a baby and organizing at the same time.

She shrugged into her coat and tied her wool bandanna under her chin. Walking out of the house, she felt a cool refreshing release from the heat, tension, and intensity of a successful birth. But also intense joy. Then the inexorable arithmetic came back. The refreshing feeling from moist air and dripping trees gave way to anxiety. She was now twenty, the ideal age, her mother used to say, for having and nursing babies but too young for raising them. She said every year after twenty it got physically harder, so waiting for the right man had its costs. Say twenty-four was as far as she dared put it off. She realized she was thinking in circles. If she didn't want to get married, then she could just have a kid. But did she really want to have a baby without being married? How many men out there were like Voitto, willing to have children without being married? She laughed at herself. Lots of them. Maybe she should just tell Jouka she'd gotten scared, say yes. Why *had* she panicked so?

Then the arithmetic again. If she went to Jouka now, he'd marry her right away. But maybe she needed six months to really think this through. But what if after six months she decided Jouka was the wrong man after all? Six months to find another one. Six months to find out that this one wasn't right, either. Six months to find the next one. Six months to see if he was the right one. Two years right there.

There was another time pressure. How much longer before Rauha wanted her out of Ilmahenki?

31

The next Saturday, Rauha sent Aino into Tapiola to buy sugar cubes and baking soda, carefully doling out coins as if to a child. Rauha had delivered a baby. She was now a woman.

Walking into Tapiola carrying an empty canvas tote bag, Aino entered a patch of late afternoon sunlight. Shutting her eyes and holding her arms out wide, she stood there feeling the sun on her face. There was a rustling high above her. She watched the tops of the feathery hemlocks move with the wind, meeting, pulling away, returning, like girls in a dance line holding their skirts.

Just before she reached Tapiola, she tucked her glasses into the tote. She shook out her skirt, making sure that the petticoat beneath it didn't show; pinched her cheeks; and made sure two tendrils came down from her hair piled under her wool bandanna. One never knew.

Just as she reached Higgins's store she heard loud cursing in the new saloon, followed by two fighting loggers hurtling out the door. Several others followed, watching them until one went down, briefly unconscious, and the fight stopped. As the loggers filed their way back into the saloon, Aino realized Jouka had come outside with them and was now standing on the splintered planks of the sidewalk. He raised a glass of beer to her. She started walking toward him, admiring his blue eyes and his chest muscles pushing at his suspenders. Then he turned his head and looked up the street and her gaze followed.

It was Aksel, wearing a new pair of shoes and new wool trousers.

"Fancy new clothes," Jouka said to him in Finnish, grinning. "Matti must be paying you well."

Aksel nodded shyly to Aino, saying hello, and then turned to Jouka. "We just finished the Saaranpa site." He smiled. "We're in the money," he said in English.

"I've heard he's using a high lead with that Chinese yarder of his." Jouka turned to Aino. "It's no secret. Someday Reder will find out."

"That's Matti's business."

"And business is good." He drained his beer. "Hey Aksel, I'll buy you a beer, then you can buy me two."

Aksel looked at Aino uncomfortably. They all knew it would be unseemly for her to go inside. "Come and have coffee with me," Aksel said to Aino. "It's too early to drink."

Jouka's body tensed and it seemed to Aino as if he got bigger. She didn't like where this was headed. Not only had Aksel invited her to coffee without Jouka, triggering his jealousy, but he had criticized Jouka's drinking to boot.

"You can drink with the men or have coffee with the women," Jouka said.

Now Aksel went stiff.

She looked from Jouka, who'd thrown his shoulders back slightly, to Aksel, his brilliant blue eyes now half-hidden behind lowered lids.

Aino felt a rising panic. The locomotive was on a downhill run with no brakes. Jouka had called Aksel out in front of her. In a culture that had no other means of showing you weren't a slave except your manhood, Jouka's insult required a response.

"Right here. Right now," Aksel said in Swedish, pointing a finger at the ground. Jouka coolly drank the rest of the beer and set the schooner on the boardwalk. He stepped into the muddy street. She wanted them to stop but knew if she intervened, they'd never forgive her.

At this moment, a logger came out of the saloon. Turning his head back toward the dark interior he gave a sharp whistle through his teeth and shouted, "Finns against Swedes! Right outside!"

Aksel and Jouka had moved to the center of the street, watching each other warily, both slightly crouched. Each had his puukko sheathed behind his back.

Men crowded through the door, Swedes moving to Aksel's side and Finns to Jouka's. Then Jouka pulled his puukko out and there was a gasp of surprise mixed with a murmur of approval for blood sport. Aino covered her mouth in horror.

But Jouka had taken it out only to toss it to the side of the street, which he did, looking steadily at Aksel. Aksel drew his own puukko and tossed it next to Jouka's. The crowd murmured a mixture of admiration and disappointment.

They began circling each other, looking for the first opening. The crowd shouted encouragement. A couple of bets were made.

Aino couldn't stand it any longer. She rushed in between the two, startling them.

"Get out of here, Aino," Jouka growled at her.

She turned to Jouka and put her hands on his chest, but at the same time she turned her head back toward Aksel, engaging him even though she also spoke to Jouka. "You're friends. You'll hurt each other." She turned to Jouka. "You've been drinking. I don't want you fighting over something so stupid."

"We're fighting over you," Aksel said.

She stepped back from Jouka and took her hands off his chest. "Don't fight."

Jouka nodded and stood straight; his arms came down. Aino turned to Aksel and walked toward him. The entire street was quiet, so every word could be heard. She held Aksel's upper arms with each hand. "You're a fine young man, Aksel Långström. Someday you'll find a woman worthy of you. It's not me. Jouka and I are going to be married."

Jouka looked dumbfounded. The crowd gasped, then broke into shouts and cheers.

"Jouka gets the red!"

"Hey Jouka, did you propose or did she?"

"You're in for it now, Jouka."

Aino went to up to Jouka, stood on her toes, and looking him in the eye said, "My answer is yes." She turned to the crowd, most of whom she knew. "The fool has asked twice before. You all know I don't give in easy."

The crowd laughed and then roared approval. Someone shouted, "I'll drink to that!" And the loggers headed back inside, laughing and jostling each other, shouting that Jouka was buying, although no one believed anyone had enough money to do something like that.

Aksel, forgotten in the drama, stood there, hands at his sides. Jouka put his left arm around Aino's shoulder and held out his right hand to Aksel.

Aksel's face was stone cold. He walked over to Jouka and shook his hand. He raised his own hands up, as if to take Aino's head and pull her toward him to kiss her, but he stopped, putting them back at his sides. Addressing them both, he said, "I hope you're happy." He wasn't sarcastic and it wasn't taken that way.

Aksel turned his back on them, picked up his father's puukko, and walked down the street and out of town.

32

In September 1909, having seen what Matti and Aksel had done with Ilmari's timber and the Saaranpa purchase, Higgins gave 200-Foot Logging a contract to log some timber he had purchased ten years earlier from a man who'd bought a large tract from the Northern Pacific Railroad. The railroad had been given its thousands of square miles of timber free by the U.S. government as an incentive to lay tracks. The man had logged the easy stuff and sold the rest to Higgins cheap.

There was a reason it was cheap. The tract was way up the Klawachuck River, the next large river north of Deep River. Klawachuck meant "slow river" in Chinookan. The Indians had named it with their tongues firmly in their cheeks. The timber was on impossibly steep terrain. Impossible to most people but not Matti Koski.

Matti and Aksel winched the cobbled-up steam donkey up the Klawachuck with new cable, no longer restricted to moving in two-hundred-foot increments. By late September, the donkey was in position. First, they built a small sauna next to a creek. They slept in it while they built a crude log cabin, cooking their meals on a fire outside because the sauna had no chimney. They got their water upstream from the cabin and shit downstream.

Matti convinced Higgins to provide payroll. To find loggers, he posted notes in general stores and churches. He sneaked into bunkhouses, feeling like a subversive like Aino. He, however, could offer no good food and no good quarters. No one was willing to wait, like Aksel, until profits came in. He changed to saloons and whorehouses.

There he found experienced loggers: experienced alcoholic loggers, experienced sex-addicted loggers, experienced half-crippled loggers, experienced loggers who'd gotten blacklisted. There was no shortage of experienced loggers. Some left after the first payday. One left before, stealing an ax as his pay.

The brightest moment in the hiring process came when a twelve-year-old boy tugged on Matti's shirt in a saloon in Willapa. It was Kullerikki. He'd managed to shed the diminutive, but he was still known by his nickname, Kullervo, instead of his given name, Heikki. He begged Matti for a job. Still not big enough to log, he'd been working for food and a place to sleep under the bar during the morning daylight hours. Matti said he would feed him and put a roof over his head in exchange for chores.

Aksel and Matti worked so hard it made their days with Reder Logging look like indoor work. On some days, they could fell and buck three or four trees. Other days, they didn't get one down. They sometimes just left larger trees that took too long to fell and were too expensive to move.

Sometimes they would have two additional loggers, sometimes four. Some days there was no one except Kullervo. It was always Matti and Aksel working as a team. They would start by chopping out an undercut, the two of them standing on their springboards six or eight feet above the ground, swinging alternately with their axes, and then trading sides to swing with their opposite arms. Their shoulders and arms grew strong and thick. So did their calluses. After getting the undercut sufficiently deep, they would move to the other side of the tree and saw through to the undercut, each pulling one end of a twelve-foot-long crosscut saw, cursing it when it bound, freeing it by driving wedges into the cut, greasing it with oil, and wiping their sweat from its handles. Then came the thrill.

The saw would start to tremble. Pulling the saw clear, jumping to the ground from their springboards, they walked coolly—running could kill them—to one of several preplanned safe spots. There they watched the tree go down, hearing the wood creak, then crack, then sigh, the tree gaining momentum, falling faster and faster, the air rushing through the branches, the wood at the hinge where the saw cut had almost reached the undercut cracking and squealing with the force of hundreds of tons of wood that for several hundred years had fought against gravity and was now hurling toward the ground from where it came. The ground would shake beneath their feet and the air would vibrate as the giant met its death. Then, they would set to work with their sturdier eight-foot-long single-handled bucking saws. The huge logs would loom above them, like rounded cliff faces. If they chose the wrong place to cut, the log could roll and crush them.

Some of the giants produced forty-foot logs so heavy they would defeat the old steam donkey. When that happened, they would laboriously auger holes into the log, forming a line down its length. They would then tamp pieces of dynamite into the holes and set them off simultaneously with electric blasting caps. The straight-grained old-growth logs split beautifully, halving the load on the donkey.

They both carried dynamite in their back pockets and kept blasting caps close by. If it was too hard to get a choker cable around a log, they would blast a hole underneath it and bring the choker through the hole. They could also be crushed doing this. If they misjudged placing the blasting caps they could lose a hand. Misjudging the powder charge could kill them.

Once the choker was hooked to the main line, Matti would handle the steam donkey, watching Aksel's hand signals. If Matti jerked the cable too hard or loaded it beyond tolerance, the cable would snap. Several tons of steel rope would whip through the air. Another way a logger could die.

Using block and tackle, sniping the forward edges of the logs so they would skid along the ground easier, sometimes cutting small trees to make corduroy roads across difficult spots, constantly repositioning the steam donkey and resetting the blocks to get different angles, they moved the logs to the Klawachuck. There, just before rolling the logs into the water Kullervo would mark the ends with the 200-Foot Logging flottningsmärke, the Roman numeral for two hundred, CC, hammered into the wood using a steel stamp like a cold branding iron.

33

On December 10, Matti and Aksel hiked out to the bay and caught a boat for Willapa. They had been invited to Aino and Jouka's wedding the next day at the office of the justice of the peace. It surprised no one that Aino had refused a church wedding.

Jouka's mother and two of his sisters were there. His brothers were logging and couldn't get the time off. Ilmari, Rauha, Matti, and Lempi stood as witnesses.

After the ceremony, as the *Shamrock* steamed south for the mouth of Deep River, Jouka stood at Aino's side. He hugged her in close to him, protecting her from the wind-driven drizzle. She would occasionally look up at him and smile, as was expected, but as she watched the shoreline pass by, all she could see were stumps and abandoned and rotting oysterman shacks dwarfed by piles of oyster shells twelve to fourteen feet high. They disembarked in the dark, even though it wasn't yet five, and the wedding party walked the eight miles back to Ilmahenki in the rain.

Waiting for them were Jouka's band; Reder loggers; neighbors, most of whom were members of Ilmari's church; the girls from the henhouse; and even Ullakko and his children. Rauha and Lempi had prepared coffee the previous day, as well as sandwiches, cookies, and loaves of pulla or nisu, the traditional sweet cardamom bread. The henhouse girls gave Aino a real silk scarf. Lempi added the personal gift of a rolling pin, joking that it wasn't just a kitchen tool but could be used occasionally to knock some sense into Jouka. Then Lempi grew serious. "Oma lupa oma tupa," she said, meaning, loosely, "My kitchen, my castle." It really meant no one messed with a Finnish woman in her own kitchen, including her husband. "Now, I give you a tool of a mature woman and wife," Lempi said. Then she grinned. "Girlhood is over."

Jouka's band members had all chipped in on a bottle of rye whiskey, from which each took a swig before they started to play.

About an hour into the gathering, Aksel somewhat awkwardly presented Aino with a set of large spoons and ladles he'd carved.

At the end of a break, when the band started to reassemble, Aino saw Aksel speak to the accordion player. The man nodded. He did a quick flourish to get everyone's attention. "We have a request for a waltz," he announced. Before Aino had time to even think about it, Aksel was in front of her. "May I have a dance with the bride?" he asked politely. She turned to Jouka, who smiled broadly. She was glad to see that he was genuinely happy Aksel had come. She was also glad that the bottle of rye whiskey had been stoppered and Jouka wasn't drinking. Ilmari would have thrown them both out. She turned to Aksel and offered her hand. "Of course," she laughed. "But it won't be the Grizzly Bear. Not at Ilmahenki."

It was "Lördagsvalsen." Aksel guided her to the center of the living room floor. Rauha had sanded the planks and removed the braided rag rugs. Off they went on the magic circle path.

They danced in silence for a moment. "Do you remember?" Aksel asked. "Midsummer night?"

"We were children. You're so sentimental," she said, kidding him.

"Yes." He blinked several times. "I am sentimental. Our first dance."

"A fight with the Russians."

She smiled, trying to keep things light, but was touched by sadness. They had danced this waltz together before they lost Gunnar and Voitto.

Aino wished the reception could go on all night but for the wrong reason.

* * *

They arrived at the hotel in Knappton just after midnight, Jouka only slightly tipsy from finishing the last of the rye on the way. Neither Aino nor Jouka had ever stayed in a hotel before. The bed had enough room around it to get in on either side and was covered with crisp, dip-starched sheets and solid wool blankets under a light brown bedcover with eyelets and lace trim.

Aino's brief feeling of enchantment turned to dread at the sound of the door closing behind her. The memory of the closing cell door started her trembling.

Jouka, thinking it was bridal jitters, took her gently in his arms. She stayed there, trying to calm her breathing as he kissed her. Then, he began fiddling with the buttons on the dress she had made with Rauha's help and Rauha's sewing machine, a gift from Louhi.

"No. No, Jouka. Let me." She gently pushed him back and went to her valise of green canvas covered with red roses. She pulled out the cotton nightgown she'd ordered from Sears Roebuck, again with Rauha's help, just for the occasion. She held it up to him and peeped at him over its top. She nodded toward the door and he smiled. She went down the hall to the privy. She sat on the narrow bit of wood between the bench's edge and the hole that opened to the river below. She was trembling fiercely, trying to focus on Jouka, who she knew was a good man, but she could not.

She remembered her sisu. Straightening her shoulders, fighting down the urge to cry, she stepped out of her dress. She loosened her corset strings, unhooked the corset busk, and stepped out of her pet-ticoat. She left on her new open-crotch cambric drawers, edged with nearly an inch of lace. She still hadn't succumbed to the odd custom of American girls who wore closed undergarments. She and Lempi had often joked about the trouble they went through to pee. She slipped the nightgown over her head. Then from her toiletry bag she took one of several balls she'd made of carefully dried and powdered cow dung, honey, and sodium carbonate. Feeling the cool river air against her bottom, she inserted the pessary into her vagina, pushing it as close to her cervix as she could. Her body heat would cause the mixture to melt and run, coating her vaginal walls as well as forming a barrier to the cervix itself. She wondered briefly if she should swallow the Queen Anne's lace seeds, also in her toilet bag, but worried that they might make her nauseated. Taking the poisonous seeds afterward might be more effective.

She'd thought about asking Jouka if he had a condom, but he'd wonder why. They were married. Didn't she want children? She returned to their room, worried that when it was over he would notice that there was no blood. She crawled between the damp sheets, fighting dread.

When he drew her in close to him, she tensed. He pulled back. She forced out a smile and loving words. This was Jouka's marriage bed, too, and none of it was his fault.

As soon as Jouka finished, he wanted to do it again. She excused herself, shyly saying there was a little blood to take care of, thanking the darkness for covering her lie. She inserted another pessary and returned. When the third pessary disappeared, she began to worry. She'd never imagined someone wanting to do it four times in a row. She realized that she'd never imagined Voitto doing it at all. As Jouka came for the fourth time, exhausted and sleepy she just stared at the ceiling. He saw this. His face flickered. Embarrassed, maybe even a little humiliated, Jouka rolled off on his side facing away from her. They remained like that for over half an hour, until Aino carefully touched him on his shoulder as if to apologize. She spooned next to him tucking her knees behind his knees and they fell asleep just as the gray of morning began to lighten the room.

The newlyweds awoke to the sound of people in the hall. Aino carried her clothes to the common washroom to dress. She washed her face and put her hair up before slipping on her chemise and corset. Tugging at the strings behind her back, she caught her image in the mirror. There she was, as usual—glasses, thick black hair up in a chignon, the plain cotton corset supporting her breasts—but she felt that something had forever changed. As a girl, she had dreamed of her wedding night, of her new husband gently undressing her, of giving herself to him wholly and finally becoming a woman. She pulled the loops tight and tied them. She pressed the cool cotton of the chemise against her vulva. Then she straightened herself. It hadn't worked out as she had dreamed. What she'd wanted to give, and what Jouka thought she'd given him, had long ago been taken from her.

While Aino was down the hall dressing, Jouka dressed and walked to the dirty window and looked east, up the river. He could see several headlands that formed bays on both sides before the river merged in the gray clouds. He had often thought about making love to Aino, and he guessed that he had; only it hadn't felt the way he had imagined. He'd been with prostitutes in Nordland several times and once he'd gone into Astoria with Aksel to the Lucky Logger. Certainly it had felt different from that, but . . . He shrugged into his Sunday coat. She had been so tense, as if she were afraid he was going to hurt her. Then, that last time, she'd just lain on her back looking at the ceiling, as if she weren't there. As if *he* weren't there. He felt a wave of shame. She had just lain there—maybe every time.

On the trail to Reder's camp, Aino fell in behind Jouka watching his broad back and wide shoulders as he moved so full of power and ease on the trail. She wished she had his confidence. She still wasn't sure how Reder felt about her coming back to Camp Two, despite Jouka's assurances that Reder preferred to put up with Mrs. Kaukonen rather than lose Mr. Kaukonen.

She wished she could just get Jouka to sing, but they were silent all the way to the camp.

Even though it was no surprise, the crudity of their new cabin still dismayed her. It was surrounded by the chaos of logging slash and mud. They had to pick their way across downed trees and around stumps to reach it or take the train tracks. She knew Jouka had managed to get one of the cabins with a roof instead of just a canvas tarp, and she was grateful. The floor, however, slanted enough to make a yarn ball roll down it, as one of the two logs the cabin sat on was slightly downslope from the other. The cabin hadn't moved since it had been lifted off one of the railcars. The train tracks were about ten feet from the single door set in the middle of the single room. A sink and a small woodstove were to the right of the door as she went in—a small table in front of them with two plain wooden chairs. To her left was an iron bed with the mattress rolled up against the simple headboard.

Ilmari had made her a cedar chest as a wedding gift. Matti and Aksel had hauled it from Ilmahenki to the camp and placed it against the far wall, leaving a note for the newlyweds. She opened it and inside found her everyday clothes, two cotton sheets, and two wool blankets—more gifts from Ilmari and Rauha. She looked at the rough planks on the floor. Dirt from the previous inhabitants had caked into the cracks—probably good to keep the floor draft down. She sat on the bed. Jouka went over to the window and managed to open it by hitting it with the heel of his hand. Light came through several places in the wall where a batten either was missing or had warped off one of the one-by-eight boards.

Jouka went to the stove and shoved the clinker bar in and out to get some of the damp ashes to move into the ash box. Their acrid smell filled the small space. He turned to her. She was staring at him.

"What?" he asked.

"It's going to need a lot of work."

He blinked a couple of times. "Yoh," he said, then went outside with the ashes and started making kindling. When he returned with a large armload, Aino had made the bed and changed into her everyday clothes. Sitting at the table, she looked blankly at the bare wall opposite the door, the light from the single window catching the nape of her neck and showing stray hair that escaped the braids of her chignon.

"What's for supper?" he asked.

The rocky start was smoothed with routine. Arising in the dark, shivering in the damp cold, Jouka would get the fire going in the stove and then go out to split wood and bring in water, while Aino made eggs or heated oatmeal or beans. Jouka no longer had to pay Reder for food in the mess hall, but Aino struggled to feed them both for the same amount. Jouka would pull on his caulk boots, sitting on the floor in the doorway, his legs outside in the cool darkness. They would kiss, and he'd walk to the waiting cars that now took the men nearly a mile from camp to where they were logging. Aino would watch him swing onto a car with the other loggers streaming from the mess hall. When she saw Lempi standing at the rail of the mess hall porch and they waved to each other, she realized Lempi probably envied her. Jouka was a good man, a good worker, and she knew he loved her.

But, many a day, she envied Lempi, who still lived and worked with other girls. Aino missed making cracks and giggling about the dirty bathwater. The few other married women kept their distance, polite and cool—Aino bore the double burden of being a red and dancing the Grizzly Bear. She was woman with whom any decent woman would not keep company. And Jouka didn't provide much relief for her loneliness—even when he did come home at night, he came home exhausted. He fell asleep soon after dinner, often during the meal, and sometimes even while Aino was talking to him.

She'd always worked as part of a team: for the striking loggers, the IWW, the farm in Finland, Ilmahenki, even for Ullakko and the children. She was used to hard work, but that hard work was always done with others, in a community, talking, sharing. Now the hard work kept her isolated. It was just the work and nothing else. And it was never-ending.

On Monday, she spent hours carrying water to the washtub, heating it, mixing in the soap flakes, wringing, hauling more water, rinsing, more water, rinsing again, and then hanging clothes to dry. They hung there for days, always brushing her face and head. In winter, damp was as dry as clothes got. Her hands were red and raw by the end of wash day. She envied Lempi on ironing day when she'd just get the iron hot on the woodstove and put it down on the clean shirt or sheet, and it would smudge black. That would put her back to a secondary wash day and scrubbing the iron and reheating it to try again.

On baking days, she struggled valiantly to remember how Maíjaliisa did it. Maíjaliisa didn't even have store-bought yeast. Aino would work fast, furiously even, because she'd been told store-bought yeast shouldn't rise all night. But it wouldn't rise at all if the room was too cold or if she put it too close to the stove and it got too hot. Jouka ate the bread without saying anything, which was good. Then again, it wasn't. Why didn't he say anything?

There were no saunas in the camp. People talked about building one, but Reder wouldn't put up the money, and the loggers were too tired to do it. So, on Saturdays she would sit in the washtub, after Jouka had used the water, her knees to her chin. Scrubbing herself with the huge bar of laundry soap, she valiantly tried to stay warm in the tepid water. Jouka would often put the kettle on and when it was hot, slowly pour the water in between her feet. It was as close to heaven as she got during the week.

The kerosene lamp blackened the chimney when the wick went low, so it had to be cleaned daily along with the smudge on the ceiling above it. The woodstove covered everything in fine soot—the wood-work, the cupboards, table legs, walls, under the bed; it even got under the sheets and on the cotton-stuffed mattress.

Every day was scrub-the-floor day, on her knees, trying to avoid splinters from the soft fir planks.

Sunday was not a day of rest. She almost became a Christian so she could walk to Ilmari's church and sit still for two hours. Instead, Sunday was when she cleaned the fireboxes in the stove, shook down the soot in the chimney to avoid a chimney fire, the constant dread of all the wives. Sunday afternoon, however, when Jouka would work on his violin or practice on it, she would wash her hair and try it in dif-ferent styles that she saw in catalogs and magazines. Sometimes Lempi would come over. Aino would nearly weep when she left.

She never imagined getting married would make her lonesome.

In February, she missed her period. When it still hadn't come by March, she began secretly eating the seeds of Queen Anne's lace that she had carefully been drying and storing in her cedar chest. On the twentieth of March, she felt a change. On the twenty-third, lying on the cabin floor between the sink and the table, she delivered an eight-week fetus. She wrapped it in some rags and cleaned up the blood.

She left Jouka a note, drawing a simple map of the farm on Deep River with two stick figures of Rauha and Ilmari. When she reached the banks of Deep River, she buried the unborn child, about the size of a kidney bean, just upstream from Ilmahenki beneath a stately cedar on the south side of the river. It was a spot where she sat often, as close to home as she could get, missing her mother, feeling her presence in the river that nourished her brother's farm, just as Maíjaliisa had nourished them all. She marked the spot with stones in a pattern that would look random to anyone but her. Then she cried.

PART THREE

1910–1917

Prologue

On May 10, 1910, in Yukon, Pennsylvania, a crowd of striking miners, who were protesting a 16 percent cut in their piecework wages, began making fun of twenty-five sheriff's deputies who were searching their boardinghouse. The deputies opened fire on the crowd, killing one and wounding thirty. That same month, some of the striking miners got too close to coal company property and twenty sheriff's deputies and state policemen attacked and severely beat them, killing one miner who was trying to protect a child in his arms. On July 28, a worker picketing against the American Sugar Refining Company in Brooklyn, New York, was shot multiple times by the police. During the garment workers' strike in Chicago against Hart Schaffner Marx in December, two strikers were shot by private detectives. Everywhere that people rose to right the balance, the forces of "law and order" rose to reset the balance back. Laws designed for completely different problems were applied to stop labor. Workers walking together on a public road after a union meeting could be put in jail for "contempt" or forced to pay a fine equal to a month's wages. Labor organizers or people identified as "ringleaders" were savagely beaten and tortured by deputized private detectives or the police. Who do you turn to for protection if it's the police who are attacking you?

1

A nswering that question, among many, kept Aino organizing. Freed from the pregnancy and freed from working long hours in the dining hall, she began widening her contacts with other Wobblies, as IWWs were increasingly being called. All spring she'd tried to keep up her duties at home, leaving only for a day or two three or four times a month to help sign up new members. She knew that it was hard on Jouka, and she felt a little guilty about it. Jouka came home in the dark, ate dinner, and collapsed into bed, only to get up the next morning in the dark. He rightfully expected breakfast and a packed lunch.

She would ask Lempi or some of the other wives who were more sympathetic to the Wobbly cause to check in on Jouka. She felt burdened, not by Jouka, but by a system that kept wages just high enough to keep her and Jouka alive, both working constantly but unable to save anything. Exhausting as organizing was, she saw the One Big Union as the only way out for her and Jouka and everyone like them.

Membership was a key component of union power. Even at Reder Logging, despite all her efforts, only a third of the loggers secretly carried the IWW's red card. From members came money and money was what sustained strikes. She'd learned this the hard way at Camp Two. She'd also learned that striking against a single owner was far less effective than striking an entire industry.

Month after month, sleeping on the floor at fellow Wobblies' homes, talking her way on to boats for free rides, occasionally splurging on a rail ticket, but mostly doing a great deal of walking, she signed men up to carry the red card of the One Big Union.

Aino kept up with events through *Työmies* (the Worker), a Finnish-language labor newspaper printed in Hancock, Michigan, which several of the Finns in camp had pitched in to get. Several others had jointly subscribed to the *Industrial Worker*, the IWW newspaper printed in Spokane. The papers passed from hand to hand, becoming tattered and torn with use, but they provided the only countervailing voice to the capitalist-controlled press. The news was rarely good. Sometimes Aino felt so oppressed by it—by the overwhelming odds labor faced—that she wished she didn't have to read it. Sometimes it made her just damned mad and got her sisu up.

Women conquered their fear, just like the men. The men could not let fear of death or crippling stop them from providing for their families. The women could not show their fear for their men or their fear of the very real consequences for them and their children of death or crippling, lest it weaken the men's resolve. The dangers of logging were faced with a united and silent front.

In late June, a logger named Hendrickson lost an arm. Aino had helped Mrs. Hendrickson deliver her fourth child just four months earlier. Now she was helping her move out of the company shack. The Hendricksons, all six of them, were moving to Portland, hoping there would be work for a one-armed man or that Mrs. Hendrickson could get domestic or cannery work.

Aino got home from the Hendricksons' after Jouka that evening, so dinner was late. Jouka, as usual, was ravenously hungry. Although he said he fully understood Aino's wanting to help the Hendricksons, she felt his resentment. Knowing that the resentment was to a large measure left over from previous neglect didn't abate her own annoyance with Jouka's seeming indifference to anything except his stomach.

"How can you just sit there, eating? Hendrickson's arm is gone and they're going to be starving in Portland. Reder and all the other owners take no responsibility."

"He's the one who stuck his arm where it shouldn't have been stuck."

"So, it's his fault?"

"Yoh." Jouka took in another bite of stew. "Logging's dangerous. Hendrickson knew that when he signed on."

"He didn't sign on to be so exhausted three-quarters of the way through the day that he can't think straight."

"Being tired isn't an excuse."

"No! It's a cause!"

Jouka stopped eating. Looking at his plate, as if explaining to a child, he said, "If we don't log as fast as we can, Reder Logging goes out of business. Reder Logging goes out of business, we don't eat. It's not anyone's *fault*."

He started to eat again. Aino put her hand over his bowl. He looked up at her.

"I don't want to lose you," she said.

He put his hand on hers, took it up, and kissed it. "Aino, I'm a good logger. It won't happen to us."

Aino looked over her shoulder through the window. Down the railroad tracks she could see several bundles of the Hendricksons' belongings waiting to be loaded on the next train out.

2

In August, Aino was loading her own belongings onto a train. Reder decided to take advantage of the long days and warm weather to move the camp to better timber above Grays Bay. The dishes, cups, and glasses had all been carefully packed in crates with straw to protect them from the shaking that was to come. The closet Jouka built on his Sundays off had been laid sideways on the floor, filled with bedding and clothes. The kitchen table was turned upside down and chairs were lashed inside the upturned legs along with the chamber pot, washing basin, and water pail. The wedding picture, carefully wrapped in towels to protect the glass, lay on the floor covered by the mattress, itself covered by the upside-down bed.

Blocks and steel cables were strung from a makeshift boom and connected back to a steam donkey. Jouka and Huttula, pulling on steel cables hanging from the butt rigs, set chokers around the four ends of the two parallel logs upon which the little shack sat. Jouka gave a signal, answered by a toot from the donkey, and the lines went taut, pulling the little house right up into the air. Huttula and Jouka joined two other loggers standing by with a cable looped around the middle of the log nearest the train track right beneath the front door and guided the house to the waiting railcar. Another signal for slack and the house was placed on the car and the train moved forward to pick up the next house.

That afternoon, Aino sat on the stoop of her shack's open front door, feet dangling, and watched the stumps and slash slide by. As the train rumbled across the high trestle, she caught a last glimpse of the old camp, empty rectangles of darker earth now marking the place where the shacks had stood among the jumble of bleached slash and stumps. Occasionally, at a long bend, she could see all the shacks, each on a railcar, moving in a long line. She gazed at the skyline of the denuded ridge to the north of the old camp. As far she could see the forest was gone, replaced by slash and straggler trees too small to bother with.

Soon, the train was moving through dense old-growth forests, first downhill in gentle switchbacks, then uphill in more switchbacks, recrossing what she presumed to be the same stream, until the train arrived at the new camp surrounded by huge trees. The mess hall had already been built, as had the new henhouse, and she could see Lempi and the other flunkies hard at work preparing the first meal in the new camp.

Reder's Camp Three had been born, eight miles southeast of what would soon be called Old Camp Two. New rail line had been laid from the new camp a little over a mile to a small bay that Reder had named Margaret Cove, a heretofore quiet and unnamed backwater on Grays Bay, which was on the Columbia River's north side, a few miles upstream from Knappton. The log booms would grow until ready to be towed to a mill.

As soon as the steam donkey unloaded the shacks and placed them helter-skelter, wherever somewhat level ground could be found, the loggers set up the donkey to the west of camp on a small hill and began yarding in the huge logs the felling crews had already laid down. Three days later, the operation boomed in high gear, whistles blowing, cables screeching, exposing the dark, secret places of the ancient forest to the harsh daylight of modernity.

The cabin floor now slanted even more than it had at Old Camp Two and despite Aino's complaining about it for nearly a week, nothing was done to level it. Aino felt no one gave a damn about her having to work with a floor that made her ankles hurt by nightfall—not even Jouka. Coming home exhausted after spending fourteen hours trying not to get himself killed while negotiating steep hillsides, brush, and slash,

Jouka didn't have a lot of sympathy and resented her for somehow making it all his fault.

One day, Aino attempted to put some tall wildflowers in a jar on the floor, where Jouka could see them when he came home. The hem of her skirt touched them and they tipped over. She screamed with frustration at the mess, leaving it there for Jouka to see when he got home.

"He pays you nothing and we're supposed to be grateful for this—this lopsided kennel," Aino steamed.

"Go stay with your brother, then," Jouka said. "I'll happily go back to the bunkhouse. At least there'd be someone there at night."

A sudden feeling of fear that he'd leave her swept tightly across Aino's chest and settled into her stomach. She started adding up the times she'd been gone. Twice to Portland to the IWW hall; twice up to Nordland, where they met in a private home; once to Willapa. Then there was the Astoria trip, which had embarrassed him more than the others. He'd made his own breakfast but had forgotten to make his lunch, so everyone knew Aino wasn't at home taking care of him.

When fear struck, the only option for Aino was taking the offensive. "You'd get more drinking done," she said tightly.

But Jouka was a Finn, too, and a fight between a Finnish couple was like a fight between glaciers. Only the occasional sound of the cracking of ice revealed the power of the opposing forces.

"I'd get better sex," Jouka said.

"Go get it then."

Aino reached into the unfinished wardrobe and threw Jouka's clothes on the floor.

"Might as well be in a pile," Jouka said. "They're never ironed."

Aino walked over to the stove, picked up the flatiron resting there, and threw it on top of the pile.

Jouka walked over to the shelf above the stove, took the tobacco can that held all their cash, and threw it on top of the pile, daring her to pick it up. "I work fourteen-hour days for that," he said.

Aino picked up the half-empty bottle of whiskey and tossed it on the pile without saying a word.

"It will keep me warmer than you do." Jouka said.

"Get out."

"I will." Jouka picked up his clothes, with the bottle and the cash box among them, and walked out the door.

Aino came to the door and threw a can at his receding back. "And you can grease your own boots."

Jouka bent down and picked it up. "You've greased my boots three times. Other men's wives grease them several times a week. But you're off with your red friends. At least, when you were midwifing, you brought in some money."

Aino went inside, slamming the door behind her.

Jouka drank the rest of the bottle in the bunkhouse that night and worked the next day with a horrible hangover. That same morning, Aino pulled out the small purse that she hid beneath the shack and caught the steamer for Ilwaco at Knappton. At Ilwaco, she caught a ride to Nahcotta on the Ilwaco Railway, a narrow-gauge railroad whose timetable had to coordinate with the tides. From Nahcotta, on the east side of the peninsula, she paid for passage on the *Shamrock* to Willapa, where she knew Wobblies who worked in the sawmills.

After a few days, the wives began to make clear she was welcome for a night or two of speeches, but not more.

Four days later, on Saturday, she spent the last of her money for the boat to the Deep River landing where she talked her way onto a small steamboat carrying building supplies for Higgins's new hotel in Tapiola. She decided to walk to Ilmahenki before heading on to Camp Three. When she arrived, Ilmari said, "You just missed Jouka."

"He came looking for me?"

"No. He came to help with the milking."

Ilmari rarely used sarcasm. It hammered his anger home.

"Where have you been?" he asked.

"Willapa."

"He loves you and he's a good earner."

"What? And I'm a fool?"

"Yoh."

*   *   *

Rauha, definitely showing the baby expected in October, fed Aino some warm, freshly made bread, which made her feel even worse. She knew Jouka would be playing at the dance in Knappton that night but couldn't face him.

The bunkhouse was deserted when she walked into camp, as was the henhouse. Only Alma Wiitala, standing on the porch of the new mess hall, saw her coming. Alma gestured for Aino to join her. She was setting out coffee when Aino knocked on the side of the open door.

"Sit down," Alma said, not unkindly but with the authority of the queen of the mess hall. Aino sat down.

"My husband says you and Jouka are fighting over who greases his boots."

Aino looked down at the table. Put that way, it seemed so trivial. She said, "It's not about the boots."

Alma nodded sympathetically. Then she said, "Are you *so* unhappy?"

Aino's lip started to tremble. She hid it with her coffee cup.

"Put the cup down, Aino," Alma said. Aino put it down and was met by Alma's warm blue eyes, almost soft violet in the lantern light. "He's a good logger and a good man. You give him a child and he'll stop drinking."

"How can you know that?"

"He'll be a family man. That's more than a married man. You'll be a mother. Neither of you will have time for selfishness about who's on top."

Aino went to the bunkhouse and found Jouka's caulk boots and clothes. She also found the cash box under the mattress. He had spent none of the money. She carried everything home, made bread, greased his boots, and put the boots by the door where he would see them.

She waited, watching by the window, all Sunday morning. Some of the loggers had gone to Tapiola for services at Ilmari's church and she heard them talking as they pumped the speeder back up to camp. Jouka was sitting with them. She opened the door and stood in the doorway, waiting for him to see her. When he did, he stopped talking. They looked at each other for half a minute as the speeder was pumped onto a spur. The other loggers jumped off and headed for the bunkhouses. Jouka stood there, tall and straight. Aino's pulse was in her throat.

Then Jouka gave her that big grin of his, shook his head as if in wonder, and came toward her. She rushed inside, hung her apron on the peg, and poured the waiting coffee into a cup. She ladled the already made pannukakku batter onto the already heated skillet and its custardy aroma filled the small cabin as Jouka walked in the door. She looked over her shoulder at him. "How was church?" she asked.

Jouka laughed out loud. He threw his violin onto the bed and hugged her off her feet.

For several weeks, there was an era of good feelings. Aino stayed home. Jouka knew that Rauha's due date in early October had some influence on this, but he hoped that there was more to it, that Aino truly loved him and cared for him. When news came of a big IWW rally to be held in Nordland on October 15, he could feel her rising impatience. She expressed this as impatience for Rauha's delivery. He knew better but said nothing.

Then, on the first of October, a bomb was set off, killing twenty-one newspaper workers in Los Angeles, and another bomb partially destroyed the Llewellyn Iron Works in the same city. The IWW was blamed. This sent Aino into high gear. The era of good feelings was over.

Aino traveled nearly every day to make speeches trying to prove that it wasn't the IWW, making it clear that the IWW condemned violence. Still, some men tore up their cards, which represented weeks of her hard work. Loggers were increasingly afraid to have the cards. Owners could rifle through loggers' belongings because the loggers were on the owners' property. If they found a red card, the logger was fired. Aino was constantly exchanging new cards for cards that could barely be read, because loggers kept them in their pockets while they worked. She'd joke with the men about the owners' at least having to stop short of groping in pockets.

When Ilmari galloped up on his horse shouting that Rauha was in labor on October 9, Jouka sadly watched Aino's back until she, Ilmari, and the horse disappeared in the trees. He knew that there'd be no keeping her from Nordland. Now that Rauha's baby had come, Aino would go.

Ilmari named the girl Helmi, for the beautiful amber of the Baltic.

When Aino arrived in Nordland, she noticed groups of sullen men watching her from in front of the saloons. They weren't workingmen. She felt a twinge of fear.

At the IWW hall, workers were coming in from the mills and logging camps in the hills north and east of Nordland and up the Chehalis River. Aino got a stack of pamphlets and immediately began to recruit. She loved it. She was helping the union grow and it felt good to banter with the men, arguing with them, hearing them laugh at her witty retorts and admiring her. She'd made a wool suit with Rauha's help and she knew it fit perfectly.

In the late afternoon, she saw Joe Hillström coming from the train station. She couldn't help feeling a flutter of excitement, standing a little taller, sensing his gaze. She met his shining eyes proudly. He nodded his approval, flashed her a grin, and disappeared into the hall. She unconsciously smoothed her skirt over her bottom.

The rally started at seven in front of the saloons. All around them were recently deputized policemen, citizens who hated the IWW, and thugs hired by owners, all under the eye of Chief of Police Bill Brewer.

Hillström was magnificent, witty, inspiring, and daring. However, when he started lampooning the government, Chief of Police Brewer had what he needed. He shouted, "Clear 'em out." The police and hired thugs waded in.

Aino refused to run. A deputy stood in front of her, smiled, and struck her right shoulder with an ax handle. She went down to her knees in pain, raising her arms to ward off the next blow, an agonizing crack of the ax handle against her forearm. The deputy ran off. Using only one arm, she tried to get up, but she went down again face-first in the reeking sawdust when another deputy slugged her across her back.

He kicked her head. If she hadn't been facedown in the mud, the blow could have snapped her neck. Dazed, she was barely conscious of being handcuffed with her arms behind her, jerked to her feet, and herded into a small corral next to a high-walled cattle chute behind a slaughterhouse. It reeked of blood and the watery shit of frightened animals. The last thing she remembered was two men trying to climb the high fence and being clubbed back into the pen.

She came back to consciousness with her head in Hillström's lap, her arm and back aching, her wrists raw from the handcuffs. She looked up into his face, which was swollen and bruised. There was dried blood beneath his nose.

"Welcome back to the land of the free and the home of the brave," Hillström said gently in English.

Aino rolled back from his lap, placing herself beside him, her back against the wall of the slaughterhouse. "Could be worse," she said. "They could have thought we were communists."

Hillström laughed. Then he sobered and said, "I've seen worse."

"Me, too." She took in an unexpected quick breath, then consciously released it.

Hillström looked at her quizzically. "Where?"

She hesitated, then said, "Finland," making it clear she didn't want to talk.

They fell asleep, leaning their heads together, slumped against the wall.

Aino woke up shivering in a cold rain. It woke Hillström. Opening his coat, he pulled Aino in next to him. She felt his heat. It felt good.

She touched his left knee with her right hand, a silent thank-you. He put a hand on top of hers. She did not pull her hand away.

3

She could hide her bruises from everybody except Jouka. When he first saw them, he went very quiet. He gently put his hand on the bruise on her arm, then withdrew it. Looking her in the eye he said, "Now, are you really done?"

She couldn't answer him and said nothing.

Winter in the Deep River valley settled in, weeks of cold rain and short days. Christmas at Ilmahenki was a bright spot. Both Matti and Aksel came down from the Klawachuck. Midnight services with candles at the little church were followed by ginger cookies and glögg, sweet hot wine punch garnished with raisins and slivered almonds. Ilmari objected to having alcohol in the house, but he was overruled by everyone else. He didn't seem to mind too much. Jouka and Ilmari played until four in the morning, Jouka getting increasingly inebriated until he collapsed asleep in the corner, his fiddle on his chest and his bow in his hand. Aino put a blanket over him and crawled into bed with Ilmari and Rauha.

January was worse than December. It brought a wet sluggish snow that made Aino long for Suomi. It gave Ilmari more time to see Vasutäti.

Throughout that January, Jouka would come home soaked through, his boots leaving puddles overnight from water that seeped out of the leather. In the morning, he put them on over dry socks, which turned wet within minutes. In early February, however, Jouka came home with a ray of sunshine.

He burst open the door to the shack, the inrushing cold air making the kerosene lantern waver and Aino jerk back from the list of
IWW card carriers she was updating to send to Portland.

Sitting on the doorsill, pulling off his caulk boots, he said, "Reder's
going to buy a Shay!" He turned to look at her, excitement on his face

"OK, what's a Shay?" she asked, smiling. She knew full well it was
a type of logging train engine but didn't want to deprive Jouka of whatever it was about one that excited him.

He grinned, turned around, and continued pulling off his caulks.
"It's a locomotive that uses a gear to move the power from the main
shaft to the drive wheels instead of using reciprocating arms like what
we have now."

"I assume that's good."

"You bet it's good." He grunted and tugged his second boot off. "It
can take sharper curves and go up steeper inclines. Saves lots of money
building tracks." Jouka came over to the table, leaned over her, smelling
her hair and holding her shoulders. "I'm going to learn how to run it.
I'll be the engineer." He moved to the sink, where he poured water into
a bowl and splashed his face and hands.

"Did Reder give you the job?"

"No, no. Not yet. And I'll probably be up against the donkey
punchers, because they already know steam. But no one knows how to
run a Shay or even more important how to fix one."

"Why not give the job to Dale Swanson?"

"You heard he had that blackout last month."

"Yoh."

"He's getting old. Reder thinks it's his heart. Reder will sell Old
Number Two and put Swanson in the machine shop."

"Just like that. One blackout."

"He's not going to risk a new Shay on an old man." He poured
coffee and sat down. His clothes were starting to steam and were still
covered with dirt and duff.

"You need to change clothes."

"No. You don't understand. An engineer can get double what I'm
making now. He works out of the rain. It's like an indoor job!"

"You need to change your clothes." She looked up at him as she was unbuttoning his shirt. "How are you going to learn how to run the Shay? Give me your shirt."

Jouka slipped his suspenders down and unbuttoned his wool shirt as he talked. "I'm going to order books about it."

"Jouka," she said. "You can't *read*. What foolishness is getting into you?"

He stood up and now hopping on one foot tugged off his trousers. "Aksel told me once . . . when we were both in the bunkhouse . . . the technical manuals have pictures and diagrams. You don't need to know how to read."

"Aksel's a dreamer and you know it."

"But, Aino, I saw the technical drawings for Old Number Two. Swanson let me look at them and . . ." He walked over to the stove and handed her his trousers, which she hung next to his shirt. There was no use washing them, she thought. They'd only be dirty again the next day. Jouka was still talking. "I understood them! Just looking at the drawings. Aino, I *understood*."

She'd never seen him as animated and she was happy for him, but she feared that his bubble would be burst by harsh reality. She couldn't imagine learning anything from a book without being able to read words. All the donkey punchers were Finns from Finland, which Jouka wasn't. They could all read.

"Your long johns are wet, too," Aino said.

Jouka turned his back and pulled his arms from the top of the long johns and then pulled the rest from his feet. He handed the long johns to Aino and stood there naked, looking at her.

She had to smile at him. "Get dressed, for heaven's sake."

He got his other pair of long johns out of the bureau and put them on as she fired up the stove.

"Aino," he said. "I can make headway. I know I can."

A month later the diagrams for the Shay arrived along with two books on steam engines. Jouka cleared the table after dinner every night and pored over the diagrams, occasionally asking Aino to read something.

He sometimes crawled into bed after midnight, getting only four hours of sleep before heading back to work at 4:30. He constantly sketched machine pictures from memory, looked at diagrams, and then corrected the sketches. He still played at the Saturday dances, but he was home right afterward, needing to sleep so he could get up with the light on Sunday and keep at the books. He'd stopped drinking.

One Sunday evening Aino returned after dark to find Jouka at the table with the kerosene lamp. He looked up at her when she came in the door. Something had changed in his face these past couple of months. There was a maturity she hadn't seen before—or maybe it had just arrived. She hadn't even got her coat off when he said, "There's going to be a test."

"What kind of test?"

"The Lima Locomotive Works representative gives it. They build the Shays. Whoever passes gets certified. Reder says that whoever gets the best marks will get to run the lokie." He used the logger slang for locomotive.

"How are you going to pass a test if you can't read the questions?"

"Reder says he'll ask the Lima representative to do it orally."

"Are you still up against the donkey punchers?"

"Yoh," he said in a lower voice. Then he brightened. "You know how much time I've been spending with Swanson on Number Two. I've taken it apart and put it back together at least three times. None of the donkey punchers have done that. *Can* do that."

"Maybe they don't need to." She watched Jouka's face change. She'd gone too far trying to protect him.

"Aino, I can do this. I know that lokie so well now."

She knelt beside him. "I just don't want you to get hurt."

"I know," Jouka said. He gently stroked her hair. "I know," he murmured. "You just couldn't say it."

She put her cheek on his leg. This closeness between them, so rare.

The Lima representative had been up to Camp Three two times already. Jouka told her he was clearly in the lead. Still, she remained worried that he was just heading for an embarrassing disappointment.

Certainly, he had a way with engines and boilers. Even Matti commented on it. She wondered if she should risk talking with Margaret, but she quickly shut the thought down. She didn't want any favors from Margaret, and if Jouka ever found out, there would be hell to pay.

He came in for lunch on the day of the test and changed into his Sunday clothes. They were both aware that the test was going to cost them half a day's pay. She kissed him goodbye and he headed to the dining hall where the Lima rep would be giving the test. She watched him as he made his way on the path through the slash. She looked around at the tumble of shacks; the mud; the six-to-ten-foot-high stumps dead in the ground; the litter of cables, tin cans, and broken boxes.

She looked over at the mess hall, which reminded her of working there. That made her think of Lempi. Aino knew Lempi was being courted by Huttula—an old man like Ullakko, in his late thirties—but Lempi didn't seem to mind his age. Aino had hoped Aksel would come to his senses, but Lempi just flat out told her she'd given up on him. Huttula was a good worker and she wanted a baby. Boys could wait. Girls couldn't.

She walked back inside the shack. The letter Ilmari had walked up to Camp Three last Saturday was still on top of the bureau. Word had come from a released prisoner that their father had died in a Siberian labor camp sometime around 1908. He'd lasted three years. He would be fifty-nine now. She felt like crying for the futility of it all: Finnish independence, the revolution, Jouka's plans, Matti's plans, the One Big Union. Vanity of vanities, saith the Preacher, vanity of vanities; all is vanity. Ecclesiastes, 1:2.

She closed the door, shutting out the mud and smell and noise and dead stumps. Now, even her best friend, Lempi, was going to get married and have children. The image of the little disguised grave by Deep River hit her. She laid her head on the table and cried.

The test was over just before dark. She had made riisipuuro, a thick rice and cream pudding, flavored with blackberry jam, a favorite of Jouka's. He ate it, saying nothing, and she feared the worst. When he finished, she asked, "Well? How did it go?"

Jouka leaned back, wiping his mouth with the back of his hand. "There wasn't a goddamned thing on that test that I didn't know." He broke out in a huge grin.

She smiled at him, greatly relieved. "Good," she said.

Three days later, the letter came certifying him as a qualified Shay engineer. Jouka had Aino read it aloud to him three times before he took it over to Reder's office. Then he made a frame for it and put it on the wall just opposite the door. One night after dinner he took out his fiddle and made a song up about a brave Shay engineer, moving around in rhythm, swinging his body with the music. They both were laughing by the time he finished and together they tumbled onto the bed.

Reder paired Jouka with Dale Swanson for three days on the old locomotive, then moved Swanson to the machine shop, leaving Jouka on his own until mid-April when the Shay was scheduled to arrive. He tasked Jouka with training his best donkey puncher on the old locomotive, freeing Jouka for the new Shay.

Moving huge logs to water is extremely difficult. Moving a thirty-five-ton Shay locomotive from water to railroad tracks is more difficult.

The Shay had arrived by barge, towed and pushed by river tugs to where it now sat, gently moving with the remnant of swell from the wide main course of the Columbia in Margaret Cove.

Jouka stood next to John Reder like an anxious father, looking at the black giant, its boiler already fired and its steam up, soon his to run. The rail line had been completed from the new show to Margaret Cove and now the final piece of track was being finished. Set on pilings, it led right onto the barge.

Reder looked at Jouka. He had chosen to supervise the transfer himself. Jouka understood. If this transfer from barge to rail line went badly, it could bankrupt Reder Logging and end the job of Jouka's dreams. He climbed into the cab.

The locomotive had been set on rails on the barge. The barge's rails had to be lined up perfectly with the shoreline rail spur. Cables had been rigged on both sides of the barge's bow, which had been winched tight to the shoreline, as insurance in case some vagary of wind or tide forced the barge out of line. This, however, was only some insurance against the barge drifting horizontally. The Columbia River had swells. Even though Margaret Cove was sheltered from the main channel of the river, the remains of swells washed up against the beach, making the barge subject to vertical movement should a large swell come into the bay and lift the stern or, worse, move the bow vertically. One slip, one faulty rigging job, one bad or misunderstood signal, one cable snapping, one large swell and the locomotive could go plunging into the deep bay, taking Jouka with it.

Reder looked at Jouka. "Here we go," he said. He started off toward the boom where he could see everything better.

Jouka peered out the right cab window and then the left, watching the rigging crew manning the cables.

Reder, looking at the river, timing the swell, gave a vigorous hand signal. Jouka, slowly eased steam into the pistons. He tried to become part of the locomotive instead of just being on it. The Shay quivered. More steam. The Shay moved. Barge crewmen on both sides gave him the signal that the wheels of the Shay's leading bogie had moved onto the land-linked track. Now, came the critical moment. The front of the locomotive hit track on the temporary pilings, taking weight off the barge and causing it to move upward. If Jouka didn't get across the juncture between barge and pilings fast enough, it would be his first and last time at the throttle of a locomotive, maybe his last time ever. He added power and speed.

The nimble Shay hit the rail line on the pilings at about ten miles per hour, which seemed to Jouka like a hundred. He heard a cheer from the barge crew behind him at the same time he felt the difference in motion beneath him. He was on the pilings now, hoping they had been placed firmly enough so the rail line wouldn't move as it bore weight. Within seconds, he hit tracks on solid ground. His felt a wave of relief and satisfaction. His heart was pounding. He'd done it.

He stopped the engine and gave a long shrill toot on the whistle. Reder ran down the temporary tracks and climbed into the cab. He pounded Jouka on the back and grabbing the lanyard of the whistle pulled a series of short toots, grinning like a schoolboy.

*   *   *

Over the next two days, as the same procedure unloaded the railcars, Jouka brought the engine up to full pressure several times and then ran it by itself all the way up the line.

The felling and yarding operations were already running at full speed when Jouka brought the first train of empty cars to the landing. With a long blast on the engine's whistle, the first load started to the cove where the temporary spur had been replaced by logs laid side by side, perpendicular to the rail line and going down underwater in the bay. These logs formed a sturdy ramp for other logs to be rolled from tiltable car decks to go smashing into the water, raising spectacular fountains.

Jouka lay on the whistle all the way down to the water, bringing in the first load.

4

For Matti and Aksel, the months of hard, relentless work on the Klawachuck and some occasional blowouts in the whorehouses and saloons of Nordland came to an end in March 1911. They'd logged the show out. Aksel's boat fund had grown but was still not large enough. He refused to follow Matti's advice and get a loan. For his part, Matti had something else in mind. He figured he had enough money to get married.

Matti decided against looking for a bride in Nordland because, as Aksel said, it was nothing but sawdust, shit, and hookers. So, they decided on Astoria, which Rauha said was filled with salmon packers who smelled like fish guts in addition to sawdust, shit, and hookers. Matti took heart from Aino, however, who said there were more Finnish girls there than anyplace else on the lower Columbia and surely he would find someone.

As Matti walked off the *General Washington* he smelled the creosote on the thick timbers that formed the streets and the pitchy tang of smoke from burning sawdust. Fishing boats swung easily on lines tied fore and aft to wharves and pilings. Astoria thrived on lumber, plywood, and salmon. The population had grown to more than seven thousand. Salmon-canning plants lined the river from Youngs Bay on Astoria's west side to Tongue Point on its east. The plants were interspersed with smoking wigwam burners and stacks of lumber and plywood waiting to be loaded on one of the many waiting ships. Like Knappton, Astoria was built on pilings.

Matti had a plan. Women shopped.

He began by wandering up and down Commercial Street, where there were shops in abundance. He lasted about five minutes in Grimson's Ladies Apparel, unable to answer the saleslady's questions about his wife's size and what color she wore. Lunch at Moberg's Café proved futile, because he just sat at the counter, afraid to talk to any number of apparently single women who were sitting together at tables. He tried standing in front of girls walking down the street and tipping his hat, but got only puzzled or annoyed looks.

By three in the afternoon, he became convinced the plan had failed. Women shopped, but he was hopelessly inept at shopping for women. The *General Washington*'s last departure was at 4:30, so to avoid a fruitless trip, he decided to buy new caulk boots. The sign on the Tenth Street shop read: SAARI SHOES. Even he knew enough English to know the name was unfortunate, and it made him smile. In the display window another sign read: BUY ONE PAIR AND GET A SAARI SHOES WOODEN NICKEL FOR 10% OFF YOUR NEXT PURCHASE. He walked through the half-glass door, ready to do business.

The blond girl behind the cash register looked at him with soft green eyes. She smiled and the room became three shades lighter.

"Can I help you?" She asked in flawless unaccented American. His heart sank.

"I wanting good shoes for verking. Caulk boots . . . for . . ." He trailed off, embarrassed because he didn't speak good English, and because he had a Finnish accent as broad as the hindquarters of a cow in June.

In unaccented Finnish the girl asked, "Are you looking for ones that just cover the ankles or ones that go up over the calves?"

He became aware that his mouth was open and he shut it. He looked at his shoes.

She cocked her head just slightly and with a twinkle in her eye said, "You're definitely Finnish." She wore a green cotton dress that had a pattern of small tastefully scattered pale-red roses and closed at the back with mother-of-pearl buttons. She had a slender figure and a graceful curve to her hips.

She motioned him to follow her to where boots were displayed on individual shelves on the wall. Looking over her shoulder, she asked, "You still want to buy boots?"

He lurched forward, feeling entirely clumsy and totally in love. Back aboard the *General Washington* he couldn't stop admiring his new dress shoes. His new caulks were in a bag along with his old dress shoes. He hoped the new caulks he bought Aksel would fit—and the dance shoes he'd bought Aino. He had no idea what he could possibly spend the fourth Saari Wooden Nickel on.

It took Matti several weeks to get his affairs in order and the yarder back to Ilmahenki, but the day Jouka landed the Shay, Matti was on the *General Washington*, his clothes in a carpetbag and all the cash from the Higgins job pinned to his long underwear. He checked into a poikata-loja, a boardinghouse catering to single Finnish men, and worked up another plan—a full-frontal assault.

Matti's initial intelligence gathering determined Kyllikki Saari had graduated from Astoria High School the previous year, which made her eighteen or nineteen. Her father and mother, Emil and Hilda Saari, had arrived in Astoria when she was three; this explained her unaccented American. Emil Saari owned Saari Shoes, as well as Saari Marine Chandlery, the name of the business he had owned in Kokkola before he sold it and took his pregnant wife and young daughter to America. He wanted his children to grow up with all the rights and freedoms of the American Constitution and Declaration of Independence—copies of which he kept on the wall behind the cash register at the chandlery. Hilda Saari delivered a son who died of influenza when he was three. The Saaris had no more children. Whoever married Kyllikki Saari was marrying not only a beauty but an heiress, although the word "heiress" had a different connotation in Astoria, Oregon, from in Newport, Rhode Island.

Matti's opening move was walking into the shoe store and asking Kyllikki if he could take her for coffee.

"I suppose that would be cheaper than buying more shoes."

He nodded ruefully. "Yoh." She still hadn't answered his question. Finally, she broke the silence. "There's a dance every Saturday night at Suomi Hall. I usually go."

"So, you won't have coffee with me now?"

"Yes, I won't have coffee with you now. I don't even know you."

"My name is Matti Koski."

"Well, Matti Koski, unless you're buying shoes, I look forward to seeing you Saturday night."

Saturday night, walking up the twelve-foot-wide stairs to the second floor of Suomi Hall, Matti felt out of place. Everyone was Finnish, but at least half of these Finns were socialists and communists—Aino's people, not his.

The stairs ended at a large, narrow room on the east side of the building where tables held coffee, pulla and other kinds of coffee cake, and punch. The women forbade alcohol, so any drinking was done outside the building or in the tavern across Marine Drive next to Union Steam Baths, which declared itself with the sign: THE HOT-TEST SPOT IN TOWN.

He walked through large double doors and found young women chattering on the edge of a large oak dance floor. Boys and girls, age five to seven, were darting into, out of, and under red plush curtains drawn across a stage at the river end of the dance floor.

He returned to the social room where women with faces flushed from the woodstoves in a good-size kitchen with windows facing the river served food and coffee from huge blue-and-white-flecked percolators.

Matti went outside and around the back. Looking across the river in the waning light, he rolled a cigarette, smoked half of it, then stubbed it out, putting the remaining tobacco back into his tobacco pouch. Returning to the front of the building, he saw Kyllikki walking up the street with her mother and father.

He took off his hat. Her eyes changed—encouraging, but the introduction was formal.

"Mr. Matti Koski," she said. "My father, Emil Saari; and my mother, Hilda Saari."

Matti shook Mr. Saari's hand and made a slight bow to his wife. Emil Saari's hand was strong but soft, an indoor hand. Matti felt he could crush it if he wanted. Then he looked into Mr. Saari's eyes and the brief feeling of superiority fled. The eyes were those of a man of authority and power.

Matti glanced at Kyllikki. She hadn't missed a thing. She and her mother lifted the hems of their dresses and turned to mount the steps, followed by Mr. Saari. Matti caught a glimpse of Kyllikki's ankles and petticoat. She looked over her shoulder at him and smiled as if she knew what he was thinking. She continued up the stairs but pulled her skirt against the back of her thighs. He felt himself blush.

When Kyllikki wasn't dancing, she was drinking punch and talking to whichever young man brought it for her. Finally, Matti just pushed in and asked her to dance. It was the only dance he got.

The next Saturday night, Kyllikki's parents were coolly polite. He got only two dances with Kyllikki. At the end of the second dance he asked her out for coffee after she got off work. She said no.

On Monday morning, he walked into the shoe store. She was there, as he expected, but so was her mother, who he had not expected.

"Mr. Koski," Mrs. Saari said. "How can we help you?"

"You know I'm not here to buy shoes," he said.

"Yes. I do know." She actually softened before delivering her next line. "I know you're sweet on Kyllikki, but you need to be realistic. We expect a better life for our daughter than being married to a gyppo logger."

"We're small now," he said. "But there are a lot of trees out there and I'm good at cutting them down."

"Yes. We've asked around. You and your partner, and no one else." She looked at him. "Go find a nice Finnish girl in Tapiola."

He knew that if he didn't stand up to the mother, he would never have Kyllikki's respect.

"This is America. Parents don't decide."

"They sure as hell do."

The swearword, coming from a woman, took him aback. Masking his discomposure, he turned to Kyllikki. "Do you want to have coffee after work?"

She looked at him, suppressing a smile, then looked right at her mother, and back to Matti. "I would love to," she said. "I'm off at six thirty."

"Kyllikki Saari!" her mother said.

"Yes?" She answered coolly.

"We forbid it." Mrs. Saari turned to Matti. "I have nothing against you, but if you don't end this, her father will."

Matti's heart was pounding, but he looked at her steadily. "I hope it doesn't turn out that way." He turned to Kyllikki. "At six thirty then?"

"At six thirty," she said. "At Moberg's."

Mrs. Saari flounced to the back room.

"You may have pushed too far." Kyllikki said.

"Yoh."

Over coffee at Moberg's Café on Sixth Street, Matti proposed a picnic on Sunday afternoon and she accepted.

On Wednesday, Aksel arrived at the poikataloja, saying he would need to dip into his boat savings if they didn't get another show.

"Give me two more weeks."

"OK," Aksel said. "But in two weeks I go looking for work."

"For slave wages."

"For feed-my-mouth wages."

Sunday at noon Matti knocked on the Saaris' front door, picnic hamper in hand. Mr. Saari answered, told him Kyllikki wasn't home, and that Matti needed to leave or he'd call the police.

Matti walked across the street to a neighbor's lawn where he carefully laid out the picnic and began eating. He saw Kyllikki in the living room window. She was replaced by her scowling mother, who pulled the venetian blinds shut. He took two hours to eat the picnic, waving to Mrs. Saari whenever he saw her peeking out the window. Once he caught a slight movement of curtains in a second-story window. Kyllikki was looking at him thoughtfully. He stood up, took off his hat, and made a sweeping bow. The curtains shut, but not before he saw her suppress a smile.

That night he counted his money. He didn't want to lose Aksel or dip into his double-drum-donkey fund. Courtship, love, marriage, the one:

they were all very romantic, but in the real world he had limited time and required money. He needed to act.

He bought a small cart and a very old horse and began making firewood. When Aksel returned after the two weeks, the two of them just carried on the partnership, Matti sending flowers to the Saaris' house, Aksel going to the Lucky Logger.

Emil Saari sent the police to tell them that if they didn't go back to the Washington side, at the slightest wrong move they'd be thrown into jail. The two of them pretended they didn't understand English.

The next day, Matti gave a boy a dime to deliver a note to Kyllikki, asking her to meet him at eight o'clock on the *General Washington*'s wharf, a public place that would not stain her honor. When the passengers from the last run were climbing up the gangway, he saw her emerge from the fog wearing a hat and a long coat with a fur collar that was cut to hint it covered lifelong enchantment.

He wasn't sure he should kiss her.

When she reached him, she quickly looked around to see if they were alone. Then she looked up at him, her lips slightly parted, and he was suddenly sure. He kissed her and held on to her as the fog swirled across the wharf in the light from the single new electric street lamp.

They sat on a bench and she snuggled her coat around them. The talk was delightful and happy, ranging from their hopes and fears to their likes and dislikes, intertwined with occasional kisses. They were in a bubble of light. Around them whispered the wind and fog and the quiet ebb of the river. He was aware of their touching thighs.

The bubble burst with a loud exclamation from the land end of the wharf. "I knew that son of a bitch was with her." It was Mr. Saari and two Astoria policemen barreling down on them. Saari grabbed Kyllikki by the arm, jerking her away from Matti. "I'll have you jailed for this."

"I do nothing wrong," Matti said gravely. His sisu was up and the mask on his face in place.

Mr. Saari turned to the policemen. "Arrest this man. He's, he's . . ." He was searching for a law being broken. "He's defaming a young woman." Matti noticed that the two policemen gave each other a look. "He's corrupting youth."

"I'll be nineteen next month," Kyllikki said to the police.

One of them turned to Mr. Saari. "Now that we found her, she looks perfectly safe." He paused, then said, "And unabducted." He nodded to his partner and they both walked back toward the lights of the town. One of them laughed, which infuriated Mr. Saari.

Breathing hard, he said to Matti in Finnish, "I have other ways to stop you from harassing my daughter and I'm not afraid to use them."

"Father, calm down. I came here of my own free will."

"You'll get back to the house. Your free-will days are over."

Kyllikki pulled gently on her father's arm. "Father, let's talk about this at home." She gave Matti a have-patience look. Then she turned to walk toward the town, leaving Mr. Saari no choice but to follow her.

Alone on the wharf, Matti was in awe of the way Kyllikki defused the situation and handled her father. Unlike Aino, who was like the roaring rapids of their name, Koski, Kyllikki, whose name meant "a woman," was like a flood tide.

Two days later, three hard-looking men approached the wood yard, but when Matti and Aksel split apart, pulling their puukkos—just the opposite of what amateurs would do—the three walked away.

The small boy who'd delivered Matti's first note brought a note that read: "Back door of Roth's Drugstore at three."

Matti was there at two thirty. When the back door opened, he felt his breath shorten. She had done her hair differently. He knew it was for him.

"You've got to leave," she said after a brief kiss. "Father's contracted—"

"I know. We met them this morning."

"I can't see you anymore. I don't want you hurt."

"Marry me."

"I hardly know you. Are you crazy?"

"Marry me."

She looked around as if for help. "I can't. You know that."

"Marry me."

"We can wait a year. Until your business grows."

Matti just looked at her intensely.

"It's crazy, Matti. Please. You'll get hurt."

"More than this?" He turned abruptly, leaving her at the back door of the drugstore.

Two nights later, just outside the poikataloja, the three men struck with baseball bats. Matti was alone, his puukko under his coat. Before he could get it, he went to the ground, bleeding from the face and spitting out a tooth. Then, berserker fury took him. The only way to fight people armed with clubs was to get inside their swing. Matti rolled toward the men, screaming, his puukko out, aiming for legs. One thug hit him on the back of his head, but the bat couldn't get any speed. Still, Matti saw stars. Enraged, he slashed down on the man's arm, then waded directly into all three, the puukko flying, occasionally cutting through a thick coat to reach flesh. One of the men shouted, "He's crazy" and began to back away. Matti immediately turned to the next man, who'd hesitated between attacking or falling back. Matti's puukko stabbed instead of slashed and went deep into his belly. The man screamed, dropping his bat, clutching at the wound, stumbling backward. Matti kept following, knowing he couldn't give them room to swing their bats. The door of the poikataloja opened and several residents came running toward them. The three assailants ran, two of them helping the third. Matti kept screaming and running after them, his puukko pumping before him as he ran, until one of the men from the poikataloja tackled him.

"The jig's up," Aksel said in English, using a newfound expression, as he stitched the cut on Matti's head. "If they go to the cops, we're going to jail."

Matti said nothing, nauseated from concussion. Aksel doused the stitches with rubbing alcohol. He stood back.

"They won't."

Matti sat there, brooding. Then he came to a resolution. "Go back to Ilmahenki," he said. "Fire up the yarder to the highest pressure you can. Have Ilmari fix any leaks or weak points." He smiled. "Tell him I'll pay him."

Aksel nodded.

"The jig's up," Matti said in English and they both laughed.

In the morning Aksel caught the first boat for Knappton. Matti went to the shoe store. He shut the door and put the CLOSED sign in the door window. Kyllikki winced when he turned his face to her. "My God."

"I'm going to marry you no matter what," he said. "But if I wait any longer, I'll lose my partner and best friend. And probably my business."

Kyllikki nodded.

Matti held up two tickets. "The boat for Knappton leaves in twenty minutes. You can stay with my brother in Deep River or with my sister at Reder's Camp."

He felt as though Kyllikki was boring into his brain with her eyes. He knew that they both knew there would be no going back, whichever way she chose.

"I know my father hired those thugs," Kyllikki said. "And one of them is in St. Mary with a knife wound in his stomach. You're lucky he's not talking to the police."

"They came at me with baseball bats."

"You nearly killed him."

"What? Three against one and I'm bad for defending myself?"

"Of course, you had to defend yourself. But the word around town is you went crazy. They had to tackle you to stop you."

He avoided looking at her eyes.

She touched his cheek to make him look at her. "I have no intention of raising a dead man's children. You've got a temper. There's even a story about you back in Finland."

Matti held his hands open. "They were Russians. In our *home*."

Kyllikki said, "If I marry you, I will marry you for life. I asked you to leave so I *could* marry you for life. You risked it all by staying."

"I couldn't risk losing you."

"So, you risked *me* losing *you!*"

"I didn't think of that."

"When you get married, you stop thinking about yourself. You think about your partner."

Matti was silent. Then he said, "Marry me."

She smiled, shifting her body, opening herself to him. "On one condition." Matti waited. "The puukko stays home when you're not working. You must give up fighting and behave like a husband and father. Go to the police if there's trouble."

This time the silence was long. Kyllikki was asking him not just for a change in behavior but for a change in identity.

Matti loosened his belt, slid off the puukko sheath, and rebuckled it. He held the puukko in front of him, but he held it in his fist with his fingers closed around it. "I have one condition as well."

She waited.

"You'll dance with no one without my OK."

"I will never dance without you there," she said quietly.

He held the puukko out in front of him, his hand open. She took it. "I'll marry you," she said.

They looked into each other's eyes. When she was satisfied that he understood her completely, she handed the puukko back to him. "Quit standing there like a lunkhead and kiss me," she said. "We only have ten minutes to catch the ferry."

Holding hands on the stern of the *General Washington*, they watched Astoria recede. A strong swell from the mouth was tilting the boat to starboard and port as the swell hit from the west side and then passed beneath it. They said nothing, watching the tops of the ridges to Astoria's south appear one by one as the boat moved away. Soon, Saddle Mountain appeared, formed from the remains of massive lava flows that had poured down the old Columbia River valley. At over three thousand feet high, it dominated the surrounding land. It was a rare clear day with a strong west-by-northwest wind. Far upriver, to the east, Mount Saint Helens rose above the land, brilliant white and perfectly symmetrical.

Kyllikki turned her eyes from Astoria to it.

"The Indians call it Loowit, a beautiful maiden," Kyllikki said.

"With a temper," Matti said.

Kyllikki looked at him and smiled. "Not a temper. Heat."

* * *

Aino was cutting potatoes to add to the steelhead stew when she heard Matti's voice. She looked out the window to see him and a girl in an expensive coat with a fur ruff, her city shoes soaked, the hem of her dress brown with mud. Lempi had told Aino that Matti had gone to Astoria for a wife, but she'd discounted it. She took off her apron and put her glasses on the top of the dresser. Checking her hair in a small mirror by the sink, she went to greet them.

The girl was bedraggled—and beautiful.

Matti was grinning like a ten-year-old who'd just won the blue ribbon. "Aino," he said. "This is Kyllikki Saari. We're going to be married."

"I heard that you went hunting for a wife." Aino turned her eyes on Kyllikki.

"And I bagged him," Kyllikki said with a smile.

Well, Aino thought, maybe there was some spirit inside the pretty package. The girl was radiant and so fair next to her dark brother, with a perfect oval face, deep-green eyes, and small, perfectly formed ears. At the sight of Matti beaming beside the girl, a brief pang of jealousy hit her. Aino felt dark and unattractive.

Suddenly, memories of Mielikki and Lokka, her sisters, overpowered her. She felt the empty ache they had left in her heart all these years.

"Looks as if you left in a hurry," Aino said. Matti smiled and said nothing. The girl looked down at the skirt of her dress and smoothed it. She looked up and took Matti's hand. "We're eloping. My parents had someone different in mind." She looked up at Matti.

"I don't have a good situation," Matti said.

"And he's hotheaded."

"They're right on both." She smiled at her brother affectionately, then turned back to the girl. "The men will be coming off work. I'll throw in some more potatoes and carrots." She looked at Matti. "Jouka caught a nice steelhead on Sunday."

The girl sat on the bed with Matti, watching Aino augmenting the stew. She offered to help, but Aino made it clear that she didn't want any help.

The clear and musical sound of someone whistling came from outside the plank door. "That'll be Jouka," Matti said.

"He's a musician," the girl said with authority.

"Yes, he is," Aino said. She opened the door and the cool evening air came in, mixing with the air heated by the woodstove. Aino called, "Jouka, we have company."

Jouka stopped and looked at her, puzzled. "Matti and his new wife, well, soon-to-be wife." She turned back into the single room of the shack and Jouka followed her up to the doorsill. He stopped there and broke into a grin as Matti arose and came over to shake his hand. The girl rose and stood next to Matti.

"Jouka," Matti said. "This is Kyllikki Saari."

"Welcome," Jouka said. Aino could see Jouka's practiced eye take in the girl from head to toe and she knew that Jouka was smitten. How could any man not be? "If you don't get married and soon," he said to Matti, "they'll have you for kidnapping."

"I'm almost nineteen," Kyllikki said.

Jouka looked at her. "Oh, a full-grown woman."

"Woman enough for Matti."

After supper, Matti and Jouka set off in the dark for Knappton to get word to Pastor Hoikka.

Aino borrowed a blanket from the henhouse and, laying it on the floor with all of their jackets, made a bed.

"Until you two get married, you can sleep with me," Aino said. "Jouka can sleep on the floor and Matti's still got friends in the bunkhouse."

"I thought you were a red. Free love and all that."

"Oh God, that one." She looked up at the ceiling. "They all wish." Then she got serious. "If you want to get along with the women around here, Matti will sleep in the bunkhouse."

Kyllikki laughed. "Just like Astoria," she said.

Aino went outside to the community pump, came back with a kettle of water that she set on the hot spot on the stove, and threw in some kindling.

Kyllikki took Jouka's and Matti's socks and started to wash them in the warm rinse water remaining in the dishpan. "You have anything else?" she asked.

"Yes, but you don't need to."

"I want to chip in."

Aino took a wicker basket sitting at the end of the bed and dumped its contents on the sink counter, looking at Kyllikki. "You're not afraid to work. I was worried when I saw your coat."

"It's a nice coat," she said. "I like it." She wrung out the four socks and hung them on the line over the woodstove.

"Matti can't afford coats like that."

"Not yet." The girl dumped some long underwear and a pair of Aino's stockings and a petticoat into the dishpan and began scrubbing the clothes together. "You have a washboard?"

"Outside. I take the stuff to the creek when I have to."

"No soap?"

"There's a bar by the washboard."

"It's bad on the hands. My mother uses Ivory Flakes."

"How *in*teresting," Aino said.

Kyllikki turned to her slowly, her eyes flashing with anger. "I'm trying to be a friend here. It's called small talk. It doesn't convey information. It shows intent. Don't you have any girlfriends?"

Aino colored. "I'm sorry. I have a wicked tongue."

"I've been told."

The two were silent for a while.

Kyllikki hung the rest of the wash without saying anything.

The water started boiling. Aino threw a mixture of a few ground coffee beans and roasted barley into the bottom of a large enameled coffeepot. She smashed an egg, shell and all, into the grounds until she had a black sticky glob. She poured the boiling water over it and stirred hard. With her back to Kyllikki, she asked, "Do you love him?"

"With all my heart."

Aino poured two cups and they sat down at the table.

"I want to be friends," Aino said.

"Me too."

"I lost my sisters."

"I lost my brother when I was six."

Aino nodded, saying nothing.

Then Kyllikki said, "Matti told me what happened."

"Did he tell you anything else?"

"That you lost your love."

Aino nodded, a barely perceptible nod. They drank their coffee without talking.

When they both had finished, Kyllikki said, "Matti told me that you're a midwife."

"I learned from my mother."

"This is awkward."

"What is awkward?"

"I don't exactly know what to do. You know, about . . . that. I . . . well . . . I didn't have time to talk to my mother."

Aino watched Kyllikki blush. She touched her hand. "Nature will find a way. And if she doesn't, Matti will."

Kyllikki laughed a full-hearted, earthy laugh and Aino joined in.

"Do you want to have a baby?" Aino asked.

"Certainly, yes. Why do you even ask? Isn't that what happens when you get married?"

"Oh dear, we've got a lot of ground to cover."

Matti and Kyllikki were married two days later, the earliest they could get Pastor Hoikka across the river. Aino stood by Kyllikki as matron of honor, with Aksel the best man, feeling that this was as close as he'd ever get to Aino and an altar.

For their wedding gift, Ilmari and Rauha gave the newlyweds an acre on Deep River at the northeast corner of Ilmahenki. Matti, Aksel, Jouka, and Ilmari all pitched in to build their new sauna the next Sunday. Safely sheltered in the sauna, Matti and Kyllikki began building their new house on the first of June, 1911. Because the house sat on a shallow bend in Deep River where the current slowed, they named it Suvantola, for the slack water.

5

Summer for Aino and Jouka meant more daylight to get more chores done. Aino was darning one of Jouka's wool socks by the window, while he was outside splitting firewood, stacking it in long parallel rows covered by chunks of bark. There, it would dry over the next year. Dry wood burned hotter and reduced creosote buildup, which led to chimney fires. The shack required no heating in summer, so wood was needed just for cooking until at least October. She heard Jouka shout a hello and the murmur of his and a woman's voice. Then she heard the striking of his splitting maul start again and almost immediately a knock at the door. It was Lempi. She had a wicker basket of three different colored yarns and a half-finished sweater in it. She'd come to talk.

Aino got Lempi coffee and Lempi knitted while Aino darned. Sitting at the table in the Sunday quiet—with no screeching steel cables, no rumbling railcars outside the door, the husbands safe for the day, her friend Lempi wanting to bring up whatever it was—she felt calm joy.

"More coffee?" she asked Lempi in Finnish.

"I'm good. Thank you," she answered in English.

It was good Lempi refused. She wouldn't have to make a second pot for Jouka's Monday morning cup. They could afford an extra Sunday pot of coffee now that Jouka made good wages running the locomotive, but old habits, especially ones involving money, die slowly. She realized Lempi had been talking to her. She recalled the words that she had unconsciously recorded in her mind, recovered, and responded as if she'd been listening all along. "Huttula asked you to marry him?"

Lempi nodded, a smile on her face.

"And . . .?" Aino asked.

"I said yes."

So, Aino thought, she couldn't wait for Aksel. Probably wise. Aksel was a loner at heart.

"I know he's old," Lempi said quietly, interpreting Aino's lack of an immediate response as disapproval. "But he's making two and a quarter a day now on the steam donkey and he even told me he loves me."

He was making almost as much as Jouka, Aino thought, then rebuked herself mentally. It was insidious. Here she was comparing scraps from under Reder's table with her best friend. If any of them would just put their noses above the tabletop, then they would see the truth—a table groaning with more food than the few diners could possibly eat in a week or even a month.

"Yes, but he still pays Reder a dollar and a quarter for room and board," Aino said.

"We'll be able to get a company house."

Aino looked up and all around the small one-room shack with exaggerated disdain.

"It's better than the henhouse," Lempi said.

"I suppose so. If you prefer smelling long johns"—she nodded toward Jouka's underwear hanging from a line above the stove—"to drying menstrual rags."

"Oh, Aino . . ." They both laughed. Then they looked at each other, the steady sound of Jouka and his maul coming through the single open window. "Aren't you happy for me?"

Aksel hung in the air between them, between the sounds of the maul. A girl had to make choices.

"He's a good man," Aino said. "He will be a good provider."

"Yes," Lempi said, instead of "yoh." She hesitated. "Would you be my matron of honor?"

"Is it going to be a church wedding?"

"Well, Huttula *is* a Lutheran."

"What about you?"

"Of *course*, I am. Oh, Aino, I know what you think about religion, but I just never imagined my wedding any other way and certainly not in some government building. I'm not like you, that way. No one is," she added.

"Oh, Lempi. Of course I'll be your matron of honor."

She and Lempi smiled at each other. Aino certainly didn't feel a need to be more demonstrative. "Big white dress and all?" Aino asked.

"Well," Lempi said. "*That* is another question."

They decided a suit would have more use than a bridal dress, even one that could be remade into a day dress. The suit would take Lempi's savings, but then all her savings would go directly to something just for her and not have to be spent on joint things like dishes or bed linen. That could all come out of Huttula's savings—if he had any. They both speculated that he did, because he hardly ever went to Nordland or Astoria and didn't drink.

They set the wedding for four thirty in the afternoon of Sunday, October 3, so people would be off work and Pastor Hoikka would have time to get across the river.

Sitting in the little church on the day of the wedding, about to watch Lempi marry Huttula, Aksel knew it was his own fault. He'd stayed stupidly in love with Aino when Lempi would have married him in a heartbeat.

Ruusu Pakkanen started the Bridal March from *Lohengrin* on the little organ and everyone rose to face the back of the church.

Lempi stood beside her favorite uncle, who worked in a mill in Westport and had come to give her away. She wore a new suit and a beautiful new hat. Huttula was standing at the altar with his brother from Bellingham. As Lempi went by Aksel in her slow, stately walk, her eyes flickered from Huttula to him, then went quickly back to Huttula.

Two weddings now at the wrong end of the church, Aksel thought. He'd been smiling at Lempi, not knowing if she'd seen him.

He wondered if she had any regrets like his. Huttula was old but a good man in a less dangerous job. Huttula could very well live to see his and Lempi's grandchildren.

Lempi reached the end of the aisle and her uncle went to his place at the front left pew. Pastor Hoikka motioned them all to be seated and the ceremony began. "Dearly beloved . . ."

Aksel wasn't listening. He was looking at Aino and Lempi standing together, standing up there with Jouka and Huttula. That's when he remembered Lempi asking him about his swamping ax. What a fool he was. She didn't give a damn about the ax. He wanted to bolt from the church in his shame and misery. Shame for being so stupidly callous about Lempi's feelings for him and hurting her. Misery, this terrible loneliness, when it could have been otherwise, simply by opening his heart to Lempi.

6

After the wedding, Aino refocused on her letter-writing campaign, doing it during what wealthy people called spare time. For Aino, it was sleep time. Since being jailed in Nordland, she had tried to get off two letters a night once Jouka fell asleep. She'd written over five hundred letters, urging other Wobblies and sympathizers to come to Nordland on November 22 to exercise their constitutional rights to assemble and to speak freely. At two cents a letter, that was over a week of Jouka's wages. This concerned her more than it did Jouka.

As the word about the next free-speech fight got out to Wobblies, it of course got out to the good citizens of Nordland. The Nordland city council, reacting to people's fears, quickly passed an ordinance shutting down the IWW Meeting Hall and prohibiting the IWW—and only the IWW—from speaking or assembling on city streets. The council also deputized several hundred "prominent and professional" men to protect the town. Jouka urged Aino not to go. Louhi increased her beer inventory.

On November 20, Aino pressed her blouse and long skirt, took in her coat a little at the waist, and left for Nordland. She got off the boat on November 22 wearing her good shoes, which were soon wet with mud and damp sawdust from the streets. She immediately began buttonholing loggers and mill workers outside the saloons and barbershops, handing out leaflets, urging them to attend the rally that night on Crane Street. One of the speakers was to be Joe Hill, Hillström's latest pseudonym. Aino could never think of him as anything other than Joe Hillström.

The citizens of Nordland were scared. Wobblies had been arriving by train, climbing illegally onto the cars, hanging from the iron rungs that formed the ladders up the sides of the boxcars, clinging to the floors of the flatbeds, huddled on the narrow plank walkways that ran down the center of the roofs of boxcars.

Chief of Police Brewer, basking in his role as protector of civilization, passed out the usual ax handles and wooden wheel spokes to other recently deputized protectors of civilization.

Aino felt like a nesting robin beneath a circling hawk.

The afternoon of the rally, the hawk struck with ruthless efficiency. Hillström, still singing, was frog-marched to jail by four police officers. Angry men grabbed Aino's bundle of red cards, ground them into the mud, and dragged her to jail as well, but not before beating her with ax handles and billy clubs.

Thrown into a cell by herself, Aino was flooded with memories of the prison in Helsinki, hanging by her wrists from the ceiling, shivering with cold. She backed into a corner of the Nordland cell, clamping her jaw against the pain from the beating, fighting the urge to crumple to the floor in a fetal position. Then she heard the singing coming from the other cells at a volume that sounded as though each cell held several men. Aino walked to her cell door, put her hands on the bars, and joined in as loud as she could sing.

By nightfall, the jail was overflowing. She was now packed in with twelve others, including Hillström. Sympathizers pushed sandwiches through the outer window of the cell but were soon driven away.

When there was no more room to house more of the arrested Wobblies, the deputized citizens simply started dragging men out of jail and beating them. They would herd these men—or if the men were unconscious, throw them—into wagons and haul them out of town, telling them that if they came back it would be even worse for them. They came back.

Louhi watched the whole affair somewhat philosophically, noting that when you have power, you don't want anything to change, and when you're powerless, you can't change anything. She stopped her philosophical musing when Belle Sorenson, the manager of Tannika House, came to her with declining sales figures. Louhi sent for Drummond.

"Goddamnit, Al, it's plain bad for business. Three-quarters of this town is male and if my arithmetic is still good that makes at least half of the men single. But now three-quarters of *them* are out there singing songs and making sandwiches for a bunch of communist rabble-rousing antibusiness . . ." She controlled her temper. "No one's screwing. Bar receipts are in the shit house. They're all high and mighty about One Big Union and solidarity with these communist . . ." She caught herself. "Al, you need to carry two arguments to the city council. First, the city is acting illegally. Don't think these Wobblies can't bring in some highfalutin do-gooder lawyers to take the city to court. And the city will lose. It screwed the Wobblies out of their right to have a meeting place. That's unconstitutional. Then the city screwed them again by making ordinances about where they can gather and give speeches on the streets. That's also unconstitutional."

"OK," Al said, a little bemused. "Why this sudden concern for the Bill of Rights?"

"Because those stupid knuckleheads in the city council, and that includes you, don't see that if we double these workers' wages, we double our profits. Where in hell are eight or ten thousand single men going to spend that extra money? They sure as hell aren't buying ency- clopedias and Bibles."

Aino spent Christmas in jail.

Matti and Kyllikki, with considerable trepidation, went to spend Christmas in Astoria.

It had taken Kyllikki's mother several months to get her father to agree to let "that goddamned Koski" into the house. Matti had stood his ground firmly, saying, "He can come to my house if he wants."

The women saw it as just another bump in the road of managing their men for their own good and went to work on it with relish. Kyllikki getting pregnant in early June had lent considerable strength to their arguments for making peace. Still, two stubborn proud men, she mused to herself, watching her husband's face as he looked at the river, and she wouldn't for a moment wish them to be any other way. It was like choosing to ride a spirited horse. You knew what you were in for before you got into the saddle, but you still wanted to ride. She smiled and put her hand on her increasingly round tummy. She hoped it was a girl, someone to talk with when she was doing the chores, Matti being gone from dark to dark. Matti wanted a boy, someone to go logging with. She worried about Matti constantly. Someone died in Chinook and Clatsop Counties nearly every other week fishing or logging. And she couldn't imagine a son going logging. It really wasn't inconsistent. Her job was protecting her children. His job was protecting her—and that included providing.

"Why do you keep smiling?" Matti asked.

"Just thinking about our baby."

Matti did not respond.

"What's on your mind?" she prompted.

"I was just thinking maybe I could bid on some forty-year-old second growth. Pilings are being used building docks, and that seining ground out to the west of us must have one hundred pilings. Second-growth trees might be just the right size. Way easier logging. There's also government money in pilings: public docks, bridges."

"Do you ever stop thinking about logging?"

"In bed," he answered.

"That had better not be because you're asleep."

She saw his pleasure in his eyes.

When they reached her house—as she still thought of it—she noticed that her mother had put a beautiful wreath on the door. She hesitated to knock. Even she was nervous. One spirited horse she could manage. Two, with one of them still clinging to the notion that both mares belonged to him, she wasn't so sure about.

Her mother opened the door. She could see her father through the door of the living room, looking at the river. The foyer had been garlanded with fir boughs and holly. When they walked into the living room, she let out a little squeak and clapped her hands, beaming at her mother and the beautiful tree. It had all the old familiar ornaments in the little crèche beneath it that she had known all her life. Unlit candles were attached to its branches, waiting to be turned into light. "Oh, Mother, it's beautiful."

Her mother beamed. Then Kyllikki gave her father a hug and stood back. He was stiff as a fence post and sunk in deep.

He didn't offer his hand to Matti. Matti stood there saying nothing.

Her mother began bustling around, getting her and Matti seated, asking about coffee. Her father had settled into his usual chair.

Her mother brought coffee in silence.

Well, Kyllikki thought, time for some gentle heels to the flanks. "Isä, I'm sorry we ran off." She looked over at Matti, smiling. "Aren't we, Matti?" There was not a sound from Matti. Damn him he could be stubborn and after they had talked about it and agreed. She didn't want to use spurs. "Matti," she said quietly.

Matti put his coffee on the end table by his chair. "We're sorry."

She allowed herself a moment of triumph, then took a breath. "But we wouldn't have had to if you hadn't been trying to do everything you could to stop us."

Her father put his coffee cup down. So far, they were still both sitting. Her heart rate was picking up. This couldn't be good for the baby. Oh dear, now what?

Her mother broke in. "We want to apologize for that, don't we, Emil?"

Good old Mom. She had just reined Daddy around to face a united front. One thing her father never did was disagree with her mother in public.

"Matti," her mother said, "You're going to be the father of our grandchild." Her mother looked right at her father then. She was leaning over the horse's neck and using the crop on both flanks. Here we go. "Emil, you apologize for sending those thugs."

"I did no such thing."

"Emil."

"I only did it because I wanted so much more for you," he said to Kyllikki.

Oh, dear, she just got put back in the saddle. "I know, Daddy. I know."

He looked around, anything to avoid looking at a person. "I only wanted them to rough him up. Discourage him. They didn't have any weapons and he nearly killed one of them."

Matti stood up. "You don't call a goddamned baseball bat a weapon?" he said way too evenly.

"Matti, please sit down," Kyllikki said.

Matti walked over to the window instead.

"I don't want some killer in the family," her father said.

Kyllikki stood up abruptly. "No. Neither do I," she said. "He's no killer. It was three to one and they had baseball bats."

Her father now stood up saying, "He could've run."

Matti turned around. There was cold fury in his eyes. Oh, God, his sisu was up and so was her father's. She glanced at her mother with a pleading look.

Hilda Saari placed herself between Matti and her husband. "Don't either of you move or say a word." Then, to Kyllikki's horror, her mother left the room.

All three stood, silent. She felt her heart hammering.

Then her mother returned. She held a puukko that Kyllikki had never seen before out in front of her and walked slowly over to her father. Whatever she was saying to him, she was saying it without words. They were just looking at each other.

"You've kept that?" he asked. "All these years?"

She nodded slowly.

She watched some struggle play itself out on her father's face. Then it softened. "Go put it away," he said quietly. Her mother looked at him with love, nodded, and left the room. He was still struggling with something when she returned.

"Why don't we all sit down," Hilda said.

"No," her father said. He straightened and addressed Matti. "I'm glad you didn't run. I wouldn't have either." He paused. "Didn't."

Kyllikki looked at him. She knew this was all he was ever going to say about whatever it was.

Then he smiled and reached out his hand to Matti. "But that puukko of yours cost me one hundred dollars to pay the hospital bill, another fifty dollars each, and one hundred dollars for the man you nearly killed."

Matti shook his hand. "I shouldn't have sat outside your house eating that picnic," he said. "It was childish."

Something passed between them. Kyllikki didn't know what exactly, but it was something like a secret handshake. Matti; seeing that knife; her father saying, "Didn't." It was all done without explicit words, but suddenly it was as if they were on the same team.

Both men sat down. It was over. They started talking about lumber prices and the growth prospects of Astoria and the lower Columbia region. She looked down at the promise of the new child. She had to laugh at herself. She had a long way to go before she could ride like her mother.

Reder Logging shut down at Christmas because of snow and mud and Jouka visited Aino in the Nordland jail on Boxing Day. He brought an orange and some pulla that Lempi had baked for her. He was subdued. He said he'd had Christmas dinner at Ilmahenki, but Matti and Kyllikki had gone to Astoria for Christmas with the Saaris. After struggling for an hour to make conversation, he left.

Aino spent twelve more days in jail, each day a battle against memories. She held on, sustained by the righteousness of her cause and the support of so many comrades in jail with her.

Ashamed of the way the city was handling the situation, many citizens started to pressure the city council to back off. Drummond rallied business owners who were seeing sharp decreases in sales. They put additional pressure on the council. When the city treasurer pointed out the costs of jailing so many people, the councilors crumbled. On January 7, 1912, they repealed the ordinance banning speech and assembly and even paid some money to the IWW for shutting down its hall.

It was a complete triumph.

Aino, however, returned to a family that was embarrassed and an unhappy husband. Jouka, who had always supported the cause, didn't make a scene. He just said, "Why can't you be a normal wife?" and then came back long after dark on Sunday, smelling of whiskey.

Aino vowed to focus on the marriage.

7

Focusing on the marriage did not mean giving up reading the *Industrial Worker*, the IWW's newspaper. In March, Aino read that on January 1, 1912, while she was in jail, twenty-five thousand women in Lawrence, Massachusetts, went on strike against the American Woolen Company under IWW leadership. They were followed by eighteen thousand textile workers in Lowell. The state legislature had passed a law reducing the workweek from fifty-six hours to fifty-four hours and the mill owners retaliated by lowering wages to make up for the lost production. The state militia was called out. The usual mass arrests and beatings soon followed.

When the IWW attempted to transfer the children of the striking workers to sympathetic homes in Philadelphia, both the mothers and the children were assaulted and beaten to stop the evacuation. One of the beaten women miscarried. When Aino read that, she sat on the edge of the bed, her head bowed down in her hands, for nearly ten minutes. Slowly the sorrow for the woman and the lost baby turned to anger and resolve. She took out her anger on the woodpile.

The news continued to be grim. The striking women in Lowell had refused to pay fines levied on them by the courts, many going to jail with babies in their arms. The brutality brought national attention and a Senate investigation.

Aino, keeping to her vow to focus on Jouka and the marriage, read the news, simmering, but she stayed home. This combined with Jouka's natural good nature had things back on an even keel.

There was good news in March. On Thursday, March 14, the American Woolen Company settled. On that same Thursday, hundreds of sawmill workers went on strike in Nordland, asking for a 25 percent wage increase to two dollars and fifty cents per day. Aino knew that this was at least in part because of her efforts to sign up members. She wanted desperately to be there, but Matti and Kyllikki's baby was due any day. She was stewing, torn between her own marriage, Kyllikki's delivery, and just packing up and leaving for Nordland, when the dreaded constant tooting, signaling an accident, cut through the air of Camp Three. Women came out of their front doors, some holding small children or babies, others drying their hands on their aprons. The constant clatter of the logging operations ceased. Silence.

It was nearly four, the tenth hour of work, when fatigue dulls judgment and reflexes, breeds carelessness and inattention to detail. This is the most likely time for the choker bell to come out of its socket and several tons of bucking logs to go free from the main line and slam against a stump—or a man. This is also when it is most likely a cable isn't slackened soon enough or a small fray in the cable goes unnoticed and within minutes causes a cascade of breaking wire, until the line snaps and hundreds of pounds of steel crack through the sky like a bullwhip, its flying tail lashing through brush, cutting small trees—or a man.

Aino saw Lempi standing at the door of her new shack across the rail line and about a hundred yards toward the bay side. Lempi gave a tentative wave and Aino waved back. After another five minutes came the toot of the steam whistle and the operation started up again, slowly gaining speed until once more the distant clatter, shouts, whistles, and crash of falling trees and giant logs bucking their way to the landing filled the evening air. The women went inside, preparing dinner, each wondering if her husband would be the one not to come home.

At quitting time, Aino watched the body coming to camp on top of the wood box just behind the cab. Jouka was in the cab and Aino sighed with relief. The train stopped. Women gathered below the load as two loggers dragged the body off the engine, trying to achieve some sort of solemnity as they laid it on the ground.

It was Huttula. His head was a bloody pulp, his face nearly unrecognizable, the result of a flying cable. The women turned in relief and pity as Lempi screamed and went to her knees cradling Huttula's mutilated head.

Aino ran to squat down beside her. Lempi was kissing Huttula's face. She turned to look at Aino. Smearing the blood on her hands over her own face, she looked up at the gray sky and howled like a wounded animal.

That cry ended any doubt in Aino's mind about leaving home. She told this to Jouka bluntly, her anger barely under control. He understood. To fight her would feel petty and selfish, but he wished it were otherwise.

Jouka helped sell Huttula's tools and Aino helped Lempi pack. Lempi would not go back to the henhouse. Nor could she afford the rent for the shack, fifty cents a day. Finished with the packing, Aino sat with Lempi on the stoop of the empty shack under a somber April sky and waited for Jouka to come by with the train. When he arrived with a full load of logs, he hopped from the cab and walked along the line to where Lempi and Aino stood with Lempi's bag. He took it without a word and started back to the engine.

Aino walked silently with Lempi, following Jouka. He tossed the valise into the arms of his firemen and waited for the two women.

Lempi, Aino, and Kyllikki decided Lempi's best bet was Astoria. The canneries hired women to pack salmon, paying them by the can. The work involved extremely sharp knives in the hands of women driven to pack as many cans a day as they were physically able to. If a woman was fast enough, she could earn fifty to seventy-five cents a day, and she was sure to make at least forty-five cents if her legs held out and she wasn't too inept with a knife. Chinamen previously did the work, but they had been driven from town because they worked for even lower wages than the women and, besides that, were dirty, smoked opium, and associated with criminal tongs called Provident Societies that kidnapped white girls and sold them into slavery.

Aino looked into her old friend's sad blue eyes. "Good luck to you, Lempi. I'll come see you."

"Sure. Astoria's not so far."

Neither said anything else. Then they heard Jouka clearing water from the cylinder cocks. "I guess Jouka has to get the load down to tidewater," Lempi said with a wan smile.

"Yoh."

"Aino?"

"What?"

"I'm two months pregnant."

Aino was in a frenzy of indecision over whether to go to Nordland to help with the strike, or stay to help deliver Kyllikki's baby, which was due imminently. Kyllikki and the baby came through, solving the problem. A girl, Suvi, was born on March 17, 1912. The birth was normal—terrifying, painful, long, and filled with joy. Aino saw Kyllikki through it with aplomb and left for Nordland the next day to throw herself into recruiting and organizing the wives to distribute food and medicine.

The strike widened to neighboring towns. Having seen the tactic of deputizing solid citizens turn ugly, the mayor of Nordland instead deputized city employees, ordering them to break up the strike, figuring they'd do as they were told. Most employees quit, leaving the city stranded, with the opposite outcome from what the mayor wanted. Angry citizens formed a citizens committee. They trashed the IWW hall and arrested strikers at random, taking them into the forest and clubbing them senseless. Aino and the other women made bandages, collected iodine, and tended to the wounded who were lodged with local strikers. The citizens committee upped the pressure by forcing 150 strikers into boxcars to deport them, injuring scores more in the melee. Sympathetic railroad workers intervened, refusing to move the deported workers, unless they were Finns and Greeks, who had a reputation for being more radical than other ethnic groups. After that, the vigilantes focused on "non-Americans," deporting several hundred, many split from their families. When she was accosted, Aino barely escaped, cursing them soundly in Swedish.

Finally, the pain on both sides began to tell and an agreement was made. The mill owners raised wages to two dollars and twenty-five cents per day and promised to give preference in hiring and pay to native-born Americans. Aino was shaken by the way the American-born workers had turned on the Finns, convincing her more than ever of the need for solid funding for strikes. She committed herself to organizing, focusing on increasing membership and the consequent cash flow.

The people at Camp Three were mostly sympathetic to the cause of the IWW, but they were also increasingly sympathetic to Jouka, who had clearly been abandoned by his wife.

Aino traveled a lot that spring, her reputation for successful recruiting growing along with the IWW's growing membership. Just by being a healthy woman she attracted more potential members than any male recruiter did, and once she had them in front of her, the combination of her quick wit, ability to explain the workingman's situation, and passion won many over. Portland headquarters could now pay for train and boat tickets. Coming back from one of her trips by train, she set out to find Lempi. She located her in a women's boardinghouse. They talked until long after dark, a single candle lighting Lempi's small room. Aino slept next to her that night, both giggling occasionally about stories from the old days.

There was a sad undercurrent. Lempi was alone in a tiny room without a child. Aino suspected she had gotten an abortion. Aino never asked her.

8

On Sunday, March 31, Matti and Kyllikki traveled to Astoria to show her parents Suvi, with an additional item on the agenda.

"Go on, tell him," Kyllikki said to Matti, rocking Suvi gently in her arms.

Matti turned to her father. "If there's war in Europe, everyone knows lumber prices will go up. But there's something less obvious. Airplanes are starting to be used for artillery spotting and reconnaissance. Someone's going to use other airplanes to shoot them down. Then the other side's going to want to build airplanes to shoot those airplanes down." He paused, letting her father catch on to the implications. When Emil Saari nodded, Matti went on. "They're all made from spruce."

"Yoh," her father said evenly.

"I need a loan for a new yarder. It would double our speed getting logs to the landing. With that rusted tin-can yarder I've got now, we'll stay a two-bit gyppo outfit no matter how high the prices."

"But that wood will aid our enemies," Hilda Saari broke in. "Germany's our only hope to break free of Russia."

"I'm a logger, Mrs. Saari, not a politician."

"But you're a Finn!"

"I'm an American," he replied.

"Your father gave his life for Finnish independence!"

"Please," Kyllikki said. "We're talking business here." It was at this moment that one of her breasts started leaking.

"But the business will hurt Finland!" her mother cried, looking to her husband for help.

Emil Saari took a deep breath. "If America sides with Russia, we side with Russia."

"If that means we're nothing but money-grubbers, then by God I—"

"Hilda." She stopped talking. "All Finland ever did for us," Emil said, "was freeze us in the winter, starve us in the summer, and draft our boys in the spring and fall."

"The Russians drafted our boys." She walked to the kitchen muttering, "Business, business, business."

"She's a patriot," Emil said.

"A Finnish patriot," Kyllikki said.

"Maybe Aino has it right," Matti said. "Patriotism is a con job. I don't care if the lumber goes to the English or the Germans. Patriotism just cuts the market in half."

"Yes," Kyllikki said. "But without that 'con job' there'd be no war and no rise in spruce prices."

Both Mr. Saari and Matti looked at her, momentarily stopped.

"Patriotism exists," Matti said. He turned to Emil Saari. "We can make money on spruce."

"But we'll be making profits from war," Kyllikki said.

Matti turned to Kyllikki. "What governments do is none of my business, which means none of *our* business."

Kyllikki made no reply.

Matti and Emil Saari agreed to a loan of five thousand dollars, four for the yarder and associated equipment, another thousand for working capital. Emil had only part of it, but he agreed to talk to Jamison, the manager of the Astoria branch of the First National Bank of Oregon. He put it in writing. Matti signed and looked at Kyllikki with triumph in his eyes. She felt a sudden apprehension. She gave Matti an encouraging smile despite her misgivings. She'd never take a risk like the one he was taking. That's one reason she married him.

*   *   *

Three days later, Matti was in Nordland with its stench of smoke from a dozen mills, garbage floating around the docks, tidal flats gone to cesspools, and half-rotted sawdust paving the streets. Rauha's town. More important, Rauha's mother's town.

He took a deep breath, sighed, and made his way to Louhi's office, which was across from the Bank of Nordland, upstairs in a two-story wood building with a dry goods store and a butcher shop on the ground floor. When she opened the door after his knock, her face was impassive, so he didn't know if she was happy to see him or not.

"I'm in town to bid on a logging job. I thought I'd say hello."

Louhi motioned him to a chair. He shut the door and sat down, balancing his new fedora on his knee.

"Coming up in the world," she said. "Businessman's fedora, a coat that fits, and wanting to bid. Congratulations. You've arrived. How is Rauha?"

"She's fine. She wanted me to say hello."

"And so, you're doing that for her?"

"No."

It was no mystery where Rauha's ice came from.

"I heard you got married."

"Yoh."

"A sweet little thing from Astoria."

"Yoh."

Louhi laughed. She went to a sideboard. "You drink?"

"Sometimes. Not much."

"Wastes money?"

"Yoh."

She opened a bottle of rye and poured two glasses. Handing one to Matti she said, "This one is on me, so drink up."

He looked at her, looked at the glass, raised it in a toast to her, and said, "Kippis." He emptied it with one gulp. She matched him and asked if he wanted another. "No, thank you," he said.

"Even if it's free?"

"Nothing's free."

She laughed again, took his glass, stoppered the bottle, and then sat back down at her desk. "You know, Matti Koski, I might even come to like you someday."

At this, he laughed.

"So, Rauha could have written a letter. What do you want?" Her face was polite but revealed nothing. What a poker player she must be.

"I'm bidding on a contract on a section of land above Grays Bay. It's owned by Al Drummond. Rauha says you know him."

Now she really laughed, surprising him. "Yes. Intimately," she said, her previously careful and measured eyes twinkling. "He's a son of a bitch. Watch out."

"Son of a bitch, how?"

"Well, first you'd better make sure he's actually got the title. People have logged for Al Drummond before and found themselves sued over cutting someone else's timber."

"Oh."

"Just check the title on your way back through Willapa. He probably got it from someone like Weyerhaeuser."

"Where did they get it?"

"Probably from the Northern Pacific, which bribed members of Congress to give it to them for free. The goddamned government gave the railroads a slice of land forty miles wide clear across America and all they did was slip some money into a few politicians' pockets."

"He doesn't seem like much of a friend. You call him a son of a bitch."

She laughed. "Hell, Matti, I like sons of bitches"

Louhi wrote an introduction note to Drummond and two less intimate friends in the timber business. Matti wasted no time meeting them and by late afternoon he'd learned the structure of the mill ownership in western Washington, the state of the market, and that Reder had been in town two days earlier, bidding on the same Drummond acreage.

When Matti was ushered into Drummond's office, Drummond offered him a cigar. Pulling on his own cigar until it was glowing,

Drummond shook the match out and threw it to the floor. This shocked Matti as much as anything he'd seen in Nordland.

"Bank gets cleaned every night. Avoids having to empty ashtrays," Drummond said. Then before Matti could speak, he said, "Your brother married Louhi's daughter."

"Yes."

"God help him."

"Rauha's OK," Matti replied carefully.

"Don't mean to bad-mouth your sister-in-law, but she can be a mean little bitch."

"I came here to bid on a logging contract."

"Strictly business. OK." He leaned back and blew smoke toward the ceiling. "What's your offer?"

Matti gave him a price. Drummond rejected it. Matti gave him a lower price. Drummond rejected that, too.

"If you want this job, Koski, you're going to have to beat John Reder."

"I can beat any price Reder gave."

"Can? Without knowing the price? Without laying track?"

"I can beat Reder."

Drummond wrote a number on a piece of paper and handed it to Matti. "Beat this by a nickel a thousand board feet and you got the job, but with two provisos."

Matti knew it was unethical to undercut Reder without giving Reder a chance to amend his bid. He took the paper. It was possible that Drummond was lying about Reder's bid, but then, knowing Reder Logging Matti didn't find the bid unreasonable.

"You said two provisos."

"Lumber prices are going through the roof on nothing but war speculation. Everyone's going to get rich on the misery. I think so, but not for a couple of years and certainly not by the end of August. This bubble will burst, like all of them. I want my timber delivered to a mill of my choice by September thirtieth, or I don't pay you."

"What about paying me for the logs I do deliver?"

Drummond drew in on the cigar and let the smoke out. He watched Matti through it, smiling. "Well, Mr. Koski, I can make a deal like that with John Reder. And for just a nickel more a thousand board feet, I take considerably less risk. Reder's proved himself many times and he can do railroad logging. You, on the other hand, have proved you can log your brother's land and do a two-bit, one-crew job on the Klawachuck for the owner of a general store."

"The creeks will still be low at the end of September. I won't be able to float the logs to tidewater. You'll have all your logs by the fifteenth of November."

"Not good enough."

Matti hesitated only a moment. "OK, October thirty-first." Seeing Drummond's smug face was enough alone to make Matti promise anything.

"Agreed."

"The second proviso?" Matti asked.

"Given you and I just cheated on John Reder's bid, I'm assuming you're one of us."

"What do you mean?"

"You know, *business*men."

The way Drummond said "business" put Matti on alert. He smelled money. He'd also lost his temper and made a bid he wasn't sure he could deliver on. "I'm listening."

"My property and Reder's adjoin for about a mile. A mile will border twenty-six one-acre plots. We both know there's around a hundred and ten to a hundred and twenty thousand board feet per acre up there." Matti nodded. "At today's prices a mile's worth of acres will yield around twenty-eight thousand dollars." Matti did the math. That was around a year's salary for fifty loggers. "If you happen to stray over the line, say by fifty feet, move a few surveyor's marks, a little judicious cutting won't even be noticed. That would yield seven thousand dollars. I'll split that fifty-fifty." That would pay off 70 percent of the loan.

"Why wouldn't I just do that myself?"

"Because I know about it."

* * *

"Saatana," Aksel whispered, upon hearing the deal. Matti said nothing. They were standing on top of the ridge running north and south on the west side of Grays Bay. Between them and the bay were several hundred acres of old-growth Douglas fir that had thrived in open ground cleared by a large forest fire several centuries back. There were some western red cedar with a sprinkling of Sitka spruce in the bottoms and some annoying hemlock, most of which they'd have to log around because it was worthless. A strip of stumps and slash about a quarter of a mile wide hugged the shoreline. "I see why they stopped," Aksel went on.

Matti, of course, had seen the timber before he had bid the contract. Twenty years earlier an outfit had stopped logging because it became too expensive to move the logs to water. Back then, it was done with oxen, corduroy roads, sweat, and ingenuity. Timber too far from water was one reason Reder had so much money tied up in railroads. Railroad logging was way out of 200-Foot Logging's league.

The new double-drum steam yarder floated on a raft about a mile away and five hundred feet below them. The elation of winning the contract had been replaced by cold reality—and apprehension. He would never tell Aksel, or even Kyllikki, that he might have underbid the job. No, *had* underbid the job. Failure would be the end of 200-Foot Logging. He would be back to working for wages. He had his ace up his sleeve, however, the agreement with Drummond to fudge over the line. If *that* ever came out, he'd never be able to look Kyllikki in the face.

Silently, they calculated how best to get the yarder up to where it could go to work.

"Saatana," Aksel said again, speaking Finnish. "It's going to be a son of a bitch."

"Yoh," Matti answered.

"You must have had *some*thing in mind before you made the bid," Aksel said. "Sky hooks?"

Matti laughed at the old joke played on rookies, but this show would be no joke.

"You didn't mention time," Aksel said. Matti made no reply. "On the Klawachuck show we didn't have a deadline," Aksel went on. "What have we got on this one? Six months?"

"Six and a half."

"Oh. I breathe easier."

Kullervo, now a skinny teenager, nearly fifteen, arrived with the new crew of ten. Because Kullervo couldn't hear on one side, the result of one too many corrections by his mother, Matti set him building a lean-to that would serve as the kitchen and mess hall. Reder had fired two of the ragtag crew for getting drunk in Nordland and coming back four days late. Another had a serious limp and couldn't move fast enough for most logging but could fell and buck the small trees for fuel and could also be used to manhandle the logs down the creek. Three others Matti found down to their last dollar in saloons in Astoria. The remaining four—two Finns, a Swede, and a Norwegian—had never logged and couldn't speak English. If they lived through the first two weeks, Matti figured he could make loggers out of them.

A woodstove was disassembled and barged to the beach, then reassembled in the lean-to, along with a week's supply of eggs, bacon, beans, flour, potatoes, beets, carrots, canned beef and salmon, and the other ingredients needed to keep everyone fueled for the six-day work-week. It lacked only the cook, who soon arrived: Kyllikki, a knapsack on her back, filled with what she called essentials, and Suvi in a sling.

That night, Matti left them sleeping. Silently he made his way west, past where he'd already set four of the crew felling, until he reached the surveyor's mark that had been driven into the ground. It took several hours to move it fifty feet farther west, along with a second stake and the ribbons that had been tied onto tree branches. He was back before sunrise.

9

The crew soon settled in: fed by Kyllikki, coached by Aksel, and motivated by Matti, not only by example. Kyllikki was breastfeeding Suvi, who by August was robust and healthy, living in plain air, and adored by thirteen men. On August 1, 1912, Rauha provided Suvi with a boy cousin, Jorma. Aino was there to help along with Kyllikki who took on Mielikki, three and a half, and Helmi, now nearly two.

Jorma's christening was on August 11. After the service, everyone was invited to Ilmahenki for coffee.

Rauha's curtains hung straight in open windows with an occasional gentle movement from a lazy air current. Deep River flowed sparkling and well contained, rocks unseen in the spring now showing along its edges.

When the nonfamily guests left, there was an afternoon miracle. All the children went down for their naps simultaneously. Aino found herself at the kitchen table with Rauha and Kyllikki, who'd come in from the show with Matti and Suvi. The men were sitting on the river-bank, smoking and talking, suspenders off their shoulders.

"So, Aino, when's it going to be?" Rauha asked.

"When's what going to be?" Aino answered. She knew full well but had learned that playing dumb about questions she didn't want to answer gave her time to think of answers she usually didn't want to give. She glanced at Kyllikki, suddenly feeling alone, the dark one next to these two fair women. At the christening, she had noted with some pleasure that Rauha's brilliant yellow hair had turned darker.

"A baby," Rauha answered. She wasn't one to be circumspect. Then, neither was Aino.

"When we want to."

Everyone silently sipped coffee. Then Kyllikki, trying to be kind, said, "You know you can't put it off much longer."

"If there isn't some other problem," Rauha said.

"What do you mean by that?" Aino shot back.

"You know he's been seen carousing around when you're away."

"So, he drinks a little with his friends after dances. Jouka likes to have fun."

Another awkward silence.

"Maybe, you know . . ." Kyllikki offered. "If you were home more often."

"Then, what?" Aino retorted. "We would make love more often and that's what's stopping the baby?"

The sharp answer peeved Kyllikki, who was only trying to help. "You have to spend time together," she said tightly.

"We spend plenty of time together."

"So then, maybe it's something else," Rauha said, glancing at Kyllikki. "Maybe he can't, you know."

Kyllikki quickly shot back: "That's private business."

"Sure, but people are talking."

"What about?" Aino asked.

"Well," Rauha said, primly setting her cup in its saucer with both hands. "You *are* gone a lot. They wonder if maybe there's trouble."

"There's no trouble," Aino said.

Rauha gave her a come-on-I'm-no-fool look.

Aino was tired of always defending herself. It was none of anyone's damned business whether she would have a baby, whether she and Jouka were getting along, or what her absences and his late-night drinking meant. She was most tired of always being the one at fault.

"Well," she said. "I don't want to talk about it. But with my sisters . . ." She managed to get tears in her eyes. "I just don't know what to do. He comes home drunk and I try to be there ready. And, well, I hate to say this. Don't you dare say anything. But Jouka does have trouble."

Rauha looked as though she had just been fed steak. Kyllikki gave Aino a what-are-you-doing look.

"I've tried. I've really tried." She was getting into the role. "He starts off OK, but . . . Don't you dare say this to anyone, even my brothers. Promise me."

A murmur of "We promise" followed, with a nodding of heads in sympathy.

"I've heard that oysters are good," Kyllikki said.

"I think it's something in his head," Aino said. "You know that he used to go to Astoria and Nordland before we were married."

"What man didn't," Rauha said.

The men came back into the house, smelling of cigarette smoke and sweat. Shirts and Sunday coats went back on, babies were picked up by the women, and formal goodbyes were said.

As Aino and Jouka walked back to Camp Three in the evening stillness, the strip of sky above them dark blue against the nearly black green of the shadowed treetops, Jouka asked, "What were you women talking about?"

"Oh, you know, girl talk. It drives me nuts," Aino said, suddenly feeling deeply ashamed of herself, ruining her walk home in the summer twilight.

That summer had been one of the best in memory. The North Pacific High had settled into its dry season position off the coast and the line of multiple breakers shone brilliant white in the clear sky and steady northwest wind. Inland, sheltered by the coastal hills, the air lay warm and cozy in the river valleys. All along the trails and new roads around Tapiola, blackberries had changed from their hard green of June to softer and plumper red by the end of July. They now hung juicy and black, vines drooping with their weight. Women and children filled buckets and old coffee cans to the brim with them for pies or to be eaten at breakfast with cream. A few late red huckleberries winked out from the undergrowth and blue huckleberries grew in profusion in the sunlit logged-off areas. Little boys with blue-smeared faces went from farm to farm selling them for five cents a pound or hounded Higgins to stock his grocery store with them.

Until this night, Aksel had enjoyed the weather like everyone else. However, walking back to the show by himself, he felt uneasy. He wasn't hearing the usual rush of the creeks. He knew there had been less rain than usual. He didn't know why. It was because when Matti had made his deal with Al Drummond in April, El Niño had already arrived.

Keeping his counsel, Aksel said nothing until one morning in late August. He was up before dawn, the morning air cool but lacking humidity. Dew didn't even form on the steel cables or the saws. He fired the donkey's boiler. Then he waited for Matti, sitting on one of the skids, smoking, while the steam pressure rose.

When Matti arrived, Aksel threw the butt of his cigarette into the firebox. "We need to talk."

"After work," Matti said.

"Now."

Matti jumped up on the donkey and pulled on the whistle. He was ready to work. Where was everyone else? "What?" he asked.

"We've got a lot of logs to move and the creeks are going dry," Aksel said.

Matti's face darkened. Aksel knew he was forcing Matti to face what Matti already knew. "It'll rain," Matti said.

Aksel looked pointedly at the clear sky, then gestured at the large number of logs yarded in various spots. "I talked with Old Cap Carlson at Knappton. He's fished the river for years. He says that after a first summer that's drier than normal, the fall will be drier than normal, too."

"Cap says that, huh?" Matti said.

"Cap says that."

Aksel lit another cigarette, took a draw, and handed it to Matti. "If we don't get rain we won't make the deadline. You need more help."

Matti took a deep drag and handed the cigarette back to Aksel. "I'm out of money."

"And time."

"I'll get it logged."

"Will you get it moved?"

Matti was quiet, thinking. "I'll offer the crew a bonus, a big one, when we sell the logs."

"We're already working summer hours. Push these loggers any harder and they'll start making mistakes. Remember what happened when Reder started highballing?"

Matti grunted.

Aksel pressed on. "You need more loggers."

Matti sat quietly, his lips moving just slightly in and out, a sign he was thinking hard. Aksel waited. No sense in prompting a Finn.

Matti climbed to the ground. "Come with me," he said.

Matti took him downstream. "We'll build it right here," he said.

Aksel looked around. Two hills came close to the stream at this point. They had small trees on their slopes, not worth logging.

"It'll have to be plenty high to back the water all the way up to where we're logging now," Aksel said, knowing exactly what Matti had in mind.

"No higher than we can build it."

"We," Aksel said, pointedly. "*We* are on the absolute edge."

"I only need a week and enough money for five loggers." Matti looked hard and steadily at Aksel.

"No!" Aksel said. "Goddamnit, Matti. Not my savings."

"I'll give you double back."

Aksel walked over to another viewpoint. Matti joined him. Aksel was feeling the old excitement he first felt in the redwoods. Like what a poker player must feel before a high-stakes game, he thought. Double his poke and he would have his boat within a year. He also knew an additional source of labor that Matti's pride wouldn't allow him to hire.

"Double and a half," Aksel said.

"Deal." They shook hands.

That evening Aksel walked the nine miles to Ilmahenki in the twilight and then walked to Camp Three in the dark.

Ilmari showed up before dawn with an ax and a crosscut. He was soon followed by Aino, carrying a pack made from a burlap sack. It was stuffed with clothes, blankets, a few kitchen utensils, and bars of good soap. Jouka couldn't leave work. Rauha had stayed at Ilmahenki with the children to supervise the sawmill, her chore workload doubling so her husband could help his brother.

Aksel didn't know which was the more beautiful sight, Aino and Kyllikki moving confidently in the makeshift outdoor kitchen, or Ilmari methodically tearing into one of the trees that would go into the dam. His contemplation of beauty was quickly interrupted by Matti shouting orders, rearranging work, and generally being a pain in the neck. Then Matti left to hire more crew with Aksel's money.

Aksel heard his name called and turned to see Aino holding one bucket of water and another of warm coffee. On her back was a packboard with a flour sack tied on it. She set it down; asked him if he wanted coffee, water, or both; and pulled out from the sack a corned beef sandwich thick with butter and laced with black pepper and salt.

"Packing it out to you will save almost two hours of daylight working time," she said. Then she laughed. "The eight-hour day doesn't apply to the Koskis."

Aksel wondered what it would be like to have her making sandwiches for him all the time.

The work, ordinarily hard until the dam building began, became even more intense. Matti had both hired more crew and promised a bonus when the logs were delivered. The loggers stumbled to their beds in the dark. The dam, constructed of stacked logs, grew daily. Matti spent hours at night doing maintenance on the yarder and other equipment. Aino reverted back to the rhythm of the henhouse, catching only a few hours of sleep, cooking pancakes in the dark, serving them cold at breakfast. No one minded, because she also turned out hot bacon and eggs at first light. Four or five times in the day, Aksel would hear her voice, turn, and see her standing there with coffee and water, glasses on, her hair piled above her sweating forehead.

On Saturday evenings Jouka showed up. The last weeks of September, the moon was waxing toward full and directly overhead around midnight, so he worked nearly the whole night and all day Sunday.

Rauha showed up with the children, and production in the kitchen went into high gear. The men were like boilers, the women stuffing them with food and water. The work never slackened. Aksel felt they had an intense joyous madness in the way they pushed themselves to see if it could be done. No one thought about wages.

The last tree was felled nine days before the deadline and hauled down to the reservoir, now a mile long and in places two hundred yards across. It was packed with floating logs. Aksel and Matti walked the creek between the dam and the bay, blasting potential obstacles with dynamite.

On October 25, everyone stood on the small hillside above the splash dam. Aksel and Matti had rigged dynamite in the dam's center. Matti offered Aksel the plunger, but Aksel offered it back. Matti looked at the crowd. "Kyllikki," he shouted.

"No," she shouted back. "I've got Suvi."

"Come on," he pleaded.

The loggers started chanting Kyllikki's name. Her face flushed, she turned and held out her hand to Aino. "It'll be like launching a ship."

Aino laughed. "No champagne from Matti."

They both made their way to the detonator. Suvi on her hip, Kyllikki knelt next to Aino. She put her right hand on the plunger and Aino joined her with her left.

"Be sure to duck," Aksel said quietly.

Aino whispered, "One, two, three," and they both shoved down on the plunger.

There was a brief muffled sound, and the dam seemed to bulge outward and upward for just a split second. Then logs and pieces of logs rose into the air with a shattering roar. Water from the reservoir pushed through the center of the dam, spilling down its face. Then, the whole dam gave way. The man-made flash flood hurtled down the nearly dry streambed and with it came tons and tons of logs. The ground trembled.

The water and logs together scoured the sides of the creek to bedrock. Small trees were ripped from the banks. The ground vibrated. Some of the crew had already been stationed alongside the streambed and now all those watching the blowing of the dam ran to help, carrying pike poles and peaveys. Logs jammed. Men jumped, balanced, lost their balance, were pulled to safety, but kept breaking up developing jams. The first logs reached Grays Bay, their momentum taking them majestically away from shore, to be gathered later into booms for towing.

On October 30, the last log was manhandled down the now slick flume that had once been the original creek and was added to the huge boom linked to a waiting tug.

Matti and Aksel rode the boom all the way to the mill, smoking and laughing. They wanted to be there when the logs were graded and scaled and to argue against any decision to cull one. Mill owners were notoriously hard on loggers when it came to grading and scaling.

Matti sent the tallies by mail to Drummond, along with the code for what had been taken from Reder. Two weeks later, a letter came back saying Drummond didn't have the money, but he was good for it—trust him.

10

Kyllikki was watching Matti pack his good shoes and clothes. "You promised me you'd leave the puukko at home."

"Except for work," he replied. "This is work."

"No," she said in English—emphatically.

Matti walked over to the kitchen sink, looked out the small window, then whirled around and savagely kicked the kindling pile next to the stove, scattering it against the wall.

"The goddamn son of a bitch." He grabbed the flatiron sitting on the stove top and hurled it, putting a deep dent in the bead-board wall.

That made her mad. He was acting like a child. Then she caught herself; he was acting like a man whose family was endangered and who was powerless to do anything about it.

Matti had gone back to staring out of the window.

"Take Aksel. He's more levelheaded and his English is better than yours. The puukko stays here."

"Aino is right," Matti muttered. He looked over his shoulder at her. "In this country, you steal five dollars and you go to jail. You steal a railroad and you go to Congress."

"She didn't make that up."

Suvi started crying. Kyllikki picked her up, shushing her gently, and walked over to Matti. "Daddy wants to hold you," she said, handing her to Matti. "Don't you, Daddy?" He took Suvi in that awkward way men have, as though they've been handed something beyond price and made of matchsticks. She watched his mood disappear, as she knew it would. Snuggling up to him, Suvi between them, she said, "We'll get through it."

He looked at her. "Yoh," he said softly.

Matti and Aksel were ushered into Drummond's office by his secretary. He greeted them like old friends he hadn't seen for years. "Can I offer you a drink?"

"Ei," Matti said. It came out like the warning growl of an aroused German shepherd.

"He means, 'No thank you,'" Aksel said quietly in English.

"Ah, yes. Well, coffee then?" He didn't wait for an answer but walked to the door. Leaning out, he called to the woman who escorted them in. "Hey, Kate, how about some of that coffee Bill Brewer dropped off?" He turned back to Matti and Aksel. "Cream? Sugar?"

"Black," Aksel said.

Drummond leaned out the door again and called out: "Black."

He sat behind his desk again. "So, I'm guessing you boys are here about the money."

"Our money," Aksel said.

"Sure, sure. Of course, it is." Kate came through the door with the coffee. She gave a slight nod of her head to Drummond as she served them. "Thank you, Kate," Drummond said, not looking at her. Aksel gave Matti a be-careful look. "But, surely, you boys understand businesses often experience cash problems," Drummond was going on. "Of course, it's your money. We just have to be a little patient is all."

Matti looked at Aksel. He understood the English perfectly well but wanted the time to think and cool down while Aksel translated, adding in Finnish: "Keep your temper."

He turned to Drummond. "We want our money, now. We're having cash problems of our own."

"Of course," Drummond said. "That's why we have banks. I tell you what, we could open a line of credit, tide you over until we get this little situation solved."

"If you have money for the loan, why not for the logs?" Aksel asked.

"You know the bank's money isn't *my* money. It belongs to our depositors." He paused, looking for some reaction. There was none. The two faces were masks, devoid of any signals. It unnerved him slightly. "You just put up a little collateral. I don't know. Maybe equipment. And the money is yours."

"Why you not borrowing money from depositors and paying us money you owing us?" Matti broke in, unable to constrain himself any longer.

"Well, come now, Mr. Koski. That's a bit unseemly." Drummond gave a chuckle. "I mean, the president of his own bank borrowing for one of his businesses. There are rules of ethics about things like that."

Matti stood and pounded his fist on Drummond's desk, making his coffee cup jump along with pencils and framed photographs. Aksel rose with him, putting his hand on Matti's wrist. Matti tossed Aksel's hand aside.

"I want my money now."

"Or?" Drummond said coolly. "We'll go to court? It'd be here in Nordland. It's what's called legal venue." He smiled. "Or maybe word would get out that some Finnish gyppo logged nearly a mile-long strip of John Reder's timber."

Aksel visibly jerked.

"And you go to jail with me," Matti said.

"Oh," Drummond said, his face mocking. "How was I to know the logs were stolen timber?"

Just then the door opened and Drummond's secretary poked her head in. "Chief Brewer to see you, sir."

Brewer and another police officer walked through the door. "Mr. Drummond," Brewer said. He looked at Matti and Aksel. "They're not giving you any trouble, are they?"

"No, no. Of course, not." Drummond leaned back in his chair. "It wouldn't cross their minds."

At dinner the next Sunday, Aino let Matti have it. "You see now, big businessman? You see where laws and government get you in a capitalist system?"

"Aino," Kyllikki said.

"Oh, sure. The big money from Astoria speaks."

"Aino," Matti growled.

"You're all damned fools. All you want to do is get into the pig trough with the other pigs."

"Aino!" Ilmari slapped the table. She stopped. "It's not about capitalism or socialism," Ilmari went on evenly. "Mr. Drummond is a bad man. Both systems have bad men."

"No, they don't." She jabbed her finger at Ilmari. "The capitalists are in it for themselves. Socialists are in it for other people. They can't be bad."

"Oh, *Aino*," Matti said.

"Oh Aino, what?" she shot back.

"Don't be a fool."

"Like the fool that bit off more than he can swallow, worked us all for nothing, owes the bank and his wife's father years of wages and his partner's fishing boat money?"

"You're all fools," Rauha said quietly. They all looked at her. "Contracts. The law. Socialism. The good of the people. Good men. Bad men." She harrumphed. "It's all foolish talk to make you believe you are more powerful than you really are. The people with the real power give us all this socialist, capitalist, legal, moral nonsense while they do what they want."

"But I have a contract," Matti said.

"I have a contract," she mimicked him. She shook her head. "A contract in the hands of someone who can't afford a lawyer is toilet paper."

Matti shoved his chair back and went outside, slamming the door.

"You're being a little hard on him," Kyllikki said.

"Reality is hard on everyone," Rauha answered.

That night Rauha wrote a letter to her mother explaining what 200-Foot Logging owed Sampo Manufacturing for her and Ilmari's direct labor at the show, for all the blacksmithing done without payment; what Drummond owed 200-Foot Logging; and what all that meant in total dollars for the major shareholder of Sampo Manufacturing.

Two weeks later, a letter arrived at Higgins's store. Higgins had secured the position of postmaster for Tapiola, eliminating the need to go to Knappton for the mail. The envelope contained a check for the full amount from some company none of them had ever heard of, but it was signed by Al Drummond. Matti took the check to Astoria where he deposited it into the account with First National Bank of Oregon. Ten days later, the check cleared. Christmas of 1912 was a good one for the Koskis.

11

Times were also good for the IWW. The efforts of hundreds of organizers like Aino were paying off. Membership was growing, as were the union's influence and its geographic reach. In January 1913, Hillström was in Mexico to help organize the revolution and IWW halls were springing up there. The IWW was organizing textile workers in the East, mostly women and immigrants. In January alone, the IWW organized sixteen strikes, ranging from cannery workers in California to lumbermen in Louisiana to hotel waiters in New York City. Aino was sent to the Willamette Valley to help the families of strikers in ten logging camps. They wanted shorter hours without lowering wages, an end to mandatory overtime, and Sundays off. Owners, helped by the railroads, retaliated by shipping in scabs by the carload. The strikes failed, but a groundswell of support for the IWW continued to grow.

In February, 25,000 textile workers in New Jersey struck, demanding an eight-hour day, an end to working multiple looms, and age restrictions on child labor; 1,850 strikers were arrested and jailed. That same month 400 rail workers struck against the Pennsylvania Railroad, asking for a raise from a dollar seventy-five to two dollars and ten cents per day for a ten-hour day.

In April, sawmill workers struck in Pilchuck, Washington, asking for the right to organize, sanitary bunkhouses, decent food, and fire escapes. Aino spent three days there, organizing the food and using the strike to gain membership.

In May, sawmills in Marshfield, Oregon, went on strike. When loggers sympathetic to the IWW were fired, IWW Local 435 in Coos

Bay went on strike in sympathy. When the IWW in Portland asked for her help, Aino refused. She'd stretched Jouka to his limit.

In June, however, because of her experience with loggers and lumbermen, union leaders in Portland implored her to help with recruiting in Centralia, Washington, a mill town in the middle of timber country. The IWW was building a new hall there, three blocks from the train station.

She dreaded bringing the trip up with Jouka. She knew she would be gone at least three or four weeks. When she finally got up her nerve to tell him, his reaction frightened her. He didn't seem to care.

When Aino got off the train in Centralia, however, all feelings of guilt vanished. That night was to be the grand opening of the new hall, and an itinerant logger told her that Hillström was going to be there.

Upon reaching the hall, she set down her valise, shook the hem of her dress to get the dirt off, carefully put her glasses in a case, and tucked the case into a side pocket of the valise. Just outside the new hall, she greeted several comrades from the Nordland free-speech fight. Her people. She felt good—at home. She walked inside, adjusting her eyes to the dark. A general murmur in the hall died down. Women in the logging and mining camps were rare and women Wobblies even rarer. She hated it when everyone looked at her, but she also didn't like it when no one noticed her.

A man who'd been talking to a small group came toward her. She smiled, remembering not to squint, wondering if she knew him.

"The Elizabeth Gurley Flynn of Chinook County," the man announced. It was Hillström. He kissed her hand ironically. "Our own Finnish rebel girl." Two years earlier, in 1911, Hillström had written a popular song about Flynn called "The Rebel Girl."

She felt more than saw the twinkle of humor in his eyes. "If I could speak like her," she said, "I'd be in Chicago not Camp Three."

"Have you ever heard her speak?"

"No."

"Then how do you know you can't speak like her?"

She knew it was flattery, but she still felt as if she'd just been asked to dance—and she felt like dancing.

"Come on," he said, taking her hand. "Let me introduce you around."

She grabbed the valise and followed his lead. She didn't like how Hillström didn't even ask if she wanted to be introduced. But when he began introducing her in English, she liked it.

The opening ceremonies went reasonably well. After five or six speeches, Hillström got them singing and laughing at his clever parodies. Nervous policemen stood silently at the back of the crowd.

After the last song, Hillström gave an impassioned and, at the same time, humorous speech about how important it was for all working people to join the One Big Union and finally gain the power to end the constant pitting of immigrants against immigrants, craftsmen against laborers, man against man that the capitalists employed to keep them in poverty and under control. Aino could see he connected with the crowd by the nods and occasional murmurs of agreement. It excited her to know Hillström. She wanted everyone to know he was her friend.

"And I want to introduce you all to Aino Kaukonen, our own little Finnish Elizabeth Gurley Flynn from Chinook County who led our strike against Reder Logging. She's been organizing loggers and mill workers from the Willamette Valley to Nordland. And I must add," he said, letting them in on a secret, "an absolutely delightful person to share a cell with."

The crowd laughed. Heads turned to look at her. She felt herself flushing. She wished he'd stopped short of the crack about sharing a cell.

Wives had set up coffee and a potluck dinner. Many of the women introduced themselves to Aino, seemingly making polite small talk. They'd ask questions, however, some that went all the way back to the failed strikes of 1907, over five years earlier, and the free-speech fights in Nordland. Almost all made vague references to Joseph Hillström. She realized they were trying to ascertain her relationship to him. Many Wobblies said that relationships should be free and the business only of those involved, but she knew most—especially the women—didn't believe it. She understood. There was theory, and then there was practice—the talking of the mind and the feeling of the heart.

With people heading home, Hillström came quietly beside her and said in a low voice, "You want to get some air?" She nodded and put her empty coffee cup on the rough boards of the trestle table at the side of the hall. She felt people watching her leave with Joseph Hillström. She felt guilty. What if Jouka found out? She also felt the excitement of doing something risqué.

They walked on a trail worn by mill workers along the banks of the Skookumchuck River.

"The place is humming," Hillström said.

"Full employment," Aino agreed. "Lots of potential members, but less incentive to join."

"Surely, even fully employed men want higher wages and better working conditions."

"Sure, they *want* that. But what will they *fight* for?" She paused. "Honor and dignity rule men and work," she went on. "Money is secondary." Ideas were tumbling together in her mind. "Honor keeps them at their jobs, supporting their families, showing their courage. Honor makes it hard to organize. In fact, working under horrible conditions *increases* their honor."

Hillström chuckled, nodding his head.

"At some point, however, living without dignity and respect will overcome honor. We organize to give them dignity. With the red card, a man holds his dignity in his hands. The red card tells the world: 'Respect me. I am not a slave. I am not a machine.'"

Hillström took her hand. "My rebel girl, you're not only beautiful, you're a deep thinker." She felt herself blushing in the dark.

They walked side by side, hips and shoulders often touching.

He stopped and faced her. "Where are you spending the night?"

She felt a quiver of excitement and danger. "At the hall."

"On the floor," Hillström stated.

She nodded.

"Why not stay with me at Michael Tierney's? You'll sleep a lot better than on a cold floor. There's a lot of work to do tomorrow."

He'd given her an excuse, but she couldn't quite give in to herself without some sign of resistance. "I don't want to impose."

Hillström smiled. "You're worried about what your husband will think," he said.

"Yes, a little."

"You believe in all that marriage stuff?"

He'd given her another argument, one her pride didn't allow her to counter. How could she admit that she wasn't a modern socialist woman? "Of course not." She saw him smile. "It's just that Jouka does. It'll hurt his feelings."

"If he ever finds out." He let that hang in the air. "Look, Tierney's married, with two kids. His wife, Kathleen, will be there the whole time. Her brother Jack's staying there, too. The Tierney place is a well-known roost for all of us IWW organizers."

She said yes.

On waking, even before she opened her eyes, she breathed in the wonderful smell of him, the pungent odor of his skin, the soft remains of yesterday's hair tonic. She kept her eyes shut, lying on her side, her back to his side of the bed, reliving the jumble of images—him singing, the crowd looking at her, the women curious about her and him, the long river walk, the quick trip to the hall to pick up her valise, walking outside to him, his gentle but assured hands unlacing her. She rolled over to snuggle in close to him.

He wasn't there.

She saw his valise and heard sounds from the bathroom. The feeling of sleepy contentment was replaced by a feeling of loss—and guilt.

He came into the bedroom in his undershirt, suspenders hanging down from the waist of his trousers. He'd just finished shaving.

"Where are you going?"

"South. I'm at Eugene tonight, then Roseburg, then Klamath Falls. Big sawmills."

"When are you coming back?"

He looked at her and smiled. "Not soon enough, I assure you."

"No, really, when are you coming back?" She realized she was sounding needy and switched to a more businesslike tone. "I thought you were going to be here helping with the organizing."

"Nope. I'll leave that in your very capable"—he walked over to the bed and took both her hands in his—"and beautiful hands." He then went back to packing his bag. She sat on the edge of the bed, unable to speak.

She threw herself into organizing, up early in the morning at the house and back later at night to sleep in the same bedroom. Tierney's wife, Kathleen, made breakfast for Aino; her husband, Michael; her brother, Jack Kerwin; and her two young children. When her husband went off to his sawmill job, Aino and Jack left with him. Jack focused on loggers, so because of the distances he would often not make it home at night. Even though Aino focused on closer sawmill workers, she would often come in after the family was asleep. She always found supper left in the warming cabinets along the top of the woodstove, slow heat radiating gently from embers in the firebox.

During the day, she would stand just outside the property of sawmills, catching workers as they went to their shifts or, better, when they were leaving, as that gave her more time. Mill owners called the sheriff to eject her several times and she had to scramble to an obviously public place where she had a right to be and where, in full view of others, she'd be less likely to be beaten. The sheriff would leave her with a warning. The next day, she'd be back at the edge of the mill property, preaching her gospel of dignity. She helped put together pamphlets, giving her ideas to people who could write English. She then carried the material from the printers to the hall. She went to barbershops, only to be run out by irate barbers. She stood by saloon doors, only to be threatened by bouncers. The police got to know her. Sometimes they would simply say hello and talk. Sometimes they would tell her to get her red ass out of town before they threw her into jail for vagrancy. One day, they did throw her into jail charging vagrancy, but the city attorney, a man named Polly Grimm, said to release her. He didn't like Wobblies, but the law was the law. She had a right to speak her mind in public places and if she had a place to live, she was no vagrant. This outraged the wife of a prominent lawyer. The woman beat Aino with an umbrella, shouting that she was a disgrace to women, un-American, and should go back to Finland along with all the other reds ruining the country. She was propositioned by drunk, or not so drunk, loggers and mill hands and occasional upstanding citizens of Centralia. Once a woman asked if it was true Wobbly women had their ovaries removed so they could make love without the fear of getting pregnant. Aino replied she'd gladly lift her skirts so the woman could take a closer look and see that she had no scars. The woman hurriedly left.

The work was hard, but it was paying off and not just in Centralia. By the end of June over fifty lumber camps in Washington State were on strike, around five thousand loggers. It seemed that they were at a turning point. She decided to stay longer than the three weeks she'd told Jouka.

Two weeks later Hillström returned, bringing the embarrassing question of sharing the room.

"They're already calling me a red whore," Aino said to him as he stood just inside the door.

He took her in his arms. "Sticks and stones," he said.

She wriggled free. "Easy for you to say."

"Are you still mad about me leaving?" he asked, as if it were inconceivable.

"You could've told me before."

"And what? We wouldn't have made love then? Aino, I leave all the time. I go places." He smiled warmly at her. "Aino, I'm organizing. I'm doing the *work*. Just like you."

"You should've told me," she said, somewhat mollified.

He took both her hands. She let him. "Come on. I'll sleep in the hall. We're comrades, aren't we? We must support each other, not fight."

She wanted to ask him to stay—but she knew that this would hurt the cause more than anything else she could do. "OK, friends," she said.

"Comrades," he replied, just as Kathleen Tierney entered the living room.

He picked up his bag and cheerfully said goodbye to Kathleen, who shut the door and leaned against it, looking at Aino until one of the children ran into the room and broke the uncertain spell.

The police began patrolling around the IWW hall, showing up at rallies and speeches in greater numbers. Aino felt an ominous chill watching them silently watch the crowd. As the audiences grew, the police added more deputies.

"I say let's have it out," Hillström said. It was close to eleven at night and the leaders had returned to the new hall after a well-attended rally. "Let's show them we're an international union, a force to be reckoned with."

There were murmurs of assent.

"We shouldn't be pushing so hard," Aino said. "At some point the deputies wade in with ax handles, and people get scared and tear up their cards."

"We've all faced ax handles," Michael Tierney said.

"I'm not afraid for ax handles," Aino said. "If you weren't a man, I show you my scars."

That got a laugh.

"Weeks of recruiting work will be wasted because workers afraid of cops using ax handles."

Murmurs of assent arose for her side as well.

"A big rally gets us in the papers," Hillström said. "We'll sign up new members from Canada to Mexico."

"Joe's right," Tierney said. "We let people know Joe's going to be speaking and singing and we can draw a really big crowd."

"Big crowd of cops," Aino said.

"Come on, Aino. It's just what we want. We'll be in newspapers all over the country."

"And capitalist newspapers making us look like crazy dangerous people, scaring everyone. Making recruiting harder."

The image of Voitto passionately arguing his case before the raid came unbidden. She tried to focus, struggling with the images and the English.

"We recruit here already over three hundred. They recruit others. In a year, we have every worker in Washington on our side. Then we have power. Then we shut down entire lumber industry. Direct action! Not newspaper stories."

"Theory," Hillström said dismissively.

"Yes. Like the laws of Newton," Aino shot back.

"OK, OK," Tierney said. "We'll put it to a vote."

Aino knew she would lose. She did.

Pamphlets were printed and distributed. Signs posted. Aino traveled by train and walked miles on dirt roads to logging camps and mills, restaurants and saloons, barbershops and tobacco stores, advertising the rally. But advertising reaches everyone.

On the day of the big rally, Aino noticed burly men coming in on trains and going to the police station. Mill workers and loggers came into town as well, going to the saloons, getting drinks before the night's entertainment.

She watched the happy jostling crowd with a sinking heart. Most of them were here for the spectacle. She recognized many that she'd talked to and hadn't convinced to carry the red card.

After brief introductory speeches, Hillström mounted the platform to applause and cheering. He asked for quiet and began one of his great speeches, cutting through the fog of befuddled sociology and economics that held them in thrall. He got cheers. He got laughs. He led a few songs. Organize. Show these capitalists and their captive politicians and police what real power is. Join the Industrial Workers of the World. Get dignity, get a fair deal, and lose your chains. A cheer arose.

Then someone threw a bottle at one of the cops.

A whistle shrilled three times and the surrounding line of police and deputies stormed into the crowd, batons and ax handles flailing. People tried to defend themselves or get away. Women screamed. Men went to the ground, both police and Wobblies, and both were kicked as they lay there by other policemen or workers. Hillström ran off the stage toward the hall. Aino raced after him, but someone tripped her and she went down. A man stomped on her below her right shoulder, making her gasp with pain and briefly lose her vision. She struggled to her feet, petticoat and skirt wet with mud, her hair loose and falling over her shoulders. Fighting her way through the crowd toward the hall, she reached its doors. Men with pistols were standing guard there. She rushed past them, looking for Hillström. He was gone.

She left the hall several hours later, her blouse showing a patch of blood, her back aching. Jack Kerwin offered to walk with her to his sister's house. He had coagulated blood in his hair and on his face and walked with a limp.

They moved through the area where the rally had been held. The platform stood empty. On the ground were letters, flyers, food, lost hats, even a shoe—and torn-up and trampled red cards. No one would risk going to jail with one of those in a pocket. Months of recruiting, lying in the mud.

Furious and frustrated, her back throbbing, Aino sat at the kitchen table as Kathleen carefully tended to her brother's head wound and her husband's cuts and bruises. Kathleen moved quietly between the water heating on the stove and her brother and husband. She occasionally looked at Aino, who was staring at her coffee mug saying little. Once their eyes met. Kathleen looked down at the bloody rag in her hand and then back at Aino, her eyes sad. "I heard Hillström hopped a freight."

Aino held her gaze momentarily. She looked down at the floor, murmured, "Yoh," and walked from the room out into the night.

Off to the northwest there was still a faint hint of light from where the sun moved beneath the northern horizon. She'd spent six weeks away from Jouka doing what she'd done to end up where she was. Now she had to go back and face him.

12

When Aino returned from Centralia in mid-August, Jouka was working. All he said when he came home was: "You're back." He said nothing about Centralia and Aino wanted nothing said.

By the end of September the heady feeling from the strikes of spring and summer was gone. The lumber market was turning down. Owners were less motivated to settle. When strikes were called, the IWW organizers found it difficult to get men for the picket lines. Too many of the loggers, itinerant and single, simply moved.

On the second Sunday of Advent, December 7, 1913, the family gathered at Ilmahenki. Ilmari had lit the candle of hope on the Advent wreath the Sunday before and was now lighting the wreath's second candle. "Today we light the Bethlehem candle of preparation for the celebration of the birth of our Lord, Jesus Christ," he said softly. As the candle came alive, it lit his usually solemn face, which, like that of a child, was filled with wonder at the miracle of fire and the hope of returning light.

Aino looked at Jouka, whose blue eyes reflected the candle flames, and then at the faces of her family, shining out of the darkness. Even the little children were grave and thoughtful, watching the wavering candle-light grow stronger. She saw little Helmi's eyes stray over to the warming cupboards above the stove, which concealed a pie Rauha had made using apples from the cellar dug into the hill on the other side of the sauna.

Aino thought about her parents and snowy Christmases back in Finland. She thought of her father, dying who knows where, like many who had gone forward alone, so the rest could follow better off than before.

She said softly, "The voice of him that crieth in the wilderness, prepare ye the way of the Lord ... Every valley shall be exalted, and every mountain and hill shall be made low."

"And the glory of the Lord shall be revealed," Ilmari continued. "And all flesh shall see it together." He smiled at her. "You still remember your catechism."

"It was beaten into me," Aino said with a laugh. "Literally."

Her brothers laughed. No one who failed to get the lesson right escaped Pastor Jarvi's loving hand.

Matti managed to say through a biscuit in his mouth, "So, Isaiah was a Wobbly?"

Aino and the others laughed. "Well, at least a Marxist," she quipped back at him. "He prophesied the coming classless society." This begat more chuckles. She loved them all.

After the meal—the dishes washed and dried, everyone drowsy—Aino put on her coat and scarf and grabbed the galvanized bucket of kitchen scraps, saying she was going to the compost pile. After turning the compost to oxygenate it, she walked to the river. She watched the roiling water, in full flood after the fall and winter rain, remembering lighting the Advent candles and the glow on her mother's and father's faces that Christmas before they lost her brother and sisters; remembering kissing Voitto in the falling snow; thinking of Hillström, of Aksel. Maybe Aksel and Lempi? Huttula was close to forty when he died. She was twenty-four and childless. Do you defeat death by giving birth? Would a child fill this emptiness? Was that just another delusion?

She turned the compost pail upside down and sat on it, tucking her skirt tight against her ankles. She wondered if Vasutäti was sitting alone in front of her little shelter. She must have been married when she was younger. Ilmari had told her Vasutäti lost all her children to measles. So much for the bearing of children as the answer to death.

Aino picked up a stick and threw it awkwardly from her sitting position into the dark river where it was whisked downstream and lost in the churning current. On its way to the ocean, she thought. You die. You're buried. You leak horrible liquids and it all ends up in the ocean. We're small sticks torn from the tree of humanity by the storms of winter. She wished she had Ilmari's faith. Delusions, she thought. She laughed out loud with no mirth.

She stood and looked at the glow from Ilmari's house in the late-afternoon gray. Why was she always outside, looking in? It would be dark in an hour and a half. Jouka had brought their lantern, so the seven-mile walk to Camp Three wouldn't be quite so frightening. The forest still scared her. To Jouka, Matti, and the others like them, it held no mystery at all. They just turned it into logs.

Three weeks after Christmas, Aino read in the *Astorian* that Joe Hill had been arrested for murdering a grocer and the grocer's son in Salt Lake City. He'd been found wounded on that same night and the prosecution claimed he was shot by the dying son. Aino argued vehemently that Hillström had been framed by the capitalists and their stooges in the legal system. Hillström claimed someone else shot the two men and his wound was the result of a dispute about a woman whose name he didn't want to reveal. That certainly seemed credible to Aino. It did not to a jury. On July 8, 1914, Hillström was sentenced to death.

She worried about the IWW's growing reputation for violence. The horrible mining wars in Colorado and northern Idaho years ago between Bill Haywood's Western Federation of Miners and the owners had been punctuated with dynamite and killing. Many of the miners joined the IWW with Big Bill, bringing their reputation with them.

She fought this temptation to violence herself. People were rightly angry. She was angry. She carried one scar on her forehead and another on her right shoulder, where she had fallen to the man beating her with an ax handle in Nordland. But in Nordland and at all the other free-speech fights, the IWWs had folded their arms in accordance with the strongly held belief that although violence was the basis of every political state in existence, it had no place in the foundation or super-structure of the IWW. So far, she and the union had remained true to this ideal, but they had failed to communicate this. The bosses and their newspapers had successfully labeled the IWWs as violent anarchists, creating a false image that fed people's fear and undermined popular support for the cause. The American people, she mused, espousing an ideology of rugged individualism, the mythology of "Don't Tread on Me," were as twitchy as chipmunks.

She suspected that Joseph Hillström unconsciously wanted to be a martyr. It would suit his romantic temperament, which is what likely got him into jail in the first place, fooling around with that woman. She laughed under her breath; it also beat hard work. Then she felt ashamed of herself for thinking such things. Hillström had heart and his heart was in the right place, no matter his flaws.

She was overtaken by sadness and empty loss. They were going to kill Hillström whether he had killed someone or not.

The specter of violence also haunted the international news. The arms race in Europe that Matti had predicted grew throughout the spring. On June 28, Gavrilo Princip, a radical anarchist, shot Archduke Franz Ferdinand of Austria and his wife, Sophie, fueling anger in Europe and fear of mad and violent anarchists in America.

On Sunday, August 2, Aino was sitting in the afternoon sunshine on the beach in front of Ilmari's house knitting a hat, her naked nieces and nephews jumping into and out of Deep River. She heard a horse galloping and turned from the river, shading her eyes, following with her ears the hoofbeats coming from the forest. Higgins burst into view. He reined up next to the men helping with the winter wood supply. Kyllikki and Rauha were chatting on the porch in the shade, also knitting, preparing for winter. "The Germans have sent the Belgian foreign minister a letter," he shouted. "They claim France is about to attack Germany by crossing through Belgium and Germany has to enter Belgium to defend itself. It's a load of nonsense. It means war between England and Germany."

Kyllikki and Rauha ran toward Higgins with their knitting and balls of yarn in their hands. Aino watched Matti's and Ilmari's faces light up; she knew about their purchase of the timber rights to several hundred acres of spruce near the south end of Willapa Bay. Excited, Matti asked Higgins, "Where is Finland?"

"The same place as Ireland," Higgins replied. "On paper, Ireland will fight alongside England, but the people won't be gulled. Both of those bastard monarchies will be hard-pressed to get good Irishman and Finns to do their dirty work for them, by Jesus."

"No need to swear," Ilmari said.

Aino joined the group, trailed by naked, dripping children. "It will be the same in England, France, and Germany," she said. "No working-man will kill a fellow worker for a war between capitalists over imperialist greed. This war will be over in a week."

Higgins looked at her, sadly. "I don't think so, my proud firebrand." He rode off, leaving the men to speculate among themselves what war would mean for logging, sawmilling, and farming, never slacking on putting the wood away. The women returned to the shade, Aino with them. She sat down on a crate, holding a skein of wool between her raised hands while Kyllikki wound it into a ball. Kyllikki gently shook her head at her, looking into her eyes. "Higgins is right on this one, Aino," Kyllikki said. "Patriotism trumps class."

"Not this time," Aino said.

"Every time," Kyllikki answered. "Patriotism makes us all feel like one people. Class divides us."

"Marxism is changing that."

Kyllikki began singing, "We'll have pie in the sky when we die."

Aino threw the skein at her.

13

The business cycle bottomed out in December, but spruce prices kept rising, as Matti had predicted. French and English purchasing agents combed the Pacific Northwest. Two-Hundred-Foot Logging was making money. Then, a series of bad storms in February shut even Matti down. Aksel asked for a few days off.

After two nights at the Lucky Logger, Aksel decided to go to the Saturday night dance at Suomi Hall. When he reached the reception room at the top of the stairs, he saw Lempi talking with two other women at the far end by the kitchen window counter. Their eyes met. The distance between them vanished.

Lempi was clearly no longer the girl he'd first known at Reder's Camp. Her eyes spoke of sorrow—and depth into which he felt himself plunging.

Lempi looked away first. The other women looked at Aksel, made a quick appraisal, and then quickly looked at Lempi to try to guess the relationship by the expression on her face. One of them whispered into Lempi's ear.

Good old Lempi, Aksel thought. It had been three years since Huttula had died. She had probably been right here in Astoria all along. Everything came clear; he knew he was going to marry her.

Six weeks later, he proposed. She agreed, provided he quit logging.

Two days after the wedding, Aksel went to Knappton and found Cap Carlson at the docks washing out his boat's fish box. Cap was alone, raising Aksel's hopes. Maybe he needed a boat puller, so called because the job involved pulling the boat forward under the heavy net, the only way to get it back into the boat, while the captain focused on untangling the salmon.

Carlson looked up. His smile, warm and broad, showed a couple of gaps where decayed teeth had been pulled.

"By golly, Aksel," he said in English. "What brings you to Knappton?"

Cap started hauling on the stern line, which ran through a pulley on the wharf and then above the boat to another pulley attached to a piling opposite the boat's bow. Aksel climbed down the ladder and waited for the boat to get close, his feet only two rungs above the water. He jumped nimbly to the deck.

"This calls for a smoke," Cap said in Swedish. He pulled out his pipe and Aksel rolled a cigarette. It was only after they had their first long pulls that Aksel answered Cap's question in Swedish.

"I got married."

"Who to?"

"Huttula's widow, Lempi."

"That was a tough one," Cap said. He drew a long pull on the pipe. "I didn't know Huttula." They were both respectfully silent. "I remember her," Cap went on, "when she first came to work up at Reder's. Thirteen or so. Orphan girl."

"She hasn't had it easy," Aksel said. Again, the calm silence, smoke rising to the wharf above them. "She's a good worker and she's a good dancer."

"What more could you want?" Cap said.

Aksel laughed. "I'm happy."

"So, you came to Knappton just to tell me wedding news?"

"I wondered if you could take me on as a boat puller until I learn the river and then help me get a cannery boat."

"I thought you and Matti Koski were doing OK in the logging."

"Lempi doesn't want me to log."

"Huttula," Cap said.

"Ja." Aksel waited while Cap thought things through.

"Ja. OK," Cap said.

* * *

Cap took Aksel to meet the Knappton supervisor, Gerald Gleason, a man known on both sides of the river for his callousness and ability to get things done. It was mid-May, the very end of the spring Chinook run. Gleason wasn't encouraging. "How do I know he can fish?" he asked, ignoring Aksel.

"He grew up fishing."

"Where?"

"The Gulf of Bothnia," Aksel answered. "Like Cap."

"That ain't the Columbia."

"I'm good at finding fish. I can handle a boat."

"You vouch for him, Carlson?"

"Ya, you bet."

"You take him on as a boat puller for the blueback. Teach him the river. He can have Number Twenty-Seven if he convinces me he can handle her." He turned Aksel. "You'll sign a contract saying you'll work day and night, no days off, until the run is over. We'll pay you after the run."

Aksel agreed.

The run was a delirium of struggling, slippery fish and lack of sleep. The tides ruled all. There was no starting time or quitting time. Sometimes drifts set at night or in dangerous waters caught nothing. Often, however, drifts were rich with blueback hitting the gill net at full speed, pulling down the cork line with deep thumps—the sound of money.

At the season's end, Gleason paid Aksel off and Aksel showed him how well he handled Cap's double-ended gill net boat alone. Gleason was visibly impressed, and Number 27 was Aksel's. Cap shook his hand a little sadly. "Not going to find another boat puller like you," he said.

Aksel and Lempi found a company shack at the south end of Knappton, just above high tide. It smelled of mudflats, dead plants, dead fish, and garbage, but Lempi soon had fresh curtains on the two small front windows—she had bleached the smoke-stained curtains and resewed them with ruffles along the edges—and, after four days of hard work on the floor and walls with apple cider vinegar, bleach, lye soap, and elbow grease, she had the interior smelling clean. She covered a large burned patch caused by a chimney fire behind the stovepipe with a baby quilt she'd made. There was an iron bed frame, a cooking stove, and a table. Lempi sewed a mattress from some sailcloth scraps, filled it with sweet-smelling straw, and made sheets from flour sacks, which were the finest woven cloth she could find.

There were always fish to be caught, even between the runs, and Aksel soon proved he could find them. When he was home, he and Lempi would sit on the threshold, watching the tide coming in and going out, listening to the slamming of heavy boards and whine of saws coming from the mills, watching the seagulls and hell-divers doing their own fishing, feeling the great river in their bodies and souls. They both knew the gods had given them a gift. They were thankful and happy.

Aksel renamed Number 27 the *Lempi*. He'd always imagined naming his boat after Aino. Now, however, for the first time in a decade, he'd stopped thinking about her. Except for not having his own boat and net, Aksel felt content. He fished the *Lempi* by himself, a not unheard-of decision for a man of exceptional skill and strength. Handling the boat alone in rough weather was more dangerous than having a boat puller who could double the boat's power by adding two more oars in rough weather. But boat pullers had to be paid. Men like Aksel, with confidence in their own skill and stamina—who knew how to work with currents, weather, and tides instead of against them—saved the money. They also took the risk.

The blueback run in June had been good with lots of June Hogs, big Chinooks spawned in Canada and Wyoming, weighing in frequently at more than 120 pounds. There was nothing, however, that could compare to the August Chinook, and that August the Chinook run was one of the best in memory. They would lie offshore by the river's mouth, waiting for the tide to slacken its flow, and then come teeming across the bar, silver scales flashing beneath the water as the huge fish—not as huge as the June Hogs, but still weighing up to a hundred pounds—hit the fresh river water, full, fat, and strong from four years of feeding in the North Pacific, honed by evolution to carry their eggs and sperm hundreds of miles up the Columbia and her tributaries to make new life.

In concord with the salmon, and in accord with her name, which meant love, Lempi became pregnant in August.

Aksel learned the basics of the river quickly: the main channels, the changes in the currents with the tides, the shape of the bottom, the sandbars, where the seals and sea lions lurked, the taste and temperature of the water. He knew where the fish would be forced to swim, and with each changing tide, the edges of his sail vibrating just right, he sailed there. On many days he was top boat at the cannery.

When he had to catch a night tide, Lempi, her long hazelnut hair in braids, fixed him breakfast of eggs and pancakes or reheated salmon stew from the day before. As they kissed goodbye in the dark, he would feel her breasts beneath her flannel nightgown against his chest. Just before he lost her from view, he would look back to see Lempi standing in the shack's door, silhouetted by the kerosene lamp on the table behind her.

Hugging herself against the cold, Lempi would stare at the empty space Aksel left for some time before turning back into the shack. She tried to make light of her fear. Wives worried when their husbands set out alone in the dark on uncertain water to find and bring in the fish. They would break the round of cooking, laundry, gardening, tending to kids by walking to the river. There, they would peer into the distance, waving to the one or two other wives doing the same thing, looking for the boats to come back—looking for that one boat upon which rested not only their children's lives, but, if they were among the lucky ones, their very happiness. Wives never talked about it.

The days grew shorter, Lempi grew rounder, and soon it was Thanksgiving Day, 1915. As was customary, Ilmari said the Thanksgiving prayer from the head of the long table he'd made from Oregon oak inlaid with red alder along the edges. The children ate on temporary two-by-twelve trestles: Rauha and Ilmari's Mielikki, nearly seven, Helmi, four, and Jorma, three; Matti and Kyllikki's Suvi, three, and Suvi's brother, Aarni, seven months, who lustily banged his hand on Kyllikki's chest wanting to nurse.

The prayer over, the conversation turned to one thing they were truly thankful for: spruce.

"I heard there's four or five buyers down here from the Royal Flying Corps," Matti said. "If it weren't for the British blockade, we'd have buyers from the Imperial German Flying Corps. The more one side builds, the more the other side shoots down."

"Men die in those airplanes," Aino said.

"They volunteered," Matti said.

Aino gave Matti a look that said she wasn't going to lower herself to answer that.

Then Rauha said, "Men die here, logging that spruce, one every four or five weeks."

"That's why we need the eight-hour day," Aino said.

"If Aksel and I worked eight-hour days, we'd still be logging Higgins's stand on the Klawachuck," Matti said. Aksel nodded agreement.

"Can I suggest," Kyllikki said, "no war, no labor politics when we're having Thanksgiving dinner."

Then Ilmari said, "Mmm," which he did when about to speak seriously. "The Germans shoot down a British airplane; another British pilot dies," he said, looking far beyond the walls. "The Royal Flying Corps sends another order for spruce to America. Purchasing agents dole out the order to people like me, who buy logs from people like Matti and Reder. Jouka makes good wages hauling logs to tidewater. Aino eats because of his wages, which Reder pays with money squeezed out of British taxpayers or borrowed from American banks. No one is clean." He paused, then continued. "At the base of it all is the forest: planted, tended, and grown by none of us."

Jouka broke the ensuing silence. "Ilmari, you do have a way with words."

This brought chuckles and people resumed eating and talking. Ilmari said that he'd seen a copy of the *Astorian* at Higgins's and that the radical agitator Joe Hill had been executed by a firing squad in Utah.

Aino put her fork down slowly.

Kyllikki shot a look at Lempi.

"Well, he murdered that grocery store man over some woman," Rauha said.

"They executed him because he was dangerous to capital," Aino said. "The charges were trumped up."

"Remember, no war, no labor politics," Kyllikki said brightly. She smiled and stood, collecting her plate, Lempi and Rauha rising with her, collecting dishes. Aino didn't move.

When the three stood by the kitchen sink, Rauha whispered, "I heard they were all over each other at Nordland and they slept in the same house in Centralia."

"I'm sure it was innocent," Kyllikki said quietly. She reached for an apron.

"You know those Wobblies always put each other up," Lempi said.

"I'm just saying what I heard," Rauha said.

"Leave her alone," Kyllikki said. "At least think about Jouka," she whispered, nodding toward where the men were talking.

"And Ilmari wonders why there's no baby yet," Rauha said.

Aino came into the kitchen with more plates and Rauha busily put on her apron. Kyllikki could see that Aino's nearly black eyes were troubled and sad in her stoic face. She gave Aino an encouraging smile.

The men were still talking logging over their coffee and cigarettes at the end of the table while the women were washing and drying the dishes, except for Kyllikki who nursed Aarni and walked him back and forth behind them, trying to get him back to sleep. With the last plate returned to the shelf next to the water pump, Aino said nature was calling and went for her coat.

"Me too." Kyllikki said. She followed Aino outside. As she suspected, Aino went nowhere near the outhouse but instead stood watching the river in the late afternoon gloom, her hands thrust into her coat pockets. She'd shaken her beautiful dark hair loose and it hung down against the back of the coat except for a thick strand she'd started to braid but now just silently stroked as it lay on her chest.

Kyllikki joined her regarding the river. She'd caught a glimmer of tears in Aino's eyes. Aino quickly blinked them away and resumed braiding her hair, her face stoic, her eyes searching beyond the river.

How to begin? She looked across the river as well, joining Aino. "Are you OK?" she asked, not looking at her.

"Ei." Aino tugged on the half-plaited strand and said, "Workers are dying in Europe, they're dying here because they are worked to exhaustion, and all anyone talks about are lumber prices and money. My own brothers."

Kyllikki waited to see if Aino had any more to say. She didn't. Then Kyllikki said, without looking at her, "You slept with him, didn't you?"

Aino had taken another one of her braids down from atop her head and it now hung nearly to her waist. As she was still braiding, her jaw started to tremble. She flung herself against Kyllikki, letting out a long, anguished cry as she shook with sobs. "I'm such a fool. I'm so ashamed."

Kyllikki held her close, stroking her hair and the back of her neck. "Yes, Aino, you are." she said. "A fool with a big heart that's just the right size for breaking."

14

The days continued to grow shorter. Unlike summer fishing, with gentle swells and short nights with temperatures in the midfifties, winter fishing meant large, fast-running swells and rainy nights with temperatures just above freezing. If Aksel brought in a hundred pounds, mostly silversides and steelheads, he had a good day. Risking the net for so few fish made sense only because every month he owed rent money for the *Lempi,* the net, and the shack. He felt compelled to go out in all sorts of weather to "maintain headway." Lempi's swelling belly also encouraged him each time they said goodbye and each time they said hello again.

Aksel never worried about the danger. He could barely settle himself to eat and often would scald his tongue drinking his coffee too fast so he could get to the *Lempi.* There were fish to catch and the runs didn't last forever. He knew well the aphorism that time and tide wait for no man.

Nearly seven months along, in early March, Lempi couldn't help smiling as she watched Aksel at supper, squirming in his seat from barely suppressed excitement. He wolfed down the fresh rieska she'd baked at midday while he slept, one of the rare times he wasn't sleeping in the boat. He always put the entire flat, round rieska loaf in the crook of his arm, pulling his puukko toward him to cut large slices. It looked unsafe—she always sliced the bread on a breadboard—but Aksel never once cut himself.

"Where tonight?" she asked. Aksel had been trying different places nearly every night. The spring Chinook were due any moment.

He'd already brought in a few early ones, so she knew his blood was up. When the big run hit, he wanted to be there from the very beginning and in the right place.

"McGowan, then the north side of Desdemona Sands if McGowan isn't working." He pulled the thick wool sweater she had knitted him over his wool shirt and wool underwear. Wool kept in body heat when wet better than any other material. She looked out the window into the gloom of the dying day. A light rain was falling.

"What you think?" she asked. Aksel was putting on his boots.

"Don't worry. Should be all right."

He stood and kissed her on both eyes. She loved the feeling of his lips, warm against the lids. It made her wish she wasn't pregnant, so she could get pregnant again. She laughed aloud at the thought.

"What?" he asked. They usually spoke Finnish, as Lempi's Swedish was only fair, but they often spoke English. They didn't think about it; it just came out the way it did.

She stood on her tiptoes, kissing him gently on the lips. "I'm thinking about when you come home."

Aksel smiled and looked pointedly at her swollen belly.

She smiled, looking into his eyes, and touched her forefinger to his nose. "We can work that out," she said in English. She could still make him blush.

He turned to wave when he reached the bend in the road; as always, she was there. He felt close to crying as he walked to the *Lempi*, as if warm water were overflowing from his heart. As he was untying the *Lempi*, a gust of wind hit his face, coming from the southwest. The rain changed angles with it. He looked out on the river and saw whitecaps.

He'd been skunked on his first drift off McGowan and could no longer see the shore in the dark, so he tacked south against the rising wind to just north of Desdemona Sands, where he knew there were no rocks. On his second drift there, a sudden gust of wind heeled the boat over, vibrating the furled sail on its mast. Aksel ignored the danger to himself of being blown up against unseen rocks in the dark on a lee shore or swamped by swells that turned suddenly into breakers or not seeing one of the many half-submerged logs. His fear was for the net and the boat.

He heard several solid thumps as an early Chinook hit the net, so he knew he at least had something to show for the night. He had a lantern, but lanterns always seemed to flicker and die just before they were needed. He worked his way forward against the chopping motion of the deck to untie the cork line and put it over the roller fixed on the starboard fore gunwale. A sudden breaking swell twisted the deck from beneath him, leaving him momentarily airborne. He slammed to the deck hard, landing on his left flank as the boat rose up. The suddenly howling wind pushed the *Lempi* faster than the net, which hung heavy in the water out of the wind, forcing him to furiously pull in the water-soaked net so the boat wouldn't overrun it. Then the gale hit with its full force. The breaking swells would raise the *Lempi*, nearly pulling his arms from their sockets as he hung on to the cork line while the swell passed under her, pulling her away from the net like a frightened horse pulling back on its halter rope. Aksel hung on fiercely so he wouldn't let any of the cork line pay out and lose ground getting in the net. Then the boat slammed down, threatening to throw him over the gunwale into the dark water, jarring his spine and teeth. Then the next swell.

When he finally pulled in the net, salmon were still fouled in it, kicking fiercely in the tangle. He was so exhausted he could hardly put his oars in their locks. Each oar was easily double his height. He got the oars into the water and, sitting on athwart amidships, holding the thick round ends, heaved with everything he had to keep the *Lempi*'s double-ender stern slightly into the wind. Pulling on one oar, then another, fighting to keep himself from being thrown from the boat, he was pushed by the wind through the darkness to he knew not where, except it would be the north shore of the river. Aksel had been tested to his physical limit, but he was big, was rock hard from both logging and fishing, and had just turned twenty-four.

Cap Carlson was fifty-one and his boat puller was weakened by alcohol addiction.

* * *

Aksel and the other Knappton fishermen waited six hours after the storm abated, but there was no sign of Cap and his boat puller. Looking for them was pointless. There was too much river and there were too few fishermen. Gleason would also fire anyone who missed the next tide. Knappton Packing owned the boats.

So, they fished, vaguely hoping Cap and his boat puller had made it ashore, hoping they might find a body, but knowing neither was likely.

Two days later, a Chinook Indian said he'd seen a boat on the beach just upriver from the Chinook village and had been told there was a body on the beach down toward Baker Bay. Gleason and another manager took the company's single-cylinder, steam-driven launch, returning two hours later with Cap's boat. Aksel and several others waited at the dock as the two men tied the boat and came up the ladder.

"Where's Cap?" Aksel asked Gleason.

"We own the boat, not him," Gleason replied and walked toward the office.

Aksel pretended he was setting out for a drift but went looking for Cap instead. He found him that afternoon. He and a kind old Chinook Indian buried Cap on the beach next to the river he loved. They never found the boat puller.

15

During Lempi's last trimester, Aino visited her weekly, taking the log train down to Margaret Cove and catching a ride with a fishing boat or tug to Knappton. Several days before the new moon on May 13, Aino moved in with her. Maíjaliisa always said a new moon was nearly as good a stimulator of birth as a full. Aksel slept under a tarp in the boat so Aino could sleep in the bed with Lempi.

Lempi was nervous. Aino suspected the nerves were related to what happened with her first pregnancy as much as the coming birth, but Lempi never spoke of it.

The first contractions came at around six in the evening on May 15, 1916. The tide was flooding, so Aksel was downstream of Knappton on the north side of the river where the salmon would try to catch the tide going upriver. The water was shallow there, so they couldn't pass easily under the gill net. The setting sun glowed on the sails of the returning boats lined up to have their fish boxes lifted and weighed.

Lempi was doing fine, so Aino went to look for Aksel. She recognized him immediately, focused on bringing his boat into the dock in a light wind. He dropped the sail and rowed the boat up to the standing lines coming from the wharf. He heaved on the stern line, pulling up close to the ladder, and then hopped lightly up the ladder using only one hand. The other held one of the wool sweaters Lempi knitted for him and his lunch pail. He had seen Aino waiting on the wharf and came running.

"Is she OK? Is it happening?"

"She's OK. It's happening."

He ran to the shack. Aino smiled at his receding back. A small pang of envy went through her. Maybe it was her fault she and Jouka didn't have what Aksel and Lempi had. Jouka loved her and she didn't love him—not the way Lempi loved Aksel—and that was that. She walked to the shack. Unlike Aksel, she knew there was plenty of time before the baby came. Another long night. She thought of her mother. Maíjaliisa would have known what could go wrong with an abortion and how it might affect a later birth. She, herself, knew nothing about what happened past the cervix. She paused, watching the long shadows of the hills darken the water. Far off to the east, Mount Saint Helens glowed orange. Behind it, even farther east, she saw the last alpenglow off Mount Adams, tiny in the distance, a nub against the gathering dark from the east. It was a rare day, to see all the way to Adams. She hoped it was a good omen.

By midnight, Lempi was in trouble. She was dilating, but the baby simply wasn't moving down. Something was in the way. Lempi started bleeding.

Aino kept Aksel busy, washing out bloody cloths, boiling them, drying them over the woodstove, sometimes frying them right on the hot metal. The little cabin became overheated. She opened both small windows and the door. Cool air off the water kept the temperature down, but it made the lamp flicker, which made it even harder for her to see. She apologized to Lempi and put her hand in as far she could, trying to feel for the blockage. Lempi clamped down on one of the freshly washed cloths. A wave of contractions hit her and nothing moved. She screamed. The pain passed. She was sweating profusely even with the door and windows open.

The last scream brought Mrs. Leppälä from the hut next door. She carried her nine-month-old, and her three-year-old daughter clung to her skirt. Her husband had gone over to the Hammond side of the river for the night, hoping to catch the next flood just outside the shipping channel.

"What can I do?"

"Hold her head. For comfort. There's not much else."

"What's wrong?" she mouthed to Aino from behind Lempi's head. Aino shook her head and nodded toward the door.

"Are you OK, Lempi?" Aino asked. "I need a little air."

Lempi shook her head no but gasped, "Sure. OK."

Outside, Aino gave Mrs. Leppälä the best explanation she could.

"She needs a doctor," Mrs. Leppälä said.

"You have one in mind? You know what the wives of the mill workers call that shoe clerk the sawmill hired."

"The Handyman," Mrs. Leppälä answered, as if she were spitting.

"She needs a real doctor."

"If she could afford a real doctor, she'd be in Astoria right now. Besides, she doesn't have anyone to stay with; they'd have to pay that bill, too."

When Lempi started screaming again, Mrs. Leppälä took the children away. Her daughter was crying with fear at the screaming and her nine-month-old son was crying because his sister was crying.

At around 2:00 a.m., the blood flow overwhelmed the bandages and soaked the bed. Aksel was holding Lempi's left hand with both of his hands and pressing it to his face, kissing her fingers. Aino stuffed bandages, still not dry, up as far as she could, but the bleeding was deep inside where no pressure could be applied.

This was far worse than Margaret Reder's delivery. Margaret wasn't bleeding like this. She wanted desperately to tell Aksel that she didn't know what to do. She'd only heard her mother talk about such things. She wanted to tell him it was beyond her, to tell him how scared she was that she could do something wrong and kill her best friend. But Aksel was focused on Lempi, as he should be. She was alone in this. No one was coming.

At 3:00 a.m. Lempi's face had gone from bright red with exertion to sweaty pale. Aino had trouble finding her pulse. Aksel looked at Aino. Without saying a word, she knew he understood. She nodded at him and he nodded back, then returned to stroking Lempi's hands and belly.

Aino stepped outside and breathed in the cool damp air and all the smells of the river. She straightened her skirt, smoothed her apron, and then put her palms on top of her head and shut her eyes, just feeling the river moving past her. She brought her hands down and looked at them, dimly pale in the darkness of the new moon. She had her hands. Men and women have had their hands forever. Some prayed with them. Not her. She consciously squared her shoulders and went back inside. She knew what had to be done. She didn't know if she could manage to do it.

Aino set Aksel to work heating two kitchen knives red hot. She used Aksel's sharp puukko and a straight razor to cut vertically through Lempi's abdomen, cauterizing the blood vessels with one glowing knife, switching it with the second knife when the first cooled. Then, she spread apart Lempi's abdominal muscles to expose her womb and cut again. Massive amounts of blood gushed out. The baby was dead.

It took nearly an hour to sew Lempi up. During that time, Aksel held the dead baby, a little boy, looking at his face. When Aino was finished, he placed the baby on Lempi's chest. Lempi fell asleep and Aino took the baby and wrapped it in a towel.

As early daylight filtered through the window, Lempi suddenly woke up. She turned toward Aksel and threw her right arm across his shoulder as he bent over her, his knees on the floor. She pulled his head down tight against her chest—holding him as if she'd never let go—and then she let go.

That evening several women from the old henhouse group came by to get the body ready for the viewing. When they were done, they left Aksel and Aino alone. The sunset was beautiful, the high clouds above the river turning into islands of orange and then blood red.

Aksel lit a candle and puddled wax on the headboard to hold it over Lempi.

Worn with grief, lack of sleep, and a vague sense she'd done something wrong, Aino walked to the river's edge. The river brought life to parched uplands. It fed verdant marshes. It pulsed with salmon as they surged toward their birthplaces. The river, however, flowed in only one direction, toward the sea. She felt that Lempi and her baby were

flowing there now, flowing with the great river, toward the only destination of everyone.

She heard Aksel, who'd come up behind her. She faced him. His
eyes were dull with grief. Although they were close together on that
narrow beach, the space between them was huge. Putting one hand
under her chin and his other on her shoulder, he tilted her head up.
"Aino," he said. "It wasn't your fault."

She sobbed and hugged him. Her relief was palpable. As they held
each other in their pain, Aksel murmured into her ear: "Some wrongs
even you can't fix."

Aksel had Lempi buried on Peaceful Hill just outside Tapiola, her dead
baby tucked in her arms.

Aino went over the birth, again and again. If she had only made
Lempi tell her about the abortion. Had Lempi bled during that, too? If
she knew, she'd have forced her to go to a doctor in Astoria, hang the
cost. She hadn't known, but maybe she still should have forced Lempi
to go to Astoria. But not even a doctor could stop interior bleeding. The
ifs and buts of a crisis endure forever.

A week after the funeral, Aino made the journey back to Knappton.
Aksel's clothes were gone. Everything else was left behind—Lempi's
clothes, pots, dresser, glasses, tableware; the lantern on the table; the
drawer that held Lempi's underclothes, which she had prized so highly.
The bed showed only the springs.

Aino walked to the dock and saw the *Lempi* swinging gently up
and down on her pulleys, only she was no longer the *Lempi*. Gleason,
Knappton Packing's supervisor, had already repainted Number 27 over
Lempi's name.

In July, Kyllikki gave birth to a healthy baby girl, Pilvi, in St. Mary
Hospital. The river flowed on.

PART FOUR

1917–1919

Prologue

Ilmari dreamed that he stood high above the spire of the little church that he had birthed, and all around him the sea surged before a mighty storm, and the sea flooded the Columbia River and drowned Astoria, and it flooded the Chehalis River and drowned Nordland, and it came flooding into Willapa Bay and then he was inside the little church, and Deep River overflowed its banks and flooded around the church, its waters red with blood, its surface burning with fire. Bullheads threw themselves up onto the land, flopping there, unable to breathe in the bloody water, unable to breathe in the fiery air, choking and dying there, between elements suddenly hostile to life.

And the mighty storm hit the little church and he was standing in the aisle, the congregation around him, fearful in the night, as the windows shuddered and the walls rocked. Flames in the lamps flickered as the pressure inside the church seesawed between windblasts.

And the women were weeping, and the men were looking down in sorrow, and a coffin was being borne up to the altar, its lid closed, because Pastor Hoikka had not wanted anyone to see the mutilated body that everyone knew was someone's son but not whose, and they each wept for all.

And Ilmari wept for the sorrows of life and was glad for life's brevity.

And he looked down and the offering plate was in his hands and he looked up and Matti and Aino stood opposite each other across the aisle, looking furtively at the offering plate as he held it up to the altar.

And there was a rending and tearing of tortured wood as a huge tree came crashing through the roof above the altar, throwing Hoikka into the pallbearers, and the shrieking of the wind mingled with the screams of the women. The lights were blown out and there was darkness.

Half-awake, Ilmari understood that there would be war. Fully awake, he forgot the details of the dream, but knew there would be great demand for floor joists for army barracks. That meant maximizing the output of fourteen-foot two-by-tens.

1

After Lempi's death, Aino focused relentlessly on organizing. In mid-June, she boarded the train for Portland, still feeling the loss but also having a sense of urgency. She'd learned from the last failed strike that striking when prices were down was a bad idea. But now, because of the war in Europe, prices were climbing and owners were pulling in money. More important, there was full employment—no hungry, out-of-work loggers and mill workers needing to feed their families and therefore willing to scab. The IWW's time was now.

Thirty miles north of Seattle, in Everett, shingle workers were striking at that moment, demanding a return to the 1914 wage scale they had conceded when prices were low. Forming a cartel called the Commercial Club and allying with local politicians and police, the mill owners were refusing to budge.

Aino arrived at the Portland IWW hall to be greeted by compatriots, friends she'd made in Nordland and Centralia. When she joined the small group of women folding pamphlets and getting a lunch buffet ready, one said sarcastically, "Well, if it isn't our own Elizabeth Gurley Flynn from downriver."

The women were cool. She was sure they all knew about her and Hillström, but because of his martyrdom they kept a lid on their stuffy morals. Aino joined a group of men talking and smoking outside on Burnside Street.

At the meeting, the IWWs decided to get involved with the strike in Everett, particularly since it seemed that the AF of L was getting all the publicity—and if the strike was a success, would also get the credit.

They decided to send Jim Rowland, one of their best, to Everett. Aino returned to Camp Three to focus on organizing the lower Columbia counties.

Throughout the summer and early fall, Rowland and other IWW organizers held meetings and rallies, but after several months there was still no progress. In late October, Rowland asked for volunteers to add some weight.

They were met by Sheriff McRae and several hundred armed, deputized citizens, who took the arriving Wobblies into the woods and nearly beat them to death. That enraged Wobblies from all over the West and on November 5, 250 Wobblies boarded a ferry in Seattle and sailed for Everett, just twenty miles north on Puget Sound. When they arrived, somebody fired a weapon.

The news of the Everett massacre hit Aino the next day like a sledgehammer to the abdomen. Five Wobblies, including two she knew, were killed, and one deputy. Twenty-seven Wobblies and twenty-four deputies were wounded. Seventy-four Wobblies were arrested for murder.

She grabbed the hatchet used to split kindling. Striding to one of the large stumps next to their shack, using both hands, she hammered it with the hatchet's blunt end until exhaustion finally brought her back to her senses. She then screamed and buried the blade, leaving the hatchet for Jouka to work free.

She lost no time using her and the men's outrage to start organizing the next strike for late spring.

While Aino was traveling daily, organizing from Nordland to Neawanna, loggers were traveling from as far away as Louisiana and North Carolina to find employment in the booming Northwest timber industry. They all needed to be fed. Rauha's beef business boomed.

She'd started with five heifers in 1907, just after marrying Ilmari. She'd planted clover and alfalfa among the stumps left from logging. She fenced meadows with brush and when money was available from Sampo Manufacturing, she put up barbed wire, often by herself. The herd had grown to sixty head and even Rauha couldn't keep up. She hired help. None stayed long. Rauha was a tough taskmaster. She asked no more of her helper than herself. The difference was that Rauha cut corners, often to the helper's detriment. After a few weeks, the helper would demand better pay, be refused, and move on.

After Sunday dinner on a particularly cold and wet February day, Rauha's issue came up in the sauna with the brothers. "She's just too hard on the hired help," Ilmari said.

Matti muttered a barely discernible, "Yoh." With that one word, he managed to convey "I agree," "I'm not surprised," and "I told you so."

Ilmari and Matti were lightly switching their own backs with branches, Ilmari on the bottom bench, Matti on the top one, from old habit. When Matti was little he had to prove he could take the heat better than his older brother.

"She doesn't like Americans," Ilmari said, "because they're spoiled and don't work like Finns. She doesn't like Italians or Greeks or Bulgarians because they're dirty. She certainly would never consider hiring an Indian or a Chinaman."

"So, find her a good Finnish boy," Matti said.

"Easier said than done," Ilmari said. "If they can stand on two feet and breathe, they'll be logging for better pay."

Silence followed. Ilmari ladled water onto the glowing rocks in the fire pit. The sudden steam, hot and piercing right to the soul, made it momentarily impossible to talk.

Finally, Matti said, "I know someone. And he's a Finn, but he was born here."

"Who?" Ilmari asked.

"Heikki Ranta. We used to call him Kullerikki at Reder's Camp, because trouble seemed to follow him everywhere. He was a whistle punk when I worked for Reder. He must be around nineteen or twenty now. People still call him Kullervo."

"So why isn't he working for you?"

"His mother used to box his ears," Matti said. "Some nights he would return to Reder's Camp and curl up on his bed with his hands on his ears, trying not to cry."

The two brothers thought on this. Life was hard. Some people had it harder than others.

"He can't hear in one ear," Matti went on. "He'd be dead in a month if he went logging. Or someone else would be."

"How would he be for helping Rauha?" Ilmari asked.

"He's scrawny, but he's scrappy and tough. Even when he was a kid, he'd fight grown men. He nearly killed a man at a dance when he was fifteen, some insult about his sisters growing up to be whores like their mother."

"That's sufficient cause," Ilmari said. "The man he nearly killed?"

Matti smiled and shook his head. "A logger. Outweighed him by fifty pounds."

"Humans outweigh cougars by fifty pounds. I'd bet on the cougar."

"Yoh," Matti said.

They pondered this for some time.

"Sounds like a hothead," Ilmari said.

"Well, you'd have a temper if your father and mother both beat you," Matti said.

Ilmari picked up a small branch and was lightly switching it on his back. The sweat glistened on his face glowing red from the coals. "A child has only two choices," Ilmari mused aloud. "He can knuckle under, convince himself that being hit is love, or get angry and fight back. The first will make you crazy and the second will get you in jail."

A week later, Rauha hired Kullervo for three bits a day plus room and board. Room was the sauna. It was the board that wasn't nailed down. Kullervo expected logger-size meals; Rauha resented every potato.

2

Mielikki had turned eight in January and, at her own insistence from an early age, Ilmari had started taking her to visit Vasutäti, who was more like a grandmother to her than Louhi was. One Sunday afternoon in March, he and Mielikki trudged through the sodden forest, Mielikki barefoot, Ilmari with water squishing from his shoes, to Vasutäti's little camp. Up until recently, Vasutäti had let Mielikki play at helping with basket weaving. On their last visit, however, she'd put Mielikki to work, bending the cedar-bark strips to crack and then peeling off the outer layers, leaving moist flexible wands. Vasutäti then let her work the fresh wands into a basic twill pattern, over two, under two, over one, forming the base of a basket she was making to sell. Mielikki felt proud of being able to contribute to Vasutäti's income.

On this day, Vasutäti met them as they emerged from the forest. She was carrying a hatchet. "Today," she said to Mielikki, "you learn how to accept the gift of the tree of life." She looked at Ilmari, smiling. "You call it western red cedar and I need your help. Too old to accept gift by myself." She handed Ilmari the hatchet.

After ten minutes, she stopped in front of a young cedar. "You cut here," she said. "Not more than two women's hand wide. Then you grab and pull cedar bark as high up as you can. I will sing a song thanking the tree." She snorted. "Too old to do anything else."

Ilmari pulled off a strip of wide bark about twenty feet long. They hauled it back to the campsite, where they converted it to basket wands and sorted them by width and color. Then Vasutäti went into her shelter and returned with an old, beautifully crafted but very simple basket.

"This was my mother's," she said to Mielikki. "You put wands under it, make twill pattern base, and bend up. You copy this exactly." She emphasized the "exactly."

Mielikki's first basket would be molded on a basket made by Vasutäti's mother. Even at eight, she knew she was entering sacred and adult ground.

That spring, on April 6, 1917, Aino heard the constant tooting of Jouka's Shay long before she could see it. She stepped outside into the rain and looked down the tracks. Other women had done the same, some with shawls over their shoulders and bandannas on their heads against the driving rain, others, like Aino, just accepting getting wet. Aino knew Jouka had passed by their shack with a load just two hours ago and nothing was wrong then; if something had gone wrong, it most likely would be down at the log dump and booms at Margaret Cove. The whistle kept tooting. This was different.

The train came around the first dump-side bend, moving slowly uphill. Jouka was still laying on the whistle. By now, the cook crew, the flunkies, and even John Reder had come outside. Reder happened to be in his office instead of supervising operations as he usually was. Reder had plenty to supervise. The crew had grown to over a hundred and he had two rail lines that split off just north of Camp Three going to two different shows, each with two yarders.

Jouka jumped from the back of the cab onto the coal deck where he could be seen and heard. "We're at war with Germany!" he shouted. Aino's heart sank. The murmuring of the crowd died. It looked to Aino as if Jouka were elated. Not only were the European workers killing each other; now American workers would be fighting German workers alongside Finland's enemy, Russia.

Crossing the tracks and running up to the train, Aino asked, "Will we be fighting Finnish boys?"

"I hope not. The Finnish volunteers are mostly on the eastern front, fighting the Russians."

"But, Jouka, this is crazy. We could be killing Finnish boys who volunteered to fight Russia with the Germans."

Reder ran up to the engine. "Was anything said about the army's response?" he asked. "Expansion at Fort Lewis? A draft?"

"I just know what the Knappton Packing's telegraph operator knows. No details."

Reder was silent, thinking. "It's time to punch a line into that stand up by where your brother-in-law was logging." He looked up at Jouka, excitement showing in his eyes. "OK. Better get going. We're going to be moving a hell of a lot of logs."

The train chugged off, leaving Aino staring at the empty cars as they clacked by her, just five feet from her face. When the last car went by she crossed the tracks to their little shack, working out what going to war meant for workers and the IWW. Prices were sure to go even higher, meaning extra shifts. Boys would sign up to fight, just like the fools in Europe. Both factors would make labor scarce. The bosses would be far more likely to settle rather than stop the money flowing in. The army would be desperate for war materials. Now was the perfect time to strike. But if they did strike, they would surely be accused of sabotaging the war effort, being unpatriotic—or worse. Up until now, labor's war had been against the bosses. Now, it might be against the United States government. She straightened her shoulders. So be it.

3

Four days after America declared war, Kyllikki Koski was feeding Matti a good last supper before he would leave at three thirty in the morning. Word had quietly been passed that there was to be a secret meeting of owners, large and small, in Nordland to discuss "the timber industry's contribution to the war effort." Matti knew that this was the political way of saying how to stop Aino's IWW without violating the Sherman Antitrust Act.

"Aino said that the Wobbly river workers' strike in Montana is spreading to the sawmills on the east side of the mountains," Kyllikki said, pouring Suvi and Aarni their buttermilk. She'd just finished breastfeeding Pilvi, who was asleep. "Even to some logging camps."

Matti's body tensed. "Is that all Aino said?"

"Aarni, both hands." She turned back to Matti. "She said the owners will want to get in bed with the federal government."

Matti carved off a slice of rieska. He buttered it lavishly. He took a bite, chewing slowly. She could almost feel the gears turning.

"She's right."

"It's sour. I don't want it," Suvi, nearly five, said, in unaccented English.

"It's called buttermilk," Kyllikki said, also in English. "It's good for you. Now drink it."

"No."

Kyllikki looked over at Matti. He looked back, annoyed that she was sending the problem to him. "You drink it," he ordered Suvi in Finnish.

"No." This "no" wasn't quite as forceful.

Matti rose from his chair and reached across the table, taking Suvi's buttermilk. He started drinking it.

"That's mine," Suvi said.

Matti looked at her around the glass as he emptied it. He put the glass down on the table with an exaggerated satisfied sigh. Matti quietly resumed eating. Suvi stared at the empty glass.

"That was my buttermilk," Suvi said.

Matti looked at her, saying nothing. Aarni quickly started drinking his own buttermilk.

"It's not fair!" Suvi shouted.

"You want a spanking?" Kyllikki asked her. Out of the corner of her eye she watched Matti deep in thought. For some reason, she felt a shiver of foreboding.

"No," Suvi said quietly.

"If you don't drink your buttermilk," Kyllikki said, "someone else will."

"It's not fair," Suvi whispered.

Aarni held his now quarter-full glass out to Suvi.

"I don't want any," she said to him fiercely.

He looked up at his mother and father, his feelings hurt by the rejection.

"The Bible calls it casting your pearls before swine," Kyllikki said, barely containing her amusement.

"His stupid buttermilk isn't a pearl," Suvi said.

"And you're not a swine, just pigheaded," Kyllikki said quietly. "Get ready for bed or I'll tan your backside."

"Aarni has to come, too, or it's not fair."

"He will, when he finishes his buttermilk."

Suvi stomped off and Kyllikki gave Matti a quick look. "She's clearly your daughter," she said to him in Finnish.

When Kyllikki returned from settling the children, she asked Matti, "Why are you going? Even John Reder isn't in the same league."

"I'm an immigrant. I have a Wobbly sister. Aino's crowd *will* strike. It'll bring in the government. If Two-Hundred-Foot isn't clearly with the government and the big boys, we'll never sell another log."

"None of our loggers are Wobblies. I don't see how Aino's politics—"

Matti cut her off. "The army will be putting a lot of contracts out for bids. Every competitor will tar us with being friendly to the Wobblies. I need to be at that meeting."

While Kyllikki was finishing the dishes, she could hear Matti packing. She walked into their bedroom just in time to see the puukko and its sheath go into the valise.

"No, Matti. We agreed."

"It's work. We agreed. And it's Nordland."

Kyllikki couldn't argue with the latter point. Nordland was notoriously dangerous.

"Take your Sunday shoes," Kyllikki said. "You can at least look like an owner. Are they shined?"

"They'll do."

She gave him the look that brooked no comeback.

"OK, I'll shine them," Matti said.

"No. I'll shine them. I don't want some Nordland whore thinking you're not married."

Two days later, John Reder was making small talk with a group of mostly middle-aged and well-dressed men in the Tyee Room of the Gray Hotel in Nordland. They were all waiting for the arrival of George Long, Weyerhaeuser's general manager, the unofficial industry leader. Reder, however, was waiting for the arrival of Matti Koski, and he was seething.

The day after the declaration of war he'd gone with a supervisor to plan a rail line to his timber next to the stand Koski had logged for Drummond several years earlier. In the old days in Michigan, he'd once "inadvertently" gone over the line and gotten away with several hundred dollars' worth of timber that wasn't his. Ever since, he always buried his own markers near the surveyor's marks.

The surveyor's marks had clearly been moved—as well as several thousand dollars' worth of timber. If he accused Koski, Koski would point to Drummond. If he accused Drummond, Drummond would point to Koski. If he went to court, he couldn't prove conclusively that the original stakes had been moved. The opposing lawyers could claim the first survey was in error and he'd buried his own markers after the fact. This crime needed to be paid for outside the legal system.

When Matti arrived, Drummond and Reder were both there, along with around twenty other men, a few representing the giants, a few representing medium-size firms, and some small owners like himself. When he shook hands with Drummond, he got a poker face. When he shook hands with Reder, he got civil hostility. He knew then that Reder knew. How?

He looked at Drummond, his eyes very briefly flickering to Reder and back. Drummond was showing just a shadow of smugness. Matti realized that Drummond knew that Reder would be unlikely to do anything about it—legally.

Then George Long walked into the room and it went silent.

Drummond, ever the party host, began identifying the men in the room. The group included two army officers in civilian clothes. When he got to Matti, he said, "This is Matti Koski. He owns a little outfit logging around Grays Bay."

A man who seemed to be around fifty looked at his cigar and said, "I'm Julius Bloedel. How many loggers work for you?"

"Fifteen."

That brought smiles.

"Two years it was me and one."

"Well, we're prospering, I see."

Reder broke in. "Before Mr. Koski became the head of his own show, he worked for me." People nodded. Reder looked hard at Matti. "Along with his red sister."

Long cocked his head questioningly.

"She's a Wobbly organizer," Reder said. "She's married to one of my locomotive engineers."

"He must be a hell of an engineer," Long said.

Everyone chuckled except Matti and Reder, who they were locking eyes.

"Koski, did you ever formalize your citizenship?" Reder asked. He turned to the group. "Mr. Koski, here, married a genuine American beauty. A pathway to both citizenship and her father's money."

Matti was barely keeping himself under control. Wrenching his eyes from Reder's, he addressed Long. "Yes. My sister is a Wobbly. Yes, I am married to an American. I am an American and proud to do my part for the war effort." He felt he was licking the floor with his words. He glanced at the two army officers, for whom the speech was meant.

Both nodded, smiling. "We won't hold your sister against you, Mr. Koski," one of them said. There were more chuckles. Matti smiled, his mouth closed, his teeth clenched.

The meeting got down to business and Matti and about half the men in the room were virtually ignored. The business was, as Matti had thought, how to stop the IWW from shutting down the woods.

Matti ended up at the far end of a long bar in one of the main Nordland speakeasies with several of the smaller owners. Already on his third whiskey, he was trying to fit in, nursing a grudge over Reder's nailing him with Aino and implying he'd used his wife's money to get ahead. His humiliation and anger were made worse by his guilt over drinking his and Kyllikki's hard-earned cash, which explained his overreaction to a whore trying to pick up business. He'd shouted at her in Finnish to go to hell and the word soon passed to the other whores to watch out. There's a drunk, angry Finn at the bar.

He was halfway through his fifth whiskey when Reder came into the speakeasy with Al Drummond and another man from the meeting, all of them already well liquored. The men drinking with Matti all looked at him. They knew Reder had tried to humiliate him but not why. Matti knew that they expected him to uphold his honor.

Reder, Drummond, and the other man ordered bottles of Olympia beer, prized like a rare Northwest vintage since statewide prohibition had closed the brewery down just over a year earlier. In making their way to a table, Reder and the others almost walked right past

Matti. Then Reder saw him. "Well, looky here. If it isn't our Finnish Frederick Weyerhaeuser."

Matti turned back to the bar. He slugged down what was left of his whiskey, his shame and anger at his humiliation rising. His drinking companions started moving away.

"Come on, Koski. Buy me a drink." Reder said. "Would it be with your wife's money or mine?"

Matti swung and connected squarely with Reder's nose. Blood spurted.

John Reder was no stranger to bar fights. Snarling with pain and rage, he smashed Matti across the temple with his beer bottle, causing Matti to see stars.

Matti didn't think; his body just reacted. The puukko came from its sheath and into Reder's ribs. As Reder buckled to the floor, Matti made a wide sweep with the puukko, forcing people away, and ran for the door.

He ran for the river. He knew his life had been changed, just like that—in an instant. If Reder died, he'd never see Kyllikki or his children again.

He heard distant shouts. "There he goes. The son of a bitch is over there." He ran—and he was a good runner—soon leaving them behind. He headed north of town, away from the water, the most likely escape route. He settled into a loping run, heading in a wide arc toward the mouth of the Chehalis River and the sea. The April night was cool. A waning half-moon moved behind and out of high clouds. He hit the river, put his shoes and clothes into a bundle, and swam for the south shore. He felt bottom after about half an hour of hard kicking and waded quickly into the muddy marsh grass. He was shivering with cold. He had to hide. He had to reach Kyllikki. He didn't know where or how. By instinct, he moved south, in Kyllikki's direction, crossing the hills separating the Chehalis from the north end of Willapa Bay.

After hiding in the brush the entire next day, he again went in the water, this time striking out across Willapa Bay for the Long Beach peninsula that separated the bay from the sea. He ran down the beach on the Pacific Ocean side making good time, the hard, flat sand perfect for running. Just south of where he figured Oysterville would be on the bay side, he cut across the low-lying dunes and through the shore pines and salal until he reached the mudflats on the east side of the peninsula. It was about a two-mile swim from there to Long Island—an island logged off near the water, but with thick old-growth forest still left in its interior. He knew the island was uninhabited except for infrequent visits by a few oystermen, and probably safe.

Over the next two days he built a shelter using his puukko and scoured for clams and oysters, eating them raw. By now Kyllikki would have heard the news. Was she married to a murderer?

Initially, he wanted to throw the puukko away, but it was too useful. And, of course, the problem wasn't the puukko; it was him.

Sitting on the rocky beach on the north side of Long Island, staring into the gray sky above the gray-green water of Willapa Bay, feeling a vast distance from his wife and his children, seeing a future as bleak as the cold waters before him, Matti almost cried for the first time since he was a child.

Already a little worried, because Matti should have been home by now, Kyllikki saw Aino at the front door of the house she and Matti had built on Ilmari's land gift. Aino's normally impassive public face telegraphed bad news.

When Aino came in, she put her hands on Kyllikki's shoulders and, looking into her eyes, said, "Matti stabbed Reder in a saloon. Reder's alive, but Matti ran and probably doesn't know it."

Kyllikki stood still, thoughts of Matti in jail, Matti killed by the police, her children without a father, her own dread for Matti's life, and anger over the stupid stabbing flooded through her. She took Aino's wrists and pulled them together in front of her. Her eyes still fixed on Aino's, she said, "Do you want coffee?" The time for sisu had come.

After coffee and much speculation about where Matti had gone, Aino walked over to Ilmahenki and found Rauha lecturing Kullervo on the virtues of promptness. She and Rauha told Ilmari about Matti at lunch. No good would come from interrupting a morning's work.

Rauha sent Kullervo into Tapiola for news, but he learned only that a manhunt over Pacific and Nordland Counties was in progress. Over supper, the family tried to work out a plan. Until Matti made contact, not much could be done. It went without saying, Kyllikki and the children would never want for food and shelter. Ilmari would see what could be done with Matti's current logging operation. Aino stayed the night with Kyllikki. The next morning, she helped with the children, then left to get back to Jouka.

Just after Aino left, Sheriff Cobb came with a search warrant. Kyllikki sent the children to Rauha. She watched stoically as the sheriff and a deputy went through their belongings. Then Cobb put the deputy outside the door and explained to Kyllikki that the charges would be attempted murder and assault with a deadly weapon. If she cooperated, told them where Matti was, he would do all he could to reduce the sentence. Matti could be out in ten years, maybe less.

Kyllikki offered him coffee.

Two days later, a Chinook boy of about twelve arrived at the house with a piece of alder bark rolled into a tube. He told her a man had come out of the woods on Long Island and given him the bark along with a silver dollar. The man said if he told no one, he would get another silver dollar upon delivery. Kyllikki gave the boy the dollar and then the boy gave her the alder bark. Carved inside was a big oval with an X on the top left-hand side, a half sun with an up arrow on the left, and another half sun with a down arrow on the right. Matti would wait on the northwest shore at sunrise and sunset. She served the boy fresh bread with blackberry jam. She said bad men were looking for her husband, but if only the two of them knew the location, he could come every month for jam, cake, and a silver dollar. If he told anyone, she would find out and have him and his family killed.

That night Jouka and Ilmari searched the woods to make sure no one was spying. Then, leaving the children with Rauha, Kyllikki rowed Ilmari's boat to the bay and then south along the shore. When she could just make out Long Island, dark in the starlight to the west, she rowed across the channel to its north side where she beached the boat. Unable to drag it into the woods, she disguised it with driftwood.

At sunrise, Matti woke her, kissing her on the face and neck. She reached up to him and they rolled together on the ground, holding each other as if for the last time.

She told him that Reder was alive.

"That's good," Matti said as he was wolfing down a whole loaf of rieska and nearly two pounds of cheese.

"They'll only put you away for ten years for assault."

Matti didn't reply.

"If you'd left the puukko at home . . ." She started, but he put his finger on her lips.

"It's not the puukko. It's my hot head."

She realized this was as much of an apology as she'd get.

That night she reversed course and reached Ilmahenki at dawn. A week later she made the same journey, this time with blankets, a hatchet, and a fishing line and hooks, along with the food. The next week, Aino made the journey. Matti, lean before, was now leaner but healthy. As he told her, fishing and trapping didn't burn much energy.

Kyllikki returned to Suvantola, where one by one, Matti's loggers showed up to say goodbye and get their pay. It was the last of their cash.

4

When he arrived at Kyllikki's door the second week in May, Reder still wore bandages and had trouble breathing. "You tell me where the son of a bitch is hiding!"

"If you find out, let me know."

She looked over Reder's shoulder and saw Sheriff Cobb and two deputies. "It takes four of you to ask me a question?"

Reder turned to Cobb. "Read it to her."

Cobb pulled papers from his jacket pocket, unfolded them, and began to read. "The Espionage Act of Nineteen Seventeen," he started. After a paragraph of government jargon, Reder cut in.

"Just tell her about section four."

"On June fifteenth, we will have the right to arrest, imprison, fine up to ten thousand dollars, or deport anyone interfering or thinking about interfering with the war effort."

"That means your red sister-in-law," Reder said. "And anyone the sheriff here thinks might be thinking about doing something to hurt the war effort."

Stunned, Kyllikki said, "I don't believe it. You can't arrest someone for thinking about a crime."

"When the country's at war, you bet your bottom dollar we can," Cobb said. "It's a matter of national security."

Reder said, "You'll for sure believe it when we start rounding up all you reds to send you back to Finland. Stockades are being set up all over the state right now."

"I am an American citizen and it's unconstitutional."

The sheriff with his two deputies walked up to her. He held out a piece of paper. "This is a warrant to search your house. It's constitutional."

"You already did that!"

"We have reason to believe we might have missed something." He brushed past her. She ran in behind him, jostling with the two deputies, and gathered up Suvi, Aarni, and Pilvi, holding them close to her as she watched the three men ransack the house.

When they left, she followed them out. Lighting a cigarette, Reder looked at the burning match and then casually tossed it against the side of the house. "You tell me where he is and this all stops."

With fierce love in her heart and cold steel in her voice she said, "You go to hell."

Kyllikki left the children with Rauha and walked to Camp Three to tell Aino about the Espionage Act.

Aino already knew. "National security. Bullshit. As if the kaiser's army is about to storm our beaches. *We* went over *there*. Just like the stupid song says. Land of the free and home of the brave," she said. "They throw away the land-of-the-free part the instant someone threatens them."

"Aino, I'm scared. For all of us."

"That's exactly what they want."

"Well it's working."

The two women alternated visits to Long Island to minimize suspicion, going on random days, always having a reason to be away from home and telegraphing it well. They planned their next six trips, three each, just in case they couldn't meet.

When Aino was visiting Suvantola after one of her trips to tell Kyllikki how Matti was doing, Kyllikki said, "I guess you heard that the Nordland AF of L has denounced you people as unpatriotic. You could be arrested if this Espionage Act goes into effect."

"Toadies," Aino answered.

"You grew up in a country governed by a foreign power. You underestimate American patriotism. Those AF of L workers in Nordland aren't toadies. That's the way they see you. They're genuinely patriotic."

"As long as they're getting their money and security," Aino said. She whispered, as if to some spirit unseen, "I told them in Portland they'd hang us with this." She turned to Kyllikki. "Patriotism is going to kill us." She again looked out to the unseen spirit. "We have to kill patriotism."

"Blind patriotism," Kyllikki said.

Sheriff Cobb came with a new warrant every Monday afternoon. Kyllikki would put the house back in order, weeping. On the third Monday, Rauha waited with her. They watched the deputies destroy the interior of the house.

Rauha spit at the sheriff's heels as he left. He whirled on her. He was met by the hardest icy-blue eyes he'd ever seen. He was used to violence and not without courage, but this was a power with which he had never before contended. Quickly deciding that upholding the honor of his office would prove counterproductive, he let the insult pass and walked away.

The day after the Espionage Act went into effect, June 16, 1917, Sherriff Cobb came to the house with three deputies and another search warrant. He informed Kyllikki that he had reason to believe that material pertinent to the case was hidden in the garden. The deputies destroyed the garden, essential for getting through the winter.

"Nothing, boss," one of them reported.

Cobb looked around. "Hmmm. Maybe we got the wrong garden." He looked at Kyllikki and shrugged. Then they all left.

Three days later, Reder came to the house, alone. He was breathing better and the bandages had been removed.

"I assume they don't give warrants to private citizens," Kyllikki said.

"They don't," he answered coolly. "We don't need them as long as the police do our work."

"You smug bastard."

Reder chuckled. "That's not very ladylike, Mrs. Koski."

"What do you want?"

"I want you to come to your senses. They're going to start rounding up you radicals by the carload now that the act is in effect."

"I'm an American citizen. I'm not a member of the IWW. My father is a businessman in Astoria and belongs to the chamber of commerce. My husband owns a logging company. We're hardly communists. That oppressive act can't touch us."

"That's exactly why I'm here. Oh, we'll get that red sister-in-law of yours, the instant we hear a single word that hurts the war effort. But you—we'll have to get you another way. I've come here to give you one last chance."

"Or?"

"When we do find him, we'll throw the book at him. You and your children won't see him for decades." Kyllikki was glad her skirt hid her shaking knees. She reached for her sisu.

"Mr. Reder, I have chores to do. If you'll excuse me." She turned into the house. She felt Reder's eyes on her back. She turned to him. "You know my husband's hotheaded. He didn't mean you harm."

"I know he's hotheaded. So was I at his age. But the son of a bitch nearly killed me. I lost ten days of work. I can't let it go."

"Why not? We can pay you for your lost work. Pay you double."

"You don't just owe me for lost time."

"What do you mean?"

Reder told her exactly what he meant—including interest.

She whirled away from him, slamming the door. Shaking with fear and anger she walked into the bedroom and began packing for Astoria. She didn't tell Aino when she skipped her turn to go to Long Island.

The first day, Matti thought she was delayed. He hid near the beach until sunset, the other designated time. When she didn't show up and it had been dark for several hours, Matti's mild anxiety moved into worry. She wasn't there the next day—or the next.

When Aino arrived on her scheduled visit, she told Matti that Rauha said Reder came to the house and that same day Kyllikki and the children moved to Astoria.

Matti was now beside himself, torn between hiding and worry about why Kyllikki was in Astoria.

Kyllikki came the next week. He rushed to kiss her, but she turned her back on him, pulling the rowboat onto the beach. When he touched her on the shoulder, she whirled around and slapped him.

"Don't you dare tell me you did it for me and the children."

Matti said nothing, rubbing his cheek.

"Goddamn you, Matti Koski. You think I'm the kind of woman who will just spend her husband's money and not ask any questions?"

She threw the food onto the beach and rowed away.

5

While Matti was hiding, the IWW had been acting. On April 16, just ten days after the United States declared war, the union led out over six hundred paper mill workers in Camas, Washington, demanding fifty cents more per day for eight hours' work. IWW log drivers in Brief, Washington, left millions of board feet of logs, critical to the war effort, floating in the rivers. The owners immediately met their demand of five dollars for an eight-hour day. There was a war on and money to be made. The union's strategy of taking advantage of this situation was successful—until it wasn't.

Under an onslaught of bad press, mostly organized by the government and ownership, strikers were painted as siding with Germany and damaging the war effort to line their own pockets. In late May, when the IWW led thirteen hundred miners in Bisbee, Arizona, on strike, protesting dangerous conditions and poor pay, retaliation was swift and brutal. Goaded by the press, two thousand deputized citizens—full of patriotic fervor and armed with machine guns paid for by the mine owners—herded the strikers into manure-strewn cattle cars. They were transported without water or food to the desert town of Tres Hermanas, New Mexico, and abandoned there. Angry citizens everywhere began attacking picketers as traitors.

At Reder's Camp, the loggers were also divided over the question of sabotaging the war effort. To win them over to striking, Aino focused on the ethical question at the root of the conflict: why were they—working people, loyal American citizens—being asked to sacrifice for the war effort by accepting low wages and dangerous and appalling working conditions, while owners were making money from the war and sacrificing nothing?

The government didn't care. It wanted lumber, no matter what. There were rumors that it was willing to send in the army to do the logging if the IWW struck. Owners were focused on costs, not ethics. The IWW was asking for three dollars for an eight-hour day and clear safety rules to stop the horrifying maiming and deaths. It wanted an end to cramming twenty loggers into leaky bunkhouses designed for eight. Often, the younger boys slept three to a bed. It wanted clean quarters without lice and flies and the outhouse shit limed every day and then buried when the pit was full. For the big boys, these demands would hit only earnings per share. For smaller outfits, survival was at stake.

On June 12, Reder asked Aino to talk with him in his office.

"I've been invited to another industry meeting in Nordland on Friday. The big companies are going to ask all of us to form a united front."

"So?"

"You'll be facing the combined power of the government, the timber industry, the banks, the newspapers, and an outraged patriotic public."

"We know that."

"You'll lose, not just to the industry. The IWW's image will be forever tarnished in the eyes of loyal Americans."

Aino knew that as well. She'd argued the very same case to IWW leadership to no avail, but she stayed silent.

Reder put his large forearms atop his desk. "Once I attend that meeting in Nordland," he said, "there will be no way you and I can make a separate deal. If I don't go along with whatever is decided, no one will buy my logs. I'm out of business." He waited for that to sink in. "I'm open to a deal now. What will it take to avoid a strike?"

"You know what the IWW demands are."

"You're asking too much. It'll put me out of business."

"Not if the whole industry bears the same costs. All we're asking for is fairness and human dignity. If we don't get it, we're prepared to fight for it."

Reder looked at her like a father trying to reason with an intelligent teenager convinced of her moral superiority. "The meeting in Nordland will definitely ensure labor costs are the same: low everywhere. Compromise with me."

"Mr. Reder, if I compromise, I'll be a scab."

Aino read Reder's appeal for a compromise as a sign of weakness and held a rally in the dining hall when he left for Nordland. Reder found out when he came to Camp Three on Monday morning.

When Jouka brought in the Shay that evening, Reder shouted from the office steps to come see him. It could only be because of Aino.

"I've tried to reason with her," Reder said. "Now, you get her under control."

"Mr. Reder, she's no horse."

"And if you can't control your wife, you're no man."

Jouka knew the loggers often laughed at Reder, who had trouble controlling Margaret. That was the point, however. They laughed. Jouka felt deeply shamed.

"I want her to stop haranguing my loggers or you're fired and she's evicted. You're only here because she did us that good turn at my daughter's birth."

"I'm here because I'm the best engineer in long-log country," Jouka said quietly.

"Yes, Jouka, you probably are," Reder said, softening. "But this is a business. I don't need the best. I only need one good enough to get the logs to tidewater and you know there are plenty of those. If my loggers go on strike, I'll by God fire you and blacklist you in a heartbeat. And you also tell her, we'll find that son of a bitch brother of hers."

Jouka felt a dark curtain falling on what had been the most satisfying act of his life. He had respect. He had good wages. If Aino would just stay home, he could even have a real wife and maybe someday children.

"Please, Mr. Reder. I worked nights and Sundays learning the mechanics. We haven't had to send for repair parts since I started running the Shay." He hated this groveling. It shamed him nearly as much as the taunt about not controlling his wife.

"One more speech and you're both gone."

"I'll see what I can do, Mr. Reder." Jouka stood there for just a moment longer, fully understanding powerlessness.

Jouka usually whistled when he walked from the rail yard to their shack. Aino watched him walking along the railroad tracks, his head down. The Shay had come in some time ago. She suspected he'd been called in to talk with Reder.

He didn't announce he was home or come in. She opened the door to his back. He'd taken off his boots and was sitting there, looking down the tracks to where the Shay stood in the yard. She wanted to touch his shoulders, but she was afraid. Those shoulders, usually broad and strong, were slumped. Was he fired?

She went inside, saying nothing. After about ten minutes Jouka came in, his shirt off, his suspenders dangling from his waist. He walked over to the stove. "The coffee's cold," he said.

"I'm saving wood. You know that."

He turned to her, the pot in his hand, and he slowly and defiantly poured it out onto the floor. Then he hurled the empty pot at the wall behind their bed. The violent action made her flinch, but she wasn't going to back down. Reder had probably laid down the ultimatum that she knew one day had to come.

Jouka was staring at the pot that now lay on the bed, a brown stain slowly growing around spilled wet grounds. Then quietly, as if talking to the air, he said, "If you make one more speech, I'm fired and we're evicted." Jouka sat on the edge of the bed, his forearms on his knees, looking at the floor. Aino's whole body was tense, anticipating an explosion. She'd seen him fight. If he lost his temper, really lost it, he could kill her.

He looked at her. "All my life, Aino, I was ashamed because my father left us and I can't read. I married you, an educated woman. I worked hard, and I passed the test." He was looking at his clenched right fist. "When I blow that whistle steaming through camp, I blow it for you, to let you know I'm coming through. I'm running the engine. It fills me with pride." He looked up at her. "You're going to destroy that."

She felt herself trembling. She always knew there would be sacrifices. It had never occurred to her that the sacrifice would be someone she loved.

"Do you really want men like Huttula to die so Reder's grandchildren will never have to work? What about our own grandchildren?"

Jouka came to his feet, "We won't have any without having children first." He walked out, slamming the door behind him.

Jouka returned about two in the morning, drunk. She was under the covers, awake. She heard the door shut and his breathing. She smelled the whiskey and the cigarette smoke on his breath. She stayed still, as if somehow staying under the wool blankets would protect her from Jouka's anger. She heard him stumble against one of the chairs at the little table. Then she heard him cursing, picking up the chair, and smashing it against the door. He smashed it repeatedly until it splintered in his hands and he could smash it no more.

"Great," she said aloud. "I assume you're going to be the one who stands to eat."

She heard him breathing. Then he said, "One chair will be enough for this house." He walked out, not bothering to shut the door. She lay there, the room getting colder and colder. Finally, she came out of the warm covers, shut the door, and crawled back into bed.

In the morning twilight before the usual time to go to work, Aino made a speech outside the mess hall. Jouka was getting steam up in the Shay. He'd spent the night in its cab. He lit a cigarette and listened while Aino spoke. There had been no movement from the industry. The next day, June 20, the Reder loggers would either join their brothers from British Columbia to California or be shameful toadies of big business and government. Every logger holding the red card voted for a strike.

Eighty percent of those not holding the card voted to strike as well. Jouka's heart sank.

Reder had been listening from the office steps. He marched over to the Shay and climbed into the cab. Reder said nothing for a while, the red glow of the open firebox lighting his face. Jouka threw another piece of wood into the fire. He shut the door and turned to face Reder, knowing what was coming.

"You are to be out of the house by tonight, or I'll have the sheriff on you."

"No need for that, Mr. Reder."

Jouka picked up a rag and wiped the throttle one last time, saying goodbye.

Reder looked out the cab window, unwilling to face Jouka. "You know that I can't have her back."

"I know."

Jouka carefully folded the wiping rag, relishing the mixed smell of oil and burning wood. "Are you going to blacklist the best locomotive engineer in the woods?"

"I won't have to. As long as you're married to her, you'll never run anyone's lokie." Reder held out his hand. "I'm sorry, Jouka. I don't want there to be any hard feelings. I had no choice."

Jouka looked at Reder's outstretched hand. "All they want are safe conditions, an eight-hour day, and a living wage. You had a choice. Go shake hands with Frederick Weyerhaeuser."

Jouka grabbed his lunch pail and pushed past Reder, jumping to the ground. The tall stumps all around the camp were just visible, long ghosts emerging from the darkness.

They made two trips to Ilmahenki, the second with Ilmari's horse.

The next day, June 20, 1917, fifteen thousand loggers and mill workers all over the Pacific Northwest walked off the job. Lumber manufacturing—and that part of the war effort—ground to a halt.

A week after the big strike was called, Rauha stood with Aino looking at the ruins of Kyllikki's garden. Rauha toed a potato plant and then squatted to set it upright. "What a mess," she sighed. She turned to Aino. "Is Jouka all right?"

Aino was taken aback. "Sure. Of course. Why?"

"Well . . ." She hesitated. "You know. When he came home early this morning." Aino felt a wave of shame. They knew that she and Jouka were having trouble. "Jouka was out drinking, wasn't he."

"He's angry about losing his job. He'll get over it."

"If a man can't provide and protect, he doesn't feel like a man."

"I don't need anyone to do that for me," Aino shot back.

"None of us *need* anyone to do that. But don't you *want* someone to do it?"

Aino bent down to get a stone and threw it sidearm at Matti and Kyllikki's chimney. She missed.

Rauha picked up a stone and threw it overhand with considerable force. It hit the chimney square on. Aino looked at her with surprise. "It was my job growing up to kill the chickens," Rauha said. "I hated it. I started killing them with rocks. I got pretty good at it." She smiled, then picked up another stone and hit the chimney in the same place. "Ilmari kills the chickens in my house."

Two weeks later, Jouka didn't come back at all. He had been making a little money playing at dances, but striking loggers weren't spending much money on those. Some nights he'd come home with just twenty-five cents. He showed up around noon on Sunday. He'd clearly been out in the open all night. Aino was furious.

"You passed out, didn't you?"

"Why do you care?"

"You embarrass me in front of my family."

"Nothing more than I embarrass you?"

"No," Aino said. "Of course, I worried about you . . . It's just that—"

"To hell with you. So, I'm an embarrassment? One way to solve that. Pack my bag."

"I will not," Aino said.

He grabbed her arm, hurting her. "You think *I'm* the only embarrassment in this marriage?"

"Let go of me."

Jouka pushed Aino backward, surprising her with his anger. "I can't find any work here. Because of you. Now, pack my bag so I can go find some work and stop being an embarrassment to you."

Aino's first reaction was to dig in and fight him, but she didn't, knowing her marriage was on the brink. It frightened her. There was Jouka, the man who'd fought for her and for others less able to fight, the best engineer in the woods, the best fiddler in the woods, standing in front of her, his eyes red, his hair and clothes muddy, smelling of vomit and booze, begging for some respect.

She packed his bag.

Rauha, who'd heard the whole exchange, met them in the kitchen with a loaf of freshly baked rieska. She handed the bread to Aino and said in a low voice so Jouka couldn't hear her, "My mother once told me that sometimes by bending, we give them room to stand straight." She nodded her head toward Jouka who was standing next to the kitchen table, the valise at his feet. Aino hesitated. Then she walked over to Jouka and began packing the rieska into Jouka's valise. When she finished, she looked up at Jouka. He reached out his hand. She took it and he helped her to her feet. Then he walked out, leaving Aino with a hole of loneliness she would try to fill by dedicating herself to the coming battle.

6

By the time Jouka left, forty thousand loggers and mill workers and over 75 percent of the logging camps west of the Cascades were out on strike. The IWWs had the moral high ground and thought they were winning.

In all wars, however, both sides think they're right and can win.

On the first of August, a patriotic mob lynched Frank Little, an IWW organizer, in Butte, Montana. The United States Post Office refused to mail newspapers or other written material that any individual postmaster considered to be hurting the war effort. IWW strikers were jailed on charges ranging from disturbing the peace to vagrancy to obstruction of justice.

The most serious response was the Espionage Act. When President Woodrow Wilson urged a Democratic-controlled Congress to pass the act, he declared that "these creatures of passion, disloyalty, and anarchy must be crushed out. They are not many, but they are infinitely malignant." The penalty for violating the act was up to thirty years in prison or death.

Aino lived in fear. Every morning when she awoke, she didn't know if that night she'd be sleeping in jail. Still, every morning she went to work, traveling from camp to camp, encouraging the strikers with news of other strikers, inciting their anger with stories of brutal retaliations, helping the women organize to collect and distribute food, talking doctors into treating strikers' children for free, arguing from upturned boxes on city streets—always wording her arguments carefully so they wouldn't run afoul of the Espionage Act—that what was being done in Europe and to workers at home under the banner of patriotism was wrong. Patriotism was being used to club labor. She was arrested twice but released after a day or two, mostly because the jails were full and she was female.

On August 15, Governor Lister of Washington—under extreme pressure from labor voters on one side and the War Department and federal government on the other—offered a compromise: an eight-hour day with nine hours of pay at the old rates, around twenty-five cents an hour. Details like safety, sanitation, sleeping conditions, and lice were left out.

"No. Don't settle," Aino said to the Reder loggers. She stood in the twilight just at the edge of the bunkhouses at Camp Three, having made her way on a trail avoiding the normal approach on the rail line or the well-worn trail from Tapiola. "He's throwing you a bone so you'll stop barking," she went on. "You act like dogs. You'll be treated like dogs."

The loggers at Camp Three rejected Lister's offer as did loggers and mill workers all over the state.

Because of the strike, Aino could get food to Matti only irregularly and infrequently. He couldn't hunt, for fear of giving himself away. He tried trapping, running the makeshift traps at night. Fishing was out because he could be seen. Aino knew this and with every trip saw him grow leaner. In the last week of August, she decided to make a food run late at night.

Oskar Mannila, a striking mill worker, had gone to Long Island to see if he could get some clams and oysters for his family. He took blankets intending to spend the night and start early the next morning at low tide. Sitting with his back against a driftwood log, he was watching the northern lights—at this southern latitude more like a soft eerie glow than the curtain of colored light he'd watched in his native Finland. Aino unwittingly rowed up onto the beach in front of him. He knew her from her organizing efforts at his mill.

He shouted out her name, but Aino shoved off immediately, saying nothing. She rowed to where she and Kyllikki hid the boat on the mainland and set off overland for Chinook, the little town growing around the Indian village on the Columbia River's edge. From there she took the road to Knappton and got the ferry to warn Kyllikki that Matti's hiding place had very likely been compromised.

"How do we warn him without leading them right to him?" Kyllikki asked.

Aarni started banging a pot with a ladle and marching around the room, another pot on his head for a helmet, shouting in English, "Kill the Boche! Kill the Boche!"

"Mama, make him stop," Suvi cried out. "He took the railroad station."

"Aarni, please," Kyllikki said, moving over to him. He deftly moved in the other direction.

"Kill the Boche. Kill the Kaiser."

Kyllikki's mother appeared at the kitchen door steadying a now toddling Pilvi, a clear they're-your-kids look on her face.

Kyllikki had managed to get the ladle out of Aarni's hand and he threw the pot at her before running up the stairs, "Kill the Boche!" echoing from the upstairs hall.

Kyllikki, watching the empty space at the top of the stairs, said, "He misses his father." She turned to Aino, tears in her eyes. "I can't stay mad at him forever." Aino walked over and hugged her until Suvi tugged on Aino's skirt.

"Is Mama crying because she misses Daddy?"

That made up Aino's mind.

"If he stays where he is, he'll go to jail and we won't see him for years," Aino said quietly. "If he runs again, even if he makes it to Canada, we still won't see him. Winter's coming. He'll starve."

She walked over to the window and looked across the Columbia to where mist rose from dark hills to meet the low clouds that had infiltrated from the ocean.

"I've got to talk to Margaret Reder," she said quietly.

"She must hate you," Kyllikki said. "And Matti, too."

Aino looked at her. "She doesn't hate me; she just thinks she should." She paused. "Just the way I think I should hate her."

Kyllikki was puzzled.

"She wanted to be my friend. It was impossible. Still is." She was already walking to get her coat. "But she'll make a deal."

When Margaret opened the front door, she was astounded to see Aino Koski. Aino was no longer the idealistic girl she'd first seen reading Lenin in Russian over ten years ago. Nor was she the young woman who'd saved her and her baby's lives. She was now a mature woman—with considerable power. She still had that direct bearing all the Finns shared. Aino told her once it was from standing up to winter. Margaret suspected it was also from standing up to more powerful neighbors. "Aino, my God. If John sees you here, he'll . . . he'll . . . I don't know. What on earth are you doing here?"

"Matti can't hide much longer. Winter is coming. He has a wife and two children." She looked coolly at Margaret. "I'm here to make a deal."

"You have a nerve to think there will ever be a deal. Your brother nearly killed my husband and you've done everything in your power to kill our business." She noticed that Aino was wearing her glasses. That happened only when her guard was down.

"We can talk out here or inside," Aino said.

Margaret remembered why she used to like this woman so much. However, she would not give in to that. "Neither place," Margaret replied. "We don't have anything to talk about."

"We do, and you know it."

Margaret opened the door and stood aside.

When John Reder came home Margaret met him on the porch. "Aino Koski is in the kitchen," she said.

"Goddamnit, Margaret . . ."

Margaret put one index finger up and then put it to her lips. "Outside."

The wind was backing off to the northwest where the sky was turning a brilliant orange. Upriver, the clouds glowed soft pink. Reder had his back against the porch railing, his arms folded. She took a deep breath. "She wants you to drop the charges against her brother."

Reder exploded, as she knew he would. "Drop charges? I'll have that son of a bitch hung. You tell her to get out of our kitchen or I'll—"

"John." Margaret moved in front of the door. "I won't throw her out of the kitchen before you talk."

"I'll have the sheriff—"

"What? Ransack her other brother's house?"

"That had to be done."

"I understand that. Doesn't that make you even?"

"No, by God, it doesn't. I'll have that hotheaded bastard in jail if I have to turn this county upside down. I'll have Pinkertons—"

She put her hands over her ears. He went silent.

"John, we're on the edge of financial ruin. The big boys, Weyerhaeuser, Simpson, Bloedel . . . they can weather the storm."

"I can't make a separate deal," Reder said. "They'd ruin *us* instead of the Wobblies."

"She knows that," Margaret said. "She's not asking for a separate deal."

Reder was silent. Then he said, "What's she asking for?"

"She's confirmed that the War Department is putting as much pressure on the owners to settle as it's putting pressure on the Justice Department to round up Wobblies under the Espionage Act. There's going to be another offer. The unspoken alternative is that if both sides don't come to terms, the federal government will step in and nationalize the whole industry."

"That's socialism."

"Ironic, isn't it."

Reder didn't laugh. "You still haven't told me what she's offering."

"Aino will forcefully and publicly argue to return to work. Then, she'll move across the river and cease all organizing activities north of it."

Reder said nothing. Margaret was used to this. Wheels were turning.

"One more thing, John. You did break a beer bottle over his head." She saw that this hit home. One of the many things she loved about him was his innate sense of justice. It's what got him nearly cuckoo over private-property rights—and it was what made him respected by laborers and owners alike.

"OK," he said. "But her brother moves south of the river with her. He promises never to log in Chinook, Wahkiakum, or Nordland Counties."

"Won't work."

Reder was taken aback.

"She won't deliver until he's home," Margaret said.

"I can't gamble on that."

"If she doesn't deliver, you have him arrested. A word-of-mouth deal with a Wobbly will mean nothing to the courts. She'll be taking the gamble, not you."

He pondered on that. "OK." He smiled. "That son of a bitch is the best logger I've ever seen. And he learned it all from me."

Aino retrieved Matti on August 30. After coffee at Ilmahenki, he walked over to Suvantola. It smelled of neglect. There were mouse droppings on the floor and kitchen counter. He returned outside and saw the ruined garden. He was seized with an ache for Kyllikki that was palpable. It was like a vacuum in his heart and stomach, pulling him toward Astoria.

He said goodbye to Ilmari at the mill. Then he went to the house to say goodbye to Rauha. He found Rauha castigating Kullervo for something. When Kullervo walked away, he said, "Go easy on him, Rauha."

"I don't know why I ever let you talk me into hiring him."

"Because no one else in the county will work for you."

She walked away angry, leaving Matti with a slight smile on his face. Welcome home.

He caught up to Kullervo and said, "Don't mind her."

Kullervo had grown tall and filled out since logging the Klawachuck.

"She's a bitch. Worse than my mother, and I'd kill my mother if I knew where she was."

"You don't mean that."

Kullervo gave him a look that chilled him. He thought back on the many times he, Aksel, and Jouka had patched up the boy's bruised and broken skin.

"You need to go easy on each other."

"Maybe I'll join the army."

"Don't. It's not our fight."

"But we're in it."

"Who's 'we'?"

"Us. Americans."

"Well then," Matti said. "*We* are stupid to be over there. I don't see any German gunboat steaming up Deep River." Matti looked around him at the forest-covered hills; at Deep River, placid in the summer; at smoke coming from the chimney of his brother's house as Rauha made supper.

"I heard about your fight," Kullervo said. "Too bad you didn't kill the bastard."

"No. It was too bad I knifed him. My family's uprooted. I have to start all over again in Oregon."

"Let me work for you."

Matti felt sorrow for the little whistle punk he'd met a decade ago, but even he wouldn't hire the rangy twenty-year-old time bomb. "Let me get something going. We'll talk." He watched Kullervo's eyes go to the ground. He knew. "Got to go," Matti said, trying to cover the awkwardness. "I haven't seen my wife in months."

"That's not what I heard," Kullervo said with a smile. He got quiet. "Someday I hope to find a woman like your wife."

"You and every sane man."

7

When Matti knocked on the Saaris' door, Hilda Saari opened it. She called out, "Kyllikki, your children's father is here." She left him there.

Kyllikki came from the kitchen, wiping her hands with a towel. Before she said anything, Suvi, now five, burst through the door from behind her, squealing with pleasure. She was up in Matti's arms, kissing him repeatedly on his cheeks, when Aarni, now three, came through the door, a wooden spoon in his hand. Matti put Suvi on the floor and stood tall, reaching out to Aarni. Aarni pointed the spoon at him, said, "Bang," and ran back into the kitchen.

"You're dead," Kyllikki said, looking at Matti.

Matti opened his arms to her. She folded hers. Suvi, clinging to Matti's trousers, alternated between looking at Matti and looking at her mother.

"If it wasn't for the children . . ."

"I'm sorry."

"Never. Never again, with the puukko."

"Never again."

Matti began to move into the doorway, but Kyllikki didn't budge. "Never again, cheat on a business deal, cheat on anyone."

Matti looked down at his shoes. He looked into her eyes. "Never."

"Suvi," Kyllikki said. "Show your isä his bed." She walked back into the kitchen. Suvi looked up at her father, smiled somewhat tentatively, and then led him by his hand down into the basement.

For Matti, starting again from the bottom took on a whole new meaning.

Four days after Matti's homecoming, on September 5, 1917, the Justice Department raided forty-eight IWW halls across the United States using the Espionage Act for its authority. In Chicago alone, the department indicted 160 IWW leaders for "interfering with the war effort." All faced long prison sentences; those born in other countries faced deportation.

Stories circulated in newspapers about strikers being financed by German gold and being organized by German spies. Thugs were hired to beat strikers on the picket lines. Local police forces arrested strikers under any number of pretexts. As the numbers of arrested strikers rose, the authorities resorted to building bull pens to hold them, as they'd done during the free-speech fights. False stories were published in newspapers saying that strikes were being broken and loggers returning to work elsewhere, so strikers would lose heart. Union halls were ransacked. Angry citizens threatened strikers' families. One striker in Troy, Montana, was burned alive in jail.

Aino knew that she was performing a delicate balancing act. On the one hand, she had to deliver a settlement for Reder to keep Matti free. On the other, she did not want to sell out the strikers, throwing months of fear and hardship under the wheels of the capitalists' and the federal government's freight train. She needed a way for both sides to claim victory. After considerable thought, she knew her course.

She started with the family men. All Camp Three families were short on food and, although food could be supplemented with hunting and fishing, winter loomed. The family men would support Aino against the hard-liners. In addition, she made sure that news about the constant arrests of organizers under the Espionage Act was always in front of the men—and always with the carefully worded innuendo that strikers at Camp Three would be next. On September 12, when the Camp Three strike committee met, she was pretty sure the vote on her proposal would go her way.

"We are going to pretend we agree to the next proposal," she said. "We make sure everyone knows we're doing this because we're loyal

American citizens and are totally behind the war effort. If it were not for our willingness to sacrifice for the war effort, we would still be on strike." She paused, looking at each hard-liner in turn. "Then, we're going to work like Hoosiers and shoe clerks and eat the bosses' food." There was a moment of silence, then a few people who got the strategy laughed. As others caught on, the room started to buzz. Anyone who couldn't log was either a Hoosier—a dumb farmer—or a shoe clerk: a city boy.

"The bosses will know what we're doing, but they'll never be able to buck the pressure from the army. They'll happily take some logs over no logs. Meanwhile, we get paid and fed by Reder."

There were smiles of approval, a few choice ideas about how to work like a Hoosier, and the vote went her way.

Aino's idea spread quickly to mills and logging camps all across the region. When the expected government offer arrived a week later, Reder's loggers didn't make a single protest, nor did loggers from the other camps. The big timber industry strike was "settled" under the approving eye of the United States Army. Owners had to accept so as not to appear unpatriotic; they wanted to accept to avoid losing their army contracts.

Trees went down and logs moved to the mills, but there was a dramatic rise in fouled cables, logjams, slipping chokers, logs dropped from too high onto railcars and damaging the undercarriages, lost tools, conferences to plan how to do something that'd been done a thousand times, leisurely lunches, being unable to understand what a head push wanted, and inability to understand English. The owners knew what was going on, but none of them were going to buck their biggest customer, the U.S. government. And—they were making money again.

Watching from the deck of the *General Washington* as the houses and steep hills of Astoria came ever closer, Aino was despondent. She'd freed Matti and she hadn't betrayed the cause. Some concessions had been made, but they fell far short of what the loggers needed and she regretted what the strike had cost. She knew many of the imprisoned Wobblies. Public opinion, usually sympathetic to the plight of the workingmen, had turned against them as she'd predicted. The tactic of working like Hoosiers was a balancing act: the pressure had to be kept on owners, but stopping or slowing work too much would be seen as unpatriotic.

The late-September light and crisp air, the water of the great river sparkling in the sunshine, the leaves of the oaks and alders turning yellow with the occasional brilliant red of a vine maple peeping through—all went unnoticed. Amid this beauty, she came ashore on the Oregon side, her new home, carrying the weight of the strike's biggest cost: Jouka and her ruined marriage.

It took her until sunset to find Jouka at the Desdemona Club, a proud workingman's club with a sign outside offering its members coffee, tea, and fellowship. With regular monthly payments to the Astoria police and several judges, everyone could enjoy tea and fellowship without interference. Prohibition had been voted in, primarily by Oregon women. Most men didn't give a damn about it, including the police who let the Desdemona Club alone. Half of them drank there themselves.

The bouncer at the door was surly. There was certainly no law against women being in the club; lots of women were in the club, women of a certain type. But he knew Jouka was inside, so he let her in.

It took a moment for Aino's eyes to adjust to the low light of three electric bulbs just over the bar. Some of the tables still had kerosene lanterns. The smell of stale tobacco smoke and spilled beer hit her as if she were coming into a warm barn from a cold Finnish night. The open door had briefly cast bright light against the near wall, but now it was closed. Gradually she could make out the bodies and faces of the men and a few working girls. At the far end of the bar, three full and two empty shot glasses in front of him, sat Jouka, staring at the glasses. The Jouka she'd known—bigger than life—looked older and smaller, bending over his drinks as if guarding them instead of tossing them down with laughter. Her heart lurched.

She worked her way through the standing people and touched her hand to his shoulder. He turned toward her, his eyes bleary and slightly bloodshot. "So," he said. "You gave up organizing for your brother."

But not for him, she filled in silently.

Jouka pushed a glass toward her on the bar. "Sit down. Welcome to Astoria. Have a drink."

"You know I don't drink," she said.

"Oh, yeah. How could I forget?" He picked up the glass he had offered, gulped the liquor down, then held it in front of her face. "Only half an hour of work on the docks, when I get work." He signaled with his hands to the barkeeper for two more shot glasses. "You want a beer? Lime phosphate?"

"I want you to come home with me."

"Where's that?"

"Well, where are you living now?"

"I'm living in a poikataloja on Fourteenth Street. Three to a room. My roommates will be delighted."

"Jouka, look at me, please." He did. "I want to try again. I want to make everything right."

His face, lit by bare, low-wattage bulbs in ceiling fixtures, was stoic and sad.

"I'm sorry," she said.

His face contorted, holding back tears. She touched his knee. "I'm so sorry," she repeated putting her forehead on his thigh.

"Oh, Aino," he moaned. He came to his feet, pulling her up with him and holding her close. "Oh, Aino. Why does it have to be so hard?"

They talked for over an hour. The poikataloja was out as a place to live for several reasons: it had only a three-holer in the back, no running water, no place to cook, and was occupied entirely by single men. She didn't want to bring Jouka to Kyllikki's house, because he smelled. It was awkward enough to impose on your sister-in-law's parents without that. Jouka had put aside seven dollars in the time they'd been separated. Aino had fourteen dollars left from Jouka's wages and an additional ten from her midwifery business.

Earning a living as a midwife was no longer an option in Astoria. There was a hospital, and local doctors were increasingly putting pressure on women to avoid midwives, claiming they were untrained, unhygienic, and unsafe. However, with the lumber strike settled, longshoring was picking up. They could get by as long as Jouka's number got called often enough. To ensure this meant supplying the right people with bootleg whiskey and other gifts, all expensive. They agreed that Jouka would stay at the poikataloja and Aino at Kyllikki's until they could find a place to rent.

When they left the Desdemona Club it was full dark. The night was clear and cold. The polestar could be seen hanging at the end of the Little Bear's tail just above the dark hills on the Washington side of the river, but the city's new electric street lamps made the Little Bear increasingly difficult to see. The Milky Way was undiscernible, lost in a foggy yellow glow.

Jouka walked Aino to the Saaris'. She'd just shut the door when Kyllikki came down the stairs after putting the children to bed.

Kyllikki's nose wrinkled. "So, you found him."

Aino nodded.

"At the Desdemona Club," Kyllikki said.

Aino nodded again, pushed herself off the door, and began taking off her scarf and shawl.

"Come into the kitchen and sit down," Kyllikki said. "We'll have coffee. Everyone's asleep. It's just us. Like old times, when we first moved in with you and Jouka."

Aino knew Kyllikki was trying to assuage her pride, reminding her that she and Jouka had put Kyllikki and Matti up.

"So?" Kyllikki said. "Tell me all."

"Not much to tell."

"He walked you home."

"Yes. I feel like a schoolgirl talking to her mother. Stop it."

Kyllikki laughed. "I will, if you talk."

So, Aino did. It felt good talking with Kyllikki, so different from the earnest discussions with fellow Wobblies—even the women Wobblies—about ideas, tactics, strike funds, and the myriad of injustices.

"I told him I was sorry," Aino said. "Twice. What more can I do?"

"We're going to need more coffee for this one," Kyllikki said. She poured Aino and herself another cup. Aino noticed that the coffee contained no roasted barley.

"He doesn't want an apology. Men will say they want an apology, but what they really want is for you to love them."

Aino sat silent.

"Do you love Jouka?" Kyllikki asked.

Aino didn't answer for some time.

"In the way you're talking about, the being-in-love whirlwind . . . I used to."

"You might find it surprising you're not alone."

That lightened Aino up a little.

"Do you respect him?" Kyllikki asked.

"Other than his drinking. He's a good man, a hard worker. More than once I've seen him wade in to help the underdog. And when he dances . . ." Her eyes brightened with the memory of dances at Knappton when she was a girl. "It's like being no longer of the earth; you never want to come down, and you're perfectly safe." She paused. "He puts up with a lot from me."

"That he does," Kyllikki said.

The two were silent.

"I can't love him if I don't," Aino said.

"Then act as if you love him. Love is expressed by actions. The feelings behind the actions are yours."

"I want to live my life not act it."

Kyllikki studied Aino. "Do you want to save your marriage?"

Aino looked down at her coffee, chagrined. "Sure, I do." She looked up at Kyllikki, her eyes moist. Kyllikki touched Aino's hand and Aino almost wailed, "I do."

Kyllikki waited for Aino to get back under control. "So, what does he want?"

"He wants a good job and a family and a normal wife who wants to be married to him."

"Of course, but you know there's more." Aino didn't answer. "Aino," Kyllikki prompted. "I know you know."

"He wants to hold his head up again," Aino finally said. Aino looked at her coffee. She wiped a tear away.

"Aino, what do you want?"

Cradling her coffee cup, Aino said, in a barely discernible voice, "I want a baby."

8

The next day, when Jouka finished work, he saw Aino waiting where the wharf joined Marine Drive. She stood alone against a stream of chattering women coming from work in the salmon-canning plants. She wore the black wool skirt that brought out her waist and hips and a soft purple blouse he'd not seen before. Her glasses were off, so he knew she couldn't recognize him from a distance. He stopped. Her hair was up, but she'd framed her face with curled tendrils. She'd done it for him. She looked like a schoolgirl wanting to be called on but afraid she might have the wrong answer. Her vulnerability made his heart ache.

With gratitude for her effort and feeling protective, he approached her. She looked up at him and said, "I found a place."

The apartment was in the basement of a three-story Victorian sitting on the hillside about halfway between the city center and Alderbrook, the little fishing village to the east of town. The clatter and ringing bell of the new electric trolley line two blocks down the hill symbolized city life—a new life far from Camp Three, from logging, from the IWW.

With the increased shipping for the war, longshoring work was plentiful. Jouka soon learned how to bribe the foreman to get a high card number. The small bribes, combined with his charismatic good looks and charm, which worked on men almost as well as on women, ensured that Jouka worked almost every day.

City life was way easier than life in Camp Three. The electric lights didn't need kerosene, the walls didn't have a coat of soot, the floors didn't have mud in the cracks, the wind didn't come in through the walls, and the heat came from a radiator without their having to build a fire. Aino didn't have to kill the chickens, butcher the meat, collect the eggs, or grow the vegetables. Someone else did all that for her—as long as Jouka brought home the money. Aino and Jouka were more dependent on others, but these were others neither of them knew or even saw. They lived in the illusion of independence.

Aino had the shopping done and the apartment cleaned by mid-morning. The mending, washing, and ironing were finished by lunch-time. She spent her much-expanded free time looking for work at the salmon-packing companies lining the river. Within a couple of weeks, however, she knew she had been blacklisted. With time on her hands, she began to frequent the office of the Astoria Finnish socialists, the ASSK. Unlike with the IWW, at first, she was barely tolerated, because she was a woman. However, discussing news, arguing socialist theory, speculating about how to move forward, she soon worked her way into being accepted. She avoided the local Wobblies, even walking on the other side of the street from the meeting hall. Too much was at stake.

The socialists, however, were very different from the Wobblies. To her, they seemed to live more on hope than action. *Someday* they would become a viable labor party. They didn't see that once their politicians got into the system, they would become tools of the system like any other politicians. All they seemed to do was talk. However, that was also what Aino liked about the socialists; they talked. The Finnish was flying with an intensity of feeling that reminded her of Voitto, his face shining as he talked socialism back in Kokkola. She could argue without having to guess at meanings or sounding hesitant because the English eluded her. It felt good.

She was always home before Jouka to have dinner ready.

When Aino missed her October period, she was sure the night of con-ception was Sunday, October 7. When she missed her November pe-riod, she told Jouka. He was elated. Aino's change of heart about their marriage filled him with purpose. Although he knew longshoring was nothing compared with running the locomotive, he left each morning whistling. He started playing his fiddle in the evenings. Aino spent a lot of time with Kyllikki, helping her with the children, knitting with her in the rare quiet moments, talking, getting sick.

One evening at a formal business meeting of the ASSK, her frustration at the organization's lack of action boiled over when a member said something about violent Wobblies. "The Wobblies are being clubbed, jailed, and even deported, while you just talk, talk, talk."

"The chair recognizes Aino Kaukonen," Alvar Kari, the president, said drily.

"It's not funny, Alvar. What are we accomplishing here having coffee and coffee cake?"

"We're working to elect socialist candidates to the legislature."

"Don't you see it? We can't beat the system. We have to change it."

"How do you propose to change the system, Mrs. Kaukonen, really?" Kari asked.

"By blowing people up with dynamite," someone shouted from the rear.

That brought Aino to her feet. "No Wobbly has ever, *ever* been found guilty of dynamiting or any other act of terror." She was sick of the constant and false hammering. She turned to better face the membership. "That's the work of anarchists and lunatics. Look what we did last summer."

"Lost a strike," the same voice from the back yelled.

She turned in the direction of the voice. "We didn't lose. We *turned down* the best offer that has been made in the history of the industry. Did you or your socialist candidates get that? No. Did the toadies for the AF of L get that? No. *We* got it, the IWW, through direct action."

The same voice came from the darkness in the back. "You got it because the army's back is against the wall to get spruce to fight the Germans. The kaiser's done more direct action than any of you rabble-rousers."

"OK, OK." Kari was banging his gavel amid the laughter. "Order. Order."

She sat down, angry at these socialists who clung to the myth that they lived in a democracy ruled by the people for the people.

* * *

After the meeting, Kari brought her a cup of coffee and a small plate
with some pulla on it. He was an older man, well into his fifties. He
ran the head rig for Astoria Lumber and Plywood and had logged,
fished, worked green chain, and raised five children. He'd been an
active socialist in Helsinki. "Come and sit, Aino." He lit a pipe while
she settled with the coffee and pulla. Then he said, very calmly, "Aino,
the government is going to crush the Wobblies. The people hate them."

"Over half the loggers west of the Cascades hold the red card."

"And when the army lowers the boom, there will be torn-up red
cards all over the woods."

She remembered the torn-up cards in the mud in Centralia and
said nothing. The feeling of a heavy iron door closing hit her again. She
rallied. "Then there will be revolution, like in Russia."

"Where workers have no alternatives and no hope. Here, they
have both."

"Pie in the sky."

"Stop being flippant." Kari took a puff on his pipe. "It's a very real
pressure-relief valve."

"But it's *false*. 'Everyone is equal' is as good a myth as Christianity and heaven. It's economic Calvinism. If you're one of the elect,
the right parents, the right schools, the right connections, you get into
capitalist heaven. The rest are damned at birth."

Kari smiled at the image, then became serious. "I know you can
organize. Suppose, instead of overthrowing capitalism, we workers
become capitalists ourselves? We all chip in and build a sawmill, our
own company."

"Cooperatives are nothing new."

"But they're new here. And it's something we can do. If God grants
us just one or two small victories, we'll be way ahead of the game. We
can throw our lives away trying for the big victories."

That night, she couldn't sleep. All would chip in equally. They
would buy or lease land and sawmill equipment, manufacture and
sell lumber, and equally share the income. The co-op members would
vote on what decisions required a vote of everyone and what decisions

could be delegated to the board or managers, also elected by the members. Instead of involving a whole industry, all the organizing would be local. She could still have a family.

That morning at breakfast, Jouka listened to Aino with a sinking heart. When he asked her why she couldn't wait until the baby was well along, he saw the flash of anger quickly masked, followed by assurances that all the organizing was local and wouldn't interfere with the baby. He felt powerless in the face of her excitement. It made her happy and he wanted her to be happy. How could he ask her not to get involved? He kissed her goodbye at the bottom of the stairs that led to the street level. As he walked to the docks, no tune came into his head and he did not whistle.

Aino rushed through the dishes and making the bed, put on her new blouse and best wool skirt, and set off for Manion's Realty. The sawmill would need land and she took it upon herself to find some before the next meeting. She knew the Seattle, Portland, and Spokane rail line had been extended sixteen miles south to the little coastal town of Neawanna. The tracks ran alongside Youngs River for several miles and land was still plentiful there. She took the trolley to the end of the line and walked down the rail tracks, humming to herself, filled with energy.

She managed to get home in time for Jouka's dinner, totally worn-out. She tried to listen to stories about near accidents, one that really happened, what ships were in from where, but she was thinking about how to present her ideas that night to Alvar Kari. She forced herself to clean up after dinner and put up her hair. She left Jouka where he'd fallen asleep in their single armchair, still in his working clothes, and where she would probably find him when she returned. Struggling to drag herself up the stairs, she reached the street and threw up her dinner. She looked at the river below her and asked it for strength. She waited, feeling its dark water rolling toward the sea in the ebb. Then she wiped her chin and lips and set off for Suomi Hall and the first board meeting of what they would name that night the Workingman's Lumber

Manufacturing Cooperative, with Alvar Kari as president and Aino Kaukonen as secretary.

Two men who worked with Alvar at Astoria Lumber and Plywood were there. Sitting in the social room, the four of them calculated the cost of the minimal equipment to get started. Aino had located two potential parcels earlier that day that could probably be leased and perhaps someday owned by the co-op. With fifty workingmen, all contributing a hundred dollars, they could start. Convincing fifty workingmen, and—more important—their wives, to leave good jobs when prices were climbing because of the war wouldn't be easy. On the other hand, it was a good time to start, for the same reason.

The three men's jobs would primarily be acquiring and setting into operation all the equipment once they'd selected a site, after which, if duly elected, they would manage operations. Aino's primary job would be recruiting. She was also to create a legal entity to buy and sell lumber, pay bills and wages, and have a bank account, all without having to pay a lawyer. Once the co-op was in operation, if duly elected, she would manage the office. Finns in the Midwest had formed co-ops. She could write to any of them for advice. It didn't seem too daunting. The daunting part would be talking Jouka into putting up a hundred dollars.

She served him his breakfast and sat across from him, smiling, pouring them both coffee. She first talked about the excitement of the idea of worker cooperatives, how all workers could be owners, no longer exploited. He understood that. It was a good cause. He just wasn't quite as excited about it as she was. Then she talked about the opportunities of being an owner/worker in a sawmill. He pointed out that he really didn't much like the idea of working in a sawmill no matter who owned it. She felt this was selfish on his part and pointed it out to him. He responded by pointing out that risking her and the unborn baby's health by running around organizing, trying to be a big shot, was selfish. She had her priorities backward. What about a family? What about him? She came back with it being no different from any other local job. She could easily take care of him and the baby. She knew it was a sacrifice for him to get the money at the docks, but think of it as a real investment in their future—as a family.

"Money? Investment?" Jouka asked.

"Sure. You think these things start for nothing?"

"How much?"

"A hundred dollars."

He stood up, nearly shouting the price, several times. She stood up and shouted back at him that he was acting like a child.

He walked off to the docks without finishing his breakfast.

When Jouka finally came home around midnight, reeking of alcohol, he flopped facedown on their bed without even taking off his boots. The next morning the previous night's dinner of cold stew was still on the table. Aino poured a cup of coffee and set it next to the cold stew. Jouka poured the hot coffee on top of it.

"Childish," she said.

"Like leaving cold stew."

He left.

She cleaned up, made the bed, put on her new blouse again, and went to the county courthouse to start researching. She thought briefly of doing abortions to get the hundred dollars. Doctors weren't doing that, at least not openly. The memory of Lempi, however, put a quick stop to that. If she had to crawl to Matti and Kyllikki, she would. She would never crawl to Jouka.

She came back to the apartment in the early afternoon and baked bread and pulla, setting them both out with coffee cups, ready for Jouka when he came home. Then she sat down and stared at the set table. Nausea hit her again. How did the baby fit into all this? The Indians worked all day with their babies right there, strapped to their backs or cradled in front of them. Those women could do it. Could she? But they worked together and took their babies to work with them. She rushed over to the sink and threw up.

9

Aino and Jouka were civil with each other when they went to the Saaris' for Sunday dinner. Matti had found work busheling for Warila Logging, an Astoria-based gyppo. Busheling meant getting paid by the tree, not the hour. A busheler could make triple what an hourly logger made, but it required skill, stamina, a good partner, and speed. Speed was dangerous. Matti was complaining that his partner was too slow.

"There's not a logger in the county that you wouldn't find too slow," Kyllikki said, holding Pilvi as she passed a plate of pot roast from where her father was carving down to where Hilda Saari sat, flanked by Suvi and Aarni. Matti had worked his way out of the basement, but only after Kyllikki had asked for, and gotten, a vow about temper and theft, which she said was as serious as their marriage vows, because their marriage depended on it.

Hilda Saari was cutting Aarni's meat, while Suvi watched with a slight pout.

"Grandma, I want you to cut my meat, too," Suvi said in English.

"Talk to your grandmother in Finnish," Kyllikki said quietly. She slipped another spoonful of riisipuuro into Pilvi's mouth.

"That's old-country language. Mary Peterson told me."

"Suvi, we're Finns. We speak Finnish here."

"*I'm* an American," she said in Finnish.

"Well, cut your own meat like a good American then," Kyllikki said.

Suvi gamely went at the meat with her table knife, only to have it slip off the plate onto the tablecloth. She looked up to see if she was in trouble. Kyllikki simply nodded at it indicating that she should put it back on her plate, which she did.

"It wants a puukko," Suvi said.

"American girls don't have puukkos," Kyllikki said.

Suvi's jaw went out and she looked at her father. "She's right," Matti said. "Only Finn girls have puukkos."

Hilda Saari reached into her dress pocket, pulled out her woman's puukko, and started to cut Suvi's meat with it. "Maybe," she said in Finnish, "if you decide to be a Finn girl, someday you can have this one."

"I can?" Suvi asked.

"Maybe. But you have to be a good Finn girl."

Suvi looked at her grandmother, then stabbed her fork into one of the pieces of cut meat. "Americans don't need puukkos," she announced. "They get their meat cut at the store." She looked puzzled when everyone laughed.

When the laughter died, Matti asked Jouka, "Why not go logging with me?"

"I haven't been on the wooden end of an ax for years."

"You're only thirty-two. You'd soon get back in shape, just like the Reder days."

"Not so very long ago for me."

Kyllikki broke in brightly. "How are the soldiers doing, Matti?"

In October, the federal government, desperate for spruce, had sent in the army to overcome the lost production resulting from the work-like-Hoosiers tactics. It had proved a dangerous failure.

Matti laughed. "We sent five of them back for sky hooks on Friday. They're about one-third the speed of real loggers."

"One-third the speed and three times the wages," Aino said.

"I'd draft loggers," Matti said. "They'd make better wages as army privates and the army would get a lot more wood."

"I'd happily run a locomotive for army wages *and*," Jouka emphasized, "army hours."

"I can go one better than the army," Matti said. "You know those two parcels of spruce by Bean Creek on the Washington side? Well, the deal worked out by Aino and Kyllikki"—he smiled at them to show his appreciation, which in turn was appreciated—"I can't log in Washington so I sold them last week."

"To Reder," Kyllikki broke in, giving a what-can-you-do gesture with her hands.

"Oh, Matti. no," Aino said.

"Aino, money's neutral."

"It's not neutral. You got started because the government gave Ilmari a timber claim of thousands of board feet for free," Aino said.

"I got started because I took thousands of board feet of worthless wood sitting there for centuries doing no good for anyone and got it to a mill where it was turned into houses."

"Enough," Emil Saari broke in.

"I'm tired of busheling," Matti said. "And I have enough money to get started again. I need a real partner, a logger who can do everything. What do you say, Jouka?"

The look of gratitude and pride on Jouka's face would have brought tears if everyone at the table weren't a Finn. "We'll call it Two-K Logging, Kaukonen and Koski."

"Too bad Aksel's not here," Kyllikki said. "It would really be like the old days."

"Yoh," Matti said. "No one knows where he is."

Aino saw in her mind the open door to Aksel's and Lempi's empty shack.

At that very moment, Private First Class Axle Langston of the United States Army's First Infantry Division shivered in the dark in a trench in the Sommerville sector of the lines, ten kilometers southeast of Nancy, France. After he left Knappton, he sought solace drinking bootleg liquor in Nordland. He then sought solace with prostitutes in Seattle. Finding none, he made his way to New York City on freight cars, found the city intolerable, and so headed to Florida because he'd never seen a palm tree. Out of money and ideas by the spring of 1917, he still couldn't face returning home and the memories it would evoke.

The army offered a new start, guaranteed room and board, distraction, the possibility of excitement, and, most of all, a legal path to citizenship. Two months after he joined, the United States entered World War I. The first three promises had been delivered. The path to citizenship, however, was fraught with peril.

10

During the summer strike, General of the Army John J. Pershing brought a favorite officer, Brice P. Disque, out of retirement, made him a lieutenant colonel, and told him to solve the labor mess in the Northwest—by any means. The army needed ten million board feet of spruce every month. The disgruntled loggers were producing two million.

After several fruitless months of negotiating with both sides, Disque realized that unless the loggers got more pay, better living conditions, and safer working conditions, they would never log fast enough to meet production requirements. He also saw that the owners would never knuckle under to the IWW. Unable to break the impasse, he convinced Pershing to send in the army.

It was a disaster that had all the loggers laughing and the owners totally frustrated. Out of the disaster, however, both management and labor could see that the government was willing to throw millions of dollars and thousands of drafted men at the problem, no matter how inefficient that solution was. Both the IWW and the owners would be sidelined.

A week after the soldiers started logging, Disque and a small group of business and AF of L leaders met in the office of University of Washington president Henry Suzzallo. They formed a new union, firmly anti-Wobbly, called the Loyal Legion of Loggers and Lumbermen. "Loyal" was the key word. All its members would be required to swear a loyalty oath stating they would "stamp out any sedition or act of hostility against the United States government."

Disque then convinced the War Department to form the Spruce Production Division and to draft loggers to fill its ranks. This put the entire industry under military law. Loyalty to any union attempting to slow production would be a court-martial offense.

On November 7, the Bolsheviks seized power in Moscow. The American public welcomed the sweeping changes in government power, giving no thought to their effects on personal liberty.

Aino knew they'd won a tactical victory; their demands were mostly met. But they had suffered a severe strategic loss. The government of the people, by the people, and for the people had ensured that workers would get fatter crumbs from the capitalists' table but never be seated there. The sole bright spot was Russia. When the revolution spread to Finland, she was filled with hope.

"Now we can all go back to Suomi," she said to Kyllikki, her eyes sparkling. "We'd be part of building the new world."

"Aino," Kyllikki said, pouring coffee while Suvi held her by the back of her skirt, pressing a cheek against her hip and staring at Aino. "You're married to an American and you're pregnant. You're living in the new world already." Kyllikki pulled up a chair, dragging Suvi with her. "Suvi, you go play with Aarni. If you want to stay here with us, you have to be quiet." Kyllikki waited for Suvi's decision, which was to run off to her brother. "People are starving in Helsinki. Only a moron would go back."

"Food will be distributed for free once we take full control."

"Russia's headed for civil war. Finland won't escape it."

"Capitalist propaganda. How can there be a civil war when ninety-five percent of the country is working people?"

"Yes, and two-thirds of them are farmers and ninety percent are Lutherans, just like Ilmari and my father. He *hates* what is happening in Finland. He wants General Mannerheim to stop the disaster that you call paradise."

"Well, he'd better get used to it, because it's going to happen here, too."

"Aino, revolutions require visionary leaders. In America, the visionary leaders go into business."

On December 6, Pehr Evind Svinhufvud declared Finnish independence in Helsinki. Two days later there was a celebration dance at Suomi Hall. Many of the women hung hand-sewn flags showing various sizes of light blue cross on a white background in the style flown by Finnish fishermen and other private boat owners. Others showed crosses or designs of red and yellow, the colors of Finland's coat of arms. Still others, however, showed a yellow hammer and sickle on a red background. Suomi Hall nearly became the first battlefield of the Finnish Civil War.

Emil Saari and Alvar Kari took the stage to try and calm things. Alvar held a small copy of the flag imposed on Finland by Russia, the hated orjalippu, the slaves' flag. The crowd hushed. With great solemnity, Emil struck a match and set the flag on fire. The crowd roared as Alvar waved the burning flag over his head, scattering smoking pieces. The band began playing "Finlandia." The harmony was short-lived.

Fueled by illegal alcohol from hip flasks, unconscious rivalry over still-scarce women, growing news of atrocities in Finland perpetrated by both sides, and just plain old grudges for any number of previous slights and injustices, a fight broke out between several ASSK socialists and some loggers and fishermen who begged to differ with their politics. It started on the dance floor but quickly moved into the reception hall where two tables filled with hard-earned and diligently prepared food collapsed in a crash of crockery. The younger women and girls watched from the walls with their hands over their faces, some covering their fear and horror, others covering their excitement. The older women, who'd done most of the work and known many of the fighters since they were little boys, waded in with iron soup ladles and large wooden mixing spoons. This galvanized their husbands to restore order.

Aino found Kyllikki holding the pieces of the beautiful porcelain serving plate she had risked taking to the hall to display her pound cake. Furious, she thrust the pieces toward Aino. "Politics," she said.

*   *   *

On Sunday, eight days after the celebration of Finnish independence, Matti answered the door, having successfully dodged the weekly Saari trek to the Evangelical Lutheran Church. Standing before him was a rather unimposing-looking man in civilian clothes. The man put his hand out. "I'm Captain Ed Denning. I work for Colonel Brice Disque, commanding officer of the Spruce Production Division of the Aviation Section of the U.S. Signal Corps. I assume you know all about us."

Matti shook his hand. "Yoh," was all he said.

"May I come in?" Denning asked.

"Yoh." Matti showed him to the living room.

"Your family, Mr. Koski?"

"At church."

"Of course, it's Sunday."

Matti said nothing.

"Mr. Koski, we're both busy men. I'll get right to the point. People tell us you're the best logger in two states. We want you to join the Spruce Division as a senior sergeant. We need men who know how to log and how to handle loggers."

"I have my own company."

The man took in the steady gaze. "I'll make no bones about it," he said. "We have the power to draft you, even if you're not a citizen. I'd rather you volunteered to serve your country."

Matti said nothing.

"If you volunteer, you'll have a senior sergeant's pay and be able to send every penny of it home to your family, because the army will provide for all your needs. You'll have a clear path to citizenship."

Matti watched the man's face carefully. This man, perhaps in his midthirties, had the full backing of the United States government. Not only could Matti be drafted, but he could also be deported. The government could make sure nobody would buy his logs at any price.

Then Captain Denning coolly delivered the coup de grâce. "We can have you jailed for obstructing the war effort under the Espionage Act."

Matti thought about the power behind this man. He thought about his family. Then he said, "I have a partner, Jouka Kaukonen, who's the best locomotive engineer in the Northwest. Same deal for him?"

There was no hesitation. "Same deal."

Matti told Kyllikki that night. He told Jouka at work early Monday morning. Two days later, Jouka and Matti were heading east on the Spokane, Portland and Seattle train to Fort Vancouver just across the Columbia from Portland. The headline on the small article on page three of the *Astorian* read: FINNISH FAMILY SENDS VOLUNTEERS TO SPRUCE DIVISION, followed by, "Mr. Matti Koski and Mr. Jouka Kaukonen, of Two-K Logging, have volunteered to help bring sound logging practices to the newly formed Spruce Division. They will be stationed at one of several division camps west of Port Angeles. In an interview just before the pair boarded the train for Vancouver Barracks, Mr. Koski said he did it because he loves his newly adopted country and he loves to log. He and his brother-in-law, Jouka Kaukonen, will add much-needed skill, many years of experience in the woods, and their spirit of patriotism to the American war effort."

Kyllikki, with Aarni and Suvi holding her skirt on each side; and Aino, standing to Suvi's left, holding Pilvi's hand, stoically watched the train disappear. Neither of them knew when they would see their men again. For Kyllikki, Matti had just returned from months of hiding, but neither of them would risk deportation or jail. Aino wanted to make the marriage work, but with Jouka in the army, that effort stopped. She also faced carrying, delivering, and parenting the baby alone. On the other hand, there would be a steady government paycheck and she could focus everything on recruiting for the co-op.

11

Knowing it would be gauche to try recruiting at Christmastime, Aino reluctantly left for Ilmahenki on Christmas Eve. It seemed such a backwater now. She loved being in the thick of things. She loved being the one the men came to with the myriad problems that had nothing to do with manufacturing—problems she could solve with solutions she controlled. She feared that this would be lost when the baby came.

She smiled graciously at the congratulations from Rauha and Ilmari about her pregnancy. She basked in the bustle, the children, the food, seeing Ilmari so full of joy at Christmas. Kullervo came for a Christmas dinner of baked ham, rutabaga casserole, and beetroot salad. He entertained them with stories from the old Reder's Camp days with Matti, Aksel, and Jouka and of logging on the Klawachuck. It felt good to hear the stories, but it also heightened the effect of their absence.

For dessert, Rauha served her star-shaped puff pastries with plum jam and poured coffee for all, including sweetened coffee with half milk for the children.

Then, as if she couldn't stand the good feelings, Rauha shooed Kullervo out of the house to go tend the cattle and got on Aino about the new co-op being more competition for Sampo Manufacturing.

"It's going to increase log prices and lower lumber prices," Rauha said. "Am I not right, Ilmari?" She looked at Ilmari for support, making him squirm, not wanting to be caught between the family hard rock and flat place.

"Well, it's a big market," Ilmari said.

* * *

Aino returned to Astoria and Kullervo to his lean-to. January was typically cold and wet, with occasional slushy snow that would melt after a few days, the temperatures never climbing out of the low forties. Rauha seemed to begrudge every meal she provided to Kullervo, and Kullervo became increasingly disgruntled with her and the weather.

On the last day of January, Kullervo sat on his haunches, the ground far too soaked to sit on directly, smoking the second half of the cigarette he had rolled that morning. He was shivering. He did some jumping jacks, cigarette in his mouth, and then squatted again. He'd asked the ice queen for a coat and she told him if he saved his money instead of throwing it away on cigarettes and Saturday nights, he would have one of his own. A spatter of rain came on a cold gust and hit his back.

He walked over to throw some wood on the smoldering fire in front of the makeshift lean-to where he slept. He squatted with his back to the fire, looking toward the north end of the meadow where a broad muddy path had been trampled alongside the small stream that ran from the meadow through a cleft between two hills and then fell rapidly toward Deep River. Rauha Koski would be coming up that path with his food, he hoped. She was supposed to have been here yesterday but hadn't showed up.

The cattle all lifted their heads toward the gap. Kullervo quickly ground out his cigarette and put the remains in his shirt pocket. He grabbed his cattle goad and was walking along the south side of the herd when Rauha, panting with the short climb, emerged into the meadow carrying a dinner pail.

He watched her make her way around the herd, bundled in one of Ilmari's coats, which she easily could have lent him. He also watched her counting the herd as she moved along.

A fine rain fell straight and soundless in the cold air, so still he could hear the large drops that had formed in the boughs of fir and hemlock trees smack onto the leaves of the underlying salal and Oregon grape.

Rauha held the bucket out to him and said, "Here."

Kullervo took the bucket without speaking and opened the lid. Inside was a congealed glob of boiled potatoes and parsnips set next to some hard-boiled eggs. He looked at her. "This is it? What about dinner?"

"Plenty there for lunch and dinner."

"You said room and board." He pointed to the rough shelter. "That's not room." He poked his finger into a boiled potato and held it in front of her face. "This is not board."

"And what you do is not work."

God damn her. He felt the anger tensing his entire body. "I want Ilmari's coat," Kullervo said. "I'm freezing to death here."

"Use the blankets. I gave you two."

"If I use the blankets outside, they get wet and are no good for sleeping. If I use them in the shelter, I can't watch the cattle."

"Use one for rainy days and then the dry one at night."

The comment evoked a memory of his mother telling him to shut up when he'd begged her one rainy cold night for blankets for him and his sisters. No matter what he asked, no matter what he said, she gave an answer that belittled and mocked him. The rage of a little boy, rage that had to be buried so he wouldn't be hit, so his sisters wouldn't be hit, took him over. He slung the lunch pail at Rauha, hitting her full on the side of the head. Rauha screamed and slapped him across the face. Then her face turned into his mother's and he hit her with the cattle goad—and hit her again—and again.

The rain was still falling soft and silent. Depending on one's mood, it could feel like a mother cooling your feverish forehead or like the Chinese water torture. The rain never changed.

It wasn't his mother; it was beautiful, cold, blond Rauha Koski, crumpled and lifeless in front of his knees. Blood from her face and head slowly dissolved in the mud. He knelt beside her body and looked at the cold, gray sky and cried the cry of all who are pushed beyond the point from which there is no recovery.

He jabbed the cattle goad into his thigh and the pain coursed through him, meeting the terrifying rising panic. He then leaned over her and wept, repeating, "God, God, God . . ."

He dragged Rauha's body to the muddy path between the hills and laid it in a fetal position on its side, the arms over the head, as if trying to protect it. He took two pitch-laden limbs that he sometimes used for light at night and put them in the fire. When they were blazing, he ran into the herd, separating yearlings from cows, making the cows nervous. Their rolling eyes reflected the firebrands. They began lowing and bumping into each other. He ran to the south end of the meadow, screaming, cougar-like, screaming his madness. He rushed again and again at the herd. Again and again, waving the firebrands above him, stabbing at their eyes, screaming, he got three cows running. Within seconds, the lowing had turned to bawling and, as if united by a single, crazed mind, the cattle stampeded for the narrow pass.

When it was over, Rauha's body lay in the mud, recognizable only by the bloody, trampled clothing.

The cattle had come running down the bank of Deep River and had slowed to a walk by the time they passed in front of Matti and Kyllikki's empty house, moving to their familiar pasture in Ilmahenki. Ilmari heard them lowing. Wondering why Rauha would want them down from the meadow, he stood up by the head rig, looking. The cattle seemed to be milling aimlessly. Seeing neither Kullervo nor Rauha, he immediately knew something was wrong. He walked to the house where Jorma, age five, looked up at him from where Rauha had set him cleaning the kitchen stove's firebox. Mielikki and Helmi were both at school.

"Where's your mother?"

"She took Kullervo's dinner."

Ilmari ran. Dodging the occasional stray cow that had lagged behind the herd. Ilmari turned up the creek from Deep River, following the ever-increasing violence of the churned mud. He found Kullervo weeping over Rauha's body. His face and hands were badly bruised. Blood was slowly oozing from a bad gash on the back of his head. He was covered in mud.

Ilmari went to the ground, soundless. He lifted Rauha's smashed head from where it had been pulverized into the rocks and mud and held it gently against his knees. He looked up at the gray sky in anguish, saying nothing. Then he buried his face on Rauha's chest and said the Lord's prayer. "... Thy will be done ... For Thine is the kingdom and the power and the glory forever. Amen."

He stood looking down at Rauha's body and then, turning to Kullervo, said, "Let's take her home."

They laid Rauha's body in the empty living room of Suvantola and covered her with a sheet. Ilmari asked Kullervo to inform the sheriff of the death. He then waited for the girls to come home from school, helping little Jorma with the firebox chore, treasuring him, seeing Rauha in his face and hair. When Mielikki, just turned nine two weeks earlier, and Helmi, seven, came home from school, he sat the children down and told them that their mother had been trampled and died. They sat in stunned silence until Helmi started to cry. Mielikki put her arm around her sister, pulling her head into her own body to muffle the tears. Little Jorma just stared at his sisters, too young to understand. Then Ilmari pulled Jorma in next to his sisters and the four of them swayed together, close, and silent. Then Ilmari said, "Äiti's happy and safe with the angels. No need to cry." He stepped back. "I have to go tend to your Äiti now. I want you to stay here. Mielikki, can you get started with supper?"

Mielikki nodded, fully aware she'd just stepped into her mother's shoes.

At Suvantola, Ilmari laid Rauha's body on boards across two saw horses. He washed the body, nearly alabaster white where the sun never reached, and then he washed the mud from Rauha's shining hair, drying it with towels before combing and braiding it. Leaving the doors and windows open to keep the body cool, he left her under the sheet, with a single candle burning at her head.

He checked on the children. Mielikki already had them in bed. Then he walked through the dark into town. There he sent telegrams from Higgins's store to Louhi and Matti, including Kyllikki and Aino in the greeting, saving the cost of one telegram, but adding the cost of two words.

He set the funeral for Sunday, three days hence, so no one would miss work.

He worked all night in the barn making a coffin. When he'd finished, he walked into Tapiola to arrange for burial on Peaceful Hill. He passed the little church. It stood there, forlorn and empty. He looked down and kicked a small rock. When he looked up, tears were streaking down his cheeks. He looked up to the steeple and beyond it into the gray clouds and beyond the gray clouds. In anguish, he cried out, "Miksi, Isä?" Why, Father? Then he stood there, waiting. There was no answer.

12

Aino and Kyllikki caught the *General Washington* on Saturday afternoon and made their way in the dark to Ilmahenki. Louhi arrived two hours later, having caught the last boat from Willapa to the mouth of Deep River, walking the rest of the way, alone with her thoughts. Ilmari suggested she not open the coffin, but she did anyway and sat on the porch all night with a single candle looking at the trampled beauty of her daughter.

Pastor Hoikka gave the funeral service on Sunday afternoon.

That night, Louhi slept with Mielikki. The next morning, as she was leaving, she told Ilmari that as had been agreed when Sampo was formed, Rauha's share of Sampo had passed to her and she now was the majority shareholder. Still, he was to run it as he had all along. Ilmari pointed out that with Rauha's share of the profits now going to Louhi, there would barely be enough to keep the children and the farm going.

"They're your grandchildren," Ilmari said.

"You didn't need to make them," she replied and left.

Ilmari stopped going to church. Instead, on Sundays that weren't too wet and miserable, he would take the children to see Vasutäti. Helmi and Jorma would do what most children did in the woods: dam the creek, look for birds' nests, dig up licorice root, throw things. Mielikki stayed at the camp along with Ilmari, who took on chores that Vasutäti had difficulty doing.

Vasutäti was moving Mielikki into increasingly beautiful patterns and designs—each basket assigned being correspondingly difficult.

Mielikki would bring the basket she'd been working on during the week. Vasutäti would inspect it carefully, pointing out flaws, treating Mielikki as an adult with pudgy fingers. The Ini'sal had little room for a long childhood. Vasutäti taught Mielikki basket weaving the same way she taught Ilmari to enter the space between the kantele notes, guiding Mielikki into the spaces between the basket wands. Being nine and gifted, Mielikki could absorb Vasutäti's teaching at an uncanny rate.

Being nine, she also could get tired and frustrated. One day she threw her basket onto the ground and sat down abruptly on a log. "When is a basket good enough for you?" Mielikki asked, near tears.

Vasutäti sat down next to her. "There are three good-enoughs in basket weaving. The first is that your basket does the job it was made for." Mielikki nodded. "The second is that your basket will hold water for a year." Mielikki showed despair. "The third is when you can make a basket without worrying about whether it is good enough. The third one is hardest."

Mielikki rubbed away a tear with the back of her hand and smiled.

When Ilmari finished the chores, he would sit by the fire meditating while Vasutäti and Mielikki worked together at the entrance to the shelter. When Ilmari entered that world, that space between moments, even the children's interruptions were simply part of the whole.

Members of the church came by Ilmahenki on several occasions. Mielikki served coffee, as was the duty of the woman of the house. Ilmari was polite but adamant. If there was a God, He or She or It—as Ilmari mildly put it, knowing this would disconcert them—wasn't around Deep River.

"Why don't we go to church anymore, Isä?" Mielikki asked one day.

Ilmari put his hand on her head, as if in blessing, and said nothing for a long time. Then he said, "I don't know."

Mielikki, hugged him around the waist and put her cheek on his stomach. "Don't be so sad, Isä. Please don't be so sad."

Two months after Rauha's funeral, Louhi was back, sitting next to a driver in a black 1915 Dodge touring car. Convict labor had helped push a gravel-and-rock road south from Nordland all the way to Ilwaco, but Tapiola was still connected to that road only by the old wagon road, muddy most of the winter and spring. The going was slow and rough. Still, what had taken two days a decade earlier now took only six or seven hours.

Ilmari watched the car lurch across the field between Ilmahenki and the mill. Maybe he would get an automobile someday. A Packard—he'd seen a picture in a newspaper—now *that* was a real piece of machinery.

Louhi got down from the car with a valise and leaned in to say something to the driver. He drove off. She waved at Ilmari, shouting, "When you quit work."

He was proud of Sampo and had wanted to show it to her in action, but she was already disappearing into the house. Sampo Manufacturing wasn't Pope and Talbot, but it was profitable and the eleven men he employed in two shifts liked working there. The old waterwheel had been replaced by steam boiler, so the mill now ran at full speed winter or summer. Hard shovel work had enlarged the millpond the previous summer. That got the log inventory out of the river, which ranged seasonally from gentle stream to roaring torrent. Now, instead of wrestling the current to move the logs to the chain conveyor belt that lifted them from the water to reach the head rig, the first and largest saw in the mill, they could move logs around in still water and sort them by length and grade to maximize mill profits.

As he lined up the next big log, doing the geometry nearly unconsciously to maximize the value of the cut, he wondered why Louhi was here. Prices for two-by-tens were up—floor joists for barracks. Rotating the log to maximize for two-by-tens, he committed to the first cut. The steam belched out of the boiler, the leather belts roared, the chains clattered. If he made the first cut wrong, he could lose half the value of the log. What did Louhi want? Profits were good. To see the grandchildren? Maybe. She was getting on and he'd heard women sometimes changed when they became grandmothers. He wondered if his mother had changed, but then Maíjaliisa had never seen her grandchildren, other than the pictures they took in Astoria at Palmer's Studio and mailed to her two years ago. Sure, some people called Rauha an ice queen. But she was a queen, a beautiful queen—and a good worker who took care of the kids. Why did God take her? And that time God took his sisters, Mielikki and Lokka; and his little brother, Väinö? The end of the log slammed into the big saw and the screaming shut out all thought. The saw came clean out of the other end of the log, the heavy carriage slammed back, and the millpond man set the dogs to hold the new face of the huge cant ninety degrees to the next cut. Ilmari was again doing the geometry.

When he turned the mill over to the night shift along with the cutting instructions, he washed his face and hands before walking up to the house. Set an example for the children. Grandma didn't visit often, maybe once in the summer and then again at Christmas.

Mielikki was making dinner. She had quit school to take on the work of the house and the care of Helmi and Jorma. The herd was neglected; leaving everyone in the lurch, Kullervo had joined the army. Requiring nearly five million men, over half of whom had to be drafted, the army didn't seem too concerned about his hearing.

Ilmari felt bad about all the children having to take on Rauha's jobs, particularly Mielikki. Rauha had been a good mother, lack of public displays of affection notwithstanding. He and the children never expected otherwise. If he remarried, Mielikki could go back to school. Maybe one day. God willing. God. A real puzzle.

He watched Louhi setting the table with Helmi who would be eight in October—the same month he would be forty. Old to have such young kids. Couldn't be helped. Took time to get established. Now there wouldn't be any more. Jorma was cutting kindling from larger pieces of firewood that Mielikki had selected for their straight grain. He used the hatchet with both hands, but he still did good work for a five-year-old. All three kids were good workers. Rauha had seen to that.

Louhi was helping Mielikki with ladling the stew and had silently acknowledged his entrance. They all sat. Admonishing the children to sit up straight and have good manners in front of their grandmother, he said grace. Louhi motioned for them all to pass their bowls to her and she ladled out the stew. If Louhi's hair were as blond as Rauha's—maybe in ten years Rauha would've looked like her. He wished his mind would just stop going that way.

Leaving the girls and Louhi to finish the dishes, he went to split more firewood from the rounds he'd sawed several days before and to tend to a bad hoof Helmi had spotted on a heifer. Jorma tagged along after him in the dark. Maybe Jorma could handle the farm when he got old. They returned to find Louhi reading the girls a story from one of the books she bought for them last Christmas. Jorma snuggled on the floor next to her feet to listen as well. They now had three books. The children knew the stories practically verbatim. After Bible reading came bedtime. Then it would be time to talk to Louhi. Time was something Louhi never wasted.

"I'm selling the mill."

It stunned him. "Why? We're making record profits. The mill's in good condition, the crew well trained, none of them likely to get drafted."

"The war will be over by next year, maybe earlier."

Ilmari just blinked at her. She sighed, then she smiled. "You're a good blacksmith and you've built a fine little mill, but you're a lousy businessman, Ilmari. Without Rauha, well, I don't have time to run the business myself."

He kept quiet.

"The barracks are built. We've got airplanes coming out of our ears. Prices will start to fall before peace, not after. Mills will be going down like hay in August. We sell now. When the prices are high."

He couldn't help looking across the fields to the mill—clattering and screaming—electric light from a small generator making it possible to run the night shift. It was all part of Ilmahenki.

"I don't want to sell it."

"I figured. I'll put a third of my shares into a trust for the kids. It would've been that way if Rauha had lived. The cattle are yours."

"I suppose that's fair."

"Fair," she harrumphed. "That's why you're not a businessman. Ilmari, it's generous. You can hire someone to help with the kids or get remarried."

"I'm not. I—"

"Mielikki needs to go to school."

Ilmari went out on the porch. Some stranger would take part of Ilmahenki. Worse, a legal document called a corporation, without even the decency to be a stranger. He looked at the mill for about ten minutes, then he walked back inside.

"You're the majority owner."

"Yoh."

The Dodge returned early the next morning and Louhi left.

13

Some sounds are always there and go mostly unheard: the wind moving the treetops two hundred feet above, Deep River's quiet rippling and small slaps against the bank, its rushes over stones in the shallows, the chirping and chattering of squirrels and chipmunks, birds raucously warding off intruders but going quiet when feeding their chicks. Up until now, the sound of Sampo Manufacturing had been part of it: the boiler hissing, saws screaming as they bit into wood, the slapping of lumber and timbers being pulled from the green chain and stacked in the yard. Now there was just the quiet of nature as Ilmari watched Mielikki make sure Helmi was scrubbed and her dress spotless before sending her off barefoot to the new one-room schoolhouse. It seemed, for now at least, Mielikki had put aside the sadness of having to quit school. Now was her time for sisu.

A half-finished basket was on the kitchen table. Mielikki had been working on a new pattern that Vasutäti had shown her. She worked on her baskets at night, after Jorma and Helmi went to bed. It was the best time for basket weaving or carving or working leather, snug in the kitchen, the rain pelting on the roof, the sound of the coyotes signaling each other, warning about territory violations, the hooting of owls doing the same thing or seeking mates in late winter.

Ilmari followed Helmi out the door, picking up his ax where it was struck into the chopping block. There was alder to cut for firewood. He watched Helmi disappear down the road and his mind went back to the happier times, when he and Rauha had helped with building the little school the previous summer on a small hill at the edge of Tapiola on land donated by Higgins. The men arrived after church—whether they'd gone or not—and within minutes they would be formed into teams, hammering, sawing, hauling, climbing: all working furiously, competing to see who could get his wall up first or get his quarter of the roof shingled first. The women didn't work in teams, competing, but split up the work to be done, talking and laughing as they prepared food or made coffee, which they walked over to the men.

The men would work until darkness made them quit. Then all would eat what the women had made, telling jokes, laughing at stories they had heard at least three times before.

The mill had been sold to Western Washington Lumber Products, a growing company with three—now four—mills in Washington and one in Oregon. It had an eye on the vast amount of timber in the Willapa Hills that until now had been too expensive to get to market. With rail lines, however, all that timber could be harvested and Sampo was on the south edge of it.

So was Vasutäti.

Ilmari didn't want her to leave, but he felt it was his duty to warn her of what was coming. The forest would be logged. The government was consolidating the small coastal tribes into one larger tribe inland by Chehalis. Vasutäti's time was ending.

One warm Saturday in May, Ilmari took the children with him to visit Vasutäti to see if he could convince her to move while she was still spry.

He realized he should have known better.

"Everything changes," she said, almost as if comforting *him*, talking to him in their own language of Chinook jargon, English, and Finnish.

Ilmari looked at her fondly. "I hope you don't live to see the day," he said. "You can always live with us."

She looked away. After a moment she said gruffly, "You take the children home. Leave me with Mielikki. She's ready for the next design."

14

The first car in Tapiola was a used 1913 Ford Model T that Higgins converted to a small truck. The truck still took nearly an hour to get to Willapa Bay from Tapiola, but it could do so no matter what the tide or weather.

Ilmari's Packard was the second, arriving in Tapiola on April 24, 1918. He'd left Ilmahenki with Mielikki to go fetch it in Willapa where it had arrived by train. The children heard the horn honking well before the huge roadster came roaring up with Ilmari grinning at the wheel. They rushed the car, the girls shrieking, everyone fighting to sit in Ilmari's lap behind the steering wheel.

When Aino came to visit the next Sunday, he took her for a ride. When they got back, he patted its large hood. "Twin sixes. That's twelve cylinders."

Aino only said, "How much?"

"Two thousand six hundred dollars."

Aino gasped. It had to be close to everything he got from selling Sampo.

This peeved Ilmari. "I can't have some fun like everyone else? I'm a dirty capitalist now?"

"You're a materialistic consumer," Aino said.

"Welcome to America."

Aino didn't answer for a moment. Then she asked, "What about the kids? I mean, the money."

"I'll still be blacksmithing."

Aino touched the heavy black paint, wanting to see if it gave at all. It didn't.

"Guaranteed not to rust," Ilmari said proudly.

"In Detroit," Aino replied.

"Horseradish. You're just jealous."

"Ei." Aino muttered under her breath. She watched Ilmari bump and jolt the Packard through the field toward the mill, which was once more screaming and clattering, smoke rising from the new wigwam burner merging with the overcast. Sampo Manufacturing was now Western Washington Lumber Products Number Four.

A week after Aino left, Ilmari missed dinner. At first Mielikki didn't think too much of it; work had to be done when it had to be done. But after she'd put her little brother and sister to bed, Ilmari still hadn't shown up. By ten that night, she was very worried. She had no idea what to do. All she could think of was to walk to Higgins's store to find help, but that would mean leaving Jorma and Helmi. If she woke them to come with her, it would scare them. She tried to read the Bible by the lantern. She felt a hole filled with anxiety growing larger by the hour.

Finally, there was the sound of a motorcar. She rushed outside with the lantern and saw the headlights of the Packard. Two men were hauling her father out of it. She ran to them, crying aloud.

"He's OK," Matti Haapakangas said. She saw that the other man was Antti Salmi. Both were founding congregation members. "A logger from Camp Three was in town late," Mr. Haapakangas said. "He spotted the Packard parked in front of the church and got me."

"But what—" Mielikki started.

Mr. Salmi put his hand up, silencing her. "Too much to drink," he said.

The two men hauled the unconscious Ilmari into the house and put him on the bed, and Mielikki, who'd kept coffee hot hoping for her father's return, served them instead.

The next morning, Ilmari didn't get out of bed until nearly noon. He smelled and so did the Packard. He went to the sauna, and when he returned he tackled the vomit in the car. He said nothing to Mielikki, who said nothing to him.

The next day, he stayed in his bedroom all day, coming out only to go to the outhouse. Mielikki dutifully made him his meals, but he didn't eat. On the third day, Mielikki tried to get him out of his bed, but he just rolled over and put the pillow over his head. Now frightened, she got Helmi off to school, telling her to take Jorma with her and tell the teacher there was an emergency and to watch Jorma. When they disappeared, Mielikki ran to find Vasutäti.

Vasutäti handed Mielikki some dried plants. "Make tea," she said. She walked into Ilmari's bedroom.

It stank. He hadn't shaved in several weeks. The sheets hadn't been changed.

"Get out of bed," she said.

Ilmari groaned.

Vasutäti pulled the covers back. Ilmari was fully clothed and still smelled slightly of vomit and whiskey. Ilmari snatched feebly at the blankets and Vasutäti took them entirely off the bed.

"You sit, now," she said.

Ilmari managed to sit on the side of the bed, his head down, looking at his shoes, also still on his feet. Vasutäti watched him silently. Mielikki came in with a cup of the tea. On Vasutäti's nod, she gave it to her father.

"You drink," Vasutäti said. She nodded her head toward the door and Mielikki left.

When Ilmari finished, she waited again. Ilmari rolled back down on the bed and Vasutäti walked over and grabbed his shirt and pulled him up, surprisingly strongly for such a small woman.

"Now you sit, and you look at yourself through my eyes."

Ilmari looked at her blankly. "Breathe, like I taught you." Then, as if a whip had cracked, she said, "Now."

Ilmari put the empty cup down on the mattress. "Look at yourself through my eyes," Vasutäti said again.

Ilmari did. She watched the subtle changes in his body. "Mielikki is nine," she said. He was moving through despair to shame. He squirmed and she pulled him back. "Through my eyes."

Then, she saw that he was looking at her through his eyes but was now present, there with her.

"You are sad," she said.

Ilmari nodded.

"You have a shiny new car outside. You think everyone thinks you bought that car to replace Rauha." Ilmari nodded. "I know your heart. You bought that car because you're mad at God."

Ilmari looked away in shame. Then he said, "Maybe there is no God."

"No God the way *you* want."

Ilmari snorted. "How do I want God?"

"You want a God that is good." Her merry laugh rang out clean and clear. "That is what they taught us at the mission school. All wrong." She laughed again. "In this world"—she looked at her open left hand—"good is good." Then she looked at her open right hand. "And bad is bad. In the other world, where God lives"—she clasped her hands together—"there is . . ." She searched for some words, then putting her clasped hands directly in Ilmari's face, said, "There is one thing, goodbad-badgood, not two."

Ilmari looked at her, puzzled. She laughed again. "It solves the stupid problem." She went into a whiny tone of voice, "Why did God let Rauha die? Why did God let little children suffer?"

Looking at the ground, Ilmari had to smile at her antics.

"Christians only want Christmas not Good Friday." She went into the whiny voice again. ""God is bad, boo-hoo." She looked him in the eye. "God is the center of the world, not you. You grow up."

She let that sink in. Then she went on. "You are God. I am God. Everything is God. *Everything* means everything: good and bad, too."

"But, how can you say we're God? We're nothing like God."

She thought on this. "So, a baby in its mommy's womb is part of the mommy, right?"

"Yoh."

"But a baby in its mommy's womb is also different from the mommy."

"Yoh."

"So why is this so hard? You have no trouble with a baby being part of mommy and not being part of mommy at the same time." She laughed. "We are all babies in God's womb."

After Vasutäti's visit, Ilmari was up every morning. Mielikki gave her father Vasutäti's tea, one cup a day. She also wrote a letter to her Aino-täti.

Aino read the letter three days later. That evening she was knocking at Kyllikki's door. "This just came from Mielikki," she said, handing her the letter. Kyllikki looked at the childish handwriting asking for help. "We need to get Ilmari married," Kyllikki said.

"Yoh."

"You have anyone in mind?"

"What about Alma Wiitala? It's been nearly two years since her husband died on that logjam on Grays River. She doesn't have any kids and she's a good worker."

Kyllikki considered it. "You want to go see her on Sunday?"

"Yoh."

Kyllikki met Aino for the first Sunday sailing of the *General Washington*, having left her children in the care of her mother. The two women walked the six miles directly to Alma Wiitala's farm, set on the north bank of Deep River, west of Tapiola. When they arrived, they looked at each other and nodded silently. Brush and small trees had sprung up in once neat fields. The vegetable garden had weeds. The paint on the house was peeling and moss and several inches of fir and cedar needles covered the roof.

They scattered chickens as they walked to Alma's front door and knocked. She opened it slowly, then broke into a huge smile and threw it open wide.

As Kyllikki and Aino crossed through a tiny parlor to a larger kitchen located on the back side of the house, they again exchanged silent glances. The interior of the house was spotless.

Alma made fresh coffee while the three of them caught up, also sharing a few stories about the old days at Reder's Camp. When the first cup was drained, Kyllikki got right to business.

"You know Ilmari's Rauha has been gone nearly four months."

Alma nodded her head.

"Now, I know," Kyllikki went on. "Ilmari went sort of haywire. That big Packard. The money from selling Sampo burning a hole right through his pockets. But he isn't really that sort of spendthrift. Is he, Aino?"

"Just the opposite," Aino said.

Alma said nothing.

"You know he's always been a good worker," Kyllikki broke in.

"Still is," Aino added.

"Some sort of screw went loose when Rauha died," Kyllikki said. "But he's blacksmithing again."

"He's making good money," Aino said.

Alma simply nodded her head, taking it in.

"He's a good man," Kyllikki said. "Kind."

"And he doesn't drink," Aino said.

Alma nodded.

"Mielikki is nine," Kyllikki said. "She's had to leave school."

Alma shifted in her chair. "She's very pretty," she said. "Like Rauha."

Kyllikki saw her opening. "The three children need a mother."

She watched Alma struggle for control. She achieved it. "How old are the others?" she asked.

"Helmi will be eight in October and Jorma will be six in August."

Alma's eyes moved to the window. "Anneli would be twenty and Aapu would be eighteen," she said quietly, still looking out the window. She took a deep breath, then picked up her coffee cup.

It was clear to Kyllikki that Alma wasn't going to make any precipitate moves, but the rest of the negotiation was going to be about details.

"He owns his farm free and clear," Aino said.

"I own my farm, too," Alma said.

"Free and clear?" Kyllikki asked.

Alma's cheek muscles made just a flicker, indicating to the two envoys that her farm was on the edge.

Kyllikki touched Alma's hand. Alma pulled it back. "Every month you miss the payments, you own less of it," Kyllikki said softly. "You don't have to struggle like this."

Alma just nodded her head, waiting for more.

"You could sell the farm and come into the marriage with the equity," Aino said.

"An insurance policy," Kyllikki said. "In case Ilmari goes haywire again."

Alma took it all in. "Does he sauna regularly?" she asked.

"Every weekend. Without fail," Aino said.

"And you know he goes to church," Kyllikki added. "Well, he used to—regularly."

"Does he snore?"

With that, Kyllikki knew they had her.

That afternoon at Ilmahenki, Aino and Kyllikki laid the deal out on the table before Ilmari.

"You know she can cook," Aino said. "She's fed a whole logging camp."

"Does she like children?" Ilmari asked.

"She lost two babies and after that she and her husband tried through three miscarriages," Aino said. "And she mothered the entire henhouse when I was a girl."

After taking a slow sip of coffee, Ilmari set the cup down. "I haven't seen her lately," he said. "How does she look?"

"Ilmari," Kyllikki said firmly. "You're nearly forty. You can hold out for someone younger and prettier and die a lonely miserable old man."

"She's a good worker," Aino said.

"She will love your children," Kyllikki added.

"I need to think about it," Ilmari said.

The two emissaries looked at each other. Then, they simply sat there, waiting, saying nothing.

"I said I need to think about it," Ilmari said.

"So, think," Aino said. She poured them all another cup of coffee and sat down again across from Ilmari. She and Kyllikki sipped their coffee, while Ilmari stared at his.

"Yoh," Ilmari said.

"We'll stop by Alma's," Aino said, loving her brother with all her heart.

15

Ilmari and Alma were married on May 26, 1918. Aino and Kyllikki and the children all returned to Astoria that night under a full moon that painted an arrow of white gold across the river. The next day, Aino was back recruiting for the co-op.

She was eight months pregnant, and the effort exhausted her, but they were still short of their recruiting goal, which meant short of money to buy the equipment. She was on her feet twelve hours a day. She came home wearied, often throwing herself onto the bed without taking off her clothes.

On the third Sunday in June, Kyllikki walked to Aino's basement flat, leaving the children with her mother. Aino was slow answering her knock, so Kyllikki opened the door a crack and called Aino's name.

"Hätähousut," Aino's voice came from inside. She heard Aino grunt and the bedsprings squeak. She walked in.

Dishes were unwashed. The air was damp. There had been no fire in the woodstove for some time. Aino was sitting on the edge of the bed in her night shift, bending backward on her elbows. The sheets on the bed looked as worn-out as she did.

"Are you OK?" Kyllikki asked.

"Sure, sure. Why wouldn't I be?"

"Oh, maybe because you're eight months pregnant."

Aino grunted.

She launched herself to her feet. Kyllikki noticed that her breasts were larger and seemed to rest on her distended abdomen. Aino pulled off her night shift, slipped on a light cotton undershift, and reached for her support corset. She pulled up on her belly and settled it into the pouch of the corset, then turned her back to Kyllikki, who started lacing it. She turned Aino around. "Feel OK? Not too tight?"

Grunting a reply that Kyllikki took to mean it felt OK, Aino reached for her skirt, pulling it up over her belly. The front of the skirt hung way higher than the back. Aino pulled the back to the same level, but that exposed too much of the back of her legs. She let the skirt drop back. It occurred to Kyllikki that someone ought to make clothes that fit pregnant women so at least the hems stayed even.

"It kicked a lot last night," Aino said.

"Probably a dancer like her mommy and daddy."

Aino laughed. "Were you at Suomi Hall last night?"

"Ei," Kyllikki said, no. "There's no men. Besides, I promised Matti."

"Why does he care? It's not like you're going to run off with someone."

"It's sort of a bargain between us. You know, about the puukko."

"*He* took it to Nordland," Aino said. "I'd say you're free to go dancing."

"Two wrongs don't make a right."

"You're just afraid of his temper."

"He'd never hurt me."

"I know that," Aino said.

Kyllikki nodded, then she said, "I'd hurt him." They both laughed.

Kyllikki bustled around the tiny apartment, washing the dishes, stripping the bed, and putting the sheets to soak in the washtub, while Aino gamely went outside and split firewood.

"Maybe you should be doing the cleaning and I'll split the wood," Kyllikki shouted to the street level where the wood was stacked against the house's side.

"It's summer. Don't need much," she heard Aino reply.

"It's summer in *Astoria*," Kyllikki shot back and heard Aino laugh. It was good to hear. Aino was too quiet, clearly bone weary. Jouka was making good wages. Why she pushed herself with this co-op idea made no sense—and it worried Kyllikki.

When Aino returned, a load of kindling in her arms, Kyllikki said, "Father says the new head rig is coming by barge next week. His bank manager told him you people bought the head rig from a Scappoose bank that foreclosed on a company whose mill burned down. Doesn't that mean you've got the money? Why are you still pushing?"

There was an awkward silence.

"Is that why you're here? To tell me to stop pushing?"

"Aino, come to our house or go to Ilmahenki. What if the baby comes early?"

"Not likely."

"Oh, yes. Dr. Midwife." Kyllikki said. "Has it occurred to you that you're not in charge? This baby will come when *it* wants, not when you want."

"Did you come here to tell me that or to stop pushing?"

As much as Kyllikki loved her, Aino could be infuriating. "Aino, Father says the co-op is launched. What is this, this obsession?"

Aino was uncharacteristically slow to answer. "Poverty makes desperate workers compete for jobs. That leads to low wages and more poverty. To break free, they need to share in the wealth they produce. This co-op will break some of us free in Astoria. That's the obsession."

Kyllikki didn't know whether to scream at Aino or admire her.

"We all die," Aino went on softly. "Organizations don't."

"Organizations are abstractions, made up of people who die and who can be ignorant, greedy, cruel, and selfish. Why is this organization going to be so different that you'll risk killing your baby?"

"You sound like Aksel."

"Aksel's right." The two women were locking eyes. Then Kyllikki softened. "You know he's in the fighting, don't you?"

Apprehension briefly flickered across Aino's face. "How do you know that?" she asked.

"Jens Lerback, you know, from Camp Three. He wrote to his mother and said he saw Aksel." She walked over to look at Aino and

Jouka's wedding picture. "Jens is in the fighting, too," she said. "I'm glad Matti is logging. No fighting and so far, no Spanish flu at their camps." Both women were silent at the mention of the pandemic. It was generally not spoken about, as it held even more terror than the fighting. No one knew its cause or its cure, and it was spreading everywhere. "It's killing more of our guys than the Germans," Kyllikki went on. "You must feel lucky that Jouka's with Matti."

"Lucky our men are gone because of a capitalist war that pits workers against workers?"

Kyllikki could take no more. "It's always capitalists, toadying politicians, One Big Union. Aino, get down to reality. A reality for which you should feel everlasting gratitude that Matti and Jouka are logging instead of fighting like Jens and Aksel. Gratitude that you're not Jens's mother. That you're not Jens."

Aino was biting her lip. Kyllikki didn't know if it was because she was angry or ashamed. She didn't care. What was at stake was clear. "You are risking killing your baby." She grabbed her shawl and opened the door. "A live, human baby, Aino. Not an abstraction." She slammed the door.

Two days later, Aino was at Ilmahenki. And it was a good thing, because on the evening of June 22, just four days later, she went into labor, two weeks early.

Laying out Aino's midwife kit on the kitchen table—stethoscope, suction bulb, scissors, forceps, two metal trays, thermometer, safety razor and blades, cords, clamps, urinary catheter, and some sort of arm cuff that measures blood pressure that she didn't know how to use—Alma kept reminding herself that she had already delivered two healthy babies of her own and she had Aino to talk her through the process. If Aino could talk. When she was sure no one could hear her, Alma would pray in a whisper, "Please, dear Lord, make it all right" over and over. It calmed her.

Aino was fully dilated at midnight. Ilmari, quiet as usual, was standing at the bedroom door looking in on them. He'd just finished carrying Mielikki to her bed. She'd wanted to stay up for the birth and

Ilmari and Alma both thought it would be a good experience for her, but she had fallen asleep. The way things were going, Alma thought, it may have been a blessing.

"All the children are asleep," Ilmari said.

"Good," Alma said. She looked at him for a moment, as if on the verge of asking something, swallowed unconsciously, and returned to dabbing Aino's head with a wet cloth.

Ilmari went to Aino, who was lying on the bed covered in sweat. He touched her forehead and looked at Alma. Alma shrugged her shoulders, her face solemn.

Aino cried out as another contraction hit her.

Ilmari turned to Alma. "What do you think?"

"She's going to be all right," Alma said. She gave a plucky smile.

Two hours later, Aino was still in agony and nothing was moving. Ilmari squeezed Alma's shoulder and walked out, saying nothing.

Alma wanted to scream at him, but she had to deal with Aino, whose eyes were rolling. She grabbed a wet cloth and rushed to put it on Aino's forehead, talking to her, trying to soothe her. Oh God. Maybe it wasn't going to be all right.

Alma could clearly see light outside the window when she heard footsteps on the porch in spite of Aino's cries of pain. The door opened to the morning, revealing Ilmari and Vasutäti.

Vasutäti dropped several bundles of herbs and roots on the kitchen table. She turned to Ilmari. "Build a really hot fire. Boil two small pots of water." She turned to Alma. "It will be all right," she said.

Alma wanted to hug her.

Vasutäti was at Aino's side, then at the end of the bed, looking up at her vulva, then palpating her womb, feeling for the baby. Aino let out another scream.

Vasutäti smiled at her. "Now, you use sisu." Aino clamped her jaw tight, her eyes bulging. Vasutäti turned to Alma. "Help me get her up."

"Get her up?"

"Get her on her feet. Earth pulls baby down. If Aino lies down, hole in Aino not where earth can pull baby. You help her up."

Alma did as she was told. Aino didn't fight, didn't say a word, just kept her jaws clamped. Vasutäti put one of the roots she had brought between Aino's teeth and she clamped down on it hard.

"We hold her now. Let earth pull baby."

The two women supported Aino, who went into a squat, her knees spread wide. Vasutäti kept repeating some word in her language, which Alma could only think must mean push—and Aino obviously thought the same.

Aino bit right through the root. She spit it on the floor, rose slightly, then squatted again and pushed.

The baby's head crowned. Vasutäti shouted at Ilmari, saying, "You help hold." As soon as Ilmari was in place to help Alma, Vasutäti put her hands on the baby's head and beamed at Aino, saying the Indian word for push over and over. And Aino came through. And the baby came through. It was a beautiful little girl—Jouka and Aino combined—with auburn hair and light eyes, maybe blue, maybe hazel.

Vasutäti made sure the baby was breathing and then began to gently rub the vernix into her skin. She put the little girl up against one of Aino's swollen breasts, and the bud-like lips were soon tight around Aino's nipple. After the little girl had drunk her fill, Aino, exhausted and glowing, settled her in the crook of one arm.

Ilmari had come quietly into the bedroom. Aino looked up at her brother. She had never felt so proud in all her life. After all the deliveries, hers, her mother's, at last, here she was, through the trial and found worthy. She moved so Ilmari could see his niece. "I'm naming her Eleanor."

"Good American name."

Aino looked down at her daughter's tiny face. Inexhaustible love was pouring from her entire body straight into Eleanor's eyes and heart. Ilmari touched Eleanor's forehead—then her little bright-red lips. He looked at Aino with his dark soulful eyes. "Would you give her away, ever, even for a million dollars?"

"No. Of course not."

"Then you're a millionaire."

16

Aino tried to keep that in mind when she took Eleanor back to Astoria a month later in July. Ilmari had telegraphed Jouka and Matti about the birth, and she'd gotten letters from both. Jouka's was written by his commanding officer, who added his own note of congratulations. Jouka sent home almost his entire paycheck. He was now a sergeant, running a locomotive hauling logs to a mill in Port Angeles and making more money than he ever made working for Reder.

At the new mill site, the men were polite, but it was clear that Eleanor didn't fit in. She would cry without regard for the mill's operation. Aino had to supervise the loading of the railcars, carrying Eleanor. If a railcar didn't show up or went astray, it required walking into town to the SP&S rail station, carrying Eleanor. Despite his romantic idea that Aino was a millionaire, she thought ruefully, Ilmari didn't calculate the debits against the credits. Another irony, she thought: a committed communist thinking about a baby in terms of debits and credits. Even though the workers owned the mill, it was in a capitalist economy. When the debits outweighed the credits too long, the law closed you down. Caught up in the system, people inevitably started thinking in terms of hours at work, debits and credits, assets and liabilities, instead of Eleanor's pretty mouth. Alvar suggested she wean Eleanor and look for a babysitter. He gave her three months, pointing out that if it weren't a co-op and she weren't an officer, she'd have to quit her job. Jouka, after all, was making good wages.

Coming back to the mill from the SP&S freight office, where she'd begged the manager for more railcars, made scarce by the war economy, she paused to nurse Eleanor, looking at the huge Youngs River estuary where it joined the Columbia just at the west end of the Astoria hills. She could see smoke from the Hammond Mill to the west. A shipbuilding factory had started just a half mile down Youngs River from the co-op mill, working on a large order for wooden mine-sweepers for the navy. She saw two freighters moving up the channel to Portland. It was all so busy—and yes, efficient. But it wasn't like farming, where Ilmari and Rauha and now Alma could raise their children with the rhythms of nature—and humans. Alma worked her tail off, but she worked figuratively and often literally alongside her husband. She thought in terms of good crops or hard winters, not debits and credits. There were no time clocks on Deep River.

Aino looked north across the Columbia, but it was too wide for her to see the old Chinook village. Then she looked south to where the co-op's new mill stood between the railroad and Youngs River. Logs bobbed in the river, waiting to be hauled into the mill. Rudimentary buildings, open on all sides, with corrugated steel roofs to shelter the saws and conveyers, were surrounded by a large yard that held stacks of lumber, sorted by length and dimensions. She could see the men hauling newly sawed lumber off the green chain, the final phase of the intricate conveyer system that moved a log and then a cant through the various saws that turned it into lumber. Green lumber was heavy and wet. It had been part of a living tree just days ago. On the other side of the yard were the railroad tracks on which she stood. Logs in from the river—lumber out to build houses or barracks—money in to pay for the logs with some left over for the workers. At the base of it all—timber. The forest was like a giant farm that nobody had planted and nobody replanted. From this immense cycle of pay and get to get and pay, here she was standing on a railroad track that just a few years before didn't exist, looking down the track to the new mill, looking across the Columbia to the hills that hid Deep River from view, feeling like a leaf in a roaring creek in full flood with the war, heading where?

She gently popped Eleanor's mouth from her nipple and resettled her in the carrier.

She could just go to Deep River, lead a quiet life raising her daughter. But they needed her at the mill. She was useful, even important. Secretary of the co-op. Half of her made fun of the corporate title, but the other half was proud. She'd been instrumental in forming that bunch of buildings, saws, and conveyer belts. The men even used that word, "instrumental." She thought about Alma saving flour sacks so she could make the children's undergarments. She thought about the times when she, Kyllikki, and Rauha would sit with the coffeepot on, making socks for their husbands and children. Then she thought how here in Astoria, all she had to do was walk a few blocks to a store and buy what she needed already made.

Years later, she would always remember that moment of standing between Deep River and the co-op. Just as planetary conjunctions occur only for a moment and then years go by before the two planets once again align, so it is with life's major decisions. You can't just change your mind to make it good; you must wait for the next conjunction. Aino chose to keep walking toward the mill.

After Aino and Eleanor left, Ilmari went to see Vasutäti.

"Thank you for coming, you know, that day."

"I like new wife. Good head."

Ilmari smiled. He knew Vasutäti wouldn't acknowledge the thanks.

"Alma. She's a good woman."

"A good woman wants a good man," Vasutäti said, but there was wistfulness in her voice.

She served him some soup and indicated that he should meditate, which he did. When he'd first started learning from Vasutäti, Ilmari knew she was a shaman, just like the old ones in Suomi. He, however, had thought that the lessons would be about magic herbs and magic incantations. Vasutäti didn't like magic. She said it existed, but she never practiced it. Instead, she made Ilmari focus on sitting still and breathing—for hours. He'd practiced daily before bed—until Rauha died.

He broke the meditation and found Vasutäti watching him closely. She grunted, disappeared into her shelter, and returned with some dried mushrooms in her hand. He recognized them: they were a common variety, easily found in meadows where elk and increasingly cattle grazed.

"What's this?" Ilmari asked.

"If you had just like these in Finland, maybe Finns not have so much sisu when not needed." She laughed her ethereal elvish laugh.

"Now serious," she said suddenly. "You have mind strength; many practice sessions not thinking. So now we take risk."

"Are they dangerous?"

"Not dangerous for the body, dangerous for the mind. You weren't ready until now."

Ilmari knew this was a threshold in his tutelage. The old people, who kept the old ways, talked of journeys with spirit animals—journeys from which some never came back to their ordinary senses and from which no one returned unchanged. He was afraid.

Sensing this, Vasutäti said, "Now is time for sisu."

He held out his palm. She put the mushrooms in it, closed his fingers on them, and then closed her hands over his. She nodded, encouraging him. He swallowed the mushrooms.

"I'll be with you," she said. "If you get in trouble, I'll pull you out. Just like I did from fancy car." She laughed, her deep brown eyes sparkling with love.

He was building a fishing boat that he launched onto a gray choppy sea. He sailed and sailed, heading ever northward, sailing, until he landed on a rocky beach. He pulled the boat up onto the shore. He knew he was to meet someone here. So, he sat still, just as with the no-thinking practice.

He waited for a long time. Then the trees moved with a sighing of the wind. His heart began to pound. He tried to still his fear. The trees moved, and he heard the understory crackle with the passing of some great body.

Emerging from the woods, taller than the trees yet smaller than a child, a figure stood before him. Ilmari was filled with awe and fear. Fir trees grew on the giant's shoulders, the haunt of squirrels and owls, oaks grew from his brows, hemlocks grew like whiskers on his chin, and his teeth were like cedar trees.

He knew it was Antero Vipunen, the god of the forest. He wanted to run but remembered Vasutäti telling him now was the time for sisu and he sat, trembling, rooted to the ground. Antero Vipunen thundered, "Slave to humanity, rise up from the ground, from sleeping so long." He took Ilmari's right wrist and attached it with a rope woven from cedar bark to a young birch tree. Then he attached the left wrist to a second birch, and then his feet to two others. With a wave of his hand, the birches began to lean away from each other. Ilmari tried to keep from squealing with the pain and fear, but the pain and fear grew as the birches leaned farther away, pulling him in four directions. He screamed, trying futilely to fight the birches back to avoid being torn into four pieces.

Then Vasutäti was there—Vasutäti as he'd never seen her before, Vasutäti naked and young, her skin smooth, her body slender—her eyes sparkling with love.

"Now, you must hold the center," she said gently, stroking his forehead. "Now you must hold still and not fight the birches. Now you need sisu. Now you do not-thinking."

He breathed. He breathed in agony and fought panic. He breathed, trying to remember his father and mother. He looked into Vasutäti's eyes, as if the love there were a rope, pulling him from drowning in the pain, pulling at his navel like an umbilical cord attached somewhere in the heavens, attaching him to some vast sky placenta that covered the earth with blood and strength and life.

Then, focusing on the love in Vasutäti's eyes, he accepted the pain and consigned himself to being torn apart.

The pain ceased. The birches stood upright and still. Antero Vipunen, terrible of strength, terrible of manly beauty, stood before him. Vasutäti stood behind Ilmari and whispered, "Now you ask him questions."

To ask a question? What question? To know. He wanted to know the secret of existence. He asked, "How does the universe work?" And Antero Vipunen said, "The wind chases the wind." And it made wonderful, beautiful sense. He *understood*, truly. Then he asked, "How did it all start?" And Antero Vipunen said, "If nothingness is something, then nothingness exists. Nothing exists, always." And Ilmari wept with the terrible beauty of it all.

He awoke next to the fire, under a full moon that couldn't be seen but whose pale light filtered through the trees. The Vasutäti he'd always known was ladling crawdad stew into a bowl. He ate ravenously.

"You were with the forest god," she said. "We have a different name for him."

"How do you know that?"

She laughed. "Do you not remember? I was there."

He was silent for some time. "Antero Vipunen. We call the forest god Antero Vipunen." He fell silent, taking several more spoonfuls of stew. "He told me something, something that answered my question, *really*, really answered it and I understood, but now it doesn't make any sense." She waited for him. He said softly, "He said the wind chases the wind." He looked up at her, helpless. "It's like having an enormous shattering dream, but when you wake up you're struck dumb and can't tell it to anyone."

"It's like that."

"Is he real?"

"As real as Jesus."

"Do you mean Antero Vipunen is real or that Jesus isn't?"

She smiled at his obvious consternation. "God is like a rushing waterfall. If you stand in it and try to drink, you will be smashed into the rocks and lost downstream. Antero Vipunen and Jesus are also God, but they are the slow streams at the waterfall's base that allow us to drink."

Ilmari wept. He'd lost the awe and the beauty of Antero Vipunen's answer and here he was—again—nowhere special.

Vasutäti touched him tenderly on his cheek. "I too am sad to leave the world where I am beautiful for you. In this world, I am too old to make children, to give you pleasure." She laughed. "Too old to give me pleasure."

"How old are you, Vasutäti?" Ilmari asked.

She smiled the smile that helped the sun rise. "Same as you." She laughed. And when Ilmari understood what she was saying, he laughed, too.

"I've never asked. What is your real name?"

She smiled. "Mowitch. It means deer."

They were silent for a while. Then Ilmari said, "I was frightened."

"An appropriate response."

"If I go there again, will you be there?"

Vasutäti motioned for Ilmari's empty bowl. She set it aside, then held out both her hands to him. He hesitated, then joined their hands. She looked up and he followed her gaze to where the near-white moon danced with the branches of the firs and the scudding clouds. They watched it together for a time, then she squeezed his hands and looked into his eyes. "If we're ever apart," she said, "know I'll be looking at the same moon."

17

The forest god that reigned west of Port Angeles, Washington, was Brice Disque, commanding officer of the Spruce Division. To Jouka it seemed that whatever Disque wanted—rails, locomotives, saws, men, food—he got.

One of the locomotives was Sergeant Kaukonen's. He'd proved his reputation was deserved in the first week and made sergeant immediately. In the engine cab, right above the throttle, was a tiny snapshot of Aino holding Eleanor in front of the Saaris' house, too small to really see what Eleanor looked like, but he found it comfortable and reassuring. What money he kept, he'd been saving to go see them on his leave, which was granted for five days, starting August 21.

On the day before he left camp, Tuesday, August 20, his commanding officer, an affable National Guard captain named Royce, helped him write a telegram that he'd have the signal officer send to Aino, saying Jouka was on his way.

He arrived at the Astoria train station about seven thirty Wednesday night, proudly wearing his uniform. He could see the great river from the station platform, the Washington side so far off that the hills were a two-dimensional monochrome darkness between the river and the sky. He felt a tug of nostalgia as he tried to make out Margaret Cove.

Aino wasn't on the platform. Of course, she'd have Eleanor where it was warm. He rushed for the waiting room, imagining Aino, her black hair flowing over her shoulders onto their daughter. He chuckled. Aino would never wear her hair down in public. He burst into the waiting room.

Aino wasn't there.

He shouldered his knapsack and walked to the little basement apartment. Should he knock? No, of course not. It was his place, too. He straightened his shoulders and strode through the door, grinning. A startled teenage girl shrieked, her book flying. Eleanor, tucked in a bureau drawer on the floor next to the bed, started screaming.

"I'm sorry," Jouka said in English. "Where's my wife? So, this is my daughter?" He took the crying baby up by her armpits and held her in front of his beaming face. "Don't cry, don't cry," he cooed in Finnish. "Daddy's home." It sounded so wonderful and strange to hear himself say that. He pulled Eleanor in closer. Her grimacing face was red from crying, but he knew she was the most beautiful little person in the world.

He turned to the girl, asking in Finnish, "Where's Mrs. Kaukonen?"

"I'm sorry . . ." her voice trailed off. "I can't speak Finnish."

He held Eleanor out from him and did a dance turn. Eleanor stopped crying. "Where's Mrs. Kaukonen?" Jouka asked in English.

"She's at work," the girl said, puzzled by the question.

"But isn't work over by now?"

"Well, you know, everyone's the boss at the co-op. No union hours for them." She smiled at her joke. "Here, let me have her." The girl put Eleanor against her shoulder.

"But the captain sent a telegram. She knew I was coming," Jouka said.

"I sure didn't."

"You stay here," Jouka said. "I'm going to get her mother."

The late-August sun was going down across the Youngs River, lighting Saddle Mountain with orange, and the second shift was in full swing when he walked into the office.

"Jouka! My God." She was alone and clearly surprised. Something must have gone wrong with the captain's telegram. She rose. "You're home."

"And you're not."

"I . . . I'm working."

"I send you good wages every two weeks. There's no need to work. But, I came home to . . . I wanted to come home to . . ." He'd rehearsed the speech all the way to the mill, but now the words just stopped. He sent her nearly everything he earned. It felt as if she was throwing the money in his face.

"I was there at dinner to nurse Eleanor. She's—"

"I want you home, not some babysitter."

"Let's not fight. Please."

"OK, let's go home."

"Just give me a second." She started to rearrange something on her desk. Jouka exploded. Screaming, he swept the top of her desk clean and she stumbled backward in fear. He picked up the typewriter from the floor and threw it through the window. He stalked past several workers who'd been attracted by the noise.

Aino assured them it was just a marital spat, but knew she was trembling and it showed. She cleaned up the mess and walked home in the twilight, her stomach in a knot of— what? Guilt that she'd hurt him again.

Aino paid Mary Alice and tidied the apartment. Several times she went out into the dark, hoping he'd be coming up the hill, wanting to see her, wanting to see Eleanor. Deep down, however, Aino felt sick with dread. She knew she could probably find him at the Desdemona Club, but she couldn't go there with Eleanor.

Aino was right. Jouka was at the Desdemona Club, well on his way to a drunk the likes of which he hadn't seen since the Old Camp Two bachelor days.

"Hey soldier, don't I know you?" He turned to see Jane Townsend. She'd started at the Lucky Logger, but when Oregon prohibition shut it down, well, the prostitutes improvised.

It felt like driving pilings—and it was no fun. To his surprise, she seemed genuinely to like it.

"Trouble at home, soldier?" She was lighting a cigarette.

"Jouka. My name's Jouka Kaukonen."

She blew out a cloud and gently picked a bit of tobacco off her tongue. "I do know you. You used to play fiddle at dances. You were good. You're married to that Wobbly."

"Aino."

"What's it like being married to one of those free-love reds? Not so good I guess, given you're paying for it here."

"She's no free-love red, just red."

"That's not what I heard."

Jouka had been putting on a shoe. Her words stopped him short. "What did you hear?"

"Well," she smiled, almost wickedly. "You remember, before the war, when this Wobbly called Joe Hill got framed for murder down in Utah?"

Jouka just looked at her.

"Well, just after they shot this Hill guy, one of the Wobblies who comes in here said he'd been sweet on some Wobbly girl from across the river. He thought they'd gotten together. Was it Nordland? Maybe Centralia? Anyway, one of those free-speech fights."

Jouka stood. He carefully counted out the two dollars, but his hands were shaking.

Two hours later he was let-it-all-out, confessional drunk, venting his anger and hurt on all who would listen. They delighted in telling their wives.

Jouka didn't come at all the next day, or the next. Aino called the police and they found him unconscious, his pockets empty, vomit on his uniform, lying where the bouncer had thrown him in the early morning hours. They brought him home and deposited him facedown on the bed. Aino dragged Jouka onto the floor, throwing her coat over him.

When Jouka awoke, the apartment was empty. He went through the usual places, found a dollar and a quarter, put on his civilian clothes, and went back to the Desdemona Club. There, he bet a man a quarter on a pool shot and won. The man doubled down and lost, leaving Jouka with two dollars, a dollar of which he doubled on several poker hands, giving him three dollars, which got him into a quarter-ante poker game. By six that evening, he had enough for a five-cent hamburger from the grill behind the bar and a whole night of drinking.

He returned home about two in the morning. He switched on the single bulb hanging over the kitchen table, waking Aino and Eleanor.

"You're drunk," Aino said.

"Yoh."

He threw his shirt onto the table and shrugged out of his suspenders.

"You're not sleeping in this bed."

He laughed. "You're right." He kicked off his trousers. "I'll go to other whores. They'll only take part of my paycheck."

"What do you mean?"

"Oh, sorry. You're not a whore. Whores charge for it."

She knew that Jouka had found out about Hillström. She also knew that Jouka was never coming back—even for Eleanor. Never. It hung like a life sentence. She had never really loved him, but he'd loved her. He was a good provider. They danced together so well. And always his whistling and singing . . .

She took it head-on. "Yes. I slept with Hillström. It was a mistake." His face was a mask. She reached to touch him. "I'm ashamed."

He shook her hand off. "When?"

"At the Centralia rally just before he was framed in Salt Lake City."

"Everyone knew but me. Have you not shamed me enough?"

"I told you I'm sorry."

"He's a murdering, whoring red, and you slept with him."

She knew she'd slept with a flawed man who was not her husband and she would regret it all her life, but he was a man who gave everything for what he believed in and was not a murderer. The words seemed to fly from her mouth as if it belonged to someone else. "At least he's not a drunken toady to any boss who'll let him play with a steam engine. He died for a cause. He gave his life for a cause. He was twice the man you'll ever be."

She braced herself, holding Eleanor, and wondered where she had found the arrows.

Instead of retaliating, Jouka was putting on his shoes, as if she weren't in the room. He stuffed his uniform into his knapsack. "I took a dollar and a quarter from the coffee can behind the dresser." He threw two dollars on the table. "Keep the change."

Four days later, Jouka went to Captain Royce for help with the divorce papers. Sitting in front of Royce's desk, he carefully wrote his signature. Rain slashed against the single windowpanes in the raw wooden headquarters building.

Jouka pushed the papers across the desk and walked into the rainy twilight. The melody to "Påskliljan Schottis" and its G-major chord progressions flooded his mind along with memories of the feel of Aino, her dark hair and eyes, how light she was on her feet, that first night they'd danced at the Knappton net shed. What had happened? Was it he who turned her so cold? Was it because she'd become even more of a red? Somewhere, he had fallen short—or failed. She took this Hillström, this "Joe Hill," over him. Hillström probably had never held a decent job. As for Hillström's songs, Jouka shook his head. Clever lyrics, but he stole the melodies.

He was walking by his locomotive, number 12. Twenty trucks were neatly lined up next to the rails. They could carry only one log or two logs each but didn't need rails. Cheaper to operate, if you could punch the roads in. But they'd never replace trains. Just think of the inefficiency—one engine per log versus one engine for fifty logs.

He remembered staring with wonder into Eleanor's hazel eyes. He imagined her in a little calico dress playing jump rope. Maybe her auburn hair, seemingly a cross between his blond and Aino's black, would grow rich and full like Aino's. He remembered the heft—that was it—the *heft* of Aino's long black hair. To hell with her. He'd see Eleanor. Take her for ice cream.

Rain still slashed across the compound as he walked to his sleeping quarters. One thing for sure about the army, they lived like kings, right down to the lowest buck private. Sheets! Rich khaki wool blankets.

Stoves in every bunkhouse. Outhouses all over the place and away from where they slept—and an eight-hour shift. He wished the war would last forever.

The divorce papers reached Aino a week later. She'd gone with them to the county courthouse on Commercial Street but stood outside holding Eleanor, unable to go in. No wind. A light rain drifted down, like fog with tears.

She tried to tell herself that a divorce was as bogus as a marriage, but it didn't feel that way. It had been gut-wrenching enough when he'd walked out the door of their flat, but this . . . It felt more final than the wedding. She took in a deep breath and turned away toward Kyllikki's house, stuffing the unsigned papers into her purse.

The war ended two months later, on November 11, 1918. On hearing of the armistice, the Spruce Division loggers had literally dropped their tools where they were working. They left behind vast amounts of train track, cables, yarders, trucks, empty barracks and mess halls, huge unyarded logs and cold decks of giant spruce, as if a sudden wind had simply swept through the woods, silencing all.

18

A cold February rain slanted at a forty-five-degree angle across Commercial Street as Aino lugged Eleanor, now eight months old, wrapped in the shawl against her chest. She was on the lookout for a baby carriage that the better-off women used to trot their infants around town, but lumber prices were dropping, and her share of the co-op earnings dropped with them. To her relief, Jouka never asked for his half. She didn't even know where he was. He never went back to work with Matti.

She passed the empty IWW hall with its broken windows. Someone had written TRAITORS in white across the front.

Aino reached Matti and Kyllikki's new house, a modest place two blocks up the hill in Uniontown, which Matti and Kyllikki bought using Matti's army savings for a down payment. She was happy she didn't have to visit at the Saaris' anymore. Emil and Hilda Saari were polite, but she never felt welcome—particularly since the Red Terror in Finland last summer had killed one of Hilda's brothers. As if it were somehow Aino's fault. Well, Hilda needn't have worried. The whites, mostly farmers, churchgoers, and members of the middle class loyal to the Finnish senate, were now getting even with the reds, mostly industrial and agrarian workers loyal to the radical faction of the Social Democratic Party. The Red Terror had become the White Terror.

When Aino knocked on the door, Suvi opened it, squealing with delight, "Aino-täti, Auntie Aino." She still wore her church clothes. Kyllikki came to get Eleanor while Aino struggled out of her wet coat and scarf.

"Guess who's here," Kyllikki said, smiling with delight.

"How would I know?"

"Aksel."

She didn't move, then remembered Eleanor and took her back. She followed Kyllikki into the living room with its single window looking on the river. Matti and Aksel both stood up from where they'd been sitting in the two armchairs.

She was first struck by Aksel's being older—older than herself, older than anyone else in the room. She smiled brightly. He smiled a bit awkwardly and his eyes went to the floor. Some things didn't change. Then his eyes rose to meet hers. They moved constantly, disconcertingly, so she looked away herself this time.

"When did you get back? It's so good to see you." It *did* feel good to see him.

"Last week. Left the army in New York, and they paid for my train fare to Tapiola. Too bad the train doesn't get that far." He laughed.

"Never will," Matti said, sitting down and thereby inviting everyone else to sit. Unfortunately, there was only one other armchair.

"Why not?" Aksel asked, remaining standing.

"Trucks and automobiles. Cheaper to build a road and let people put up their own capital for the cars. Except for heavy freight, railroads won't compete."

Kyllikki disappeared into the kitchen, returned with two straight-back chairs, and disappeared again. Aksel took one, offering the vacant armchair to Aino. As she moved toward it, Eleanor reached a tiny hand toward Aksel. He smiled and reached for her. Aino hesitated. Aksel quickly withdrew his hands and sat in the straight-back chair. "What's her name?" he asked.

"Eleanor."

Aksel was always so open. Holding Eleanor by her armpits, Aino grinned at her saying, "It's long-lost Aksel-setä. He's been in the army."

Eleanor leaned back away from Aino's chest to take a closer look at Aksel and again reached out one hand to him. Making a sudden decision, Aino handed her to a surprised Aksel. At first, he held her away from him, his arms stiff, but then he put her on one knee and started quietly bouncing her up and down saying, "El-a-nor, El-a-nor," raising his knee with each syllable. Eleanor giggled with delight.

Kyllikki arrived with the coffeepot, followed by Suvi with four cups. A wind gust rattled the house, vibrating the floor. Aksel walked over to the window, holding Eleanor so she could look out at the river. It was so wide one never sensed that it was moving, but Aino knew that its dark power carried the weight of mountains.

Smiling, Aksel said to Eleanor in English, "When it's better weather, you can come fishing with me." Aino realized Aksel had been gone over two years, probably never speaking Swedish or Finnish. He pulled Eleanor back to his chest and stood there, looking quietly at the great river like a man looking at his sleeping beloved.

Matti spoke in Finnish. "Do you want to come logging with me? A share of the profits. We get big you can quit and go fishing."

Aksel said nothing, staring out at the river so shrouded in rain that the north shore was hidden. Then he turned, still slightly bouncing Eleanor. "That's a very generous offer, Matti. But I don't know what I want to do. I'm not even sure why I came back. Wages are good back east."

"Wages?" Matti asked. "But, there's no good logging back east anymore and the fishing's all Wops and Portuguese."

Aksel laughed. "Not all Wops and Portuguese," he said. "From Boston up it's mostly Americans." He paused. "But I'm not thinking about fishing or logging. After I got hit," he said with only a slight hesitation, "I was transferred to an engineering outfit. Turns out I made a pretty good carpenter."

"Carpenter!" Matti said it as if carpentry were illegal.

Aksel chuckled. "How do you suppose all that lumber gets used?" Then from out of nowhere he asked, "Where's Jouka?" Everyone looked at everyone else.

"I guess you don't know," Aino said. "We got divorced. Well, everything except the paperwork."

Aksel just blinked a couple of times, taking it in. "OK"—again the American expression. "Still, where is he?"

After an embarrassed silence, Matti said, "We don't know. We think he's drinking. Every once in a while, people say they saw him at the Desdemona Club."

More silence.

Aksel's eyes, constantly scanning the room anyway, looked for amplification from someone. None came. "I guess I shouldn't be surprised," he said, looking straight at Aino. She felt all the condemnation. "Did Jens Lerback make it back?" Aksel asked, trying to change the subject.

"Yoh," Matti said.

Aksel waited. "Yoh? That's all?"

Kyllikki broke in. "His mother says he's kind of restless."

"Restless," Aksel repeated, then chuckled sardonically.

"He shows up at home occasionally, but she doesn't know where he goes. Won't go to work for Reder, for anyone."

"I saw him over there a couple of times," Aksel said quietly as if he were talking to the window, lost in the memory.

"We know," Aino said.

"You know?"

"His mother told us."

Aksel gave a brief laugh, saying, "It figures."

"You could have written, you know," Aino said.

"Who would I have written to?"

"Me," Aino said. Everyone looked at her. "Lempi was my best friend, you know," she added lamely.

Aksel left Matti and Kyllikki's in midafternoon, taking the venerable *General Washington* as far as Rosburg, the next landing after Knappton. It was dark and raining when he came ashore. Still in his uniform, the only clothes he had, he headed along the road on the south side of the river, not knowing or even caring where he was headed. When he reached a covered bridge that crossed the river, he wrapped his woolen army greatcoat around him and slept. It was drier than the trenches and no one was shelling him.

He awoke at dawn and continued north, vaguely seeking the upper reaches of Deep River. There, he found a well-sheltered site on a tributary creek that rushed between hills rising over a thousand feet on both sides. He made several trips to Rosburg and Tapiola, spending his army savings on camping essentials, fishing gear, and a rifle. He built a canvas shelter covered with cedar bark that was snug against both wind and rain. He built a smokehouse and it was soon filled with fillets of Chinook salmon.

One day, in early April, on the North Fork of Deep River, his solitude came to an end. A man was fishing at one of Aksel's favorite spots.

Aksel's first reaction was to chamber a round in his rifle. The man whirled to face him. Aksel raised his rifle above his head and the man raised his empty right hand. Aksel was about fifty feet from the man when they recognized each other. It was Kullervo.

Kullervo threw his pole to the ground and stomped through the rocky shallows, grinning with delight. They shook hands, looking into each other's eyes. After a little talk about the fishing, Aksel asked Kullervo, "Were you overseas?"

"Yoh," Kullervo answered. "Infantry."

"Me, too," Aksel said.

"Get hit?" Kullervo asked.

"Yoh," said Aksel.

"Me, too."

That was all they ever said about it.

Kullervo had been knocking around the river towns doing odd jobs before deciding he'd rather live off the land. He'd ended up in roughly the same place as had Aksel, for the same reasons: good fishing, good hunting, steep hillsides, big trees for protection against the wind, and no one to bother him. Aksel's campsite soon had a second bark-covered shelter and they had more salmon smoking than they could possibly eat in a year.

They both had pocket watches but didn't wind them. They only kept a calendar, so they'd know when it was Saturday night. Then, they'd shave, wash their armpits, put on their Saturday shirts, and head for Tapiola or Knappton to seek what all young men seek.

On the last Saturday in April, Aksel and Kullervo struck out for Tapiola. They stopped by Ilmahenki to drop off smoked salmon. Alma fed them hot coffee and warm biscuitti, the Finglish word many were now using for pulla. They walked on the new plank road to Knappton. Mill workers, loggers, fishermen, and a few men of uncertain occupation were roaring in the old net shed. A small band played some of the old familiar schottisches and polkas, but it also played what was called by a new word: Dixieland jazz. As usual, the men outnumbered the women considerably, but the crowd was noticeably more balanced than it had been in the old Reder's Camp days. Aksel and Kullervo had no trouble finding dance partners.

It was well past midnight when the pair ended up in a new saloon that had been built on pilings just south of the hotel. They would never spend their money on a hotel room, preferring to find a place to hole up on the way back to their campsite, but they would spend money on illegal whiskey.

The saloon was crowded and lively. The few women were there to work not play. Aksel and Kullervo got a shot of whiskey at the bar and made their way to a corner that had a window looking out to the river. There, at a table, were three men still in uniform. This usually meant more than the obvious—that they were veterans. It also meant they'd come home not in their right minds, or they didn't have any other clothes, or probably both. One of the men was Jens Lerback from Camp Three. He and Aksel shook hands, grinning.

Jens introduced Aksel and Kullervo to his two friends, Heppu Reinikka, who'd been raised on a farm downstream from Tapiola; and Yrjö Rautio, a former mill worker from Willapa. With a few words, it was established that all five had been in combat, although Jens received a bit of ribbing from the others because he'd been in a new kind of unit called armored and avoided the trenches. Jens had already established himself as a good mechanic before going into the army, so Aksel wasn't surprised that armored was where he'd ended his war. Heppu Reinikka, a solid man with thick forearms that he rested on the table in front of him, had done his time in the trenches as had Aksel and Kullervo. Yrjö Rautio, on the other hand, said he *wished* he'd done his time in the trenches. He'd joined the Marine Corps. In an organization famous for expert riflemen, he had been singled out because of his skill with the M1903 Springfield. He'd spent his war as a sniper, outside the trenches. All five had gone through their fifth round of whiskey. It being Kullervo's turn to buy again, he made his way to the still-crowded bar. Waiting for his order in a pleasant alcoholic haze, he began to listen to several loggers drinking at the bar next to him. They'd been in the Spruce Division and were comparing experiences, mixed in with the usual mild boasting. Then one of them said that it was too bad the war ended. He'd never made so much money.

Kullervo didn't even think. He hit the man with a right cross that made his knees buckle. The logger tried to stay upright by clinging to the bar, but Kullervo grabbed a shot glass and pounded his fingers, screaming curses at him. The man crumpled to the floor. Kullervo kicked him, calling him one more name.

The man's friends stared at Kullervo, momentarily stupefied. Then, with a scream, two of them came at Kullervo, swinging. Aksel, seeing that Kullervo was under attack from two men, ran to the bar. He took on the closer one with a furious combination of lefts and rights, unleashing the pent-up rage of war.

Jens looked at Yrjö and Heppu. Heppu shrugged his broad shoulders and stood, nodding his chin toward where Aksel and Kullervo were now fighting several men each. Without debate or reflection, the three veterans chose sides and joined the fight.

Outnumbered nearly two to one, they were saved by the bartender, who fired his shotgun out of an open window toward the river. He didn't want to mess up the inside of the bar. The five veterans backed out of the door, warily watching for someone to jump them. When they reached the street, they turned and ran.

Panting from the steep uphill run from town, lying on the wet ground next to the plank road, looking up in the dark, the unseen rain hitting their faces and soothing their cuts and bruises, they began to talk about how it was for them coming back home. Jens told the old joke that he wouldn't trade the experience of war for a million dollars, but he wouldn't pay a nickel to do it again. Heppu said he was tired of farming. Yrjö said he didn't feel that he counted anymore. Lumber got made whether he showed up for work or not. In the war, people died if he didn't show up.

Then Aksel told them about the little camp on the upper reaches of Deep River. "We can live off the land. We work for no one. We watch out for each other."

No one said anything.

They all fell into a drunken sleep. Upon waking, the rain still falling on them, they rolled over, struggled to their feet, held their heads, threw up, and followed Aksel to his campsite. There was no vote, no discussion. They formed a squad and Aksel was the unquestioned leader. It was the hunting group—and it was the first time since any of them had returned home that things felt right again.

No one heard from Aksel for a couple of months, but in early summer he started showing up occasionally at Ilmahenki, sometimes with a nice steelhead, Chinook, or blueback. He smiled enigmatically when asked where he caught it. As far as anyone knew, he didn't have a job—but rumors were flying. He and his squad of veterans often showed up drunk at dances and always left together. The local girls started to call them the Bachelor Boys. No one knew where they lived or what they were doing for money, although one obvious possibility was bootlegging.

They weren't bootlegging, but they weren't about to tell anyone what they were really doing.

It had all started when Kullervo found a thousand or more elk skeletons, scattered over several square miles. Why, how, or when so many skeletons ended up in roughly the same area, they weren't sure, but elk herds, before the Europeans came, could get quite large and elk, like all ungulates, were particularly susceptible to disease because they lived in herds. Kullervo's find was only mildly interesting.

It became far more interesting when Jens Lerback came back from a visit to the Desdemona Club in Astoria.

"This guy was showing off this big elk whistler on his watch fob because he's a member of the Elks Lodge," Jens said.

"What's that?" Heppu asked.

"The Benevolent and Protective Order of Elks. They have clubs in every town in America. They sort of look out for each other. And they're growing. Lots of veterans joining since the war."

"They drink trouble-free," Yrjö said. "No cop will bother them."

"So, did he say how much he paid for this tooth?" Aksel asked.

"Eight dollars."

Several of them whistled.

"It probably included the setting and chain," Jens added. "And it looked like a tooth from a cow."

"Still," Aksel said. "A bull whistler could be worth twice as much."

On his next visit to Astoria, Aksel went to the Desdemona Club after visiting Matti and Kyllikki. The girls there stacked up favorably with girls in similar clubs in France, with the added feature that they spoke better English. Upon finishing his business, he sat at the bar for a last drink before catching the boat. Sitting at the end of the bar was the man with the elk-tooth watch chain.

"Nice-looking watch fob," Aksel said. He pointed to the tooth. "What's that?"

"It's an elk whistler. Some people call 'em buglers. I'm a member of the Elks Lodge." The man held the tooth up for Aksel's closer inspection. "Pure ivory. The only ivory in North America except for walrus."

All elk had two vestigial tusks in about the place where a cat's incisors would be. Why people called them buglers or whistlers, Aksel had no idea. They had nothing to do with how elk bugled.

"Really?" Aksel said, pretending that this was all news to him as he examined the beautiful piece of ivory.

"All other elk teeth are just enamel."

"No kidding. Where'd you get it?"

"Mail order."

"Who from?"

The man told him the name of the company.

Aksel wrote a letter. The company was indeed interested in a supply of elk whistlers. It would pay anywhere from a dollar and a half to four dollars for whistlers or buglers, depending on size, age, and general condition.

That averaged around two days of a logger's pay per tooth. All they needed were hammers and pieces of wood to knock out the whistlers without damaging them. The Bachelor Boys were in business.

19

That summer of 1919, lumber prices hit bottom. The co-op teetered on the edge of bankruptcy. Aino struggled with the unremitting workload and constant cash crises. Eleanor was down to one or two breastfeedings a day and toddling. Aino relied increasingly on Kyllikki to watch her but felt guilty.

One Sunday in July at Ilmahenki, Aino was helping Alma do the dishes. She surprised Alma by asking her if Eleanor could stay with her for the next week. Alma didn't answer. "To get to know her cousins better," Aino added.

Alma could see that Aino was exhausted and, to ask this, desperate. She looked at her husband's sister, wanting to help, but for Alma it was Eleanor who took precedence.

Alma said carefully. "Aren't you still nursing her?"

"She's down to just one or two a day. One really," Aino added quickly.

Alma tried to be diplomatic. "I think Eleanor still needs her mother." Then she quickly added, "And you'll miss her."

"I will, of course, but Alma, just this one week. I'll pay you."

Alma took a silent deep breath. One second she was loving her sister-in-law, feeling empathy for her plight, and then out of her mouth came something that simply infuriated her. That was so like Aino. Alma said very slowly, "She's my niece." She let that sink in until Aino's eyes went to the dishes.

"Sorry," Aino said.

"Don't hear that from you very often," Alma said, smiling.

Aino laughed.

That was Aino, too.

Aino returned to Astoria with Eleanor and set about weaning her. She knew weaning at twelve and a half months wasn't ideal, but she didn't see any way out. She was exhausted. No good to Eleanor, no good to the co-op, no good to herself. The last weekend in July, she left Eleanor with Alma and Ilmari. She'd have paid far more than aching breasts to finally get some rest.

She picked Eleanor up the next weekend and brought her back to Astoria for the week, but when she went to Ilmahenki the following weekend, she left her for another week. It was rational. Eleanor could grow up in the country. She was the pet of her cousins—well, at least of the girls. She got fresh vegetables and milk. Why would anyone want to raise a child in the city? Of course, she missed Eleanor, especially at night, but then she was soon asleep and up at five to get to the mill by six. She didn't want to think about Eleanor missing her mother. She watched every sales order closely, always inspecting the railcars for better ways to load the lumber. Sales kept falling. The co-op missed two payments for logs and the entire management committee had to crawl to the company in question offering a workout plan. Paying the monthly lease for the land was always a near thing. And the wages— the good wages of the war, the eight-hour day—were killing them. In desperation, Alvar Kari called a general meeting and explained the situation. The nearly sixty members, including spouses, sat in stunned silence. He offered two paths. Everyone could take a cut in pay, or people could leave with a promise from the co-op that their share money would be returned when things got better. Everyone took a pay cut. Because everyone earned the same, everyone's pay cut was the same. Justice, however, was a poor substitute for money.

20

The steady northwest wind of the North Pacific High was sparking up whitecaps on the river. From the deck of the *General Washington*, Aino watched high clouds scudding through the blue sky, disappearing over Saddle Mountain. It was late Saturday afternoon and she was going to see Eleanor at Ilmahenki, which made her very happy. The troubles of the co-op, being alone, and missing her daughter were lost in the great river, running to the sea as it had done, as it would do, for millennia. Life was brief, she mused, and it ended. She didn't for a moment believe, as Ilmari did, in its continuance after death. This was it—as hard, as sad, as joyful as it was. The future to strive for was a better, more harmonious humanity, not heaven.

As the boat came around the point to the Knappton docks, she felt the comforting smells, sounds, and emotions of home, a pleasant surprise; home used to be Finland. She had always expected to return after the revolution, but Mannerheim had crushed the revolution in Finland and there were disturbing stories coming out of Russia. She walked by the old net shed, remembering dances, tired happy walks back to Reder's Camp on Sunday mornings, the girls in the henhouse—Lempi.

She wondered where Aksel was. Alma said he and his friends, the Bachelor Boys, were constantly mentioned in the gossip of the unmarried girls—and frequently of the married women. It was said they lived in a mysterious camp deep in the forest, hunting and fishing. The five would show up at dances as far away as Skamokawa or Willapa, wild as any loggers, spending money, dancing—but none of them were logging. They must be bootlegging.

People could make mysterious heroes out of the most ordinary men, Aino thought. Bootleggers. Nonsense. Just young men back from the war who didn't want to rejoin the same wage-slave system—the system that sent them there for no good reason in the first place. The slaughter had been horrible beyond what anyone could have conceived five years earlier. The three-hour walk to Ilmahenki got her there at sunset, a little tired. City life, she thought. She was also thirty-one.

Deep River, running slow and revealing lots of rock with the summer dry season, was cast in long shadows from the alders growing among the stumps on the Ilmahenki side of the river. Across, on the north side, was the tall old-growth forest. Logging operations on the north side had started downstream near the mouth, but when the war ended, so did they. Temporary reprieve, she thought. Someday, Vasutäti would have to face reality and leave.

A Ford Model T was parked next to Ilmari's Packard. Unusual. She walked into the house. Relatives never knocked.

Ilmari rose from the table. "We just sent word for you. I drove to Ilwaco to get the doctor."

Aino hurried into the children's bedroom without saying a word. The doctor was putting away his instruments and Alma was holding a wet rag on Eleanor's forehead. Alma stood quickly, stopping Aino's rush toward the bed. "She's going to be OK," she said.

Aino pushed around Alma and knelt beside Eleanor, who radiated heat and smelled like vomit, just like Aino's little brother, Väinö, when he died.

"You're the mother?" The doctor asked in English.

Aino simply nodded.

"She has the Spanish flu. I'm afraid it's finally reached us here in Chinook County."

"Is she going to be OK?" Aino asked.

"Better chance than if she were older. Odd for a flu." He sighed. "Wish I could be more positive." He was counting out a pile of white tablets. "One every half hour."

Aino picked up one and looked at him. "Aspirin," he said. "The latest thing to keep fevers down." He was shrugging into his coat.

"Every half hour. Without fail. If the fever gets worse, you might add a second one."

Aino took over holding the wet rag, feeling guilty for not being with Eleanor sooner. Alma quietly left with the doctor. When Ilmari was paying him in the kitchen, she heard the doctor say, "Keep the other kids clear of the house. I'd let her mother do most of the nursing. No sense risking your wife. We're losing people all over the county. It's killed over half a million here in America alone."

Aino dabbed at Eleanor's rosebud lips, listening to the Model T rattle off toward Tapiola. Eleanor started vomiting and Aino picked her up so the vomit wouldn't clog her trachea. Alma came back with a basin of cool water and knelt beside Aino. The retching abated. Aino laid Eleanor down and started taking off her encrusted nightgown. Eleanor reached her hands out for Alma.

The fever got worse. After several hours, Aino doubled the aspirin, grinding the pills into powder, stuffing it deep into Eleanor's mouth with her finger.

The fever continued, mottling Eleanor's face, coloring her body red, making it glisten with sweat. Occasionally she would try to throw up, but nothing came. She wailed in misery. Aino walked her on the porch in the cooler air. A memory of walking with her dying baby brother crowded in. She thought of praying but then thought that one might as well shake rattles at Eleanor.

Although they kept up the pace with the aspirin, the fever seemed to be getting worse. Eleanor's little face was contorted with pain and her tiny arms and legs jerked. Aino felt panic rising in her gut and curling up to her throat.

Ilmari came into the bedroom, touched Eleanor's forehead, then felt for her pulse. "The aspirin doesn't work," he said. "It could be making it worse."

That made her temper flare. "When did you get your medical degree?"

Ilmari pointed to the single armchair.

"Rest."

"No."

"Aino, it's going to be a long night. I'll watch her. You get some sleep."

"How can I sleep when she's . . ." The fear rose from her stomach, past her heart, and she barely stopped herself from screaming.

Ilmari understood immediately. "We don't know if she's dying. That will be revealed. We do know the fever is worse."

Aino compulsively started grinding more aspirin tablets.

"Don't give it to her."

"She's my child."

"Stop. It's too much."

Aino started to cry. She clamped down. No one would see her cry, not even Ilmari. She stubbornly started putting the powder into Eleanor's mouth. She heard Ilmari walk out the door.

Aino jerked awake on her knees next to the bed, her head resting only inches from Eleanor's hot body. There was noise on the porch. She began again bathing Eleanor.

She could smell Vasutäti before she turned to see her standing next to Ilmari. She had a basket filled with God knows what. Strange roots and flowers. "You keep that stuff away from Eleanor," Aino said. She turned back to her daughter. She fought fear and despair. The fever wouldn't break, the doctor was gone, and now Ilmari had shown up with Vasutati. The old Indian certainly knew how to midwife, but midwives didn't know about disease, and Indians didn't go to medical school.

"She came to help."

"You went and got her."

"Yoh."

She could feel both pairs of dark eyes looking at her, noncommittal. They were so alike!

"Just let her look at her," Ilmari said. "What can it hurt?"

Aino stepped away from the bed. Vasutäti immediately went to Aino's former position, her liver-spotted dark hands gently prodding

Eleanor's body. She stood and picked up one of the aspirin from the pile. "What this?" she asked in English.

"Medicine," Aino said. "The doctor says for her to take one or two every half hour."

Vasutäti carefully bit off a little piece and rolled it in her mouth. "It has willow energy."

"Willow energy," she said to Ilmari in Finnish. "Jesus Christ almighty." She was aware that she was cursing like a logger's wife.

Vasutäti was looking at her with that steady nonjudging regard. "The willow spirit is making her sick more than the flu," Vasutäti said.

"Superstitious nonsense." Aino's face was contorted.

Vasutati turned her head to Ilmari at this, her eyebrows questioning.

"Aino, listen to her. She's a true shaman, a healer."

"Superstition."

Vasutäti looked compassionately at Aino. "Stop the willow medicine or the baby will die."

"The 'willow medicine' is aspirin and it's been prescribed by a medical doctor trained at the University of Washington."

"Trained in science?" Vasutäti asked.

"Yes, not mumbo-jumbo."

"But you just *believe* this doctor. That's religion."

"Get her out of here," Aino said quietly to Ilmari in Finnish.

Vasutäti calmly laid out some roots at the end of the bed. "Boil these in water, not too long, and make tea. Give the tea to the little girl. Stop giving her white pills."

She looked at Ilmari. "Your sister is very afraid and not thinking. She's giving her daughter too many white pills. A little willow spirit helps; too much will kill her. Talk Finn to her. She doesn't trust me."

"Aino, listen to her," Ilmari pleaded.

"Get her out or I'll throw her out," Aino said through clenched teeth.

Ilmari looked calmly at his sister, working something over in his mind. "Yoh," he said. He escorted the old woman out of the house, talking to her in a low voice in the pidgin language they used with each other.

Ilmari came back. "She's gone. You treated her badly, but she knows you're frightened."

Aino was again kneeling at the bed. She looked up. "I'd be a lot less frightened if we just stuck to what the trained medical expert says instead of 'willow energy.' What in hell is that?"

"You want an answer or are you just complaining?" He gently put a hand on the top of her thick hair and dug his fingers down through it and slowly rubbed her scalp.

She stiffened for a moment, then seemed to collapse, wailing, her face buried in the blankets. "Oh, Ilmari, I'm so scared."

Ilmari knelt beside her and pulled her close to him. She stopped her crying.

After another five minutes, Ilmari still gently digging his fingers into her hair, her head nodded with exhaustion. She jerked it back. Then she felt Ilmari helping her to the floor, covering her with a blanket. "I've got her, Aino," was the last thing she heard.

Aino woke with a start and threw the blanket off. The bed was empty. She screamed with rage and tore into the kitchen where Alma was feeding the children breakfast. "Ilmari's gone crazy. Get the sheriff. He's taken Eleanor."

Alma just stood there with a spoon in her hand. The children watched their aunt Aino with their mouths open.

"Kidnapped!" Aino shouted. "He and that Indian are going to kill her."

"Calm down," Alma said.

"Eleanor is dying. I'm getting the sheriff."

"Your own brother?"

"My own child!"

She ran all the way to Higgins's, called the sheriff, and then ran back to the river. It was low, reaching only to her breasts at the deepest place, and the slow current allowed her to keep her feet until her weight began to bear again. She climbed up the bank, her skirt easily thirty pounds heavier. She took it off, wrung it, threw it over her shoulder, and ran up the path to Vasutäti's place.

It was impossible to surprise Ilmari in the woods, and, as she had expected, he met her at the edge of Vasutäti's little clearing.

"She's OK. She's inside with Vasutäti."

"You get out of my way."

"You're irrational with fear. The aspirin is making it worse. I had to stop you."

"I sent for the sheriff."

Ilmari looked at her sadly. "Bad idea."

"I'll get her back."

"No. You'll just force me to face him off with my rifle." He turned. She darted past him, but he tackled her and rolled her to a stop beneath him, letting her kick and struggle. She knew he could hold her all day. She stopped.

"Put your skirt on. I don't want you in your underwear when the sheriff comes."

Well into the afternoon, Ilmari stood guard at Vasutäti's dome-shaped hut, keeping Aino out but letting Vasutäti go back and forth. At midafternoon Aino saw Ilmari become alert and pick up his rifle. A few minutes later, Sheriff Cobb and several deputies emerged from the forest. They stopped short, seeing Ilmari in front of Vasutäti's shelter with his rifle.

The sheriff smiled. Two more men joined him from the forest. The sheriff turned to Aino. "You goddamned Koskis seem to like to stand me off with rifles." There was some nervous laughter. "Is the child in there?"

"Yoh," said Ilmari.

"I need to see she's safe."

"She's safe." He said something to Vasutäti who came out of the door with a bedraggled and sweaty Eleanor in her arms.

"Baby safe," Vasutäti said and disappeared back inside.

"Is that your daughter?" the sheriff asked Aino.

"Yes. They've kidnapped her."

"Well." The sheriff looked genuinely puzzled. "It seems more like a custody dispute."

She heard the rifle cock. She turned to see Ilmari calmly pointing it at the sheriff's feet.

"The baby stays here," Ilmari said. "You have to shoot me and Vasutäti both if you want to take her away."

"Now, Ilmari, goddamnit," Cobb said. "There's no need for that."

"Good. You want coffee?"

The posse, if it could be called that, moved to the fire.

Aino knew Ilmari had them in a standoff. She glared at him. "Eleanor dies," she said in Finnish, "I'll kill you. I swear."

"Eleanor might die," he answered in English. "But at least not from aspirin poisoning." He sat down cross-legged, the rifle cradled across his thighs, cocked.

"Why don't you help the sheriff and the boys get some coffee," he said in Finnish.

At about four in the afternoon, Aksel and Kullervo broke into the clearing.

"What brings you boys here?" the sheriff asked. "I don't see a still." He looked around exaggeratedly. "But then I never see you boys by a still. That's why you are still out of jail." He laughed, proud of his pun.

Aksel turned to Aino. "What's going on?"

She told him. Then Aksel asked Ilmari the same question. Ilmari told his side. Aksel was quiet for a moment. Then he looked at the sheriff. "Custody dispute, right?"

"I'd say so, but she's claiming kidnapping."

Aksel muttered something about stubborn Finns and turned to Kullervo. "You get two fresh horses to meet me at the Knappton dock." Then Aksel ran into the forest.

"What the hell?" Cobb sputtered.

Kullervo smiled. "I think Sergeant Långström has a plan." Then Kullervo ran after Aksel.

Cobb and the lawmen huddled around the fire through the night, while Ilmari sat cross-legged, silent and meditative, in front of Vasutäti's hut with his rifle across his lap. He was still there as a cool September dawn moved west through the high trees.

When Aksel and Jouka walked out of the woods into the growing light, leading two horses, Aino gasped. Jouka looked as though he'd been dragged out of a swamp. He was not just thin, but gaunt, unshaven, his eyes sunken and bloodshot from drinking.

"Sheriff," Aksel said. "You know Mr. Kaukonen. He's the child's father."

The sheriff grunted and rose to his feet.

Then Aino knew. She shouted, "No! No! Goddamn you, Aksel Långström. You can't do this." She turned her attention to plead with Jouka. "You can't listen to Ilmari. The doctor told us to use aspirin to break Eleanor's fever. The doctor from Ilwaco, not the quack from Knappton Mills."

Jouka walked slowly over toward Aino. "She's my daughter, too."

"He doesn't even know her," she moaned to the sheriff.

"He's the father," the sheriff said grimly. "What the father says goes. It's the law."

"I'm the *mother*," she shrieked. She frantically grabbed a chunk of wood from near the fire, only to have her hand caught by Aksel before she could hurt anyone. Aksel held her, letting her kick him and scream, but she could no more break free than could a mouse from an eagle's talons.

Jouka went into the hut and came out several minutes later. "My child will stay under the care of her uncle and this Indian woman," he said to Cobb.

Aino screamed at them. "You arrogant, superstitious bastards are going to kill my daughter."

"Well, boys, in the state of Washington, the father has custody," Cobb said. "We're through here."

Just before he disappeared on the trail, he turned. "I hope to hell that baby lives."

Still being held by Aksel, Aino relaxed her body a little and felt him reciprocate. "I want to see my daughter," she said quietly. Aksel looked at Ilmari, who looked at Jouka. Jouka nodded.

Ilmari looked at Aksel, who released her. "My child dies, I'll kill you *and* Ilmari *and* Jouka," she said in a low, even voice. She meant every word.

"We all hope she lives," Aksel replied calmly.

She pushed past Jouka, saying nothing, and entered the shelter. A small fire glowed beneath a smoke hole in the low ceiling. Vasutäti was sitting next to Eleanor, singing softly. Aino touched Eleanor's forehead and pulled her hand back sharply. "She's burning with fever." Aino started to wail. "I can't believe you're doing this."

"A small fever is good," Vasutäti said in English. "It kills the little animals that cause sickness."

Aino stood there, helpless, feeling the calm gaze of the Indian woman. Then Vasutäti picked Eleanor up and handed her to Aino. Aino immediately clasped Eleanor close to her bosom. Eleanor began to reach a hand out, her mouth seeking the familiar breast.

"It's good if child sucks," Vasutäti said.

Aino looked at her questioningly. "She's weaned. No milk."

"No milk is OK. She feel better. Big help for her live."

Ilmari quickly left. Aino unbuttoned her blouse, put Eleanor's mouth to her nipple, and once more felt the insistent sucking of her baby.

For the first time in days, it seemed that everything might just work out. Then she realized Vasutäti had suggested nursing as much for her as for Eleanor. She looked at the old woman, who simply nodded at her, smiling. Our secret, she seemed to say.

Eleanor's fever broke late in the afternoon. Holding Eleanor, Aino slowly turned around and around, her eyes closed, savoring the child's now comfortably warm little body. When she opened her eyes, Ilmari and Vasutäti were looking at her, smiling.

"I—" Aino didn't know what to say. "I can be so stubborn," she said, holding back tears, her jaw trembling. Ilmari and Vasutäti both nodded their heads, accepting her halting apology.

Aino was too relieved to notice Aksel and Jouka quietly leading their horses away.

21

A ino stayed at Ilmahenki until the next Friday. She gave Eleanor a last kiss and handed her to Alma. It hurt to leave her, but it was better than leaving her in that dingy downstairs apartment with strangers.

All the way to Astoria, her mind was on the quarterly Saturday night membership meeting. A proposal to hire new workers but just pay them wages and not allow membership was on the table. Many current members saw it as a way to increase their own share of the co-op's surplus. She was utterly opposed. It defeated the entire purpose of a co-op. Labor was only a "factor of production," and there was a "labor market" where prices, called wages, were bid up and down, only because the culture saw people the same way it saw machines.

Everyone voting on everything had started to bother her. Voitto had once told her that it was dangerous to let a group of fools make important decisions—and it got more dangerous the more fools there were. That was why, he said, Lenin made the party the vanguard of the proletariat. She didn't like that either. A few powerful party members making decisions for the workers were no different from a few wealthy owners making decisions for the workers. She laughed at herself. She wanted everyone to vote but vote her way.

When Aino reached the mill in the afternoon, Alvar Kari nervously told her that there was talk, mostly among the wives, that a divorced woman shouldn't be on the board. She knew it was Alvar's kind way of saying that if the co-op were to be in good standing in the community, it shouldn't have an adulterer who abandoned her baby and who was a member of a traitorous radical organization on its board. The wives of the board members were invited to discreet coffee klatches by concerned women over the next two weeks. Then the coffee klatches were expanded to the wives of key workers. Aino chose to leave.

Per the bylaws, the co-op would refund Aino's original membership contribution and retained patronage—over a ten-year period. She left with nothing, feeling enormous anger about the unfairness of it all.

She stopped by Matti and Kyllikki's little house in Uniontown on her way home. Kyllikki, strands of hair sticking to her sweaty face, was washing clothes with Pilvi.

"Why aren't you at the mill?" Kyllikki asked as Aino walked in. "Pour yourself some coffee." She indicated the stove and went back to pounding the clothes with a solid round stick in a large galvanized tub of water she kept reheating with water from the big kettle on the woodstove. She had all the windows open. Pilvi, who had her own little stick, was pounding away at the tub with Kyllikki.

"I quit before I was voted off the board. I'm a disgraced woman."

Kyllikki stopped pounding. "Gossiping hypocritical old biddies." She smashed the washing stick down hard, startling Pilvi. Aarni came in with another load of kindling for the firebox. "Why don't you go see if Billy Haskins can play," Kyllikki said. Aarni bolted out of the house with Kyllikki shouting after him: "And if he can't, go find Suvi at school and . . . Do you want a nickel?" Aarni came back in a flash. Fishing out two nickels from the penny jar on the shelf above the stove, Kyllikki said, "And tell Suvi to take you both to Roth's for a phosphate." She paid the bribe and he went running down the street. Pilvi looked between her mother and aunt, not quite sure how to react to seeing her brother and sister get a nickel. Kyllikki picked her up and set her at the table, whispering in her ear, "If you can sit here like a big girl and not interrupt us, I'll let you have some girls' coffee with a sugar cube."

"Talk," she said to Aino, having cleared the way for action.

"The drumbeat was it didn't look good for the co-op to have a divorced, unpatriotic Wobbly on the board."

Kyllikki took that in, then asked, "Did it have anything to do with Hillström?"

"That was years ago."

"Yes, but it's today's news."

The two sat in silence, taking it in, Pilvi looking wide-eyed, sensing something but keeping quiet.

"I'm going to Portland," Aino said. "There's serious work to do."

"What?"

"I've been wasting my time with that stupid co-op."

"I hardly call creating jobs for thirty men and having Eleanor wasting time."

"Depends on how you look at it."

As soon as the words were out, Aino felt a shift in Kyllikki to something deep in her core. It was a mother bear standing firm over her cubs. It was deep roots that allowed the grass to move with the wind, but never lose its grip on the earth. It was Kyllikki's power, so different from Matti's power.

"How you look at things determines where you're standing to look."

"I don't need a lecture."

"No. You need a kick in the rear." Kyllikki leaned across the table. "You have a child and you almost lost her. And you want to leave her again?"

Aino bristled. "I'll send for her as soon as I'm settled."

"Aino, you might find this hard to swallow, but sending for her isn't the issue. Putting her second is the issue."

"Letting her stay with her uncle and aunt for a couple of weeks isn't putting her second."

"Stop dreaming!" Kyllikki slapped her hand on the table, making the dishes rattle. Pilvi's eyes grew wider. "The Wobblies are done. Finished. The government, the owners, and the people, Aino, *the people*, see you as traitors. Your leadership is all in jail. It's a wonderful dream, Aino, One Big Union, but it's a dream butting up against reality. The AF of L has it right."

"We've got to change reality! Lenin has it right."

"You can't serve God and mammon. Jesus had it right."

"Matthew, chapter six, verse twenty-four," Aino said sarcastically. "Don't preach to me about money. You and Matti are trying to get rich as fast as you can. If Astoria had a country club, you'd join it."

"Mammon's not just about money, Aino. God's about love and mammon's about the ten thousand petty things that get in love's way. Yes, money's one of them, but the expression is the *love* of money is the root of all evil, not money itself. And if you tell me you love the IWW, I'm telling you that you're fooling yourself. You can't love an ideal. You can only love people."

"Oh, great, you love concrete things, not ideals. So, do you love this?" Aino indicated the room all around her. "Concrete things like your washtub of dirty clothes, your dances on Saturday nights, your little house on the hill. My *ideal* is making history. You and your *things* . . . you're going nowhere."

Aino immediately knew she'd overstepped—again. It had been mean. She watched Kyllikki struggle for control and then gain it.

Aino sighed. "I didn't mean it. I'm sorry."

"Oh, Aino, Aino," Kyllikki was shaking her head. "We're all going to the same place, Aino, the grave. All that you or any of us will take with us is love."

"No one takes anything to the grave."

"You need to choose either Eleanor, your living, breathing daughter, or the IWW."

"I can do both."

"It's not the doing, Aino. It's the attitude or priorities. It's the . . ." She was searching for words and although Finnish was her first tongue, her adult vocabulary was English. "It's like the position you choose to see things from, your stance in life. Matti can be motivated to make money because he loves logging or because he loves money or because he loves his family. The logging's the same." Kyllikki smiled affectionately thinking of Matti. "He got over money when he nearly killed Reder and, but for you, would have gone to jail."

"Right there! John Reder can throw poor people in jail or throw you and Matti out of Chinook County with impunity because of this rotten-to-the core system."

"Poor people all over Russia and Finland have been thrown in jail because of the rotten-to-the-core system you reds came up with."

"Yes, people are angry on both sides, but communism is about helping others, while capitalism is all about helping yourself."

"Isms!" Kyllikki nearly spit the word. "Social*ism*, commun*ism*, capital*ism*. All *isms* are about words and people worship the words the same way other people worship God."

"One Big Union isn't an *ism*. Direct action isn't an *ism*."

"Helping your friend, caring for your child, *that's* direct action. The *isms* just wrap the desire for power, money, and security in pretty words." Kyllikki gave a tired sigh. "Who's going to run Finland if the reds take over? Who's going to run the One Big Union, Aino? Grow up."

Aino shot to her feet. Pilvi pulled her girls' coffee up tight to her chest. "I choose the IWW." Aino was nearly spitting, trembling.

"You get on that train to Portland instead of the boat to Knappton and you'll regret it the rest of your days."

"Don't talk to me about regret." Aino reached into the washtub and pulled up one of Matti's long johns, the water streaming from it. "This is the life *you* chose." She dropped the wet long johns back into the tub and stalked out the door.

22

ino took the first train to Portland. She walked to the IWW hall on Burnside Street and rented a room from a fellow Wobbly. That night, she wrote to Ilmari and Alma, saying she would come for Eleanor as soon as she got settled.

She found part-time work waiting tables where she got one good meal a day. She joined the effort to organize the workers in the sawmills just downstream on the Willamette River. It was an uphill grind. Even though the Wobblies had championed and won the eight-hour day, many of the mill workers held a simmering resentment against the Wobblies for striking in America's hour of need.

This issue of patriotism brought her to her feet at the last weekly meeting in October. "We need to show we are not un-American," she said. "We need to be at every Armistice Day parade, any celebration with those who served during the war in uniform."

"All you're doing is pandering to nationalism," someone pointed out.

"No one pandering to anybody," she shot back. "Wobblies obeyed the draft and fought in the war, whether they believing in it or not. People need to know that. We must make clear we are not against the United States."

People broke into arguing. The local president banged his gavel for order. When it returned, he asked, "Your ideas, Aino?"

"Two years back, hired thugs smashed up our hall in Centralia and beat fellow Wobblies on the street. The Centralia Wobblies have made a new hall in an old hotel. There's going to be a big Armistice

Day parade. We need to make clear solidarity with the Centralia Wobblies and show the American Legion and National Guard they weren't the only ones *over there*." She paused, afraid someone would make a wisecrack about the last time she was in Centralia. No one did.

On the morning of November 10, 1919, she took the train north. Sitting on the left side, she could see the Columbia intermittently until it turned westward, disappearing into the Coast Mountains, rolling west to the Pacific, to the big timber and the noisy clanking operations cutting it down, to Astoria, to Knappton and the little trail, now a plank road, that led to Tapiola and Deep River.

She reached the Roderick Hotel, serving as the new IWW hall, in the afternoon. She was pleased to see Michael Tierney and his brother-in-law, Jack Kerwin, there. Jack had logged for the Spruce Division and knew Matti.

The place was in a furor and Aino was immediately engulfed in rumors. The American Legion would be armed. Thugs had been hired to beat up Wobblies. They were going to shoot Wobblies for being traitors. They would all be jailed like the fifteen Wobbly miners in Colorado.

At the root of the rumors, it was always "they." Who were "they"? The government? The capitalists? John Reder? His sheriff? Margaret Reder? Matti and Kyllikki?

She staked out a place on the floor to spend the night and began producing leaflets for the next day's parade. A nice kid named Wesley, still wearing his army uniform, helped her by turning the hand crank of the little printing press. He had a good sense of humor and the time passed quickly as they worked together.

Aksel, Kullervo, Jens Lerback, Heppu Reinikka, and Yrjö Rautio were also wearing their uniforms. Many veterans did so, not for nostalgia, but because the uniform was high-quality wool and free. Feeling the need for something more exciting than fishing, hunting, and getting drunk at dances, they decided to join the festivities at Centralia. The American

Legion had formed in Paris when they were still overseas. Although they weren't members—there was no Legion post closer than Willapa or Astoria—they thought they might run into some old comrades since legionnaires were coming to the big parade from all over. They arrived on the train around seven, long after dark, and quickly found a speakeasy. The tension over the next day's parade was palpable. The feeling of the speakeasy crowd was that the Wobblies were Bolsheviks who wanted to overthrow the United States government and needed to be run out of town. The local American Legion commander, Warren Grimm—a war hero as well as a lawyer—said they had every legal right to remain in town, even though he didn't like Wobblies. His brother, Polly, the city attorney, agreed with him. It outraged many of the veterans. They'd fought a war to defend American freedom and values, and the law was protecting Wobblies who wanted to destroy them.

The Bachelor Boys simply looked at each other over their drinks. It wasn't their fight. They had formed their own society, self-sustaining and, in their opinion, superior to the one to which they had returned.

They bedded down in a pasture by the Skookumchuck River, wrapping themselves in army surplus wool blankets and rubberized ground cloths. After the trenches, a November night in a cow pasture didn't even seem like camping.

Kullervo woke Aksel by kicking him gently and handing him a canteen of hot coffee. Aksel liked Kullervo but was always a little wary of him. It wasn't just Kullervo's explosive temper. Hell, Aksel thought, since the war they all had explosive tempers. It was also that Kullervo idolized him the way he himself had idolized Gunnar. Aksel felt the admiration was misplaced.

"Thanks," Aksel said in English. English was the natural default because Jens's first language was Norwegian, Heppu's and Yrjö's was Finnish, and Aksel's was Swedish. Kullervo had learned Finnish and English simultaneously.

"The parade starts at noon," Kullervo said. "The legionnaires will be packing live ammunition. The Wobblies are coming armed. They won't back down the way they did in seventeen." Kullervo was bouncing on his haunches with excitement.

"How do you know that?"

"I went back into town. You know"—he smiled—"Eve's Garden."

Aksel laughed and took a sip of the scalding black coffee. Heppu and Jens awoke and stood side by side, peeing about five feet from Aksel and Kullervo, who hardly noticed. Yrjö had moaned and rolled over in his blanket. It seemed he might have been at Eve's Garden, too.

"You think there will be a fight?" Kullervo asked Aksel. "I mean a firefight?"

"You want one?"

Kullervo looked away. When he looked back, Aksel could see that he did.

"Those bastards beat hell out of the Wobblies back in seventeen," Kullervo said. "This time, the Wobblies will fight back. They're going to have guys with rifles posted outside the Roderick Hotel, so if the legionnaires rush their hall, they'll take fire from both directions."

"The boys learned something in the war," Aksel said.

"Only it won't be legionnaires rushing the Roderick," Jens said. He, Yrjö, and Heppu had joined Aksel and Kullervo.

"Who, then?" Aksel asked.

"They call themselves the Centralia Citizens' Committee—thugs paid by the president of the Eastern Railway and Lumber Company."

Kullervo licked his lips. "Should have brought my Springfield."

"Hell, Aksel's tommy gun," Yrjö chimed in.

After eating pork and beans out of cans, they walked along the Skookumchuck into town. When they began walking up Tower Street, they could feel the tension. Jens touched Aksel's arm and nodded toward a hill just across the river. On it were armed men, probably Wobblies. They would have an unobstructed field of fire along the entire street. Eyes darting now with the increasing tension, the Bachelor Boys began to pick out riflemen on the rooftops. The Wobblies truly weren't going to be pushed around this time.

The legionnaires loosely formed into their local posts. All carried rifles for the parade. Many nervously fingered clips in their pockets. Several had already seated their clips in their rifles. Others were carrying rubber hoses and gas pipes. Nervous deputies and city police stood around armed with pistols.

The Bachelor Boys fell into old habits, moving as a unit, but not too close to each other. Although they had been in the trenches, they had spent many of the final months attacking Germans in French forests where they felt at home.

They walked by the old hotel that served as the IWW hall since the original one had been burned down. A couple of Wobblies in uniform leaned against the outside walls and more stood inside the door. All carried pistols. Aksel noticed at least three Wobblies in the doorway of another hotel just across the street. Well, he thought, no way in hell anyone was going to burn this Wobbly hall down.

Then he saw Aino emerge from the Roderick Hotel's door, that unmistakable carriage, the wire-rimmed glasses, her heavy black hair piled on her head, and, after all this time and the baby, the same fine figure that first took his breath away when he was a boy. He looked away. He didn't want to be seen for some reason. He moved closer to Jens, always reliable in serious trouble. Having logged together before the war, they'd been in a band of brothers already.

"These Legion boys look trigger-happy to you?" Aksel asked.

Jens looked around as they walked. "Hard to tell. Could just be carrying rifles for the parade. So far mostly without the clips in."

"Yeah, but we know how many clips you can carry in your pockets."

"We do."

They had arrived where the parade was forming. Different Legion posts were squaring themselves into formation, unfurling flags, adjusting their staffs into leather pockets attached to shoulder belts.

Aksel asked the post from Olympia if they could form the back row. They could hear the spatter of snare drums, like nervous hail on a tin roof, the occasional bugle calls and short scale runs.

Unseen, far ahead, a band struck up "Under the Double Eagle," and everyone straightened in anticipation. A marching band from a company town just in front of them started "The Stars and Stripes Forever."

For a time, the parade moved along in the usual fits and starts. At the corner of Tower and Second Streets, however, as a result of poor planning, the head of the parade ran into its own tail. Aksel heard several men shouting, "The sons of bitches have changed the parade route!" Then he heard a round being chambered up above him. Everything stopped—right in front of the new Wobbly hall.

Aksel thought he saw movement up ahead and behind the Centralia legionnaires. He heard the commander of the Centralia post shout, "Halt! Close up!"

Aksel went flat on the ground before he became conscious of hearing a single shot. All the Bachelor Boys were down on the ground with him.

Then, hell broke loose in Centralia.

23

Aino heard the shot. It seemed to have come from the Avalon Hotel across the street from where she was standing by the door of the Roderick. She remained standing, stunned, having seen the legionnaire who had just passed an order for his post to close up go down wounded. Fire erupted around her. Men on both sides were pulling back the bolts on their Springfields and Enfields, levering their Winchesters, firing six-cylinder revolvers and .45-caliber automatic pistols they'd brought home from the war. She was tackled from the side and went down to the concrete sidewalk—hard. She felt the lean body and coarse wool uniform of a soldier lying on top of her. It was Wesley, the young man who had helped her yesterday. "Stay on the ground," he said. "Don't move."

She lay there, her eyes shut, her hands over her ears, feeling the protective weight of his body. When she opened her eyes, the street was covered with people who'd also gone to the ground. The windows of the hotel had been shot out. Wobblies and marchers were down and bleeding. So much destruction and carnage in just seconds was staggering. Wesley rolled off and said something urgent. She couldn't hear a word, deaf from the firing.

Wesley pointed toward the hall with a pistol. Pulling her to her feet by her hand, he jerked her into the hotel. She thought she heard him shout, "There's going to be hell to pay." But she couldn't be sure. She and Wesley emerged into the back alley. Wesley shouted, "Come on. There's cover by the river." She didn't know what he meant by cover and stood frozen there. Wesley jerked at her arm and her natural inclination was to pull her arm back. He looked around wildly, shook his head at her, turned, and headed east toward the river. She came to her senses watching him run from her. She followed her instincts and ran in the other direction.

The instant the firing died down, Aksel rose and ran hard, jumping over prone bodies, brushing past fleeing women and children, many of them screaming. He reached the door of the hotel looking wildly for Aino. The combat veterans among the legionnaires had reverted to instinct and training. Caught in the killing ground where fire was coming from the hill down Tower Street and from the rooftops all around them, they charged both the Avalon and the Roderick, firing their rifles. Several were already inside the hotel lobbies firing round after round. Askel quickly saw that Aino was not lying on the ground, although plenty of wounded men were. He crouched to the floor and backed out of the hotel.

A horse galloped down the street, a deputized man on its back. As he thundered past Aksel and the Roderick Hotel, he fired three pistol shots through the broken front window. A black Liberty Six with four men in it roared up behind him. The men wore badges pinned to their chests but no police uniforms. "Keep the bastards penned in there," one of them shouted, taking cover behind the car. The others joined him, throwing themselves to the ground. "We'll get the sons of bitches, by God."

Aksel saw the Bachelor Boys running toward him.

"You boys get out of the line of fire," one of the deputies shouted. They ignored him, running straight up to Aksel.

"Help me get some of the wounded to safety," Aksel said, already dragging a wounded legionnaire by his feet away from the fight. Heppu and Kullervo together started pulling a large man by each leg, following Aksel to cover in an alley west of a dry goods store. Jens, with a wounded man in a fireman's carry, came stumbling after them. They all set to work tearing the men's clothes to make bandages for their wounds. Aksel ran into the store, grabbed three bolts of cloth as the clerk yelled, "Looters! Looters!" Aksel put a bolt under each man's feet, elevating them to help stave off shock.

Firing erupted again although it was now sporadic. Again silence. Then Aksel heard someone shouting, "He went that way. Stole three of my best bolts." Three legionnaires, all with rifles, stormed around the corner into the alley. They stopped short, seeing the Bachelor Boys in uniform and wounded men with their feet on the bolts. The man in the lead smiled. "That clerk thought you were looters," he said. "You boys armed?"

Aksel shook his head and sat back away from the wounded man, still applying pressure to the wound. "They'll be all right," the man said. "We need every able-bodied man to hunt these bastards down."

"It's not our fight," Aksel said quietly to the leader. He pulled out a cigarette.

"Well, it should be. We don't stop the sons of bitches now, we'll have the bloodbath they got in Russia. We're going to hunt these bastards down and then we're going to hang 'em." He turned to his companions. "Come on, these boys are cowards." The men disappeared.

Aksel stopped Kullervo from going after them. Lighting his cigarette and slowly exhaling smoke, he passed it to Kullervo. "Even cowards need a smoke now and then."

Kullervo laughed and took the cigarette, then handed it to Heppu who had a drag and then said, "We need to get these guys to a hospital."

"Not our problem," Aksel said. "Kullervo, go back to that dry goods store and tell that whiny clerk we need blankets. No. Just take 'em."

Heppu passed the cigarette to Jens and left with Kullervo. Jens took a last draw and held up the glowing butt to Aksel, who shook his head no. Jens flipped it to the damp ground and they watched it slowly burn out as they waited for Kullervo to return with the blankets. When he did, they wrapped the wounded men in them. Aksel stood up. "I saw Aino Koski standing by the door of the Roderick," he said.

"That woman can sure find trouble," Jens said, shaking his head.

"These people are in a hanging mood," Aksel said. "Because she's a woman they may not grab her, yet. But she's pretty well-known around here and if they do grab her . . ." Aksel ground the dead cigarette butt under his boot. "I'm going to look for her."

"To do what?" Kullervo asked.

"Don't know for sure."

The other Bachelor Boys glanced at each other. "Still soft on her," Kullervo said.

"I like her brother," Aksel said.

"Doesn't have nearly the chest," Kullervo quipped. The others laughed. Even Aksel smiled. The smile, however, was from a memory of dancing the Grizzly Bear with Aino.

Aksel ran back to the chaos of the Roderick, followed by the Boys. He didn't see Aino. He sent Heppu and Jens to search Tower Street heading north, reminding them that they looked like legionnaires, meaning a Wobbly could try to kill them. He told Yrjö to go south on Tower, keeping close to the buildings on the east side so he'd get shelter from anyone firing from the hill across the river. He kept Kullervo with him and headed west up Second Street.

Aksel and Kullervo found Aino hiding behind garbage cans in an alley. Aino scrambled to her feet. Aksel pushed her down, hissing at her to be quiet. Then he turned to Kullervo. "Go tell everyone we found her and to assemble here." Kullervo ran. Aksel spotted discarded curtains next to the cans and he threw them on Aino. She started to push them off, but he just shoved her head down underneath the curtains and she stopped. Then he sat on her and started rolling a cigarette as four legionnaires came running up the alley.

"You see any of those Bolshevik bastards coming this way?" one of them shouted.

The wiggling underneath Aksel stopped.

"We got one of them trying to cross the river," the man continued, panting for air. Another one, also panting, said, "The red bastard shot Hubbard," as if Aksel would know who that was.

Aksel simply shook his head no and struck a match on his shoes. He knew the legionnaires could see the ribbons on his chest and would trust that he told the truth. They ran off, just as the other four Bachelor Boys came running back.

"Where is she?" Jens asked.

Aksel nodded down at the pile of curtains beneath him. All four of them broke into grins.

"We have to get her out of here," Heppu said.

There was silence. Then Kullervo said, "I have an idea. Aksel, you stay here with her." The Bachelor Boys looked at each other, then followed Kullervo.

They returned, walking under a long, rolled carpet. They dropped it at Aksel's feet, smiling. Yrjö said, "We took it from the lobby of the Roderick. Told the cops we were from the Willapa Legion post and were taking it as a fair exchange: Wobbly Hall to Legion Hall."

Nodding at Kullervo and Heppu, Aksel said, "Security." They ran to stand guard some distance to the east and west of the others. He pulled the curtains off Aino. She was hugging her knees in a fetal position. She struggled to sit upright, adjusting her glasses, slightly bent by Aksel sitting on her. "Did they get that boy Wesley?" she asked. "He had a pistol. I came this way. He took off toward the river."

"Don't know him and don't know," Aksel answered. "All I know is they're rounding up every Wobbly they can find and they're in a lynching mood."

"Bastards," she muttered.

"We have to get you out of here."

"My place is with my comrades."

"Your comrades are going to be arrested and then killed."

He watched her blanch, then struggle to control her fear. She stood erect. "I'll not run."

Aksel could see that her sisu was up. He gave a quick whistle and Kullervo and Heppu came running. Aino looked at Aksel belligerently, as well as with a little puzzlement. "Time to go," Aksel said to the four Bachelor Boys. They grinned and started unrolling the rug.

Aino suddenly understood. "No, goddamnit. No. You're not putting me in that." She tried to run.

Aksel jumped her, pinning her arms behind her, taking her to the ground. She tried to kick and bite him, but within seconds she was being rolled up in the rug, screaming in a blind panic, out of control. Aksel had never seen her like that. He realized this was panic from beyond what was happening now. Panic or no panic, it couldn't be helped. He squatted next to the end of the rug. She tried to spit on him but couldn't roll her head back far enough to do it. The spit hit the leading edge of the rug in front of her face. Aksel then lay on the ground, his face close to hers. "Shh, shh," he whispered, as if to a child. He touched her hair. "Shh, now. You'll be safe. We've got you." He smiled at her. "Think of Eleanor."

She stopped her wild struggling.

"We're going to the train station," Aksel said calmly. "Shh, now. You make a single sound, you'll be in jail and likely dead by morning."

No sound came from the rug.

Aksel loosely stuffed some of the curtains above her head and the five of them spelled each other, walking casually toward the train station. They were stopped twice, but both times gave the same answer, Wobbly rug to Legion Hall rug, and they were not stopped. At the station, they set the rug down, Aino's end of the roll toward a wall. They took the curtains out, giving her some air.

They were on the platform two hours, smoking, laying their heads on top of the rug, joking with passing legionnaires, until the train from Tacoma arrived. National Guardsmen piled out, moving into ranks on the station platform. As the troops started moving toward town, Aksel found the conductor, who was looking at his pocket watch. "We've got a rug here for our Legion Hall," he said. "Going to Castle Rock. Where should we put it?"

The conductor indicated a baggage car and they casually dumped the rug in it, Aino still inside, and walked off to a passenger coach.

At the Castle Rock train station, they retrieved the rug, carrying it into the woods out of sight. Aksel again sent Heppu and Kullervo out as security. Then, he nodded at Jens and Yrjö, and the three of them quickly unrolled Aino onto the ground.

At first, Aino wanted to scramble to her feet and curse them, but she was so stiff she couldn't move and so grateful to be unconfined again that she quickly forgot the impulse. Even more urgently, she needed to pee.

Aksel pulled her to her feet. Those bright-blue eyes were laughing at her. She couldn't hold on any longer and she hobbled off a few steps, lifted her dress, parted her split drawers, and peed. She wanted to sigh with relief but wouldn't because she assumed the men were watching her. Embarrassed now, she adjusted her drawers and skirt and turned to face them, her chin up. She saw only their backs.

"You can turn around now," she said in English.

Five grinning faces. God. Men could be such boys, she thought.

"You have any money?" Aksel asked, again speaking Finnish.

"My purse is back at the hall. I had a return ticket to Portland."

Aksel reached into his pocket and pulled out two five-dollar bills. "You can pay me back later."

Aino took the money. "I will," she said. She looked up at Aksel and then at the Bachelor Boys, who were all watching her, their faces kind but otherwise uncommunicative. "I—" she started. She looked down at her shoes. The tears came. She lifted her chin. "Kiitos," she said to Aksel, thank you. "Kiitos," she repeated to the watching Bachelor Boys. She then looked to Aksel for some sort of help. Kullervo, Heppu, Yrjö, and Jens walked across the street and lit cigarettes, leaving the two of them alone.

She and Aksel stood looking at each other, saying nothing. Finally, Aksel said, "I was at Ilmahenki last Wednesday."

"Did you see Eleanor? How is she?" She suddenly worried that Aksel, too, would harbor accusations that she'd abandoned her child.

"She's fine."

"I'm going to get her as soon as I'm settled."

"Well, get settled soon."

The way he said it took her aback. It sounded nonjudgmental, but she knew he was delivering a message about the direction she'd chosen. Before she could think of a response, he walked away to join his friends. She boarded the train for Portland, alone.

PART FIVE

1919–1932

Prologue

Leaving himself on his bed, Ilmari walked to Deep River and waded out from the shore. The tide was ebbing fast, running past Stanley Point and Long Island, where Matti had found refuge; passing Needle Point where it was joined by the waters of the Klawachuck and the three Nemahs; past Goose Point, which sheltered the mouths of the Palix and the Niawiakum; and then past Leadbetter Point, where the waters joined with the water of the Willapa and the Cedar and where the fresh water of the land met the salt water of the sea. He went with the power of the many rivers and was swept into the deepest of waters. Then, growing afraid, he struggled against the current, but when he grew tired, he sank into the darkness and drowned.

There, deep in the ocean, the Salmon People came and took him to their village beneath the ocean, a village that looked like the villages of the Chinook and the Chehalis, the Clatsop and the Clatskanie, the Cowlitz and the Tillamook. They did not use their bodies, for they had left those behind for the human people and the animal and bird people to eat.

Ilmari joined them. Now he belonged to the Salmon People.

When they reached their village, he heard a child crying. The child was at the breast of its mother, but the mother looked up at Ilmari with hollow cheeks and sunken eyes and he felt her deep sadness because she had no milk. He watched the returning Salmon People enter their own lodges, but he saw that the lodges were no longer strong. The cedar-bark roofs needed repair and the smoke from the cooking fires, instead of rising into the clear air-like water above, seeped down from the smoke holes and lay along the paths and the meeting places where it stung the eyes and burned the nasal passages.

He entered a dancing ground in the village center and an old man and an old woman, elders of the Salmon People, invited him to sit before them. The old woman said her people's milk would not flow until the bones of her people were returned to the sea. The old man said the lodges would not be made strong until the entrails of his people were returned to the sea. And Ilmari understood that his people should not take more than they needed from the Salmon People, lest their gift be withdrawn. The old woman said the women's milk would not flow until her people's eggs could be planted in clean gravel. The old man said the smoke would not rise above the village unimpeded until his people's children could return to the sea unimpeded. And Ilmari understood. As a woman dips water from a stream for her use but the stream flows on, so too must flow the cycle of the Salmon People.

Then Ilmari heard children laughing and he walked to where a stream within the ocean flowed past the village and children of the Salmon People swam and splashed and laughed, moving like flashes of sunlight on the water. The old woman said, "Look closely." And Ilmari looked beneath the surface of the water and saw that the children were missing feet or hands. "If you hunger, you may eat our children, but if you do not return their bones and entrails with respect, they will be reborn crippled and eventually they will die, and you will have eaten a child who can never be replaced."

Ilmari stayed the winter with the Salmon People, learning their lore. When it was again spring and time for them to return to their birthplaces in the small creeks that flowed over the rocks into the deep currents of the great rivers, he swam, too, for he now belonged to them.

He swam to the opening at the end of the long north-running peninsula. The Great River had carried sand ground from the rocks of the mountains to the sea. The sea had carried it north and dropped it there, forming the bay that his former people called Willapa. Now, smelling Deep River, he found its mouth, and then smelling Ilmahenki, he found the beach in the slack water. There, Vasutäti caught him in her net.

When she pulled him from the river, she saw his dark eyes and broad chest and knew it was him. She took him to her campsite and held him, singing to him, until he began to shed his skin. On the third day, he was again human. She sat him down before her and said, "I will not stay with you much longer. You must remember what I have taught you."

He walked to Deep River with her and stood at her side looking across to Ilmahenki and the smoke from the stove where Alma made breakfast for his children and he was filled with longing to cross the river and join them. Then he saw a huge salmon, an old tule who had fought the battle upstream to spread his milky sperm and now, spent, drifted slowly with the current, his flesh turning red and soft with decay, back toward the sea. He saw it was his own soul. He turned to Vasutäti, who nodded solemnly and handed him a spear. He thrust the spear into the old salmon and Ilmari died, as we all must.

Then he awoke, as we all do.

1

The next day in Portland, November 12, 1919, Aino read the headline: MASSACRE IN CENTRALIA. WOBBLY HUNG. MORE ARRESTED. Her heart pounding, she read that Jack Kerwin was arrested and charged with murder along with many others. The young soldier, Wesley Everest, was lynched. The legionnaires had broken into the jail and hanged him from the Chehalis River Bridge. The paper said he shot a deputy named Hubbard while trying to escape across the Skookumchuck River.

The last paragraph said the police were looking for a female accomplice in the murders of the five legionnaires. She had been seen with Everest several times, the last time fleeing with him from the Roderick Hotel. She felt her stomach lurching with fear.

She couldn't stay in Portland and she was afraid to go home. All she could think of was to flee to Chicago where the IWW was large and active, where she could find comrades to hide her. She ran to her rooming house to gather her things, not knowing if she would ever see Eleanor again.

Just before Christmas, Kyllikki and Matti received a letter postmarked Detroit with no return address. One day later, Alma and Ilmari received an almost identical letter. Alma read it first and then passed it over to Ilmari who read it, said nothing, and went to do the milking.

After the children, including Eleanor, were put to bed, Alma sat down with her knitting. She was working on a sweater for Eleanor. Ilmari picked up his carving; he was working on a cedar salad bowl.

They usually had these fifteen or twenty minutes together before going to bed themselves. No use wasting the kerosene and time doing nothing practical.

"Why won't she tell us where she's living? I don't think it's Detroit," Alma said, at the same time keeping count of her knit-and-purl stitches. She watched Ilmari as he carefully made a wood shaving curl with a new gouging tool, hollowing out the bowl from a single block of fine-grained cedar. She knew he was thinking, not ignoring her.

"She got into trouble with the police in Finland, you know," Ilmari finally said.

"Yoh."

"She's frightened."

"Yoh."

They both continued working.

"Do you think she's in Detroit?" Alma asked.

"No. She's in Chicago."

"Why do you think that?"

"I don't *think* that," he said.

Well, Alma thought, that makes it clear. She's in Chicago.

After another long silence Ilmari asked, "Do you mind having Eleanor?"

"No. I love her."

"We might have her a long time."

"Yoh."

Spring came but was very different from Alma's and Ilmari's memories of it's arrival in Finland. There, the water would start to trickle in the afternoons and freeze again at night on the deeply frozen rivers. Around Deep River, snowfall was unusual by March. Only on rare occasions would ice form across the river. Spring was about more daylight and getting things done.

Nature's colors came earlier in Deep River than in Finland and lasted longer. By February, the dark-green branches of the conifers would start to show tiny chartreuse feathers of new growth, bright yellow-green jewels like earrings on the tips of the branches. Blue-violet lupine and starbursts of purple camas came into view. The low, muddy ground near rivers and streams pushed up the dark leaves and yellow cornucopia flowers of skunk cabbage. Then, most secret and special, the first glorious trillium raising its delicate but brilliant white petals from dark humus, braving the still-cold rain of early March, announced that winter was not yet vanquished but would be vanquished once again. In April, the promise fulfilled, new vines and bushes seemed to grow as you watched them. In May, the pale yellow-orange and watery salmonberries ripened. In June, translucent red huckleberries. In July, deep-red thimbleberries, used by little girls to color their lips, and with wonderful tiny seeds to chew into mash. Finally, in August, the blue Cascade bilberries, wild strawberries, and three varieties of black-berries: wild mountain, evergreen, and Himalaya.

On an early Sunday morning in May, Ilmari decided to visit Vasutäti. Mielikki, now eleven, grabbed an unfinished basket, so she could get Vasutäti to solve a particularly difficult problem with a pattern. She'd long ago moved on from her first fumbling attempts with a child's hands. Even Vasutäti had told Ilmari that the girl had a gift for weaving. Ilmari knew that Vasutäti was teaching Mielikki everything she knew about weaving. Helmi, nine, and Jorma, seven, came as well, leaving Alma with Eleanor.

The children scampered barefoot on the moist needle fall of the previous winter, the girls hunting for trilliums—mostly past, but occasionally a late one could be found—and Jorma hunting for food. Sheep sorrel, its soft trifold leaves tasting like little bursts of lemon candy, or young fiddlehead ferns, with their musty asparagus-like flavor—or the occasional squeal of delight at finding a good licorice root—kept them all chatting and happy. They all loved visiting Vasutäti, and Ilmari loved taking them.

About halfway to Vasutäti's campsite clouds darkened the sun. The children hardly noticed. In these forests, the passing of the sun into and out of clouds barely registered on the forest floor. But Ilmari felt this one more than he saw it, and it chilled him.

He picked up his pace and Jorma started to lag. Ilmari swung him up onto his shoulders.

Mielikki hurried up beside Ilmari. "Why are we going faster, Isä?" she asked.

Ilmari stopped. He looked down at her and smiled. "Good question," he said. He looked off into the darkness of the deep forest. "No good reason to hurry. No reason at all."

Mielikki's hands suddenly went to her mouth and her eyes grew wide. Ilmari nodded slowly at her and put a finger to his lips. Then he knelt in front of her and hugged her. When he stood up again, she was struggling against crying. He laughed and tousled her hair. "Vasutäti would say now is not the time for sisu."

Ilmari crawled into the little bark-covered shelter and in the dim light could see Vasutäti lying on her beloved bearskin blanket in her deerskin ceremonial dress with the Hudson's Bay beads she'd sewn on it herself when she was young. Her hair was combed and flowed unbraided over her chest, adorned with a single owl feather over her right ear. Her twinkling eyes and merry laugh flooded his memory. She was dressed for a wedding, not a funeral.

2

Business was good for the Bachelor Boys in May 1922. A single day working on whistlers earned the equivalent of five days' pay for logging. They'd work only when the money ran out. Right now, they were flush and girls at the dances were wearing skirts that showed their knees when they spun.

All five of them had washed, shaved, and walked to Tapiola. There was a buzz when they walked into a dance. The girls would look at them quickly, look away, start whispering to each other, fuss with their hair, and smooth their skirts or dresses. The Bachelor Boys knew people said they were bootlegging. Wanting to take advantage of the rumors and also protect their source of income, they kept the elk bugler business secret. They, however, were unaware of a downside to this strategy. Not only did the local girls think they were bootleggers, but bootleggers from Nordland thought so too.

When Aksel walked into the dance hall above Higgins's, his eyes—always scanning—stopped on five well-dressed men, not loggers. His eyes went back to the girls. Tapiola now had a high school with twenty girls in it and several of the older ones were here, too young for him and the other Bachelor Boys but still nice to look at.

At the next break, Aksel and Jens were smoking by the stairwell when Kullervo came over to them with three giggling high school girls in tow. Yrjö and Heppu were talking with their current partners on the dance floor. Aksel and Jens rolled their eyes at each other before turning and smiling politely.

"They wanted to meet you," Kullervo said in English. He'd been drinking, and he introduced the girls with a broad possessive hand motion that made Aksel smile. "Sylvi, Martha, Sandra, these are Aksel and Jens, two of my business partners." The three girls giggled. Aksel made a slow bow and Jens followed suit. Sylvi, obviously the leader of the pack, smiled and went into a perfect curtsy, coming up with her eyes sparkling, looking straight at Aksel.

"We've always wanted to meet you," she said.

Aksel looked at her more closely. "I think we've met before," he said, a little uncertainly.

"You've seen me before, but we've never met."

Aksel looked at her, exaggerating puzzlement.

"I'm Sylvi Wirkkala. Alma Wiitala is my mother's sister."

Aksel grinned. "I saw you talking to her at Higgins's."

"And we didn't meet."

Aksel chuckled. "So, now we meet."

Sylvi looked at her friends for help, but none was forthcoming. Amused, knowing why the girls wanted to meet them, Aksel waited. Finally, Martha burst out, "Are you really bootleggers?"

"Martha," Sylvi said, embarrassed by her bluntness.

Martha looked back at her and then repeated to Aksel, "Well, are you?"

"If I said no, you'd think I was lying," Aksel answered. "If I said yes, I could end up in jail."

The girls looked at each other, not knowing quite how they should take the comment.

Aksel took in the flirting with a smile. Then he shook his head. "How old are you?" he asked.

"Almost seventeen," Sylvi answered.

Aksel nodded slowly, still smiling. "I'm thirty."

Sylvi's face showed exaggerated disappointment. "Oh," she said. "We thought you were more mature."

Aksel and Jens both laughed out loud.

The band started playing and Kullervo, who'd all this time held Sandra's hand, took her out to the floor. This left the four of them looking awkwardly at each other.

"Oh, OK," Aksel said. He looked at Jens, who looked at the ceiling. He held his hand out to Sylvi. She took it, raised it above her head, and twirled beneath it. Jens and Martha followed them onto the floor.

All three girls were good dancers, but Sylvi was very good, a delight to lead, responsive to the slightest signals. She and Aksel danced another dance and then Aksel, concerned that she might be misinterpreting signals he was trying not to send, escorted her off the floor. She was clearly disappointed. Sensing this, Aksel said, "You're a wonderful dancer. You're sixteen."

"I know," she said, then looked up at the ceiling in mock despair. "It just was never meant to be."

Aksel started to leave her. "It'll only be ten years," she said quickly to his back.

He turned back to her, puzzled.

"You know the old-country formula," Sylvi said. "If the girl's half the man's age plus seven, it's ideal to marry and have children."

Aksel took half his age in ten years, added seven, and got twenty-seven, which was seventeen plus ten. The girl was quick.

"It's twelve years for a sixteen-year-old," he said.

"I can wait."

"You'd only have to wait three years for Kullervo. He'll turn twenty-two next week."

"I'd have to be as crazy as people say he is."

Aksel laughed.

Sylvi looked pointedly toward the dance floor where Kullervo and Sandra were slow dancing. "She'll only have to wait two years. She's already seventeen, but I don't think she wants to wait."

Although the words came out of Aksel's own mouth, they took him completely by surprise. "Some people wait a lifetime."

The sudden overwhelming sadness made him look away from her to hide the tears rising in his eyes.

Kullervo came over with Sandra hanging on his arm, followed by Jens, who was politely but firmly escorting Martha off the floor. Aksel and Jens thanked them for the dances and were leaving when Martha blurted out. "Why do you live in the woods?"

"Who told you we live in the woods?" Aksel asked.

"Everyone knows it," she said, looking to Sylvi for support. "We even know you're up on the North Fork."

"Hmm. Famous, are we?" Aksel said. He turned to Jens. "Why do we live in the woods?"

Jens smiled, shook his head, and shrugged his shoulders. Aksel turned back to the girls. "You see. We don't know."

"Is it because you're wolves and can't live with domesticated dogs?" Martha asked.

There was a silence. Jens said, "Never thought of it like that."

Then Sylvi said in her even, quiet voice, "It's also like an animal that goes off to lick its wounds, isn't it?"

Jens found someone else to dance with and Aksel went outside to smoke. Leaning against the wall, he became aware that the five strangers had followed him out. They surrounded him. Adrenaline started flowing, but he knew action would only lead to pain. "Can I help you boys?" he asked.

"Yeah, squarehead. You can." The man who spoke was heavyset and had a diamond stickpin holding his tie to his shirt. "You and your pals can get out of our turf."

"What?" Then it dawned on Aksel. "You think we're bootleggers?" He laughed.

"Very funny, wise guy." The man turned to his friends, a slight but vicious smile on his face. He whirled his whole body around, driving a fist into Aksel's stomach. Aksel doubled over in pain, only to be hit with an uppercut to his chin. He went down. The man kicked him in the head and Aksel saw stars. He tried to get to his feet but got only as far as his knees when he was kicked in the kidneys from both sides by two other men. He blacked out from the pain. He came to consciousness with the leader squatting down, holding him up by his shirt. "You have a week." He drove his fist into Aksel's face. "To get out"—he hit him again—"of our turf." He hit him twice more and let go. Standing up he said, "You're still here next week, you and your pals are dead." He stomped on Aksel's face and then kicked him in the groin. As the four men walked away, the one man who hadn't gotten in any licks kicked Aksel in the ribs. Aksel blacked out again.

Two other smokers found Aksel and one went to get the Bachelor Boys. A small crowd gathered behind the building, some muttering: "Rival bootleggers. Serves him right."

They managed to get Aksel back to their camp.

"If the girls know where we live, those boys know, too," Heppu said. "We should move camp."

"Let's kill the bastards," Kullervo said.

"We'll have the sheriff on us," Jens said. "You have to assume he's on the take. They've been selling alcohol for a long time."

They were all silent, agreeing.

Aksel painfully shifted his body, the effort causing him to breathe harder, which caused him more pain. "Everyone thinks we're bootlegging. Might as well be hanged for a sheep as for a lamb," he said. He winced. "Why not tell *them* to get out of *our* turf?"

"You'd have to be willing to kill them," Jens said. "Otherwise it's an idle threat."

Aksel didn't answer Jens. The thug had kicked him in the groin when he was defenseless.

He coldly outlined an attack plan. "The situation is that if we stay, we'll be attacked, probably killed. They have the protection of the law and the law will assume we're rival bootleggers so won't care anyway." He looked around him, pointedly. "Unless we act first, we'll be on constant alert and vulnerable to surprise attack. Our current position is indefensible. We're surrounded by higher ground and the sound of the river will mask their approach."

He waited for comment. None came.

"Our mission is to kill those bastards or drive them away. If we succeed, we remain vulnerable to a repeat of this same situation, whether from them or other bootleggers." He paused to let that sink in.

"Unless we run, we are in the bootlegging business whether we like it or not." He felt himself starting to tremble. "I am not going to run and I'm going to kill the son of a bitch that kicked me."

They determined what was needed for support and how the five of them would communicate before and during the coming fight. Aksel was selected to do reconnaissance by talking with Louhi. With her saloon and whorehouse intelligence network, she would know who they were up against and whether these bootleggers were connected to a larger mob or operating independently.

He set out immediately, walking with great pain. They had only a week's time—if the bootleggers kept their word.

Aksel reached Nordland late the next day having slept just one hour. He was ushered into Louhi's office with no delay.

"You look like hell," Louhi said, speaking English. She studied him while a woman poured coffee for them. When the woman left, she said, "I heard you're bootlegging."

He outlined the situation for Louhi, including the elk whistler business, which made her laugh out loud. When he'd finished, she was quiet. "What do you want?" she asked him.

"Intelligence. Who are they? Are they connected? What do you know that we don't even know enough to ask about?"

"I buy my booze through the Seattle mob. They buy it from dealers in Vancouver, where it's legal. It's shipped down from Canada any which way. Sometimes it comes to a beach in Puget Sound and gets here by truck. Mostly it comes direct on a boat just outside the twelve-mile limit where it's transferred to a barge, totally legal. The barge is covered with gravel, sawdust, or whatever, to cover the hatches. The barge comes here or into Willapa Bay, depending on orders. Whatever is on top is delivered. There's a false bill of sale for a full load. That covers the local cops who can claim to be bamboozled." Aksel shook his head, smiling.

"Those toughs that beat the hell out of you are customers of Seattle, just like me," Louhi continued. "They live in Willapa. If you hit them, it's unlikely you'll be retaliated against by the Seattle boys. However"—she paused and looked at him—"it is likely you'll go to jail unless you step in and keep the payments up."

Aksel took it in. "If we stay," he said, "we're in the bootlegging business. We're all veterans. We've got good," Aksel paused, "operational skills." Louhi chuckled at this. "But we don't know anything about the business."

Louhi walked over to the window and looked out silently for a long time. She turned to Aksel. "You'll need a truck, weapons, storage facilities, and protection from the law. I can provide all of that. You'll pay me back double in four months for the loan to buy the equipment. I'll get five percent of everything you sell for my contacts and protection. You'll buy directly from me and I'll buy from Seattle." She smiled at him. "Otherwise, how do I know how much five percent is."

"Does that mean we work for you?"

"Can I fire you?"

Aksel laughed. "No."

"Can I mess you up?"

Aksel looked at her sardonically. "Oh, yes."

"Keep that in mind."

Aksel returned to Tapiola in a 1920 Chevrolet 490 half-ton truck, carrying five war-surplus Springfield rifles, one fitted with a sniper scope for Yrjö, five war-surplus Colt .45-caliber automatic pistols, a Thompson .45-caliber submachine gun with four hundred-round drum magazines, plenty of ammunition, and several cases of dynamite, along with electric blasting caps and thirty-two 1.5-volt D batteries. He also came back with half a ton of scotch and Canadian rye.

It was relatively easy to get word to the Willapa gangsters that they would leave but wanted to discuss terms.

They met behind a speakeasy in Willapa. The man who'd beaten Aksel so savagely was all buddy-buddy. "No hard feelings, Swede, huh? Strictly business." He offered his hand.

Aksel didn't take it.

"We'll agree to leave," Aksel said. "But you have to buy our inventory at cost."

"Or?"

"Or we fight you."

The man almost sneered. "You and what army?"

"There are four of us and five of you. Someone is guaranteed to get hurt or killed."

"We hear there are five of you."

"Yrjö got scared and ran."

This was met by derisive chuckles.

The man scuffed his shoes, pretending he was trying to decide. "How much have you got?"

"Forty-one cases of bourbon, twelve cases of gin."

"Huh," the man snuffed. "American stuff. No wonder we never run into you."

Aksel waited. "Well?" he finally asked.

"No hard feelings," the man said. "We don't want a fight." He paused. "We'll give you six hundred dollars."

Aksel feigned outrage. "That's not even a dollar a bottle."

"My next offer will be fifty cents," the man replied. "I'm only giving you that because I'm a nice guy."

"And don't want a fight," Jens said.

The man looked at him. "OK, a thousand bucks, that's two fifty for each of you." He looked at his friends again. "That'll get you to wherever you go." He turned, his face suddenly hard. "Final offer, Swede."

Aksel nodded for Jens to huddle with him away from the group. "These dumb fucks," he whispered. After a suitable time, he returned. "OK. We agree." He still wouldn't shake hands.

The transfer of inventory would take place at dawn, Sunday, May 21, 1922, in an open field on the dirt road that now went down the east side of Willapa Bay, linking Willapa with Tapiola.

The five Bachelor Boys got there just after dark and carefully began placing the dynamite in strategic spots, hiding the detonation wire, linking it to the batteries, and rigging triggers that were concealed just beneath the ground and could be set off by foot. Four of them would detonate two charges of dynamite each. Yrjö hid where he could survey the entire field.

The Bachelor Boys waited by their truck in the middle of the field as the bootleggers from Willapa drove up the unpaved road. The Boys had stacked fifty-three cases of the whiskey where they could be seen but so that the labels didn't show. The truck from Willapa slowly drove onto the field and came to a stop in front of the Bachelor Boys—right where they wanted it. With a swagger, two men got out of the cab and three more got out of the back of the truck. They had their pistols out. "Sorry, Swede," the leader said. "I think we'll just take the inventory off your hands. Hate to slow down your departure."

The man's head exploded blood before anyone heard the crack of Yrjö's rifle. Then, the Bachelor Boys detonated the dynamite. The bootleggers threw themselves to the ground in terror. The Bachelor Boys were all accustomed to artillery fire and knew that they might suffer mild concussion but that there would be no shrapnel. The dynamite had been set just far enough away from the trucks to allow them to remain standing. Pistols out, they quickly disarmed the stunned bootleggers.

"We have four more men in the woods," Aksel said, shouting so they and he could hear above the roaring in their ears. "There are eight of us. We know where you live. You will be out of Chinook County by tomorrow or we will hunt you down and kill you, just like we did this dumb son of a bitch." He toed the man's bloody head so they could see the exit hole.

Kullervo had gone back to the Chevy 490 and returned with two shovels. "Bury the bastard," he told the bootleggers.

On their first day of business, the Bachelor Boys increased their assets by five revolvers and a 1921 Ford Model T delivery truck.

Aksel and Jens drove the two trucks and the whiskey inventory to Higgins's large two-story house, which was just northwest of Tapiola, within walking distance of his store. The old Irishman's eyes sparkled when he saw what they were asking him to store. "It's good I'll be doing for the community," Higgins said. "But I'll not be doing it for free." He looked at the Bachelor Boys.

Aksel and Jens looked at each other and shrugged. "What's the going price?"

"Well then. At the end of each month I'll count the bottles. You'll pay me ten cents a bottle on the average of that and the previous month's count."

After some debate, they approached Ullakko, asking if he had room in his barn for one of the trucks. He did, for fifteen dollars a month.

First Louhi's cut, then Higgins's, then Ullakko's. The Bachelor Boys were learning about the cost of doing business.

They decided to drive the Chevy to the closest point to the North Fork camp. As they passed the big snag, Aksel noticed that salal bushes had grown around it with the passing of time and almost all the bark was now sloughed off. They hid the Chevy and started walking. When they got about a quarter of a mile from the campsite, Heppu swore he smelled apple pie. A hundred yards from camp, they all smelled it.

They chambered rounds. With hand signals, Aksel placed Kullervo on point, since he was the youngest and had the fastest reaction times. He motioned Heppu to walk in the water on their left flank and put Yrjö on their right flank, paralleling the trail. Since Yrjö had the toughest going, they slowed their pace to match his.

Kullervo went to the ground and crawled forward just before the camp clearing. He stood and turned to them, smiling. "You won't believe this," he said.

The Bachelor Boys moved into the open. Standing by their cooking fire were the three high school girls in their Sunday dresses. A Dutch oven containing an apple cobbler was nestled in the glowing coals.

The girls could easily see the evidence of the recent fight. Aksel told them the whole history, from the beginning of the elk bugler business to the misunderstanding with the Willapa bootleggers. He swore them to secrecy, threatening to ruin their reputations by telling everyone they had visited the Boys unchaperoned.

Kullervo disappeared into the hut he shared with Yrjö and returned with three beautiful ivory elk whistlers attached to thin leather strips. They nodded their heads, thinking he was showing them proof. He surprised them by placing one over each girl's head.

"You have to swear on the elk whistler over your heart that you'll tell no one. Our lives depend on it."

The girls put their hands on the whistlers and on their hearts and swore.

"You can't come here again," Aksel said. Again, the three girls nodded silently. Heppu and Aksel took the girls home, dropping them off away from their houses.

On the next Sunday, Sylvi showed up by herself.

"We told you never come here again," Aksel said.

"You is a difficult word," she replied, carefully unpacking eggs from a cloth satchel. "It can mean, you, several persons; or you, one person." She picked up the coffeepot and looked him right in the eye. "We interpreted it as *you* several." She continued, emphasizing the word "you," "Someone needs to look after you, whether you like it or not." She smiled. "And we know you like it, no matter what you say."

She got no objections.

"If any of you so much as whisper a word about what the three of us are up to, so help us, we'll ruin *your* reputations."

From that day, on most Sundays, one of the girls would come with pulla or korpu or fruit in season, and the Bachelor Boys attended coffee at camp as regularly as the rest of the valley attended church.

3

A s Ilmari somehow knew, Aino was in Chicago. She'd found a job in a bakery in an Irish neighborhood under the name Ina Virtanen. The baker was kind as were most of the neighbors. All, however, were strongly Catholic, anticommunist, and anti-Wobbly. She sold bread, smiled a lot, and kept her IWW life quiet.

When she'd arrived in December, the IWW was staggering from the severe blows of the Palmer Raids. The nation, fearing a spreading Bolshevik revolution, was already primed for action against the IWW when on June 6, 1919, Galleanist anarchists exploded eight bombs, one of them in the home of the attorney general of the United States, Alexander Mitchell Palmer. Palmer seized the moment by blaming the bombing on the IWW. He then appointed a skillful, enthusiastic, and some would say fanatical man to head up FBI intelligence to help him destroy the union. The man's name was J. Edgar Hoover.

By May, under Hoover's onslaught, over three thousand Wobblies had been arrested and held without warrants, including over two hundred IWW leaders and organizers in Chicago alone.

Working all her evenings and Sundays, Aino joined the effort to free the two hundred imprisoned Chicago Wobblies. She soon found use for her recruiting skills, focusing on unskilled laborers, mostly immigrants who lived in grinding poverty and were ignored by the AF of L. Recognizing her ability, the Chicago leadership increased her funds to focus on recruiting women when Tennessee ratified the Nineteenth Amendment, women's right to vote, on August 18, 1920.

Over the next two years, never knowing if the FBI was about to knock on her door, she helped recruit thousands of women working primarily in the clothing industry. All the while, she ached for Eleanor's little warm body next to hers. Often she'd wondered if Jouka ever saw Eleanor. She knew she'd hurt Jouka badly but consoled herself by thinking she'd used him for a good cause. Deep down, however, she knew that she was engaging in sophistry. She often thought about the last time she'd seen Aksel walking away from her at the Castle Rock train station and wondered what he was doing.

Aino had been working at the bakery since four thirty on the morning of December 9, 1922, when her attention was drawn to a newsboy shouting something about Astoria. She walked to the front door. The newsboy walked by bawling in his high-pitched child's voice, "Astoria, Oregon, is a fire ruin! Coast city wiped out! Read about it here. Thousands homeless!"

The paper said nothing about deaths. She was anxious all night, but the next day it seemed only one person had died. But what about Matti and Kyllikki's house and Kyllikki's parents' house? She had no way of knowing.

Within days, Astoria was no longer in the news.

By the spring of 1923, the Cleveland Shirt and Dress Company had expanded from Cleveland to Chicago, St. Louis, and Denver on the backs of the women who did the sewing and cutting and the men who did the pressing. By the time a woman reached forty, her hands were arthritic and her sight was damaged. They worked ten-hour days six days a week and made roughly fifteen cents an hour—roughly because they were paid by the finished garment, not by the hour. When Aino walked to work she saw barefoot children going through garbage for food. Their mothers weren't home. They were working, but their work couldn't adequately feed, clothe, and shelter the children. Those who had working husbands could scrape by. Those who did not were desperate.

Fueled by the plight of these desperate people, Aino committed herself to organizing the Cleveland Shirt and Dress Company workers into an IWW local. Many of the company workers were immigrants who didn't want to be perceived as disloyal to the United States. Many couldn't speak English. All the workers feared retaliation. Their fear was not unfounded. The day after the local was formed, one of the men who handled the massive presses was severely beaten after work for having joined the union. The next day, another presser who'd joined was beaten. On the third day, a third. Each day more men joined—and more men went to work, each not knowing if this was the day he'd be beaten nearly to death. Yet on each day when more joined, they all went to work, and one of them took the beating. Aino visited the men's homes, using her midwife skills to treat open wounds, concussions, and severely bruised bodies. She managed to engage the help of a sympathetic doctor to set a broken arm. She helped the men's wives care for their husbands and children and brought food to compensate for the days each man lost in work and wages. The retaliation against the women who joined the union was less physical. Instead, large numbers of the garments made by the women who joined were rejected by management for trumped-up quality issues, effectively cutting their pay in half or worse.

The workers stayed with the union, and with every man beaten and woman sent home with half pay anger grew. Aino used that anger to overcome their reluctance to retaliate with the only weapon they had: the strike. Still, they would not strike, hoping that management would relent.

Then, in April 1923, one man had four of his front teeth broken off at the roots by a man wielding brass knuckles. That night, after an impassioned speech by Aino, the workers voted to strike, asking for an eight-hour day at twenty-five cents an hour, nearly double what they'd been receiving.

Management retaliated by switching work to other factories.

Aino quit her job and, relying on fellow Wobblies to give her food and shelter, took the train to St. Louis, the site of one of the company factories to which management had diverted work. She had the St. Louis workers organized within a week. When she returned to Chicago, she spent hours at the Western Union office, coordinating the Denver

Wobblies to get the Denver workers to strike the company's remaining factory. She and her fellow Wobblies enlisted the help of teamsters and railroad workers in every city where Cleveland Shirt and Dress operated. Cleveland Shirt and Dress shipments languished in warehouses and on loading docks; boxcars with Cleveland Shirt and Dress shipments got lost or hooked onto trains going in the wrong direction.

Faced with being outmaneuvered by the IWW, and with pressure from sympathetic AF of L workers, Cleveland Shirt and Dress resorted to other more sophisticated forms of counterpressure: politics and public relations.

By late May the strike had gone on for several weeks. Aino spent a lot of her time making sure that the picket lines were manned. Picketers brandished signs calling for an end to slavery. Aino usually joined the picketers before and after work, carrying a One Big Union sign. She and all the other Wobblies took pains with their apparel. Even though temperatures were in the low eighties, she wore a tight-fitting jacket over her dress.

Tensions were mounting. May was when Cleveland Shirt and Dress had orders to fill for the summer line—and the buyers would be putting pressure on the company to deliver as promised. Every day was a day of lost revenue at a peak buying time and a day where the competition would steal market share. Management, who had previously weathered two strikes without meeting workers' demands, began a public relations campaign. A firm was hired to write and place newspaper articles with appropriate stories. It seeded bystanders with people paid to reinforce management's message, physically if need be.

Aino was unsurprised when the hired public relations firm planted stories and slanted the news. But she hadn't expected it to undertake direct action of its own. One morning, she faced an unusually sullen and hostile crowd. The morning had started with the usual taunts: "Traitors, you all ought to be in jail" or "Commie bastards, if you don't like it here, move to Russia." This was standard anti-Wobbly fare, the old red menace fear combined with lingering anger over the perceived and much-advertised traitorous sabotaging of the war effort.

This crowd was different. Aino could see the police looking nervously at their supervisors. Something was up. Her anxiety started to grow into fear. She walked from picketer to picketer, steadying them, warning them.

The first hint of what was to come was a rock hitting Aino's sign, hurled by a boy of about ten. Then she saw other boys, about the same age, running out from the crowd, throwing their rocks, then scampering back to where they couldn't be seen. The rocks pelted down on the picketers, who tried to shelter behind their signs.

A boy with thick red hair came out of the crowd, hurled his stone, and started back in, but Aino ran for him and caught him just inside the line of the gathering crowd.

"Let me go! She's kidnapping me! Let me go!" The boy shouted, obviously enjoying himself.

"I won't until you show me the man who's paying you."

The boy struggled. Aino held on. Then a woman's voice said, "You leave that child alone!"

The boy, sensing victory, started shouting, "Help! Help! She's trying to kidnap me."

"You let him go," the woman said. She didn't wait for Aino to release the boy. "Police! Police!"

Two policemen from the line that separated the crowd and the strikers started toward Aino. She panicked and ran for the picket line, the two officers in hot pursuit. Several of the male garment pressers from the factory moved into their path, letting Aino inside the line. The police started hitting the men with their billy clubs.

At first, the rest of the policemen didn't know what to do, but someone in the crowd shouted, "They're attacking the police! Get the Bolshevik bastards!"

The crowd surged.

Aino was put in an ugly little cell in the Cook County jail, along with two other women picketers. Once again, her back was a mass of welts and bruises, blood showing at the roots of her hair by her right ear. The only light in the cell came from a single window, high above them, so covered with grime they could not see the sky. Her cell mates were huddled on the floor against the wall, both clearly frightened, one occasionally bursting into tears. They were garment workers, not organizers.

Aino stood away from them, pushing her back against the cold stone wall, struggling to contain her panic, consciously trying to keep herself in the present. Being in jail was no longer new. Still, every time, it raised the ghost of Helsinki.

She sat down next to the woman who'd been crying. "Everything going to be OK. They just scaring you," she whispered.

"They're doing a great job," the woman whispered back.

They always do, Aino thought, cradling the woman's head against her shoulder.

They were left in the cell for hours, having to share one bucket to relieve themselves. Around midnight, they heard keys jangling and the lock turning. Two guards, followed by a supervisor, came into the cell.

"It stinks in here, ladies," the supervisor said. The two guards chuckled. The supervisor stopped in front of each woman, exaggeratedly wrinkling his nose. He turned to the guards. "Take the other two, leave that one." He pointed at Aino. She felt her heart lurch. She struggled not to show it. They had singled her out.

The two guards roughly grabbed her cell mates. The one who'd not been crying protested. "Where are you taking us? What's our crime? You can't hold us without—" She was cut short by a backhand slap from the supervisor. "Are you going to be a troublemaker?" he asked her. She lowered her head and the supervisor grunted approval.

Aino pushed herself up against the wall with one forearm held up against her breasts and the other held down in a fist protecting her vulva. Her hands were shaking. She knew she must act, say something to show she wouldn't be intimidated. By sheer will she lowered her arms and straightened her back. "What crime have we done? What is going to happen to us?"

The two guards looked at the supervisor to see if he would answer. He nodded for them to get on with their business, which they did, taking the two women away. He turned to Aino. "Not us, princess, you. We've found no record of an Ina Virtanen. Those two women are United States citizens. Unless you have proof you are, and even that may not save you, you'll be sent back to Finland under the Espionage Act."

"We not fighting in the war now."

The man laughed. "The war's over, yes, but the Espionage Act is here to stay." He leaned in so their faces were only inches apart, making Aino press back against the wall even harder. "You and your communist traitor friends are not."

He walked to the door, then turned to look at her. She could see his body and head silhouetted by the naked lightbulbs strung down the corridor. Then he shut the door and she was in darkness, all alone, again.

Panic grabbed her. She fought it back, trying to take regular deep breaths. She failed. She rammed her fist into her mouth and bit down, hard. The pain brought her to the present.

She squatted against the dank wall and wrapped her skirt tightly around her ankles to keep out rats. She could hear her own breathing and occasional clangs, clanks, and the voices of guards. Then she heard sharp claws skittering across the stone floor. She rose to her feet, her heart pounding. Maíjaliisa would say now was the time for sisu. Ilmari would say now was the time to pray. Matti would say now was the time to kill rats. It was too dark, however, to see the rats, and she did not want to have to feel for them. What she said to herself was that now was the time to endure.

She pulled her skirt tightly around her legs against the rats, fighting what she knew was a pull into insanity. She was in Chicago, not Helsinki. Americans don't torture people. She realized she was moaning.

She finally exhausted herself and went unconscious. When she awoke, looking up at the window she guessed it was still early morning. She tried to remember everything about Eleanor: how she smelled after breastfeeding, how she looked sleeping, how soft the skin on her face felt, her perfect fingers with their tiny perfect fingernails, the sound of her laughter. She imagined Eleanor with Alma and Ilmari. She imagined walking with her brothers and Eleanor on the banks of Deep River. She remembered that day walking back to the mill when she'd turned her back on Deep River. For the co-op? For the One Big Union? For her own feelings of worth and, yes, power? Fighting for a worthy cause? Oh, the cause was worthy—but was it worth it?

She remembered her argument with Kyllikki. Had she put Eleanor first, she wouldn't be here now, terrified. It occurred to her to pray. Oh, how easy it would be to take it all to the friend we have in Jesus. Bring it to the Lord in prayer. She laughed at herself. Then she started thinking: What's wrong with comfort in hard times—even comfort based on a fairy tale? Why did she have to be the one who put aside her life and the people she loved for the betterment of society? If people like her didn't do it, the world would surely be run by the bullies and tyrants, whether political or economic. When was it time to pass on the torch? She was suddenly tired of being tough-minded. She wished Aksel and the Bachelor Boys would come storming through the door. She smiled at the scene she'd just constructed with herself, Aino, the damsel in distress. Then she wondered: What's wrong with that? It's what she was.

She didn't exactly pray, but she did make a promise—to who or what she did not know, but to something more than just herself. She promised that if she ever got out of this alive, she would put Eleanor and her family first. She would be the best mother Eleanor could have, a mother with a capital M—and she would go back to Deep River.

The keys in the door set her heart thumping again. The single pane high above her showed a dirty gray-brown light. She braced herself.

The man who stepped inside carried a briefcase and wore a neat business suit. She heard the guard say, "Twenty minutes."

She backed up against the wall. There was no escape.

"Well, Ina," the man said. "I'm Albert Angell." He smiled. "I'm not, however, an angel. I'm a lawyer."

She said nothing. This might be a ruse.

After several minutes of calm talk, he eventually gained her trust. He was from a prominent Chicago firm but did pro bono work for the IWW, lately trying to get its leadership out of prison.

Aino wanted to hug the man but knew it was undignified.

She told him everything: her real name, her involvement with radical socialism in Finland, her family, her marriage to Jouka, her divorce. He questioned her in some detail about what happened in Centralia when she told him she'd been there during the massacre. Then he switched to another line of questions.

"You say you're divorced."

She nodded. "My husband is not living with me," She hung her head, unable to look at him.

"What jurisdiction?"

She looked at him, puzzled.

"What court? Where did you file the papers?"

"I didn't file them."

"So, you're not divorced?"

"Jouka doesn't live with me anymore."

"That's called a separation." He paused and took a small breath. "Is Jouka a U.S. citizen?"

"Yes. He was born in Washington State."

Angell smiled as if he'd just won a poker hand. "Fact is," he said, "as far as the law is concerned, you're still married." He paused for effect. "To a U.S. citizen." She looked at him questioningly. "They were thinking of deporting you. I think now they'll have a hard time. You're a U.S. citizen, too. All but the paperwork."

"I ran from the law in Centralia. My name is in newspapers as an accomplice."

"Accomplice?" He looked at her, thinking. "As far as the state of Washington is concerned, they've imprisoned everyone who's guilty." His jaw tightened. "Unjustly. With shockingly unfair sentences." He brought himself back to the cell. "I'll check to be sure, but my guess is that no one's looking for you."

She wrote to Matti, Kyllikki, Alma, and Ilmari to tell them she was coming home as soon as she earned the fare—and she was coming home to stay. She hesitated but plunged in, telling them about the strike and being thrown into jail. That night she slept, troubled by dreams of frantically searching for Eleanor. She woke several times, wondering if Eleanor remembered her. She'd left her a toddler. She'd be five by the time she returned. Could she ever make it right?

4

.

uring Aino's lost years in Chicago, the Bachelor Boys had moved from subsisting on elk whistlers to thriving in the liquor business. Jens, Yrjö, and Heppu sent a lot of money to their families. They were all content with using one of the trucks for personal affairs, but they rarely needed transportation for personal affairs because the Bachelor Boys as a group had all chipped in on a deep-burgundy, four-door 1923 Oldsmobile Sports Touring car with black trim, solid burgundy wheels, and black leather seats. Being behind its steering wheel was sheer exhilarating joy and being in the back seat with no control was sometimes sheer exhilarating terror. There was no road in Pacific and Nordland Counties that tested its maximum speed. Police departments didn't have the budgets to buy vehicles that could compete.

Because Aksel was the leader, he drove the Oldsmobile most often, using it on a regular basis to drive to Nordland to make deposits in the Nordland Bank. Just another year or two, he figured, and he'd have the finest gill net boat on the Columbia, made to his specifications with a four-cylinder gasoline engine. Matti was investing in the stock market and that looked like a smart thing to do, but Aksel wasn't interested in getting rich. Even though the stock market seemed to do nothing but go up, he didn't want to risk the boat. He wanted money in the bank.

He, however, had a problem: income tax, which could lead to other charges, confiscation, and even jail time. He couldn't show large deposits in his name.

Louhi used Al Drummond to launder her earnings for the same reason, so Aksel went to Drummond. Aksel knew Drummond was slippery, but anyone who laundered money was slippery by definition. In addition, Drummond was the only game in town. He and the sheriff kept out all the competition. Aksel figured that along with his connection with Louhi, better the devil he knew.

Al was only too happy to set up a savings account under a false name for him, for a mere 2 percent per year on the balance, paid directly to the bank every three months. The account would yield no interest. Another cost of doing business—illegally.

The account grew and one night at their camp Aksel asked the Bachelor Boys to sit with him by the cook fire. When Aksel opened a bottle of scotch, they knew the meeting was serious. They never drank inventory.

In the twilight that still lingered even though it was after ten, they passed the bottle around like a peace pipe, saying nothing until everyone had taken a sip. When it returned to Aksel he placed it carefully in front of him and took a deep breath.

"I've decided to quit," he said. "I've got more than enough for my boat."

Everyone took it in.

Jens motioned toward the scotch. He took a swig and said, "Maybe you should wait a bit."

He passed the bottle to Heppu, who said, "That'll only leave four of us. Holding the turf with four is going to be harder." He passed the bottle to Yrjö.

Yrjö took a drink, said nothing, and passed it back to Aksel.

"You can have the Oldsmobile," Aksel said. His meaning was clear. He passed the bottle to Jens and it went around the circle until it was empty.

Aksel left in the Oldsmobile the next morning, getting to Nordland late in the day. The bank was still open.

He walked in, put his savings book in front of the teller, and said he wanted to withdraw all his money. The teller looked at the sum in the book, blinked, regained his composure, and said, "Certainly, sir. Can I just see some identification?"

Aksel blinked. When he regained his composure, he asked, "Isn't the savings book enough?"

"No sir, I'm sorry. It could be stolen." He hastily added, "I'm sure it isn't, but we need to protect our customers. You understand."

Aksel took three slow breaths. Then he asked, "Is Mr. Drummond in?"

"I'll see, sir."

The teller left. When he came back, he said, "Mr. Drummond asks who you are."

Aksel stormed into Drummond's office without knocking. Drummond looked up, surprised, then immediately became the genial banker. "Aksel Långström," he said. He rose and extended his hand. "What a pleasure. I hear you boys are doing pretty well for yourselves," he added, pointing a conspiratorial finger at him and grinning. "Coffee?" He pantomimed someone looking conspiratorial. "Drink?"

"No," Aksel said. "My money."

"Your money?" Drummond asked. "Is there something wrong?"

"The teller says he can't give it to me without identification papers."

"Well, he's right." Drummond looked at him innocently.

"You know I put it there under a false name."

"That was certainly your business."

"You tell him it's mine."

Drummond sighed and sat back in his swivel chair. "Aksel," he said, as if explaining something to a child. "How can I do that? We have rules in place to protect the depositors. People like yourself. What kind of a bank would I be running if any old anybody could just walk up to a teller and tell him to hand over a large amount of the depositor's money to someone the teller doesn't even know."

"You son of a bitch."

"Careful, Långström. You threaten me, and I'll call for Chief Brewer."

"We pay him."

"No, Louhi pays him. So do I."

"That's my money."

"That's money made illegally." Drummond tsk-tsked, shaking his head. "Of course, since it's under a false name, the law would have a very hard time prosecuting." He paused. "Unless someone like myself and my teller told the court that you asked for the money under the false name, but we both knew you under another name. It wouldn't be hard to find people to testify that you sold them illegal alcohol." He smiled. "After all, Bill Brewer is very keen on keeping our community safe from drunkenness and the ravages of alcoholism."

"You'll pay for this."

"Ah, a threat. Funny, I've been threatened by petty criminals before. So many of them disappear or do jail time." He pushed a button on his desk. "I think this meeting is over."

A secretary came to the door. "Mr. Drummond?"

"Show this gentleman out, please."

"Certainly." She motioned to Aksel. "Sir?" Over her shoulder Aksel could see two hefty uniformed bank guards coming down the hall.

When he returned to the camp, he told the Boys what happened and said, "I'm back in the business." They found him the next morning with his legs in the river, passed out by a nearly empty bottle of scotch.

They hauled him into his hut. Jens called a meeting. Within an hour they were driving the big burgundy Oldsmobile north to Nordland.

One of the unsolved mysteries of the Nordland business community was the disappearance of Al Drummond. There were rumors. He did have enemies. Was known to be involved in shady stuff. Someone claimed to have seen a shanghai gang hauling a well-dressed body, which was very unusual for that trade, aboard the *Olivier* out of San Francisco. It was bound for Yokohama with high-grade mountain hemlock. That rumor was met with wry jokes. If it was Drummond, in his shape, he wouldn't last past the first storm. The shanghaiers probably had to pay the first mate of the *Olivier* to take him.

That was true.

5

Aino took the train from Portland to Astoria on July 2, 1923. She didn't know what to expect. Some passengers said the fire was worse than reported in the papers; some said it wasn't as bad. As the train moved along the ever-widening river toward Astoria, she felt its strong current pulling her home, filling her with hope, while at the same time she grew increasingly anxious, fearing there would be no home left.

When she walked around the west side of the train depot, she was shocked. She could see nothing but burned hulls of buildings and entire streets that had been made of creosoted planks and pilings that were burned through, showing the water and mudflats beneath. Great gaps appeared in the lines of buildings where frantic citizens had used dynamite to stop the fire. She hurried, picking her way through and around piles of burned buildings, moving up the hill toward Duane Street, which was on solid land and not pilings. The fire had been in December. The eight to ten inches of rain that fell every month had battered the charred remains of Astoria into low, stinking piles of ash.

Everywhere she saw groups of men rebuilding. Instead of a city defeated and in mourning, there was a bustle. There was self-respect. There was sisu.

The country was booming, and Astoria was determined to catch up. Many of the canneries and sawmills had burned out, but the guts of these businesses, the metal machinery and the workers, had been put back to work immediately. Through gaps in hastily thrown-up walls she saw women canning fish at tables rigged on burned planks. She saw fishing boats tied to burned-out pilings being readied to head out for more fish. She could hear the whining saws of the mills. She saw a charred, burned-out city sucking in logs and fish, converting them to lumber and money, and bootstrapping itself back to wholeness. She felt proud to be one of these indomitable Scandinavians.

When she reached Matti and Kyllikki's house, she found the roof gone and the house empty, smelling of wet, burned mattresses and carpet. Most of the windows had been shattered by the heat.

Matti's equipment would have been spared, so he must be working, but where was the family? She nearly ran to the Saaris' house, only to find nothing but the chimney sticking up. It looked like those photos of the French and Belgian villages destroyed in the war.

Her only remaining hope was that she'd find them safe at Deep River, in that little valley behind the hills on the north side of the great protecting river. No fire could cross it.

She reached Knappton by five, having spent nearly all her money on the ticket for the new ferry, a sixty-foot diesel-driven boat that could hold fifteen cars, most of them belonging to people bound for the Long Beach peninsula for summer vacations. She walked from the ferry landing at Megler to Knappton, then started for Tapiola along a much-improved plank road. A salesman returning from a call on one of the Knappton mills stopped for her in his new black Model T Coupe. There wasn't room inside because of his samples, but she could throw her bag on top of them and ride on the running board, talking to him through the window. He told her all about his four-cylinder twenty-horsepower engine, his business, his trips to Seattle, shouting over the noise, while she clung tightly to the wood frame around the window as the floor rattled and bounced across the thick wood planks. It was all noise, something she thought she had left behind in Chicago, but here it was, Chicago coming to the old trail she had taken to dances, feeling its cool earth and soft fir needles under her bare feet. Progress, she thought.

The car passed what looked like the trail that led to Camp Two, but she couldn't be sure because the alders, salal, young hemlocks, and firs hid everything she could remember. The salesman left her off at Higgins's and she started the mile-long walk to Ilmahenki with her valise on top of her head and hope in her heart.

* * *

She arrived around nine o'clock that evening. The sun had set, but everything she remembered was still visible, illuminated by soft glowing light from beyond the horizon. She emerged from around the bend in the road, now widened and graveled, to see Ilmahenki and Suvantola before her with Deep River just beyond. Electric lights from the Western Washington Lumber Products sawmill blazed in the gathering darkness; the roar of an electric generator and saws echoed around her.

Her heart started to pound with anxiety. Eleanor would surely be asleep long ago. How would she react? Should she wake her up? Would Alma be angry with her? She lifted the valise off her thick bun, took out her hat, and adjusted it on her hair so she would look nice when she reached the house.

To her great relief a lantern was lit in the kitchen and she heard Ilmari's voice and his kantele. As he always put it, a little music for the soul just before sleep. She fought back tears, now uncertain whether to knock like a stranger or walk in like family. She did both, opening the door and knocking at the same time.

"Aino," Alma gasped. She bolted to her feet. "Ilmari, it's Aino!" she shouted. Ilmari came to the kitchen door, kantele in his hand. He stood there, motionless.

Somebody should say something, Aino thought, but she didn't know what to say. She just stood there with tears running down her face.

"Have some coffee." Alma said. She began putting kindling into the firebox.

"We got your letter," Ilmari said. "You're here to stay." It wasn't a question.

Then Alma said, "Eleanor sleeps with Mielikki and Helmi." She smiled. "Jorma's going to be eleven next month and has a room of his own."

Ilmari nodded toward the stairs. Aino set down her valise. Ilmari handed her a candle and she went up the stairs.

The size of the three children stunned her. Mielikki, asleep in the top bunk, looked so much like Rauha, as beautiful and nearly as tall. It took away her breath. Sleeping beneath Mielikki on the bottom bunk was Eleanor, one arm sprawled over her cousin Helmi. She'd last seen Eleanor when she was sixteen months old. Now she was a healthy girl of five, a heartbreakingly beautiful amalgam of Ilmari's iron and Matti's mercury, with Jouka's copper shining through in her hair. And herself? Was she there? Would Eleanor recognize her when she woke up? Of course not.

Her throat aching from the lump in it, she knelt beside Eleanor and put her nose on her back. She could feel the heat. The memory of Eleanor held to her breasts took hold of her. Once again, she could smell the sweet warm odor of breast milk. She stayed on her knees for minutes, nuzzling her nose into Eleanor's hair, ribs, and back, whispering over and over, "I'll never leave you again. I'll never leave you again."

Finally, she rose to see Ilmari standing by the doorway. She didn't know how long he'd been there, silently watching her. She felt wax from the candle on her hand. Reluctantly, she moved past him, and he followed her down the stairs.

Alma had coffee ready—and pound cake. They sat down, silently drinking their coffee, Ilmari still taking it through a cube of sugar from the saucer. After he'd had his cup, he told her that Kyllikki and the kids and Hilda Saari were at Suvantola, their old house by the river, until they could move back to Astoria. The people who were renting Suvantola had found another place.

"Renters," Alma huffed. "We spent a week cleaning up after them."

Ilmari smiled and shrugged his shoulders, communicating *It's money.* "Mr. Saari stayed in Astoria to get the business back on its feet. Matti is logging on the Oregon side."

"How are they?"

"No one was hurt."

"Matti should come over for the Fourth," Alma said. "For the picnic in Tapiola."

They again lapsed into silence. Aino basked in it.

"Are the skirts really that short in Chicago?" Alma asked, nodding toward Aino's skirt.

"Well," Aino said, tugging at the hem, which was at her knees. "They're actually back to the ankles this year. I just can't afford the latest style."

"Stand up; let me see."

Aino stood. Alma fingered the hem, tugging at it gently. "My, oh my," she said. "Are you really going to wear that to the picnic?"

"It's what I have."

"But how do you? I mean, men can see up your legs."

"You just keep your knees together," she said with a little laugh.

Alma frowned, looking doubtful. "Seems awkward," she said.

Ilmari watched his wife and sister with joy.

Alma laid three rag rugs on the living room floor as a pallet, then she and Ilmari disappeared with the lamp into their bedroom, leaving Aino alone in darkness. The second shift at the mill had just ended. The air was still. Aino could hear the river, a calf's low soft bawl. From way off in the distance, on the north side of Deep River, came the sound of a coyote, yearning for the moon.

She awoke to the noise of children in the kitchen, pots rattling on the woodstove. She dressed and walked into the kitchen. There was a sudden hush. Mielikki was dishing mush to the other girls. Jorma was absent, probably out helping Ilmari with the cattle. Eleanor looked up at Aino over a steaming bowl. Aino's throat caught. Eleanor's large eyes were intense hazel, neither Jouka's blue nor her own nearly black brown.

Alma bent over behind Eleanor, her hands on the girl's little shoulders, and spoke into her ear with a happy chirpy voice. "Eleanor, this is your äiti."

Eleanor's lips parted, her head went down, and she stared at her mush.

"Eleanor," Mielikki said, setting another bowl in front of Helmi. "Say hello to your äiti."

The little intensely red lips pushed out in a pout, she muttered, "Päivää."

"Hyvää päivää, for a grown-up," Mielikki corrected her.

"She's not my äiti," Eleanor said sharply. She looked down again at her bowl.

Aino felt as though she'd taken an arrow through her heart.

The children started with their chores. Aino walked to look at Deep River, now in the middle of summer showing rocks and expanses of open beach that were usually underwater most of the year. She stood quietly for a long time, wanting the river to take her sorrow to the sea. She walked upstream to Matti and Kyllikki's little house. Aarni, now nine, was outside splitting wood. He looked at her, a little puzzled, then he ran into the house. Kyllikki emerged, a dish towel in her hands, Aarni beside her, pointing at Aino; a young girl, who must be Suvi, now eleven, looking from behind Kyllikki.

Kyllikki shouted, "Aino!" and started running. Aino was forcing a smile, afraid of all the negative possibilities. Her forced smile was shattered by joy when Kyllikki ran to her, hugging her close, tears gushing from her eyes. Aino stiffened just slightly and Kyllikki quickly stepped back, a little embarrassed. "I am *American*," Kyllikki said, smiling.

Aino laughed and they both hugged again. Then they stepped back to really look at each other as only sisters can.

Kyllikki shouted at Suvi to put on the pulla and coffee and they walked side by side, shoulders touching occasionally, into the kitchen. There, Kyllikki's mother stood next to the stove, little Toivo stacking mill ends from the sawmill at her feet. Kyllikki had been pregnant with Toivo when Aino last saw her. Toivo was now three and a half. He stood, as he'd been taught, and said, "Hyvää päivää." Then he sat back down and resumed stacking the mill ends, clearly not understanding who Aino was.

"He's fascinated by the sawmill," Kyllikki said. "He's gone missing twice. Both times we found him at the mill." She paused and gave a mock frown. "After around an hour of panic." She looked at Toivo warmly. "The louder the noise, that's where he goes."

"Sounds a little like my brother," Aino said.

Kyllikki gave her a mock dark look. "One in the family is enough," she said.

6

Matti arrived at midmorning on the Fourth. Operating once again as 200-Foot Logging, he was running a show south of Svensen on the upper reaches of the Klaskanine River, doing difficult logging for Western Cooperage. Cooperage could not punch a rail line into the stand cost-effectively, so the company put the logging up for a bid, assuming some fool might take it on. If the fool went bust trying, Cooperage would still own the trees and they'd still be there for the next fool. Matti won the bid at a price Cooperage management thought foolishly low. Matti knew where there were hundreds of trucks left mothballed by the Spruce Division, trucks he bought for close to nothing and used instead of punching in a rail line. In the dry summer months, it took only a bulldozer and some rock to build a road that would last long enough to haul the logs out on trucks. Matti was making a killing.

Kyllikki and Alma marshaled their children to help them make the Fourth of July picnic, which would include chicken fried in fat drippings collected in a coffee can over the past month and a new gelatin dessert Higgins brought in called Jell-O.

Aino was grateful for the chance to stop feeling helpless and took over the making of the potato salad. She looked up to see Eleanor looking at her from the doorway. She smiled at her, but Eleanor looked away. Eleanor followed the other children without looking back.

Alma saw the stricken look on Aino's face and said, "Give her time."

Aino knew the advice was sound, but it was hard to follow. She felt the need to make up so much time. Eleanor's childhood was already almost a third gone. She wanted to run outside and hug Eleanor, but it was like stalking a very shy bird—one clumsy move and the bird would fly away.

As Aino took up the potato salad preparations, she had to ask where everything was.

The food was loaded into several large baskets Mielikki had woven into artistic and intricate designs, all learned from Vasutäti. They piled the food into Ilmari's wagon and set off for Tapiola, the girls larking around it in freshly pressed dresses, Jorma and his uncle Matti walking behind. Matti was showing Jorma how a spring worked. Toivo, fresh from a face scrubbing by Kyllikki, ran to catch his brother, Aarni, and his cousin Jorma.

The children all walked like their mothers and fathers, shoulders relaxed; head, neck, and spine aligned; their young muscles lean and toned from constant hard work; their posture proud from constant reminders. The girls were like aspens and alders to their brothers' young firs and oaks.

Aino trailed behind them with Kyllikki, feeling an immense pride in all of them, and a little left out—or maybe it was left behind.

They spread blankets in the large field behind Higgins's store. Higgins had personally scythed and raked the field with three friends to get it ready for the Fourth. The blankets evened out the tufts and soft July stubble, the grass cut young and green before it went to hay. The band from the Deep River Legion Post 112, which combined Knappton, Tapiola, and the logging camps all around, warmed up. The musicians marched and practiced every Sunday afternoon, rain or shine, mostly the former.

A large touring car, its canvas top pulled back, spattered with new mud up to the running boards, came bouncing over the unpaved wagon road from the direction of Skamokawa. Aino felt her breath stop just for an instant when she recognized Aksel at the wheel and the Bachelor Boys on the dark, nearly black leather seats. The car bounced over the field, roared up to them, and stopped. Aksel grinned from beneath a working-man's leather hat that showed just a bit of his blond hair, trimmed short above his ears, the brim mostly hidden by the flat overlapping crown. She saw Jens, Yrjö, Heppu, and Kullervo climb from the car, looking around as if now that they'd arrived the festivities could begin.

Aksel was walking toward them. His brilliant-blue eyes seemed to laugh with the obvious joy of seeing Aino and the family. She felt a sudden lightness, as if he were about to ask her to dance.

He'd filled out and filled out well, she thought, from the too-lean and restless man who'd carried her away from Centralia. He looked like a man who'd gotten used to being in charge. He and the others still carried the aura of danger. She was sure they were bootlegging. That car looked expensive.

Eleanor screamed with delight, "Aksel-setä," Uncle Aksel, and ran straight for him. He caught her with ready hands and threw her squealing high above his head. Aino saw that it was a well-practiced move, which made her both happy and jealous.

She turned to Kyllikki and Alma, who were drinking coffee from one of those new thermos bottles Ilmari bought in Portland. All the married loggers were getting them for Christmas and birthdays.

"Aksel come around fairly often then?" Aino asked.

Alma nodded. Aksel now had Eleanor by the arms and was swing-ing her around, her legs and skirt horizontal to the ground. Pilvi ran up, jumping up and down for her turn.

"Jouka?" Aino asked.

"Not so often," Alma said. She looked quickly at Kyllikki, who nodded go ahead. "It's . . . the drinking."

"He loves Eleanor. He really does," Kyllikki broke in. "But . . . there's been some trouble."

"Several times in jail," Alma said. "Caught with booze on the street." She sighed sadly. "He was a good logger."

"And dancer," Kyllikki added.

Aino wondered if they blamed her. Jouka had been drinking long before she even met him, but she said nothing.

"What in the world is Aksel doing to get such a fancy car?" Aino asked. Matti had joined them and was squatting, reaching for a piece of chocolate cake.

"That's an Oldsmobile with a 233-cubic-inch V-8 engine. It'll outrun any cop car on a paved road. It costs more than a logger's annual salary. What do you think he's doing?"

Aino didn't answer.

"War changed him," Matti said.

Aksel put Pilvi down and came walking up to them. What hadn't changed were his radiant blue eyes.

"Päivää," he said. He shook Matti's hand and then made a slight head nod to the women, repeating, "Päivää" to each of them. "When did you get back?" he asked Aino in Finnish.

"Two days ago."

"The heat's off then." It wasn't a question.

She nodded yes.

"We missed you."

"Come for dinner," she blurted out. She quickly looked at Alma, who smiled approval. Aksel gave a look toward the Bachelor Boys, who had dispersed among the picnickers. "They can come, too." Aino said. "I owe all of you."

Matti had already left to look at the Oldsmobile. Aksel smiled at Alma and Kyllikki. "We'll tell the story over dinner."

The younger children had to go to bed after supper, but Mielikki, Helmi, and Suvi got to stay up. All of the Bachelor Boys came, except Kullervo. He assured everyone he really liked Ilmari and Alma, but he always had some reason to stay behind. Ilmari had made a violin just three years earlier and was already a fair player, but it turned out Jens Lerback was a master, so Ilmari just did chords on the kantele and everyone danced with everyone. The three girls were trying hard to be grown-up and the Bachelor Boys were being gallant with dance partners whose faces touched just above their belly buttons.

Aino saw Aksel whisper to Jens, who laughed and said in English, "Name me a Scandinavian fiddle player who doesn't."

Aksel walked over to Aino, and Jens began playing "Lördags-valsen." Aksel held out his hand. Aino took it and she was filled with memories—of Midsummer's Eve, of Knappton and Lempi, of Jouka, and of Aksel. The memories were like bright beads on a somber necklace. Her heart filled with longing for those moments and the people she shared them with. She could only conjure at the edges of memory the time between the beads, time not specifically remembered, but felt now, in this room, in her brother's house, with Aksel reaching out his hand, here, now, sharing this moment. She knew she'd come home.

The Bachelor Boys left in the Oldsmobile as the sun was coming up. The adults had coffee.

"Good dancer, isn't he?" Kyllikki said to Aino.

"Who?"

Kyllikki rolled her eyes.

The room was silent as everyone drank coffee. The cows would need milking, the younger children would need feeding, the soot would need to be dusted from the walls, firewood would need to be cut. The life of the farm was relentless and sweet.

Ilmari cleared his throat, a sign something serious was coming. "Aino," he said. "We've been talking."

"I hope you're not sending me to Ullakko," she quipped. Everyone but Ilmari chuckled.

"No, but it's the same problem. You could stay and help Alma with the house, but—"

"We would drive each other crazy," Aino said.

"Yoh," Alma agreed.

There was a pause.

"So," Kyllikki said brightly, "almost all the poikatalojas in Astoria were burned out. The lumber and logging business has been good. We own the land, so instead of rebuilding our house, we're buying the neighbor's lot to build our own poikataloja."

"We're going to wire it for electricity," Matti said.

"Where will you live?"

"We're going to build a new house on my mother and father's land," Kyllikki said. "They'll live with us."

Aino waited.

"So, Matti's logging. I'll have my hands full with the kids and my parents. We want you to manage the poikataloja."

"I don't know anything about running a poikataloja."

"You worked in the mess hall at Reder's Camp. You can cook. You can handle single men. You ran the business end of the co-op. You'd be perfect."

"It will have an electric stove and electric lights," Matti said. "Way less cleaning."

"No fear of fires," Kyllikki added.

"But . . . I'd just be a . . . a maid for fifty bachelors. I, I'll midwife instead."

"The doctors have shut the midwives down," Matti said.

"I need to think about it."

"Aino," Ilmari said quietly. "Now is not a time to be proud."

Aino accepted. While the poikataloja was being built, she helped Alma at Ilmahenki and Kyllikki at Suvantola. She fished for crawdads with Eleanor. She took her into Tapiola for candy at Higgins's. She told stories from *The Kalevala*. Gradually Eleanor started warming to her. But when the poikataloja was finished and the day to move to Astoria arrived, it was clear she hadn't warmed enough. Eleanor ran away.

After five hours of frantic searching and calling out her name, Jorma and Aarni found Eleanor at Vasutäti's old campsite, which had become a secret hideout for the children, huddled against the back wall of the little bark hut. They told Eleanor that her mother said she could stay, and it was OK to come home.

She was furious when she found she'd been tricked and bolted for the door, but Jorma and Aarni stopped her. Aino reached out to take her arm, but she twisted away and ran to Alma, burying her face in Alma's skirt. Alma looked awkwardly at Aino. She knelt, both knees on one of the many rag rugs, and hugged Eleanor. Then she pushed her back so she could talk to her.

"Eleanor, your äiti loves you. She wants very much for you to go with her to Astoria."

"I don't want to go to Astoria."

Aino went to her knees beside Eleanor and Alma. She knew she was begging this tiny person who held her happiness in her power. "Please, Eleanor. I want you to come with me. I know it will be hard to leave Alma-täti." She again reached out to her, but Eleanor pulled away saying, "I hate you."

"Eleanor," Alma said, kneeling down to her level.

"What," came a little voice.

"When we face hard or scary things, what do we do?"

Eleanor said nothing.

"What do we do?" Alma insisted.

"Remember our sisu," she said without looking at her.

Alma waited for Eleanor to do what needed to be done.

Alma had woven a beautiful little wicker suitcase with two colors and a little latch she had ordered by mail. She helped Eleanor pack, Aino anxiously looking on, and walked with her to the front porch. "You'll see Matti-setä and Kyllikki-täti every day. Astoria has stores even bigger that Mr. Higgins's and a school with lots of rooms where everyone in a room is the same age, and lots of girls to make friends with." She bent down and hugged Eleanor into her skirt, letting her bury her face in it. "I'll always be your täti," she said, holding her close against her legs. Then, bending down and nuzzling her nose into Eleanor's thick auburn hair, she said, "I will miss you and I will always love you." She stood and tried to smile but turned and walked back into the house.

The children lined up. The boys shook both Aino's and Eleanor's hands and the girls gave Eleanor a flower crown to wear to Astoria. Then Ilmari pulled up in the wagon and they got in. Eleanor dived to the floor, burying her face against the rough wood of the wagon, saying nothing. Even with Ilmari's coaxing, she wouldn't wave goodbye.

7

The poikataloja was full within two weeks of opening. The economy was still good; work was plentiful and places to live were scarce.

Kyllikki helped Aino with the little basement apartment they'd designed for her, making curtains, lining shelves with paper, and making two new rag rugs. Eleanor had her own bed for the first time in her life.

It didn't make Eleanor happy.

Nor did school. Aino decided to send Eleanor to first grade, even though she was five. It was better for her, Aino figured, since she herself was busy all the time running the poikataloja. There was a further problem. Eleanor didn't speak English.

On the first day of school Eleanor came home at lunchtime crying. Aino spanked her, because she felt it was required for good mothering. She marched her back to school, telling her stories of brave Finnish girls who helped beat the Russians.

Eleanor sat tight-lipped and angry in the front row where Mrs. Hawkins placed her to keep an eye on her. She hadn't gone to the toilet all day, because she couldn't see any outhouse and didn't know how to ask where one was. Desperate, she finally wriggled into bushes at the side of the playground. Her mother had put her into panties, like all the American girls, and she didn't quite know how to manage. She spent the rest of the day ashamed and scared that someone would smell them. When she came home she quickly pulled them off and hid them. When

Aino found them and confronted her with them, Eleanor grabbed them and threw them at her. She got spanked for that as well.

She finally made friends with a Finnish girl named Jenny Pavola. When Jenny asked Eleanor to come to her house to play, she couldn't, because Jenny's parents were whites and those kinds of people did terrible things to true Finns. When Eleanor reluctantly told Jenny why she couldn't come to play, Jenny said it was all right, because her mother said they didn't want any girl from a red family in their house. The reds had killed some of her aunts, uncles, and cousins in Finland and didn't believe in God. The girls still played at school, but the budding friendship struggled.

By Thanksgiving, Eleanor could make herself understood in English and could understand most of what Mrs. Hawkins said. By Christmas, she spoke better English than Aino. She also learned that you spoke "old-country language" only to parents.

She eventually worked out the complicated social issues.

She could be friends with Finns and other Scandinavians, talk with Greeks and Italians at school, and smile and be polite to the Chinese but stay clear of them. Their tongs were vicious secret societies that would sell a little blond Scandinavian girl into a brothel, whatever that was.

She could play with friends at school, but she could never play at their houses and they could never come to her house, whether they were red or white, because she was from a broken home—as if anyone would want to come to a hole in the ground underneath a bunch of smelly bachelors. Even worse than being a child from a broken home, she was a child from a broken home whose mother had done something bad. Jenny told Eleanor that her mother said that Eleanor's mother had gone to jail. Eleanor said that her mother went to jail because she helped working people, and mean bosses paid the police to put her there. Jenny believed her. She and Jenny would meet downtown and window-shop and stare at sailors, but they couldn't play with Jenny's dolls.

She hated it.

At Christmas, they went to Ilmahenki where everyone was red— or at least no one was white except Matti-setä, but he didn't exploit people, so he was an OK white. When Aksel-setä came for Christmas glögg, she asked him if he was a red or a white. He said that he was an earthling, which she knew was a joke but didn't understand. On Christmas Eve, they went to Ilmari-setä's church and even her mother came. They put out all the kerosene lamps and everyone lit a candle. They sang her favorite carol, "Hiljainen Yö," which meant "Silent Night" in English. Helmi said it was a German song, but we Americans had beaten them in the war and even Martin Luther was a German and not a Finn, and it was OK to do mixed-up things like that in America. When she walked sleepily into Alma-täti's house, Ilmari-setä lit the candles on the Christmas tree and everyone got an orange from California that Matti-setä bought in Astoria. Everyone said that Matti-setä was making good money, so he could afford to do this.

She slept with Helmi and it felt warm and snuggly. She helped Alma-täti make rieska and pulla and even helped Mielikki make a basket for next Easter. She thought Mielikki—who now had breasts—was beautiful and she and Pilvi went into her room and found a brassiere, which was a risqué new kind of underwear. They both tried it on, giggling, until Mielikki came in and snatched it away from them.

Even though Jorma teased her about being a city girl, he let her help with the milking. He and Aarni let her fish for steelhead with them. They even told everyone she landed one all by herself, although it was a lie. Jorma had stood behind her guiding every move, helping with the reel, but it was a good lie.

She knew her mother was trying, but she still felt Alma-täti was her real mother, her cousins were her brothers and sisters, and Astoria was unfriendly, lonely, and far away from everything she loved.

She ran away when it came time to go back.

This time they didn't find her. It was dark and cold by four o'clock, so she came in on her own. Alma-täti hugged her and said she'd scared everyone and they'd been frantic with worry, although Eleanor saw no reason why. Her mother hugged her, too, and then said, "I'm trying so hard." She felt bad her mother felt bad, but then Alma-täti never had to try hard.

So, because she didn't want her mother to feel sad, she went back with her to the poikataloja and the smelly bachelors.

February was miserable in Astoria, gloomy at noon and dark sixteen hours a day. The rain slashed down with one southwest storm after another. Even Captain Elving's ferry, the sixty-foot *Tourist*, stayed tied up at the dock several days, bucking at the heavy ropes as swells moved upriver, breaking over its decks. Because no one's parents would let her play at their houses, Eleanor had only her little doll, Kiki. Ilmari-setä had carved her head and Alma-täti made her body and her clothes. She tried to cheer Kiki up, serving her coffee, talking about summer at Ilmahenki with Mielikki, Helmi, and Jorma.

One day at school, Ilona Salminen said her mother told her that Jouka Kaukonen was Eleanor's father. Eleanor said, "So what?" Ilona said that her mother said that Jouka Kaukonen was a drunk. She shoved the stupid girl and when Ilona hit her back, she grabbed Ilona's arm and bit her as hard as she could. Ilona ran crying to Mrs. Hawkins, who took Eleanor to see the principal who asked why she bit Ilona. When she told him, he had looked out his office window at the river for the longest time. Then he turned and said two wrongs don't make a right and wrote a note for her to take home to her mother.

When her mother opened the principal's note, Eleanor thought she was going to be spanked, but her mother just sat down and put her head in her hands. So Eleanor spanked Kiki instead and then felt bad because Kiki didn't bite Ilona. She made it up to Kiki by having a tea party. Eleanor pretended that her father, Alma-täti, Ilmari-setä, and Aksel-setä had all come. Kiki got mad at Eleanor's father and it ruined the tea party. When her mother returned from making the bachelors' dinner, the tea party was all over the floor and her mother shouted at her and sent her to bed without supper.

That Saturday morning, she pretended to be asleep when her mother went to the kitchen to make breakfast for the bachelors. She knew that after breakfast was cleaned up her mother would go shopping for dinner and Sunday breakfast. So, with her and Kiki's clothes in the little two-colored wicker suitcase Alma-täti had made for her, Kiki safe and warm under her coat, she went to the coffee can her mother thought was secret, took four quarters from it, and walked to the *General Washington*.

When she gave the man the quarters for her ticket, he asked her where she was going. She said in English, "To Knappton. My uncle Ilmari is meeting me there." It was another good lie.

When the *General Washington* tied up at Knappton, one of the crew helped Eleanor up the ladder because it was low tide. She sat on her suitcase, cradled Kiki in her lap, watched the river, and waited.

Several men and two women asked her why she was sitting there. She told them that she was waiting for her uncle Ilmari.

Just before dark, she heard someone walking behind her and she turned her head. It was Ilmari-setä. She knew he would come. He did.

When Aino found Eleanor gone, she ran through the poikataloja, searching the rooms. Within minutes, the bachelors who were off work joined the search. She ran to the police station and the word went out. When the rest of the bachelors got off work, they formed an organized search, fifty men covering every street.

Mielikki arrived around midnight, having talked a gillnetter into taking her across the river, and told her that Eleanor was safe at Ilmahenki. Aino quivered between relief and despair. She'd gone to the police and all the bachelors in the poikataloja had joined the search. She thanked all the bachelors and she and Mielikki walked over to tell Kyllikki and Matti that Eleanor was safe. Aino pleaded with Kyllikki to mind the poikataloja for a couple of days and she and Mielikki took the first trip across the river in the morning.

Aino saw Eleanor coming from the barn with a wicker basket of eggs and rushed up to her, nearly breaking the eggs when she hugged her close. Eleanor returned the hug, as best she could.

At supper, Aino watched Eleanor eat as if every bite would be the last she would see. Eleanor, focusing on her stew, drinking her winter milk, less creamy than the spring and summer milk, asking Ilmari to cut off a slice of rieska for her, buttering it with care, was unaware of her mother's aching heart.

That night after the children went to bed, Aino asked Alma and Ilmari how much they would require in cash to feed Eleanor. Alma protested they needed nothing, but Ilmari said five dollars a month and Aino was grateful. Ilmari and Alma would hardly notice what Eleanor ate, but Ilmari knew Aino needed to send that five dollars every month to keep herself connected to Eleanor as well as hold her head up.

The next morning Aino packed her overnight bag in the dark. She heard the rooster cry, imagining him seeking the dawn and not finding it. Rain drummed on the thin single-pane windows. An occasional gust of wind rattled them. Ilmari started the fire and Alma soon had mush and coffee going. Aino wondered if she could face saying goodbye to Eleanor, who was still sleeping. Maybe she should slip away. She watched Alma laying out the mush bowls and spoons for the children. They would walk to school in Tapiola in the dark. When they came home the girls would help Alma, churning butter, making balls for knitting from wool skeins, cleaning up after meals. Jorma would help with the cattle. He was learning how to blacksmith. Here, Eleanor counted. In the city she was just an added mouth. Here on Deep River, Eleanor had Alma, Ilmari, and her cousins. Here on Deep River, there was no stigma of divorce, no red versus white; there were no hours spent alone without friends while her mother worked. This time, what was truly good for Eleanor filled Aino with aching sadness.

She lit a candle and climbed the stairs to where the girls were sleeping. Eleanor was curled up next to Helmi, her auburn hair in nighttime pigtails loosely tangled with Helmi's yellow pigtails. Outside, the rooster crowed again.

"Eleanor," she whispered, touching her gently. "Eleanor, Äiti's going." Eleanor stirred and opened her hazel eyes.

Rubbing her face and gently untangling her pigtail from Helmi's, Eleanor sat up. Aino hugged her awkwardly with one arm, still holding the candle. She pulled back, looking into Eleanor's beautiful little face. "Last chance. Do you want to come with me?"

Eleanor looked down at her chest and shook her head no.

"Well, then, you be a good girl for Alma-täti and Ilmari-setä. Be a good worker."

Tears welled up from Aino's eyes. She reached out for Eleanor once more and smothered her hair and face with kisses. Then she stood and whispered, "I'll come whenever I can."

Eleanor looked solemnly up at her, her face reflecting the candlelight, and nodded.

Aino held herself together until she reached the plank road to Knappton. She'd believed she was being a good mother but in truth had not been thinking of Eleanor's happiness at all. Eleanor left her. Now she was leaving Eleanor, but this time it was for Eleanor's happiness, truly. Aino howled in anguish, no less seeking the dawn than the rooster.

8

Aino worked, visiting Eleanor throughout the spring and summer whenever she could. It was hard, prosaic, daily work that was never finished and never varied, but it was essential to the lives of everyone living there. She counted. Here was no great cause—other than earning room and board and Eleanor's keep. However, why wasn't this as great a cause as any? Who passed judgment on whether causes were great or small? Yes, there were no great debates, like syndicalism versus socialism. There were only small ones. Should she order navy beans or pinto beans? Should she try to move Ojala, who'd lost his leg to a flying cable, to the ground floor? Should she let him stay until he could get a job? The tasks were set before her—every morning, ever the same—like seeds spilled across a board that she had to sort, and after having them sorted into various piles by the end of the day, she awoke to find them scattered again, and again she set about sorting. There was no goal. There was no end point. There was just this daily living, this daily sorting of seeds that was the very life of the poikataloja and the men who lived there. She lived like a circle instead of a line. Since what she was doing didn't matter in terms of power, politics, and history, it didn't matter what she was doing. It felt peaceful.

She finally confirmed her citizenship at the courthouse. She'd been married to an American citizen for over fifteen years. A month later, she turned in her divorce papers and her divorce was granted.

Most of the bachelors at the poikataloja were in their late teens and twenties. They came to her for help with writing letters, advice on what color tie to buy to go with a new shirt. Some paid her a nickel to grease their boots, darn a sock, or patch a shirt. They talked to her some nights like a surrogate mother and other nights like an intriguing divorcée.

She worked under the single electric ceiling light late into the night, reconciling accounts, making lists for tomorrow's shopping, repairing her own clothes. She found herself writing letters home for her boys, as she came to think of them, in Finnish and Swedish.

Aino used her mending money to buy gifts for Eleanor but soon learned the gifts made her cousins envious, so she began taking something for every child. Eleanor was happy. Aino realized that the happier Eleanor was, the more joy it brought herself.

Eleanor responded. She talked more with Aino on her visits. She shared more of her life at Ilmahenki. It was clear, however, that Ilmahenki, not Astoria, was home.

Spring moved into summer. Lumber prices had been falling since the summer before and the single men moved out of town, looking for work somewhere else. Aino and Kyllikki both had to spend time advertising, talking to prospective boarders.

She began to submit articles to *Toveritar,* the Finnish-language women's socialist newspaper, and within a few weeks had a weekly column explaining different aspects of Marxist theory. The paper circulated only in Astoria and nearby towns and she knew that the women cared more about recipes than Marxist theory—so one day she added a recipe and did mental gymnastics to relate it to Marxist theory. It elicited positive letters to the editor. She gradually changed the column to one called Recipes for Working Families, which included food recipes focusing on cost and nutrition but also "recipes" for raising families with social consciousness with object lessons that were increasingly brought to her attention by readers.

After three months of dry summer weather came nine months of wet winter weather and then three more months of dry weather and the beginning of another nine months of wet. New boarders came as old boarders left. Squash in the summer, turnips and rutabagas in the winter.

Apples in the fall, fresh fat cream in the spring. Socks darned, trouser knees patched, letters written, breakfasts and dinners cooked, plates and pots washed, sandwiches made for lunch buckets, toilets cleaned, dances at Suomi Hall, and every week another column for *Toveritar.* Time seemed to stand still, punctuated by holidays that themselves seemed to never change, and Aino, now thirty-seven, sorted the seeds of a woman's life.

That Christmas she had small gifts for everyone, which she toted aboard the *General Washington* in a large canvas shopping bag. The sun had just set, leaving orange-pink traces. A nearly full moon was rising far up the river, pale white in a sky that stretched, darkening, into empty space. She felt the vibration of the boat's deck and then she sensed the vibration moving into the river and the river flowing from the moon, flowing to the sea, flowing through her. She, small and alone, was yet part of this vast animated soul of a river, a flowing, vibrating, moving stillness.

Christmas Eve was wonderful. Alma had outdone herself preparing the food. Her niece, Sylvi, had come by to help with the pies and other baking, which puzzled Alma a little, but then she wasn't going to turn down the help. Even Aksel stopped by, leaving candy he said he'd bought in Portland. He, however, seemed preoccupied, saying vaguely that business wasn't as good as it used to be. Kyllikki told Aino that when Matti came back from the sauna, he said that Aksel had a new scar.

The only slight imperfection in an otherwise near-perfect Christmas was that Mielikki got a toothache when she ate some of Aksel's candy. Ilmari said he would be happy to yank the tooth with pliers, making Mielikki blanch. Alma came to her rescue, saying her father might be a good blacksmith but was no dentist. Everyone laughed.

Of course, the cattle didn't know it was Christmas, so Ilmari stood up from the table and excused himself to check on them.

Outside, far above the stillness, in air so high above the earth there was no warmth, he heard the honking of geese flying south, the last of them getting out before winter. He stood quietly, waiting. The honking got louder until he saw the first of the huge undulating chevron, like a giant heart, pulsing in the sky. He watched a single goose, suddenly an individual, hurrying to regain its place in the whole. It disappeared into the flock, a single goose no more, but the flock continued. For nearly an hour, he watched individual chevrons, obviously insistent on some destination far from Deep River because the leaders were keeping them so high. Then, as mysteriously as they'd come, they were gone.

Then he heard it: wind stirring the tops of the trees two hundred feet above the edge of the hard-won pasture, like the sound of rapids in a distant unseen canyon, a sibilant echo of air and forest beings. He looked across Deep River and saw the tops of the trees moving wavelike in the ominous-feeling air. Cold dread seized him, and a dark spirit passed over him like the wings of the Angel of Death.

Its next visit would be soon. On that visit, it would not fly over Ilmahenki like the geese.

9

The bootlegging business wasn't so good. By early March 1925, the Seattle cartel, which had been immune to problems with the Seattle police because its boss was a former police lieutenant, was coming under increasing scrutiny by a fanatical branch of the FBI, an organization that apparently was impervious to bribes. Liquor continued to flow from Canada across isolated beaches and bays into the hands of customers, but because of increased federal pressure the smugglers were asking for more money to deliver. Local law enforcement at the retail end, aware of the margins the bootleggers were making, had upped the price of protection. Aksel was paying Louhi nearly double what he'd been paying her when he started the business.

He was getting squeezed on the demand side as well. Some buyers reacted to the higher prices by driving to Portland, loading up their cars, and smuggling the liquor into the Bachelor Boys' turf, putting the Boys into the role of customs agents. In addition, many people were becoming adept at making bootleg beer or whiskey themselves. Although nowhere near the quality of smuggled alcohol, it got people safely drunk at half the price. Ironically, the Bachelor Boys found themselves trying to shut down illegal stills, mostly through intimidation but sometimes through confrontation that ended in gunfire. These firefights were short. Still operators weren't gangsters; they were farmers and loggers making money on the side. No one was killed in these fights, but Aksel got winged before Christmas and in February Heppu got a bullet that went through his right upper arm. It had exited without serious bleeding, the usual cause of death, but he was out of commission for over a month.

Just before April, Aksel was summoned to Nordland.

Louhi wasted no time. "Seattle gave notice that they'll only sell me liquor I retail myself. They know about our deal and they also found out about some of my other wholesale deals." She humphed. "Their margins are getting tight and they're consolidating. In short, cutting out the middleman. That's me and you."

Aksel nodded his head. He knew it had been coming and he was more vulnerable than Louhi. Through her saloons, she was a major retailer in her own right and far more nuanced in the human end of the business, mainly political. One of the costliest lessons of his life was not having asked Louhi first about doing something illegal, like depositing under an assumed name.

"You've got three options," Louhi said. "You go to work for the cartel, you go back to logging, or they'll come gunning for you. You know the ship from Vancouver leaves in two days. If you don't stop the order, the Seattle people will find out and assume you're challenging them."

"So, it's war or working for wages," Aksel said.

Aksel relayed the business news to the Bachelor Boys the next day. Louhi needed their decision in a week.

"That's just before the shipment from Vancouver," Jens said. "We've already paid half of it. That's money we'll never recoup."

"That ship leaves Vancouver tomorrow," Aksel said. "We don't stop it and take the loss, Seattle will know and assume we're still in business."

"Are we going to let these bastards in Seattle push us around and steal our money?" Jens asked.

The discussion didn't go on much longer after that. The other Bachelor Boys' blood was up and so was their pride—three Finns and a Norwegian. When the vote was taken, it was four against one. By the next evening, the ship literally had sailed.

* * *

Its destination was a beach near the mouth of the Niawiakum River, just south of the marshlands of the estuary. Second-growth timber, already over thirty years old, came right down to the water.

The Bachelor Boys parked the trucks close to the beach. It was raining the soft misty rain that felt as though one had walked into an atomizer spray. Gray turned to black.

About midnight they heard the motor of a tug. As arranged, Yrjö signaled with a flashlight from a small promontory at the south edge of the beach. The tug was moving very slowly, pushing the barge, feeling its way down the bay, a man at the barge's bow throwing a lead line.

Aksel smelled the tidal flats to their north and the marshland of the estuary, pungent in the cool mist. Then he saw a light wink twice and Yrjö signaled back. The sound of the motor rose as the captain brought the bow of the barge in to the left of Yrjö's light. There was a soft sliding impact and the barge came to rest on the beach.

They went to work, shifting the load of gravel to uncover the hatches, then struggling from the barge to the beach, each man carrying two cases. Aksel knew that he should have set one of the boys back toward the road as security, but faced with the need to rapidly unload the cargo he didn't—an understandable choice but a mistake.

They all saw the brilliant white flashes and heard the whip-crack sonic booms of the bullets before they heard the gunfire. They were on the ground, Aksel and Heppu going underwater, when the hammering air-pulsing sounds of rifles and Thompson submachine guns hit their ears. One crewman and Jens went down. The engine on the tug revved up and crewmen were scrambling to climb aboard as the captain backed the barge off the beach.

The Bachelor Boys, with no verbal command, formed a line perpendicular to the beach and parallel to the line of fire coming from the trees to take the attackers under fire without shooting each other. It saved their lives.

Jens screamed that he was hit but could still shoot and kept shooting. Aksel fired quick bursts from the Thompson and the other three coolly fired their Springfields, taking aim at the flashes of light. The ambushers' fire slackened. Aksel shouted at Heppu and Kullervo to crawl forward with him. Yrjö, who was on the far end of the line, crawled in the direction of the road. Using the darkness as cover, he rose to a crouch and scrambled toward where he'd seen the flash that indicated the end of the ambushers' line. He reached the tree line and slowly worked his way toward the flank of the ambushers' line. He saw a face light when the man's rifle went off. He fired his own, ejected and chambered, and fired again. There was no more firing. He stumbled on the body in the dark, put a bullet in the man's head to make sure he wouldn't come after him, and moved toward the next flashes.

Aksel knew what Yrjö was doing the instant he heard the two rifle shots. He loaded another drum and directed a short burst of fire just ahead of Yrjö's advance. There were another two cracks and flashes from the right side and then silence. The gunfire from the left of the ambush was now sporadic. There was another single shot from the right side. Then the firing stopped completely. All they could hear were the muffled shouts of men running for their lives, never having expected such a disciplined reaction.

Yrjö signaled the letter Y for his name with his flashlight. Aksel, Kullervo, and Heppu joined him. They shouted for Jens, but there was no answer.

"You find him," Aksel told Heppu. "We'll cover."

Heppu took the flashlight and, covering it down to a sliver with his hand, found Jens unconscious and bleeding badly from near the hip. He ripped Jens's trousers down and got his belt right up in Jens's crotch and then twisted it around his thigh using a stick to turn it as tight as he could. Aksel and Heppu joined them, and the three of them hauled Jens to the Ford and got him to a doctor in Willapa.

He lived but would walk with a considerable limp for the rest of his life.

Over the next week, they sold all of their inventory. Then Aksel took the other truck to Nordland where he asked Louhi to broker a peace.

"You killed two of them," she said. "And you wounded two more. They won't be in a peaceful mood."

"How many were there?"

"Eight. They said there were twelve of you." Louhi shook her head, smiling.

"Jens will never walk right again."

Louhi took that in. "Do you quit?"

"We quit."

"OK. Let's keep them thinking there are twelve of you. The Seattle boys are mad but they're not stupid. They'll happily take over your turf without having to fight twelve damned good fighters for it."

The Bachelor Boys were out of the bootlegging business.

10

The week after the Bachelor Boys' last fight, Mielikki complained again about the tooth, an upper bicuspid. Two days later, she was running a fever, but no one thought it was related to the toothache; it seemed to be just a touch of flu. The next day, she couldn't get out of bed. Ilmari came in at lunchtime and put wet towels on her forehead. He tousled her blond hair, thinking for a moment about Rauha. Then Alma came bustling into the room with some hot chicken soup and he felt Mielikki would be OK. He went back to the mill.

Around three in the afternoon, Mielikki's fever soared and she was covered in sweat. As the sun was setting, she grabbed Ilmari's hand when he put another wet compress to her forehead. He knew then that he would lose her. He fell to his knees beside the bed, holding her hand to his face, kissing it again and again. She looked at him with her clear blue eyes, smiling at him, loving him. He lay down beside her on the bed, her small left hand held between his two large blacksmith hands. That's where Alma found him, lying on his side, looking at Mielikki's beautiful face.

Once again, Ilmari made a coffin, working alone through the night. Occasionally, tears would hamper his work and he would walk outside into the cool night to regain control. He reflected, breathing deeply, listening to Deep River running to the sea, how God's ways were unknowable and terrible. He remembered Vasutäti telling him to grow up. *For now we see through a glass, darkly; but then face-to-face: now I know in part; but then shall I know even as also I am known.* Maybe, maybe not. For now, he had the task that God had set before him.

He finished the coffin and was sitting next to it when he looked up to see three of the women from the church, Ruusu Pakkanen, Linna Salmi, and Lilo Puskala, standing quietly in the rain outside the barn door. Tears flooded into his eyes and he wiped them away. "Come in. Come in," he said.

Ruusu took his hand. "We're so sorry," she said.

"Won't you bury Mielikki next to her mother?" Lilo asked.

Linna added, "We all want you to have her funeral in the church."

Aino arrived from Astoria with Matti, Kyllikki, and their children. Louhi got there several hours later. They all assembled in the living room, along with members of Alma's family, the Vanhatalos and Wirkkalas, and they paid their silent farewells to Mielikki, who lay in the open coffin in her church dress holding a bouquet in her hands. Ilmari had tied in her hair a blue ribbon that had belonged to her mother. The children sat quietly, those who had them wearing their shoes, all of them in their church clothes, all bravely holding back tears. The pallbearers—Ilmari, Matti, Ullakko, Aksel, and two of Alma's brothers—carried the coffin to the old wagon. Everyone followed the horse-drawn wagon to the church on foot. No one could imagine putting Mielikki in a motor-driven truck.

At the funeral in the little church, when it was Aino's turn to view the body, she had an urge to kiss Mielikki's face. Instead, she touched her over her heart. For a moment, she thought Mielikki was breathing. Then, the illusion left her. She was bewildered by the pain of life, by the utter finality of death that cut off all future possibilities, leaving her with the paltry few possibilities she'd made manifest in her brief time knowing Mielikki, somehow never imagining that there wouldn't be time enough later. She lifted her hand and glanced over at Eleanor, who was sitting with her cousins: stoic, bearing the pain as they all must. She straightened her shoulders and joined her brothers.

When the last of the viewers was seated, Ilmari rose. He moved to the coffin and looked up toward the ceiling of the church. His deep voice quavering, his words coming slowly and in short phrases, yet penetrating every heart in the church, he spoke to Mielikki as if she were standing across a small field from him. "I see you . . . looking over your shoulder . . . holding out your hand to me." He was looking beyond the ceiling. "Because of you . . . I lived in sunshine, no matter how dark the day . . . My love follows you, but I must remain." Then he straightened his back. He looked down at her face and touched her cheek. Then, he walked with slow dignity to take his seat with his family. As he did, he looked on all the members of the little church, seated solemnly before him. He knew then that he no longer had to look for God, as if God were somewhere up in the sky. He knew Vasutäti was right. Ruusu Pakkanen playing "Beautiful Savior" on the organ, Abraham and Tuuli Wirkkala, Antti and Linna Salmi, Matti and Henni Haapakangas, Lilo and Kalle Puskala—all tributaries of the waterfall of God.

At the graveside on Peaceful Hill, family and friends walked by, each in turn gently tossing flowers onto Mielikki's coffin, which had been lowered into the grave. Ilmari, who'd waited until the last flower was delivered, knelt and reaching down into the grave carefully laid several sheaves of basket wands on top of the many flowers. He stood and looked at the hills surrounding the little valley, knowing that Vasutäti's knowledge, which she had passed on to Mielikki, was now lost, returned to the earth.

His eyes brimming with controlled tears, he took the shovel and tossed dirt into the grave. The dirt hit the coffin and flowers with a short, scattered thump.

One by one, the people of the Deep River valley walked by, each adding a shovelful or a handful of earth until the coffin, the flowers, and the basket sheaves were lost from sight.

Ilmari wanted to walk back to Ilmahenki alone. Mielikki his dead daughter. Mielikki, her namesake, his dead sister. Suomi, ordered, placid summers and fierce winters. Here, wild, cool summers and cooler winters. Rauha. He found himself looking at the old snag. It had once been nearly three hundred feet tall; then one day everything changed.

The tree became a snag. Eventually, the snag would decay, fall to the ground, and become a nurse log for new trees. The new trees would grow, some to be three hundred feet tall, some to perish for lack of sunlight, and maybe someday there might even be another lightning strike and another snag. He'd first seen the snag as something dead. Now, he saw constant change and life everlasting.

11

A ksel and the Bachelor Boys came to the funeral. As was the custom, coffee, cake, and biscuitti were served at Ilmahenki. There, the women of the family talked about children, people at the funeral they hadn't seen for a while, who was seeing whom and where it might lead, and a kitchen in Astoria that ran completely on electricity, including the stove. The men talked logging and lumber. Matti had an idea of how to power different, more efficient yarders with diesel engines, which had been perfected during the war. He'd already converted two steam donkeys from wood to oil by mounting big oil tanks on the back of the skids and eliminated two men, no longer needing anyone to cut and split wood.

Matti had put most of his and Kyllikki's savings into the stock market and the market had gone up. He figured he could sell some of his stock at a good profit and use that money to buy the new diesel and necessary components for the new yarder and still leave him with more money in the stock market than he'd originally invested. If it all went as planned, it would be like getting a new, more efficient yarder for free. What a country this was.

Matti made up his mind to put money behind his ideas when Jens Lerback answered his question, "What are you up to these days?" by saying, "Not much, looking for a new line of work." Jens already had a reputation for gasoline engines. It wouldn't take him long to get up to speed on diesels. He'd had some sort of accident and walked with a decided limp. One arm wouldn't rise above the level of his shoulder, but Matti had no doubts he could run a yarder. Heppu Reinikka and

Yrjö Rautio were known to be good loggers. Matti knew that Aksel was the finest high rigger on the long-log side of the mountains, even with a shoulder wound. As for Kullervo, he was a hard worker and the experience of the others could mitigate his hearing problem. Anyway, it clearly was a package deal.

He offered the Bachelor Boys fifty cents an hour for an eight-hour day. They would need to move to the Oregon side of the river, because of Matti's deal with Reder.

They went outside to talk it over. No one talked. Aksel and Jens lit two cigarettes, took deep drags, and passed them on in different directions. Heppu took a deep drag on one and blew the smoke upward, looking at the clouds. "It's fair wages," he said. Looking at the burning end of his own cigarette, Yrjö said, "I swore I'd never again be a wage slave," and he passed it to Kullervo.

They all kicked at the ground, passing the cigarettes along, squinting in the smoke.

Finally, Aksel said, "If you work for Matti Koski you aren't a wage slave; you're a logger."

They all took that in, passing the cigarettes along until they'd smoked them to the point of burning their fingers. Jens flipped a smoking butt away, shaking his fingers where it had burned him. "I'm in if you're in," he said to all of them.

Everyone looked at Aksel. He nodded his head and they went back inside.

It didn't take Jens long to figure out how to hook up a diesel to power the big cable drums of the old steam donkey. He removed the boiler and the steam pistons and bolted down the diesel in the boiler's place. Then he linked the drive shaft of the old cylinders to the diesel's power takeoff. Everything else remained the same, except the throttle.

The Bachelor Boys moved to Svensen, Oregon, a settlement close to Matti's new show. They and the new diesel yarder were in operation three weeks after Mielikki's funeral.

There was only one thing wrong with the new workforce: they were out of shape. No one had given it a thought, especially the

Bachelor Boys. By midmorning on their first day, everyone was thinking about it. Hands had grown soft along with muscles. Reflexes were still fast, but not lightning fast—and in the woods lightning fast saved your life.

At first Matti worried a bit; then it got downright funny. They all had the brains of loggers, but the bodies of shoe clerks. He watched Yrjö and Heppu wolf down a large lunch and then walk somewhat stiffly back to the show. A huge log temporarily hung up, then jerked over the obstacle and came hurtling right at them. They both sprinted for a shallow dip in the ground and threw themselves into it as the log careened over their heads and up the hill to the landing. The sprint had been too much for them. They both poked their heads up from the indent with vomit on their chins and shirts. Matti laughed out loud, drawing a middle finger from Heppu.

A lot had changed in the high-rigging game since Aksel had last done it. Now, high climbers had spurs, much like those worn by electric linemen, only with way longer spikes. The extra length was needed to penetrate the thick unstable bark to reach solid wood. The flip line was a rope with a steel core, a safety measure against a badly aimed ax stroke that had been learned the hard way. Harness and saddle combinations of varying designs had also been invented.

He flipped the line, it caught, and he dug in his spikes. At the first limb, his hands were shaking from the exertion and beginning to blister. He was breathing heavily. He steeled himself for the job ahead and took a moment to regain some strength by holding closer to the trunk.

From far below he heard Matti holler, "Rig it, Aksel. Don't make love to it."

He moved.

When the tree narrowed to about three feet, he began sawing. Sweat stung his eyes. He was gasping. His shoulder ached from the wound he never talked about.

There was a light cracking sound. The top of the tree began to move. Aksel dropped down quickly, jamming his spikes into the trunk. In a slow majestic fall, the top swept past him, falling away, growing smaller and smaller. The delimbed spar suddenly lurched to the side, then came whipping back, its speed vastly accelerated with the tension of the entire trunk, moving nearly twenty feet before whipping back in the other direction. It was like being on a mainmast in the highest wind imaginable, only three times higher up.

He slowly made his way to the ground, then staggered off to get the small 50-pound block they would use to haul up the massive 350-pound bull block that would do the real work.

When he finished the day, his hands bleeding, his feet aching, he was totally spent. He hadn't felt like this since his first day at Reder Logging. He would have preferred to be back in combat.

Aksel and the other Bachelor Boys piled into the Oldsmobile. They all lit cigarettes. They carefully drove the Oldsmobile over ruts and pot-holes and through the mud to their boardinghouse in Svensen, where they collapsed in their cots without taking off their clothes. It was a stiff and sober crew that arrived the next morning.

In three months, as Matti had expected, they were all fully productive—and each about fifteen pounds lighter.

12

Walking to work in the dark on Wednesday, January 6, 1927, with Oregon mist drifting from leaden skies, Kyllikki's father, Emil Saari, died of a heart attack. He was buried on Sunday in Pacific View Cemetery, located just below the mouth of the Columbia River on a hill overlooking a small lake nestled between two lines of sand dunes. Beyond the westernmost dune line, the rolling surf of the Pacific Ocean thundered onto a beach stretching for seventeen miles, unbroken by a single home or river, from the mouth of the Columbia south to the little town of Neawanna, hugged in close to Neawanna Head, a promontory with thousand-foot-high basalt cliffs pushing westward from the coastline nearly a mile into the sea.

As expected, Hilda Saari put out coffee and cake for everyone at the house.

Aksel squatted next to Eleanor, who was looking out the window at the river. Aksel was looking fine. Six months of logging could erase years of soft living. He and Eleanor watched the river together, talking quietly. Aino knew that Aksel saw Eleanor whenever he stopped at her brothers' farms, and the brief thought occurred to her: maybe he was trying to get closer to Eleanor so he could get closer to herself. Then Eleanor laughed. Aksel grinned and Aino had the horrific thought that he was doing it just because he liked Eleanor—period. Then it dawned on her how much she liked Aksel. She fled into the kitchen to help Hilda Saari.

* * *

The nonfamily guests left. Aksel already had his coat on and the Bachelor Boys were at the door saying goodbye to Kyllikki and Hilda when Matti walked up to the group. "You know I have two parcels of spruce left over by Neawanna. I've got another diesel yarder coming in the next couple of weeks. I want you boys to run the show."

The Bachelor Boys looked at each other, quickly nodding their approval to Aksel. Aksel said, "We don't mind, but it's a long way from Svensen."

Before Matti could open his mouth, Kyllikki said, "You can stay at the poikataloja. We'll give you free rooms." She looked quickly at Matti. "And board."

"Wait a second . . . Kyllikki, I . . ." Matti was spluttering.

Kyllikki touched him on the arm and with her back to the group looked up at him and made eyes toward the kitchen and then toward Aksel. Matti looked up to heaven for help. Kyllikki grinned and squeezed his arm. Turning around with a bright smile, she said, "So, it's a deal then. You'll do it."

The Bachelor Boys just looked at each other. It seemed the deal was done. Aksel suddenly caught on, started to shake his head no, and Kyllikki looked at him with that look that told a man: "This is my department. I know it's good for you, so you might as well enjoy the ride, because you're on it." Aksel and Matti just looked at each other, suppressing smiles. Sometimes being manipulated for your own good felt like being loved.

"OK, it's a deal," Aksel told her. Then he turned to Matti. "Can you come outside with us?"

Kyllikki, knowing her job was finished, smiled and went back into the house, leaving her husband and his friends to finish whatever job was on their minds.

Aksel led Matti to the big Oldsmobile, looked around, then reached into the back seat and pulled out two very heavy army surplus duffel bags. Matti looked at them, puzzled. "If we're going to move to the poikataloja, I'll need you to store these for us. We can't have them at the poikataloja."

"What's in them?"

Aksel hesitated.

"Rifles," Jens said.

"Rifles?" Matti repeated.

"And some pistols and a tommy gun," Aksel added. "You know, from the old business."

"Some ammo," Kullervo added.

"Why not sell them?"

"Maybe we'll need them someday," Aksel said. Aksel transferred one bag into Matti's arms and the weight made Matti buckle slightly for a moment.

"It's not illegal," Jens said. "It's in the Constitution."

"Yes," Matti said. "But if one of the kids finds them and then Kyllikki finds out—"

Aksel said, "Just do it for me."

Two weeks later, the big Oldsmobile roared up in front of the poikataloja with the Bachelor Boys and their gear. Aino showed them to their rooms. When she held the door open for Aksel to get his suitcase through, it bumped against her right thigh. Aksel mumbled a quiet apology, but she saw his eye travel down from where the suitcase had bumped her. Hemlines were even shorter now than they'd been in Chicago. She'd bought silk stockings at Grimson's Ladies Apparel two days earlier, and when she put them on that morning she was taken by surprise at how she wanted Aksel to notice. His eyes rose quickly to hers but took in all of her on the way up. He hadn't looked at her like that since before Jouka—and Lempi. It was more than desire. It was delight. It was appreciation. He certainly noticed the new silk stockings.

13

By February 1926, 200-Foot Logging—still tiny compared with operations like Tidewater, Western Cooperage, and Weyerhaeuser—had become a healthy gyppo outfit. Matti had three yarders, one diesel and two oil-burning steam, operating on two Klaskanine shows and a new diesel yarder on his own timber just north of Neawanna. The Neawanna show straddled a ridge running north-south from the top of which you could see the long line of white breakers to the west, multiple white lines of combers rolling in from the Pacific, stretching from Neawanna Head to the Columbia. Saddle Mountain could be seen to the southeast—on a clear day. In February, northwesterners see mountains mostly with their imaginations.

The spruce on the Neawanna show were so big and thick that their needles turned the usual coastal fog into rain even in summer, supplying nearly half of the trees' total water. Sometimes if it did rain, no one on the ground far below was aware of it.

The first job on the Neawanna show required felling these big trees to make a road to get the yarder in position. Aksel and the Bachelor Boys started on the east side of the ridge and worked their way west and uphill, pushing the line of standing trees before them. Matti, supervising over on the Klaskanine shows, scheduled his trucks to service both operations efficiently. He put Aksel in charge of the Neawanna show along with the Bachelor Boys, two other loggers, and the new diesel yarder; 200-Foot Logging was moving forward.

* * *

Aino's business also moved forward. Matti and Kyllikki replaced the big woodstove with one that used propane. This meant Aino no longer had to clean soot from the walls and ceiling and pay someone to split wood. It also reduced the fire hazard. People grumbled that you could blow yourself up with propane gas, to which Matti replied, "You can, if you're stupid."

Aino had dinner ready every evening at seven. The boarders were usually asleep two hours after dinner, exhausted. Aino would have liked to do the same, but she had to do the prep work and set out the table for breakfast at 5:00 a.m. The boarders would leave for work in the dark. Aino would clean up breakfast, then do the shopping for dinner and the next day's breakfast. The rest of the day was spent preparing dinner, making sure the outhouse was serviceable, sweeping the halls and stairs, and whatever chores weren't daily, like washing windows. The meals she served were the meals she'd learned to make when working at Reder's Camp, twenty years earlier.

Almost all the boarders were loggers and worked eight-hour shifts, thanks to the IWW. Aino worked sixteen hours, albeit at her own pace and without a boss. Some days there was time to do personal shopping, visit Kyllikki, or even get a brief nap. She was thankful that at her poikataloja, the boarders took care of their own rooms and laundry.

Aksel asked Aino to a dance at Suomi Hall a couple of weeks after he had moved in. He could still dance so well that Aino felt both the joy and the envy of the other women watching them. He occasionally took her to the Liberty Theater to see moving pictures. Kyllikki and Matti often went as well and Aino and Kyllikki, over coffee at Matti and Kyllikki's house, would discuss—even marvel at—the risqué clothing and makeup of the actresses.

Then, one Sunday in April, Kyllikki was wearing lipstick.

"Oh, my God," Aino said. "Where did you get that?"

"At Woolworths. You know they've had it for several years now." Kyllikki grinned, pursed her lips, and then licked them slowly.

"What does Matti think about it?"

"Matti doesn't mind. I think he even likes it, but he wouldn't say."
Then she put her face right up close to Aino's. "See anything else?"

Aino pulled back abruptly. "Your cheeks are rouged."

Kyllikki grinned again. "You wear this and men will see you clear
across the dance floor and the women who don't have it will be feeling
like farmhands." She walked back to the stove. She looked mischie-
vously at Aino. "You want to try some?"

Kyllikki made up Aino the first time, talking her through the process,
just as the salesgirl at Woolworths had done. When Aino looked in
the mirror with Kyllikki smiling over her shoulder, she felt she'd done
something illicit. The face looking back was, of course, hers but certainly more dramatic—highlighted. She moved her facial muscles and
lips. She looked younger.

"Do you think this makes my lips too obvious?" she asked.

Kyllikki turned her around and gave the question serious consideration. "I don't think so, but if you do, just go to Woolworths and get a
color that fits you better."

Aino turned and looked in the mirror again. She grinned and gaily
opened her fingers in a "Voilà!" gesture. You just go to Woolworths. As
easy as that.

Not entirely. Deciding among five different colors took consultation
with the Woolworths salesgirl and considerable time. And it wasn't
cheap. Still, she put on lipstick for the Saturday dance, as well as a light
dusting of powder the girl also sold her and just the slightest brush of
rouge. When Aksel knocked on her door, she panicked. He'd think she
was a whore. He'd think she looked like a clown. She took a deep breath
and opened the door.

Aksel's first reaction was to ever so slightly pull his head back and
blink several times. Then he smiled—and then came that look.

He walked her home that night after the dance and they kissed
for the first time.

14

The next day, Aino was making riisipuuro for Sunday supper when Kathleen Tierney walked into the kitchen. It had been thirteen years since she'd stayed with Kathleen while organizing in Centralia. She was momentarily flustered.

She quickly made coffee and finished making the rice porridge, the first step in making riisipuuro, while they caught up. Then Kathleen came to the real reason for the visit.

Ever since the Centralia Massacre, her brother Jack Kerwin had been in prison in Walla Walla, unjustly accused and sentenced with six others.

Kathleen's chin started to tremble. "It's so unfair!" Her eyes filled with tears. Aino reached across the table and touched her hand. "Aino, there's going to be a big May Day rally in Olympia, International Workers' Day."

"For those killed in the Haymarket Massacre. It is also Vapu, Finnish May Day."

"No one even remembers the Haymarket Massacre," Kathleen said. "What about the Centralia Massacre? What about my brother and the other Wobblies? They didn't do it, Aino."

"There's plenty wrong in the world," Aino said.

"Do you remember Elmer Smith?" Kathleen asked.

"Sure. The Centralia local's lawyer."

"He's heading up a campaign to get the sentences overturned."

Aino waited.

"Will you speak for their cause in Olympia? We've all heard you speak. You're good!"

Aino shook her head gently. She'd promised Eleanor no more jail, ever. If ever there was a risk of jail, it was defending accused traitors. "I can't," she said.

"Who then? I don't know anyone else!"

As Aino put the riisipuuro into the oven of the electric stove, she could feel Kathleen silently begging her. She knew prison. She knew ax handles.

Kathleen pressed harder. She outlined her plan to apply for a permit for herself to make a speech about the Bill of Rights. At the last minute, she would get sick and Aino would step in.

"Please, Aino," Kathleen said. "Please."

Aino thought about how Eleanor would see it. She remembered Maíjaliisa once telling her when summoned for what was sure to be a very difficult birth: "Sometimes God just puts things on your plate that you have to eat."

The first thing she did was seek support from the Finnish Brotherhood, the social entity behind Suomi Hall. Representing Suomi Hall would give her more clout than just going up there alone. It was, after all, Vapu and there were lots of Finns in Olympia. It would also make it clear that she was no longer representing the IWW.

Aino went to the board, telling the officers that the speech would not only be about the seven men unjustly imprisoned by the state of Washington for the deaths in Centralia, but also show solidarity with all class-war prisoners serving time for crimes they did not commit, such as the fourteen IWW leaders in Chicago still serving twenty-year terms for violating the Espionage Act.

When she finished her pitch, the officers were silent. Finally, Alvar Kari said, "Aino, all these people were convicted in courts of law."

She maintained control. "In the case of the Centralia men, there was no evidence. In the case of the Chicago men, the law they were convicted of violating is both unjust and unconstitutional."

"How is it unconstitutional if it was passed by Congress?"

She replied, as levelly as she could, "Because it violates the Bill of Rights. How is forty years in prison on flimsy evidence not cruel and unusual punishment? How can you say we live in a free country when it is illegal, illegal to"—she put her fingers up to show quotation marks—"'honor, print, write, or publish any disloyal, profane, scurrilous, or abusive language about the armed forces, the flag, the Constitution, or democracy'?" She brought down her hands. "How does that not violate the freedom of speech?"

No one answered.

"If they were serious about this law being for everyone and not just aimed at the IWW," Aino said, "they need to arrest every soldier and sailor for any"—again she used her fingers as quote marks—"profane, scurrilous, or abusive language about the army and navy."

That got a laugh, especially from the veterans in the group.

Alvar Kari quieted them and said, "Aino, we need to be good Americans."

"Good Americans defend their constitutional rights!"

"We don't want any trouble," Kari said.

"Trouble is here, now. These people are in jail. They have families. Forty years. We need to stop it."

A motion was made to take her proposal under consideration.

When she showed up three days later with her finished column for *Toveritar*, Alvar Kari told her the Finnish Brotherhood couldn't be seen supporting people convicted of being disloyal to the United States.

Small towns have no secrets. Some members of the Finnish Brotherhood were also members of the American Legion and the Veterans of Foreign Wars. Even Aksel belonged to the American Legion. There, he could talk with men who understood war—even if they never talked about it directly or just told funny stories about their time overseas—and he could also drink without fear of being harassed by the cops. Many of the police and city officials also belonged to the Legion for the same reasons.

On Saturday night, a week before May Day, Aksel, Yrjö, and Heppu were having a quiet drink in what was known as the "back room" but on Saturdays was really the busiest room in Legion Hall.

Kullervo and Jens had gone to Neawanna for the weekend, primarily to see if any Portland girls were there. Fred Dahlquist, the current post commander, owned the Chevrolet dealership, was a friend of the mayor, and was a man who took civic duty and citizenship seriously. After all, he would often say, he fought for democracy and a lot of men died for it. Those deaths would be in vain if the living didn't fulfill their duty to the republic. As far as Aksel was concerned, it was a fine sentiment, but he could see no way to construe that Germany and Austria-Hungary threatened American democracy. He fought the Germans because he was heartbroken and hadn't much cared if he died over there. Joining the army also helped solve a nagging problem resulting from jumping ship in San Francisco. Two years after joining, he became a citizen.

Dahlquist asked if he could sit with them. They pulled up a chair, all without speaking. Fred took no offense. He knew lots of Finns. He also knew the average Finnish man's disdain for small talk. "You know Aino Kaukonen, don't you, boys?" He included all of them in his words, but he was looking at Aksel.

"Yes," Aksel said.

"I'm not trying to put my nose into anything here, but, well, I got wind of something."

The Bachelor Boys just looked at him, no expression on their faces.

"I happen to know she's going to try and stir up trouble in Olympia about those Wobblies thrown into jail for murdering legionnaires up in Centralia."

"How do you know this?" Aksel asked.

"I heard she went to the Finnish Brotherhood to try and get support for a speech about those murderers. I have a good friend on the board."

The Bachelor Boys regarded him without affect.

"I've also got a friend in Post Three, up in Olympia," Dahlquist continued. "Served with him in France, good friend. So I called him, and he called back saying there's a permit application for some woman named Tierney to make a speech about the Bill of Rights. It's a cover." He said it as if he'd just exposed a spy network.

"Can't she say what she wants?" Jens asked.

"Well, of course. She's got a right to talk about whatever, but people talk about all sorts of things."

The Bachelor Boys said nothing.

"There's a limit. Don't you agree?"

The Bachelor Boys neither agreed nor disagreed.

"While we were over there fighting and dying, those Wobblies were back here sabotaging the whole war effort. Cowards and traitors. That's what I say."

"You've got a right to say what you want," Jens said.

There was now an awkward silence. "Can I buy you boys a drink?" Dahlquist asked.

The boys gulped down their drinks and held their empty glasses out to him.

"You boys know her," he said after buying the round. "I just think, you know, there's going to be ... Now, I know you boys are all veterans, but my friend, well, he told me"—he took a drink—"there's going to be a lot of legionnaires and folks who support them up in Olympia and if she tries to spoil Americanization Day, well, they're not going to like it."

"The Finns will be celebrating Vapu," Aksel said. "It's sort of end of winter and Labor Day combined."

"Sure, sure. That's the point, isn't it? We call it Americanization Day because it's how all of us, labor, owners, immigrants, natives, hell even Catholics, we're all Americans."

"Yes. We are," Aksel said.

Aksel could also see Dahlquist was trying to do what he thought was right. "So you want me to ask Aino to back off," he said.

"Well, Aksel, we wouldn't want it to be as direct as that. Heaven knows," he chuckled, "the American Legion isn't exactly against the Bill of Rights."

"No. We aren't."

"I mean it's just working people celebrating, together. Sure it's a socialist holiday, too. I know that. But hell, no one in Astoria's going to have a problem with that. Half of Suomi Hall are socialists, good hard-working people, good citizens."

"Fred, I've known her for years. Asking her to back off is like asking a she-bear to back off from her cubs."

"Yeah, I know her reputation. Active back in the free-speech fights. A Wobbly herself, right?" Dahlquist leaned across the table. "Aksel, you and I, we fought. They stayed home and did everything they could to harm the war effort. They deserve prison."

"I think they just wanted higher wages and didn't give a shit one way or the other about the war."

"Did we refuse to fight because we weren't paid enough?"

"Hard to do when you're drafted," Heppu said.

That stopped Dahlquist for a second. "Will you help out?" he pleaded. "My friend, he's the post commander. He just doesn't want any trouble."

"I tell you it won't do any good."

"Aksel, a lot of our boys will have had a couple of drinks." The jocular tone was gone. "You know what happened back in nineteen between the legion boys and the Wobblies up in Centralia. We don't want a repeat of that, do we?"

Breathing hard from the uphill climb to the poikataloja, Aino saw the electric light from her room spilling a glow down the steep hillside toward the river. Had she left it on? Opening the door, she saw Aksel sitting at the table.

"What are you doing here?" she asked.

"Pretty good speech," he said, pointing to the handwritten pages on the table. "It's a long way from platitudes about the Bill of Rights. It's going to enrage a whole lot of people."

"As if *our* enragement at totally unfair imprisonment counts for nothing?"

"I didn't say that." He put the speech back down, neatly aligning the pages. "Aino, please sit down. I've been talking to Dahlquist."

"Capitalist toady."

"Aino, this is too serious for name-calling. Please," he said, but the "please" had a ring of command to it. "Sit down."

She sat down.

"Dahlquist has a friend in the Olympia Legion post," Aksel said. "The guy's worried."

"I hope so. He needs to be."

Ignoring the statement, Aksel said, "The American Legion is calling May first Americanization Day."

Aino shook her head, puzzled.

"Americanization Day," Aksel repeated. "On the surface, it means we're all coming from the old country and are now here, Americans all of us." He paused. "Underneath, it means if people don't look like Americans and *behave* like Americans, they shouldn't *be* Americans."

"I don't understand."

"Aino. The Espionage Act you are so against is still on the books. You *can* get arrested for being un-American. This could land you in jail."

"I'll have a permit. I won't go to jail."

He still looked at her. "Can't you just see people instead of sides?"

"I see people just fine. Jack Kerwin is my friend's brother. I see *people* unjustly thrown in jail. It's capitalists and you legionnaires that don't see people."

"Ah. Now we're 'you legionnaires.' That's just what I'm talking about."

"People choose sides and live with the consequences."

"We didn't choose a side. We drink there and tell stories."

The two of them sat silently.

Aksel sighed and began talking, she felt, as if to a child. "There will be drinking. A lot of men will be armed. You are going to tell inebriated armed men that people who they consider to be traitors to their country, people who they consider to be murderers, have been put in jail unjustly. What you are really saying is that those armed men, most of whom fought a war that they believed was to make a better, more just world, a world that is safe for democracy, a world their friends died for, were on the wrong *side*." He spit out the last word. "You're going to light a fire you can't control."

"I can't believe this! The American Legion is against me. The VFW is against me. The good citizens of Astoria are against me. I come home to see you sitting smug and cozy in my room and all you're doing here is to tell me you're on their side."

Aksel was silent, collecting his thoughts. Now he spoke very carefully. "My own brother died because he chose sides. When his side came to power in Finland, they imprisoned, starved, and executed thousands of people without trial. When the other side took back the power, they did the same thing." Aksel stood. "I'm choosing you, not because you're on one side or the other. I'm tired of watching you expose yourself and the people you love to danger."

Very coolly she said, "You go to hell."

Aksel was on her, pulling her arms, forcing her to face him.

"You listen to me," he said. "You're going to get someone killed and it could be you."

She wriggled free, hissing at him.

"Aino, I don't want you to get hurt." Aksel was pleading, something she'd never seen him do. "Don't go."

"Don't treat me like a child."

"I'm treating you like a man trying to protect his woman." He left, slamming the door.

Aino sat down and looked at the pattern in the tablecloth for a long time. His woman.

The next morning, she saw that Aksel's door was open. His sheets were neatly stacked on the folded mattress; his clothes were gone. She had never seen an emptier room.

15

Aino went to see Kyllikki to talk out the fight.

"But you're still going to do it," Kyllikki said.

"Yoh," Aino answered.

Kyllikki nodded. "OK," she said. "What are you going to wear?" That was the second agenda.

"Can I borrow your green dress?"

"It's short."

"So?"

"You need to shave your legs."

"Why?" Aino asked.

"It looks better."

As she watched Kyllikki fill her coffee cup, she was struck by how wonderful it was just to sit with a sister and talk; her body felt happy, as when she was pregnant with Eleanor. Her brothers talked to get things done or to pass on information. She, Kyllikki, Alma—and even Rauha— talked because it was part of who they were. Woman talk could be banal, mean, and vicious, but it could also be like this talk now with Kyllikki, as if nature wanted her to do this, to bind the tribe. Here, in talk over coffee, the roots of family, not the visible leaves and branches, got tended to.

Tending to the details of the poikataloja had changed her. Organizing was still important and she would never quit, but her attitude had changed. It wasn't more or less important than tending to the roots over coffee.

Men got the hard, physical things done—logging, building dams and roads, moving things that looked impossible to move. She'd always felt vaguely inferior because nature hadn't designed her to do those things. But after these months of doing "unimportant work," she'd come to realize that nature designed her for subtler but equally important things—that decisions about finding a new wife for a lonely brother, freeing up young girls for love, bringing together families and neighbors were as important as the things men did. Too many people—men and women both—didn't see it or even count it. She looked at Kyllikki, who was pouring the coffee. Here was solidarity as fine as any she hoped for with the One Big Union.

Aino went home and thought about it for a few days. Then she shaved her legs and bought a bra that showed off her breasts. She took the train to Olympia two days later, on April 30, 1926. She'd arranged to stay with Kathleen Tierney's sister. That night, she went to Sylvester Park, which was in the center of town next to the capitol building, to get the feel of the bandstand.

Looking out over the park in the darkness, the cold drizzle on her face, she imagined the crowd and went through the carefully prepared speech, whispering it, making sure that her English was flawless even if her accent wasn't.

On May Day morning, she washed her hair and carefully put it up. All the younger women were bobbing their hair. She didn't feel like doing it, despite all the talk about emancipation and ease. She liked her hair long. She carefully ironed Kyllikki's dress and attached the brooch Jouka gave her when she had Eleanor. She shined her new shoes. She'd bought them wholesale at the Saaris' store. The two-inch heels made her look taller and her legs longer—important now that legs were showing so much.

Kathleen was scheduled to go on at two in the afternoon, so Aino would have half an hour before she had to yield the bandstand to the Sons of Norway dance competition. She noticed nearly as many women present as men—so different from the old picnics at Tapiola. Ilmari had once said, "Build them houses with feather beds and the women will come." Companies still had logging camps with bachelor bunkhouses, but the tiny shacks by the railroad tracks had curtains in the windows and there were plenty of feather beds in the cities and towns. Lots of Finns were present. She couldn't tell whether they were reds or whites. They were all drinking sima, a lightly fermented and just slightly alcoholic drink made from brown sugar, lemons, and yeast. There was a prayer by a local minister followed by a speech by the mayor, all about Americanization. Then there was a local politician talking about the contributions of American labor and the Finnish and Scandinavian communities.

While listening to the speeches, Aino became increasingly aware of men wearing VFW and American Legion overseas caps starting to assemble in front of the bandstand. Her butterflies grew. The speech before hers, also about Americanization, delivered by the local commander of American Legion Post 3, was met with loud applause and some cheers. Several legionnaires standing by her gave her a look. She felt a tingle of fear, a memory of wheel spokes, billy clubs, boots, and ax handles.

An official came onstage and announced that Kathleen Tierney couldn't make it and Aino Kaukonen, a veteran of the free-speech fights before the war, was going to say a few words on the Bill of Rights. Aino winced at the reference to free-speech fights. The announcer had intended to set her up as a Wobbly.

She straightened her dress, patted her hair, reset her hat for the tenth time, took off her glasses, and mounted the stairs.

"Go back to Russia, you red bitch," someone shouted.

"Yeah. Go back where your Bolshevik buddies are creating the workers' paradise."

She had heard worse. She glanced around for the cops. She saw six of them, in pairs, nightsticks at their belts. It wasn't anything like the free-speech fights with dozens of cops and scores of recently deputized citizens encircling the crowds. Still, the mayor had planned for trouble.

She drew herself up straight. She began with the 112 Wobblies imprisoned under the Espionage Act. That number had been 113, but Big Bill Haywood had escaped to Russia.

She continued, "The jury deliberated fifty-five minutes." She let
the shortness sink in. "Judge Landis gave fifteen of the men twenty
years in Fort Leavenworth prison; another thirty-three, ten years; the
rest up to five years."

"They should be hung for treason," someone shouted. "Jail's too
good for 'em."

Her first instinct was to engage the heckler in debate, but then she
kept to the prepared speech and launched into the specific case of the
seven Wobblies unjustly imprisoned in Washington.

A legionnaire started singing "God Bless America." Others joined
him, drowning out her words. People who'd been picnicking were joining the crowd. The policemen, their nightsticks at the ready, looked
around nervously.

"Please, please." She raised her hands for quiet. "I have a right to
speak."

The singing grew in volume. Kathleen promised there would be
lots of support, but any supporters were by far outnumbered.

Someone threw a chicken bone. She ducked. She stood up again,
straight and tall—and alone.

"Please," she said again, as loud as she could. "Let me speak." The
singing swelled along with laughter. She was providing entertainment.
The crowd pushed against the bandstand. It would be only minutes
before someone leaped onto the stage.

She saw people at the edge of the crowd looking toward the street.
A big deep-burgundy, four-door 1923 Oldsmobile Sports Touring car
with black trim, solid burgundy wheels, and black leather seats swerved
off the street onto the grass of the park. Suddenly, the crowd grew
silent as the Bachelor Boys, all in their uniforms, stepped out of the car.
People knew a big expensive car when they saw one, and they knew
what kind of men drove such a car, especially if there were five of them
in it at the same time.

Aino watched Aksel, Kullervo, Jens Lerback, and Heppu Reinikka
wearing their American Legion caps and Yrjö Rautio wearing his VFW
cap walk calmly onto the bandstand to stand in a line to her right.

Aksel stepped forward slightly. "Fellow citizens, fellow veterans," he began. His English was now very good though still lightly accented. "I'm not a speech maker. I only ask you two questions. For what did we fight and for what did many die, if not the right to speak freely?" He paused. "Are men who faced German fire really afraid of words?"

He paused amid a murmur of agreement.

"Let this woman speak. She has fought, more than most, for that right. Not just for herself, but for all of us."

He turned to the Bachelor Boys, gave a nod of his head toward the steps, and the five men calmly left the bandstand. Aksel didn't even look at Aino. The five nonchalantly settled on the fenders and running boards of the big Oldsmobile to listen. The crowd stopped looking at them and turned to Aino.

Aino took a deep breath, squared her shoulders, and finished her speech. At the end, there was loud applause from some, but the majority were silent.

She looked for Aksel, but the big Oldsmobile and the Bachelor Boys were already out on the street and pulling away.

When Aino got back to Astoria late the next afternoon, she found a small box and a note on the kitchen table. The note read, "For Miss Sisu." Inside the box lay a beautiful, dainty lace handkerchief. She couldn't imagine anyplace in town that would sell such a thing. Aksel must have bought it when he was in France and kept it all this time.

16

Aksel pitched a lean-to by the river on a narrow rocky beach close to Tongue Point. The beach was sheltered from view by salal and salmonberries growing under alders that had sprung up after the old-growth trees had been cut down in the 1880s. He joined a small tent city of itinerant loggers, hoboes, sailors—merchant and navy, American and otherwise—who'd jumped ship or whose contracts had expired and who chose not to sign on again. Although June gloom had set in, the occasional rain was light. Astorians called the month Juneuary. The ground above high tide was slippery with mud or river slime only for a day or two after a real rain, but otherwise solid, if not dry. Bluebacks were running and a short walk took a man into good deer hunting. So, mingled with the smell of cigarettes, bootleg whiskey, and alder smoke came the good rich smell of venison on a spit or salmon pressed to cedar boards and arranged to roast in a circle around the fire. An old rowboat had been beached there and Aksel used it more than most.

Matti had moved Aksel to running the diesel yarder, a physically easier job. This left him with enough energy to fish at night and most of the day on Sundays. Whenever he hooked into a particularly nice salmon or sturgeon, he cleaned and butchered it into steaks and dropped some off for Matti and Kyllikki's family as well as his friends still at the poikataloja. On occasion, he left a nice cut in Aino's sink but only when she wasn't around.

* * *

One Sunday in July, Kyllikki invited Aksel to stay for her special fish-head stew after he dropped off a beautiful fourteen-pound summer-run steelhead.

"Where'd you get the fish?" she asked casually. His Sunday clothes smelled like wood smoke.

"Up by Tongue Point, just off the railroad trestle."

"Long way upriver for a rowboat," she said easily.

Aksel hesitated and then said, "Oh, you know fishermen. We'll go anywhere and tell no one."

She knew something was amiss.

That evening, she put her young ones to bed and told Matti and the older children that she was going to visit Aino-täti for some just-woman time and she walked to the poikataloja. The gloom of the morning and afternoon had been driven off and the river stood clear in the late summer evening all the way to Cape Disappointment at the north side of its mouth. The air smelled of tide flats and woodstoves. The sun seemed to hang suspended above the river's mouth over the unseen ocean as if reluctant to set, as if not wanting to end one of the year's longest days.

She found Aino cleaning up after supper.

"What was for dinner?" Kyllikki asked.

"The usual stew."

"We had a nice steelhead stew at home tonight."

Oh." Aino was now on the alert.

"Yes. Aksel brought us a nice fourteen pounder."

"Nice of him."

"I thought so. I gave him the eyes."

"Nice of you."

Aino returned to scrubbing her pots. Kyllikki went over to the stove, picked up the two-gallon blue-and-white-speckled coffeepot to ascertain its contents, got two cups, filled them, and set them on the end of one of the long dining tables. "You going to join me?" she asked Aino.

"Looks like it," Aino said. She dried her hands and sat down.

Kyllikki looked at her and saw suffering. "Aino, what happened?" she asked. "Aksel isn't living here, is he?"

"Does Matti know?"

"Not yet."

"Did Aksel tell you . . . anything?"

"No. I smelled tide flats and alder smoke on his Sunday clothes this evening. Where is he?"

"I don't know," Aino said miserably.

Aino told Kyllikki the whole story, including the fight, the May Day speech, and the delicate handkerchief from France.

"I've said it before," Kyllikki said. "You're the smartest fool I know."

"I am." Aino nodded her head in agreement. After a moment she said, "Can you make a guess where he is?"

"From the smell, I'd say he's living rough somewhere along the river. He said he got the steelhead off the trestle by Tongue Point, so I guess somewhere around Alderbrook."

"Do you think he'll come back?"

"If you don't act, he won't. I guarantee it. To him it'll feel like crawling. And it would be. Now, it's your turn to go to him."

"I don't crawl."

Kyllikki exploded from her seat, slapping her hand on the table. She had never been so angry with her beautiful, proud sister-in-law. "You goddamn stubborn Koski."

Aino started to speak.

"You shut up and listen."

Aino shut up.

Kyllikki was surprised at the fury she felt, and it came boiling out in words. "You broke that man's heart when you married Jouka. Then you broke Jouka. Then Aksel had his heart broken again when he lost Lempi and the baby. And you . . . you . . ." Words failed her.

She sat down and leaned across the table. "Aino, this is it. That man needs his heart back and you, by God, you will go to him with your heart in your hands and you will offer it to him and if you don't, you will live with a stone in your chest for the rest of your miserable proud life." Kyllikki's own heart pounded. She saw she'd actually frightened Aino. Good! Good, good, good!

Aino opened her mouth and closed it. Her face had gone pale. It was the face of someone frightened to her core that she might have lost everything.

Kyllikki rose and walked behind Aino. Putting her hands on Aino's shoulders, leaning her head close beside Aino's, she felt her magnificent black hair against her own soft blond. She nuzzled her cheek against Aino's head just above her ear and said softly, "Go find him. I'll finish up here."

Aino took her wool shawl and head scarf to ward off the chill air coming off the river. She also took a kerosene lantern. She began walking upriver, starting at Fourteenth Street where the ferry docked. Soon, she came to the end of the plank streets built up on pilings. She reached the railroad tracks and continued on them, moving eastward, looking for shanties or tents. When she spotted a little bunch of them, she would find men sitting by fires, smoking, talking in the lingering twilight. The twilight shifted north, outlining the Washington hills as the hidden sun moved around the pole. By midnight, only the faintest glow in the north showed beneath a clear night sky. Standing on a log railroad trestle she saw the embers of dying campfires across the tide flats, glowing on a beach just downstream from where Tongue Point joined the river's south shore. After an hour of backtracking she found a way to reach solid ground. She then walked back upstream to where she'd seen the glow of the dying fires.

Her wet shoes and stockings smelled of what the river left behind as it ebbed. She picked her way between embers and dark tents. She found two men drinking from a single bottle. They looked at her in surprise.

"I'm looking for Aksel Långström," she said.

"Next to the water"—on of them pointed—"over there."

She continued, leaving the faint red light of the dying fire behind, moving again into darkness, only a sphere of lantern light moving along with her, casting quavering shadows. Up ahead, she saw the faint glow of a cigarette. Her pulse quickened. She moved toward it, hope rising. She saw the outline of a tarp lean-to and the figure of a man leaning back against what looked like an upturned rowboat. The man turned to look at her.

The lantern lit Aksel's face so that it seemed to glow in contrast with the dark tarp behind it and the night all around. She stood still, looking at that face, for the first time really seeing it. All these years. All these wasted years. And now, this beautiful strong human face she truly saw for the first time.

"Aino?" Aksel asked.

Aino held the lantern to her face. She felt the tears streaming down her cheeks as he rose to his feet. She put the lantern on the ground and ran to him, squeezing him against her, and all she could do was say his name over and over again and, "I'm sorry. I'm so sorry," kissing that face everywhere until he stopped her by putting his hands on her head and holding her still and kissing her long and slow and so tender.

17

Aksel moved back to his room at the poikataloja. That summer was the best summer for years. The northwest wind blew steadily and the sky was clear. There were even a few days when the temperature soared to the mideighties. Lumber prices were also soaring. Matti had his crews on overtime, something new in an industry that used to pay by the day. Aksel and the Bachelor Boys were making money. Matti was making a lot of money. He invested it in the stock market and timber. The sawmills and plywood mills all along the river ran shifts into the night; darkness was no longer even the slightest impediment to production, because of electric lights. The salmon run was strong, although not as strong now as a quarter of a century earlier, but the catch was up because the gill net boats were now powered by internal combustion engines instead of sails. The nets cost less, so they were longer and heavier but could now be handled, along with all the fish in them, by the newly powered boats. The canneries hummed with the sound of conveyor belts and hundreds of women cutting the fish, packing the pieces into cans, and chattering as they worked at the long cutting tables.

Aksel came home exhausted but content. Every morning he arrived at work and the smell of the forest made the air sweet. The days were filled with problems of rigging and yarding and the contentment of working with a crew that was savvy and strong and could develop wild satires the equal of any comedian's on the vaudeville circuit.

And he could come home to Aino. He remembered watching her with longing as she worked in the dining hall of Reder's Camp. Now, as he watched her working, his only longing was to get her alone, just the two of them. And that longing was fulfilled every night but never by sex. They would talk—sometimes in his room, sometimes in her basement apartment—and occasionally touch or kiss, but that was where it stopped.

Aino, despite an occasional crack about free love and the idiocy of marriage in earlier days, deep down never really believed what she was saying. Her single indiscretion with Joe Hillström had left her feeling flat and used, not only costing her job but also bringing pain to Jouka and the child she loved. She still thought society was cruel and petty; what she had done wasn't morally wrong. It was, however, psychologically and emotionally wrong—at least for her.

Aksel, who in his younger days had been with every whore at the Lucky Logger and prostitutes up and down the coast all the way to Nordland, learned the sweetness of love with Lempi. He wanted that sweetness again with Aino. He wondered when he should ask her to marry him and she wondered when he would ask.

On Saturday nights, they danced at Suomi Hall. Now dances like the Charleston and the Black Bottom mixed in with the schottisches, hambos, and polkas. Then, one Saturday in September brought a new band from Portland, Big John and the Jazz Syncopators. John was reputed to be one of the hottest jazz trumpeters in the Northwest—and people said he was a Finn, which made him even more intriguing. When the musicians walked out from behind the curtains to take up their positions at the bottom of the stage, Aino gasped and covered her mouth with her hands. Aksel broke into a broad grin. Taking Aino by the hand, he pulled her willing or not—and about that she wasn't sure—but suddenly here she was, holding Aksel's left hand while Aksel shook Jouka's hand with his right.

She looked into Jouka's eyes and was flooded with memories of dances at the Knappton net shed. There was no bitterness in his eyes. He seemed genuinely glad to see them both.

"Hello, Aino," he said in English. "How are you? How's Eleanor?"

"I'm fine." She squeezed Aksel's hand. "We're fine," she went on in Finnish. "She's good, too. I see her most weekends. She's with Ilmari and Alma right now."

Jouka nodded with a wistful smile. He turned to Aksel, staying in Finnish. "You fishing yet?"

Aksel shook his head no. "Not yet. Had the money. Lost it."

"How?"

"Long story. Better told elsewhere."

Jouka nodded knowingly.

"Working for Matti," Aksel said.

"How is he?"

"Same as ever. Logging. Making good money."

"Times are good," Jouka said. He began to touch the valves on the trumpet, impatient to start. It was then Aino noticed that his left hand was crushed and missing three fingers. She gasped.

Jouka looked at her and then at his arm, which he raised, as if it no longer belonged to him. "Yeah, hurt it on a show down by Roseburg. Stumbled. Reached out to catch myself. Caught a moving cable drum instead. Wrapped the hand right up with the cable." He laughed—the good sport. She winced inwardly with pain.

Jouka raised the trumpet in his right hand. "Hey—everything for the best, right? You only need three fingers for this thing."

Nobody spoke. "Well, gotta go. We owe the brotherhood four hours."

She reached out suddenly and kissed him on the cheek. He smiled, moved by the gesture. She smelled the whiskey on his breath.

Even though Aksel and Aino were a known couple, men constantly asked Aino for a dance—and, having grown to manhood in a time and place where women were scarce, Aksel didn't mind. Now that women were no longer scarce—at least in the cities and towns—he danced with other women as well and the women, both married and single, were delighted.

They talked with Jouka again during the break. At the last dance he called out, "And now, a special request. From me." He turned to the band, counted a three-four cadence, and played "Lördagsvalsen," his trumpet sweet and clear, filled with joy, sadness, and nostalgia such as only a superb musician could evoke. For most of the people in the room it was a beautiful old-country waltz played on jazz band instruments. For Jouka, it was a blessing given—and for Aino and Aksel, a blessing received.

They were mostly quiet walking back to the poikataloja, Aksel holding Aino in close to him, both not wanting to spoil the mood set by Jouka's blessing. The air was autumn crisp. Stars shone brilliantly, the waning moon having set an hour earlier. The Milky Way looked as though a child had splashed light right across the center of the sky. Aksel looked for Arcturus, feeling that he wanted to share his happiness with his star, but Arcturus had set. He turned to find the Big Dipper, found it just about due north, just above the Washington-side hills, and he quickly traced the pointers to find Polaris. Finding it, he turned his gaze back to the electric streetlights, showing yellow puddles that could never rival the sky.

They ended up lying together on top of Aino's bed, both clothed, looking at the ceiling. Aksel smoked while he talked until he stubbed it out on a saucer on the floor beside him. The mood had been set for intimacy and sharing.

"Do you think Jouka will be OK?" Aino asked.

"He's still drinking."

"I know. Sometimes I feel it's my fault."

"Everyone knows he drank before you met him."

"Yes. But . . . him being . . . You know, out there on his own."

"Don't torture yourself. We all have regrets."

"What are yours?" Aino asked. She turned her head to Aksel just as he turned his head to her. This made them both smile with a quiet joy. "You go first," Aksel said.

They started small. She would share one and then he'd share one. She felt aglow with the honesty, the openness. Here was a man with whom she could live her life out. She hesitated when she got to Joe Hillström but plunged in. She turned again to see his reaction. He was looking up at the ceiling.

"You don't mind?"

"It's no secret, Aino," he said with a sad smile.

"I guess not," she mumbled.

"It's OK. Hell, I screwed every whore in the Lucky Logger, more than once. A lot more."

"Did you ever cheat on Lempi?"

"Do you wish I had?"

"In a way," she sighed. "Well?"

"I didn't."

That was the answer she wanted to hear but didn't want to hear. Her guilt was hers alone.

"What was it about him?" Aksel asked. "There were rumors of you two at the Nordland free-speech fight as well."

She had to gather her thoughts.

"He was just like Voitto: clever, committed to the cause, alive." She gave a short chortle. "Good-looking."

"That was a hard time. Back in the old country."

"It was."

"You were in Voitto's cell with my brother, Gunnar."

"I was."

"Did he die in the raid?" Aksel asked.

"Gunnar?"

"Voitto. I know Gunnar's story." He swallowed a little nervously. "I know it very well."

Now the silence was a waiting silence, a pregnant silence.

"I think I killed Voitto," Aino said in a whisper.

Aksel squeezed her hand, brought it up to his mouth and kissed it, then put it back and looked her in the eyes. "How? How could you have done that?"

"I was arrested right after the raid."

"I know. Matti told me."

"Did he tell you they tortured me?"

"It was only implied."

She felt herself starting to tremble. She couldn't stop it. She felt his grip firm on her hand. The tears were building, like a thousand logs against a splash dam about to be exploded with dynamite.

She told him every detail.

Aksel crushed her in his arms, as if protecting her. The sobbing was beyond her control. "I told them the name of the man hiding Voitto. They found him. Oh, God, Aksel. What they must've done to him." He was smothering her face with kisses, wiping her tears gently, and then kissing her again.

The sobbing stopped. She felt him roll off her and lie back beside her again. They were quiet for a long time.

Then he said very softly. "I killed my brother, Gunnar."

Now she felt him heave slightly. Then she felt a dark premonition, something lurking in the shadows of her intuition, and she didn't want it to come to light

"I couldn't stand the thought that Finnish people, our own aunt, could be killed," Aksel said. "I found the dynamite. I . . . I was fourteen. I hit him with a rock. I tied him up and tried to send a note to the Finnish workers." He looked at her in anguish. "Oh, Aino. I'm so sorry. I had no idea what would happen. To my brother. To you."

She gasped as her dark premonition came to light. She moved away from him. He looked at her, his eyes imploring her for something—some forgiveness, some understanding.

The anger came like the rapids of her name. It caught her like a small twig and she went whirling down the rocks into a chasm. She had loved Aksel. Right up until this moment when he revealed he was the one man she swore she could never forgive.

He stood. "Aino, I'm so sorry."

She was shaking her head, murmuring, "No" over and over.

"Aino—"

"Go away. I, I've wanted to kill you for twenty years. I wanted to torture you the way they tortured me. I wanted you to feel all the pain of hell. And now . . . It's you!" She started for the door and then realized she was in her own room. "I've got to think. You've got to go. Just go." She grabbed his coat and hat and stuffed them against his chest. "Get out." She felt hysteria rising. She fought it, choking off the rising scream. "Get out before I go crazy."

She saw Aksel start to say something but stop. She opened the door and then stood next to it with her face to the wall. She heard him walking toward her. "Go," she whispered through clenched teeth, her forehead on the wall, tears streaming down her face. She felt his hand on her shoulder and then he was gone.

18

Aksel tried several times to talk with Aino. She had politely but firmly said she needed space to think.

Throughout the summer he'd seen ads in the *Oregonian* for carpenters unafraid of heights. Seattle City Light was building a dam. It was going to be the highest dam in the world. He gave Matti several weeks' notice, said a formal goodbye to him and Kyllikki at Sunday dinner, and on Friday, October 22, 1926, after his last day of work, Aksel boarded the train for Portland. There, he took the Union Pacific to Seattle and then north to Mount Vernon, Washington. He caught the Seattle City Light bus that worked its way on gravel roads up the Skagit River to Diablo Canyon, deep in the Cascade mountains.

Aksel reached the sprawling camp of workmen at the base of Diablo Canyon in the evening darkness. The huge project, already in its ninth year, had started with boring a tunnel through the basalt roots of the North Cascades. Then, slowly and steadily, form by form, scaffold by scaffold, concrete pour by concrete pour, the Diablo Canyon Dam rose ever higher toward its planned 389 feet. Seattle City Light planned on having it provide enough power to light the bulk of the rapidly growing city by the early 1930s. For now, power at the construction site came from a small temporary dam on Newhalem Creek, several miles downstream. It lit the mess halls, the workshops, and the work site. The rest of the camp was lit more softly by low-watt electric lightbulbs, the occasional old kerosene lantern, and new Coleman gas lanterns.

Aksel looked north and skyward. He could see the Little Dipper above the dam and just the tip of Boötes rising above the ridge to the east that hid Arcturus. The partially completed dam from this angle just blocked Polaris. He looked up at the east ridge again, reassured knowing that Arcturus would be in the sky within a couple of hours. Some things were still right in heaven. He'd heard that the dam was built upstream from the major salmon spawning sites. If it wasn't, no salmon would make it past this point. At least it would never happen on the Columbia, he thought. No one could dam a river that big.

Aksel didn't show up for the Christmas holidays and then Aino refused to go to the New Year's dance to welcome in 1927. Kyllikki could stand it no longer. On January 3, the first day the children were back in school, she knocked on Aino's door as she let herself in.

Aino emerged from her bedroom, disheveled, a book in her hand. That wasn't a good sign; she'd normally be up and working by this time.

Kyllikki waited. "Are you out of coffee?"

Aino shook her head. "Sorry. Not thinking clearly."

Kyllikki rustled up some biscuitti while Aino brewed coffee. Then, the preliminaries out of the way, Kyllikki plunged in.

"Why did Aksel leave?"

"We had a fight."

"You kicked him out, didn't you? Why, for God's sake?"

Kyllikki watched Aino's face cloud with grief. She decided to ease up.

"Has he written?"

Aino opened the drawer of the bureau and picked up a stack of letters and postcards.

"Do you answer them?"

She shook her head.

"What is wrong with you?"

Aino couldn't look her in the face. She got up, agitated, walked to the door, then walked back and sat down.

Kyllikki asked her again, gently. "Aino, what's wrong?"

Aino slowly shook her head back and forth. Her eyes were tearing. "I can't tell you," she whispered.

Kyllikki reached across the table and gently touched Aino's hand. "Hey. It's me, Kyllikki. There's nothing I won't understand."

Aino started with Voitto. As she slowly told the story of her involvement with Voitto's organization, the man from Helsinki taking control, the raid, and Aksel's part in its betrayal, Kyllikki found herself holding Aino's hands in hers, giving her all she had in her heart. Then, Aino began to talk about the torture. Kyllikki wanted to let go of her hands and cover her own ears, but she did not. She held Aino's hands firm and opened her heart. Aino was sobbing openly now—for a quarter of a century she had been holding in the horror only to find that the man she loved was the man she'd hated all that time. The sobbing grew to uncontrollable bawling with Kyllikki holding Aino's body close to her own, letting her shake but never letting her go.

When the storm finally passed, Kyllikki looked into Aino's eyes. "You've lived with this alone for a long time. I don't know how you bore it." Then she said, "Aksel's lived with it alone just as long."

There was a soft grunt of understanding.

"Maybe if you two could share the burden . . ." She left that dangling in the air. When there was no response, she turned Aino's face to her and said, "Forgive him. You were both children. Maybe if you forgave him, you could both find peace." Aino remained with her head on the kitchen table, listening but not responding—not wanting to respond. Kyllikki knew how hard it was to forgive. "You need to go up to the Skagit and tell him."

"No," Aino mumbled into her arms. "I can't."

Kyllikki gently moved so she could lift Aino's face from the table. Holding her beneath the chin, forcing Aino to look at her, she gently said, "You've always been a strong woman, Aino. But now, it's time to be a woman of strength."

After a silence, tears still running down her face, Aino said in a small voice, "But he's a white and a capitalist."

"Aino, he's a fisherman."

Aino started to laugh through her tears.

19

ino boarded the train for Portland the next morning after stops at Woolworths and Grimson's Ladies Apparel. She hadn't seen Aksel in nearly three months. Kyllikki moved into Aino's apartment to cook for the bachelors, leaving Suvi to watch the younger children under her grandmother's eye.

When Aino arrived at the dam site, she could only gape. The dam towered over everything. The workshops, machinery, sounds of hammering and sawing, screeching of engines and cables, men shouting, took her back to the early days at Reder's Camp. For a moment she reveled in the sight and sounds of big work being done by big machines. She also had to admit that in spite of being in love with Aksel, she'd forgotten how good it felt to be one of a few women among so many men, who were all trying not to stare at her.

Everyone knew Aksel and simply pointed toward the face of the dam when she asked where to find him. She reached the downstream side and squinted skyward to the dam's horizon. She thought she recognized Aksel high on a scaffold, moving nimbly and seemingly without fear, doing his work. She watched him for some time, wrapping her coat around her in the cold air, her shoes wet from the snow and mud of the construction site. On the way up to the site, she'd caught glimpses of the high granite mountains of the North Cascades, different from the volcanic mountains she could occasionally see from the Columbia River or from the top of a logged-off hill. Now she felt their presence, wild in a roadless wilderness, stretching north, east, and south of her, unseen because they were obscured by low clouds and the steep walls of the deep canyon that would soon be a deep lake.

She began to shiver with the cold and shouted up at him. She might as well have been shouting into a typhoon. She found a huge wooden cable spool, climbed up on it with her suitcase, and sat there, dangling her legs, watching the action, looking up constantly to see if Aksel saw her. At one point, she saw a makeshift elevator move up the face of the dam. It was designed for carrying materials, so it had no handrails. A man sat nonchalantly on the deck, his legs dangling into space, smoking a cigarette. The man got off and walked over to Aksel. The man pointed down at her. Aksel turned and saw her. She felt her heart leap and jumped to her feet, waving her arms, wishing they were wings. He waved back broadly and joyfully. She kept waving, making little jumps up and down on the cable spool. They finally stopped waving and Aksel went back to work. She knew he could not see her until after quitting time.

She settled in again on the big wooden cable spool. Men would stop by, offer her coffee from their thermoses, ask her who the lucky man was. All of them knew Aksel and it made her proud to be Aksel's— what? Girlfriend? Hopeful fiancée? Wet snow fell occasionally, just on the edge of being rain. It didn't stick but merged with the mud. She tried pulling the burgundy felt cloche hat lower around her ears. She'd been assured it was the latest style by the saleslady at Grimson's and that it went perfectly with her dark hair and eyes. Right now, however, she wished she'd worn her old wool scarf that not only covered her head but also kept her neck and face warm. She occasionally stood on the huge spool, stamping her feet. She was cold, but she didn't mind. She couldn't imagine waiting someplace where they couldn't see each other.

It was dark by 4:30. The men worked with gas lanterns and under lights powered by the small temporary dam downstream. At 6:00, she saw Aksel on the open platform of the makeshift elevator. He rode it down hanging on to one of the cables, watching her watching him. When the platform reached bottom she was there to meet him.

Aksel hugged her, whirling her around so her legs swung out behind. Her burgundy flannel velour dress had cost her nearly a week's wages. The latest fashion, its skirt only just covered her knees when she was standing and for a moment she feared it would fly up and expose her thighs above the welts of her stockings or even her new champagne-colored silk teddies. Then, she didn't care. She had her arms around his neck and she never would let go again, never, ever. He stopped whirling, her legs dropped to the ground, and they were waltzing, Aksel singing "Lördagsvalsen" in Swedish, while his fellow workers grinned, lit cigarettes, and watched with amusement—and some envy.

"Kom följ mig nu Aino lägg armen om min hals!
De ska'g å undan uti slygande fläng I denna vals."

Aino, follow me now; put your arm around my neck. This waltz insists that we whirl together.

They found a cheap hotel in Newhalem, a town of nearly a thousand people that had sprung up downriver.

That night, Aksel pulled a small box from his pocket, took out a thin gold ring with a small single diamond set in it, went to one knee in the traditional manner, and asked if she'd marry him. She said yes with no hesitation in her heart. Her yes felt right, as if there were no other choice, just this acceptance. How right everything was.

Aksel slipped the ring onto her finger, whispering, "This was in my pocket that night."

"I'm glad you didn't pawn it," Aino said.

They both laughed and held each other as if they could stop time.

They agreed on a June wedding date and then they agreed it was moral and right to sleep together. Kyllikki had lent Aino a soft cotton nightgown, low cut and trimmed with lace that flowed to her ankles and made her feel beautiful. She let Aksel take off her new teddies.

They talked and made love then made plans and made love again. Aksel was sure that this time, when the dam was finished, he'd have enough money for his boat. They'd live for a while at the poikataloja and then, when the money from the fish came in, they'd buy a house, maybe in Alderbrook where land was cheaper and where Aksel could moor his boat and walk to it from the house. After a long discussion, they decided

Aksel shouldn't wait for the project to finish but instead stay and work just long enough to buy the boat. In the dark early morning hours, she stood with him, bundled against the chill among men stamping their feet in the cold and the glow of cigarettes and she said goodbye. She had been away from the poikataloja three days and it was time to return. It was like a small death, an emptiness that could be endured only because of the promise of reuniting.

Aino was filled with ideas about how to make the basement of the poikataloja more of a home, with thoughts of getting Eleanor to stay with her, them, and with dreams of the fishing boat and maybe, someday, a house of their own—and perhaps children, their children. She would turn thirty-nine in March, she mused, but why not?

Aksel would also find himself daydreaming about life with Aino. He'd been promoted to crew supervisor and was making good wages, almost all of which he was saving for that future life. He was in such a lulling state when he hopped onto the platform of the elevator that would take him to his current place of work, high up on the dam. The elevator had a load of iron rebar, a maximum load, to minimize the up and down trips. As the platform climbed the face of the dam, Aksel heard a thin *tink* as one of the strands of the cable he was grasping broke. Apprehension filled him. There was another *tink*. He began shouting for the operator to stop. He couldn't be heard. The platform with its heavy iron load continued up the face and the *tinks* became a whirring noise of breaking strands of wire. The cable snapped. The platform lurched to hang from the three other cables, dropping Aksel, holding a stub end of the cable in his hand, down the face of the dam, the rebar flowing after him as there was no retaining wall or handrail.

Aksel had been writing several letters a week and Aino had answered every one of them. Then, his letters stopped.

She wrote to him every day but no answers came. She grew increasingly uneasy.

On Friday, April 8, a letter came in a Seattle City Light envelope, addressed by typewriter. She put it on the table, not wanting to open it. After half an hour of agony, she read the letter, informing her Aksel had fallen, jamming his right tibia up past his knee and into his groin area. They amputated just below the knee. The letter was signed by a company nurse. At the bottom scrawled in a shaky hand, Aksel wrote, "God gave me two legs for a reason. I can still work."

But he couldn't work at the dam site. They let him go without any compensation.

20

Aksel returned to Astoria without enough money for a fishing boat—and even if he'd had the money, he wasn't sure he could fish with just one leg. He was even more uncertain whether Aino would want to live with him. When he reached the station in Astoria, she was there waiting with Kyllikki. Matti would, of course, be working. She rushed to him and nearly knocked him from his crutches. He barely recovered his balance, then found himself being hugged close, her face buried in his chest. He dropped the crutches and clung to her, leaning on her for support, holding her tight.

Kyllikki picked up the crutches and waited until Aksel and Aino came up for air to hand them back to Aksel. She told Aksel that he could stay at the poikataloja for free until he could get on his feet and was immediately embarrassed by the poor choice of words. Aksel laughed, easing the sudden tension by saying, "At least I can't put my foot in my mouth."

Matti, Kyllikki, and the Bachelor Boys all chipped in to get Einar Karlsson, a master boatbuilder, to make him a wooden leg. Meanwhile, Aksel gamely clumped around on crutches, trying to keep everyone else's spirits up, especially Aino's. As for his own spirits, he sank into deep despair at night yet awoke every morning renewing his vow to find work. It was simply unthinkable to him that Aino—or any woman—would marry a man who couldn't provide for her and her children, despite Aino's assurances that it didn't matter. Maybe it didn't matter to her. It mattered to him.

But what could he do? Aksel's skills were all highly physical—and extreme physicality was demanded by all the jobs he knew. Even punching the yarder, with its heavy iron levers, gears, and roaring cable drums, was beyond him. Within a month of returning, he had his new leg, a simple long peg attached with a lined leather cup and straps to his stump. He walked on it for an hour before the stump started bleeding. He laid off it for a couple of days and picked up a little money helping mend nets, sitting on a box he could move along the net racks. Aino came by his room every night after she'd finished feeding and cleaning up after the boarders with Aksel doing what he could to pitch in. They would lie on his bed and just talk about making things work out. Neither would speak about their fears.

Coming back to the poikataloja one evening in June, with a few quarters in his pocket from mending nets, Aksel felt particularly down because he realized the fishermen asked him to help with the net mending because they wanted to help him, not because they wanted him to help them. He went back to return their money, but they'd all gone home and he was left standing on his stump on the splintered planks of the net rack pier, the river lapping up against the pilings beneath him, the gill net boats moving up and down with the gentle swell, their mooring pulleys squeaking plaintively. He looked at the last of the sunset beyond the mouth of the river. The air moving in from the Pacific, sweet and cool, was pregnant with the promise of teeming salmon and their eternal cycle of living and dying.

The brightest stars and planets already shone down. He looked up the river, searching low in the eastern sky, and found Arcturus, which connected him back to Finland and his parents, still living when he got their last letter; and his sisters, all married, with children. He thought of Gunnar. He looked at the emerging lights of the houses on the hillsides above him and he thought about Aino being home, cleaning up now after the evening meal, and his heart ached. He thought he was failing her.

He limped slowly toward his room smelling the smoke of late cooking fires. Then it hit him. His first job in America was chopping wood on the journey north from San Francisco. He'd started logging by chopping wood for the steam donkey. By God, he would restart life, as a one-legged, used-to-be fisherman and logger, chopping wood.

The little money he'd saved for the fishing boat bought a cart, a lame horse, an ax, two wedges, a splitting maul, a large one-man crosscut saw, and some low-grade logs the sawmills didn't mind selling. It took his entire savings. On the side of the wagon he carefully painted: ASTORIA FUEL COMPANY, AKSEL LÅNGSTRÖM, OWNER. ALL YOUR HEATING AND COOKING FUEL NEEDS SUPPLIED.

He stepped into Aino's kitchen still carrying the paint bucket and brush and called out to her, holding them up for her to see, "Now I'm a capitalist!"

She put down her towel and walked over to him. He couldn't hug her because his hands were full. She reached up to hold both cheeks in her hands and pulled his head down toward her for a kiss, whispering, "You're not a capitalist. You're a petit bourgeois. And I love you."

The fuel business grew. Aino waited. She knew Aksel wouldn't set the wedding date until he was sure he could support the family— including Eleanor, who they both hoped would now move back home. Aino knew Aksel's dream of a boat had been thwarted once again and she worried he may have given up on his dream altogether, for her. It made her feel grateful, loved, and sad. She'd made his dream her dream, whether he had given it up or not.

One dreary evening in late August, he came into their flat changing the entire feeling of the room when he crossed the threshold.

"What's the matter?" She asked, putting his dinner in front of him.

"Nothing."

He was just like her brothers. Pride and custom forbade men to complain or brag. Since they all believed that life consisted of 95 percent things to complain about and maybe 4 percent things to brag about, this left them with little that was fair game.

She remembered Kyllikki explaining it to her. Ilmari and Matti had accidentally killed a cow that wandered too close to a stump they'd dynamited. A wood splinter had gone through the cow's eye.

"Sure, they should have seen the cow," Kyllikki said. "But they didn't. Both feel ashamed for not being competent. So now we play hide-and-seek."

"Hide-and-seek?" Aino asked

Kyllikki laughed. "That's what I call it. The men hide their feelings and the women seek to find them."

They both laughed.

"Why do you let them play the game?" Aino asked.

"Aino, if they felt their fear or lack of confidence or sadness at failure, they couldn't function out there."

Then it hit her—out there, where it was dangerous and they were alive. She sat down across from Aksel and looked into his eyes. "The August Chinook are running."

"Yoh," Aksel answered. They always spoke Finnish when they were alone.

She ladled salmon stew into a bowl for him. He had slumped into the chair, his peg leg straight out to the side of the table.

"You wish you were fishing," she said.

"No. Not anymore," he answered. "We're OK with the fuel business."

She poured two cups of coffee. He ate silently.

"You'll be back out there someday," she said.

Aksel stared at his stew, his fork held upright in his hand next to the bowl. He looked up at her. "I said I'd never fish for the big canneries. I did for Lempi. I'd do it for you, but they won't hire a one-legged man."

"I know you'd do it for me," she said. "I know what you're doing now is for me."

He took a couple of deep breaths, then it came out. "I was a high rigger! I did what few men would dare. The most dangerous and highest-paid job in the woods. I can find fish anywhere! I could bring in enough fish to buy two houses. Now I'm watching the shit running out of a lame horse's asshole and selling bits of wood for pennies like some goddamned lame, useless cripple." In a sudden fierce move, he turned the fork upside down and started jabbing into his lame leg.

Aino rushed around the table and knelt next to him, hugging his leg, forcing him to stop. Looking up at him, his pain and his shame bringing tears to her eyes, she said, "I love you. I love this." She was kissing the blood that had oozed up to mix with the wool of Aksel's trouser leg. He leaned over and smothered his face in her hair and the pain and disappointment poured out as he said her name over and over.

The next day Aksel loaded the wagon with wood and heaved himself up onto the seat. The horse shit. For a moment, he stared at the greenish brown feces plopping quite contentedly to the ground, then he started to laugh. He rubbed his trouser leg and felt the bandage that Aino had put on the wound the night before. Still laughing, he clucked the horse forward.

That night, he asked Aino if four weeks from Sunday would work for the wedding, and on September 18, 1927, Aksel and Aino were married in the little church that Ilmari built. Kyllikki and Matti were witnesses. Eleanor, now nine, helped her mother get ready.

At the reception at Ilmahenki, put on by Alma and the girls, they had cranked up the new gramophone Alma and Ilmari had bought as their wedding present to themselves and everyone danced, Aksel doing an amazing job on his peg leg and everyone at ease with it. Eleanor undertook teaching Aksel how to Charleston. "Everyone is doing it," she'd said solemnly.

The newly married couple took the train to Neawanna where they stayed two nights at the Neawanna Hotel and walked on the beach at low tide. They found a little restaurant on the corner of Broadway and South Franklin Street called the Little Gem, owned by a Greek family by the name of Mavromichalis. They were served by the Mavromichalises' young son, Elias, who seemed to be about Eleanor's age. Contrary to Aino's suspicions, the restaurant was clean, tidy, and the food good. On the second evening they ate across the street at the Clam House, owned by another Greek family, named Galanis. Demetrius Galanis was the man Jouka defended so many years ago at the dance at Knappton, and he recognized Aino and remembered Jouka fondly.

He challenged Aksel to try his famous chili. Aksel did and, like a true Scandinavian, he never tried it again.

That Christmas was remembered as perhaps the best one ever by almost everyone. Ilmari had returned to the church a week after Mielikki's funeral and one month later he was back on the church council. He never talked about his absence and no one asked. He believed Jesus was God, so he could honestly say he was a Christian. He felt no need to tell others that they were God, too. Thus the whole family attended the Christmas Eve candlelight service, together for the first time in years. Helmi had come home from Portland where she had undertaken a business and secretarial course. Her prospects looked good, but the prospects were all in Portland and she would have to choose to leave Ilmahenki permanently. Business was good for everyone. Matti had made a toast to "the roaring twenties," and even Ilmari had joined in, although with apple juice.

On December 26, Aino and Aksel were packing when Eleanor came over to Aino and looked up at her. "Are you going away for long, Äiti?" she asked.

Aino went to one knee. "Not long. I'll come whenever I can. For sure, I'll be back for New Year's."

Eleanor said softly, "New Year's must be a lot of fun in Astoria."

Aino's heart started beating in her throat. "Do you want to come to stay with us for New Year's Eve in Astoria?"

Eleanor nodded yes.

21

Eleanor welcomed 1928 at Suomi Hall with her mother, Aksel, and her aunt Kyllikki and uncle Matti. Her cousin Suvi— fifteen, a sophomore at Astoria High School, and in Eleanor's eyes sophisticated and beautiful—was there along with her brother, Aarni. An eighth grader at John Jacob Astor, Aarni was OK when he was alone with just Eleanor. Her favorite cousin was Pilvi, eleven, who was like a big sister. She mostly ignored Toivo, a year younger than her and a child. She and Pilvi constantly watched Suvi to see which boys asked her to dance, commenting on the old Finn ladies dressed in their finest but with no sense of style whatsoever and sneaking coffee to keep themselves awake for the New Year. At midnight they went into the cold night air, carrying pots and pans, ladles and serving spoons and beat them all together, howling at the waxing half-moon darting into and out of rugged scudding clouds—blown by the last breath of a fierce southwest storm that had flooded streets, toppled trees, and sent logs bursting from rafts down the rivers and creeks all over the county.

Her mother asked if she would like to stay and go to school in Astoria. While she wanted clothes like Suvi and ice cream and movies whenever there was a spare nickel, memories of cruelty from the other children and the freedom and usefulness she felt at the farm won her over. Deep River was home.

Matti and Kyllikki said Aksel and Aino could continue to make the poikataloja home for free, but Aksel said no. He was earning a living and they could rent their own place. So, he and Aino found a little house in

Uppertown that had been made into a duplex and they signed a one-year lease. It was only blocks from Aksel's wood yard and a mile and a half from the poikataloja, which Aino quite enjoyed walking to once she could do it in daylight. She was OK at night but was always happy when Aksel walked her home. She knew Aksel wasn't as happy as she was. When spring Chinook started running in March, she would sometimes catch Aksel staring at the river, smoking a cigarette.

With new houses all over and these new huge buildings called sky-scrapers in the east and even in San Francisco and Portland, all of which required lumber, the logging business was booming. Matti and Kyllikki sold the ship chandlery business just a year after Kyllikki's father died because Matti said he wasn't a shopkeeper and knew nothing about it. The money paid off the loan for the poikataloja. They kept the shoe store, primarily because Kyllikki felt she knew about shoes and her mother felt useful working half days.

The heating business always slacked off around May, giving Aksel more time in the wood yard to build inventory for the next year, while still supplying the constantly growing demand for wood to fuel cooking stoves that went into the growing number of houses. Astoria's population had nearly doubled from eight thousand when Aino first saw it to over fifteen thousand now. They made their lease payments every month and had enough left over to buy a Philco radio as a Christmas present to themselves.

Because the Chinese had been forced to California, the salmon-canning factories always had jobs for women on a piecework basis. Every morning and evening, women could be seen moving in small groups, their hair under white kerchiefs, long white aprons covering their clothes, chatting and talking on the way to and from the factories, while the men went out daily for the fish or into the woods to feed the sawmills.

The slowdown in business in 1927 had turned around. The good times rolled. The economy roared, the stock market soared, the trees fell, and the money flowed in. Matti and Kyllikki paid off their house, and their savings—in the form of bank deposits and stocks and bonds—grew with the economy.

Then in the late summer of 1929, lumber prices started falling again. Matti, who had bought two stands of Douglas fir and another three trucks with free money from the stock market, suddenly found sawmills backing out of orders or delaying payment. He laid off eight men in early September. He laid off another eight at the end of the month.

22

On Tuesday, October 29, 1929, the good times stopped rolling. Business in Astoria didn't die on the day of the crash. Wild tales, however, abounded of men in New York and Chicago jumping from skyscrapers, the concrete forms and interiors of which only months before had been a major market for the lumber from Matti's logs.

Over the months following the stock market crash, the initial financial panic settled into gloom and a business depression all over the country. Trees already cut had to be left in cold decks on the show sites because mills refused delivery.

Most of Matti and Kyllikki's wealth vanished with the stock market crash. Matti had kept some of the wealth in cash in two bank accounts. One of the banks failed, cutting the cash savings in half. Kyllikki tried not to show fear but failed. Matti showed none, but Kyllikki knew he was hiding it. He'd spent more than a decade building the business back. Now, cash was going out faster than it was coming in. Banks were making no working-capital loans. For several nights, Kyllikki sat down with Matti and the account books.

Matti and Kyllikki put the poikataloja up for sale. There were no buyers. Loggers and mill workers all over the county were being laid off, and every week the poikataloja had another empty room with the mattress folded on the cot. The residents had declined from thirty-five to eight, only five paying full rent. What Matti and Kyllikki had considered to be a solid asset was close to worthless. Aino agreed to continue to work for the right to take home a share of the poikataloja food.

Days of tense worry passed as they read the paper, talked to mill owners. In March, Matti closed two sides and let everyone go. This left two of Matti's three yarders and the equipment that went with them sitting silently next to piles of undelivered logs; 200-Foot Logging was down to Matti, the Bachelor Boys less Aksel, Matti's two best loggers, and the diesel yarder that Jens both ran and repaired. In April, 200-Foot Logging couldn't make payroll. Matti reverted to what had built the company in the first place. He promised everyone a generous share of the profits when they came in. He put up the Bachelor Boys in the poikataloja for free. The other two loggers were married, and he paid them enough to make rent and fed them and their families at the poikataloja.

Word got out that some families were living at the poikataloja for free, their children sleeping on the floor. Desperate men and women started to knock on Matti and Kyllikki's door. It didn't seem fair to charge rent to the few who were paying it, so Matti and Kyllikki gave everyone free rent. Whenever a room came open, there were several families on a waiting list wanting to take it.

Word came to city hall that families were living in intolerable conditions. The City of Astoria sent the police. The police talked to the families. The police talked to the mayor. The families stayed. Matti was asked to join the Astoria Rotary Club. He did.

On Deep River, Ilmari put the sawmill on a single six-hour shift. Business revenues shrank to about a quarter of what they used to be. When he wasn't running the head rig, he did any blacksmithing that came his way. Horses still needed shoes. Machinery still broke down. He'd even had a couple of jobs modifying truck bodies. To make up for money spent on oxygen and acetylene used by the new oxyacetylene welding torch, Ilmari reverted to doing any blacksmith work he could the old-fashioned way, with Alma helping keep the kiln hot and oxygenated by pumping the bellows. Alma's main job, however, was food, the old-fashioned way: hard work in the garden, baking from scratch, canning meat and vegetables. She was also good at setting baited hooks, periodically checking on them for a fish, and keeping the alder fires in the smokehouse going, so she could preserve what they couldn't immediately eat.

The wood-fuel business in Astoria was deteriorating. People still needed to cook and heat their homes but wore heavier clothes indoors and skimped on cooking fires. Those homes with unemployed fathers, a third of Aksel's customers, quit buying his wood altogether. The unemployed fathers foraged for downed trees and abandoned logs and cut their own firewood. Aksel dropped his prices until he told Aino that he felt he was working for free. He'd gone back to saving the tobacco from his cigarette butts.

They had signed another one-year lease on their house. Aino tried to take on as many mending jobs as she could, even going to other poikatalojas to find business, but a lot of bachelors were darning their own socks. The end of each month consisted of ever-increasing worry about the monthly lease payment, until it was paid and followed by a brief day or two of respite from the money worries. Then, the worry would start to build again until the next month ended.

During the good times before the crash, they'd managed to save a little money and vowed never to use it to make rent. It was in cans, buried in the backyard. Neither of them trusted banks. Aino mistrusted them because she thought they'd be the first of the capitalist institutions to collapse in a crisis and she had lived through several runs on banks already. Aksel had told her about being cheated of his savings by a bank in the bootlegging days by the same guy who'd tried to cheat Matti on the Grays Harbor job. She knew Drummond had disappeared. Aksel swore he had nothing to do with it and she believed him. She was less sure about the Bachelor Boys.

Aino would occasionally soothe her worries about money by telling Aksel that they could always go to the farm on Deep River. Ilmari and Alma weren't making much money, but their farm made them less vulnerable than workers to the vicissitudes of the economy. Eleanor had food to eat and a roof over her head. Deep River was Aino's rock. There, they wouldn't starve. Aino knew as well as Aksel that she was saying it out loud to make herself feel better. Aksel would tell her not to worry; it would never get as bad now as when they were children in Finland. Aino knew, however, that even though Aksel never let on that he worried about the money, he increasingly went outside before bed and watched the river, the red reflection of his cigarette on the smoke that floated around his head.

After dinner one night in early May 1930, Aksel finally started to talk about what was on his mind.

"These panics always turn around. It's called the business cycle."

"Maybe not this time," Aino said. She was making a rag rug. "It might just be the end of capitalism."

"The way it ended in Russia?"

She ignored the comment and resumed braiding and sewing. Making rag rugs was when she thought best. She ripped another rag into a long strip. The individual. The group. You couldn't make a rag rug without individual strips, but if the individual strips weren't woven together, you still couldn't make a rug.

She put her work down. "I don't think you want to talk about capitalism and communism."

"No," Aksel said. She waited, her work in her lap.

"When this panic is over," he started, "people won't be going back to wood heat."

"How do you know that?"

"People want to avoid unnecessary work."

Aino, on full alert, waited.

"All these cars . . ." Aksel started and stopped. She waited. "Cars keep coming. Airplanes too. They'll require more and more oil. It's just like logging. Nature puts it in the ground and men figure out how to use it."

"And the Weyerhaeusers and Rockefellers keep ninety percent of nature's free wealth."

"Couldn't resist, could you?" he said, but he was smiling. "When I got here in 1905," Aksel went on, "we thought we could never cut the forest faster than it grew. Then we invented high-lead logging, better locomotives, diesel yarders. Matti told me about a new gas-powered saw with a continuous chain of teeth. He says a two-man crew in less than an hour can fell trees that used to take two of us several days." He paused. "We're going to be flooded with cheap oil, same as cheap lumber."

"So?"

"That oil gets refined into gasoline. What's left over is too thick for anything except burning." She looked at him. "For heat," he said.

"It will kill our business."

Aino felt a sinking anxiety.

"I can get in on the ground floor," he said. "I know every customer in Astoria. We get a franchise to sell oil stoves and then," he grinned, "we sell them the oil forever."

"You've been talking to Matti. You're not him." She saw his disappointment, maybe in her. "I don't mean you can't run the business. But Matti *loves* business and you don't."

"It's called work because we don't do it for fun."

"I didn't mean you aren't willing to work, but you don't love the fuel business. You loved fishing and logging."

He started pounding his wooden leg with his fist. "I *can't* fish *or* log!" He looked at her, his face contorted with pain.

She took a deep breath. "I can't support this, Aksel."

"I'm doing it for you and Eleanor. Don't you see that?"

"I see it. I'm grateful."

He waited.

"It'll kill you," she said. "It'll kill us."

"I'm dying now!" He clubbed the open door with his fist and it banged against the wall. "The business will be dying next. You think we have choices? How many options do you think a one-legged man has?" He put on his coat and stomped out of the front door, again slamming it behind him.

She waited until she could no longer hear the thumping of his wooden leg. She assumed he wouldn't be back for a long time; he'd taken his coat. She sat there fighting back tears. She knew that he'd given up the dream of the fishing boat not only for her and Eleanor but also because the dream had become too painful to bear. "You block-headed Swede," she said out loud. "You know what's good for me and Eleanor but not for you."

She was still for a long time, then she thought of her mother. She could almost hear Maíjalüsa telling her to stand straight and throw her shoulders back. She sat up straighter. Sisu was also about holding on to dreams.

23

ino went to both banks in town. She used her connection to Matti and through him to Kyllikki and her father's reputation. She shamelessly dropped the names of Rotarians and anyone she thought the bankers might know. It was of no avail. The manager at the First National Bank of Oregon was polite, even kind. He told her that with no assets as collateral, no bank would make a loan on a boat that wasn't even built, particularly if it was being built for a fisherman with one leg, no matter how good his previous reputation. That left her only one alternative.

It took a few weeks to set everything up, getting ahead at the poikataloja as much as possible, and on Sunday, June 8, 1930, she was ready to go. Aksel was up at five, as usual, and she fixed mush and rieska with hot bacon grease and cold salmon. She also started a cake.

"What's the cake for?" Aksel asked.

"A hen party over at Kyllikki's," she answered.

Aksel grunted, downed his coffee, lit a cigarette, and went out the door. He had been subdued since her "no" to him but didn't seem to hold a grudge, unlike her brothers who suffered the common ailment of Finnish senility, forgetting everything except the grudges.

When the cake was done, she carefully wrapped it, packed her valise with a change of underwear and stockings, and set off for Kyllikki's.

Kyllikki had offered her coffee after agreeing to cover the poikataloja while Aino was gone. She did not ask why Aino was going to be gone for three days; Aino let her believe it had to do with Eleanor but hadn't actually said so. Kyllikki did ask what the cake was for. Aino replied, "For an old hen."

Aino took the ferry to Megler, carefully counting coins she had been squirreling away ever since her refusal to help with Aksel's business idea. She had also secretly dug up one of the cans and taken one hundred dollars in five- and ten-dollar bills, half of the savings.

The *Tourist II* was only half-full of cars, but at least the ferries still operated, albeit on a curtailed schedule because of the business collapse. When Aino walked off the ferry on the Washington side, she was startled to hear her name called. A man walked up to her, his face unshaven, his clothes dirty. She figured him for a hobo, but how did he know her? When he got closer, she could smell him. Seemingly happy, he said, "Aino, it's great to see you." She couldn't place him. Then he said, "Michael Tierney, from Centralia."

She felt embarrassed she hadn't recognized him. He'd been so kind to her, sharing his home. Clearly, he was out of work. She hesitated to ask about his family. He saved her the trouble. "Kathleen is still in Centralia. She and the kids are living with her mother. We lost the house when I went to jail."

"They sent you to jail with the others? How did you get out?"

"They charged me with obstructing justice and assault. I did my time, two years."

After talking for a while, Aino started feeling nervous. "I'm really sorry, but I've got to get the bus. It leaves in twenty minutes and I need to buy tickets."

"You have some money then?" Tierney asked.

"Well, enough just to get where I'm going to and back." She felt terrible lying.

"Look, Aino. You know me. I'm no bum, just been out of work. Came here on a rumor they were hiring over to Ilwaco." He shrugged. "Wasn't true. But they said maybe the next week. Wasn't true, either."

She made sympathetic noises.

"I just need enough to get across the river and maybe a little food. I can ride the rails to Portland, then home to Centralia." He smiled.

"Of course, if you could help out with a little money for food. I haven't eaten in two days, except some apples. Those watery Yellow Transparents they grow around here. Salmonberries, you know."

"I hear St. Mary on Grand helps out with food. Also, the Finnish and Norwegian Lutherans."

Tierney's face no longer showed an affable familiarity. "Aino, I hear you're working for your brother, managing his boardinghouse with Aksel. He's that Swede who along with his friends got you out before the National Guard came in. We hear he's got his own business in Astoria. You must be doing OK." He laughed. "Not too bad for an old Wobbly."

She smiled and felt sick at heart—for him and for what she knew was coming.

"You know, I haven't worked for six months. Maybe just, you know, a little something for the Mrs. and the kids. We sure as hell would appreciate it."

She could see how it hurt his pride to ask, and it made what she was going to say to him even more difficult. "What you say is true, but the business is barely feeding us. And the *management* job pays the equivalent of room and board."

"Yeah. OK." She watched Tierney's expression move to sullen resentment.

"It's just . . . I have a kid, too, you know," she said. "And Aksel, well he lost his leg." She suddenly felt anger. Why was she apologizing? She needed the money for Aksel—her husband. "No. I'm sorry. I can't." She'd always asserted herself positively, saying yes. Saying no felt every bit as powerful.

Tierney raised himself to his full height and spit on the ground next to her shoe. She looked at the spit sadly and then at him. Then she turned her back on him and walked away.

Aino could see that Louhi had done well during Prohibition, moving into the corner office on the top floor of the Seaforth Hotel, newly built in 1926. Because hers was the only office, except for one on the ground floor labeled MANAGER, she assumed Louhi owned the Seaforth—or a large part of it.

Louhi was civil when she greeted Aino. There might even have been a hint that she was happy to see her.

Aino sat the sokerikakku on Louhi's desk. "My mother taught me."

"So did mine," Louhi said. There was sadness in her voice. Sokerikakku, a difficult spongy sugar cake, demanding lots of practice, strict precision, and loving tutelage, was the challenge and triumph of generations of Finnish women.

Louhi was speaking Finnish and it made Aino feel more confident. She hated this insecurity in her. She had faced down sheriffs with rifles and vigilante thugs with ax handles and now she sat across the desk from a small but still very attractive woman in her late fifties or early sixties, her brother's mother-in-law, trying not to show she was quivering inside. It was, of course, because much was at stake—Aksel's happiness.

Louhi called for coffee and her secretary brought in a delicate china set with cream and sugar bowls and slices of korpu, a very dry zwieback cinnamon toast, good for dunking. The korpu competed with the cake and Aino felt outmaneuvered before she started.

"We can have both," Louhi said with a knowing smile.

Aino forced a smile. She and Louhi drank several sips, dunking their korpu without speaking. Aino could see Louhi looking at her over the rim of her cup with amusement. Aino carefully set her own cup in its saucer and asked Louhi for a loan for a fishing boat. Louhi asked how they thought they could pay it off, given Aksel had lost his leg.

"I'm going to help him."

"And he's OK with that?"

"He doesn't know yet."

Louhi stood and walked over to the window. She could see the docks on the Chehalis River from it. She talked while still looking out the window. "How old are you?"

"Forty-two."

Louhi humphed. "And out of shape."

Aino bristled. Louhi laughed.

"Hell, woman," she said. "We all get out of shape. We just don't all of us try and go gillnetting."

"I can do it."

"Maybe for three or four years." Louhi stayed at the window and spoke without looking at Aino. "That man of yours gave me hell, him and his little army unit." She seemed to be talking to herself more than to Aino. "Did you know they shot the hell out of a bunch of Seattle boys? I offered him a job. We could have sewed up everything west of the mountains. But that independent son of a bitch wouldn't have it." Louhi chuckled.

This was news to Aino, but she kept quiet, hoping.

Louhi looked her right in the eye. "You've both got spunk; I'll give you that. And that man of yours can stand on his own two feet better than any man I know and do it with one leg." She sat at her desk and pulled out a large checkbook, the checks printed on perforated paper that allowed for tearing them off and leaving a stub behind for record keeping.

"I'm going to loan you the money," she said, picking up a fountain pen. "I bet on people. It's what I'm good at. I spent my life providing things that do-gooders and politicians all say people shouldn't have." She laughed. "Excepting, of course, themselves."

"Thank you."

"Get this clear," Louhi said. "I know Drummond cheated Aksel out of his money. You may feel he has some sort of moral claim on it. Neither I nor the bank ever owed him a goddamned thing."

Aino called on centuries of Finnish ability to mask feelings to control her outrage at this woman smugly agreeing to lend her and Aksel money that was Aksel's in the first place. She knew that she could rage self-righteously and with good cause against the injustice of it all, but she also knew she'd never get the money if she did.

Louhi was looking at her with a sort of detached curiosity, as if this were some sort of experiment and Louhi was just waiting to see which way the mouse would move given the stimulus. She swallowed. "Believe me, I understand that the law sometimes has nothing to do with morals."

Louhi nodded her head, approving. Then she went businesslike. "I'll loan you the amount Aksel had in his account, bank paper rate plus five percent."

"OK."

"How much can you put down on the boat? I want you to have skin in the game."

"I have one hundred dollars." Aino started to open her valise.

"You give that to the boatbuilder, not to me."

"Oh."

Louhi laughed. "Communists," she said. "God bless you, you are ignorant sons of bitches."

Aino forced a smile.

"I'll amortize it over ten years. You'll pay me monthly. You miss a payment, you pay a ten percent penalty on what's owed. You miss two payments, I get the boat."

They looked at each other.

"And keep a little back. That way if times get hard, you'll have a few months' cushion."

Aino nodded. She hadn't thought of that.

"Deal?" Louhi asked.

"Deal," Aino said.

They stood and shook hands. Instead of feeling joy, Aino felt defeated.

Louhi regarded Aino for a long moment. "You don't like feeling powerless, do you." Louhi moved to look out of the window again. She turned to Aino. "Power is the ability to reward or punish. It comes in different currencies: sex, giving or withholding; violence, actual or threatened. The best is money."

24

Aksel waited anxiously for Aino. Her note said that she'd be back in three days and not to worry but said nothing about where she was going or why. It was now the third day.

He spent the morning splitting wood, working out his anger over her refusal to support his plan and his anxiety because she was gone. The whole day, whenever he saw one of the two ferries returning to Astoria, he would drive the wagon back to the duplex in hopes that she'd be there. He made the scheduled deliveries and now sat in the new easy chair, his wooden leg stretched before him.

He heard footsteps and his heart picked up speed. He came to his feet just as Aino opened the front door. He thought there could be no sweeter joy than being reunited with a much-missed loved one.

She finally wriggled loose from him, laughing, and hung her coat and hat on the coat tree. He carried her valise into the bedroom. When he returned, she had her purse on the kitchen table and was pulling out documents.

"What's this? Where did you go?"

She looked at him and he could feel some sort of triumph in her. "I went to Nordland."

"Nordland?"

She unfolded several legal-size sheets, put the documents on the table, and then put a check on top of them. He picked it up. It was drawn on the bank that took his money for the exact amount taken.

"You got my money back? For the heating business? How did you do it?" He reached out to kiss her, but she pulled away, smiling.

"Not so fast." She handed him the legal-size papers. "It's a loan."

"A loan? But it's my money."

She sighed. "As I learned in Nordland, not anymore."

Aksel went grim.

"Just read the terms," she said. He looked at her, wondering what was up, and then started glancing quickly through the terms. He stopped, his mouth open. He looked at her with amazement. "It says here the collateral is a boat."

Aino grinned.

Aksel threw down the papers and grabbed her, whirling her around. "The boat! The boat!" he repeated. He kissed her until she pulled her head back. "You need to sign it," she said.

He went back to the documents. On reaching the last page he looked up at her, pointing to her signature.

"Yes. I already signed it. That's why we have the check. You need to sign, too, and we mail one copy to Louhi."

"The old witch," Aksel said, shaking his head. He hugged her again, reread the terms, and then laughed out loud.

Aino had poured them coffee. She set it in front of him, smiling with the joy he obviously felt. Aksel leaned back in his chair, like the captain he was finally going to be again, and said, "Hell, it was illegal money in the first place. Now I have to earn it like an honest man."

Then the joy suddenly faded as he remembered he had a wooden leg, which would slow him down in rough weather, make it difficult to keep his balance, make it impossible to get quickly from the stern to the bow in an emergency. He wasn't sure he could do it. Finding the fish was one thing, getting a hundred-plus-pound salmon, writhing with the strength that could propel it to Wyoming, into the boat was quite another. He looked at his wooden leg and then at her in despair.

"I'm going to help you," she said. "You're the captain. I'm the crew. Until we can afford a boat puller."

"But . . . what do you know about fishing? You can't pull a boat through rough water. Some of the salmon could be as big as you are. We hit rough water and you'll never be able to get the net in."

"Not by myself." He saw that rising posture of hers, as she came to her full five feet, four inches. "And you can't do it by yourself, either."

He sat silent on a kitchen chair, the loan agreement still in his hands. Then he rose and clumped his way to the dresser where he kept paper and a fountain pen. He returned with the pen, set the loan agreement on the table, and signed it. He grinned at her. "It looks like we're partners."

25

Aksel went to see Einar Karlsson, the man who'd made his wooden leg. Einar was the owner of Karlsson Boats, a designer and builder of good reputation in a market where all the buyers were boat savvy and could probably build the boats themselves if they wanted to invest in the tools. Einar and Aksel settled on a classic double-ended design, allowing the boat to slip between waves from either direction when tied to a long net. Einar had a source for Port Orford cedar, a subspecies of western cedar with remarkable boatbuilding qualities. The boat would be a carvel-built hull of Port Orford cedar planks placed on ribs of white oak. The deck, too, would be Port Orford cedar. Aksel insisted on choosing every plank and timber and came to the boatyard morning and evening. Einar liked him, so he tolerated Aksel's being pickier than he'd allow most customers to be. But also the boatbuilding business was as bad as the lumber and every other business, and Einar had already decided that with sales and production down, he would take his time. For decades, fishermen talked about having a "Karlsson depression boat" like violinists talking about having a Stradivarius.

He named her the *Aino*. She had a four-cylinder Ford tractor motor that Aksel found in Rainier through a classified ad. On the day she was launched, Aino smashed a bottle of bootleg wine across the bow and she slid into the Columbia River stern first, Aksel at the wheel.

He brought the *Aino* around, the engine almost idling, and the boat's namesake scrambled down the ladder from the wharf and into the empty net room, the open bow where the huge gill net would be folded. Aksel helped Aino negotiate the narrow ledge between the little cabin and the gunwales, and she somewhat awkwardly managed to get her feet in the stern. Aksel headed the *Aino* toward her home in Alderbrook, careful not to run her too hard until he was sure everything worked. He motioned for Aino to take the wheel. She stood on a box he had pushed beneath it. She could barely see forward above the top of the cabin, but she felt a wild excitement as the wharves and houses of Astoria streamed by the *Aino*'s starboard side. The *Aino*, she thought, named after her. She felt absurdly happy.

Aksel was absurdly happy, too. He'd hung his new gill net weeks earlier, carefully measuring the distance he tied the net to the cork line, aware that how the net hung in the water would largely determine how many fish it would catch. He'd chosen a larger-meshed net to start, knowing if Einar built the boat in time, he would catch at least the last half of the August Chinook run—and this is what he was doing. He'd often forget himself as he saw the big fish slam into the net, sinking the cork line with a sudden pop. He'd be halfway through a sandwich, hear a fish hit, and be on his feet, sandwich thrown into the water. He'd run to the side of the boat, forgetting his wooden leg, and have to be helped to his feet by Aino. Then he'd be back in the stern, spinning the wheel, turning the boat, racing to one end of the long net or the other, filled with the sheer joy of fishing again—and with such a boat. Aino had never seen him so animated and it delighted her.

As the *Aino* settled in, so did Aksel. By September he behaved much like all the other fishermen on the river, except in one way: Aksel uncannily found fish. Aino would watch him dip a hand into the river and taste the water. He'd watch the way the treetops moved and the direction of the swells, see signs of a hidden current that she couldn't see even after he'd pointed it out. He'd poke the *Aino* into eddies, let her drift, then suddenly gun the engine, heading for a spot he could see as if it were marked by flashing buoys. Whenever the *Aino* idled proudly beneath the boxes hanging on davits at the cannery weighing stations, she was always full of fish, big fish, and they were paid for by the pound.

By October, the Chinook run had abated, but there were still some late Chinook, steelhead, silversides, and even sturgeon to be caught. The two of them had moved into a routine, sleeping on the *Aino*, one of them always on watch during drifts. After they came in to deliver the catch when the boat could hold no more, Aino would return to the house, make sure everything was in order, shop for food, bake rieska, make more viili for the next outing, prepare sandwiches, have a quick visit with Kyllikki, and haul everything down to the boat. Aksel spent almost all his time on boat and net maintenance.

Aksel's enthusiasm never waned. Aino's did wane.

They fished when the tide was right, which meant if the tide was right at two in the morning, they fished at two in the morning. The smell of engine oil and gasoline permeated the cabin and made her nauseated. She'd initially solved the problem by sleeping at the fore of the net room on a little pallet she'd arranged, but as fall moved closer to winter, the rains came, driving her inside the cabin. There, she could sleep only fitfully.

Worse, with the deteriorating weather, the river grew rough. She got seasick. Eventually, the seasickness lessened, but it never went away. She also didn't like hanging her rear end over the gunwales to pee and she really hated to poop that way, especially with other boats in sight—which was almost always, except at night. She tried peeing into a pot in the cabin, enduring the fumes, but after two accidents, when the *Aino* went up and came crashing down on a sudden swell and she missed and spilled what was already there, she went back to the gunwales. Aksel said nothing to all of this, for which she was grateful. If he had said something, made one tiny joke, the crew would have mutinied and tossed the captain overboard.

In January, Aksel took the *Aino* upstream, where the river flowed between numerous islands, cutting the wind and swell and making it more likely for anyone thrown overboard to reach shore. Aino wasn't sure he'd done it for her, but she was grateful. However, Aksel brought the *Aino* back closer to the bar in March, and the heaving swells made Aino ill, on top of being miserably wet and cold. Sisu and love got her through.

*   *   *

The spring Chinook run was good. The canning factories were busy.
The price of salmon, however, was low and falling as the catch increased. At the start of the August run, all the canneries on both sides
of the river lowered their prices from five cents a pound to three cents
a pound. The prices were controlled by an organization called the
Northwest Packers Association that consisted of all the canning companies on the river. One of its board members was John Reder. He'd
sold his logging business some years earlier and moved his family to
Portland. There he had invested his money, diversifying into different
industries and serving on various boards of directors.

Fishermen of lesser skill than Aksel, although no less hardworking, found it increasingly difficult to make payments on their loans.
The Fishermen's Protective Union, organized years earlier primarily
to help the families of drowned fishermen, launched numerous com-
plaints about price fixing. Almost every lawyer in town represented a
cannery, so the union could find no one to take the case. The lawyers
who would didn't know anything about antitrust laws.

The fishermen grew desperate. In the fall of 1931, the Fishermen's Protective Union called for a strike.

26

Aksel said no to the strike and its waterborne picket line. "I'm independent. I'll sell what I catch. I never joined that union." They were on a night drift on the Washington side off Holy Water, so named because of the little pioneer Catholic church on the shore. The *Aino*'s masthead light formed a small pool in the darkness around the boat as it rocked gently in the swell. Tiny sparkles, created by the light reflecting from delicately falling mist particles, winked at them from the darkness beyond. Aino had glimpsed a set of running lights, green and red, heading south across the river in the direction of Warrenton and then disappearing in the misty darkness, but now it felt as if they were all alone in the world, rocking, rocking. Rising up with the swell, Aino felt the weight of her stomach pushing down toward her pelvis, her buttocks pressing on the fish box where she sat, her legs dangling into the net room. Then the boat would go downward and her stomach would gently rise toward her heart. Aksel stood at the bow where he had attached the net to a belaying pin on the starboard side next to the net roller. She could see the glow of his cigarette and occasionally his face, lit orange red when he pulled in another lungful of smoke.

As good as Aksel was, they were barely making it. The payments owed on Louhi's loan were relentless. If they couldn't make these, they would lose the boat. Thankfully, she'd taken Louhi's advice and set some of the loan money aside. With this strike, however, that money would be gone in three months. The lease payments on the house were equally relentless. Not making the lease payments would mean living on the boat, with its smell of engine oil and constant rocking. But that required still having the boat. If they wouldn't cross the picket lines, they couldn't sell their fish—and there was no other work, anywhere.

"I'll go to Louhi. She's family."

"No," Aksel said calmly. "If we sell what I catch, you won't need to see her."

"At three cents a pound, we'll have to catch every fish in the river."

"We only need to fill the fish box."

He was so unflappable, just like her brothers. She hovered somewhere between pride and being furious with him. "Yes, *you* can," she snapped. "What about those who can't? Their families go hungry at three cents a pound."

He struck another match and in its flare his face was white. The flare died as he lit another cigarette. "If they can't feed their families, it's not my doing."

"You were born with the gift."

"I developed that gift through hard work. I slaved my entire adult life to finally use it and"—he hesitated, stopping short of what he was going to say—"and here we are again." He stomped off to the other side of the boat.

She knew he'd never say it directly. "Here we are again" was about her strike at Reder's costing Jouka everything. She also knew that Aksel couldn't be coerced by the threat of losing her love—and she loved Aksel more than anything else, even justice.

She made her way over to where Aksel was looking at the river, standing on the deck of the net room. She stood next to him, looking at the river they both loved. She said softly, "I hurt Jouka for a cause I believed in. I wish I hadn't."

Aksel took a long pull and then looked down at the glowing tip cupped in his hand. "I know," he said. He threw the cigarette into the water and put his arm around her. She snuggled her head into the side of his chest. The only sounds were the water of the great river lapping against the *Aino*'s hull and, in the far distance, the sound of a bell buoy as it rocked in a swell.

"Look at me," he said.

She did.

"Ordinary people," he said, "the *little guy* and his wife, will be thrown out of cannery work up and down the river. Truckers will be put out of work. Restaurants and butcher shops won't have any fish. The price of fish will skyrocket and ordinary working-class housewives won't be able to buy." He gave her time to think about the chain of interrelated events. "The cannery owners will call for the National Guard. The politicians will be able to call the Guard out because they'll say *you're* hurting the little guy—and you are. And that's what they'll tell the voters. It doesn't mean the strike is wrong. Just that you need to see beyond the self-righteous us versus them. Politics is just war by another means. And there's no glory in war." He turned away from her and took a long pull on his cigarette, looking into the darkness. "Believe me."

Aino was silent, her mind moving rapidly through images of Aksel at war, the civil war in Finland—Helsinki.

"They won't bring in the Guard," she said quietly.

"They did in Centralia."

"That's because shooting and killing happened."

"Yes," he said. "Exactly." He was looking into the darkness. Quietly, he said, "Every fishing boat has a rifle onboard to kill sea lions or sharks that get in its nets or anyone corking its drift. These men don't work for wages. They aren't *workers*. Every fisherman is the king of his own country. Some will strike. Some, like me, won't. It'll be war, fisherman against fisherman."

She felt a chill.

"You'll risk getting killed crossing a picket line?"

"When I was bootlegging," he said, not looking at her, "I risked getting killed for excitement and money, trivial things compared with taking care of you and Eleanor." He turned to her. "Yes, I'll risk getting killed to sell the fish I catch. No one will stop me. Not even you."

"Don't do it for me."

"Do you want to keep the boat?"

She wanted to answer no, but she couldn't do it honestly. The boat was theirs, not just his. It was Eleanor's, too. It was what could get her to college. It was the family boat. The *Aino* was worth more than fighting injustice.

She sat on the fish box, leaned back against the cabin, aching with the sadness of it all.

Five hundred fishermen joined the strike. Aino agreed not to picket and Aksel agreed not to cross the picket lines. Both knew it meant risking the boat. They would move to the *Aino* if they lost the house. If they lost both, they'd move to Deep River. There was always shelter and food because of family.

Within days, independent fishermen with mouths to feed, bills to pay, and loan payments to meet began slipping by the striking fishermen to deliver their catch, enduring the curses and threats. Aksel knew many of them.

On a raw, windy day in mid-October, Aksel's prediction came true. Alfred Tolverson lost his temper and fired his rifle across Gregory Wycliffe's bow to stop him from selling his fish. Wycliffe turned back.

Three hours later he returned with four other boats. None of the strikers on the floating picket line were prepared for what they saw: five boats, two or three men to each boat, all armed with rifles held grimly at the ready.

Aino and Aksel watched from the wharf. Aksel looked at Aino, the set of his face and the grimness of his eyes communicating exactly what he intended to do. She nodded her head in agreement. Aksel hobbled full tilt for the *Aino* and was starting the engine when Aino climbed down the ladder right after him.

The *Aino* headed for the diminishing space between the oncoming boats and the little flotilla of strikers at full throttle, the bow wave peeling off her gracefully curved hull. Aksel threw her into reverse, gunning the engine to bring her to a complete stop. The *Aino* rocked in the slight chop, her engine idling, the line of oncoming fishermen bearing down on her, the picketing fishermen behind her. Aksel pulled himself up to the gunwale so everyone could see him.

The oncoming fishermen cut their engines. Both lines of boats rocked in the water, all filled with men aiming rifles at each other.

Aksel knew these men. Neither side would blink.

He ducked into the cabin and then climbed clumsily to its top. He raised one hand high above his head. That hand held a Thompson .45-caliber machine gun.

Aino gasped. "Where did you get that?"

"From the old days," Aksel answered, rotating with the Thompson above him, making sure both lines of boats saw it. "I stashed it with Matti," he said without looking at her. "Along with some other stuff."

Then he shouted, "This fires eight hundred and fifty rounds per minute. I have four drum magazines and every magazine has one hundred bullets." He paused. "I will shoot anyone who opens fire, no matter which side he's on."

Gregory Wycliffe yelled back: "Aksel, we don't want trouble with you. We just want to sell our fish."

"Wycliffe," Aksel called back: "Those men on strike have families to feed, just like you. Some of them, me included, have loans to pay on their boats. We're all making sacrifices."

"You sell your fish, you won't lose your boat."

"You sell your fish, we lose the strike, you goddamned scab," Tolverson shouted at Wycliffe.

That brought rifles up.

"Listen, all of you," Aksel shouted. It was hard to sound calm, shouting. He fired a burst into the air. That brought silence.

"Rifles will do nothing but kill fishermen while cannery owners get richer," Aksel said.

Aino scrambled to join Aksel and grabbed his arm, excitement on her face. "Listen. I have an idea," she whispered. In her eyes she had the fierce look that she usually carried into battle. "I don't think I'm crazy."

She raised her voice, turning her head as she did, so both sides could hear her. "Listen to me! What makes sense for all of us is to pull together!"

She knew it was a lame start, but she hadn't had time to think of anything else. "Aksel and I have been thinking." Aksel gave her a quick glance. She elbowed him. "If we had our own cannery and our own label we could tell the cannery owners to go to hell. We'll sell our catch to the people after *we* can it. We'll form a fishermen's co-op and bypass the canneries."

"I don't even own my boat," a man shouted. "How in hell are we going to own a canning factory?"

"By all of us chipping in." She turned to the striking fishermen. "There are over five hundred fishermen on strike around here. If we get two hundred of us to do this and if everyone contributes one hundred fifty or two hundred dollars, we can raise thirty or forty thousand dollars. Surely that's enough to buy some used canning machinery."

Aksel looked at her with surprise. She looked up at him, hopeful, apprehensive. She hadn't thought it through at all. He said quietly, "I'm impressed."

Someone shouted, "How are you going to get that many people to agree?"

"Tycho Finneman," she called back. "What do you think Lena would say if I asked her over coffee: 'Would you like to see Tycho dead in a fishermen's war or would you like to own a little piece of a canning factory that will guarantee you'll never have to strike again?'"

"She'd let someone shoot the dumb son of a bitch," one of the union fishermen yelled. There was laughter. Rifles were being lowered.

Tycho yelled back, "She'd say, 'Where's the money to feed the kids if we give it to the co-op?'"

"I know you'll have to dig deep. But now is the time. Sacrifice and dig now and get off this eternal merry-go-round of working for wages. Owning things gives us far more power than withholding our labor. Plus, a co-op takes all the surplus from the machines it owns and distributes it equally."

She let that sit.

"Suppose one of us is lazy or no good," another fisherman shouted. "Does he still get the same as the rest of us?"

"We can work out the details later, but one way is to keep track of how many pounds each brings in. You can be paid by the pound before the distribution. You'll still be your own men. You want to work hard, you get more. You invest in better gear, you get more. You want to loaf, you get less. You get to decide."

"What do we live on until this co-op starts selling our fish?" another man shouted back.

"If the Chinook Indians can live on salmon so can we." She turned so she could take all the boats into her view. "Most of us came from the old country. We've all seen real starvation. Don't you think two hundred determined women can find enough food in the woods and in their gardens to supplement what fish you men bring in? If we organize and share, only a tenth of you will need to fish to feed all of us. The rest can hunt, help forage, and maybe find odd jobs. We can pool the food. The issue before us is *will . . . we . . . organize?*" She paused to emphasize the words. "Or will we fall apart, even kill each other, and watch the owners squeeze us until we don't have enough gas to pass wind?"

She knew she had them when they all laughed, strikers and nonstrikers.

When the laughter died, Aksel, the tommy gun now held at his side and pointing downward, raised his voice to the would-be strike-breakers. "You all know I didn't want to strike." He turned to the striking fishermen. "But we tied the *Aino* up because we refused to cross the picket lines." He laid the tommy gun down on the top of the cabin. "Let's put the rifles down."

Tolverson, who seemed to be an unelected leader, laid his rifle down on the stern cockpit deck where it could no longer be seen. Soon, all the rifles were down.

Aksel waited to get everyone's attention again. "Let's meet at Suomi Hall at seven tonight. Call a truce for one day. Strikers"—he turned to the picketers' boats—"you, too. Choose how many need to stay on the picket line."

In the ensuing long silence, only the sound of exhaust burbling in the water from a few boats that hadn't turned off their engines could be heard.

"OK, Långström," one of the strikers yelled. "If you're so committed to this co-op idea, you tell us how you get a full fish box when most of us come in half full."

Aino stiffened. The most closely guarded secret a successful fisherman had was where and how he caught fish.

"It's a deal, Halverson," Aksel finally replied. "If this co-op idea goes, Aino and I will be in it one hundred percent. We share the profits. The more fish you catch, the more profit for me and everyone else."

"That's good enough for me," Halverson answered. He started his motor and swung his boat away from the group.

"What are we supposed to do with the fish in our boats?" Finneman shouted.

One of the strikers yelled back: "We could sure use some at our house."

At seven, Suomi Hall filled with fishermen. Wives came as well, many of them bringing what they had in the way of biscuitti or other bread. Some immediately got busy making coffee in the hall's large pots. Aino drew up a simple plan, explaining how a co-op worked, what would be required to make it work. Tolverson and a union fisherman named Alatalo were elected co-chairs. Aino was elected secretary.

There were objections and questions and some arguments as well.

"Why not just sell to the canneries while we're building our own?" someone asked.

Aino took it on. "We will only have so much processing capacity. That means we can only have so many fishermen. There will be more fishermen out there who can't join than can. They're our brothers. Their wives are our sisters. We won't scab."

"There's another reason," Aksel said in his quiet voice that made everyone listen him. "All those canneries will be our competition. If we help break the strike by selling to them, the price stays at three cents a pound, peanuts. That means we could only compete if we pay ourselves peanuts."

There was no more talk about selling to the canneries.

*   *   *

In winter, when the fishing was poor, the union fishermen would sacrifice the least. The temptation to settle the strike at any price, however, would be immense when the river was teeming with salmon in March. For those who'd joined the co-op, if the co-op wasn't running when the spring Chinook came in, it would be likely to fail. Most of the members, like Aino and Aksel, were gambling all their savings and probably what they had borrowed from relatives on its success. The cannery owners knew all this. They would do whatever they could to delay or stop the co-op's opening. The owners also knew that if they didn't settle with the union fishermen, they, too, would miss the spring Chinook. That was 40 to 60 percent of their revenue.

The owners' first move wasn't long coming. Gerald Gleason, who had worked his way up from managing the Knappton cannery of Knappton Packing, was now general manager, responsible for four plants. He showed up at the second organizing meeting at Suomi Hall.

He knew most of the fishermen. He remembered Aksel and shook his hand. Aksel wanted to shout the name Cap Carlson in his face but wondered if Gleason even remembered having left Carlson to rot.

The fishermen were uneasy. Alatalo gaveled the meeting open. "We'll dispense with the minutes. I think our visitor has something to say and then will probably want to leave." Mutterings of approval met Alatalo's intonation of *want to leave.*

Gleason was unfazed. He stood. "We're not seeking trouble," he began. "We want to settle this strike at a fair wage." Mutterings grew to hostile words. Alatalo gaveled the meeting quiet.

"I'm here to save you the trouble of trying to start this thing. More competition will not do any of you fishermen any good. It will just lower the price of salmon, which means we owners will be forced to lower what we pay you."

"That is not true," Aino said, loud and clear. "The market price for salmon is not set by Columbia River canneries alone. It is too big a market for one more cannery to affect price."

"You tell the son of a bitch, Aino," someone shouted.

Alatalo again gaveled for quiet. "Hear Mr. Gleason out," he said.

"I will be blunt," Gleason said. "We are prepared to do anything it takes to stop you from building another canning factory on the lower Columbia." He paused. "Anything it takes."

There was silence as they took in the implied threat.

"The packers are prepared to offer an additional twenty percent per pound, if you come back to work and drop this co-op idea in the garbage where it belongs."

"That's half a cent per pound," someone shouted. That was followed by howls of derision. When Alatalo had gaveled the fishermen into submission, Aino said to Gleason, "I think you have your answer."

Gleason picked up his hat from where he'd put it on his chair. He looked at it, as if studying it. Then he said, "I want you to remember that we tried to be reasonable." He walked out.

It was easy to agree on joining a co-op. When the co-op asked for money, it wasn't so easy. People had to be convinced in person.

Aino focused on the wives. She knew from hard experience that without their support the idea would fail. She also began recruiting the women to work in the proposed canning factory—not too difficult since all the salmon packers had been laid off, owing to the strike, and because of the depression there was no other work. Tolverson focused on locating canning equipment while Alatalo focused on finding a place for the factory and designing the processing. Alatalo would also focus on politics with one overarching goal: prevent the governor from calling in the National Guard to break the strike as the Oregon governor did in the fishermen's strike of the 1890s or the Washington governor did in Centralia. If the strike were broken, prospective members would fall off and the co-op, if it could get started at all, would, as Aksel pointed out, be competing with rival canneries operating with cheap labor. Timing was critical. Start before the strike ended. Start before the Chinook hit.

This made Aino and many prospective members uncomfortable. Was it wrong to hope the strike would last? Wouldn't they be abandoning their fellow fishermen? But then there was an even bigger issue. Tolverson had been up and down the river looking for canning machinery that was being sold under distress, but with the funds they hoped to raise, they could afford only equipment that would process a small amount of salmon, limiting the size of their membership more than they'd anticipated.

"We've become a country club before we've even started," Aino said at an early November committee meeting.

Alatalo, ever the practical man, said, "Right now, we don't have a problem. Why worry about it?"

"Why not turn it to our advantage," Tolverson said. "If the word gets out that membership will be closed because of processing capacity, won't that make people want to join before that happens?"

There was a murmur of agreement. Aino couldn't argue against the logic. All she could do was express her feelings. "I don't want to be part of an exclusive club."

Alatalo smiled, a little wistfully. "None of us do, Aino, but we're already exclusive. We only take members who haven't lost all their savings and can cough up two hundred bucks. That excludes half of the river."

When she went home that night and vented in front of Aksel, he took her in his arms. "We're doing our part for them by not breaking their strike." Then he whispered in her ear: "You can't save everyone." He stepped back and touched her nose. "Let's save a few. What's wrong with a small victory?"

She had to laugh.

The next morning, she was back at the membership drive.

This was difficult organizing for Aino, because not only did she have to overcome the usual objections of risking hard-earned savings or having to borrow the seed money from relatives, but she also had to overcome ignorance about how a co-op would work. Each wife wanted to know what would happen if her husband wanted out or brought in more fish than the other husbands or if her husband drowned. All the women knew that one or two men drowned every season.

* * *

Christmas of 1931 was bleak for almost everyone. Workers, even supervisors and managers, were being laid off at an increasing pace. Those who kept their jobs found wages being cut. For the families of the striking fishermen, it was the darkest Christmas in the darkest December. But no one starved.

Aino organized a collection point for food at Suomi Hall and formed a miniature food co-op. The strikers all contributed ten dollars and with that money the food committee bought sacks of staples to distribute according to family size and need: beans, flour, salt, sugar, lard—and coffee. There was no question about whether coffee was a staple.

And it was over coffee that Aino did the bulk of her work. She would often be unable to sleep at night because she was so full of caffeine. Over coffee she handed out midwife knowledge about pregnancies and a variety of women's health issues. Aino found herself drawing up family budgets, answering the question of how a family could afford a co-op membership fee. On occasion, she found herself babysitting while an essential errand had to be run by a mother.

The work was exhausting.

Every day, however, the co-op's bank account grew—sometimes by one membership fee, sometimes by four or five.

As membership grew, so did the pressure from the canneries.

27

On January 4, a train arrived with forty fishermen from San Francisco, mostly Italians. They'd been promised free use of boats and two and a half cents a pound. January fishing was mostly silverside, steelhead salmon, and white sturgeon. The canneries would take any kind of marketable fish to keep the lights on. None of them had any problem putting steelhead or silverside salmon into cans labeled Chinook.

Angry strikers quickly converged on the cannery where the Italians had been escorted by the local police. The strikers were armed. So were the police. Many knew each other.

Throughout the night, the fishermen hurled rocks at the cannery where the Italians had been lodged, breaking the occasional window. The chief of police arrived and urged calm. The sound of rounds being chambered was taken by everyone as a warning, but the point was made. The police set up lines around the cannery and pushed the fishermen back beyond rock-throwing range.

In a cold drizzle the next morning, the Italian fishermen set out nervously from the cannery with an armed police escort. They were unsure of the river and its dangers, unused to handling gill net boats, and had no clear idea of where to set their nets. These were tough, skilled, and desperate men with families to feed and no work to be found anywhere near them. They were also men ignorant of what they'd face at the mouth of the Columbia. The striking gillnetters sullenly watched them depart.

Two of the unfortunate Italians drowned in the first week. Being an experienced fisherman was only part of staying alive. Knowing the bottom and the currents where you were fishing was the other. The Italians were the former, but they did not know the latter. They were swept into the roiling water of the Columbia River bar, their bodies later found washed up on the long beach south of the jetty. They were buried there in the sand by local residents.

The fishermen took their own boats out to harass the Italians. There weren't enough police to guard every boat. One of the Italians' boats was rammed by an angry striker. It sank. The two scabs were left struggling in the water, but were picked up later by their friends.

The Italians continued to fish. The police continued to escort the Italians to their boats amid angry heckling and an occasional missile.

On January 13, John Nurmi's baby boy of four weeks died. Nurmi said it was because his wife wasn't eating well enough to feed him. Three days later, the house belonging to the owner of Northwest Seafood was torched. No one was hurt, because the family had been out. Those with a motive to burn the house, especially John Nurmi, had witnesses saying they were dancing at Suomi Hall the entire time.

The mayor and city council, now thoroughly frightened, called on the governor to send the Oregon National Guard to protect the Italian fishermen and guard the houses of owners and supervisors.

The governor was initially sympathetic to the mayor, but the co-op had prepared well. Alatalo presented the governor with the names and signatures of hundreds of members of the American Legion and VFW who supported the strike. Aksel contacted acquaintances from the old days. He learned a lot about the governor, in particular one rather sordid bit of the governor's personal history.

Alatalo met the governor and agreed to stay quiet in exchange for the governor's promise to explain to the mayor and cannery owners that it was political suicide to call out the Guard.

On January 28, Alatalo secured an old warehouse on a wharf at the end of Eighteenth Street. The owner openly defied Gleason's request that he not lease to any communist radicals from the co-op. Just two days later, Tolverson shook hands on purchasing the equipment of a canning factory that had gone out of business in St. Helens, Oregon, owing to the combined blows of the depression and the strike.

That night, co-op members celebrated. The owners, under Gleason's leadership, had failed to stop them.

Elated, Aino paid for long-distance and called Ilmari and Alma on their new telephone. When Alma finished shooing everyone off the party line, Aino told them the good news.

"Well," Ilmari said. "This calls for a celebration."

He showed up in Astoria, along with Alma and two of Alma's kermakakku—sour cream cakes—and several jars of homemade blackberry jam. It was February and the farmwork was curtailed by both weather and too little daylight, so they decided to stay a couple of days with Matti and Kyllikki to take in the big city. Eleanor, thirteen, stayed at Ilmahenki because of school. Jorma, now twenty-two, was in Tacoma at Pacific Lutheran College; and Helmi, twenty-four, was working as an office manager in Portland.

Tolverson rented an old wooden barge to transport the canning machinery from Scappoose to Astoria. With the help of twenty co-op fishermen, the barge was loaded and ready to be towed by Wednesday night, February 3. The tug, out of Longview, Washington, was scheduled for the next morning and the fishermen, in five cars, drove back to Astoria.

Later that same Wednesday night the owner of the Desdemona Club received a call from his sole liquor supplier. He was asked if he could do the supplier a favor. The favor was to pass on some information to Aksel Långström, a friend of the supplier from the old days and well known to the owner of the Desdemona. Someone was using an intermediary to hire men who would be willing to sink a barge.

The owner of the Desdemona Club was always pleased to do a favor for a gangster.

At eleven thirty that night, Aino was awoken by someone hammering on the door. She grabbed Aksel by the arm. Aksel grunted, fumbled for his crutch, and made his way to the door. Whoever it was only whispered. She heard Aksel say thank you. The light in the kitchen went on and Aksel was making coffee at the same time he was getting into his wool long johns and strapping on his leg.

"What's going on?" She asked, taking over the coffee-making job. Aksel was packing warm clothing in a haversack.

"Nothing," he said. It was that tone. There would be no more information. She started to feel uneasy but helped him put on his leg. He touched her hair and she looked up. His eyes were darting back and forth, the way they had often been ever since the war. Not a muscle on his face betrayed what he was feeling, but his eyes did. He was frightened. *That* she'd never seen. It sent her into near panic. She hugged his knee. "Don't go," she whispered.

He rose, saying nothing, and she had to rise with him. He shrugged into the coat he always wore when fishing. Then he took her with one arm around her waist and pulled her up to him, tight. He kissed her, long and hard. "I have to go," he said.

"Where?"

"Out."

By "out," he meant to find the Bachelor Boys.

Kyllikki was awoken twenty-five minutes later and she cautiously followed behind Matti to see who was at the door. She was followed by Ilmari and Alma. It was Aksel. Aksel motioned Matti and Ilmari outside and the three whispered. Matti came in, got into his warm logging clothes, and disappeared down the stairs to the basement. Ilmari went to his bedroom and came out wearing his warm clothes. When Matti came back upstairs, he had three Springfield rifles, one fitted with a scope, and two .45-caliber automatic pistols. He went back down and returned with ammunition and his own .30-caliber Winchester hunting rifle.

"What are you doing?" she asked. She turned to Aksel. "What's going on?"

She saw Aksel give Matti and Ilmari that look: keep the women out of this.

"What's going on?" she said with that voice: you'd better goddamn tell me.

"Aksel's just a little worried about the canning machinery for the co-op," Matti said. "He and Aino, and everyone else, have got their life savings tied up in it and, well, just to be cautious, maybe we'll ride along on the barge."

"Matti Koski, be cautious about what?"

"Nothing to worry about."

She looked at her husband and her brothers-in-law. "You're not going without coffee and pulla." She always had coffee ready for Matti to go to work in the morning, so all it required was heating.

Matti, Ilmari, and Aksel were standing in front of Matti's house when the big 1923 burgundy Oldsmobile touring car pulled up with the Bachelor Boys. Nine years old, showing considerable wear and tear on the interior leather, the car was kept in prime running condition by Jens. Heppu was driving. "Sorry we're a little late," he said. "Had to break into Seppa's Standard station for gas. We'll make it good with him later."

Matti and Aksel loaded the weapons and ammunition into the car's trunk and squeezed into the back seat with Jens and Kullervo, who, being the smallest, sprawled out across their laps, his head propped against one side. Yrjö was riding shotgun, with Ilmari in the front middle seat. Yrjö immediately started checking out the actions on the rifles, applying gun oil where he thought necessary.

Their first stop was the *Aino* to pick up Aksel's Thompson. Their next stop was St. Helens.

After Kyllikki got the kids off to school, she walked over to the poikataloja. Aino was cleaning up after breakfast when she walked through the door. Aino looked at her, holding a dish towel. "Where did they go? Heppu, Kullervo, Jens, and Yrjö are all gone."

"Matti said, and I quote, just to be cautious, they were going to ride along on the barge."

"Did they have guns?"

"Yes."

"I thought it was trouble." Aino sat down. She didn't trust herself to stand.

"Maybe not," Kyllikki said, following suit.

Aino looked at Kyllikki, marveling at either her optimism or her naïveté. Men didn't leave in the middle of the night fully armed if there wasn't trouble. "The cannery owners did everything they could, short of violence, to stop us," she said, "They failed."

"OK," Kyllikki said. "It's trouble."

Aino got up; poured coffee, her hands shaking; and joined Kyllikki with two cups. The two women didn't say a word. They just held on to their warm cups seeking comfort. Being married to a logger and a fisherman, they both had long ago dealt with the possibility of being widows. When it was imminent—a storm, a fire—they were scared, as they were now. No use stating the obvious. But storms and fires were indifferent, neutral. Men were intentional and far more lethal.

"We need to tell the co-op members," Aino said.

"You don't think they know?"

"Not likely," Aino said. "The man who came to the door last night was the manager of the Desdemona Club. He passed on a message. I'm guessing it was from one of Aksel's contacts from the old days."

"Yoh," Kyllikki said.

The two women left together, coffee untouched. Aino went to find Alatalo and Tolverson; Kyllikki went to the docks to spread the news.

They later met on the wharf off Sixteenth Street. They said very little but found themselves standing side by side, their arms around each other's waists, looking up the river. With those you love, you accept that there are only two ways you will not get hurt when you lose them. You stop loving them or you die first.

Aino gripped Kyllikki's hand and Kyllikki squeezed it back, sisters, both silent.

28

Aksel was smoking a cigarette, his Thompson across his lap, watching the shoreline pass by. He was near the bow on the Oregon side. Matti sat near the stern with his Winchester, his back up against the left rear tire of the Oldsmobile. Yrjö was on top of the canning equipment with the scoped rifle. Kullervo was spotting for him. Heppu, Ilmari, and Jens had the Washington side with their Springfields. The tug, on a short towrope, was moving at a steady six knots. The wood of the old barge creaked with each change of speed or direction. They'd left St. Helens around seven and passed Longview and Rainier. So far, no sign of trouble. Now, however, Aksel was growing uneasy. It was after one in the afternoon and they were moving into the narrowing channel between Puget Island and the Oregon side. They passed Westport and its huge sawmill. The distance between Puget Island and the Oregon side narrowed to around five hundred yards.

There was a slight change in the sound of the water running alongside the barge, and the bow of the barge moved up, maybe a foot, and then started back down. The tugboat's engine roared and Aksel saw the water churning from its stern as it pulled away from the barge, the towrope cast off.

"We're about to get hit!" Aksel shouted, his eyes trying to see both shorelines at the same time. "Everyone watch your sectors."

They bolted for the shelters they'd constructed for themselves on the deck, but Ilmari tripped and went down on the deck, hard, stunning himself as a powerful oceangoing sportfishing boat making thirty knots or faster came roaring out of a slough on Puget Island. The boat was throwing up a huge wake and bouncing across the water. Two men were in the large fishing cockpit aiming Thompson machine guns at the barge, each barrel held down by rope attached to a stirrup in turn held down by one foot to control the rise of the barrel. Professionals. Another man, also with a Thompson, was above them on the flying bridge next to the pilot. A fifth man was tied into the spindly lookout station that rose above the flying bridge, so he could get dropping fire that would nullify the protection of the shelters on the deck. All were firing the quick three- and four-shot bursts of pros; the heavy .45-caliber bullets thumped into the deck and wooden sides of the barge, throwing off splinters. Aksel went stumbling around the equipment to get on the attack side. Matti was doing the same. Yrjö was putting carefully aimed shots into the boat, but with the targets moving at that speed and bouncing as it was, he hadn't hit anyone yet.

Leaving Yrjö's side, Kullervo scrambled down to the barge's deck. He could see the man atop the lookout station slowly moving his Thompson's bullets in bursts of three back toward where Ilmari was lying. As the bullets stuttered along the deck, Kullervo sprinted before them, and threw himself on Ilmari's exposed body. The spray of bullets caught up with him. Kullervo's body jerked with each strike.

When Aksel reached the starboard side, he opened up with his own Thompson, using the splashes from the bullets to guide the weapon onto the speeding boat, now only ten yards from the barge. Then he saw another man, heretofore unseen, rise above the gunwales. He had several sticks of lighted dynamite held with one hand against his chest. Then one of the shooters in the fishing cockpit went down. It was Yrjö at work. Aksel fired another burst and the boat was abreast of the barge and he dived for cover as the man started hurling the lighted dynamite sticks. If it hadn't been for the Bachelor Boys' rifle fire and Aksel's Thompson putting a wall of lead in front of the barge, the speeding boat would have come right next to it and blown holes all along its side. As it was, the sticks hit the water several feet away. Still, the water served to magnify the punching power of the explosives and the old barge shuddered with each explosion. The boat sped up the river. It had all happened in about thirty seconds.

Aksel rushed to where Kullervo lay on top of Ilmari. Kullervo was conscious, but unmoving. Ilmari was gently trying to get out from under him, his clothes soaked with Kullervo's blood. Kullervo had taken three .45-caliber bullets. Aksel had seen it too often not to know what it meant for Kullervo. Even one .45-caliber bullet, hitting with the shock of a bat swung by Babe Ruth, would knock a man down no matter where it hit him. Then the shock wave it generated would shatter arteries. Aksel dropped his Thompson and took Kullervo in his arms. Kullervo smiled. "Had to do it," he whispered. Then he died.

Aksel hesitated only a moment. Last words often made no sense. He lay Kullervo back down and shouted, "Let me hear from everyone."

Three men shouted their names, then there was silence.

"Yrjö?" Aksel shouted, coming to his feet to have a look. Yrjö, who'd been in the most exposed position, said calmly, "I'm hit in my right shoulder."

Jens scrambled up to him and started to rip his shirt to apply pressure to stop the bleeding. He got a wad of shirt on the wound and calmly called out, "I need coats up here. He's going into shock."

The others took off their coats and threw them up to Jens, who was elevating Yrjö's legs. This unfortunately, put more pressure on the shoulder wound, making it harder to stop the bleeding.

Jens calmly called down. "Which is worse, shock or bleeding?"

Aksel called back. "Bleeding."

Jens got coats under and over Yrjö and lowered his feet again. He kept applying direct pressure to the wound.

The barge was dead in the water, moving with the current very slowly toward Astoria. After about ten minutes, it began to list, and after half an hour, it had sunk noticeably lower into the water. They'd left Puget Island to stern and were drifting up on Tenasillahe Island. Aksel wondered which way the river would take them, around the north side or the south side.

"How long we got?" Matti asked Aksel.

"I don't know how she's constructed," Aksel said. "The hull has clearly been stove in. I'd guess another half hour." He looked at the equipment and said quietly, "Everything we had."

The barge turned sideways, still slipping slowly along the shoreline.

Jens hollered down. "He's passed out."

"Saatana," Aksel whispered.

"He's back," Jens shouted down. "But his eyes are fluttering."

Aksel knew they had to get Yrjö to a doctor. He took one of the Springfields and started smashing at some of wooden crating protecting the equipment. The others immediately recognized he was getting wood together to build a sort of raft to get Yrjö to shore.

The barge shuddered and sank another several inches. The water was about a foot below the deck.

"Let's get him down here," Aksel said.

Matti climbed up to help lower him and Heppu and Aksel stood below to receive him.

The barge was slowly turning. Aksel could see the west end of Puget Island swing by and then the open channel to the north side of Tenasillahe. Yrjö was being lowered and he steadied himself as best he could to help Heppu with him. The south side of Tenasillahe was now in view.

The men had used their long johns to lash together a makeshift raft, just big enough to float Yrjö. Jens and Matti came down the deck. They were all shivering.

"Well, sailor?" Matti asked. "Abandon ship?"

The south channel of Tenasillahe was in the corner of Aksel's eye. He was about to say yes, but he turned and squinted into the bright gray of the sky. There were dark specks way down the channel. He paused. Then he heard a boat horn. Then he heard a chorus of boat horns.

"Would you look at that," Jens said.

Fishing boats filled the river, coming on fast, white water curving from their bows.

* * *

Nick Marincovich, a Croatian who'd installed a V-8 engine that he'd taken from an old Chevrolet Series D, reached the barge first. He immediately threw a line to lash his boat to it for more buoyancy, but Aksel threw it back. Pointing at Yrjö, he shouted, "We need to get this man to a doctor."

They got Yrjö aboard and Marincovich headed at full throttle for nearby Westport. Five minutes later, the six-cylinder boats pulled up and started lashing their hulls against the barge. The fishermen chopped holes in the barge's deck and soon had bucket brigades working to bail water. The boats with four-cylinder engines, many converted from tractors and cars, were continuing to arrive, being lashed to the barge or even to a boat already lashed to the barge.

There was a quick meeting to decide whether to catch the ebb and move the barge at night, which would be difficult and dangerous, or wait until morning. They chose to catch the ebb. Several boats hooked lines to the barge's bow and began towing the awkward flotilla of half-swamped barge and lashed boats toward Astoria.

One by one, the Bachelor Boys knelt down to touch Kullervo's face or hair and murmur something to him.

Aino, Alma, and Kyllikki had been standing on the wharf off Sixteenth Street all day. Kyllikki went back to make supper for the children, so they wouldn't suspect that something was going on. They were suspicious anyway; their mother was unusually quiet.

As soon as dinner was on the table, Kyllikki said, "I'm going to Aino-täti's," and she left.

It was dark on the wharf. Even when they could see nothing, they didn't once think of leaving. All three knew they would watch all night—until they knew. Many wives were there with them, talking quietly. All the wives were good at waiting.

At around eleven Kyllikki cried out. Coming around Tongue Point was a pair of green and red running lights. Then another set, then what looked like a pageant float of green and red running lights, all clustered together.

Aino put her arm around Kyllikki and Alma did the same on her other side. The three stood, linked, barely breathing, waiting, hope in their hearts.

Yrjö pulled through. They buried Kullervo on Peaceful Hill.

Ten days after the fight for the barge, on Saturday, February 14, Valentine's Day, the first can of Scandinavia's Best went out. It was prime Chinook, which was all the public cared about. That it was a relabeled can from the hijacking of a cannery truck in November was a closely held secret. It was sold at triple the price the association packers were getting before the strike.

Even at that price, the co-op was flooded with orders. One buyer paid a sizable sum for a guaranteed supply, giving both the co-op and the buyer leverage against the near monopoly of the packers' association.

Union fishermen started showing up at the co-op's weighing station. They were turned away if they weren't members. Many grew angry.

A group of women, wives of union fishermen, came to a co-op meeting and begged the co-op committee to be let in. Alatalo tried to explain the co-op could take no more fish than it could process. Membership was closed. Several of the women started weeping.

When they left, Aino spoke. "We can't offer them membership, but we can offer them bread."

The women of the co-op pooled resources and baked rieska all night. The next morning, there was a line outside the co-op cannery. Some wives were grateful, some resentful. They all got bread.

The co-op was the only cannery unaffected by the strike and money rolled in. The co-op committee started discussing adding another canning line.

Two weeks later, John Reder sent a telegram to Aino asking if he could talk with her in private. Reder took Aino to lunch at the Astoria Hotel, the city's business and social hub.

John Reder looked old. The man who had laid railroad tracks, built logging camps the size of small towns, logged giant trees—and who had forced her hand on a strike by threatening her brother's future—seemed subdued, even tired. It diminished the victory.

They caught up. John and Margaret had moved to Portland in 1924. John served on several boards of directors and managed his capital and timber holdings. The children were married and barely knew about the early logging days. At one moment during the reminiscing Reder slapped his hand on the table, making the plates and silver jump, and said, "Goddamnit, Aino, I miss logging. Even if it included being plagued by Wobblies like you." He said it with a smile.

"You're not logging anymore. Can we call quits the agreement that Matti stay south of the Columbia?"

"Quits," Reder said.

Aino nodded her thanks.

Reder slowly lit a cigar. He leaned back and said, "Just to clear the air, I didn't know anything about the attack on the barge."

Aino nodded. "I believe you."

They were silent for at least half a minute. Then Reder said, "The association is prepared to pay fifty thousand dollars for your cannery."

Aino studied the napkin on her lap, although she knew her answer immediately. "We will be selling Scandinavia's Best in every grocery store from Vancouver to Los Angeles. Northwest Packers Association brands won't even be on the shelf. We're already getting triple what you got before the strike."

Reder nodded for her to go on.

"We are thinking to add another canning line, not just because of the high profits. Many other fishermen are wanting joining. We will take even more of your markets from you."

Reder sat back, looking at Aino. It seemed to her that he was trying to suppress a smile.

"What?" she said. "You think I am talking foolishness?"

"No, no, Aino," Reder said. "Quite the opposite. Go on."

She checked to make sure he was taking her seriously.

"Scandinavia's Best can't can all the fish in the river. In six months, probably other fishermen will form other co-ops. That is permanent competition to the Packers Association. You don't want that."

Reder chuckled. "No, we don't."

He noticed that his cigar had gone out. He relit it and took a puff, watching the smoke rise above them. "You've done your homework, Aino. I didn't think you'd accept our offer. What will it take to settle things with the union fisher*men*, so we don't have more Scandinavia's Bests and miss the spring Chinook."

"Seven cents a pound."

"I don't think we can do that."

"The Chinook are just coming now," Aino said. "Every day, twice as many salmon as the day before. Every day you argue about what you pay the fishermen, millions of cans of salmon swimming upstream, gone. You figure out the arithmetic for lost earnings."

On Friday, March 11, the board members of the Northwest Packers Association and the owners of the canneries all along the Columbia met for dinner at the Astoria Country Club. John Reder laid out their options, including the immense loss of revenue if they missed the spring Chinook, and recommended they give seven cents a pound. They would all still make good money. While a majority agreed, those left in the minority were faced with their competitors buying salmon at seven cents and themselves getting no salmon. They quickly joined the majority for a unanimous decision.

On Monday, March 14, 1932, the canneries begin paying seven cents a pound. The next day was Aino's forty-fourth birthday.

29

Solstice in the summer of 1932 landed on Tuesday, so the Midsummer's Eve celebration took place on Saturday night, the eighteenth. It was a beautiful day, unusually warm for June in Astoria but not unprecedented and certainly not unwelcome.

Eleanor, who'd come across the river the day before, had spent Friday night with her friend Jenny. The two of them flitted back and forth between Jenny's house and Aksel and Aino's house, trying something, rejecting it, trying something else. Jenny was already fourteen and Eleanor would be fourteen on the twenty-third. They went over to Matti and Kyllikki's house two times to consult with Pilvi, who was a year ahead of them and, in their opinion, an expert on current fashion. They also wanted to make sure that Aarni saw them. He was a senior and graduating in a week. Surely, he had friends.

Matti and Kyllikki were getting ready for the dance themselves. They heard Aarni and Pilvi slam the door behind them, as usual, and smiled at each other. Then Kyllikki's lips began to tremble.

"What is it?" Matti asked.

"They've grown to be so old, but they're so young."

"What?"

"Ohh . . ." Kyllikki moaned, now very close to tears. "I was Aarni's age when we got married." She buried her face in his chest and he, surprised by the emotion, could only hold her and pat her on the back. She put her cheek against the wool of his suit jacket. "That's when I left my mother."

"Oh," Matti said. He pulled her chin up and kissed her. "It worked out, didn't it?"

She had to laugh through her tears.

Ilmari had gone out into the field after sunset. Eleanor had gone to Astoria for the dance at Suomi Hall. He was sure she would stay this time. She'd outgrown not only the local school but also the local boys—and even Ilmahenki. It had put him in a nostalgic mood, a longing for the good things of the past. It was like continually hearing the next to last chord in a familiar hymn, yet never hearing it resolve.

A full moon was rising in the sun's afterglow, so only a few stars were visible. Venus, however, shone with the intensity of a lighthouse low on the western horizon, while higher in the west hung brilliant Jupiter and, preceding the moon, low to the southeast, Saturn—brightness ascending in the descending brightness.

A drowsiness had settled over the valley of Deep River. The salmonberries and thimbleberries pulled their vines to the earth. The air, too, was heavy, but like a comforting quilt—not at all oppressive, just warm and soft, pressing gently on Ilmari's body. He heard a slight rustling. A young doe, probably born only the spring before, stepped daintily from the forest into the field. She stood there, her head raised, sampling the air. He chuckled. She had probably come for the vegetable garden. The doe looked directly at Ilmari, making him hold his breath. He felt his heart beat. She looked skyward. One of her ears twitched, as if trembling, but not with fear, with awe. She was looking at the rising moon. Ilmari joined the exquisite creature looking at the beauty—together, the two of them, in a sort of rapture. Then, the doe's other ear twitched and she bounded into the forest.

Around ten o'clock, Aksel left the dance for a smoke. He walked around to the north side of the hall and found Arcturus, despite the moonlight, hanging red and warm in the midsummer evening. He looked at the river, planning where he'd go as soon as the tide turned. Aino had become a good crew member, but she was dropping hints that between seasickness, which she occasionally still suffered in rough weather, the fumes in the engine room, her inability to sleep on deck—and an un-mentioned, but he knew strong, aversion to hanging her rear end over the side of the boat to take care of her business—she was talking about focusing a little more time on the co-op and him hiring a boat puller.

He didn't care what she did, but he knew she had to justify her decision to quit by giving him every sound reason except the real one. Eleanor had told them just before she left for the dance that she had decided to finish high school in Astoria. Aino wanted to make up for lost time.

He stubbed out his cigarette and clumped back up the stairs, no longer embarrassed by being awkward.

Aino watched Aksel talking to the band leader while the band was on break. Just after Aksel rejoined her, the leader announced, "We've had a request."

Aksel held out his hand to Aino and they moved onto the floor together. He invited her into his frame and she accepted. The band began playing "Lördagsvalsen." Aino knew it was silly to cry, but the tears kept coming as she whirled around the room, dancing, dancing in this precious moment with the man she loved.

LÖRDAGSVALSEN

N ear dark, on a gray day in March 1969, Aino sat quietly in
the armchair she and Aksel had purchased when they were
just married. She looked out on the great river through the
picture window of the ranch-style house they'd built in the 1950s.
Aksel was gone over three years now. The surgeon general's warning
about cigarettes came too late for him. He was buried on Peaceful Hill
next to Kullervo, Heppu, and Yrjö. The last two were killed in logging
accidents at ages forty-nine and sixty-three respectively. Jens was still
active with the American Legion in Neawanna, where he was the driving force behind Neawanna Kids Incorporated and the Legion baseball
team. She smiled to herself. For many years now, three bouquets would
be placed anonymously on the four graves on Armistice and later Veterans Day. She was pretty sure she knew who did it.

She missed small things about Aksel. How he would grin and
foam his mouth at her when he was brushing his teeth. His smell when
he was sweating. The heat of his body when she was cold at night. How
he cut his rieska backward, holding it against his chest. Breadcrumbs on
the kitchen counter. She even missed hearing his artificial leg thumping up the stairs from the basement where he built so many toy boats
with Eleanor's two young sons.

The spring Chinook would be running, but the Chinook were
a third of the size they had been when she and Aksel launched the
Aino. The June Hogs, evolved to survive the immense journey to their
spawning grounds at the headwaters of the Columbia and the Snake,
had been made extinct by the watershed's more than sixty dams. The

river was now a series of warm lakes. Its only remaining wild stretch ran through the nuclear waste storage site at Hanford, Washington.

The old Philco radio was tuned to KAST so she could catch the Scandinavian Hour on Saturday mornings and the news. Something caught her attention and drew her back from the river. A young woman with a beautiful clear soprano was singing a song about Joe Hill. Aino listened, then got up to walk closer to the radio.

I dreamed I saw Joe Hill last night as alive as you and me.

Says I to Joe, you're ten-years dead. I never died, said he.

Aino turned the radio off.

She put her coffee cup and saucer into the kitchen sink and clicked off the kitchen light. Click on. Click off. Easy light in exchange for Aksel's leg. Two-by-fours in exchange for dead loggers.

She shrugged into her overcoat and tied her old wool scarf on her still-thick but silvering hair. She walked into the front yard and looked west where a line of lighter gray showed where the sun was setting. Car lights winked on the huge bridge that replaced the ferries. The car lights left the bridge on the Washington side, some going east and some going west. The eastbound traffic's taillights disappeared where the *General Washington* had rounded the point to reach the Knappton docks. All that remained of Knappton were exposed pilings, moving in the gentle lapping of the river like loose teeth.

What remained of Tapiola was Ilmari's church, a few homes, and a combination gas station and grocery store.

Aarni, Matti and Kyllikki's oldest son, was coming to pick her up to go to the dance at Suomi Hall. He'd been the military attaché to Finland in the late 1940s and retired from the army in 1962. He was now running 200-Foot Logging. They would be celebrating Aino's eighty-first birthday in the social hall. Matti and Kyllikki would be there as well. Aino had now lived a year longer than her mother, Maíjaliisa, who'd died in 1938 at age eighty, spared the horrors of the war with Russia that started in 1939.

The gray band of light to the west had faded further, bringing out the lights of the Astoria waterfront, much diminished, since most of the canneries had closed. She could just make out the large buildings of the Scandinavian Cooperative Packing Company, which was sold to Van Camp Seafood in 1961 for a good price.

She felt a little lonely but content. Her mind turned to what she was going to wear tonight. She walked back into the house to get ready, humming "Lördagsvalsen." She'd had a full life.

Author's Comment

Before there was a Finland, there was *The Kalevala*. This collection of ancient songs from the shamanic past slept in the hearts and souls of Finns in the land they call Suomi. For centuries, Suomi dreamed of itself through the icy overtones of a vibrating kantele string or the songs of two old ones, who sang face-to-face, grasping each other's hand and shoulder, as they had learned from the old ones who went before them.

In the mid-nineteenth century, *The Kalevala* came to Finnish consciousness primarily through the collection efforts of a medical doctor, Elias Lönnrot. Lönnrot was stationed in the eastern and most isolated part of the Russian Grand Duchy of Finland, called the Kaleva District. He grew to love the old songs he found there, preserved out of reach of the encroachments of modern civilization. He noticed that the songs often shared the same characters, so he published these songs in the form of a single epic poem. This was in 1835 when the Finnish people suffered under Russian domination. The publication of *The Kalevala* was an important part of the awakening of the Finns, playing a key role in the revival of the Finnish language, which was under pressure from both Swedish and Russian. The revival of Finnish led to a greater identity as an autonomous people. This eventually led to nationhood and independence amid the turmoil of the 1917 Bolshevik revolution.

Before this awakening, Finnish mythical heroes were unknown, repressed by the Catholic Church of the Swedes and the Orthodox Church of the Russians. There was no Thor, no Freya, not even a Peter the Great or Catherine the Great. There was no Finland. As the yearning for a revival of the Finnish language grew, the knowledge of the heroes of *The Kalevala* grew. The sonorous names of these shamanic heroes of prehistory became part of the common language and many children are still named for them: steadfast old Väinämöinen, the lonely sage; his brother, Ilmarinen, the smith who forged the magic Sampo; Joukahainen, the celebrated minstrel of the Northland; Aino, the woman who stands alone, refusing to be married against her will; handsome, passionate, and arrogant Lemminkäinen; the sorceress Louhi, the mistress of the Northland; and many others. When Finns emigrated to America around the turn of the last century, these mythic heroes came with them.

The Kalevala has no overarching narrative structure and this novel is not a retelling of *The Kalevala* but rather a tale highly influenced by it. I've cut and combined many characters, the most painful being old Väinämöinen, who I combined with Ilmarinen, the smith, in the character Ilmari Koski.

For the sake of the story, I've condensed history in Finland somewhat. Russian troops were less a factor at the turn of the twentieth century than around the time of the World War I. Aino's part of Finland was predominantly "white," that is anticommunist, during the civil war that followed independence. As in most civil wars, atrocities were committed by both sides, leaving much bitterness. When I was a child in the 1950s, my grandmother, very much a "red," wouldn't allow me to play with children whose grandparents were whites.

I tried to set the novel in accurate history. Where I strayed, it was because of either my choice to sacrifice history for story or my ignorance. I apologize in advance to historians. The American setting is the southwestern corner of Washington state, where my Finnish relatives first settled in the 1890s and I spent much time as a child. The novel's Deep River is based on the Naselle River. Tapiola is based on my childhood memories of the town of Naselle, then a thriving logging town, now long gone except for two churches, a grocery store, and a few houses. Nordland is inspired by Aberdeen, Washington, a town known in its day for wildness. Nordland is based on *The Kalevala*'s Pohjola, which means "the Northland." It is a place of evil and darkness where the witch-woman shaman Louhi dwelled with her daughters. I've combined Raymond and South Bend, Washington, into the novel's Willapa. There is a real Deep River just east of Naselle. I simply liked the name for my novel. My apologies to locals who would prefer historical accuracy to artistic license.

Acknowledgments

Many people helped with the creation of *Deep River*. I would foremost like to thank my secret-weapon editor and cheerleader, my wife, Anne. I am blessed to have my publisher, Grove Atlantic, and my enormously skilled editors, Morgan Entrekin, Allison Malecha, Brenna McDuffie, Susan Gamer, and Paula Cooper Hughes. Risto Penttilä, Anders Eklund, and Marcus Prest furnished much-appreciated comment on the parts set in Finland. Thank you to Marsha Penti for her very helpful Finnish language suggestions. My gratitude to Bryan Penttila and George Nelson for their help on early logging, Eric Erickson for early sawmilling, and Reverend Gregory Neitzel and John and Jerry Alto for help with Columbia River gillnetting. Thank you to Chris Wick and Rick Tilghman for their help on turn of the 20th century sailing ships. I am particularly grateful for the many hours I spent with the late Rae Cheney talking about her childhood on a Montana farm in the 1920s. Further thanks to Marie Cooley of Fitting Room Corsets in Seattle for her advice on period fashion, and Sarah and Gabriel Chrisman for inviting me into their Victorian home in Port Townsend and sharing their thoughts on daily life at the turn of the twentieth century. Karl VanDevender boosted my spirits with early and constant encouragement. Karl, Josh Nogar, and Bo Sheller provided medical advice.

Many friends read drafts and provided helpful feedback. I would particularly like to thank Ed Grosswiler and LuAnn Lange for their early careful reading and detailed commentary. I would also like to thank Peter and Treacy Coates, Katherine Fitch, Mike Harreschou, Vicki Huff, Helen Odom, and Ken Pallack. My warm thanks to Cheri Lerma, of Cheri's Cafe in Cannon Beach, Oregon, for putting up with me when I was writing in a full booth during busy times while only ordering coffee.

My thanks to Sloan Harris and Heather Karpas at International Creative Management for constant encouragement and advice, both literary and business, and finally, my assistant, Halley Johnson, and Alexa Brahme at ICM for their much-appreciated support.

I want to acknowledge my great debt to and my gratitude for my grandparents, Axel and Aina Silverberg and Leif Erickson, as well as my great-uncles and great-aunts, all immigrants to the Lower Columbia region. They were loggers, fishermen, farmers, cannery workers, and hardworking and loving wives and mothers. I learned much working beside them in my childhood. I only wish I'd appreciated it back then as I do now.

About the Author

Karl Marlantes is the author of *Matterhorn: A Novel of the Vietnam War* and *What It Is Like to Go to War*. He is married and has five adult children and three grandchildren. He grew up in a small logging town on the Oregon coast and fished commercially with his grandfather as a teenager.